LITERARY EL PASO

LITERARY EL PASO

Edited by Marcia Hatfield Daudistel

TCU Press • Fort Worth, Texas

Library of Congress Cataloging-in-Publication Data

Literary El Paso / Marcia Hatfield Daudistel, editor.
p. cm.
Some texts in Spanish.
ISBN 978-0-87565-387-7 (cloth : alk. paper)
1. El Paso (Tex.)--Literary collections. 2. American literature--Texas--El Paso. I. Daudistel, Marcia Hatfield.
PS559.E6L58 2007
810.8'0976496--dc22
2009009489

TCU Press
P. O. Box 298300
Fort Worth, Texas 76129
817.257.7822
http://www.prs.tcu.edu

To order books: 800.826.8911

Jacket & Book design/Margie Adkins Graphic Design

Note to readers: We have retained the style of the original pieces in spelling, italics, capitalization, and use of accents.

For my grandparents

Patrick Duffy (1879–1974) Irish lad,
County Monaghan, Ireland

Bertie Langham Duffy (1888–1985) Texas belle,
Blue Ridge, Collin County, Texas

And their youngest daughter, my mother

Patricia Ruth Duffy (1927–)

True love never dies

Contents

Acknowledgments

Editing *Literary El Paso* confirmed my belief that writers are the most generous of souls. Nearly all the writers in the book were quick to suggest their own favorite El Paso writers and the writers who influenced their work. It was their enthusiasm and belief that this would be an important book that made this experience so enjoyable. During my years as Associate Director of Texas Western Press, the publishing house founded by Carl Hertzog, it was my privilege to help produce the books, in some cases multiple books, of some of the authors in this anthology and to serve on the Press editorial board with several others. *Literary El Paso* was a homecoming of sorts, and a happy one.

Thanks are due to James Lea for the estate of Tom Lea, Philip Sonnichsen for the estate of C.L. Sonnichsen, Cecilia Burciaga for the estate of José Antonio Burciaga, Teresa Sánchez for the estate of Ricardo Sánchez, Concha Rivera for the estate of Tomás Rivera, Ana Duran for the estate of Abelardo Delgado, and Robert Seltzer for the estate of Amado Muro for sharing their time and memories for this project. Special thanks to Dagoberto Gilb who generously smoothed my path more than once. Thanks to Robert Stakes who suggested me for this project and to Dale Walker for taking the suggestion to TCU Press. Judy Alter, Susan Petty, and Melinda Esco of TCU Press made my first experience on the other side of book publishing a very rewarding one. Their patience, good humor, and enthusiasm for the book carried it over the rough spots with ease. Susan Petty, a gifted editor, is also bright, funny, and should consider a second career in talking people off of high ledges. Karen Marasco, friend and events coordinator at Barnes and Noble, tirelessly promoted this book throughout the entire process. Claudia Rivers, head of Special Collections at the University of Texas at El Paso library, shared her encyclopedic knowledge. Benjamin Alire Sáenz, Elroy Bode, Maceo Dailey, and Nancy Hamilton offered valuable insights and suggestions for the book proposal and introduction. The UTEP community was a rich resource for *Literary El Paso*. The English Department and the Department of Creative Writing were enthusiastic and helpful. David Ruiter, Ezra Cappell, and Daniel Chacón were already suggesting events to launch the book six months before it was finished.

Feedback and encouragement from friends Walt and Vicki Fisher, Mimi and Jay Gladstein, Carl and Margaret Jackson, Robert and Cathy Nava, Charles and Gloria Ambler, Joe and Laura Gomez, Rebecca Quiñones, and Brad McLaughlin are greatly appreciated. Thanks to Harmon and Jeanne Hosch, Jack and Lillian Bristol, and Wynn and Kym Anderson for getting me out of town and away from the computer and for twenty years of great trips and great fun, and to John and Michael for wonderful times in El Paso and Los Angeles. Special thanks to dear friends Richard and Karen Jarvis for celebrating every completed phase of the book and being a tireless audience.

I am blessed with a large and noisy tribe of a family, who provides endless entertainment. Our stepfather Forrest brought our wonderful sisters Debbie Thompson and the joyous Sandy Hough to us. My hilarious brothers Michael and Brian Hatfield are relentless practical jokers. My sister Frances, boon companion, gives boundless encouragement and love in equal measure and has been there in the toughest of times, always. Leroy and Golda Hatfield have been the anchor and rock for this family. Frances, Sandy, and my childhood friend Gail Vincent Adams are fellow adventurers on our women-only retreats, and the dearest of friends. Their love is a treasure. Monte Hough, Mark Forry, and Mary Kay Hatfield are the best of all in-laws. My nieces and nephews, too numerous to name, are a joy to our family. They try hard to be as much fun as their aunts and uncles. Keep trying.

And most of all, love and thanks to Howard and my son John Patrick, who understood the year-long obsession with *Literary El Paso* and were readers, computer problem solvers, and listeners, even to my whining about the scanning process. All of that and more.

Introduction

Called El Paso Del Norte, the Pass of the North, and finally, El Paso, this region was the dark-eyed exotic stranger abducted into Texas by the treaty of Guadalupe Hidalgo in 1848. El Paso is part of the Chihuahuan desert and the adjacent Franklin Mountains are nearly the southernmost tip of the Rocky Mountain range. We are a far West Texas high-desert city with a distinctive bi-national identity. Our desert landscape seems foreign to most Texans accustomed to green valleys, flat plains and urban sprawl. Ciudad Juárez, Mexico, is plainly visible from Interstate 10; Sunland Park and Santa Teresa, New Mexico, flow seamlessly into our landscape. New Mexicans consider us Texans, Texans consider us New Mexicans, and historically, the U.S.-Mexico border has been a permeable membrane.

El Paso has been home to the Manso Indians, the Apaches, the Tigua Indians of Ysleta del Sur, Spanish explorers, conquistadors, soldiers, friars, bandits, businessmen, tubercular patients seeking dry air, newspapermen, writers, and gunfighters. Billy the Kid, John Wesley Hardin, Dallas Stoudenmire, and Pat Garrett were here. Pancho Villa and his men and General "Black Jack" Pershing were familiar faces in the city. Damon Runyon came to cover a sporting event, but wrote instead about the Mexican Revolution.

In subsequent decades, El Paso has retained an identity as an international city. Prohibition was easily circumvented since Ciudad Juárez was on the other side of the bridge with its siren call of nightclubs, bars, and bullfights. Writers and artists frequented The Kentucky Club. The clubs featured entertainers from the U.S. such as Nelson Eddy, Patti Andrews, and the Kingston Trio. Female bullfighters from the El Paso side of the border—Joy Blair, Pat Hayes, Joy Marie Price, and Pat McCormick—fought in Juárez. They met as members of the International Club at Texas Western College. Juárez was also known for quick marriages and divorces. Many movie stars obtained divorces in Juárez—Marilyn Monroe from Arthur Miller and Jayne Mansfield from Mickey Hargitay to name a few. Later, Elizabeth Taylor, as the young bride of Nicky Hilton, came to El Paso to visit her mother-in-law.

In addition to a colorful and dynamic history, El Paso has a rich literary tradition as well. Spanish explorers wrote about their findings and kept journals in the late 1500s, so El Paso has one of the oldest literary traditions in the state. In 1915, Mariano Azuela, a physician fleeing Mexico, smuggled the half-finished manuscript of the first novel about the Mexican Revolution, *Los de abajo* (*The Underdogs*), under his shirt, crossed the border into El Paso, and finished his book in an apartment on Oregon Street. Historians, novelists, poets, journalists and short story writers began to shape the literary legacy of El Paso.

A critical and significant time in the literary history of El Paso occurred in the 1960s and 1970s, during the rise of the Chicano Movement. The seeds of this movement began in 1848 at the end of the Mexican-American War when the establishment of the U.S.-Mexico border instantly created nearly one hundred thousand new U.S. citizens. In response to segregation and discrimination, organizations such as The Order of the Sons of America and the Knights of America were created in Texas to secure rights for these citizens. One of these organizations, The League of United Latin American Citizens, LULAC, established in 1929, elected Frank J. Galvan of El Paso as its eighth president in 1936-1937. Chicano activism during the 1960s and early 1970s attracted national attention and occurred at the same time as the Civil Rights Movement, which focused primarily on African Americans. During this time, previously silenced voices in the Hispanic community emerged on the political and artistic scene. Although attention to ethnic politics is usually centered on the West Coast, the first Raza Unida Party national convention was held in El Paso in 1972.

Out of this period of activism, a new genre of literature was born. Poets Ricardo Sánchez, Abelardo Delgado, who joined César Chávez in the farmworkers movement, artist and writer José Antonio Burciaga, novelist Arturo

Islas, journalist Ruben Salazar, and historian Mario T. García are only a few of these influential writers who began their work in El Paso. Rejected by mainstream publishers, they sometimes founded their own publishing houses. Then, when national attention to their work grew, they assumed their rightful place along with their contemporaries at east coast publishing houses. El Paso, along with the rest of Texas, in the 1950s and 1960s, resisted bilingualism. Schoolchildren were punished for speaking Spanish in the classroom. That has changed across the state. Still, most cities italicize Spanish in newspapers and local magazines. Our newspaper does not italicize; we are mostly a bilingual city. It is our particular bilingual and binational environment that has produced the city's ground-breaking writers.

Located on land that is now a part of Fort Bliss, the Texas State School of Mines and Metallurgy, founded in 1914, became the first institution of higher learning in El Paso. When fire destroyed the main building and all the student records, the students relocated to El Paso High. A new campus was then established on twenty-three acres of rocky hillside donated by influential families. Its unique design was inspired by images of the Himalayan Kingdom of Bhutan in the April 1914 *National Geographic*. Upon viewing these photographs, Kathleen Worrell commented to her husband, the Dean of the School of Mines, on the striking similarity between this landscape and the Franklin Mountains of El Paso. Based on this comparison, the architectural firm of Trost and Trost drew the blueprints. It took nearly twenty tons of dynamite to blast through the rocky mountainside. The Bhutanese syle of the new buildings made the school the most architecturally distinct campus in the United States. In the 1950s, the name was changed to Texas Western College, then in 1967 changed to The University of Texas at El Paso. Now with an enrollment of over twenty thousand students, UTEP is the only doctoral research-intensive university with a predominately Mexican-American student body. The five city-wide campuses of El Paso Community College also thrive.

Writers of national prominence came to teach at the University of Texas at El Paso. Raymond Carver was a visiting professor and lived here with Tess Gallagher. One of his most well-known stories, "What We Talk About When We Talk About Love," was set at a party in Albuquerque, New Mexico, but several local people remember being at that party, really held in the upper valley of El Paso, and can furnish the actual names of the characters. James Crumley, Les Standiford, James Hall, and Arturo Vivanti all taught here. The Chip Jordan Speaker Series brought Grace Paley, Gary Snyder, Robert Bly, Harry Crews, and Max Apple to the campus. Among other writers of national prominence who have lived here or presently make El Paso their home, those not featured in *Literary El Paso* are: Cormac McCarthy, Nancy Herndon, who also writes under the names Elizabeth Chadwick and Nancy Fairbanks, Janice Woods Windle, and Linda Francis Lee, among others.

An anthology, at best, is a sampling of writers. The challenge in assembling the selections for *Literary El Paso* was not to find approximately sixty writers to include, but to limit the book to that number. Every writer but one happily agreed to be included in *Literary El Paso.* The works are organized into three parts: the first section, about early El Paso, is in chronological order, of sorts, with works about the Mexican Revolution and the early citizens of the city, and a folk tale. The second section has short stories, essays, and poems about people and life on the border, and the third section is about the desert landscape and the physical surroundings that have inspired many writers.

The term "literature" can be one that refers solely to fiction and poetry, making it exclusionary. Since all writing coming out of a region is, in fact, the literature of that region, *Literary El Paso* has historical essays, journalistic feature stories, autobiography, poetry, short stories, and scenes from a play. The editor of any anthology is a target for criticism focused on who was left out. Since the criterion for the Literary Cities series by TCU is that the works represented in this anthology be about El Paso, fine writers who live here, were born here, but who did not write about El Paso were omitted. Since it was also important to feature the largest possible number of current and newer authors, some less contemporary, but certainly very fine, historians were left out, such as Haldeen Braddy, Conrey Bryson, and Francis Fugate.

Literary El Paso is a revelation in the best sense of the word. It not only provides readers the opportunity to become reacquainted with many familiar writers, but also to discover new ones. The talented writers who have made El Paso their home and the ones who live elsewhere share their affection and love for this city and their thoughts on the landscape and people that have inspired their work.

Cities give themselves nicknames. Dallas has been called the "Emerald City," and Fort Worth, the "Queen City of the Prairie." El Paso is rightly called the "Sun City." We have close to three hundred days of sunshine a year, which means we don't have to stay inside much unless we want to. It's the other days that can be a challenge. The high winds of spring stir up clouds of dust, and occasionally tumbleweeds fly around, unexpectedly landing on your car. We have very hot summers, but low humidity. Most of our annual rainfall comes during our monsoon season in late summer, so we don't keep umbrellas close at hand. We don't have hurricanes or tornadoes. We have grown accustomed to living with scorpions and the occasional coyote. We also don't need to leave a trail of breadcrumbs to find our way out of a forest here. The Franklin Mountains are our compass.

What El Paso should be called is the "City of Surprises," because most people visiting from elsewhere in Texas usually start their sentences with "I didn't know that. . . ." (fill in the blank). Despite the fact that there is only a bridge separating us from the escalating violence in Juárez, the violent crime rate in El Paso is still one of the lowest in Texas. Our scenery is surprising, too. The North Franklin Peak soars to over seven thousand feet. We see Mount Cristo Rey right across the Rio Grande. At first, the desert seems barren, but after your eyes adjust to the absence of blooming camellias and azaleas, you see native plants of many varieties of acacia, hyssop, and agave growing alongside the oleanders. Our landscape is spare, but far from stark; pine trees, palms, and pecan trees also flourish here. The sunsets in El Paso never fail to delight. The night sky is full of stars, a view unobstructed by rows of skyscrapers creating concrete canyons. Even during the fall and winter, it is comfortable enough to sit outside at night, light a fire, and gaze at the stars. We have a symphony, an opera company, and fine restaurants—if you would like to dine at a 2001 James Beard Foundation Award-winning restaurant, just go to H&H Car Wash and Coffee Shop. You can eat excellent Mexican food *and* watch your car being cleaned. In El Paso we know that chile con queso is not made with Velveeta and canned tomatoes. Salsa and pico de gallo were everyday condiments on our tables long before they became trendy elsewhere. We know that chile comes in red and green and bears no relation to the ground beef, bean, and bell pepper "chili" that most Texans recognize. Christmas here means luminarias and tamales. Groups of women gather in kitchens for tamaladas, the labor-intensive process of tamale making. Homemade tamales are an act of love.

Former and current residents still miss The Hacienda, a restaurant featuring a stuffed javelina head, looking down on diners and beer-drinking college students and professors. The live alligators in the fountain at San Jacinto Plaza in downtown El Paso are missed. Many returning El Pasoans demand to be taken to Chico's Tacos directly from the airport. Perhaps most surprising of all is the fact that we do not have to carefully plan for an arduous journey to go across town; the traffic that we complain about during rush hour is less than mid-morning traffic in Dallas, Houston, or Austin.

Houston to Austin to Dallas has been called the "cultural corridor" of Texas. Such a label does not acknowledge the rich history and literary traditions of other cities in Texas. A state as vast as Texas could never have a single passageway of artistic and literary achievement that defines culture. The road west from Central Texas is a different corridor, no less important. Next time you set out from Houston to travel along that cultural corridor, turn left at Austin. From 290, go to I-10 West, but take a detour at Balmorhea on State Highway 17. Vast areas of city lights are well behind you. Urban sprawl has fallen away, the travel pace is quiet and unhurried. In Fort Davis, the beautiful Davis Mountains rise from the desert floor. As you drive through, you will see Mount Livermore, Blue Mountain, and Sawtooth Mountain under the desert sky. As you rejoin I-10 West you're getting close to El Paso. The next expanse of lights—a huge glowing footnote to our mountains—is our city. Bienvenidos. Welcome.

—Marcia Hatfield Daudistel
El Paso, Texas, 2009

Part One

Revolution at the Pass of the North: The City Emerges

La revolución en El Paso del Norte: la ciudad surge

"A sense of history develops easily in a place where so much has happened—where so many unusual human beings have played such wonderful parts on such a tremendous stage."

~C.L. Sonnichsen, *Pass of the North: Four Centuries on the Rio Grande*

Tom Lea

Widely acclaimed artist, muralist, illustrator, and novelist Tom Lea (1907-2001) was born and raised in El Paso. Tom Lea Sr., his father, was the mayor of El Paso during the Mexican Revolution. At the age of seventeen, Lea studied under the muralist John Norton at the Chicago Art Institute and became his apprentice. He worked as a mural painter and commercial artist in Chicago until 1933 when he moved to Santa Fe, New Mexico. There Lea worked for the Laboratory of Anthropology, illustrated for *Santa Fe Magazine*, and briefly worked for the Works Progress Administration (WPA). Lea returned home to El Paso in 1936, then painted murals for the Texas Centennial celebration at the Hall of State at the Dallas State Fairgrounds and for the Branigan Library in Las Cruces, New Mexico. He won competitions sponsored by the U.S. Treasury Department, Section of Fine Arts, that resulted in the murals located in the Benjamin Franklin Post Office, Washington, D.C., painted in 1935, and "Pass of the North" located in the Federal Building in El Paso, among others. His lifelong friendship with book designer and publisher Carl Hertzog and writer J. Frank Dobie led to a career in writing and book illustration, in addition to his painting. Lea illustrated Dobie's *Apache Gold, Yaqui Silver* and *The Longhorns*. He won a Rosenwald Fellowship, but declined the honor when *Life* magazine asked him to become their accredited war correspondent. His writings and paintings were featured in *Life* from 1942-1945.

From 1941-1946, Lea traveled over 100,000 miles to the North Atlantic, on board the *Hornet* in the South Pacific, to China and the landing on Peleliu. He wrote about, as well as illustrated, his experiences in *Peleliu Landing*. During his time at war, he painted the portraits of Jimmy Doolittle, Claire Chennault, Berndt Balchen, and Madame and Generalissimo Chiang Kai-shek. However, his favorite painting remained *Sarah in Summertime*, a portrait of his wife Sarah Dighton Lea. His art has hung in the Oval Office of the White House and the Pentagon, and collections of his work can be seen at the Harry Ransom Humanities Research Center at the University of Texas at Austin and in the Tom Lea Gallery at the El Paso Museum of Art. In 1981, he was awarded the Lon Tinkle Lifetime Achievement Award by the Texas Institute of Letters. Among the many books he wrote and illustrated are:

Randado; *A Grizzly from the Coral Sea; Calendar of Twelve Travelers through the Pass of the North*; *The Primal Yoke*; *The Hands of Cantú;* and *A Picture Gallery*. Two of his novels, *The Brave Bulls* and *The Wonderful Country*, were both made into major motion pictures. He appears in a small role in *The Wonderful Country* as Peebles the barber. Lea also wrote and illustrated the two-volume *King Ranch*, a five-year collaboration with Carl Hertzog that was published in two editions, including a limited edition with a facsimile saddle blanket as a cover. *Tom Lea: An Oral History*, published in 1995, is his autobiography, based on six months of interviews by Adair Margo. His books remain highly sought after by collectors. Books about Tom Lea include *The Art of Tom Lea* and *The Two Thousand Yard Stare*. He continued his career as a studio painter until 1998 when his eyesight failed. Tom Lea, a Texas legend, died at his home due to complications from a fall.

From *The Wonderful Country*

Chapter One

An hour before daylight the wind came up and swept along the floor of the desert, moving the sand, changing the shapes of the hummocks under the dark mesquite. It blew across the bare mesas, over the summit stones of the mountains, down to a desert river flowing south through a pass where hills pitched steep to the edges of the narrowed water. Below the pass, the wind followed the stream into a valley where it found the houses of a lonely town sleeping by trees and plowed fields.

Hidden and small, four separate companies of travelers rode that morning before sunrise toward the lonely town. Unknown to each other, discovered only by the wind, they rode converging from the four compass points of the wide circling dark.

North, the wind struck a blow at the backs of three men hunched on the seats of an open buckboard headed south along the trees by the river. The wind bit at the hands of the driver holding the lines, of the man holding the rifle across his knees, of the man peering into the darkness by the mail sacks and the baggage.

West, on a long slope to the river, the wind puffed a sting of grit against the lips of six mounted cavalrymen and an officer escorting a mule-drawn ambulance headed east. The wind flapped at the fastenings on the wagon curtains; behind the canvas it brushed the face of a frightened woman alone on the jolting seat in the dark.

East, the wind stirred the dagger points of the stiff-rooted soapweed, clacking seeds in the pods dry on the brittle stalks. It blew powdery dust on an armed convoy of seven horsemen and two loaded frontier wagons headed west. The wind caught a tink of harness rings and a jingle of spur rowels in a multiple scuff of hooves, and lost them in the brush nearer the river.

South, in the twisting ruts of a road among hills and high mounded dunes, the wind cut against the moving shape of a massive high-wheeled Mexican cart. A driver with a pole walked beside the long double file of yoked oxen that brought the cart lumbering in the darkness. Two horsemen rode guarding the cart, headed north.

Chapter Two

Diego Casas, who knew the road and led the way, tightened rein and waited for the other horseman who came following the cart as rear guard.

"From here you could see the pass," Casas said. He was hoarse from the cold and the long silence. "Our animals feel the river."

Martin Brady did not answer. It was too windy and too early yet to talk. And it was necessary to be alert. He looked into the darkness and listened.

Casas spoke again, turning in his saddle, "Thanks to God—" With his chin he indicated the morning star. "El Lucero, the bringer of the light."

Martin Brady saw it. After daylight, so near the garrison, they would not expect Apaches. Until then they would.

"A long night," Casas offered. It cheered him to say something.

From far off in the noise of the wind they heard a thin howl. The horsemen stopped. The howl quavered and broke into high wobbly-toned yelps.

"Authentic. Serenade to Lucero," Casas said. He paused. "We have music but no Indians, eh Martín?"

"Not yet." The wind blew grit on his teeth when he opened his mouth.

From low beneath the morning star a luminous faint pallor climbed the sky. It marked a line in the east, then reached slowly around the circuit of all the horizon, bringing the first gray shapes to the build of the dark earth, adding detail moment by moment in the dim developing light.

The peon Pablo walking by the oxen called out to the horsemen, "There it is!" He pointed ahead with his driving pole, beyond the shelving hills, up the shadowy valley.

Martin Brady looked north and saw the pass for the first time.

Diego Casas pointed. "The butt end of that mountain, to the right of the pass—the town of Puerto is at the foot of it, where we take the ore. On the other side of the Rio Bravo. The town Del Norte is on this side."

The peon Pablo had driven oxen there before. He made another motion with his pole, and showed his teeth. "The limits of Mexico," he said, partly to himself. "Far north." He felt well about it. "Very far from Valdepeñas. —Heh!" he said to the oxen, using the pole.

Martin Brady's horse smelled the river and danced side-ward chafing, checked to the plod of the oxen by the light reining from Martin Brady's hand.

"The horse Lágrimas, he wants to see gringos," Diego grinned.

Martin Brady was not sure that he wanted to see gringos himself. Today he would see them, finally. All the way north, twenty-six days with the oxen and the heavy ore—and long before that—he had thought about it, about being again on the other side of the river. He had thought about it for years. When the *patrón* had told him to take the ore north, he wanted to go. He wanted to see what it would be like. Now he was almost there.

The wind blew harder, as if the approach of the sun were a signal. The sky in the east turned amber above the coppery dust clouded along the sunrise horizon. It grew ruddy and then red-edged as the high sky paled and darkness left the windswept hills, the speckled flats, the twisting line of the valley. The lighted tops of the mountains were pink in the first reaching rays before the sun itself came climbing fiery in the east. Then blue shadows sprang slanting far and thin from the wheels of the cart and the hooves moving along the windy slope high in the first yellow sunlight. Ahead, the bell tower of the church at Del Norte stood small and white, over the tops of the brown trees.

The sky tanned with thicker dust in the growing wind. The view shortened; the sun showed like a round burning hole in the haze. Martin Brady, with mud at the corners of his eyes, rode holding his horse to a jumpy walk, trying to see into the wind, into the grit beyond the river.

He counted the fourteen years since the night he was the scared boy leaving the country. Fourteen years in Mexico, more than half his life. There had been a long time when that night haunted him; he swam the river in his dreams, getting away, and waked up afraid. It came to him now, here at that river.

He looked over at his companion Diego Casas, thinking of the debt he owed Diego's father, old Mateo, who hid him that night. Who took him with the wagons to Valdepeñas, fed him, helped him, taught him, long ago. The old man was proud of him. "This kid Martín used his father's pistol on his father's killer," Mateo Casas boasted.

They won't remember it on the other side now, of course they won't, Martin Brady thought. It was too long ago, too far down the river. They won't remember Martin Brady from Kingdom Prairie, Missouri. They will take him for a Mexican. He guessed he was a Mexican. Not really. He discovered himself guessing it in English and he suddenly felt self-conscious about crossing the river, today. He pulled his horse toward Diego's.

"Dieguito, you can tell me now. Did we bring it to the pass?"

"I will tell you, boy. We brought it. I hope the water is low in the river. This load of rock won't swim. Anyway, our first thing is to go get the Señor Sterner from the other side. With the arrangements. With the coyote tune, at the customs house."

"I know that. Listen, Diego, what class of man is this Sterner?"

"He has the talents of his race. He will unload the cart and fill it with things of high price from his warehouse over there. Then back we go, to Don Cipriano. Before that, Martín, *yee*, we taste a cup and feel some little fleshes! They say it has a flavor in the North."

After the long desert they were near the trees. The road down the last sandy slope led them by the first mud hut on the edge of the settlements hidden in the dusty haze ahead. A shaggy dog with yellow eyes ran out barking. It came snarling toward Pablo, who picked up a rock and hurled it. Martin Brady's horse shied. The dog ran hurt, yelping into the brush.

"Ssss-s," Pablo hissed. "You won't bite now."

A wild gust bearing sharp-grained sand hit them, and Martin Brady pulled the sombrero tighter to his head. In the Mexican boots, in the Mexican stirrups, he moved his numbed toes. His feet felt the swollen sticky way they felt when they had been too long in leather. He looked down at his frayed jacket and the greasy dust caked on the hardened edges of the wrinkles in his worn Mexican breeches. With the back of his hand he brushed at the grainy wire stubble on his chin, and felt the scales on his cracked lips. He was not exactly a sweetheart going to fiestas.

At least he would find out what they thought of him on the other side of the river. And damned to what they thought. He took a hitch at the cartridge belt strapped around his belly, and turned his mind to his business coming into town. ★

Carl Hertzog

Internationally known book designer and typographer Jean Carl Hertzog (1902-1984) was born in Lyons, France, while his father was touring as a concert musician. He was raised in Pittsburgh after the death of his father. Tom Lea wrote of Hertzog, "When he was eight years old, he stuck his nose in the neighborhood print shop and smelled that printer's ink and it got him just like linseed oil got me when I was young." By the time Hertzog graduated from high school in 1919, he was qualified as a journeyman typesetter. He attended the Carnegie Institute of Technology School of Printing and Publishing, but lack of money caused him to leave after a year. While there, he worked under Porter Garnett, the founder of the noted Laboratory Press. In 1923, he came to El Paso to work for the W. S. McMath Company as a layout man. As shop foreman, he produced the books *La Lepara Nacional* by Gonzolo de La Para and *Just Me and Other Poems* by Owen White.

In 1934, he opened his own printing shop, still producing commercial publications, although his interest in fine printing continued. He met artist Tom Lea in 1937 and asked him to provide the drawings for the ads for the Paso Del Norte Hotel. Their collaboration over the years resulted in the books *The Notebook of Nancy Lea* (1937); *Randado* (1941); *Grizzly from the Coral Sea* (1944); *Peleliu Landing* (1945); *A Calendar of Twelve Travelers Through the Pass of the North* (1946); and the two volume *The King Ranch* (1957), including what is called "the saddle blanket edition," which was produced in a limited edition and a trade edition published by Little, Brown. *The King Ranch* was named one of the Fifty Books of the Year for 1957. He also worked with such writers as J. Frank Dobie and J. Evetts Haley. Hertzog and Dale Resler partnered in a printing business from 1944-1947, then Hertzog freelanced for clients such as Houston Harte, the San Antonio publisher. In 1949, he became an instructor in the Department of English and started the college print shop at the Texas College of Mines and Metallurgy, now the University of Texas at El Paso. He established Texas Western Press in 1952 to reflect the initial name change of the college to Texas Western College. Texas Western Press' first book was *The Spanish Heritage of the Southwest* by Francis Fugate, illustrated by artist José Cisneros who also illustrated several other books including *Riders Across the Centuries* for Texas Western Press. While at Texas Western Press Hertzog designed such notable books as *Bells Over Texas* by Bessie Lee Fitzhugh; *Forgotten Legions* by Val Lehman; *Pass of the North* by C. L. Sonnichsen; and *Morelos of Mexico* by W. H. Timmons; as well as two books for Alfred A. Knopf, including the classic *Goodbye to A River* by John Graves (1960). He received many awards, four of which came from the Texas Institute of Letters. His distinctive colophon graced books that still represent the most exacting standards, creativity, and attention to detail. The prestigious Carl Hertzog Award for Excellence in Book Design and the Hertzog Lectures, sponsored by the Friends of the University Library at the University of Texas at El Paso, continue to honor the work of this "Printer at the Pass."★

BOOKS
DESIGN
TYPOGRAPHY

Memo to Bob Wills

> *(Editor's Note: The* King Ranch *book project was originally scheduled to take a year, but took five years to complete. The following two letters in the voluminous correspondence from that project illustrate the difficulties in hand set type, humidity and paper and show Hertzog's meticulous attention to detail.)*

CARL HERTZOG 500 WELLESLEY ROAD EL PASO, TEXAS

January 16, 1956

REGARDING THE QUESTION ASKED YOU:

"Why does the type have to be made in San Francisco?"

The type used for the text is called "Centaur" which is an appropriate name in connection with our story. This is one of the best Roman type styles ever designed but it is not in general use, and therefore, is distinctive as well as strong, well-designed, readable.

This type was recommended by Tom Lea and approved by the Klebergs. Other type styles were presented in sample pages set to fit the scheme of the book but were rejected.

Centaur type is cast exclusively by Mackenzie & Harris of San Francisco. The mats (moulds) are made in England. M & H are in the business of making type for printers all over the country. In these days of specialization many large printers get typesetting from "trade composition shops" rather than set the type themselves, especially when unique or scarce designs are wanted.

The giant Lakeside Press in Chicago also has this Centaur type but they do not set type for anyone except their own productions. So the only source for the type selected for the K R History is San Francisco.

There is no special difficulty in this importation.* They are giving us excellent service. We got a release on the copy for the 2nd half of volume I on November 10th, and had some proofs back in three weeks. Some of the type arrived in December so that we could start processing it (unpack, correct, build into pages, etc.). By January 15th we had received all this type-65 galleys which will make almost 200 pages.

Although this is only half a book, you can use this experience for computing the time required for volume II. This was 60 days but with the momentum established we can figure on getting all the type for the whole volume in 90 days. This includes time for proofreading and correcting the galley proofs but does not anticipate any delays caused by "holes" in the copy or delays in proofreading.

This time does not include Footnotes, Appendix, or Index which will be set up here on the linotype. This can be done simultaneously if the work is organized properly.

*This size is expensive because italics have to be inserted by hand, and all alterations have to be set by hand, but Monotype permits refinements which are desirable, even though it is delicate to handle the type. ★

From El Paso's Durable Sinner

(Editor's Note: Carl Hertzog occasionally wrote articles. This essay on Owen White was published in Password, *the quarterly publication from the El Paso Historical Society.)*

ON A HOT DAY IN JUNE ALMOST SIXTY YEARS ago, I arrived in El Paso, a stranger but full of confidence and expectations. Coming out of the Union Station, I started walking toward town but at the first corner, without hesitation, I turned right and went over to West San Antonio Street. And there it was—a two-story brick building with the sign McMath Printing Company. I didn't need to ask directions; an inner force was leading me there. Maybe it was the smell of printer's ink. More likely, it was the vibrations of kindred spirits.

Mr. McMath was expecting me, as he had offered me a job by mail. The printing shop occupied the ground floor and upstairs there were four or five small apartments rented to Mexican families, except for one apartment used by Owen P. White as a studio or office. At that time he was writing a book which was to become important to all of us, especially to Owen.

William S. McMath was better educated and on a higher intellectual level than most commercial printers, especially those in the Southwest 2,000 miles from civilization. And he had imagination. He had dreamed of producing a history of El Paso because he knew how unusual the city was. El Paso *is* unique and he felt sure that a good book could be produced. The Whites and the McMaths were friends and visited frequently. They talked about the book and, since Owen was a professional writer and McMath had a printing plant, they decided to collaborate to get the job done.

When I arrived in El Paso, the book was about half done. Some pages were in type and going to press. Owen was still writing in his hideout upstairs. As I look back on those days, I realize now that I was privileged to be in on something that was important to the City of El Paso as well as to those immediately involved with the book, entitled *Out of the Desert: The Historical Romance of El Paso.*

Although I came to El Paso as a typographer and designer, and was destined to produce many books over the years, Mr. McMath was the designer of this book. He had set the style for the typography and had ordered the covers made in St. Louis. The books were hand-sewn and bound in El Paso. Both McMath and White did a good job. The book was an immediate success. The first printing sold out in a few weeks and a second edition was put on the press.

Naturally there were criticisms. The nit-pickers pointed out errors in historic facts, but the biggest noise came from those whose toes were stepped on. Owen was already exercising his ability to uncover questionable motivations, a perception that later served him well on the staff of a major national magazine. Owen had had previous journalistic experience, but *Out of the Desert* marked a turning point in his phenomenal career.

As soon as the first copies came off the press, Mr. McMath sent a copy to H. L. Mencken whose *American Mercury* was then the most distinguished magazine in the country. Mencken was intrigued and did a two column review. According to Owen, "It wasn't complimentary and it wasn't damning. It was just honest. He had my number. He said I was no master of English, but that I could tell a story, and when he got to my 'mug section' he howled with delight at the way I had soaked my fellow citizens for a hundred dollars a page and then, in my own way, had made them ridiculous . . . and as a climax to my relief that he hadn't slaughtered me he wrote and asked me to contribute an article or two to the *Mercury*." To be recognized by the prestigious Mencken* was a big step forward. Fate also favored the book at the *New York Times*. With the constant deluge of books arriving there every week an unknown had little chance of being noticed, but *Out of the Desert* was reviewed and Owen White became a writer known to the editors.

Soon after this came the election and inauguration of Miriam A. "Ma" Ferguson as governor of Texas. This was a "first" and a good news story and the *New York Times* wanted coverage. They wired Owen and asked him to cover the story for them. (In those days you didn't phone like today, you sent a telegram.) The *Times* liked the way Owen handled the story and invited him to come to New York and go to work for them.

Although busy with journalistic duties Owen began writing books for New York publishers and *Them Was the Days: From El Paso to Prohibition* was published in 1925. He did not have to do much research on a book like this, just remember his boyhood days. This was followed by *Trigger Fingers* and *Lead & Likker*, full-length books about gunfighters and escapades of the Southwestern frontier with which Owen was well acquainted. In 1929 he published *A Frontier Mother* for which he codified his flippant style to be more respectful. Owen's mother was a courageous lady subjected to the horrors and hardships of the frontier. When Owen was born they were living in an adobe *jacal* with dirt floors. His father was a physician kept busy by the violence of saloons, gamblers, gunfighters and Indians.

After Owen moved to New York, he met other editors and publishers and was soon propositioned by *Collier's, The National Weekly*. Before TV this magazine of several million circulation was popular and influential. Owen became an investigative reporter and his name was carried on the masthead. For thirteen years he was prominent in the national picture uncovering scandals (the prohibition era) and fraudulent elections. *Collier's* was fearless and so was Owen. They were crusaders for the truth. Our native son was right in the big middle of national news.

Before the books and Owen's New York experience, he had some exciting times in Mexico. Fluent in Spanish, he was an on-the-scene observer of the Revolution. His whole story is told in *The Autobiography of a Durable Sinner*, published by Putnam's in 1942. This title suggests that he was part of the scene but he was not one of the "bad guys," although he was close to them. As a young boy in the Sin City (El Paso before the coming of the railroads) he saw plenty, especially since his father was a physician who had to clean up a lot of messes. There are two kinds of sinners, he said, "The ones who are obvious: Gamblers, Gunfighters, Prostitutes and Racketeers, and the *covert* who pose as pious citizens but are wheeler-dealers behind the scenes." He exposed many of the latter long before Watergate became a dirty word.

Owen Payne White was, and is, important to El Paso. He was the first white child born in El Paso (as far as the record goes) and he recorded our early history for a wide audience. I don't know of any other El Pasoan who went so far and did his "thing" on such a nation-wide scale.

*Some of their correspondence is in the Library Archives at the University of Texas at El Paso. ★

Owen White

Native El Pasoan Owen Payne White (1879-1946) graduated from El Paso High then attended the University of Texas at Austin, but returned to El Paso after only a few months. He attended New York University to study law and served in World War I as a sergeant. In 1920 he became a columnist for the *El Paso Herald. Out of the Desert,* his first book, came to the attention of H. L. Mencken, then the editor of the *American Mercury*, which led to a long standing friendship and correspondence. The *New York Times* reviewed the book and asked White to cover the story of the inauguration of Texas governor Miriam "Ma" Ferguson. As a result, the *Times* offered him a job. In 1925, he moved to Long Island, New York, working as a freelance writer until 1940, when he became associate editor and staff writer at *Collier's*. His articles also appeared frequently in *American Mercury* and the *New York Times Magazine*. He was nationally recognized for his articles on political corruption, particularly in Texas. White's exposé of the oil industry and graft in the Lower Rio Grande Valley resulted in many threatened lawsuits against himself and *Collier's*. He is also the author of *Just Me*; *Them Was the Days*; *Trigger Finger*; *Frontier Mother*; *Lead & Likker*; *My Texas 'tis of Thee*; *Autobiography of a Durable Sinner*; and *Texas, an Informal Biography*. Incomplete at the time of his death, his final book, *Western Trails*, was never published.

From *Out of the Desert: The Historical Romance of El Paso*: The Passing of Stoudenmire

El Paso, more than any other city that we know anything about, has always lived off of and profited by the fruits of industries with which it has no direct connection. From the very beginning of its municipal existence it began to exact toll from the surrounding territory and, like a regal mistress of the Southwest, it has kept on collecting it ever since.

All that we have heretofore said with reference to the rapidity with which El Paso came to the front can be repeated, in a less concentrated and less feverish degree, in regard to the entire Southwest. For several hundred miles in all directions the surrounding territory was being settled up at the same time that El Paso was, and no sooner had each resident located himself than he instinctively turned his eyes toward this place as the fountain-head for supplies and the one centre in which he could find a sufficient and gratifying amount of recreation.

Our local population also increased rapidly and as each newcomer arrived, and found his or her niche in our social life, all seem to have placed themselves immediately in one of two categories. They either did or did not sleep late in the morning, and from this simple statement it is easy to see that ours was what is called an "all-night town." At least one-half of our population was here for the purpose of entertaining and living off of the transients and the other half.

There was not a thing in the way of commercial accommodation or of excitement and lurid entertainment that El Paso was not ready, as a kind hostess, to furnish to her guests. And, as all of these guests came into the town with their pockets full of money and their minds full of the thought that they were potential millionaires, it was no trouble at all for El Paso to collect her full dividend from each and every one of them.

We do not want to be understood as saying that we approve of this system of extortion. Today it would be unbecoming and indecorous for El Paso to reap a rich harvest by placing invitingly before its tourists, in addition to legitimate things, a complete collection of every known form of vice and wickedness and telling them to pay the price and take their choice.

But in the old days that is what we did, and it is a striking commentary on human nature—and a city is nothing but an aggregation of human beings—to note that the very vices which we invited our visitors to indulge in; the vices which we encouraged and which helped us pay our way in our youth, are today the basis of a quarrel which has been going on for a long time between us and our sister city across the Rio Grande.

Far be it from us to accuse anyone of being either insincere or hypocritical. We don't. We merely wish to call the readers' attention to the fact that it makes a vast deal of difference as to whose ox it is that is being gored. Just as long as a condition existed whereby El Paso reaped a substantial profit, taken from outsiders, from its halls of iniquity and its dens of vice, no efficient war was waged against them. The churches, of course, and people who were on the side of morality, attacked our vicious institutions and attacked them bitterly, but until the day arrived, as it eventually did, when the business men and the bankers could see that the parasites of the place were beginning to devour the citizen along with the stranger, no determined effort was made to drive these parasites out of the community.

At the time of which we are writing every saloon, restaurant and gambling house in the place stayed open twenty-four hours every day in the week. The gamblers who worked on the "graveyard shift"—two A.M. to six A.M.—had just as heavy a play to handle as did those who were on the job earlier in the night, and in short, El Paso could have advertised, as Creede, Colorado, did: "That it's day all day in the daytime and we have no night at all."

Naturally the great majority of the men who came into the Southwest when the country was young and rough and untamed were men who were in search of just the kind of an atmosphere that they found. They themselves, although they were not all rough, were young and untamed. Many came here ambitious to succeed and did so by sticking to work and taking advantage of their opportunities, but many others there were who fell by the wayside and were carried away in a whirlpool of licentiousness and vice.

For many years, even after 1881, El Paso did its part, we regret to say, in bringing about the ruination of young men, but even from this fact we have always been able to derive a grain of comfort. The men who succeeded, the men who came here and stuck it out and who resisted the temptations that surrounded them, emerged from the test each one of them ten times better than any one of the weaklings would have been.

In her own way, the Southwest in the old days, when she began to put on the garb of civilization, weeded her own garden, and thus found out for herself who the men were to whom she could entrust the task of developing her wonderful resources.

It was the knowledge that these resources existed that not only brought men into the country, but which had, in the beginning, brought the railroads themselves. Not a single one of the four trunk lines which terminated at El Paso had come here in the hope of securing any business which was here at the time. There was none. Everything in the Southwest, just as El Paso had to do, had to begin at the beginning and practically at the same time.

East of El Paso, as far as the Pecos River and away up into the Texas panhandle, men went into the cattle business. Prior to this time this industry had been one in which the dangers and the hardships were out of all proportion to the profits. Cattle had to be driven to market over a trail a thousand miles and three months long, and in addition to this the Indians had presented themselves as an almost continuous menace.

The advent of the railroad, however, changed these conditions. The Indians, who had been more than willing to take their chances against men who would meet them in the open, mounted on flesh and blood animals, gave up the fight when they were confronted by steel, steam-driven monsters. These same steel monsters transported the cattle to market in a space of time that was measured by days instead of by months.

As we have said, far back in another chapter, although El Paso is not a logical centre for the cattle business, it became, because of its peculiar attractions and its commercial facilities, the trading and the recreational centre for the cow-men. Both in the quantity and quality of its stores and in the number and ornateness of its saloons, dance halls, sporting houses and variety theatres, El Paso was supreme mistress of the border. She was both hospitable and business-like, and the result was that she won and retained the friendship of all who came in at her gates, even though a good many went out of them carrying only an empty pocket-book and a hazy memory of a very glorious and gaudy week.

But the cow-men from west of the Pecos were not the only visitors from her trade territory whom El Paso welcomed and to whom she was kind.

To the north and west, in New Mexico and Arizona, the principal occupation to which men first turned their attention was that of mining. Properties which had been known to exist for many years, but which had been non-productive because of lack of transportation, such as the mines of Santa Rita, were now opened up and extensive development work undertaken. Several silver discoveries, and a few gold ones, which attracted a great many men to the district, were made in New Mexico and the great copper deposits of Arizona, which had been discovered in the 70s, began to be worked at a profit.

All of these things, taking place simultaneously, had a beneficial effect upon the industries of El Paso. The merchants of the town, who had largely increased in number, began to carry extensive and valuable stocks of merchandise, and as freight rates at that time were favorable to this point, it became a jobbing center. El Paso's two banks also prospered and, extending the fields of their operations into the surrounding territory, gradually laid the foundation upon which the city eventually built its financial supremacy.

In all the institutions in the city the newness and the prosperity of the Southwest was reflected, but in none so much as in the gambling and sporting houses, the variety theatres and the saloons. Men from all directions, even from Mexico, came to El Paso to indulge themselves in the questionable delights of getting drunk, losing their money and associating with women of easy virtue.

The saloons and dance-halls were nightly crowded with reckless, improvident men who cared little for money when they were in search of pleasure, and who thus rendered themselves easy victims to El Paso's newly acquired parasitical citizens.

The result of this lavishness on the part of those who worshipped at the shrine of Bacchus was that El Paso's bar-rooms and bar-tenders soon assumed an entirely different aspect from the one they had worn only a year or two before. In place of a customer having his drinks shoved out to him over a pine bar by a flannel-shirted, unwashed individual, he was now served across polished mahogany, by a slick-looking gentleman wearing a spotless white jacket and, for his personal adornment, one or two thousand dollars' worth of real diamonds.

At the present time we are unable to say how many saloons were in operation in El Paso in the year 1882. We think, however, that it is safe to assert that the town was no better then than it was a few years later, and we know it to be a fact that at this later period there was a bar-room in the place for every 200 inhabitants, women and children included.

Under such conditions as these, notwithstanding its American ways, its churches, its government and its school, El Paso was still anything but a law-abiding and a peaceful community. Gun toting was still the common practice and shooting out the lights was a pastime which strangers could indulge in with only a minimum of fear.

Killings in the town were of frequent occurrence, but convictions for murder were few. Generally speaking the men who were the victims in these gun battles were either strangers in the community or were undesirable citizens of whom El Paso was glad to get rid. Hence justice was not meted out with the severity with which it would be today.

At this time the peace of the city was in the keeping of James B. Gillett, who had been appointed city marshal upon the resignation of Dallas Stoudenmire. When Gillett, who had made an enviable record for himself as a Texas ranger and also as Stoudenmire's assistant, received his appointment he says that Stoudenmire came over and took him by the hand and said: "Young man, I congratulate you on being city marshal, and at the same time I wish to warn you that you have more than a man's size job on your hands."

With this discouraging remark from the ex-marshal to cheer him up young Gillett assumed the duties of his office. From what we have seen of the lawless element in the town we can imagine that Marshal Gillett must have entered upon his official career with grave misgivings. Apparently, however, he had no great difficulty in curbing the dangerous element in the community. He was able to handle "bad men" even better than his predecessor had been and we think that we can attribute his success to the fact that he was not a bad man himself and consequently had few enemies, while Stoudenmire, who was a bully, had had no friends.

One of the things that perplexed Gillett when he first pinned on his badge of office was what to do about Stoudenmire. Stoudenmire, he knew, was going to remain in the town as a deputy United States marshal, and it would only be a matter of time until his presence here would result in serious trouble. Gillett himself, in the book which he has written, confesses that such were his feelings, and says: "Stoudenmire always treated me with the greatest consideration and courtesy and gave me trouble on only one occasion. I reproduce here a clipping from an El Paso paper of that time:

> 'Last Thursday night a shooting scrape in which ex-Marshal Stoudenmire and ex-Deputy Page played the leading parts occurred at the Acme saloon. It seems that early in the evening Page had a misunderstanding with Billy Bell. Stoudenmire acted as peacemaker in the matter. In doing so he carried Page to Doyle's concert hall, where the two remained an hour or so and got more or less intoxicated. About midnight they returned to the Acme and soon got into a quarrel. Stoudenmire drew his pistol and fired at Page; the latter, however, knocked the weapon upward and the ball went into the ceiling. Page then wrenched the pistol from Stoudenmire and the latter drew a second pistol and the two combatants were about to perforate each other when Marshal Gillett appeared on the premises with a double-barrel shot-gun and corralled both of them. They were taken before court the following morning and fined $25.00 each and Stoudenmire was placed under bond in the sum of $250 to keep the peace.'"

This little episode, to which the El Paso papers of that day paid so little attention, and upon which Marshal Gillett makes no comment of his own, was merely one of a dozen similar disturbances which occurred every week.

But as a disturbing element in the community, and as a source of annoyance to Marshal Gillett, Stoudenmire was soon removed from the scene. Ever since the killing two years before, of Campbell and Hale, and the attempted assassination of the marshal, there had been bad blood between Stoudenmire and his friends and the Manning brothers and their followers. Everybody in El Paso knew that sooner or later the climax of this enmity would be reached and a shooting affray would result. Time and again it had been imminent, but always the quarrels which arose had resulted in nothing more than battles of words which only served to increase the hatred already existing.

The end came unexpectedly and seems to have been brought about by Stoudenmire himself. Drinking one day with a few of his friends he said, suddenly, "Boys, let's go and see the Mannings and either square this thing or shoot it out." The men with Stoudenmire were agreeable and in a body went with the ex-marshal to talk it over with the Mannings. What took place at this conference is unknown to us and is of little consequence. Apparently everything between the two factions was peaceably arranged and, as no further trouble was anticipated, Stoudenmire's friends left him alone with Dr. Manning.

Between these two men there was a very striking contrast in every particular. Stoudenmire was large, over-bearing and ill-tempered. Dr. Manning was small, refined and quiet. After their friends left them the two men came down El Paso street together and went into Uncle Ben Dowell's saloon to seal their newly-made pact of friendship with a social drink.

While they were standing at the bar some word dropped by Dr. Manning angered Stoudenmire who, without any warning, pulled his pistol and fired at the little man. The bullet missed its mark but wounded the doctor in the hand. With the other hand, which had been wounded in a previous gun fight, the doctor grappled with his opponent, and managing to draw his pistol shot Stoudenmire, killing him instantly.

In this manner Dallas Stoudenmire, one of the most notorious and picturesque characters of the early Southwest, passed out of the history of El Paso.

Dr. Manning was tried for having killed him and the jury, without leaving the box, rendered a verdict of not guilty. ★

Dale L. Walker

Dale L. Walker, a freelance writer since 1960, is the author of many historical books, biographies and literary studies, including *Legends and Lies: Great Mysteries of the American West*; *The Boys of '98: Theodore Roosevelt and the Rough Riders*; *Bear Flag Rising: The Conquest of California, 1846*; *Pacific Destiny: The Four-Century Journey to the Oregon Country*; *Eldorado: The California Gold Rush*; *The Calamity Papers: Western Myths and Cold Cases*; and most recently a biography of Civil War surgeon Mary Edwards Walker, the only woman to earn the Congressional Medal of Honor. His periodical work has appeared in 130 magazines and newspapers and he has written extensively on the life and works of the American author Jack London.

Walker has served as director of Texas Western Press of the University of Texas at El Paso, books editor for the *El Paso Times*, books columnist for the *Rocky Mountain News*, and is a consulting editor for Forge Books (Macmillan) of New York. He is the recipient of the Owen Wister Award, for lifetime contributions to western history and literature, from Western Writers of America, Inc., and is a member of the Texas Institute of Letters and the Author's Guild.

The Mencken-White Letters

THEY WERE KINDRED SPIRITS, OWEN PAYNE White and Henry Louis Mencken. Both were writers, both iconoclasts, both capable of seeing high humor in all sorts of sacrosanct institutions and ideals. Their paths crossed first in the Roaring 20s and their friendship, bound together mostly by correspondence, ended only by the death of White in 1946.

A slender file of letters from Mencken to White in the University of Texas at El Paso Library Archives tells something of this friendship. The letters are a gift to the University from Owen White's widow, Mrs. Hazel H. White of

Cutchogue, Long Island, N.Y., and were presented to University Librarian Baxter Polk in 1962 by White's sister, Mrs. O. S. Osborn of El Paso.

The son of a prominent pioneer El Paso physician, Owen White was born in El Paso in 1879. His first step toward a literary career came in 1923 when he published locally *Out of the Desert*, a history of El Paso. By a fortuitous coincidence, *American Mercury* editor H. L. Mencken—even then one of America's most influential critics— took notice of the obscure book and lauded it and its author in his New York based magazine. It was the beginning of a headlong, two-decade writing career that brought White to the attention of the *New York Times* and *Collier's* magazine and which resulted in nine books,* some 140 magazine articles, and countless newspaper pieces.

White died on December 7, 1946, in the midst of work on his book *Western Trails*, the half-finished manuscript of which is in the University of Texas-El Paso archives.

H. L. Mencken was born in Baltimore just a year after White and was also the son of a prominent family—of cigar-makers. He began his writing career early, however, and published not only a volume of fugitive verse at a young age but also sound critical works on George Bernard Shaw and Friedrich Nietzsche. Mencken was really a lifelong newspaperman, however, and the bulk of his writing (outside his marvelous and lively philological study, *The American Language*, and his memorable three-volume autobiography) is made up of transient, pugnacious pieces on the passing scene. As a wit and idol smasher he was an American original and as a magazine editor and critic he encouraged such struggling writers as Theodore Dreiser, Sinclair Lewis, Willa Cather, Edna Ferber, and an impressive list of others.

Meneken died in 1956 after a long illness.

The Mencken-to-White letters on file at University of Texas-El Paso can be divided into three rough categories: those of general wry comment by the Sage of Baltimore on sundry topics, those dealing directly with White's contributions to *The American Mercury*, and letters of hypochondria. Mencken was a notorious hypochondriac with a massive, if sometimes faulty, knowledge of anatomy, physiology and pathology. Particularly pathology.

In one brief note to White, he wrote: "I surely hope the chiropractors fetched all of the polyps. I suppose you know that they are a sign of advancing senility. If a man reached 100 years, so I hear, he would be one solid polyp."

And later: "I surely hope the erysipelas is completely well, it is a great nuisance. My Uncle Wolfgang had it in 1892, and within six months thereafter had got converted to Swedenborgianism, married a widow who turned out to be bankrupt, and lost $200 playing faro."

On another occasion, Mencken wrote White:

> Lent damn near wrecked me this year. My spiritual advisor put me on a diet that was really brutal. Worse, I discovered on Easter Sunday that he had done so in violation of canon law, Article XX-A of which provides that men above 60 shall have all the privileges of pregnant women. You are still a long way from that age, but nevertheless, I advise you seriously against the practice of pious rigors.

Almost all of Mencken's letters to White are undated, short (only one runs past a single large-margin page of typing), punchy, and to the point. He was as miserly with words as he was lavish with bombast and exaggeration. As editor of the *Mercury* he developed an uncannily diplomatic method of rejecting manuscripts. He did so perfunctorily, but let the writer know his efforts were appreciated. He suggested revision and often asked for another submission, on another subject. And too, he never forgot a promised article:

> Dear White: What has become of the treatise on boozing etiquette in the Southwest? I begin to pant for it.
>
> Sincerely,
> Mencken

On a manuscript of White's accepted by the editor, Mencken wrote: "I like the piece very much, and am sending it to our genial printer at once. He will forward a proof to you anon and, at about the same time, you will receive an insult from our cashier."

Upon receiving a suggestion from White on a possible article about Wild Bill Hickok, Mencken replied: "I'll certainly be delighted to see your treatise on Wild Bill. If any American deserves proper embalming, he is that man."

And, two years later, this reminder: "Why don't you do a straight piece on Hickok? Certainly there be a dozen in him. His beginnings, true enough, were more or less accidental, but certainly he showed plenty of talent later on."

On a rejected manuscript of White's, Mencken wrote:

> I wish I could take this very amusing piece, but at the moment, I have a number of other tales and articles dealing with ladies of joy in type, and it would be imprudent of me to buy another before working some of them off.
>
> Haven't you unearthed a new lot of rich and racy Southwestern characters? I'd certainly like to get you back into *The American Mercury.*

And, on a submitted article with an unsatisfactory title, Mencken wrote: "As I read the glorious deeds of Quantrill, it seems to me that his simple name is too banal a title for his story. What do you say to 'Buckets of Blood'? I think it would be swell."

"Swell" and "grand" were favorite Mencken words for he imagined they were widely used among the Babbitt-type Americans he roundly loathed. Thus he wrote White in 1942: "My brother and I had a grand time reading the autobiography. It is a really swell book, and I hope it is doing well in the trade. I have been ill twice since Christmas and still feel somewhat rocky, but nevertheless less manage to get down a reasonable amount of malt liquor."

Some of the letters are simply exchanges on a variety of subjects that were mutually amusing to the writers. Religion in all its many forms was a source of delight for both Mencken and White. In one instance, Mencken wrote:

> The fact that you were unaware that God is an Elk really amazes me. I thought it was known to every American schoolboy. He is also a leading Moose, and was once a candidate for Supreme Worthy Archon of the Knights of Phythias.

I am sending your name to the chief body-snatcher of the International Correspondence School.

A comment on the weather was never inappropriate: "God knows I envy you your trip into the Southwest. The temperature here in Baltimore today is 25 degrees and a high wind is blowing. I am like the hippopotamus, an essentially tropical animal, and the winter always reduces me to tears."

And a fraud or hoax always provided a lever for comment: "I suppose you have heard of the outbreak of witchcraft which now afflicts Maryland. Cattle are dying in the fields, peoples' covers are pulled off them at night, and children are coming down with all sorts of mysterious bellyaches. The papers print nothing of it, but the city is all agog."

In response to White's announcement of his newest book, *Texas, an Informal Biography*, Mencken, upon receiving a copy of it, wrote:

> The book came in safely this morning and I hope to tackle it within the next few days. You are precisely the man to do a history of Texas, and I am looking forward to the reading of it with the pleasantest anticipations. I only hope that you make it clear that the Texan are diligent students of the Holy Scriptures and unfailing supporters of Christian democracy."

In 1942, Dr. Julian Boyd, librarian at Princeton University, began collecting letters of Mencken's from the Baltimorean's legion of correspondents. Dr. Boyd's intention was to publish a volume of the letters and Mencken supported the project, going so far as to write several people to assure them "that if you have any such things in your files, and he writes to you, he may be trusted reasonably."

In reply, White answered Mencken to say he would be glad to cooperate "in the plan to erect a monument to you, made with bricks of your own fashioning, that you can contemplate while you are still alive."

In another paragraph White said, "And how about a stained glass window for you in a Baptist Cathedral? Perhaps I can arrange it for you. I did it once for an old Texas cow chief and he lived to enjoy it for more than thirty years afterwards."

To this Mencken shot back:

> There is a stained glass window to me in one of the Baltimore breweries. I have left instructions that my ashes are to be deposited immediately under it. It is my hope that this window will attract many pious tourists to Baltimore in the years to come.

White followed up on his promise, not to erect another stained-glass window, but to cooperate on the Boyd project and in the University of Texas-El Paso archives is his letter in answer to Dr. Boyd's plea for Menckeniana. White's reply gives insight into the relationship of the two men that is to be found nowhere else:

> Am sorry that the most interesting and stimulating of his letters to me—those that I received in 1923 and 1924 while I was living in El Paso, Texas—are missing. As I state in my last book, *The Autobiography of a Durable Sinner*, instead of being properly ashamed of it, Mencken bragged editorially in *The American Mercury* that he had discovered me. He did. He dragged me from obscurity into the columns of his magazine; gave me a very swift and dizzy correspondence course in how to write—at times he was even openly insulting about it—and then when I had graduated, and had been offered a job on the *New York Times*, he tried his best to dissuade me from accepting and coming back East to live in the anus of the world.

Three years later Mencken told White that Dr. Boyd had undertaken the immense task of editing the papers of Thomas Jefferson and that the letter volume had been shelved. It wasn't until 1961 that a collection of Mencken's letters was published (*Letters of H. L. Mencken*, selected and annotated by Guy J. Forgue, Alfred A. Knopf, N.Y.) and even then the letters to White were not included.

Thus the Mencken-White file in the University of Texas-El Paso archives is an original testimonial of friendship between two extraordinary men—kindred spirits without doubt.

It is difficult to resist quoting Mencken's self-composed epitaph, for it could apply to both himself and Owen White: "If, after I depart this vale, you ever remember me and have thought to please my ghost, forgive some sinner and wink your eye at some homely girl."

*Among which are *Just Me and Other Poems, Them Was the Days, Trigger Fingers, Lead & Likker, My Texas 'Tis of Thee, The Autobiography of a Durable Sinner*, and *Texas, an Informal Biography*. ★

From *The Calamity Papers: Western Myths and Cold Cases:* The White Sands Mystery

Albert Jennings Fountain had enemies and knew who they were when on a late-January morning in 1896 he stepped out of his big adobe home in Las Cruces, New Mexico Territory, and loaded up his buckboard.

Inside the house, his wife, Mariana, bundled up their nine-year-old son Henry who was accompanying Fountain to court in Lincoln. She had suggested Henry go along for company despite the fact that Albert had received death threats over his relentless pursuit of cattle thieves. Mariana told her friends that nobody would harm her husband while a child was with him.

The colonel, as he liked to be called, was a tall, fit, blue-eyed man of substance and influence. The son of a sea captain, he was born on Staten Island in 1838 and educated at Columbia College. In his footloose teens he traveled to California, read law, and was admitted to state bar in 1861. That year he enlisted in the First California Infantry Volunteers and advanced from private to colonel in the regiment as it marched from San Diego and up to the Rio Grande as part of the Union's occupation force in New Mexico and Arizona Territories.

After the end of the Civil War, Fountain, now married, moved to La Mesilla, New Mexico Territory, forty miles north of El Paso, in 1874. There, on the east bank of the Rio Grande he built a fine adobe home, established a law practice and campaigned against the corrupt legislature in Santa Fé and the cattle thieves infesting the Mesilla Valley.

In the spring of 1881 Fountain was appointed as defense attorney for Henry McCarty, known by the alias William "Billy the Kid" Bonney, when the outlaw was tried for several murders in a makeshift courtroom in La Mesilla. Despite a spirited effort, the Kid was convicted, delivered to the custody of Lincoln County sheriff Pat Garrett and sentenced to hang.

By the time Fountain moved his family to the frontier town of Las Cruces in 1885, he had built a reputation as the finest trial attorney and most powerful Republican politician in southern New Mexico. In November 1888, he was elected to a seat in the Territorial Legislature and later became Speaker of the House.

He collected enemies, among which none was more implacable in his hostility to Fountain than another Albert, Albert Bacon Fall. This Kentuckian, born in 1861, had drifted to Texas as a young man, labored by day as a mucker in the silver mines in the Black Range foothills while reading law books at night. In 1887, he and his wife and children moved to Las Cruces where he opened a legal practice.

The two Alberts were at loggerheads from the start. Fall, as fierce a Democrat as Fountain was a Republican, began organizing his party in Doña Ana County and in 1893 won an appointment as judge of the Third Judicial District that included Las Cruces. This political plum elicited from Fountain a volley of frontier slander in which he described Fall as "an absconding debtor from Texas" and a "ward politician."

Among Fall's first acts as judge was to appoint some cronies, men who had served as his political bodyguard, as deputy U.S. marshals. These men, all suspected cattle rustlers, were Oliver Milton Lee, James Gililland, and William McNew.

Lee was a native Texan who migrated to New Mexico in 1884 in search of open range country. He set up his first cattle spread on the western slopes of the Sacramento Mountains in Doña Ana County, and soon acquired other outfits west of Las Cruces. A handsome, steely-eyed cowman with a brushy soup-strainer moustache, he was a staunch Democrat and among Albert Fall's closest confidantes. His rancher friend Eugene Manlove Rhodes, later an acclaimed New Mexico author, claimed Lee had killed at least eight men while carving out his cattle kingdom.

McNew and Gililland were leathery, grim-faced drifters who had taken up land near Oliver Lee's and worked for him. Both men were said to be artists with the "running iron"—the iron rod used by rustlers to change or deface brands.

After Fountain returned from Santa Fé after his defeat in 1890 he served as attorney for the Southeastern New Mexico Stock Growers' Association and wrote, spoke, and lobbied for new laws and stronger enforcement of existing ones to protect stockmen from rustlers. He often accused Albert B. Fall of gathering around him a number of dubious characters, Oliver Lee chief among them, suspected of thieving cattle from their neighbors.

The two Alberts were now embarked on a two-year collision course, the pivotal point reached when Fountain, his eight-year-old son Henry by his side, drove his buckboard from Las Cruces to Lincoln.

There, with his satchel stuffed with depositions and boilerplate documents, he presented the grand jury the evidence that resulted in 32 indictments, 17 of them for crimes against members of the stock association he was representing. Named in several of the indictments, for "larceny of cattle" and "defacing brands," were ranchman Oliver Lee and two of his cowboys, James R. Gililland and William H. McNew.

***

The grand jury work was but a step toward a jury trial and Fountain was in no mood to celebrate when he collected his son from the home of the friends, loaded the buckboard again, and departed Lincoln on January 30, 1896. He drove the eighteen miles to the Apache Agency at Mescalero and there an Apache friend presented Henry a little pinto mare.

Father and son set out again on the morning of January 31, the pony tethered to the rear of the light rig. Before they reached the town of Tularosa, when Fountain began to notice that some of the wayfarers on the road appeared to be shadowing him, he began carrying his Winchester across his lap.

At a stagecoach station about mid-way between La Luz and the southern end of the White Sands, Fountain paid the customary twenty-five cents per head to feed and water his horses and talked to stage driver Antonio Rey.

Fountain said that some riders had been trailing him all day and, "If they're after me, they'll get me sooner or later and I'm not going to show the white feather. I'll go on."

In the late afternoon of February 1, with Henry wrapped in blankets in the seat next to him, Fountain pulled his team to a stop at a point about three miles east of Chalk Hill, a small, cactus and brush-covered ridge at the southern end of the Sands. There he had a brief conversation with Saturnino Barilla, another mail stage driver who pointed out three riders off in the distance and told Fountain that he should come back with him to Luna's Well. The colonel said he had to be in Silver City on Monday and that Henry was "under the weather" with a cold, so he drove on.

It was very cold with a keen wind blowing as the buckboard bounced down the road toward Chalk Hill.

***

Mariana Fountain expected her husband and son home in the evening of February 1, and waited with growing fear all weekend, her family gathered around her. Then, at sundown on the 2nd, stage driver Barilla came to the house and said that he had last seen the judge and the boy a short distance from Chalk Hill on Saturday afternoon, only a few hours' drive from Las Cruces. Barilla said he was worried because the colonel had been followed by three riders.

Barilla's news galvanized Fountain's sons Albert, Jr., and Jack, and together with some neighboring friends they formed up a search party and rode out to San Augustín Pass and down the long slope to Chalk Hill where they made camp. Barilla sounded the alarm in Las Cruces and within hours a posse rode out to camp with the Fountain sons and awaited daybreak.

At first light on Monday, February 3, the searchers found the tracks of three horses and followed them up an old road where, about twelve miles east of Chalk Hill, they came upon the colonel's buckboard. His cartridge belt lay on the seat, his cravat was tangled in the spokes of a wheel, his dispatch box had been opened and its papers scattered. There were pieces of harness laying around, a broken whiskey bottle, tracks of a child's shoe, the imprint of blanket on the sand. Everything else was missing: Fountain's Winchester and cartridges, the horses, water, food, spare clothing.

The volunteers followed five sets of horse tracks toward the mountains and found a camp where a big fire had been built. They found cans, sticks used to cook meat, boot tracks, cigarette papers. Not far from the camp there were pony tracks headed north (Henry's gift mare was later found to have wandered back to Luna's Well), and hoof-prints of horses headed for Dog Canyon, location of one of Oliver Lee's ranches.

News of the disappearances swirled through the territory like a desert dust devil. "Murder!" in huge type was bannered on page one of the *Albuquerque Daily Citizen* on February 4 and in smaller print, "Col. Fountain of Las Cruces is missing. He was probably murdered by cattle thieves." The *Santa Fé New Mexican* joined in, calling for the discovery and "adequate punishment of the cruel and cowardly perpetrators of this awful crime."

A total of $20,000 in reward money was accumulated from the governor's office, stock growers' associations, Doña Ana County commissioners, and various Masonic Lodges.

Republicans accepted the wide-spread rumor that Oliver Lee, with his cowboys McNew and Gililland, were the probable culprits.

***

Despite the animosity toward him held in many quarters of the territory, Pat Garrett was called out of retirement to look into the Fountain case. The ex-lawman, then scratching a living on his farm in Uvalde County, Texas, agreed to Governor William T. Thornton's proposal, no doubt delighted to escape the drudgery of his patch of hardscrabble land and houseful of children.

He arrived in Santa Fé on March 3, 1896, and after a conference with the governor, moved on to Las Cruces where he instantly centered his investigation on Albert B. Fall and Fall's disciples, Lee, Gililland, and McNew.

The investigation occupied a year, then, on April 3, 1897, Garrett appeared before a district court judge asking for bench warrants for the arrests of Lee, McNew, Gililland, and another of Lee's employees, Bill Carr as "the parties who murdered Colonel Albert J. Fountain and his son, Henry Fountain."

While McNew was jailed and Carr released for lack of evidence, Garrett and four deputies rode out on July 11 the 40 miles east to Lee's Wildy Well spread. They arrived at daybreak, tied their horses some distance away and walked toward the flat-roofed ranch house, guns drawn.

What happened next remains disputed but it appears that Lee and Gililland were spotted sleeping atop the house and Garrett and deputy Kent Kearney, a cowboy and former schoolteacher from La Luz, climbed to the roof from the adjacent wagon shed. When they reached the roof parapet, Kearney yelled to the fugitives to throw up their hands. The deputy may have seen, or imagined, one of the men reaching for a gun and so fired a shot in their general direction. Oliver Lee then grabbed his rifle and shot Kearney off the roof, Garrett falling with him, unharmed.

After more shots were exchanged, Lee yelled, "You're a hell of a lot of fellows to order a man to throw up his hands and shoot at the same time."

After some loud conversation, Lee said he would come in to Las Cruces and surrender but he did not trust Garrett or his men to escort him to town.

Kent Kearney died of his wounds the next day and Lee and Gililland were charged with his murder as well as for the Fountain killings. However, while the grand jury was handing down its indictments the two accused men went "on the dodge."

After spending time in San Antonio, Texas, Lee returned to the Tularosa Valley early in 1899 and with Gililland and McNew agreed to surrender to District Judge Frank Wilson Parker in Las Cruces. On March 13, 1899, the three men were escorted to the jail in Socorro, a town on the southern edge of the Jornado del Muerto, to await trial.

The evidence against them was flimsy: the tracks leading from the Chalk Hill area toward Lee's Wildy Well ranch and the well-known rancor between Fountain, Lee, and his cohorts.

In April, Judge Parker convened his court and dismissed the charges against McNew for lack of evidence.

***

The trial opened on May 26, 1899, in Hillsboro, a mining town of 200 population on the eastern slope of the Black Range, with Judge Parker announcing, "Gentlemen coming into court will kindly leave their guns outside."

District Attorney Richmond P. Barnes of Silver City led the prosecution, assisted by two prominent Republicans who volunteered to serve without pay. Defending Lee and Gililland were Albert Bacon Fall of Las Cruces and two other eminent territorial lawyers.

The prosecution fared poorly from the outset. Fifteen of its witnesses failed to appear and many of the others offered confusing and unconvincing testimony. Much was expected of Pat Garrett's testimony but it too fell flat, too heavily tinged by his hatred of Fall, Lee and the others.

When the prosecution rested the defense proceeded to call a string of witnesses (including Lee's sunbonneted mother), all of whom testified that Oliver was at home on the fateful Saturday when Fountain and his son were alleged to have met foul play.

At 11:30 P.M. on June 12, after eighteen days of testimony, the case was handed to the jury. Eight minutes later they returned with their verdict: "Not guilty" for both Lee and Gililland.

Judge Parker ordered the defendants to be held over for the September term of court to stand trial for the killing of Deputy Kearney at Wildy Well on July 12, 1898, but the indictment was later dismissed.

***

Albert Fall quit the Democratic Party in 1902, served as U. S. Senator and in 1921 was selected as Secretary of the Interior in the Warren Harding administration. He resigned the office two years later but returned to Washington under subpoena when a congressional investigation revealed that he had leased government oil lands at Teapot Dome, Wyoming, and Elk Hills, California, to two business associates and had accepted a $100,000 payoff from one of them. He was released from prison in 1932 and died in an El Paso hospital in November 1944, at the age of eighty-three.

Oliver Lee eventually owned and operated a considerable ranching empire and was elected to the New Mexico State Senate in 1922. He died in Alamogordo in 1941.

In 1903, Jim Gililland built a successful cattle ranch in the San Andrés Mountains and operated it for thirty-seven years before retiring. He died in August, 1946.

Bill McNew died after a stroke in June, 1937.

None of the three ever spoke, publicly at least, about the Fountain case.

***

Searches have gone on periodically for well over a century but no remains of the Fountains, father or son, have ever been found.

At the Masonic Cemetery in Las Cruces, in Section A, Block 12, Lot 18-19, there is a cenotaph thus inscribed:

IN MEMORY OF
ALBERT J.
FOUNTAIN
AND
SON, HENRY,
WHO DISAPPEARED
FEB. 1, 1896

The real graves, of course, are somewhere under the White Sands. ★

Charles Leland Sonnichsen

Charles Leland Sonnichsen (1901-1991) was born in Fonda, Iowa, and raised in Minnesota. He earned his B.A. from the University of Minnesota in 1924, his M.A. from Harvard in 1927, and then taught English at the Carnegie Institute of Technology in Pittsburgh. After two years, he returned to Harvard and earned his Ph.D. in English Philology. "At that time Harvard offered no Ph.D. in English or American Literature," Sonnichsen recalled, "the degree was in English Philology, like it or not, and that was the way we had to go, though few of us wanted to make a career out of the Anglo-Saxon infinitive." The literature courses that Sonnichsen did take concentrated on English literature, particularly of the seventeenth and eighteenth centuries. Graduating in the middle of the Depression, when faculty positions were scarce, Sonnichsen accepted a summer teaching position at the Texas College of Mines, now the University of Texas at El Paso, but stayed on to become department chair of English from 1933-1960, then graduate dean. The focus of Sonnichsen's scholarship turned to regional history when he was informed by then college president John G. Barry that he would teach a course in Southwestern Literature. Barry was influenced by the writings of J. Frank Dobie and his course "Life and Literature of the Southwest" at the University of Texas at Austin. Dobie had originally suggested the course title "Literature of the Southwest," but was told there was no such thing. "You may deny that there is literature here," he said, "but you can hardly deny that there is life." Following the footsteps of Dobie, Sonnichsen became a self-described "grassroots historian," blazing the trail in Southwest lore and literature.

Author of numerous articles and reviews, he is also the author of thirty-four books including: *Billy King's Tombstone*; *I'll Die Before I'll Run*; *Roy Bean: Law West of the Pecos*; *Tularosa: Last of the Frontier West*; the two volume *Pass of the North*; *The Texas Feuds*; *The El Paso Salt War*; *From Hopalong to Hud*; and *Pilgrim in the Sun*. *Arizona Humoresque* and *Final Harvest* were published posthumously. He was past president of Western Writers of America, a member of the Texas Institute of Letters and recipient of numerous awards including the 1988 Lon Tinkle Lifetime Achievement Award from the Texas Institute of Letters. Named professor emeritus at UTEP at his retirement in 1972, he began a new career at the age of seventy-one when he moved to Tucson, Arizona, and became senior editor for the *Journal of Arizona History*. All who knew him, including a loyal legion of students, called him "Doc." His enduring legacy, besides his impressive body of work, is the people he inspired to become writers, historians and scholars.

From *Pilgrim in the Sun: A Southwestern Omnibus*: Six Shooter Capital

Nine years have gone by since the railroad opened El Paso to the world and brought the world to El Paso. It is 1890 now, and the population is over 10,000. The City of Virtue is flourishing with churches and schools, social clubs, and musical organizations. The City of Vice is doing just as well, and El Paso is known far and wide as "The Monte Carlo of the United States."[1]

The entire Southwest is booming. The ranges of New Mexico and Arizona have been stocked with Texas cattle; miners are swarming over the mountains; speculators move in and out of Mexico; and El Paso is their good-time town. Whenever anybody has a dollar in his pocket, says Owen White, "he heads hell-bent to El Paso to get rid of it."[2]

Thus there is a market for all the diversions El Paso can invent or import. These include, on the one hand, such comparatively harmless institutions as baseball, bicycle racing, boxing, cockfighting and horse racing, and on the other, gambling and gunfighting. They all are interesting to the sporting world, and the barrooms serve as centers for information, debate, and the placing of bets.

The presence of Juárez across the river is a determining factor in the situation. A sport who gets in trouble on our side takes a few quick steps and is safe on the other, and it works the same way in Mexico. The availability of this escape hatch is instrumental in attracting to the border an extraordinary group of gunfighters and fast-draw artists, some on one side of the law and some on the other, who add to our other distinctions the title of Six-Shooter Capital of the Southwest. Some people think it ought to be our pride and joy that for a few years we ranked as a murder metropolis with Fort Griffin and Dodge City, Tombstone and Tonopah.

The palmy days of the gunfighters were the middle nineties, but the breed was not disposed of finally for another ten years.

The world of the girls, gunmen, and gamblers, we should add, was on the whole self-contained. The roughs broke up no Sunday School picnics at Rand's Grove, and they mostly killed each other. As a result every survivor from those times insists that El Paso was a more secure and orderly place in the days of John Wesley Hardin than it is today. "Women could go anywhere then and be perfectly safe," says Page Kemp. "I wouldn't let my wife go downtown alone at night now."[3]

Outside El Paso as well as inside, the nineties were years of violence. Frontier conditions died out slowly, and during this time they were kept alive by gangs of thieves and rustlers who flourished in the rough country above and below town. North of the Pass toward Canutillo a band of home-grown outlaws operated out of a river-bottom *bosque* or tangled thicket. Below town a larger *bosque*, nearly ten miles long and as much as five miles wide, sheltered several hundred suspicious characters who protected each other and defied the law.

This latter stronghold was known as "The Island." In 1854 the river moved several miles north and east. The old bed was dry, except during flood times, but occasionally both channels were full of water, giving the Island its name. The International Boundary ran through the brush and cottonwood groves on the western side but the whole area was a sort of no-man's land, inhabited by people who claimed citizenship in either country as occasion warranted and who flouted the authorities of both.

It was said that by keeping to the brush and avoiding the highways, a native of either *bosque* could arrive at the other without being seen.[4]

The men who lived in the north *bosque* had a fine little rustling business going. In a canyon high up on the west side of Mount Franklin they owned a rock corral far removed from prying eyes where they could hold a few head of stock. Their favorite trick was to drop across the crest of the mountain, steal a couple of cows from one of the ranches on the east side, and drive them back through a pass so stony that trailing was impossible. This gap is still called Smuggler's Pass, though few of us know why.[5]

In 1890 the killing of Charlie Fusselman threw a spotlight on these activities. A group of thieves from the lower *bosque* on their way to the upper refuge passed the present site of Fort Bliss (then called "the Mesa"), headed for the Pass, and picked up several horses belonging to John Barnes at Mundy's Spring. Barnes got on their trail almost immediately and actually caught up with them—something he had apparently not counted on, for he was unarmed. When a "villainous looking Mexican" confronted him in the canyon leading to the Pass, he backed off and went to El Paso for help.[6]

Within a very short time he was back on the trail with two companions, policeman George Herold and Deputy United States Marshal Charles H. Fusselman of Presidio. Fusselman was in town to attend court and had time on his hands.

For some reason, perhaps a sublime self-confidence, the rustlers had gone into camp in the canyon to which Barnes had trailed them. It was said that the Bosque gangs had never lost a fight and would take on anybody from either side of the river.[7] They did put out a sentry who nodded at the wrong moment and was taken by surprise as the three officers moved cautiously up the canyon. He looked up to see three pistols pointed at his belt buckle, threw up his hands, and went meekly along. They recognized him as a well-known thief named Ysidro Pasos.

The main body of the outlaws was only a short distance away. Topping a rise, the little posse came suddenly and unexpectedly upon them. Lead began to fly at once. At the first fire Fusselman was shot off his horse and Herold and Barnes left the canyon fast, some eight or ten outlaws after them.

A few hours later Deputy U. S. Marshal Bob Ross led a ten-man squad into the hills and found Fusselman lying where he fell, shot through the neck. Well aware that they would be pursued in force this time, the thieves had decamped, leaving eighteen horses, two cows, a calf, a whole beef, and a bucket of tortillas, The officers picked up their trail on the other side of the Pass and followed them to the heavy brush along the river where the rustlers were at home and the pursuers were not. The trail led eventually to the Mexican border, and it was obvious that the fugitives intended to circle Juárez and take refuge in the lower *bosque* on the Island.[8]

No doubt existed in anybody's mind as to who was responsible for Fusselman's death. Herold and Barnes had seen a notorious outlaw named Geronimo Parra fire his rifle twice at the dead man. It took ten years to bring Parra to justice, and the man who did it was Captain John R. Hughes, a corporal when Fusselman was killed. He finally located the man in the New Mexico penitentiary but was unable to get him out until he ran down a fugitive in Texas who was wanted in Las Cruces by Sheriff Pat Garrett. According to the Captain's biographer, a deal was arranged and late in 1899 Hughes brought Parra back to El Paso, where he was tried and sentenced to hang.[9]

The story of that hanging, on January 6, 1900, is a gruesome chapter in our history. On their way to execution in the old El Paso jail, Parra and a companion named Flores whipped out improvised daggers and nearly cleaned out the El Paso Police force before the sentence was finally carried out.[10]

The canyon where Charlie Fusselman lost his life is still called Fusselman Canyon. The route of the new trans-mountain highway runs near the place where he fell.

This regrettable episode slowed the activities of the Bosque gangs for a while, but they were soon doing business as usual. The Island group was particularly troublesome. The nucleus was a family named Olguín, sons and grandsons of old Jesús-Maria Olguín[11] who in his youth had been a first-class border man himself but was now too old to keep up with his hard-riding sons.[12] During the spring of 1893 these outlaws became so troublesome that a determined effort was made to stop them. Sebastian Olguín got ten years for horse stealing; Prisciliano (sixteen years old) was sentenced to three years in the State Reformatory for stealing a cow.[13] This left Severo, Antonio, and old Jesús-Maria still at large. Severo, the most dangerous of the lot, was under indictment but still free and living in the midst of some three hundred friends and supporters. This situation was bad enough to call for drastic action, and in June, 1893, a detachment of Rangers prepared to take on the Island gang in a finish fight.

Captain Frank Jones knew what he was getting into and told the Adjutant General before he left Alpine that he would need manpower. "There must be fully 50 in the gang," he said, "and they are well organized too. They are part of the mob who murdered Howard some years ago." A small force, he thought, would "simply be murdered."[14]

Jones was a good man to take along. Thirty-six years old, better educated than most of his group, he was a brave officer and a good leader. He had been married for about a year to a daughter of the famous Ranger and peace officer Colonel George W. Baylor.[15] His presence was a great reassurance to the harried lawmen of the Valley when he went into camp with his men at Ysleta.

About the time of his arrival, as if to let the Rangers know what they had to contend with, Severo Olguín and some of his men got drunk at the little Mexican town of Guadalupe, killed one citizen, wounded three more, and rode away, unscathed and unpursued, to their headquarters at a place called Tres Jacales (Three Shacks) on the Island.[16] The news came by some branch of the grapevine to Deputy Sheriff Ed Bryant at El Paso that Severo had hunted his hole, and Bryant sent word to Captain Jones that he was ready to move. The next day, June 29, Bryant and Jones with four Rangers—Corporal Karl Kirchner, Privates E. D. Aten, J. W. Saunders and F. F. Tucker—moved out of Ysleta and stopped for the night at the old campground below Fabens. At daybreak on the thirtieth they struck out through the brush for the heart of the Island. A guide took them to the Olguín ranch, where they found nobody at home. Turning northward, they fell into a trail that followed, roughly, the International Boundary until their guide admitted that he was lost. Jones gave the order to turn back.[17]

They chose a path which seemed to run eastward toward Clint, Texas. Jones and Tucker were in the lead, Alden and Saunders, with the packmule, followed.

As they approached a tiny Mexican village, two men on horseback turned into the road and came to meet them. Realizing what they were running into, the men whirled their horses and dashed for the village with Jones and Tucker in hot pursuit. The road rounded a sharp corner at the entrance to the settlement, and when the two Rangers made the turn, they saw their quarry take shelter behind one of the houses. Immediately rifle fire burst from doors and windows.

What followed happened faster than it can be told. Tucker was off his horse first, kneeling in the road and blasting away at the hidden assailants. Before Jones could get both feet on he ground, he was hit in the thigh and a few seconds later received a bad wound in the neck.

"Are you hurt, Captain?" Tucker inquired.

"Yes, shot all to pieces."[18]

Now the other two Rangers, who had been held back by the pack mule, came charging around the curve so fast they could not stop at once. The fire from the houses grew more intense as they turned around and came back. Jones, at the point of death, told them to take cover, and when they saw he was gone, they did so, working their way through the brush and eventually making their way to Clint, where Kirchner wired El Paso for help.

Next day Sheriff F. B. Simmons and a posse demanded the body of the dead Captain, but got nowhere until the Mexican authorities were asked to help. Lieutenant Rafael García Martínez, the Juárez *jefe político*, rode with Simmons down the Mexican side of the border with a Mexican police escort. They had better luck than they expected, for not only did they bring home the body of Captain Jones, they met three members of the gang making their way out of the brush and rounded them up without a fight. These turned out to be Jesús-Maria Olguín and his sons Severo and Antonio, undoubtedly on their way to the upper *bosque*. Captain Jones had got Severo in the shoulder and Antonio in the hand. The brothers might not have been so easy to corral had they not been disabled. They wound up in the Juárez jail, but what happened to them after that we do not know.[19]

It is worth noting that a member of Simmons' posse was George Scarborough, a preacher's son turned cowboy and peace officer from the Fort Griffin country[20] who was destined to play a prominent role in El Paso's six-shooter history. Another familiar name was affixed to a telegram which came to the sheriff after his first trip to the Island: "Arriving this morning with a posse. United States Deputy Marshal Bass Outlaw, Alpine, Texas."[21]

Two results of this affair were the erection of a monument to the memory of Captain Jones in 1938 at the place of his death and the appointment of John H. Hughes, a truly great Ranger, as his successor.

The Bosque gangs were by no means the only outlaw organization in the area. The tide of violence and crime had been rising in New Mexico and West Texas since the eighties, partly, at least, as a result of a migration from farther east. Rain had fallen on the arid slopes and swales of the Tularosa and Three

Rivers country for several years and the grass was thick and high—thick, at least, for that area—and thousands of cattle were moved in to take advantage of it. The owners of these herds brought their own codes with them. They quarreled among themselves and with the people already on the ground, and things went from bad to worse. Little ranchers fought big ranchers. Cattlemen fell out with town men. And rustling became a way of life.

The Fountain murder case—the disappearance of Colonel A. J. Fountain and his little son Henry near the White Sands on February 2, 1896—grew out of these conditions,[22] and many another life had to be lost before the wild men were tamed. The shootings which made El Paso notorious in the middle nineties, however, were not battles for law and order. They involved the elimination of each other by more-or-less professional killers.

This brings up the case of Uncle John Selman, a once-notorious pistol wielder whose various lives and exploits have only recently been fully unraveled.[23] His youth and early manhood were spent in Shackleford County near Fort Griffin. There he became involved with a plausible and popular character named John Lam who married into the county's most prominent family and was for a while sheriff. When his killing and rustling activities came to light and he was jailed, a party of vigilantes, some of them supposedly his relatives by marriage, walked in and executed him. Selman, his lieutenant, was on the wanted list but fled in time.[24]

A short time later he joined a band of itinerant desperadoes in New Mexico who were murdering and stealing under cover of the confusion caused by the Lincoln County War.[25] The Rangers finally caught up with him and brought him back to his home county to stand trial. His former neighbors asked only to be rid of him, however, and he was encouraged to "escape." He went to Mexico with his second wife and stayed several years. When he thought the heat was off, he came back to the United States and after some adventures in the Magdalena country of New Mexico he became a citizen of El Paso.[26]

By now he was somewhat mellowed, as became his graying hair, and he decided to get on the right side of the law. This meant honest toil, and to make ends meet he worked for the American Smelting and Refining Company until 1889. After that he gathered cattle in the Sacramento Mountains, worked for the Mexican Central Railroad, bounced undesirables out of the Wigwam Saloon, and chased horse thieves. His activities in running down rustlers resulted in an attack on the dark streets of El Paso which laid him up for months and almost cost him his life.[27]

He finally found a place on the regular police force in 1892 when he ran for the office of constable and, to everybody's surprise, beat Republican E. C. Jones.[28] By this time he was a well-known figure in the little border town, and most people thought of him kindly although his connections were mostly among the sporting element, his best friend being Jim Burns, proprietor of the Red Light Dance Hall and dealer in liquor, sex, and political influence. John's son tells how he and his father helped Jim round up and "influence" Mexican voters who were herded to the polls to vote for the Democrats.[29] Not that the Republicans were any better, for both parties bought as many illegal votes as they could. It was just that the Democrats were able to round up more of them.

So old John became a constable in 1892, was reelected in 1894, and was still in office in 1896 when he had his rendezvous with destiny.[30] In the meantime he was probably the hardest working officer El Paso ever had. The dockets show that he was constantly bringing offenders before the courts for offenses of all types.[31] His son tells of various occasions when would-be bad men challenged him unsuccessfully, and the natural conclusion is that he showed considerable talent and energy in carrying out his duties.

The Bass Outlaw affair clinched John's reputation as a handy man with a gun, but he paid a high price for his status.

Outlaw was one of those incredible characters produced by frontier conditions. Born supposedly in Georgia, he had a good family background and a good education. He was short (about five feet four) but wiry and well coordinated, a good athlete and a famous pistol shot. He had a rather refined-looking face with delicate features and a receding chin—a face that did not go with the rest of him—symbolic, perhaps, of the fact that he was a very much mixed-up young man.

The stories say that he left his home state because he had killed somebody. In 1885 he became a member of Company E of the Texas Rangers, later transferred to Company D, attained the rank of sergeant, and in the early nineties was stationed at Alpine under Captain Frank Jones.[32] Captain Jones was not happy with him because of his one fatal flaw. A likable, friendly, winning fellow most of the time, he became a wild man, dangerous to friends as well as foes, when he was drunk. And he got drunk with increasing frequency as time went on. After repeated warnings, Captain Jones dismissed him from the Ranger Service for being intoxicated while on duty.[33]

Bass's friends took care of that. He got an appointment as Deputy United States Marshal and was so popular that large numbers of Alpine citizens petitioned Marshal Dick Ware to keep him on duty there. Marshal Ware did so, with some misgivings.[34]

Bass was in and out of El Paso during these years, and his reputation as a fast man with a gun preceded him. Some of the most dangerous characters in town were afraid to bring him to a showdown. John Watts, for instance, the iron-headed colored man who ran a Negro house of prostitution on Overland Street, was understandably resentful when Bass ended an evening of revelry in June, 1892, in bed with Watts' white mistress. After thinking the matter over very carefully, Watts filed a complaint, but when Bass sobered up, he gave the woman back with great good will and all was as before.[35]

It is said that after a few such episodes as this the El Paso city authorities sometimes assigned a policeman just to watch over Bass when he honored the town with a visit.[36]

The climax came in April 1894, when he was back as a witness in a court case. Having considerable leisure time, he employed it in getting drunker and angrier than usual. He was unhappy with Marshal Dick Ware who, he thought, had allowed another deputy United States Marshal to enter his territory to serve papers and collect the fees. The more he drank, the more resentful he became. In this frame of mind he dropped in for a visit at Tillie Howard's place, where a girl named Ruby comforted him for a while and sent him out in a better frame of mind. On the street he met Selman and Frank Collinson, to whom he told his troubles, his anger reviving as he talked. When they suggested that he go to his room and sober up, he decided that he needed Ruby's therapeutic attentions once more, and back he went to Tillie's, Collinson and Selman keeping him company.[37]

As Frank and John sat chatting in the parlor, Bass wandered off toward the back of the house, and a few minutes later they heard a shot in the bathroom. Selman looked at his companion and remarked, "Bass has dropped his gun."[38]

At that moment Tillie herself came charging out of one of the downstairs rooms, headed for the rear entrance, and began blowing her police whistle—the normal procedure for a madam in distress. By the time Selman and Collinson reached the back door, Outlaw had caught up with her and was attempting to take her whistle away.

The first notes had caught the ear of a Texas Ranger named Joe McKittrick, or McKidrict as he spelled it (it was not his right name),[39] and he came running around the corner into the back yard as Selman emerged onto the porch.

"It was an accident," Joel Selman told him. "He's all right."

McKidrict was not satisfied. "Bass, why did you shoot?" he inquired. "You want some too?" Bass spat at him, and shot him through the head. As McKidrict fell, Bass put another bullet into his body.

Selman was in action by now. Pulling his gun, he jumped off the porch and went for Outlaw, who turned and fired at him point blank. They were so close together that Selman was blinded by the powder blast, which caught him directly in the eyes. The ball, fortunately for him, whistled past his ear. Reflex action brought his gun into position and he placed a bullet directly over Outlaw's heart—then he stood there holding his eyes with his left hand, unable to see a thing.

The incredible little ex-Ranger now showed the vitality that was in him. Mortally wounded and unable to raise his pistol above his waist, he got off two more shots, one striking Selman in the thigh, the other above the right knee. He still had strength to stagger around the house into the street, surrender to Ranger Frank McMahon, and walk into the Barnum Show Saloon, where Dr. Turner came to see him. He did not die until four hours later on a bed in the back room of the saloon. His last desperate question was, "Where are my friends?"[40]

No friend was there to answer him, but Alonzo Oden mourned his passing. "Bass Outlaw is dead. Bass, my friend, is gone," he wrote in his diary. "Bass, who was so brave and kind; who could laugh louder, ride longer, and cuss harder than the rest of us; and who could be more sympathetic, more tender, more patient than all of us when necessary."[41] Outlaw was undoubtedly the only one of his kind on record about whom such things were ever said, or could have been said.

Selman was tried for murder but of course came clear.[42] As a result of this episode, however, his vision was permanently impaired—he could hardly see at all at night, says his son—and he walked with a cane for the remaining two years of his life.[43]

Selman was only one of an impressive concentration of pistol men who made El Paso and Juárez their headquarters in the middle 90s. Jeff Milton, who already had a massive reputation in Arizona as a peace officer, became City Marshal during a brief flurry of reform activity in 1894. Deputy United States Marshal George Scarborough, known as a dangerous man in a fight, was already on the ground. Several other efficient hand-gun artists were on the side of the law. On the other side were all sorts of local sports drifting desperadoes, men in flight from other regions—a wide assortment of loose-living characters who came and went in pursuit of their own nefarious ends.

A particularly interesting bunch came to town in the spring of 1895, stopped briefly, and fled to Juárez just ahead of a posse from Eddy (Carlsbad), New Mexico. There were at least four of them, probably more, their leader being a remarkable personality named Martin Morose. The newspapers spelled him M'Rose, but Dee Harkey, who helped to break up his rustling activities and rush him out of New Mexico, spells his name Morose, gives an account of his origin in a Polish community in Karnes County, southeast of San Antonio, and tells how he learned to be a cowboy at the same time he was learning to speak English. He was big, blond, crude, unwashed and immoral, but he had a gift for getting hold of other people's property and was tough enough to kill if necessary to keep what he stole. Tom Finnessy, range manager for the VVN's (Eddy-Bissell Cattle Company) and a man after Martin's own heart, hired him as a cowboy and started him on his career.[44] His prosperity began when he drove a herd to Kansas and picked up enough stray stock along the way to start him in business for himself. He adopted the Ladder brand, which would cover almost anything, and made so much money that he spruced up, began to wear boots and possibly underwear, and assumed a position of leadership among the outlaws and thieves who dominated the county.

Dee Harkey, his boyhood acquaintance, came to Eddy about this time and noted the change. The two did not have a happy reunion, however, for the legitimate cattlemen of the region were fed up with Martin and his friends and they hired Harkey to go after them. They got Dee an appointment as United States Deputy Marshal and Inspector for the Livestock Association.

There was a meeting at which Harkey met Martin and his fellow thieves, who included Tom Finnessy, a desperado named Vic Queen, and the Sheriff of the county. In all there were twenty-five or thirty hard cases in the group. Martin proposed to match Dee's salary and brand a thousand calves a year for him if he would let them alone. Dee says he refused; and during the years that followed he sent the gang off, a few at a time, to prison.[45]

Early in 1895 he ran Morose, Queen, and Finnessy out of the country for stealing horses. Finnessy and Queen went directly to El Paso and on to Juárez. Morose went overland to Midland, where he met his wife, a handsome blonde woman named Beulah whom he is said to have married in the sheriff's whore house at Eddy.[46] She had a child as a result of some former connection, and seems to have been in all ways a lady of great energy and no inhibitions. Together they took the train to El Paso, carrying at least $3,500 in cash with which they planned to buy a ranch in Mexico.[47] The news that Morose and his men were wanted reached El Paso almost as soon as he did, but he had to be run down in the interior of Chihuahua before he could be arrested and brought back to the border. Beulah was with him. True to her explosive nature, she was ready to fight the arresting officers and had to be disarmed.[48] Officer Beauregard Lee, whom she tried to kill, noted that she was carrying $1,880 in money.

The stage was now set for the dramas and difficulties of 1895. Morose was locked up. Beulah was in El Paso trying to take the heat off him. Vic Queen and Tom Finnessy, though not in jail, were pinned down in Juárez and unable to cross the international bridge. They had been joined by Sam Kaufman and a Mr. Lightfoot of New Mexico.[49] Eventually a Texas cattleman, "General" Gene Mackenzie, with whom Morose had once been in partnership,[50] brought a bag of money to Juárez and bought his friend's release from jail,[51] though he couldn't bring him out of Mexico. To add extra interest, Dee Harkey advertised in El Paso and Juárez that the cattleman's association which he represented would pay $500 to anyone who would deliver Martin Morose to the American side of the river, dead or alive.

Matters were in this situation when the greatest gunman of them all got off the Southern Pacific train and appeared on the streets of El Paso to the horror and joy of the citizens. This was John Wesley Hardin, still a great name in Texas sporting circles though fifteen years in the State Penitentiary, from which he had only recently emerged, had subtracted some of the glamour from his public image. Still, a first-class pistol man could not be taken lightly and one who had killed somewhere near forty men was certainly first class. As he appeared in the saloons and eating houses, El Paso regarded him with respectful curiosity and devoted considerable attention to him and his doings throughout the four months of his residence. Young John Selman says that the general attitude approached hero worship.

Notes

1. El Paso *Times*, November 12, 1903.
2. Owen White, *The Autobiography of a Durable Sinner* (New York: G. P. Putnam's Sons, 1942), 43.
3. Interview, June 11, 1965.
4. *Times*, July 2, 1893.
5. Laurence Stevens, April 2, 1965.
6. *Times*, April 18, 1893.
7. *Ibid.*, April 19, 1890.
8. *Ibid.*, Joe Parrish, "Ranger Killed in Gun Battle," El Paso *Times Sun Dial*, September 26, 1965.
9. Jack Martin, *Border Boss: Captain John R. Hughes* (San Antonio: The Naylor Co. 1942), 147-48.
10. Joe Parrish, "Hanged by the Neck," *Password* 3 (April 1958): 72, 75; *Times*, January 7, 1935.
11. Baylor to Mabry, July 9, 1893, Hughes to Mabry, September 6, 1893, Adjutant General's Files, State Library, Austin.
12. Walter Prescott Webb, *The Texas Rangers: A Century of Frontier Defense* (Boston: Houghton Mifflin, 1935), 442.
13. *Times*, April 4, July 2, 1893; El Paso *Herald*, June 30, 1893.
14. Jones to Mabry, April 16, 1893, AGF; *Herald*, April 5, 1893: "Body after body has been brought to town . . . not a party has been arrested."
15. *Times*, June 30, 1893.
16. Webb, 441-44.
17. *Times*, July 2, 1893.
18. Webb, 443.
19. *Times*, July 2, 1893.
20. J. Evetts Haley, *Jeff Milton: A Good Man With a Gun* (Norman: University of Oklahoma Press, 1948), 234.
21. *Times*, July 1, 1893.
22. Sonnichsen, *Tularosa* (New York: Devin-Adair, 1960), 107-201; H. B. Hening. ed., *George Curry, 1861-1947: An Autobiography* (Albuquerque: University of New Mexico Press, 1958), 100-19; A. M. Gibson, *The Life and Death of Colonel Albert Jennings Fountain* (Norman: University of Oklahoma Press. 1965), 256-88.

23. Leon Metz, *John Selman: Texas Gunfighter* (New York, Hastings House, 1966), has followed Selman's trail to the end.
24. Sonnichsen, *I'll Die Before I'll Run* (New York: Devin-Adair, 1962), 150-66 ("Justice after Dark"), covers this part of Selman's career.
25. Metz, 96-111.
26. John Selman, Jr., "John Selman of El Paso," MS.
27. Metz, 133-35.
28. *Times*, November 9, 1892.
29. Selman, MS.
30. Metz, 138.
31. *Ibid.*, 152-53.
32. Eugene Cunningham, *Triggernometry: A Gallery of Gunfighters* (Caldwell, Idaho: Caxton Printers, 1947), 236-44.
33. Metz, 146-47.
34. *Times*, April 7, 1894.
35. Metz, 137.
36. *Times*, April 6, 1894.
37. *Ibid.*
38. Alonzo Van Oden, *Ranger's Diary and Scrapbook* (Dallas: The Kaleidograph Press, 1936), 40.
39. *Times*, April 17, 1894.
40. *Ibid.*, April 6, 7, 12, 1894; Oden, 41.
41. Oden, 40-41.
42. *Herald*, June 30, 1894; District Court Minutes, 34th District Court, El Paso, Texas, Case 1753.
43. Selman, MS.
44. Haley, 229.
45. Dee Harkey, *Mean as Hell* (Albuquerque: University of New Mexico Press, 1948), 114. The Polish spelling of Morose's name is Mróz.
46. Haley, 232.
47. *Ibid.*, 233.
48. *Times*, April 12, 1895.
49. *Ibid.*, April 24, 1894.
50. Haley, 233.
51. Harkey, 131. ★

Leon Claire Metz

Historian, lecturer, and writer Leon Claire Metz was born and raised in Parkersburg, West Virginia, but made El Paso his home after his military service as a staff sergeant stationed here. He has worked in law enforcement, served as a public affairs officer for a bank, university archivist, and assistant to the University of Texas at El Paso President Dr. Haskell Monroe. C. L. Sonnichsen was a literary mentor to Metz and the editor of his book *John Selman: Texas Gunfighter*. He is the author of seventeen books including: *Trailing Billy the Kid*; *Fort Bliss: An Illustrated History*; *Desert Army: Fort Bliss on the Texas Border*; *John Wesley Hardin: Dark Angel of Texas*; *Pat Garrett: The Story of a Western Lawman*; *Border: The U.S. Mexico Line*; *Shooters*; and *El Paso Chronicles*. Metz is featured in many magazines, newspapers, and historical journals in addition to writing a weekly column in the *El Paso Times*. The *Leon Metz Show* is his popular live weekly talk show on El Paso's KTSM. He often appears on the History Channel, A&E, and the BBC's programs on the west. HBO released an original movie based on his three part series *Pancho Villa*. He is the past president of Western Writers of America, who honored him with the 1985 Saddleman Award, and a member of the Texas Institute of Letters.

From *John Wesley Hardin*: *Dark Angel of Texas*: Four Sixes to Beat

The last days of John Wesley Hardin can never be documented precisely, but sufficient evidence exists for an evaluation, and one of the best instruments for that is his Wigwam Saloon bar tab. Hardin drank in every saloon in town, and there were a couple of dozen in El Paso, at least, and plenty more in Juarez. Even taking into consideration that portions of his bar tab covered libations he bought for others, that factor is balanced by numerous people also buying him drinks.

Consider that a shot of whiskey cost between seven and fifteen cents, and a glass of beer about ten cents, maybe fifteen at the better class institutions. To consistently run up a bar bill of between one and three dollars a day, in just one saloon, indicates a hefty, two-fisted drinker.

On May 1, Hardin accumulated a Wigwam bar tab of three dollars. Considering that this figure amounted to at least thirty beers, or twenty shots of whiskey, or a combination of both, and more if he received a discount—which he probably did—that in itself represented an awesome amount of quaffing. Yet, late that night he was still tipping the glass and gambling for hours up the street at the Gem Saloon where he ultimately removed ninety- five dollars from the dealer. On the following day, May 2, Hardin paid his bar bill in full at the Wigwam, a total of $13.30 for six days of libations.

On May 8, when the state grand jury indicted him for armed robbery of the Gem, Hardin took home a half-gallon of whiskey and a pint of rye. On July 3, before John Selman Jr's. arrest of Beulah, Hardin bought "Johnny" (meaning police officer Selman), fifty cents worth of drinks. Hardin purchased a bottle of liquor for eighty cents and gave it to Jeff Milton. The refreshment helped Milton get through the 4th of July celebrations.

The record shows Hardin drinking copious amounts at the Wigwam during the last week of his life. That was the period when Beulah left, and George Scarborough marched him down to the *Times* where John Hardin scratched out his chastened public apology.

As his final days became a blur, he lost seventy dollars at cards in the Wigwam on August 18, and had run up a $3.15 bar bill by the afternoon of the 19th. The balance due had reached $198.25— the largest figure yet—and Hardin could not pay it. He had no money, he had no income, and he had no clients.

Constable John Selman accosted Hardin in the street that afternoon, snorting that he understood Hardin had threatened John Selman, Jr. Hardin allegedly called Young John a cowardly son-of-a-bitch who had arrested his woman, Beulah. When Selman defended his son and offered to shoot it out, Hardin claimed to be unarmed. Hardin said, "I'll go get a gun and when I meet you, I'll meet you smoking and make you shit like a wolf all around the block."[1]

The two men separated, Selman going off to brood, Hardin likely stumbling into the Wigwam and tanking up.

At ten o'clock on the Monday night of August 19,1895, Hardin swayed into the Acme Saloon and found it crowded. According to later testimony, Selman and an investor friend named E. L. Shackelford entered the saloon two or three times and even played a game or two of cards with Hardin. If so, they were checking positions and plotting strategy. For most of the evening, Selman sulked on a barrel near the Acme front door. At eleven o'clock, Shackelford came outside, nodded, turned around and walked back in. Right behind him, Selman put his hand on his gun and stepped through a door wide open due to the heat. He paced three or four steps quickly through the cigar smoke and haze as he focused on Hardin standing almost sideways against the bar and rolling dice down the polished counter. Hardin turned to grocer Henry S. Brown, and said, "Brown, you've got four sixes to beat."

At that instant, Constable John Selman started shooting. A .45 caliber bullet slammed Hardin in the head, and he crashed backwards onto the wooden floor. He never felt the two other slugs ripping into his body.

NOTES

1. *El Paso Herald*, Aug. 20, 1895. ★

From *John Wesley Hardin: Dark Angel of Texas*: El Paso

IN 1895, THESE GUNMEN WERE RESIDENTS OF El Paso: George Scarborough, Jeff Milton, Martin M'Rose, the Selmans (Sr. & Jr.), Tom Fennessey and the curly-wolf of them all: John Wesley Hardin.

The western frontier had vanished everywhere except at isolated communities such as El Paso. Bordertowns attracted the best and the worst, acting as magnets for ruffians one step ahead of the sheriff.

El Paso in 1895 had 13,000 people, twice as many as Ciudad Juarez, Chihuahua, its Mexican neighbor across the Rio Grande. El Paso Street served as the commercial center of town, extending from Pioneer Plaza to the Rio Grande. Most of the other streets simply branched off. A few well-to-do residents moved north of the Southern Pacific tracks into Piety Hills, as locals called it, but that area showed few signs of spectacular growth.

With the arrival of the railroads in 1881, El Paso had become "Americanized," shifting from an adobe community to one of brick and occasionally wood. Only 20 percent of the population had Hispanic surnames, which meant El Paso was an island of Anglo-Americans due to the railroad hubs and Fort Bliss, plus a strong influx of miners, gamblers, prostitutes, professional people and health-seekers.

And so it was that El Paso's two conflicting political and moral forces collided with no hope of reconciliation. One was the long established liquor, prostitution and gambling interests. The other lumped together as the Reform Movement, frequently paraded by torchlight through dusty streets to the refrain of "Onward Christian Soldiers." They demanded nothing less than the abolishment of the sinful, lustful, advocates of the devil, as represented on earth by liquor, prostitution and gambling.

***

The city of El Paso swore Jefferson Davis Milton in as police chief on August 10, 1894. Jeff Milton, born on November 7, 1861, a son of Florida Governor John Milton, spent much of his life as a lawman, serving at one period or another as a sheriff, a Texas Ranger, police chief, customs officer, and a United States marshal. Milton was chubby, dark with jet-black eyes, well-combed hair, and bushy mustache. He was a conductor for the Southern Pacific when El Paso Mayor Robert F. "Bob" Johnson wired the thirty-two-year-old Jeff Milton at St. Louis and offered him the police chief's position. Milton accepted, and later that year, at the instigation of John Selman, Jeff Milton hired the twenty-one-year-old John Selman, Jr., as a policeman.[1] The police officer would generally be called "Young John" to differentiate between him and his father, "Old John."

George Scarborough provided another link in a chain that would soon envelop John Wesley Hardin. He was born in Louisiana in 1859 and became a man of medium height with straight sandy hair, pale blue eyes, and the traditional bushy mustache. After becoming sheriff of Jones County, Texas, and killing A. J. Williams, he lost the next election and was appointed a deputy marshal for West Texas by Dick Ware. Scarborough reached El Paso during late June, 1893.

Scarborough married Mary Frances McMahan, and fathered several children. Her brother, Frank M. McMahan, also moved to El Paso, and joined the Texas Rangers in nearby Ysleta. While retaining his ranger status, he too signed on as a deputy U.S. marshal.[2]

This left only Martin M'Rose, his wife, and his nefarious friends as the final El Paso players involved in the Hardin drama. Martin M'Rose migrated out of Saint Hedwig, a Silesian settlement east of San Antonio where the family spelled the name Mroz. El Paso and New Mexico newspapers used M'Rose, Morose, and Monrose. Martin and his wife Beulah consistently wrote it as M'Rose, making the heritage look Irish or Scottish instead of Polish, but nevertheless that spelling tradition will be continued here.

He spoke with a Polish accent, and was an intelligent, stocky, dark blond, blue-eyed, nice-looking man probably in his twenties. As a youngster he became a cowboy in southeastern New Mexico. He also acquired an addiction for horses, cattle and hogs belonging to other people.

M'Rose hung around Seven Rivers, New Mexico, although he was no stranger to the Eddy County seat of Eddy (now Carlsbad), and the sin town of Phenix. The latter sprouted on the doorstep of Eddy, a transient village of brothels and saloons made possible when Eddy refused to legitimize liquor and wild women.

While M'Rose had some standing as a badman, whether or not he deserved it is debatable. He himself hinted, and even bragged about various killings, but no confirmation is on record.

Tom Fennessey and Vic Queen were two of M'Rose's closest New Mexico friends. Fennessey campaigned for Eddy county clerk in 1890, and won. He was a hard drinker and a tough, trail-driving cowboy who killed a man at Seven Rivers. Vic Queen was a medium-size, lean man with a square head, dark hair and mustache. Like M'Rose, he tilted toward blustery speech.

In 1894 or early 1895, M'Rose met and married the twenty or twenty-one-year-old blue-eyed blonde, historically known as Helen Beulah. As a prostitute working West Texas and southeastern New Mexico, she reportedly wed Martin at the sheriff's whorehouse at Eddy, New Mexico. While she has consistently been described as an "outstanding beauty," the one known photograph reveals an attractive but plain woman, thin, somewhat washed-out and showing the strains of her occupation. She had a five-year-old son named Albert, presumably fathered by someone other than Martin since the two adults did not likely meet that long ago. Helen Beulah M'Rose was intelligent, fairly-well educated, conniving, and inclined toward disorderliness. Her maiden name, and where she came from, are as obscure as whatever eventually happened to her. ★

Notes

1. Robert K. DeArment, *George Scarborough: The Life and Death of A Lawman on the Closing Frontier*. Norman: U. of Oklahoma Press, 1992, 79-81; J. Evetts Haley, *Jeff Milton: Good Man With a Gun*. Norman: University of Oklahoma Press, 1953, 211-214.
2. DeArment, *George Scarborough*, 48.

Nancy Hamilton

Native El Pasoan Nancy Miller Hamilton received her B.A. and M.A. from the University of Texas at El Paso. Following a career in newspaper reporting for both the *El Paso Times* and the *El Paso Herald-Post*, she was the first head of the media relations department of the El Paso Independent School District. She retired in 1990 from her position as associate director of Texas Western Press. Hamilton edited and wrote for the university's magazine *Nova*, and for *Roundup*, the magazine of Western Writers of America. She is the author of *Ben Dowell: El Paso's First Mayor* and *UTEP: A Pictorial History*, as well as many articles for journals and other publications, and is a past president of Western Writers of America. "El Paso's Pioneer Women" was chosen by the El Paso County Historical Society for the 2007 Eugene O. Porter Award, and her article on Alexander Daguerre won the Porter Award in 2003.

From El Paso's Pioneer Women

When she came to El Paso from Austin as a bride in 1869, Mrs. W. W. Mills rode overland in an ambulance outfitted with a berth for sleeping, making the seven-hundred mile trip in twenty-three days. Her husband had arranged for an escort of soldiers and a wagon filled with baggage, as well as having a driver and a Mexican servant. "We were in constant fear of Indians," she told the Association of Pioneer Women of El Paso in 1922. On the fifth night out, at Kickapoo Springs, a band of Indians wanted to steal the animals, but the soldiers fired at them and they left.

Her husband teased her by pointing at a primitive Mexican hut, a *jacal*, along the way, telling her that was the kind of home she would have. But upon arriving in El Paso, he took her along one of the few established streets, to his home at 312 San Antonio. He proudly showed her that it had plank flooring, the first in the town, and trees in the front yard.

Mrs. Mills learned to keep her butter and water cool by using glazed earthen vessels. "Every yard had an *acequia* with water cold as snow, as it was melted snow," she explained. She would let the water settle in a jar, put it into a porous vessel, then place it at night in a sand bank under a cottonwood tree with greens surrounding it. Glazed vessels with lids were used for butter, and an open vessel for grapes, the fruit being covered with water.

Her most frightening experience in the early days occurred when three Indians from Ysleta came to see her husband about government business. "One Indian wanted to see the squaw," she recalled. "He looked at my fingers, my arm, turned me around, looked at my hair, and talked in Spanish." Mr. Mills went to his office and one of the Indians came back to their home, drunk and riding a Mexican pony. He called to her in Spanish and pounded on the door, but she locked it and sat on the floor in fear that the man would kill her, crying until her husband finally returned. She did not know that the Indians from Ysleta were not hostile.

At the time Mrs. Mills related these adventures, she was living in Austin, where she and her husband had moved after he left the position of consul in Chihuahua City in 1907. Although she had not made her home in El Paso since his appointment as consul in 1897, she often returned to visit her many friends and kept in touch with several women's organizations, among them the Association of Pioneer Women of El Paso, which made her an honorary member. She also had been a founder of the Woman's Club of El Paso and its first president.[1]

Her lecture for the Pioneer Women was one of several recorded in the minutes of their meetings in the 1920s, when women who were true pioneers were still available to tell their stories. They shared many common experiences—living in adobe houses with dirt floors, packing mud into holes in the walls and ceilings, letting water from the Rio Grande settle in large jars, and relying on soldiers to protect the town from Indian raids on livestock.

The Pioneer Women had organized only a year before Mrs. Mills came to speak to them. Some of their group had been members of the Pioneer Association of El Paso County, which was primarily a men's organization started in 1904. Each member's name was followed by the year he arrived in

El Paso, and residence of at least twenty years was required. A later president, William I. Latham, who also once headed the El Paso County Historical Society, liked to recall that the true pioneers reached El Paso by stagecoach. Those who came on railroads in 1881 or after were dubbed "late arrivals."

***

El Paso women already had several civic-minded clubs of their own and, unlike the Pioneers who had no clubhouse, the Woman's Club of El Paso had completed its building in 1916. At any rate, the auxiliary's organizational meeting elected Mrs. I. A. Shedd as president and Mrs. L. W. Breck as secretary-treasurer, a post in which she continued to write meticulous minutes until her election as president in 1926. Those attending included some who were already Pioneer members—Mrs. Von Rhein, Mrs. Hoffman, and Mrs. Krause. Some of their dues funds were transferred to the new group by Mr. Gaal. The Pioneer Association extended three invitations to the ladies: one to a reception on October 22 to meet General Anson Mills, a distinguished former resident who had drawn the first plat of El Paso; another to an evening reception on October 28; and the third invitation was extended in order to have the auxiliary members serve the refreshments for the second reception.[2]

While there are no records to explain why the Ladies Auxiliary did not want to continue in that role, something must have disturbed them during the October reception. At their November 28, 1921, meeting in the Courthouse club rooms, the seven members present voted in favor of Mrs. C. E. Kelly's motion to have a separate organization known as the Association of Pioneer Women of El Paso, with the feeling "that an independent organization would be more effective," They would henceforth meet in members' homes. One of their objections had been financial; the men's group charged five dollars to join and three dollars a year in dues.

***

Mrs. Katie Marr told of her fear of the Indians as she journeyed to El Paso and of the corn fields around the Magoffin home in the early days. She said that at one time the Rio Grande had been dry for nine months. The first circus train in town, she noted, unloaded at Oregon Street because there was no depot.[3]

***

One of the speakers in February was Mrs. A. M. Loomis, whose husband came to El Paso by stage forty years earlier. She and her children came later by train. She spoke of the gospel tent where religious services were held with three ministers jointly, and of school being held in a tent. Like some of the others, she had two barrels of water in her kitchen, filled from the Rio Grande every other day by a servant. Wood was delivered by Mexicans. Lacking fresh milk, she used condensed milk.[4]

***

In May 1922, they heard from Miss Ellinor Porcher, who had come to El Paso in 1893 from South Carolina. The family's home being unfinished, they moved into an adobe house with a dirt floor and a leaking roof they had to stop up with mud. The water was so hard that kerosene or washing soda was used in the water when washing clothes. The road was half chuck holes, she said. There were no telephones.

"Water had to be pumped for irrigation," she related. "Benigno Alderete had wild horses which he drove into a rope-fenced space. Into this enclosure wheat was piled upon the ground and amidst whooping and yelling of Mexicans, the horses ran around the circle, thus threshing the grain. Also, during grape season a wine press was crudely constructed by suspending three dried skins from the ceiling of a house. Barefooted Mexicans tramped upon the grapes to release the juice."

Miss Porcher told the group that El Paso and Ciudad Juárez each had a population of about fifteen hundred people. Fording the river was an easy way to smuggle *serapes* and small articles. She added that cock fights were very popular in Juárez. The only American families living between Ysleta and El Paso were those of E. F. Cadwallader, J. H. Smith, the Marrs, the Tibbits, and the Hoffs.[5]

A former resident of Ysleta, Mrs. T. A. Falvey, also spoke that day. She had come to El Paso in 1881, traveling five hundred miles by stage, the mules being changed by day and at night. When she arrived, her house was not ready, so she stayed with Mrs. Magoffin and later at Grand Central Hotel—"its dirt floor was so worn it was wavelike." Food was in short supply and at times it seemed they lived on radishes and onions. When her husband became district judge in 1881, they moved to Ysleta which was the county seat. "It was more of a city than El Paso at that time," she noted. Her house had a homemade table and dirt floors covered with matting. She had two goats for milk.[6]

After a summer respite, the Pioneer Women met again on October 12, 1922. Two of them, Mrs. S. H. Sutherland and Mrs. A. M. Walthall, shared memories of early El Paso. Mrs. Sutherland came as a bride from Pennsylvania in 1883 and was "happily surprised with the conditions I found in El Paso and vicinity, as I had heard wild tales about the West." Her husband had arrived in 1880 on the Concord stage. She noted that by 1922 only twenty men remained who had reached El Paso by stagecoach. In the days when flat cars were attached to the mule-drawn streetcar, they were laden with tropical fruits in Juárez for sale in El Paso. "The now extinct El Paso onion sometimes grew to a weight of two and a fourth pounds and was of a pinkish white, with a delicious flavor," she added.

"There were many saloons and each had an orchestra, or some sort of noisy music," she continued. Mr. Sutherland and his partner Mr. Stuart had a store in a tent; it later was sold to be used for church services, with boxes from the store used as seats. A great friendship existed between El Paso and Fort Bliss at this time. Mrs. Sutherland moved to La Luz, New Mexico, where she lived for several years. Engineers who surveyed the Cloudcroft railroad stayed at her house.[7]

Mrs. Walthall came a few years later—in 1898— from Fort Worth. She recalled that there were four railroads and five or six churches. The town had no electric lights or electric streetcars, relying on mule cars connecting Juárez and El Paso. Drinking water was brought from Deming, New Mexico, by train, and delivered by wagon to one's door. The fame of Deming water helped lure Mr. and Mrs. J. H. Smith to El Paso in 1889. She told the group on November 9, 1922, that they came west from Missouri for her husband's health. Silver City, Deming, and El Paso had been recommended to them and a friend predicted that Deming would become an important metropolis. But J. B. Hammett advised them to come to El Paso, saying they could live here and drink Deming water.[8]

A visitor from Dallas, Mrs. A. H. Weekins, had attended Central School for eleven years. Bailey, at first called Mesa, and Franklin were the next schools built, she said. Myrtle Street was named for Charlie Bassett's mother, Octavia Street for Mrs. Magoffin, Florence Street for Mrs. W. S. Hills, and Ange Street for Mrs. Frank Steele, she added.

***

Professor Aoy started his school on San Francisco Street in one room, giving his services free. The school was taken over by the School Board which then paid him a salary, but he gave the funds to the poor Mexican families. He died in a charity ward in a hospital.

***

Teachers and pupils used to fish in the canal behind Aoy School, continued the speaker. There were many holiday celebrations. A notable one was a St. Patrick's Day when school was dismissed for a parade, of which a little girl said enthusiastically, "We are going to have a parade. It's Miss St. Patrick's Birthday!"

***

Mrs. C. E. Kelly, who had lived in El Paso thirty years, introduced a description of Pioneer Women at the January 18, 1923, meeting:

"P" stands for Pluck and it took pluck and more pluck and more pluck in the early days.

"I" is for Industry. It took pluck to stay here and also Industry.

"O" is not for ours but for Others. The Pioneers don't forget other people; the true Pioneers welcome others and it's their best possession now.

"N" is for Necessity. They had to go to work to obtain what they wanted and we can see the result.

"E" stands for Ears—they had to keep their ears open. They would listen for desperate men, and often they heard coyotes in the early days. They used to listen with all their might for Indians.

"E" also stands for Eyes; they looked over the mesas and saw good behind the rough exterior and saw the future. They were especially kind.

"R" stands for the Rio Grande. Sometimes it would overflow and run up by the Courthouse, and again it would be dry. The El Paso sunshine was El Paso itself, and it warmed the heart of every Pioneer; it's the emblem of sunshine always.[9]

The February 8, 1923, program featured Mrs. W. J. Fewel. She and her husband and two boys arrived September 11, 1881, on the Santa Fe Railroad, to find a small village with adobe houses, sandy streets, and not a sprig of grass. "There was nothing green except greasewood and mesquite bushes."

The few Americans, she said, "were charming and cultured people. The Mexicans were polite, always giving a salutation of some kind, often putting me to shame." There were very few streets, the main ones being Overland, San Francisco, Santa Fe, and El Paso where the businesses were located. The town was without government of any kind. Mr. Stoudenmire had just arrived as the first to try to enforce laws, but he was soon killed.[10]

Wide-open saloons were close to business houses, related Mrs. Fewel, "so one can understand why lawlessness prevailed. There was one bank, no hotel except an old adobe place with a restaurant, where my husband and little boy had their meals; meals were sent to me as my husband was not willing for me to eat there because of the odors of the people that were there."

Stores carried on a big business with Mexico, she continued, and handled all kinds of merchandise. Mr. Krakauer boasted that he carried everything in his store from a potato to the finest thing one could wear. Carriers of smallpox came from Mexico and there were many deaths from the disease among the Americans. At that time the water we had to drink was from the Rio Grande. It had to be settled, boiled, and cleared, and kept in earthen *ollas* which were wrapped in wet blanket coverings or else kept in wet sand.

After the county seat was relocated from Ysleta to El Paso in 1883, Mrs. Fewel said, improvements were rapid, due to progressive men. The gas works was built in 1883, "My husband being chiefly responsible; I lighted the first gas jet and later was asked by Mr. Neill to light the second or third furnace at the smelter. We had the first gas heater brought to El Paso put in our residence, and I still have it in my home."

When they built their home in 1882, the Fewels wanted a green yard, she continued. Bermuda was the only kind of grass to grow here, brought by express from Austin. "That was the starter of all the grass in El Paso and Fort Bliss which we have today."

Major Fewel, Mr. [Zach] White, and others organized the streetcar company to operate between El Paso and Juárez. "You have all read of that mule streetcar line and how obliging the Mexican driver was," Mrs. Fewel recalled. "If the ladies had to go through mud to reach the car, he would remove the mud from their shoes probably with his pocket knife, and was always willing to stop where the gentlemen wanted him to. I remember Major Fewel once saying of the streetcar company, 'It used to pay us two and three percent a month on the invested capital, and it was mighty convenient to be one of the owners of the streetcar line.' For instance, if we were going home and happened to meet the streetcar coming downtown, Captain [Charles] Davis and I would stop the car and have the driver take the mule around to the other end of the car and take us back home. We would go shopping downtown in the morning and send the groceries and vegetables home by the driver."[11]

The Fewel's home had the first residence telephone, Number 8. They had to ring for service then. The year before Central School was built, Mrs. Fewel's son and the Hague and Cummings children had attended school above Zach White's store where Mrs. Davis gave private lessons.

"By 1893 the real pioneer days were over," Mrs. Fewel concluded. The close sociability of those early days is a thing of the past. Prior to that time, people visited frequently, lived close to one another, and had many good times together."

Mrs. Robert L. Howze, the speaker on April 12, 1923, recalled living at the old Fort Bliss beside the Rio Grande when she was a child and her father was an army major. She said when they arrived at Fort Bliss, the Santa Fe train, which went through the parade grounds, stopped to let them off. The soldiers were busy unpacking boxes and furniture for the family. A little boy came up to her mother and she asked him for a glass of ice water. He brought her a glass of cloudy brownish liquid and she asked him, "Did you by any chance get this out of the teakettle?" At that time water was brought from the river in barrels and carried through the fort. Servants would empty it from one barrel to another to let it settle a second time, then it was put into an *olla* for drinking use. Zinc tubs were used for a bath. They were carried upstairs, filled, used, then emptied and carried down again. Her father built the quarters nearest the present—1923—viaduct and in one of the houses installed a tin bath tub and ran a pipe out of the bathroom on the second floor, thus disposing of the used water and necessitating carrying it only one way. They felt this to be quite a luxury.

At one time there was a cloudburst and "tons" of hailstones backed up in the railroad culvert. The hailstones lasted nearly a week. All ice cream freezers were rusty, but they were renovated and pressed into service, related Mrs. Howze, and everyone had ice cream made from Gail Borden's condensed milk. Lemons were to be obtained only occasionally. In the El Paso Plaza there was a fine collection of cactus plants, while the Magoffin house, she said, was a handsome residence with a patio of flowers.

Mrs. Howze spoke of the absence of snakes here now. When she was a little girl, she was not permitted to run in front of her father when they were out for a walk, as snakes were so numerous. Snakes were often killed near the smelter, and three or four times they were killed in a small cellar. There was not much beauty here, she continued, as water was too precious to use for flowers to any extent. Mrs. Howze found, on being back at Fort Bliss for the past six years, that she thought Mount Franklin more beautiful than she had remembered it from her childhood. Her husband was the general there.[12]

Owen White, El Paso's first historian, commented on the influence of the pioneer women after the arrival of the railroads. "All at once the coming into the town of such women as Mrs. W. J. Fewel, Mrs. E. S. Newman, Mrs. C. R. Morehead, Mrs. Allen Blacker, Mrs. A. M. Loomis and a few others added a new and powerful element to life in El Paso. Quiet, educated, and refined, these women, who had been reared amid Christian and civilized influences, found themselves suddenly transplanted into an atmosphere which literally reeked with the odor of the world, the flesh, and the devil. Instantly, with that intuitive, God-given instinct that good women have, they saw the path of duty that lay before them, and straightway and courageously they set out to follow it. . . . What the town needed, and what it received from these mothers, was the touch of a woman's hand; and the story of their accomplishment is one that every mother in El Paso—even the mothers of today—should read with a feeling of gratitude and appreciation."[13]

Notes

1. Married women were known by their husbands' names until late in the 20th century; men tended to use their Civil War military titles with their names. Mary Hamilton Mills was the daughter of Mary Jane (Bowen) Hamilton and Andrew Jackson Hamilton, who served as provisional governor of Texas immediately after the Civil War and then as Texas Supreme Court justice. She married William Wallace Mills of El Paso February 8, 1869, and they arrived in El Paso a month later. An Indiana native, he had followed his brother, Anson Mills, to El Paso in 1858. He was collector of customs (1863-1869) and represented the county at the state constitutional convention of 1868-1869. Mary S. Cunningham, *The Woman's Club of El Paso, Its First Thirty Years* (El Paso: Texas Western Press, 1978), 1, 2, 17; W. W. Mills, *Forty Years at El Paso, 1858-1898* (El Paso: Carl Hertzog, 1962), 81, 99; Association of Pioneer Women minutes, November 9, 1922.
2. Cunningham, 165; Association of Pioneer Women minutes, October [?,] 1921.
3. Her husband, Colonel James S. Marr, operated the El Paso Transfer Co.
4. Minutes of February 9, 1922. Mrs. Loomis's husband was prominent in the legal profession immediately after the coming of the railroads. He served on the first public school board of trustees in 1882. J. Morgan Broaddus, Jr., *The Legal Heritage of El Paso* (El Paso: Texas Western Press, 1963), 133, 151
5. Minutes, May 11, 1922. In a study of street names, Lurline H. Coltharp told how a member of the Porcher family was remembered. When J. S. Porcher's mother died in 1922, developers wanted to name a street for her. Members of the Porcher family suggested it be called "Carolina" because the family came from South Carolina. Coltharp, "Street Names," *Password* 34:2 (Summer 1989): 84. Benigno Alderete served as a county commissioner (1886-1888) and mayor of Ysleta (1890).
6. Mrs. Falvey's husband, Tom A. Falvey, served as district judge in El Paso County from 1880 to 1892, then entered law practice. Broaddus, 131-32. Mrs. Octavia Magoffin's husband, Joseph Magoffin, was mayor of El Paso (1881-1885 and 1897-1901), county judge (1876-1877), and a distinguished civic leader. Their former home is a state historical site. The Central Hotel stood at the head of El Paso Street. A second story was added after the coming of the railroads and the name was changed to Grand Central Hotel.
7. Carrie Findley Sutherland was chairman of the Civic Improvement League in 1915-1916 and was president of the Woman's Club of El Paso in 1915- 1917 when their building at 1400 North Mesa Street was erected. Cunningham, 82, 155-70. The front page of the first issue of the *El Paso Times* (April 2, 1881) carried ads for Stuart & Sutherland, one of which read: "The place to buy groceries and provisions cheap is at Stuart & Sutherland's in the Big Tent." The "preachin' tent" was used by several denominations while awaiting construction of their churches in 1881-1882. It occupied a site on San Antonio Street where the City Hall was built in 1899. William I. Latham, "Early El Paso Churches," *Password* 17:3 (Fall 1982): 100. The Alamogordo & Sacramento Mountain Railway reached Cloudcroft in 1899. Passenger and mail service ended in 1938 and the line was abandoned in 1947. Dorothy Jensen Neal, *The Cloud-Climbing Railroad* (Alamogordo: Alamogordo Printing Co., 1966), 27, 67. Mrs. Walthall's husband, Anderson M. Walthall, came to El Paso as district judge in 1899, practiced law from 1904 to 1909, then served as 41st District Court judge until 1914 when he was appointed to the 8th Court of Civil Appeals, remaining until 1942. Broaddus, 227-28.
8. Minutes, November 9, 1922. James H. Smith was city tax assessor/collector for several years and later had a real estate and insurance business with his two sons.
9. Minutes, January 18, 1923. Mrs. Kelly's husband was mayor of El Paso from 1910 to 1915 and served on the University of Texas Board of Regents. A building at the University of Texas at El Paso is named for him.
10. Minutes, February 8, 1923. The speaker's husband, Major Fewel, was a city alderman when Captain Charles Davis, Sr. was mayor, 1905-1907, and had various business interests. Dallas Stoudenmire was hired as city marshal in April 1881 to put down unrest, but was killed in a saloon shooting in September 1882. Leon Metz wrote his biography, *Dallas Stoudenmire, El Paso Marshal* (Norman: University of Oklahoma Press, 1979).
11. At the time Mrs. Fewel lighted the first gas jet, J. W. Neill had succeeded Robert Towne as head of the Towne Smelter. He resigned in 1887. Fred Morales, *Smeltertown* (El Paso: n.p., n.d.), 5. More about the early mule cars may be found in a recent study, Ronald E. Dawson, *Streetcars at the Pass*, vol. 1 (New York, etc.: iUniverse, Inc., 2003).

12. Mrs. Howze, who lived at Old Fort Bliss from 1884 to 1886, was the daughter of Hamilton Smith Hawkins, who later became a major general. Fort Bliss was located at Hart's Mill from 1880 to 1894. River flooding and the placing of railroad tracks across the parade round were among reasons for the move to La Noria Mesa, sixth site of the post. She returned to Fort Bliss in 1916 as an army wife. Three members of her family were commanders there: her father, Major H.S. Hawkins, 1884-1885; her husband, Brigadier General Robert L. Howze, 1918-1925; and her brother, Brigadier General Hamilton Hawkins, 1936. She wrote a more extensive account of her life there for *Password* 3:1 (January 1958): 30-34

13. Owen White, *Out of the Desert* (El Paso: McMath Co., 1924), 179. ★

W. H. Timmons

Borderlands historian Wilbert H. Timmons (1915-2008) was born in Springfield, Missouri, and raised in Fort Worth, Texas. He received his B.A. at Park College in Missouri, an M.A. from the University of Chicago, and his Ph.D. from the University of Texas at Austin in Latin American History after his service as a naval officer during World War II. In 1949, he joined the faculty of Texas Western College, now the University of Texas at El Paso, where he retired as emeritus professor of history after nearly thirty years of teaching. During his service as director of the Mexican Microfilm Project from 1971-1978, archives from Chihuahua and Durango, Mexico, were preserved on over two thousand rolls of microfilm at the UTEP library. Author of numerous scholarly articles, Timmons also published several books including *Morelos of México*; *Tadeo Ortiz: Mexican Colonizer and Reformer; Four Centuries at the Pass of the North*; *The Anglo-American Advance into Texas, 1810-1830*; and *El Paso: A Borderlands History*, the winner of the T. R. Fehrenbach award by the Texas Historical Commission for best Texas history in 1990. Timmons was active in many state and regional historical organizations and established the Dr. W. H. Timmons Fund of the El Paso Community Foundation. The fund underwrites the publication of area history booklets and the signage marking historic sites and buildings in El Paso. Bill Timmons was also nicknamed "Mr. History" when he visited classrooms throughout El Paso talking about historical events as part of the Four Centuries 1981 project.

From *El Paso A Borderlands History*: El Paso and Ciudad Juárez, 1910-1945

***

Although the Mexican Revolution traditionally dates from the movement initiated by Francisco Madero in 1910, significant revolutionary activity had begun along the United States-Mexican border in 1906, particularly in El Paso, because of its supreme strategic location. Here was a railroad center with links to the prosperous ranches of Chihuahua and the mines of Sonora and Coahuila; here was a large Mexican population whose loyalties had remained with the land of their birth and who still harbored resentments against the policies of the Díaz regime; here in spite of existing American neutrality legislation was a potential source of arms, munitions, and provisions; here across the river was Ciudad Juárez, with a federal garrison, customhouse, and several banks. As a center and a base for revolutionary operations, therefore, the El Paso-Ciudad Juárez area offered almost unlimited possibilities.[1]

***

Under existing United States neutrality statutes, Madero's agents could legally purchase American munitions for exportation to Mexico. This interpretation of the neutrality legislation was clearly stated on 24 January 1911 by Philander C. Knox, secretary of state in the Taft administration. Knox ruled that any individual could purchase as many guns and as much ammunition as desired and export them to any country, whether or not that country was involved in revolution or war. He added that such materials could not be used to equip a military expedition organized on United States territory to fight against a government at peace with the United States. This meant that Francisco Madero or his agents could legally purchase American munitions to outfit an army organized and maintained in Mexico. They could not, however, use the same equipment to outfit an army organized in the United States to invade Mexico or to attack the Mexican government.[2]

With considerable support for the Madero movement in El Paso, the city became a principal headquarters for the sale of arms and munitions to the Mexican rebels. Guns and ammunition were purchased from the Francis Bannerman and Sons surplus arms company of New York, shipped through Galveston to the Shelton Payne Arms Company, a sporting goods dealer in El Paso, and stored in private residences until they could be smuggled across the river. Included with these was the famous old muzzle-loading McGinty cannon known as "the Blue Whistler," which was hidden in a hole in the backyard of an El Paso residence until it was loaded with other material into farm wagons. These were then driven thirty-five miles downriver and carried across to

Mexico without incident. The Shelton Payne Arms Company did not charge the Mexican rebels a commission for handling their weapons and, on some occasions, even loaned them money to pay the freight bills.[3]

Francisco Madero, who had remained in hiding in San Antonio, New Orleans, and Dallas, decided in February 1911 that his presence on Mexican soil was needed. He arrived in El Paso, crossed the river near Ysleta, and assumed personal command of the revolutionary forces. By this time some thirty American soldiers of fortune had joined the movement, together with Giuseppi Garibaldi, grandson of the Italian liberator, and Benjamin Viljoen, a veteran of the Boer War. After suffering a demoralizing defeat at Casas Grandes, Madero brought his army to Ciudad Juárez, where he hoped to establish his provisional capital. He made camp on the banks of the Rio Grande across from the El Paso smelter. Soon a swinging foot bridge across the river carried a two-way pedestrian traffic—El Pasoans visiting Madero's camp to take pictures, and his troops coming to El Paso to buy uniforms, clothing, and shoes. Madero checked in at the Sheldon Hotel, which overnight became a revolutionary hotbed of rebels, agents, detectives, spies, informers, and newsmen.[4]

On 23 April an armistice was announced so that a peace conference between the rebel leaders and government agents could be held. The setting impressed a *Times* reporter, who wrote:

> A prettier or more picturesque spot for holding the Mexican peace conference than the one selected opposite Hart's Mill could not have been found elsewhere on the border. It is a miniature valley carpeted with green grass and shaded by a luxuriant growth of cottonwood trees. The restless murmuring waters of the Rio Grande rushing over Hart's dam, sweep along at the foot of the valley, lying within the shadow of Orozco Hill. The place will hereafter be known as Peace Grove.[5]

There was no peace, however, as federal negotiators refused to accept Madero's demand that Díaz resign. The result was military action, largely instigated by Orozco and Villa, who were convinced that the government was stalling and that the city could be taken without difficulty. The battle of Ciudad Juárez began on 8 May with rebel forces advancing on the city from all sides, followed by three days of dynamiting, shelling, burning, and fierce hand-to-hand fighting. The city's supply of water and electricity was cut off, gaping holes were made in the walls of the adobe structures, and buildings in the heart of the city were extensively damaged. For El Pasoans it was the greatest show they had ever seen. In spite of repeated city officials' warnings of flying bullets, people stood on the river banks and roof tops and on box cars to witness the action. With the taking of the federal garrison on the third day of the battle, Gen. Juan Navarro surrendered. This was the drop that overflowed the bucket, as one historian has put it, leading to Díaz's resignation and departure for Europe. Overnight the triumphant Madero became the toast of El Paso, feted and dined by city officials and businessmen at the Sheldon Hotel, and honored with a victory banquet at the Toltec Club.[6]

El Paso business interests quickly perceived that the city could play an important role in the movement Madero had initiated. Not only could it serve as a sanctuary for Mexican revolutionaries as in the past, but as a sales center for arms, munitions, clothing, and supplies, as well as providing facilities for the safe keeping of Mexican cash holdings. Thanks to the first battle of the Revolution just across the river, El Paso found itself in the national spotlight, and there was every reason to believe that the city would be making headlines for some time to come. In appreciation for the service provided by the newspapermen, the Chamber of Commerce gave them a banquet at the Sheldon Hotel.[7]

Madero became president, but lacked the strong hand and emotional stability to pacify the country. He proved to be a bitter disappointment to the El Paso business community, as anti-Madero revolutionary activities on the border continued without abatement. In October 1911 El Paso supporters of Bernardo Reyes, a former Díaz official, reportedly were planning to initiate a revolt in that city against Madero. Moreover, in Ciudad Juárez, followers of the Emiliano Zapata movement to restore the lands illegally stolen from the villages in the state of Morelos, resorted to looting and burning. But the most significant revolutionary movement on the border in 1912 was led by Pascual Orozco, the former Madero leader. Disenchanted with the slow progress of Madero's revolution, Orozco, with financing from the Chihuahua aristocracy, championed the cause of Francisco Vásquez Gómez, an early Madero leader who had broken with his chieftain when he was denied the vice presidency. Using a colorful flag as their symbol, Orozco supporters came to be known as Red Flaggers. They captured Ciudad Juárez, and the smuggling of guns and ammunition was now renewed. This time the chief supplier was Krakauer, Zork, and Moye, hardware distributors. But by now El Pasoans had become much more concerned with the safety of American lives and property than with making headlines across the nation.[8]

The *vasquista* threat in Ciudad Juárez soon had local, state, and federal officials at odds with one another. Mayor C. E. Kelly of El Paso and Gov. Oscar B. Colquitt of Texas adopted the hard line and demanded strong action by the federal government, including military intervention. In an angry letter to President Taft, Kelly attributed the "deplorable state of affairs in El Paso to the continued anarchy in the city of Juárez," and maintained that the increased United States forces in the area had been used primarily "to prevent American citizens from defending themselves." According to Kelly, federal officials spent too much time trying to avoid irritating the Mexicans rather than protecting American lives and property. "I do not propose to maintain order in the City of Juárez," Kelly concluded, "but I do intend to protect life and property in the corporate limits of El Paso, Texas."[9]

Mayor Kelly's complaints brought a show of force by the federal government. Col. Edgar Z. Steever ordered all troops at Fort Bliss into the city, and El Paso took on the appearance of an armed camp with additional units from San Antonio, plus a company of the Texas National Guard, the sheriff's posse, and eleven Texas Rangers. The Taft administration, however, resorted to economic pressure rather than military force, and declared an arms embargo in March 1912. It had the desired effect of bringing about the defeat of Orozco by government forces under the command of Victoriano Huerta, a former Porfirian general. Thus, as historians Harris and Sadler have noted, the *orozquistas* ultimately failed because they lost the battle of El Paso—that is, in contrast to Madero, they were prevented from obtaining munitions as the result of the cooperation of the United States and Mexican governments.[10]

In spite of the failure of the Orozco rebellion, the political situation in Mexico rapidly reached a crisis with the approach of the year 1913. Disgruntled army officers openly plotted Madero's overthrow, and the United States ambassador, Henry Lane Wilson, spokesman for American business interests in Mexico, made no effort to conceal his lack of confidence in the Madero regime and its ability to control the situation. The long-expected coup came on 9 February 1913 in Mexico City. This marked the beginning of a bloody affair known as the "Ten Tragic Days." It brought about Madero's downfall and the installation of the tough old soldier, Victoriano Huerta. The whole sordid affair was climaxed on the night of 23 February when Madero and his vice president, José María Pino Suárez, were shot to death. The assassination, as covered by the *Times*, was the biggest single news story in the paper's history.[11]

Taking up arms against the dictatorial Huerta was Venustiano Carranza and his Constitutionalist movement, which quickly received effective support from Alvaro Obregón in Sonora and Pancho Villa in Chihuahua. Huerta's most formidable opponent, however, was Pres. Woodrow Wilson of the United States. He denounced the Mexican president as immoral, dictatorial, and counter-revolutionary, and therefore refused to extend diplomatic recognition to his government. In the hope that he could bring about Huerta's downfall by measures short of intervention, Wilson lifted the arms embargo of the previous administration to permit the purchases of war materials by Huerta's enemies, Carranza, Obregón, and Villa. The *Times* later reported that Villa spent around $15 million a year in the period from 1913 to 1915 in arming and equipping his Division of the North.[12]

Using Ciudad Juárez as his headquarters, Villa collected revenues from confiscated cattle, hides, and cotton, from the mines of Chihuahua, and from the recreational facilities on the border. Waging fierce guerrilla warfare, his forces captured Parral and Torreón. There he extracted a forced loan of some three million pesos for the primary purpose of preparing an offensive directed at the northern frontier. Villa's spies in Ciudad Juárez provided him with information regarding the size and strength of government forces in the city, enabling him to execute one of the boldest military actions of the Revolution. After capturing a southbound government train near Ciudad Chihuahua, Villa boarded his troops and horses into box cars, forced the engineer to turn the train around, and made him send telegrams to the federal commander in Ciudad Juárez stating that the *villistas* in Chihuahua had forced the train's return. In the predawn hours of 15 November the train entered the city. Villa, with a minimum of bloodshed, quickly brought the entire area under control. The *Times's* nine "extras" had kept El Pasoans informed about one of the greatest coups in Mexican military history. El Paso now had another Mexican hero who had put the city back on the front pages and whose expected purchases of arms and equipment would provide a needed stimulant to the local economy.[13]

Revolutionary activities in Chihuahua during 1912 and 1913 brought a stream of Mexican immigration to El Paso. This time the primary motivating factor was political as opposed to the economic motives of earlier periods. Rich and poor alike came to avoid persecution, as well as the violence and destruction that the Revolution left in its wake. A number of Americans were forced to flee for their safety, and 1,500 Mormons came to escape Orozco's Red Flaggers. Thousands of affluent Chihuahua families fled, including the eighty-four-year-old Luis Terrazas, who managed to salvage a portion of his wealth and bring it to El Paso in twenty horse-drawn wagons. Don Luis rented an entire floor of the recently completed Hotel Paso del Norte prior to his move to Albert B. Fall's mansion on Arizona Street. Fall, soon to be elected to the United States Senate from New Mexico, had for years been closely linked with the Terrazas, Creel, and Guggenheim interests of Chihuahua. Others who were able to salvage something settled in Sunset Heights of Golden Hill Terrace. One of the principal streets in Sunset Heights still bears the name of Porfirio Díaz.[14]

On the other hand, Chihuahua's impoverished and destitute were forced to settle in overcrowded Chihuahuita, where conditions would "shame the holes of Calcutta." For years this *barrio*, where most Mexican-Americans in El Paso lived, had been the worst slum in the country. It was characterized by privation, starvation, disease, and crime, conditions intensified and perpetuated with the influx of thousands of destitute refugees. Although some of the older residents had managed to move out of the *barrio*, they were quickly replaced by the new arrivals. The result was that the Second Street boundary between Anglo El Paso and Chihuahuita became more firmly fixed than ever before. But it was this *barrio* that spawned the foremost novel of the Revolution, *Los de Abajo* (The Underdogs), written by Mariano Azuela, an impoverished refugee. The hero Demetrio, a Mexican peasant, was forced to join the Revolution. He fought bravely but lost everything, a victim of the historical forces around him that he could neither comprehend nor control.[15]

President Wilson's measures short of war failed to bring about Huerta's downfall, and by April 1914 Wilson's patience was wearing thin. Seizing upon an incident in Tampico involving the arrest of American sailors, he ordered the landing of marines at Veracruz, thus pushing the two nations to the brink of war. El Paso officials voiced great concern over the possibility of race riots throughout the city should Villa attack El Paso. Fears subsided, however, and the crisis passed when Villa declared, "It's that little drunkard Huerta's fight; let him fight it." Diplomatic negotiations between the United States and Mexico continued long enough to allow Constitutionalist forces, supported by United States arms, to bring about Huerta's resignation in July 1914. This was followed by the return of a semblance of calm and tranquility on the border, at least for the time being.[16]

Because of strained relations that developed between Carranza and Villa after Huerta's resignation, Gen. John J. Pershing, the ranking American officer in the area, invited Villa and Obregón to El Paso for conversations, an event which once again placed the city on the front pages. There were parades, shouts of "Viva Villa," receptions at the country club, Pershing's home, and Fort Bliss, as well as meetings with local dignitaries. Villa had become the man of the hour in El Paso and the hero of two nations. His relations with Carranza, meanwhile, continued to deteriorate, resulting in a complete break between the two leaders and several months of anarchy in Mexico as the various factions quarreled and fought. Finally, Obregón's forces defeated the *villistas* at Celaya in April 1915 and placed Carranza in an extremely favorable position to assume the executive power.[17]

In the fall of 1915 a series of incidents and developments not only strained relations between the United States and Mexico, but also fanned the flames of racial hatreds and animosities to unprecedented heights along the entire border. One of these was the revelation of the *Plan de San Diego*, a bizarre Mexican scheme calling for the "liberation" of Texas, New Mexico, Arizona, Colorado and California, followed by the extermination of all Anglo males over the age of sixteen in this area. Angry El Pasoans demanded additional troops at Fort Bliss, rapidly becoming the largest military post in the nation.[18]

Fears of a *huertista* uprising seemed to be confirmed with the appearance in the El Paso area of both Huerta and Orozco. Having been informed of secret meetings between Huerta and German agents, United States officials arrested both Huerta and Orozco for violation of neutrality laws, and they were jailed in El Paso. Orozco escaped, but was killed by a party of ranchers near Sierra Blanca, Texas. To prevent demonstrations, his body was removed from the train before it reached the Union Depot. In view of the tension in El Paso, Huerta was kept under custody at Fort Bliss, but because he was a sick man (dying of cirrhosis of the liver), he was moved to a house at 415 West Boulevard (now West Yandell). There, after surgery, he died on 13 January 1916.[19]

Villa's power and influence declined rapidly after his defeat at the battle of Celaya in April 1915. He still remained hopeful that the cordial relations he had enjoyed with Gen. Hugh L. Scott, now chief of staff of the United States Army, would prejudice the American government in his favor. In a meeting between Villa and Scott in Juárez the previous January, Villa had agreed to cancel an attack on Naco, Sonora, because it might endanger Americans across the border in Arizona. Then in August, the two met again, this time in the home of J. F. Williams on Rio Grande Street. Because Scott was one of the few men that he respected and heeded, Villa agreed to rescind an order to confiscate all foreign-owned mines and smelters in the territory under his control.[20]

By October 1915 President Wilson clearly was leaning toward Carranza. Learning of this development in Ciudad Juárez, a tired and disillusioned Villa gave a *Times* reporter what he termed "the most important interview of my life." "My own forces have recently been diminished," Villa began:

> We haven't the men and money that we once had. All the men who have made money out of our cause have left us, and they have left us because they think no more money is to be made out of it. They have gone to other lands, where they are living upon the profits which they accumulated by turning the patriots' agony and the widows' and orphans' sorrow into a means of making money.
>
> I am here in Juárez, but this is as far as I shall go—north! Mexico is my country. I shall not run away from it. Here I have lived and here

I have fought. Here I shall fight and here I shall live. Here maybe I shall die, and that probably soon, but I am content. They may kill me in battle; they may murder me on the highway; they may assassinate me while asleep in my bed, but the cause I have fought for these past twenty-two years will live. It is the cause of liberty; the cause of human freedom; the cause of justice—long delayed and long denied to my suffering countrymen.[21]

Following the recognition of Carranza's government by the United States, the wrath of Pancho Villa found expression in January 1916 in the murder of sixteen American mining engineers by *villistas* near Santa Ysabel, Chihuahua. With the arrival of the caskets, tensions in El Paso rose to the breaking point, resulting in fist fights, violence, and the city's first genuine race riot. Every policeman in the city was sent to Overland Street to control the mob; otherwise, every Mexican in Chihuahuita, Mayor Tom Lea later said, would have been massacred. Local officials and the press pleaded for calm and restraint, and the Chamber of Commerce became extremely apprehensive that the mob activity would give the city a bad reputation. Although the police were able to prevent any further attacks on Mexican-Americans, the atmosphere remained charged, a clear indication that if further trouble occurred, the city might explode again.[22]

More trouble did occur. On 9 March 1916 the *villistas* launched a surprise attack on Columbus, New Mexico, and tensions in El Paso mounted again. This time, however, there were no race riots, since it soon became known that General Pershing had been ordered to pursue Villa into Mexico. This Punitive Expedition, with some 4,000 men, including infantry, cavalry, and field artillery, was the second military intervention in Mexico by the United States within the space of two years. Relations between the two countries again neared the breaking point. Early in May Gen. Hugh Scott and General Obregón, representing the Mexican government, met at the Paso del Norte Hotel and agreed on a plan of gradual withdrawal of American forces. Although President Wilson endorsed the plan, Carranza rejected it, insisting on immediate withdrawal. The Punitive Expedition therefore remained in Mexico, where skirmishes were fought between American troops and *carrancistas* at Carrizal. Pershing's forces failed to find Villa, and with the growing possibility by late 1916 of American involvement in the war in Europe, American troops were withdrawn in February 1917. Although border conditions gradually returned to normal and tensions eased, traditional racial attitudes had been badly scarred by the events along the border during the Mexican Revolution.[23]

A decade of warfare had left Ciudad Juárez a shambles. "A few years ago," wrote Ernest Peixotto in 1916,

> the city was a thriving enough Mexican town, deriving a rather large if illicit revenue from gambling joints, a cockpit, a bullring, and a jockey club, whose activities would not be tolerated on the American side of the river. But the various revolutions have crippled it sorely. At every turn you come upon ruins—houses riddled with bullet holes or breached with shot and shell; a public library razed to the ground, a mere heap of stones; a post office badly damaged; and opposite the Juárez monument, a brick building, roofless, with gaping walls and windows.[24]

Despite the efforts of the Juárez Chamber of Commerce, business conditions during the next three years failed to improve. On 15 June 1919 Pancho Villa's forces attacked the city for the third time since 1910 and controlled the situation until Gen. James B. Erwin, the commanding officer at Fort Bliss, ordered a force of approximately 3,600, including cavalry, infantry, and artillery, to Ciudad Juárez against the *villistas* on the grounds that American lives and property were in jeopardy. This marked the third United States intervention in Mexico in five years. After twenty-four hours of fighting, the *villistas* were forced to withdraw, and a semblance of order was restored. By that time the first United States Army Border Air Patrol had been established to conduct reconnaissance flights, giving El Pasoans a greater feeling of security than they had known for the past five years.[25]

The stage was thus set for 10,000 El Pasoans to give President-elect Alvaro Obregón an enthusiastic welcome when he visited the city in October 1920. At the banquet given in the Mexican leader's honor, Gov. William P. Hobby of Texas, much to the embarrassment of the Wilson administration, called for the immediate recognition of Obregón's government by the United States, then added: "I want Mexico and Texas to be pals. In fact, I want them to be the Mutt and Jeff of the Western Hemisphere." In view of the governor's enthusiastic though inappropriate comment, a decade of bitter and bloody border conflict surely had come to a close, at least as far as El Paso and Texas were concerned.[26]

Notes

1.Estrada, "Border Revolution," Introduction.
2. Michael Dennis Carman, "United States Customs and the Madero Revolution," *Southwestern Studies* no. 48 (El Paso, 1976): 40-41; W. Dirk Raat, *Revoltosos: Mexico's Rebels in the United States, 1903-1923* (College Station, Tex., 1981), 232.
3. Carman, "United States Customs and the Madero Revolution," 51; Bush, *Gringo Doctor*, 180-85. For details on the McGinty cannon, see *El Paso Herald*, 6 June 1911; and Bryson, *Down Went McGinty*, 58-59.
4. William Weber Johnson, *Heroic Mexico* (New York, 1968), 51; Turner, *Bullets, Bottles, and Gardenias*, 50; de Wetter, "Revolutionary El Paso," 55-56.
5. Quoted in de Wetter, "Revolutionary El Paso," 56.
6. *El Paso Times*, 8-10 May 1911; Estrada, "Border Revolution," 80-84; Johnson, *Heroic Mexico*, 69; Stanley R. Ross, *Francisco I. Madero* (New York, 1955), 166.
7. Turner, *Bullets, Bottles, and Gardenias*, 70; de Wetter, "Revolutionary El Paso," 55-59; John Middagh, *Frontier Newspaper: The El Paso Times* (El Paso, 1958), 159.
8. Raat, *Revoltosos*, 243; Charles H. Harris III and Louis R. Sadler, "The 1911 Reyes Conspiracy: The Texas Side," *Southwestern Historical Quarterly* 83 (April 1980): 325-26; Estrada, "Border Revolution," 92-94, 96-103.
9. C. E. Kelly to William Howard Taft, El Paso, Tex., 11 March 1912, El Paso Public Library, Southwest Collection, Vertical File—Pioneers—C. E. Kelly; Huntington Wilson to C. E. Kelly, 20 March 1912, *Records of the Department of State Relating to Internal Affairs of Mexico, 1910-1929* (microfilm, UTEP Library, M274R17F812.00/3357); C. E. Kelly to Secretary of State, El Paso, 26 March 1912, ibid., (microfilm, UTEP Library, M274R17F812.00/3474); Don M. Coerver and Linda B. Hall, *Texas and the Mexican Revolution* (San Antonio, 1984), 44-46.
10. Coerver and Hall, *Texas and the Mexican Revolution*, 47; de Wetter, "Revolutionary El Paso," 108-9; Charles H. Harris III and Louis R. Sadler, "The 'Underside' of the Mexican Revolution: El Paso, 1912," *The Americas* 39, no. 1 (July 1982): 82-83.
11. Johnson, *Heroic Mexico*, 96-107, 108-15; Middagh, *Frontier Newspaper*, 161.
12. Mark Gilderhus, *Diplomacy and Revolution* (Tucson, 1977), 9; *El Paso Times*, 19 July 1915; Estrada, "Border Revolution," 125.
13. Estrada, "Border Revolution," 117-18; Middagh, *Frontier Newspaper*, 164.
14. de Wetter, "Revolutionary El Paso," 112, 117; Richard Estrada, "The Mexican Revolution in the Ciudad Juárez-El Paso Area, 1910-1920," *Password* 24 (Fall 1979): 66.
15. García, *Desert Immigrants*, 131, 137, 141-43; Estrada, "The Mexican Revolution in the Ciudad Juárez-El Paso Area," 65.
16. Gilderhus, *Diplomacy and Revolution*, 10-11; Shawn Lay, *War, Revolution and the Ku Klux Klan* (El Paso, 1985), 22-23.
17. Christian, "Sword and Plowshare," 333; Johnson, *Heroic Mexico*, 289-91.
18. Coerver and Hall, *Texas and the Mexican Revolution*, 85-86; Charles H. Harris III and Louis R. Sadler, "The Plan of San Diego and the Mexican-United States War Crisis of 1916: A Reexamination," *The Hispanic American Historical Review* 58, no. 3 (August 1978): 381-408.
19. Christian, "Sword and Plowshare," 344-49. For details concerning Huerta's and Orozco's last days, see Michael C. Meyer, *Huerta: A Political Portrait* (Lincoln, 1972), 221-29. Huerta was first buried in Concordia Cemetery, but later was moved to Evergreen Cemetery.

20. de Wetter, "Revolutionary El Paso," 149, 151; Middagh, *Frontier Newspaper*, 175-76.
21. *El Paso Times*, 9 October 1915; Estrada, "Border Revolution," 136-37.
22. Lay, *War, Revolution and the Ku Klux Klan*, 16-17, 25; de Wetter, "Revolutionary El Paso," 154.
23. Historians of the Columbus Raid are now essentially in agreement that it was not as irrational or irresponsible as it was once thought, but there are still differences in opinion as to its motivation. The various theses include: Villa's desire not only to retaliate against the Americans but also to provoke their intervention in Mexico, thus creating a situation on which he could capitalize; his intention to loot Columbus and the nearby Thirteenth Cavalry encampment for munitions, remounts, and provisions; his desire for vengeance against certain Columbus businessmen who had allegedly defrauded him of money and arms; and finally, the provocative theory that German agents manipulated Villa into attacking Columbus in order to embroil the United States in a war with Mexico. See Charles H. Harris III and Louis R. Sadler, "Pancho Villa and the Columbus Raid: the Missing Documents," *New Mexico Historical Review* 50 (October 1975): 343. Friedrich Katz recently has offered evidence to suggest that the primary motivation was Villa's firm belief that Woodrow Wilson had concluded an agreement with Carranza that would virtually convert Mexico into a U.S. protectorate. See his "Pancho Villa and the Attack on Columbus, New Mexico," *The American Historical Review* 83, no. I (February 1978): 102. For the Punitive Expedition, see the works of Clendenen, Braddy, and Tompkins.
24. Ernest Peixotto, *Our Hispanic Southwest* (New York, 1916), 95-96.
25. Coerver and Hall, *Texas and the Mexican Revolution*, 127; Stacy C. Hinkle, "Wings Over the Border," *Southwestern Studies* no. 26 (El Paso, 1970), 5-6.
26. Coerver and Hall, *Texas and the Mexican Revolution*, 133. ★

David Dorado Romo

David Dorado Romo was raised in both El Paso and Ciudad Juárez. He earned a degree in Judaic Studies from Stanford University and has studied at the Centro d'Attivitá Musicale in Florence and the Hebrew University of Jerusalem. Historian, essayist, cultural activist, translator and musician, Romo published *Ringside Seat to a Revolution: An Underground Cultural History of El Paso and Juárez: 1893-1923* in 2005 with Cinco Puntos Press. His essays have been published in *The Texas Observer.*

From *Ringside Seat to a Revolution: An Underground Cultural History of El Paso and Juárez: 1893-1923*: Music Across the Lines

> "When El Paso wanted a Mexican serenata given in Cleveland Square or San Jacinto Plaza, the people of Juárez would be invited to attend. Mexican officials would send a military or municipal band over to El Paso parks and they would entertain the Americans all evening. This courtesy would be returned by El Paso and they would send either a military band from Fort Bliss or the El Paso City Band to the Plaza Principal."
>
> —Ernest Schuster, Author of *Pancho Villa's Shadow*

The Mexican Revolution created major demographic shifts along the border. Large numbers of both rich and poor Mexicans refugees crossed over to El Paso and stayed for good. The influx of new residents created a boom in the city's economy and cultural life. Spanish-language movie houses, theaters, vaudeville tents and Mexican social clubs added venues in town where local musicians could perform.

The concerts held at the main Juárez plaza during the Porfiriato were simply moved across the line to Cleveland Square in El Paso. Cleveland Square, right behind the El Paso Public Library, had a long tradition of hosting the city's most important events. The McGinty Band had played there regularly; former President Roosevelt had given a speech there during his campaign to retake the White House as an independent; Mother Jones had given a wild and fiery speech there as well. But during the revolution, the city's upper-class Mexican refugees used it as their new meeting place where they could carry out the social traditions they had left behind in the old country.

Margarita Jáquez de Alcalá, a descendant of one of the pioneer families of Juárez, recalls attending the Cleveland Square concerts every Thursday and Saturday, very much in the tradition of prerevolutionary Juárez:

> There were only people we knew there. Only the better class of people—gente bien—were there. You didn't see the lower classes there—gente fachosa—no one with a sloppy demeanor. The young ladies would walk along two files, and the men in the opposite direction and through the middle. Oh! They would shower us with flowers—gardenias, carnations. The young men would arrive . . . and if we liked them we would flirt with them . . . and you'd get home with bunches of flowers.[79]

Later when things quieted down a little more south of the border, both Mexican and American bands played in Juárez as well. But the revolution had changed the nature of the audience attending the Juárez concerts. The *El Paso Herald* described how the concerts at the plaza in front of the Guadalupe Mission had changed a year after the Battle of Juárez:

> On Sunday and Thursday nights, a remnant of the old municipal band toots Mexican waltzes and Italian operas from the iron bandstand, erected by the last federal "Jefe político" just before the Madero revolution. Different from the old is the present day scene in Plaza Constitución when the band plays on. The municipal band is short handed, there is a new director, a younger one, and the old uniforms of the bandsmen are the worse for wear. One man has a jacket and no uniform trousers, another the trousers and no jacket, and another fel-

low has the cap. But they toot and bang away just as gladly, and the townsfolk swarm about as flies. But, as with the hand, the throng is different. Most of the town belles are gone, and well dressed Mexican men are fewer. They throw confetti, but there are no "gardenias" being tossed about. Yet just as heartily do vendors cry and as eagerly does the public buy "dulces" and "orchatas." The revival of the municipal music finds eager, happy listeners, if they are fewer and poorer ones.[80]

Conditions were more profitable for musicians in El Paso, where its mayor set aside a $5,000 yearly budget for the city's best bands to give summer concerts at Cleveland Square and other city parks. Concha's Mexican Concert Band was hired to play on a regular basis. So was Reymundo S. González' band—composed of two upright basses, four drums and 30 woodwinds—which rivaled Concha's band in popularity. In 1917, one number composed by González, "The Charles Davis March," was dedicated to the El Paso mayor who was footing the bill for the public concerts.[81] (History has shown that a little brown-nosing and flattery never hurt anyone's musical career.)

At least three of the most popular bands in El Paso and Juárez between 1910 and 1920 were led by former sax players in Concha's turn-of-the century Mexican Concert Band. One of them was led by Trinidad's brother, Melitón, who, played the tenor sax. Melitón was a barber by day and would lead the band when his brother was unavailable. (He was one of the music teachers of Samuel Martínez—El Paso-born violinist, Orquesta Sinfónica de Yucatan conductor, ethnomusicologist and author of three books on pre-Colombian music.) Another well-known El Paso saxophonist/bandleader was Rayo Reyes who directed the Reyes Boys Band and was a member of Pancho Villa's military band when Villa was in control of Juárez. Severo González was perhaps the most versatile of all. In addition to being a sax player, the longtime El Paso resident owned the Central Café in Juárez, and was a celebrated boxing promoter and local philanthropist. He would later organize a famous jazz band which played at the Central Café in the early 20s.

When the 82-piece Banda del Estado Mayor del General Treviño played at Cleveland Square to promote international good will, more than 20 of the band members defected and sought asylum on the U.S. side of the border. The band was composed mostly of former members of the artillery band of Porfirio Díaz. It was directed by Carrancista Major Alfredo Pacheco, whom the *El Paso Herald* called "one of Mexico's best known composers with more than 400 compositions to his name."[82] On November 5, 1916, the *El Paso Herald* reported on the mass desertion of the Mexican musicians:

> Twenty-two members of the staff band of Gen. Jacinto B. Treviño, which played in El Paso, are said to have liked this city so well that they are loath to return to Chihuahua City. In the meanwhile Major Alfredo Pacheco, the director, is in El Paso, busily engaged in an effort to gather the men's instruments and uniforms, not to mention the deserters themselves. The equipment is, of course, the property of the Mexican government and will have to be given up by the prospective El Pasoans. The men themselves, however, cannot be taken back to Mexico without an order from Washington.

The local newspaper did not report whether the musicians or their instruments were ever returned to Mexico, but it would not be the last example of music and musicians escaping the narrow confines of national boundaries. By the late teens, while revolution was still going on in Mexico, new developments in America's cultural and political climate were pushing musicians to cross the line in the opposite direction—American musicians and tourists from all over the country were pouring into Juárez by the thousands in search of sex, booze and jazz.

Notes

79. Margarita Jáquez de Alacala, interviewed by Oscar Martínez, February 16, 1974, Institute of Oral History, UT El Paso
80. *El Paso Herald*, April 15, 1912.
81. *El Paso Herald*, May 11, 1917.
82. *El Paso Herald*, November 5, 1916. ★

Cynthia Farah Haines

Cynthia Farah Haines, raised in El Paso since the third grade, received her B.A. from Stanford University and her M.A. from the University of Texas at El Paso. A photographer, film critic, and scholar, she retired as an associate professor of film studies at UTEP after ten years. Haines is the author and photographer of *Literature and Landscape: Writers of the Southwest*, which received the C. L. Sonnichsen Book Award from Texas Western Press and a Border Regional Library Award; *Colors on Desert Walls: The Murals of El Paso* with Michael Juarez, which also won a Border Regional Library Award; and *Showtime! From Opera Houses to Picture Palaces in El Paso.* Haines is a former board member of the Texas Council for the Humanities and past chairman of the City of El Paso Arts Resources Department Advisory Board. She is the recipient of the Conquistador Award, the highest honor presented by the city of El Paso for her contribution to the arts and was inducted into the El Paso Women's Hall of Fame. Currently a member of the Broadcast Film Critics Association and the Kansas City Film Critic's Circle, Haines reviews foreign, art, and independent films for the Kansas City NPR affiliate KCUR. She also serves on the Kansas Film Commission and the Kansas State Historical Society Board and Executive Committee.

From *Showtime! From Opera Houses to Picture Palaces in El Paso*: Spanish Language Movie Theaters

Some of the most famous silent film actors in the United States were Mexicans who immigrated to El Paso during the Mexican Revolution. Ramón Novarro and Dolores del Río were among a group of exiles from Durango who arrived in 1914. Novarro, born Ramón Gil Samaniego in 1899, had connections to the El Paso-Juárez community. He was the son of Dr. Mariano Samaniego Jr., a dentist in Durango, Mexico, and grandson of Dr. Mariano Samaniego, a prominent physician and politico in Juárez.

Academy Award-winning actor Anthony Quinn was born in Chihuahua but lived in El Paso while his father fought for Pancho Villa during the Revolution. One of Quinn's vivid childhood memories, recounted in his autobiography, was of the first time his grandmother took him to a movie in El Paso, probably in 1917. The film starred Antonio Moreno and it "transported" Quinn. His grandmother Sabina told him that it could be him up on that screen and that someday her grandson would be a bigger star than Moreno.

In 1936, Quinn carried his grandmother, Doña Sabina, to the balcony of the Pantages Theater in Los Angeles to watch him in his screen debut in a gangster film entitled *Parole*! Quinn played a thug named Zingo Browning and appeared in a close-up that lasted a matter of seconds. His grandmother, who was weak and suffering from cancer, said "Tony . . . you are my Ramón Novarro. You are my Antonio Moreno. You are going to be a big star. . . . Now I can die in peace." She passed away two weeks later. Anthony Quinn spent more than six decades in Hollywood, appeared in more than 150 films, and won two Oscars for his performances in *Viva Zapata* (1953) and *Lust for Life* (1957).

The Soler brothers, Fernando, Andrés, Domingo, and Julian, and sisters Irene and Mercedes, acted in and directed 520 films, which at one time accounted for 10 percent of all Mexican movies ever made. They also began their careers in the United States during the Revolution.

As Mario T. García, an historian of this era in El Paso, notes, "After 1910, Mexicans faced the acculturating influence of American mass culture through the silent movies. Although it does not appear that the early movie houses such as the Crawford, the Grand, the Little Wigwam, and the Bijou specifically excluded Mexicans, the attendance of Mexicans at the movies grew when several Mexican theaters opened by the period of World War I."

Mexican theaters in South El Paso presented "Musical variety shows called tandas de variedadas" that "proved to be popular after 1910. For 10 to 15 cents a performance, Mexican workers could sit in the galleries and be entertained by touring Mexican showpeople." The management of the Estrella claimed their theater to be "the only place in El Paso where variety shows are performed in Spanish." Although "Mexican theaters throughout the Southwest initially presented both a film and a tanda, in time, according to one critic, the moving picture superseded both Spanish-speaking vaudeville and the legitimate theater. Legitimate theater in El Paso meant that for the most part Mexican theaters appealed to the middle-class tastes of wealthier and more prominent Mexican political refugees."

By 1917, theaters catering to a Mexican clientele showed some films produced in Mexico, "but for the most part Mexican audiences paid 6 or 11 cents admission, depending on where one sat, to see American movies featuring such stars as Charlie Chaplin, Mary Pickford, and Fatty Arbuckle." The Spanish-language paper *La Patria* reviewed movies, including a Chaplin film shown at the Teatro Rex.

During these turbulent times in Mexico, impresarios such as Juan de la Cruz Alarcón, Rafael Calderón Urrutia, his brother José Calderón Urrutia, and Juan Salas Porras made significant contributions that had an impact on the motion picture business both in Juárez and El Paso. They not only built movie theaters and theater chains, they created companies to distribute films on both sides of the border. They had lofty goals. The *El Paso Morning Times* reported that Alarcón believed "American business methods and advertising are more important than art in the moving picture field . . . Alarcón has started out to revolutionize screen entertainment in Mexico and Central America. Moneymaking, he admits frankly, is an object, but the education and democratization of the Mexican people by means of the film are two more important purposes which he hopes to achieve."

Juan de la Cruz Alarcón was a printer and newspaperman in Ciudad Juárez when he crossed the border in 1913. Two years later, he was the representative of the Cinematografía Anáhuac Company, proprietors of the Eureka Theater at 315 South El Paso. Alarcón's father-in-law, Narciso Urrutia (1857-1916), operated the Anahuac, one of the first movie theaters in Juárez, which opened in 1913. He was also the uncle of Rafael and José Calderón. Alarcón told the *El Paso Morning Times*, "People laughed at me and said my ideas were crazy when I entered the moving picture field . . . but I succeeded."

In the 1918 city directory, Alarcón was listed as manager of the Alcazar Theater on South El Paso Street. Along with the Calderón brothers and others, Alarcón established the International Pictures Company, possibly also known as the International Film Company, in El Paso with offices in Mexico City. According to the Articles of Co-Partnership recorded with El Paso County, the company's express purpose was the "purchase hiring, sale and general exploitation of films in the United States and the Republic of Mexico." Alarcón served as its first general manager.

Along with the Calderón brothers and Salas Porras, Alarcón also had an interest in International Amusement Company, a partnership also formed in 1919 "for the purpose of operating certain moving picture theaters" in El Paso and Juárez, including the Alcazar, Rex, Colon, Paris, Alameda, Mexico, Ideal, Estrella, Eureka, and Hidalgo. Other partners in International Amusement Company included Luis Alfonso Calderón, nephew of the Calderón brothers, and Ysabel Urrutia de Urrutia, widow of Narciso Urrutia and Alarcón's mother-in-law. In 1921, Alarcón and Urrutia sold their interests in International Amusement Company to the Calderón brothers and Salas Porras, and the Calderón brothers and Salas Porras appear as the sole owners by 1928. Alarcón moved to Mexico City where, in 1931, he produced *Santa*, Mexico's first talking motion picture.

The individual credited with the invention of subtitles is a matter of dispute, but it appears that bilingual films could very well have been developed on the border. Alarcón claimed credit for creating the concept of following English intertitles with ones translated into Spanish. Intertitles were printed cards that described narrative action or dialogue and were inserted between scenes in silent films. Subtitling as we know it today was introduced in the late 1920s with the advent of sound. There were four "picture shows" in downtown Juárez in 1918. The February 13, 1918, *El Paso Herald* reported that a machine was being used in one of the theaters that projected a Spanish translation on the lower part of the movie screen. According to the *Herald*, "The titles are translated on a strip of celluloid three and a half inches wide and then projected by means of a special stereopticon. The device was the invention of an El Pasoan, Francisco Norte."

"This development undoubtedly went far in acculturating the poor refugees—and a few of the wealthy—to the practices of everyday life in the United States." The movies also inspired dreams of a promised land in California. As one Mexican singer explained in a *corrido*, Hollywood films had enticed him to leave Mexico: "I dreamed in my youth of being a movie star and one of these days I came to visit Hollywood."

On March 18, 1919, the *El Paso Morning Times* reported:

> American slang offers no terrors for the official interpreters who translate the titles of slapstick comedies for the movies frequented by Spanish speaking people on South El Paso Street. So successful is the work of the motion picture lexicographers what [*sic*] many Americans who are studying Spanish make a practice of visiting the theaters for the purpose of obtaining aid in the understanding of Spanish as it is spoken in El Paso.
>
> Every morning the theater translator sits down at his typewriter into which has been inserted a long film of celluloid seven inches wide. At its side the regular film is gradually unwound, being stopped at each title. As soon as the title is read the interpreter pounds out the translation in Spanish in the celluloid, then goes to another title. The Spanish titles are flashed on the screen from a special stereopticon immediately following the English title. They appear at the bottom of the screen, displacing so much of the scene by the principal of "dissolving views." The invention is the idea of a young El Paso motion expert and is now in use wherever American films are used for Spanish-speaking audiences.
>
> The intricacies of American slang become easy when the Spanish-American attacks the question. "Fathead" becomes "torpe" which means a dull, stupid fellow. "Loafer" is made into "vago" and "easy money" becomes "dinero obtenido con facilidad," "money obtained with facility." No matter what the slang may be the word artist at the typewriter always has an equivalent ready. As a matter of fact, he has to be an expert in three different languages — English, Spanish and the most difficult of all — American slang.

Alarcón contended that bad translations and worn-out movie prints doomed American movies to failure in Mexico. "'Americans are making better films than Europeans and there is no reason why the continental films should be monopolizing the Mexican field,'" he told a reporter. He also had intentions of producing films in Mexico and, as noted, subsequently produced Mexico's first sound film. Alarcón asserted, "'Mexicans have tried to produce their own pictures many times, but have always failed. The reason is that they have always paid all their attention to art instead of business."

Alarcón offered an interesting assessment of the difference between Mexican and American movie audiences:

> There are three classes of people in Mexico, the lower, middle and higher classes, instead of one as in America. The three classes have not been in the habit of associating in playhouses. By advertising I hope and I am sure of my ability to get them together. This is where the education will come in. The peon, associating with people of a better class, will take more pride in himself, dress better and more cleanly when he goes to a show, where he will also get the educational benefit of the films. I am sure that moving pictures are going to do wonders in educating the Mexican people within the next few years. Everybody in Mexico admits that education is what the Mexican peons need, but it is a case of 'let George do it.' I feel that I am going to be able to really do something along this line worth while — more than the government perhaps.

Ironically, movies originally appealed to the undereducated because they were easy to understand and were shunned by the upper classes as crass entertainment for the lower classes.

Eduardo Albafull, originally from Spain, owned two movie theaters in Chihuahua, the Salon Rosa and the Centenario, which he ran himself. He made money in diverse commercial and industrial businesses including railroads and mining. He supposedly came to El Paso dressed as a woman in 1913 in order to avoid the Mexican revolutionaries. Eventually the Villistas took over his Centenario Theater, and Albafull chose to stay in El Paso. In May of 1916, he decided to return to Chihuahua City to recover the Centenario, which he eventually rented to entrepreneurs José and Rafael Calderón and Juan Salas Porras. Albafull went back to Spain in the 1920s where he died in 1933.

The brothers Calderón along with Juan Salas Porras were among the first to build movie theaters in the state of Chihuahua. Rafael was born in 1882 in San Andres, Chihuahua (now Riva Palacio), and José, in 1887, also in San Andres, to Delfina Urrutia and Rafael Calderón. They attended school in Chihuahua, the Mexican state adjacent to Texas. After studying at the New Mexico College of Agriculture and Mechanic Arts (now New Mexico State University), they went to work for the Kansas City, Mexico and Orient Railway while living in Chihuahua City. Both brothers served as presidents of the Chihuahua Chamber of Commerce. Rafael, who was married to Estela Fischer, died in El Paso in 1970. His son Rafael took over as manager of the Colon until it was sold in 1963 to Alameda Theater, Inc. He was also the proprietor of the Cactus Drive-In Theater on Dyer Street in the late 1950s and early 1960s.

José Calderón married María Stell. He died in 1964 in Acapulco, Mexico. José's sons Pedro, José Luis, and Guillermo Calderón-Stell became movie producers in Mexico City, making many important films. Their *cabaretera* film *Aventurera* (1949) is considered one of the top 10 Mexican films of all time.

Juan Salas Porras, born in 1886 in Parral, Chihuahua, was a well-respected and successful businessman and public official. He married Sara Romero Anchondo and had two sons, Carlos and Juan, and three daughters. Juan Sr. died at the age of 65 on February 16, 1951.

In February of 1918, the Calderón brothers, along with Juan Salas Porras, formed Calderón and Salas Porras, a company to exhibit films and produce variety shows, a partnership that lasted more than 30 years. In 1919, they acquired the Alcazar Theater in Chihuahua and later the Azteca, Apolo, Ideal, and Estrella. During the same year, they founded the International Amusement Company in El Paso, discussed above.

In January 1927 the Calderóns and Salas Porras dedicated the new Alcazar Theater in Chihuahua with the screening of *Ben Hur*. The most elegant of their theaters, the Alcazar presented *The Jazz Singer* in November 1929, an event that heralded the advent of sound movies in Mexico. Besides Mexican movies, American, Italian, German, and French films were shown, which was not the case in American theaters. To this day, Mexican moviegoers are much less provincial than Americans when it comes to watching foreign films.

Many famous Mexican actors, singers, and other performers also graced the stages of the Calderón and Salas Porras theaters Local musicians were hired to provide scores for silent films. In 1925, at the Centenario Theater in Chihuahua City, *cineconciertos* were presented during which the Orquestra Sinfónica Chihuahuense (Chihuahuan Symphonic Orchestra) performed. In September 1929, the orchestra opened the Azteca Theater.

In the 1930s, the Calderón brothers and Salas Porras entered the movie distribution business by establishing Azteca Films, Inc. They had offices at 501½ South El Paso Street in El Paso, 610 Soledad Street in San Antonio, 1907 South Vermont Avenue in Los Angeles, and in Chicago and New York. The Mexican government acquired the company in the 1950s in the course of nationalizing the business of film distribution and the operation of movie theaters across the country.

The spectacular Plaza Theatre in Juárez was the last theater built by the Calderóns and Salas Porras. It occupied a city block adjacent to the city's main square and the Mission of Our Lady of Guadalupe, built in 1668. The grand opening of the theater on March 19, 1947, was a major social event. It took three years to construct the 2,500-seat theater and cost four million pesos, approximately $800,000. Three stories high, the Plaza included fountains, a bar, restaurant, and a roof garden. Artist Aurelio G. Mendoza, who supervised the decoration of the Metropolitan Theater in Mexico City, created four large murals. They depicted the four moods of women and were titled *Dance of the Hours*, *Woman Resting*, *The Hunter*, and *Fountain of Youth*. On the exterior was a tower 45 feet high with mercury vapor lamps that were visible for 64 kilometers. The movie shown opening night was *Enamorada* (Woman in Love) starring one of Mexico's biggest stars, María Felíx. In 1953, Rafael Calderón, who was also managing the International Amusement Company, announced the installation of the largest movie screen in Mexico at the Plaza. Fifty-two feet wide and 27 ½ feet high, the curved screen allowed a 35 mm film image to be enlarged 436,000 times.

The Calderóns and Salas Porras owned, rented, or otherwise operated 10 movie theaters in South El Paso that catered to their Spanish-speaking clientele. Over the course of several decades, the chain of theaters run by the

Calderóns and Salas Porras included the Colon, Alcazar, Rex, Paris, Eureka, Hidalgo, Mexico, Ideal, Estrella, and the Alameda in El Paso and the Plaza, Anahuac, and Eden Theaters in Juárez. They became actively involved in communities in both Mexico and the United States where they operated theaters.

As noted, they formed the International Amusement Company in El Paso in 1919. Frank C. Alderete served as president of the company, Rafael Calderón Urrutia was vice president, José Asunsolo was also vice president, J. Muñoz Fernández was secretary, and Manuel Salazar was treasurer. By 1924, the company was controlled by the Calderón brothers and Juan Salas Porras. Juan Salas Porras's nephew Francisco managed Azteca Films in Los Angeles beginning in 1948. He and his wife, Josefina, attended movie premieres and participated in the Hollywood social scene. They returned to El Paso in 1964.

Spanish-language movie theaters were extremely significant to the Mexican and Mexican American communities of El Paso and Juárez. Juárez's magnificent Plaza Theatre and El Paso's Colon were central to the cultural life of the huge Spanish-speaking population of the area. To this day, memorable movie images continue to play in the minds of patrons of these early Spanish-language movie houses of El Paso and Juárez. ★

Frank Mangan

Native El Pasoan Frank Mangan (1921-2009) served in the air force in England, France, and Germany during World War II. He earned a B.A. in journalism from the University of Missouri and went on to work for twenty-eight years in advertising and public relations for the El Paso Natural Gas Company. After his retirement, Frank and his wife, Judy Peterson Mangan, founded Mangan Books in 1979 and published titles as varied as corporate and military history, gunfighter biographies, and New Age Channeling. Mangan Books was the publisher of many of the books of Leon Metz, such as *The Shooters* and *John Wesley Hardin: Dark Angel of Texas.* The book *El Paso in Pictures* has been re-released by TCU Press. Among Mangan's many honors is a Texas Institute of Letters award for book design and a Border Regional Library Association Award. He was a charter member of the El Paso County Historical Society and a founder and public relations advisor for El Paso's public television station KCOS.

From *El Paso in Pictures*: The Twenties Roared

In 1920, El Paso seems peaceful at last. World War I is over, and many of the ex-doughboys who saw duty on the border come back to El Paso to make their homes in the Southwest. The city harbors many refugees from Mexico and the revolution. Cash registers jingle and El Pasoans speak with unbounded enthusiasm. By the end of the decade the population moves up to 102,000—a fair-sized city.

By 1922, Mesa Avenue is paved all the way from downtown to Cincinnati Street, and construction is underway on the mesa road from Cincinnati across seven miles of rocky arroyos to tie up with Doniphan Drive in the Upper Valley.

The slag dump from the old Federal Copper Smelter was removed to make way for the building of Memorial Park, El Paso's largest. In the early twenties Piedras Street was still unpaved, and after heavy rains flood waters washed tons of sand and boulders down from the east slope of Mt. Franklin into the Five Points area.

In 1922, the town of Newman, on the Texas-New Mexico line, was officially mapped and filed. Sunrise Acres subdivision was filed in 1929 in far northeast El Paso on the Newman Road. Country Club Acres in the Upper Valley was filed in 1926. In 1928, Mayor R. E. Thomason officially dedicated El Paso's first airport.

El Pasoans danced the Charleston and went to vaudeville and movie houses like the Texas Grand, the Crawford, the Grecian, the Alhambra, the Unique, the American, the Bijou, and the Wigwam. The Plaza Theater opened grandly in 1930. After the shows they flocked to an elegant ice cream parlor called the Elite Confectionery where the W. T. Grant Company is now located.

The Elite had a huge marble ice cream bar decorated with stained glass and surrounded by tables and booths. The management served up a heady selection of ice cream sodas and an ice cream concoction known as the chocolate-covered baseball.

The new Volstead Act outlawed liquor on a national scale and the shadow of Prohibition settled across the nation. As the sources of liquor began to dry up, the eyes of Texas and other states began to focus on Juárez. Americans were looking for a drink, and they knew they could find a legal one in Mexico. Juárez put out the welcome mat along with a diversity of entertainment unequaled on the border. And now it was Juárez' turn to boom. It changed almost overnight from a sleepy little adobe town to a Mecca for fun-loving Americans. Along with the merry makers, the bootleggers came too, and they hauled vast quantities of Mexican booze in canvas-topped trucks back to Chicago and the Midwest. Hard on the heels of the bootleggers and smugglers came a new villain—the hijacker. He merely hung around the border, and when the illicit booze was delivered to the El Paso side of the Rio Grande, he moved in on the bootlegger and relieved him of his merchandise at gunpoint. In 1921, the *El Paso Herald* reported that "mounted smugglers and Mexican river guards clashed Saturday night, 300 yards west of the east end of the 'island.' More than 50 shots were fired, according to the report given our yesterday by Raphael D. Avila, chief of the river guards."

Running gun battles were all in a night's work for U.S. Customs agents, and seventeen of them were killed in a brief five years—between 1928 and 1933—along the Texas to Arizona strip of border.

Back across the river El Pasoans talked about an exciting new form of entertainment—radio. In 1929, Station KTSM came on the air with its first show featuring live entertainment by Karl the Kowhand—better known today as Karl Wyler, president of KTSM Radio and TV. For a short time KTSM shared facilities and airtime with station WDAH which was owned by the Methodist Church. The broadcasts emanated from the basement of Tri State Music Company, next to the Ellanay Theater on El Paso Street. The letters TSM stood for Tri State Music.

The first night football game in the Southwest was played in 1928 in El Paso High School stadium.

El Paso's skyline began to take on a brand new look in the twenties. The First National Bank building, on Sheldon Alley and Oregon, was constructed in 1921. In 1926, the Cortez Hotel, designed by architect Henry Trost, opened as the Hotel Orndorff. The following year the ownership changed and it was renamed Hotel Hussmann. Fortunately, for the changeover of the large electric sign atop the building, the names Orndorff and Hussmann both contained the same number of letters. However, the name changed again a few years later to Hotel Cortez. As the decade came to a close two other new high rise buildings were beginning to take shape —the Bassett Tower and the Hilton Hotel.

And then the Great Depression closed in.

***

¡Salud!

During prohibition days El Pasoans, as well as famous visitors from all over the country, enjoyed the cultural centers of Juárez. On Saturday nights the streets of Juárez bulged with the generations of the twenties. And the fun centered around 16th of September Street and Lerdo where business boomed in spots like the Big Kid's, The Tivoli, Harry Mitchell's Mint Bar, the O.K. Bar and the old Central Café. Guest books and pictures signed by celebrities visiting the Mint and the Central read like a Who's Who of entertainers, politicians and sportsmen of the twenties. Among the famous were Jack Dempsey, Jim Jeffries, Eddie Rickenbacker, Amelia Earhart, H. L. Mencken and Mayor Jimmie Walker of New York.

Another flourishing spot, although not nearly as first class, was an adobe saloon called the Hole in the Wall. Its location alone was enough to keep it crowded for a number of years during prohibition. The Hole in the Wall was on Cordova Island west of where the foot of Piedras Street meets Paisano Drive today. Its clientele didn't bother with such formalities as U. S. customs inspections; they merely parked their cars, lifted the wire fence and walked across a plank which served as a foot bridge over an irrigation ditch. After a rain, people's feet got a bit muddy but they didn't seem to mind. After all, here they were living it up in adobe splendor and having mixed drinks within a few feet of the dry old U. S. A.

On the American side, one of the favorite eating spots was the Modern Café, located in the basement of the Mills Building. The Modern had a dance floor and dinner music combined with jazzy elegance that appealed to El Paso tastes during the roaring twenties. ★

John O. West

John O. West was born in El Paso and received his B.A. from Mississippi College, an M.A. from Texas Tech, and a Ph.D. from the University of Texas at Austin. He taught English and folklore at the University of Texas at El Paso for thirty-nine years. He collaborated with the artist José Cisneros on the books *Riders Across the Centuries* and *José Cisneros: An Artist's Journey*, which won the Twitchell Award from the New Mexico Folklore Society. Both books are Border Regional Library Association Award winners. West is the author of *Mexican American Folklore*, which won a San Antonio Conservation Society award; *Cowboy Folk Humor*; and *The Pueblo de Socorro Grant*; all three won Border Regional Library Association awards. West's articles have appeared in such publications as *Southwestern Art*, *Southwestern American Literature*, *Journal of American Folklore*, *Western Review*, and *Southwestern Folklore*. His article "The Galloping Gourmet" received a finalist Spur Award from Western Writers of America for Best Western Short Nonfiction in 1985. In 2002 West was made a Fellow of the Texas Folklore Society in recognition of his contributions to the society and its publications, and was named an "Author of the Pass" and inducted into the *El Paso Herald-Post* Writers Hall of Fame in 1995. In 2002 he retired as professor emeritus of English from the University of Texas at El Paso.

The Weeping Woman: La Llorona

Among Texas' most fascinating women is La Llorona, the focus of a migratory legend to be found in many cultures. Not a historic character like some heroes and heroines—say Davy Crockett, or the Babe of the Alamo—nonetheless La Llorona is real to many people. She fits a pattern—in her behavior, when and where she appears, and such—and she fills a need, much like defeated Southerners needed a don't-fence-me-in model like Jesse James. The Weeping Woman teaches a lesson thou shalt not fool around outside your social class—or provides a scarecrow to keep wayward children (or even erring husbands) on the straight and narrow. Although the legend of Llorona travels from place to place, she often acquires local characteristics to make her even more horrible—or like the flame that attracts the moth, even more fascinating.

Like many other dwellers in the Southwest, La Llorona is not native-born. In fact, the weeping woman garbed in white who haunts particular places—especially water—is found in many parts of the world. In Germany for example, she appears in Cologne as *Die Wiesse Frau.* She is the spirit of a peasant girl, led astray and deserted by a naughty young nobleman; in a mad rage she killed their child, stabbed the father to death with his own sword, and later hanged herself—but she comes back regularly to haunt the scene of the double murder, and woe betide anyone who speaks to her.[1] Another girl led astray was reported in the Philippines after World War II. In this case the girl, of Spanish heritage, became the prey of Japanese occupation troops—and the mother of several children. After the liberation she wanted to return to her native village, but the children were evidence of her shame, so she killed them—then went mad and sought in vain for her babies.[2]

These two stories, albeit far in scene from the Hispanic Southwest, contain most of the essential details of the La Llorona story. In both stories there is cultural or racial difference between the lovers, the girl kills the offspring, and madness results. And the typical Mexican relative of La Llorona follows much the same pattern: a Spanish nobleman and a low-born maiden fall in love and have children; when he goes to Spain on business, he's encouraged by his parents to marry an eligible lady of his own class. On his return to Mexico, he breaks the news to his mistress, who goes mad and drowns the children and kills herself—but her soul cannot rest. She must search for her children forever until she finds them.[3] Here the element of water occurs—and the basic pattern of La Llorona in the Southwest is completed.

In the El Paso area stories of the woman in white are plentiful, especially among the Hispanic population of low economic status. Told by children, they are simply horror stories; told by parents, they become obedience tales, intended to warn daughters, especially, against liaisons outside one's own social level. The pickings are rich indeed. Witness the following, collected in the El Paso area:

Late one night my uncle and one of his friends were coming home late from the cantina. *They always took too much* tequila, *you know, and so it was pretty late. All at once they saw this lady, about a block away, walking toward the canal. She really had a good figure.*

Well, you know how guys are when they've had too much tequila—*they get interested in the ladies. So they hurried to catch up and they even called to her, but she didn't wait. She walked on down by the canal.*

Finally they were just a few yards away, and they called to her to wait. Slowly, she turned around—and she didn't have any face! She lifted up her hands toward them, and she had shiny claws, like tin! And she was coming toward them, like she was going to get them, you know!

Well, they turned and ran, with the woman right behind them, 'til they got to a bright street light, where she disappeared. My uncle never went to the cantina *after that-he didn't want to meet La Llorona again.*[4]

A story collected locally by Norma Herrera, a student of folklore at the University of Texas at El Paso, has an interesting twist:

When she was born, she was a twin. She and her sister were so identical that when they were baptized, the other one was baptized twice. La Llorona was never baptized. She married when she was nineteen and had a son and a daughter. But she did not love them, so she drowned them in a ditch. When she died and went before God, He punished her by having her cry and search throughout the world for her children, until the day the world ends. Then she will be pardoned. They say that she appears where there are lakes and ditches, and her weeping and wailing can be heard.

As has been noted, La Llorona is usually found near water, and often the location is related to the crime that condemned her, like the Wandering Jew, to wander the earth searching for peace. One little old lady told the author about La Llorona, linking her sorrowful deed of drowning her children with the 1925 flood of the Rio Grande, providing believability with the detail of date—as well as making available enough water to drown any number of children.

In an occasional story told on the border, the rejected lover, crazed by the way she has been treated by her mate, kills their children and serves them as a meal to their father and his new love. Medea stopped short of making dinner of them, but not so "The Wicked Stepmother" of our Southern mountains who made the little boy into "rabbit stew."[5] And many stories have as their theme La Llorona's hatred of men, luring them to their deaths or driving them mad, much like Lilith of Hebrew tradition.[6] Kirtley finds reason to believe that although there are apparent connections between La Llorona and the Aztec goddess Civacoatl, there is much more evidence of European origin for the basic story, with local variants occurring, as is common in oral transmission, wherever a similar sort of tragedy has reportedly taken place.[7]

Along the Texas-Mexico border where a blend of Hispanic and Indian culture has dominated the scene for most of the last four centuries, it would be quite unlikely not to find the same sort of blending and variety as elsewhere in this world-wide narrative. The Lilith strain was found (with an interesting twist) by Ray Green and Federico Aguilar, Jr., in the following:

> *La Llorona hated men, especially men who have two or more women. She appears to them dressed in a white robe and makes a pass and when they follow her they are always found drowned, sometimes in the canal, but sometimes they will be in the street. They always die with their eyes open like they were looking up at something and couldn't stop.*

They also found that the death of La Llorona's children is not always deliberate, although the result is somewhat standard:

> *There was a woman who had gone out into the fields one day to help her husband with the crop. She left her children unattended. When she came home that evening, she found all of their children dead. Somehow they had poisoned themselves. When she saw this, she went out of her mind and killed herself. Since a suicide cannot be admitted to heaven, the Llorona was condemned to wander the earth.*

William Campion found a lady of seventy-two who never forgot the lesson she learned many years ago:

As a young lady I often met José in the grove of trees near the river. Much kissing and loving took place but I was always careful to leave the area well before midnight. One night shortly before my engagement, time got away from me and I failed to leave before 12:00. A cold chilling wind came up suddenly from the north with a furious intensity. A cat screamed, and a plaintive wailing sound came to my ears. It grew louder and louder until a blast of wind caused a white-robed figure to whisk past me. As the figure darted by, I saw that it had no face. I fell to my knees and sought God's help. Before long the wind stopped, and I could no longer hear the mournful cries. To this day, I have not returned to that cursed spot.

A youngster interviewed by Mary Lee Wight got her story straight from *mamá:*

My mother said to never go to the Rio Grande because if I do there will be this lady and her name will be La Llorona. My mother said if I went there the lady might drown me. She is always crying every time because she drowned her children. If you go she will drown you, too.

But another girl, who told her experience to Ralph Montelongo years later, had to learn her lesson the hard way—she got a life-long affliction of asthma from being out too late:

I stayed outside because it was too hot inside. Then I heard a howl like a coyote and I thought it was a dog. Then I heard a woman's voice scream: "Quiero mis hijos! Donde están?" *[I want my children. Where are they?]. Then a white shawl, or scarf, fell on my face and it made me take a very deep breath. The scarf smelled so bad that when I breathed in, all the odor went to my lungs. This caused me to have asthma ever since. Then it started to rain very hard and all I could do was stand there and cry. When my mother came home a few minutes later, she found me lying on the ground, all wet and cold, with the scarf next to me. Next day it was very sunny and my mother washed the scarf and set it to dry on the* tendedero *(clothesline). When she sent for it about noon, it was gone! I think that La Llorona took it back.*

Ignacio Escandon recalls from his own childhood in El Paso that children were told *"La Llorona te llevará si no te portas bien!"* [La Llorona will carry you off if you don't behave!] His memory was that

> *she had lost her sons and that if she did not find her children she would take other children . She was called by other names—Chamuco, Roba-chicos, La Llorona, and La Malinche.* Chamuco *is only a name for bogeyman;* Roba-chicos *literally means stealer of children; and* La Malinche *is used to equate with the idea of mal—evil, from mal in malinche.*

And Cathy Skender collected a differently motivated one from a boy raised in Cd. Juarez, Chihuahua:

> *A long time ago, an Indian couple was to be married, another ordinary marriage as it may appear. But as time went on, the economic status of the family went from fair to very poor. When the couple had its first baby, a boy, the father knew he couldn't feed him, so after thinking about what was best for the child, he went to the river, and after asking God for forgiveness, he dropped the child in the river. The husband believed he was doing the right thing and repeated his feat as each child was born. Each time the town's people heard the wife screaming,* "Ay, my hijo" *[Oh, my son] in an eerie tone. When her last son was born [all precious ones were boys], she was determined to have him live. She went down to the river, and after her husband dropped the boy, she went after him. Since she wasn't skilled in the art of swimming, she drowned along with her son.*
>
> *Nobody thought much of it after the death, but one foggy night, one of the farm workers saw the ghostly figure of a woman and child in the river. The woman screamed in her high pitched voice, "Oh, my son." After that night, the ghost appeared on the water and the nearby land. The husband couldn't sleep because he heard these eerie sounds. Finally the husband,*

knife in hand, jumped into the river and tried to kill the woman. After his unsuccessful try, his body was never found.

After the story was spread around, people reported seeing her in different places. But the local people said that she appeared only on rainy, foggy nights.

Rainy nights provoke another Llorona to appear, Miss Skender reports:

Well, my friends told me there once lived this lady who had a bunch of kids. Well you see, she couldn't feed these kids. So she decided to kill them. She took them to the river and told them they were going to go swimming. They believed her. She drowned them. And God punished her for this. So he said, "You will always cry when a person puts a broom in the corner and it's raining." She regretted what she had done. But every time someone puts a broom in the corner when it rains at night, she has to go out and kill someone.

In the dark of night, if one has been told often of La Llorona since early childhood, shapes and sounds bring back memories, and goose bumps go up one's neck. La Llorona wants to get even with those who are happy, this is why men—the cause of her trouble—often are driven mad by the sight of her in the night.

What does La Llorona look like? Stories vary, but generally, she looks beautiful—even enticing men closer—until one can see either the face of a horse or a blank, empty one. She dresses in long flowing robes—white or black—and her long, shiny fingernails are like knives by starlight.[8]

Several years ago, people in one of the local *barrios* kept hearing La Llorona cry about eight at night, every night. They began to group together for comfort and protection—and whoever was making the sounds of La Llorona robbed the houses people had left in fear. Such is the power of the tales of La Llorona.

But whether you think a La Llorona is only a legend or not, when you are out walking late at night, you'd better beware! She may appear to you, entice you and leave you mad. As our Mexican friends would say, *"Cuídate! La Llorona!"*

Notes

1. Johann G.T. Grässe, *Sagenbuch des Preussischen Staats*, cited in Bacil F. Kirtley, "'La Llorona' and Related Themes," *WF*, XIX No. 3 (July 1960), 158. Kirtley's fourteen-page article is packed with world-wide echoes of La Llorona.
2. Richard I. Hayden, then a radioman third class in the U.S. Navy, collected this local legend at San Miguel, P.I., in 1968 or 1969.
3. Soledad Pérez, "Mexican Folklore from Austin, Texas," *The Healer of Los Olmos, PTTS*, XXIV (1951), 73-76, brings together several variants of the Llorona story. I have synthesized the essential story from her work as well as from others collected around El Paso.
4. A student (whose name I have forgotten) at what was then Texas Western College gave me this jewel in 1963. Student-collected materials will be cited hereafter in text. They form an important part of the University of Texas at El Paso Folklore Archive.
5. Richard Chase, *American Folk Tales and Songs* (1956; rpt. New York: Dover Books, c.1971), pp. 47-50.
6. Lilith, according to Nathaniel Ausubel, *A Treasury of Jewish Folklore* (New York: Crown, c. 1948), pp. 592–554, was—or is—a female demon, seductress, and man-hater, sometimes called "The Howling One"—not too far from "The Weeping Woman"; in addition, she kills the children she bears after seducing unwary men. Lilly Rivlin in "Lilith," *Ms.*, I (Dec. 1972), 96, says "In medieval Europe (especially in Germany), Lilith became a popular man-devouring creature . . . who covets other women's children, and threatens to steal them . . . [Also] she becomes in the Middle Ages a scraggy-toothed hag. . . . Though ugly and malformed she still prevails, however, as the seductress of sleeping men."
7. Kirtley, pp. 159-162.
8. Pérez, pp. 73-74. ★

Bill Wright

Born in Abilene, award-winning photographer and writer Bill Wright began a successful business career after receiving his B.B.A. in marketing from the University of Texas at Austin. After thirty-two years as co-founder of Western Marketing, he sold the business to his employees and began his second career as an author and photographer. A familiar face in El Paso during his first career, Wright worked among the Tigua Indians for six years writing and photographing the tribe. His book *The Tiguas: Pueblo Indians of Texas* won the Border Book Award and was followed by *The Kickapoo: Keepers of Tradition*, both published by Texas Western Press. In addition, he is the author and photographer of *Portraits from the Desert: Bill Wright's Big Bend* and *People's Lives: A Celebration of the Human Spirit*, both released from the University of Texas Press; *The Texas Outback: Ranching on the Last Frontier*, a collaborative project with photographer June Van Cleef that was published by Texas A&M University Press; and *Oman*, an essay and photographic journal published by Fastback Books. Wright has exhibited his photographs in solo exhibitions and group shows in the United States and around the world. In addition, he has conducted many photographic workshops, gallery talks and lectures. He has served on numerous national and state boards and committees including: The Harry Ransom Humanities Research Center Advisory Board, The Harrington Foundation Endowment for the University of Texas Board of Directors, the Texas State Historical Association Executive Committee, the University of Texas Press Board of Advisors, The National Council on the Humanities, The Sul Ross Center for Big Bend Studies Advisory Board, and The School of American Research in Santa Fe, New Mexico, Board of Managers. His appointments include the National Endowment for the Humanities by President Reagan and the Texas Commission on the Arts. Wright is also a member and past president of the Philosophical Society of Texas.

From *The Tiguas: Pueblo Indians of Texas*

ON 17 SEPTEMBER 1540, THE INDIANS OF THE Tiwa-speaking villages near present-day Albuquerque awoke to startling news from their scouts: The long-awaited meeting with the tall, strange men from the south was at hand.

For years they had listened to stories of the disaster befalling their trading partners in the Valley of Mexico. Then around 1536, their traders returned from the land of the Jumanos speaking of a tall, bearded, light-skinned man and his black companion who healed the sick while traveling westward toward Mexico through what is now Texas. The meeting between the traders of the north and Álvar Núñez Cabeza de Vaca and Esteban, a black man from Morocco,[1] was the first recorded encounter between the people of the pueblos and the "Old World."

While the written history of the Tiguas begins with this encounter, noted in Cabeza de Vaca's journal, oral tradition and archaeological evidence push the story of the Tiguas and all Native Americans back to the day when the land stretching from the Arctic to the windswept fjords of Tierra del Fuego was populated only by plants and animals. Archaeologists now believe the first inhabitants of the Americas came across a land bridge connecting Siberia and Alaska sometime between 75,000 and 12,000 years ago. Called Beringia, this land bridge was exposed on and off during the Pleistocene, a cold period when much of the earth's water was held in glacial ice and sea level was lower than today.

BEGINNINGS, TO 1540

The newcomers migrated south through Alaska and beyond. They hunted large animals like the wooly mammoth and mastodon, many of which are now extinct, and left their spearpoints as stone calling cards, announcing themselves to modern researchers. Yet details of their movements are still controversial. The time of arrival has not been set, and some evidence suggests multiple migrations from Asia over thousands of years. Passage south was made either inland through an ice-free corridor nestled between the great ice sheets of the

Rocky Mountains and the eastern glaciers, or along the coastline in primitive boats. It seems that succeeding generations spread quickly throughout the northern continent before continuing southward, perhaps arriving at the tip of South America by 8000 B.C. All we really know is that the ancestors of the Tiguas came to the "New World" from Asia sometime in the last 75,000 years, with the earliest undisputed evidence of human occupation—the characteristic fluted points of the Clovis culture—dating from about 12,000 B.C.

By 11,000 B.C. the glaciers began their most recent recession. The environment changed dramatically, many of the large animals disappeared, and the Indians were forced to seek new sources of food and new strategies for survival. They began to rely on small game and gather more plants. Plant gathering gradually led to cultivation among some groups. Indians of south central Mexico were the first to develop agriculture in the Americas, and they apparently introduced the science to peoples of the American Southwest.[2] The southwesterners committed to a settled life as farmers in the desert, building irrigation canals and living in multi-story houses for greater protection. Some of these early apartments still stand. The people of an intermediate southwestern culture that archaeologists call Anasazi, known from the ruins at Chaco Canyon, New Mexico, and similar sites, are generally thought to be the ancestors of the Tiguas and other modern Pueblo Indians.[3]

The Place: Ysleta del Sur Pueblo, El Paso, Texas

The Ysleta del Sur Pueblo, home of the Texas Tiguas, is located in Ysleta, now a part of El Paso, Texas. The Tigua tribal members live throughout the area and the nation with some six hundred living in the HUD development on tribal lands near the Mission of Our Lady of Mount Carmel, the mission established for Indians by the Spanish after their journey to the area in 1680.

The original habitations were of mud and the branches of trees . . . similar to *jacal* structures in use today. As the development of the area continued, the Indians became concentrated in an area that was known as the Barrio de los Indios to the Hispanic population surrounding them. Later, after the construction of the HUD housing, it was called the Old Pueblo.

In addition to the homes and the mission, the Tigua Tribe operates two modern restaurants and a visitor interpretation center with historical displays, craft sales, and demonstrations. There is a regular schedule of social dances performed by tribal members during the summer tourist season.

Gran Quivira, according to oral tradition, was the ancestral home of the Tiguas of Ysleta del Sur. The pueblo was abandoned around 1675 due to encroachment by hostile Plains Indians. The Tiwa-speaking inhabitants of Gran Quivira, along with those of the other Salinas Valley Pueblos, migrated to Isleta Pueblo, near present-day Albuquerque, and to other locations along the Rio Grande and west of the mountains, some as far south as El Paso del Norte.

Because the Spanish made intensive efforts to Christianize these Gran Quivira Indians, some postulate that these peoples were more comfortable with the Spanish and less likely to revolt against the occupying forces than the older residents of Isleta, New Mexico, and constituted the majority of the group that accompanied the Spanish refugees to El Paso del Norte in 1680. Possibly they were also the group that remained in Ysleta del Sur after the reconquest of the pueblos by De Vargas. In 1718 Isleta, New Mexico, was reoccupied by the Tiguas who had dispersed during the revolt and by some who returned from Ysleta del Sur.

> This is home to me, this is really home. Just by looking at the area, you know, I hear wind. I feel at peace, I feel like I am at one with nature, and nature is with me, side by side. I could stand there and squat, and mess with the pebbles, touch the rocks, walk around, look to the horizon, and feel comfortable. I feel at peace. I feel like there are spirits around, I feel like I could communicate with them, I feel like I am understood. It's almost like a security blanket. It is a good feeling.
>
> To me, any place that I go that is a ruin, it is part of me and I am part of it, whether it is in Arizona, or New Mexico, whether it is out in South Dakota, there is a relationship. Being native, being able to relate to that sight . . . the ruin . . . the peace behind it, the understanding of the culture, the struggles. All of this old history says that this was our home, to me, Mother Earth, Mother Earth is home. This is all home.
>
> Danny Archuleta

All of the Tigua do not live in the new pueblo because of a shortage of tribal housing. The nearby Old Pueblo, or Barrio de Los Indios, as it is called, is still the location of many tribal members' homes as well as the *Tuhla*, the sacred meeting house of the tribal council.

> The guys here contribute to their own household, most of the men are like this. If something goes wrong, they get out there, they are real handymen. Most of the old homes that they live in, they built themselves. They are the ones, I would be willing to call them the backbone of the tribe, the men. Not taking away anything from the women, because they do have their own say so here and there.
>
> Danny Archuleta

> The present housing community has 113 homes, but that is not enough. My waiting list consists of over thirty families. Now, the problem is to find the land to build on.
>
> Outside the HUD housing community, there are a lot of tribal members that are renting, or they have their own homes. The ones that own homes right now, and living in substandard condition, I am referring them to the HIP program, which is the Housing Improvement Program under the BIA. The way this program works is if they qualify, if they have all the qualifications that they need to meet for the program, then the HIP will either renovate their homes or even build them a new home.
>
> Rosemary Hisa

Ritual

The Tiguas have a rich ceremonial life that has continued uninterrupted for hundreds of years. After the occupation by the Spanish, the native religion was integrated with Catholicism after many struggles with the Spanish, culminating in the Pueblo Revolt of 1680. After that time, the Indians were permitted to practice their historic rituals without harassment.

Much of the ritual is practiced in secret in the modern representation of the *kiva*, the *tuhla*. Non-tribal members are excluded from these observances but are permitted to observe the public performances which occur on the listed feast days. The principal feast day is 13 June, when the Tiguas celebrate their patron, St. Anthony. There is a mass, then a procession on St. Anthony's Day caring the image of the saint to its place in the mission of Our Lady of Mt. Carmel, which was established by the Spanish after the revolt and their retreat to the El Paso area. This followed by a ritual scourging with *varas* from the river, then dancing and a public feast.

Today, there is a movement by the Tiguas to rediscover those traditional practices which have been lost over time, strengthening their connection with the past as they maintain their identity in the modern world.

Prior to the feast day of Saint Anthony, members of the tribe gather at the home of the mayordomo to share a breakfast and then disperse in the four cardinal directions, to secure donations for the public feast to be held in conjunction with the celebration of St. Anthony.

> Every year, no matter what day of the week it falls on, Sunday or Tuesday, June the fourth is part of the preparation for the feast day, the Feast of St. Anthony. Every June the fourth, members of our pueblo go off in four different directions from a street corner out in Ysleta, corner of Old County Road and Whitney Road. That was the corner from which our people always went off into the four different directions. I think in the old days, they had irrigation ditches from the four directions that would meet at that point. The people, our Indian people, would get together at that corner. They still do today. They go off from that point as being the center, and they begin their June fourth donation seeking for the Feast of St. Anthony from that spot.
>
> Danny Archuleta

The former cacique, Trinidad Granillo (1909-1989), with members of the tribal council disperse to seek donations for feast of Saint Anthony.

Trini Granillo, who was our past cacique and his war captain right behind him, Ponciano, the one with the bandana. Together, they work hand-in-hand to make sure that everything is carried out properly. Trini was a good leader. In his own way and in his own style. Very nonchalant, low key, but always got across what he needed to get done. Ponciano was a good war captain. He has a throat! Can this guy sing! He can sing. It takes a lot of commitment to be a war captain. You're the right hand man of the cacique. Your responsibility is making sure that the ceremonial activities are carried out the way they should be. By golly, you better do it. The cacique is the spiritual leader. If he is not in good heart, the community is not in good heart. This is on June fourth. They are getting ready. They are at that corner that I was talking about a little earlier, where they head out to the four directions. They are getting ready to start collecting food on that day. Seek those donations.

Danny Archuleta

Notes

1. Esteban, or Estebanico of Azemour as he is more accurately called, played a more important role in the exploration of America than previously recognized. Anthropologist Nicholas Houser observes: "Estebanico's cultural (Moroccan) behavior reflected a tribal sense of community and native healing skills, in addition to his affable personality, linguistic abilities, and keen intelligence, which resulted in his immediate acceptance among Native Americans. This is in contrast to the three Europeans (Andres Dorantes, Alonso Castillo, and Cabeza de Vaca) who were reluctant healers and maintained an aloof presence among the Indians. Estebanico's use of colorful adornments (feathers and jewelry) and his two greyhound dogs (which later accompanied him to Zuni) strongly suggest that he recognized the Islamic concept of *bakara* (a property of holiness or state of grace which affords protection)." Nicholas Houser, "Estebanico of Azemour" (Prepared for the XII Travelers Memorial of the Southwest, An Official Project of the United States Columbus Quincentenary 1 July 1992). Also see Cabeza de Vaca's, *Adventures in the Unknown Interior of America*, Cyclone Covey, ed. and trans. (University of New Mexico Press, 1988), 65.
2. The Southwest was linked to Mesoamerica by a series of trails that served as trade routes. For further evidence of the interaction between the cultural groups of North America, see: Carroll L. Riley and Joni L. Manson "The Cibola-Tiguex Route: Continuity and Change in the Southwest," *New Mexico Historical Review* 58 (1983): 347.
3. For further reading about the prehistory of North America, see David J. Meltzer, "Why don't we know when the first people came to North America," *American Antiquity* 54 (1989) by the Society for American Archaeology. Also Linda S. Cordell, *Prehistory of the Southwest (New World Archaeological Record)* Academic Press, Inc. 1984). Other sources are: Stuart J. Fiedel, *Prehistory of the Americas* (Cambridge University Press, 1987); Brian M. Fagan, *The Great Journey. The peopling of ancient America* (Thames and Hudson, 1987), and Carroll L. Riley, *The Frontier People: The Greater Southwest in the Protohistoric Period* (University of New Mexico Press, 1987). ★

Robert Seltzer

Award-winning journalist Robert Seltzer was raised in El Paso. He has worked for the *El Paso Times* as a sports writer, feature writer, metro columnist, and writing coach. Seltzer has also worked at the *Houston Chronicle*, *Fort Worth Star-Telegram*, and the *Philadelphia Inquirer*. He has won state and national awards for his news and sports coverage, including two Texas Headliner awards and four Associated Press Managing Editors Association awards from three states: Pennsylvania, Texas, and New Mexico. In addition, Seltzer has won a national APME Journalism Excellence Award and The Nat Fleischer Award for excellence in boxing journalism. Currently, he works for the *San Antonio Express-News* and since 2004 has been a member of the editorial board. The following selection is from his manuscript in progress on the life of his father, Amado Muro.

My Father, Amado Muro

The teenager walked up the hill, and when he reached the crest, he was on top of the world, as close to eternity as he would ever get. It was breathtaking. And there, from the hilltop, he took it all in, the sky above, the lake below—a broad band of silver liquid, shimmering in the early morning sunlight. He had stood on this spot a hundred times before, and he would stand on this spot a hundred times after, but none of those experiences could rival this one moment, this one sliver of time frozen in his memory—and in his heart. And, each time he talked about that morning, he described it the same way—the morning he witnessed something beautiful, something sublime, something eternal.

That teenager was my father, and the lake was Lake Erie. It was part of his city, part of his life. My father loved Cleveland. I could tell. He described it as though it were his Oz—magical but real.

My father called himself "the old man," a term he intended to be both endearing and self-deprecating. But there was some truth in it. He lived in the past, reveled in its musty odor, its tenacious grip, for it refused to let go of him—and, yes, he refused to let go of it.

When I was six years old, the old man started giving me impromptu quizzes on mythology and ancient civilizations every day. Who was Hector? Who was Hannibal? What was the Roman name for Zeus? How many labors did Hercules perform? Where did Achilles get pierced with an arrow? But it was the Cleveland stories I loved the most, the stories from his childhood. They were the real myths, the tales freighted with humor and drama and joy. And no matter which story he related, the best character was always the town itself—big and raw and majestic, the backdrop for all his youthful adventures.

The family lived in a Tudor-style house in Shaker Heights, but his real neighborhood was the town itself, all of it, from one end to the other. Cleveland was not the center of his universe; Cleveland was his universe. He never expressed this thought, not directly, but he never had to. When he talked about his hometown, he was so passionate that I fantasized about my own life as a parent. Would El Paso—not Bakersfield—become my Cleveland when I became a father? Would I regale my children with stories from my youth? I hoped so.

Before the old man became the old man, he loved to wander the streets of Cleveland, sometimes by foot, sometimes by streetcar. He saw wondrous things, and he saw horrible things. The most horrible came during the Great Depression, when mob figures were the most successful entrepreneurs in town.

My father was a teenager. He stepped off the streetcar one afternoon, ready to roam the downtown he loved so much. Two men approached each other on a street corner; both wore black, double-breasted suits, one of them with a colorful handkerchief blossoming from his coat pocket. Mr. Handkerchief stuck his arm out, as if about to shake hands with the other man, but it was not a hand he was extending. It was a gun, and Mr. Handkerchief started firing. The other man collapsed to his knees, as if genuflecting; then his upper body crashed onto the sidewalk, his head twisting as it hit the concrete. Mr. Handkerchief walked away, briskly but casually. My father saw the murder, and he vomited, and years later, when he recounted the story, you could sense the horror—and the bile—coming back.

That was the scariest story he ever told me, but it was not the most traumatic. Before my father could become an old man, he had to become a young man, and the transition from childhood to manhood, rough and unexpected, occurred one afternoon in a downtown diner. It was during the Great Depression—why did all his memorable times happen during hard times? He met his best friend, Whitey Bimlap, and the two boys walked the streets without purpose—but, then, that was their purpose, for the greatest freedom was to act without having to act, to move without having to move.

The two boys, cherishing their youthful liberty, stopped at a diner on Euclid Avenue. The place was packed, but they found two empty stools at the counter—a spot sandwiched between two hulks who burrowed into their food like earth movers. My father and Whitey were starving, but their appetites were bigger than their pocketbooks. Much bigger. They were penniless. But Whitey had a plan.

When they finished their meals—my father a hamburger, his friend a grilled cheese sandwich—Whitey jumped off the stool, retching and groaning. He bent over, his head nearly scraping the floor—a pathetic figure folded in half, like a flower with a weak stem. Then he started screaming.

"She . . . she . . . she . . ." he stammered, pointing at the young waitress behind the counter. "She spit on my sandwich! I saw her! I saw her!"

The manager rushed out from the kitchen.

"What seems to be the problem?" he asked.

"She spit on my sandwich!" Whitey screamed, still groaning.

"OK, you two fellows can go on now," the manager said, escorting them to the door.

Then they heard him scream at the young waitress.

"And you," he said. "You're fired."

Just like that, she was gone. And with barely a shred of evidence. The manager let two boys—one a pint-sized Paul Muni, the other his silent accomplice—rage, fume and plot their way out of paying a meal. Whitey feigned illness, but when they hit the sidewalk, my father felt truly sick, his heart burdened by the injustice he helped perpetrate. The two teen-agers conspired their way into a free meal, but they cost an innocent woman her job in the process. Was she a single mother? Was she taking care of an invalid aunt? Was she working her way to a better life in California? My father would never know. The young woman was a mystery, a nameless victim. My father never told me this, and it is impossible to extrapolate a lifetime of dedication from a moment of guilt, but the incident led to his social conscience. I know it did. It must have.

"Try not to have fun at the expense of other people," he told me, finishing his tale.

"How will I know?" I asked.

"You'll know," he said.

When I became a man, I discovered that my father took Cleveland—and the lessons he learned there—everywhere he went, including El Paso. He arrived in El Paso after World War II. My father grew to love the town, just as he had loved Cleveland. He loved its people, its mountains, its sunsets, and he loved the woman who would become his wife, the woman whose name, Amada Muro, he adapted as his pseudonym.

Bias is a horrible trait, but I am proud of the bias I display in my affection toward the stories my father wrote. Would I marvel at the craft—and the decency that gleams from every sentence—if he were not my father? Who knows? I hope so.

The following stories—"Sunday in Little Chihuahua" and "My Grandfather's Brave Songs" —display his affection for art, family and tradition, an affection he expressed through prose that is almost disarmingly simple. But there was nothing simple about the craft behind the words. He would spend weeks on a single sentence, leading to an irony that would be lost on readers unaware of his work habits: The almost painful effort led to prose that seemed effortless in its grace and lyricism.

The stories also reflect his deep affection for Mexico and its culture. Yes, my father was born in Cleveland, Ohio, but geography failed to deter him. It was as if an agency more powerful than any immigration office had granted him honorary Mexican citizenship—a status bestowed upon him by virtue of his love and passion for Mexico. These emotions did not give him a double identity, for Chester Seltzer and Amado Muro were one and the same, as the following stories attest. ★

Amado Muro

Amado Muro (1915-1970) is the pseudonym of writer and newspaperman Chester Seltzer. Raised in Cleveland, he was the son of Louis B. Seltzer, the influential journalist and editor of the *Cleveland Press*. Muro attended the University of Virginia and Kenyon College. He rode freight trains, worked in labor camps, lived in the Fruit Pickers Cothouse, Red's Flophouse, and was, for a time, a seaman. While a newspaperman in Bexar County, Texas, during World War II, he was sentenced to prison at Lewisburg Penitentary for his objections to military service. After his release, Muro came to work at the *El Paso Herald-Post* and married Amada Muro, a native of Chihuahua City, Mexico, slightly changing her name for his pen name. He worked at the *St. Louis Post-Dispatch* and at newspapers in Dallas, San Antonio, Wichita Falls, and Galveston, Texas; Las Cruces, New Mexico; San Diego and Bakersfield, California; and New Orleans, Louisiana. While working for a California newspaper during the Vietnam War, Muro refused to write editorials condemning the war protestors and was replaced. His stories of his travels across the United States and in the villages of Mexico, such as "Two Skid Row Sketches" and "Hungry Men," were published in *Arizona Quarterly*, and "Night Train to Fort Worth" appeared in the *Texas Observer*. Muro's story "María Tepache" was published in *The Best American Short Stories of 1969*. He is the author of *The Collected Stories of Amado Muro*, which is widely anthologized. He lived in the Sunset Heights neighborhood of El Paso when not riding the rails or living among farm workers, strikers, and the dispossessed. Muro died of a heart attack in front of Zamora's News Stand on Paisano Drive in El Paso.

From *The Collected Stories of Amado Muro*: Sunday in Little Chihuahua

When I was a boy, not long up from Parral, I lived with my uncle Rodolfo Avitia, my mother Amada Avitia de Muro, and my sisters Consuelo and Dulce Nombre de Maria in the quarter called "Little Chihuahua" on the El Paso side of the Rio Grande.

Next door to the tenement in which we lived was a tiny café called "La Perla de Jalisco." This café was run by Doña Antonia Olvera, a jolly and industrious woman from Guadalajara, who was known throughout the neighborhood as Toña "*la tapatia*," as her townspeople are called in Mexico.

Doña Antonia kept busy all day long, humming the *Mexican Hat Dance* while she worked. Her café specialized in dishes that were seldom found elsewhere in Little Chihuahua. Toña *la tapatia* served the sugar tamales that make Oaxaca mouths water. She made the delicate, wispy tortillas, the largest and thinnest in all Mexico, that are among the great prides of Sonora. When a man tired of eating the thick, freckled tortillas of flour made by Chihuahua housewives, he would go to "La Perla" for an agreeable change, secure in the knowledge that not even the tortilla factories could equal Doña Antonia's products in fineness or texture.

Then, too, Toña served *café con leche* just as they do in the Mexico City cafés, with each cup of coffee more than half filled with boiling milk. Where, if not to "La Perla," would a man seeking a cup of hot *champurrado*, made of corn and chocolate, go on a cold winter night? And was anyone ever known to impugn the quality of the tripe which Doña Antonia put into her steaming *menudo*, a stew known to every border Mexican as the only sure cure for a hangover?

"La Perla de Jalisco" was a neat and clean café. On each immaculate table a small dish of *chile bravo* could always be found, and over the front door hung a picture of Juventino Rosas, who, besides being the composer of *Sobre las Olas*, was a *tapatio* himself.

At a front table Toña's husband, Don Ignacio Olvera, sat all day long with his books of philosophy and his bullring reviews stacked up in neat piles before him. He was the president of the "José y Juan" bullfight club and also acted as border correspondent for *El Redondel*, a bullfight magazine published in Mexico City. For his literary service, Don Ignacio received no money at all. But he did obtain passes to the fights in Ciudad Juárez each Sunday, and the satisfaction of seeing the name "I. Olvera, correspondent" at the end of his numerous and popular articles.

Between his exhaustive studies of Plato, whom he referred to as the "Divine Greek," and his equally exhaustive studies of the matador Rafael Gómez, "El

Gallo [The Rooster]," whom he referred to as the "Divine Baldhead," he managed to earn a scholar's reputation for himself in the quarter.

Don Ignacio Olvera was a short, pudgy man with deeply imbedded eyes that kept blinking constantly as though trying to beat their way out of the morass of soggy flesh that surrounded them. His cheekbones were smothered beneath puffs of suety skin that made his round face appear boneless. To the genteel residents of our quarter he was known as "The Belly" because of his bobbling paunch. But the more robust residents of Little Chihuahua knew him as "Jiggle Hips," a nickname inspired by his elephantine backside, which swayed like a woman's when he walked down the street.

Don Ignacio sat in the café all day long playing *Novillero* and Agustin Lara's *Silverio* over and over again on the jukebox while he pored over metaphysical disquisitions and bullfight reviews, gathering material for his long articles dealing with past and present bullfighters. He also wrote poems dedicated to the Mexican matadors and these, too, were published in *El Redondel.*

Where was the boy in our quarter who could not recite the verse about the day Andrés Blando killed the bull "Cuatro Milpas" with one of the mightiest sword thrusts ever seen in the Plaza of Ciudad Juárez? On that day Don Ignacio Olvera wrote:

Andrés Blando ha descubierto
Una manera de herir
Que no la comprende nadie
Ni es facil! de definir.

[Andrés Blando has discovered
A way to wound
That nobody understands
And that is difficult to define.]

And what aficionado in Little Chihuahua did not know by heart the satirical ballad he composed on the day the unhappy apprentices Juan Estrada, "Gallo," and José Lagares, "El Piti," heard the three warning bugles and underwent the humiliation of seeing the bulls they could not kill returned to the corrals by the trained oxen?

Of that unlucky day, Don Ignacio had written:

No quiero carne del toro
Que Lagares no mató.
La quiero del de Gallito
Que vivo se lo dejó.

[I don't want the meat of the bull
That Lagares didn't kill.
I want it from Gallito's
That was left alive.]

But despite the popularity of his poems, it was generally agreed that Don Ignacio's renown rested on a foundation of solid prose. His most famous article was written on the day the matador Luis Castro, known in the ring as "The Mixcoac Militiaman," cut the ears, tail, and the hoof of the great bull "Mariposa" from the herd of San Diego de Los Padres. He described the performance thus:

> [Luis Castro] fights with the gaiety and the abandon of the gypsies who dance nude amid flowering lemon trees in Seville's joyous quarter of San Bernardo, where the great bull killer Pepe Luis Vázquez was born. He smiles at the bull as Othello would have smiled had his blindness not kept him from seeing that his Desdemona was faithful. His vibrant cape rises in a harmonious curve like the swallows which make their nests in the eaves of the church of Omnia Santorum, where Juan Belmonte, 'The Earthquake of Triana,' was baptized.
>
> Plato nailed to the door of his Academy the disconcerting words 'None shall enter without knowing geometry.' And by his work with the cape and the muleta today our great military man of the bullring won the right to enter the Divine Greek's Academy unchallenged. The red ellipses of his interminable *derchazos*, the moving and deeply poetic circumference of his *pase de pecho*, the semicircular tragedy of his *larga cordobesa*, showed us that Luis Castro, too, knows geometry.
>
> Today our valiant soldier proved that his heart is as big and as round as that great gypsy moon of which the unlucky poet Garcia

Lorca has sung. So he conquered the noble bull Mariposa, who, like all true super-brave bulls, had flies on his face and defenses like the branches of the millennial ahuehuete trees in Chapultepec Park.

Thales de Mileto would have said that his movements with the cape represented a perfect conjugation of music and geometry. A poet like Ronsard would have said that the rhythm of our soldier's muleta was like the agile and beautiful flight of a bird. Becquer would have said its magic was that of a ballad heard in the mysterious depths of the Moruno Quarter of Santa Cruz de Sevilla at three in the morning, the hour when the hearts of the gypsies stop beating. For Luis Castro's muleta has that suave sweep of which the great Nicaraguan poet has spoken.

Amiable readers, today I have learned that the smell of a brilliant bullfighter is overpowering. That is because it is impregnated with the odor of greatness. When I saw Luis Castro's *farol de rodillas*, I thought that the great Rodolfo Gaona, our beloved 'Caliph of Leon,' had come out of retirement to tread the sands of the ring once more. Mariano Azuela was born to be a great writer. Rafael de Urbino was born to be a great painter. And 'The Mixcoac Militiaman' was born to be a great matador.

Luis Castro, my hand is extended to you. You have brought a new sense of joy, a new sense of danger to the ancient art of Cuchares. Matador, I salute you. *Olé*! for the profession of the thousand marvels, the most beautiful of all the fiestas.

On Sundays after the eight o'clock Mass at the church of San Juan de Los Lagos was over, the children of our neighborhood attended the Pachangas, or entertainment, put on by Don Ignacio.

This was held in the corral behind the "Perla de Jalisco." Don Ignacio would get out the brilliant cape which Luis Castro had presented to him in gratitude for his encomiastic article. He also got out a muleta which had been given to him by the matador Carlos Vera, "Canitas," in appreciation for an article in which he had compared the young bullfighter's execution of the *la sernista* pass to that of its inventor, Victoriano de La Serna himself.

On the mornings of the Pachangas Don Ignacio was as nervous as the bullfighters who await their turns in the Plaza de Cuatro Caminos in Mexico City. On the nights before, he stiffened his cape with fish jelly and on windy Sundays he weighted down his muleta with wet sand.

For his Pachangas, Don Ignacio had trained a chow dog that he called "Mariachi" to charge like a bull. He had taught the dog to follow the sway of Luis Castro's cape and Carlos Vera's muleta just as a real bull would from the herd of Corlome.

On the blistering summer Sundays when Mariachi was listless and came to the lures sluggishly, Don Ignacio heaped insults upon him. "Son of a bad cow," he reviled him. "Solemn softly, blind burro, little Sister of Charity."

But on the cold winter Sundays when the dog's body was throbbing with vigor and he came to the lures with a straight and true charge, Don Ignacio praised him extravagantly. "This is a great and intelligent bull, a rich bonbon from the herd of Corlome," he gravely informed the children. "Kids, I tell you that this brave bull knows Latin, Greek, German, Sanskrit, and Calo."

Don Ignacio wore heel-less bullfighting pumps during the Pachangas. An ancient *montera*—the traditional bullfighter's hat—battered and frizzled, surmounted his massive head. He cited the dog by patting the hardpan earth with his slippered feet. "*Ay, toro*," he bellowed at the top of his lungs. "Come, little pear in sweet sauce."

The dog Mariachi, long since grown accustomed to the vagaries of Don Ignacio's mercurial temperament, would look up at his globular master with a resigned expression. Then after a moment he would begin to paw at the earth with his hind legs just as a real bull would do.

"This one is for all of you," Don Ignacio would then yell as the dog charged the cape his corpulent master held behind him in the beautiful style invented by Romero Freg.

The delighted children would crown each pass with an "¡*Olé*!" They whooped and hollered hilariously as Don Ignacio, puffing and wheezing, lowered himself to his pudgy knees in order to execute the dangerous *cambio a Porto Gayola*.

Don Ignacio always explained the origin of every movement to the excited spectators. "Lads, this one is *la saltillera*. It is so called because it was created by our great fellow countryman, Fermin Espinosa, 'Armillita,' who was also known as the 'Maestro of Saltillo.'"

Most of us had been attending the Pachangas for so long that we knew all of the movements and passes by heart.

"You, Macario Buena," Don Ignacio would shout. "Tell me, who created the *sanjuanera* pass and how did the pass get its name?"

"Luis Procuna, 'El Caballero del Penacho Blanco' [The Knight with the White Crest], invented the pass," a small, poorly dressed boy would answer from somewhere in the crowd. "He called it *sanjuanera*, because he was born in the San Juan de Letran section in the capital."

Don Ignacio always ended the Pachangas with a suicidal pass of his own invention which he had named *la olverina*. This pass resembled an inverted *manoletina* in which the bullfighter stands with his back to the bull. For years Don Ignacio had been trying to persuade some of Mexico's most noted bullfighters to try it out in the ring. But, recognizing the pass as a certain passport to eternity, they had courteously but consistently refused.

After the Pachangas were over, Don Ignacio always started for the back door of the café, ostensibly to wash himself down. But the clamorous cries of the children and the shouts of the men and women massed on the balconies of the adjacent tenements never failed to bring him back.

"The ballad, Don Nacho," the crowd yelled. "The ballad of Niño de La Palma."

"*Ay, María, madre mía*," Don Ignacio complained every Sunday. "Boys, it's hot as three o'clock in Acapulco, and I swear by our sainted Guadalupana, the Lady of All the World and the Queen of the Skies, that I've got to dress for the bullfight."

But the children and the men and women always disregarded his protests.

"The ballad, Don Nacho," they hollered. "Recite the ballad."

Don Ignacio always ended by shrugging his shoulders and waving everyone into silence. He would take off the dusty montera, throw his head back, and square his shoulders. His stentorian voice, quivering with emotion, pierced the air like the cry of a *flamenco* singer.

All of us had learned poems by Longfellow in the American school, all of us had learned poems by Juan de Dios Peza and Antonio Plaza in our homes, but at that age of our lives no poem we had known could make our hearts beat as fast as did *Las Chuflillas del Niño de La Palma*.

With the throbbing intensity of his bass voice, Don Ignacio could make us all see the bullfighter of Ronda, son of a shoemaker and once poor like ourselves, in his great hour of victory at Vista Alegre on the day when the Bank of Spain opened its doors to him. He could make us all hear the cry of the Niño, drunk with the exultation of his triumph, as he called to the brave Campos Varela bull, challenging the fierce animal to charge and to catch him.

Vengas o no en busca mía,
Torillo, mala persona,
Dos cirios y una corona
Tendrás en la enfermería.
¡Qué alegria!
¡Cógeme, torillo fiero!
¡Qué salero!

[Come after me or not,
Little bull, evil person,
You will have two candles
And a garland in the hospital.
What joy!
Catch me, proud little bull!
How graceful!]

The deafening applause would rise over the corral in a thundering tympany. The children would sing and whistle the quick, gay *Diana*. At the Pachangas even the most melancholy of the children were laughing and happy.

Once I remember seeing Juana de la Torre there. She was the ugliest girl in our school, so ugly that even the gentlest girls in our class taunted her and called her "Juana the Female Pig." But on the day I saw her there at the Pachangas she was laughing. I could never remember seeing her laugh before.

There, too, I saw Jesús Zamarrippa. Ordinarily Jesús looked tired and sad. He was then eleven years old and he lived in an earthen-floored hut with eight other members of his family. Already he had spent a year in the tuberculosis ward at the city-county hospital. But at the Pachangas that day Jesús' face was radiant.

After the recitation was over the crowds of jubilant children began to disperse. Standing at the back door of the café, Don Ignacio watched until the last child was gone. I remember him best as he stood there with a smile on his face.

Many years later when I was a young man of twenty, I sat in "La Buena Fe" shoe shop and heard my big, burly Uncle Rodolfo defend Don Ignacio against two of our countrymen who were bitterly damning him as a preposterous poseur, a drone, and a parasite, a pickpocket who lived off his wife. "Shut up, sons of the Great Seven," my aroused uncle told them at last.

He stormed out of the shoe shop and I followed him. We walked down South Stanton Street toward Ciudad Juárez slowly. And I asked my Uncle Rodolfo why he had defended Don Ignacio Olvera against charges that were only too true, and why he had become so angry.

My Uncle Rodolfo looked at me with a sheepish expression. He started to tell me and then suddenly stopped. He took off his big Zacatecas sombrero and ran his hand through his gray hair. "Confound it," my uncle said, flushing with the embarrassment of his struggle to express an emotion that I am sure he considered unmanly.

He kept his brown face averted from mine. After a moment he got the words out. "Son," my uncle Rodolfo said slowly without looking at me. "It is just that Don Nacho can make children laugh."

He clamped his hat back down on his head. Then he looked over at me with a defiant expression as though challenging me to smile back at him in derision.

After that we walked over to Ciudad Juárez to eat *fritanga* and drink a "Chiquita Chihuahua" together. ★

From *The Collected Stories of Amado Muro*: My Grandfather's Brave Songs

My grandfather Trinidad Avitia, a gray-haired street singer, managed to make a living in Parral, Chihuahua, thanks to his guitar and the saints.

His guitar and the saints had been his best friends since his boyhood—the guitar because listeners said he played it well, the saints because there are so many.

When I was a boy, my grandfather sat on a chair in front of the Elegant Tortilla Café all day long playing his guitar and singing for every countryman who went by. Many tourists paid to hear his songs. But Mexicans celebrating their saints' days were his most numerous listeners by far, and since every day is some saint's day the demand for his songs seldom lagged.

My grandfather worked hardest on the "Day of the Lupes" and the "Day of the Juans." On those days Parral's many Lupes and Juans kept him busy singing from daybreak until long after midnight. And on those days as well as the "Day of the Pepes," the "Day of the Manuels" and many other saints' days besides, he got up long before sunrise to sing the traditional *mañanitas* (little morning songs). He sang these outside the home of the person whose saint's day it was.

Then, too, on stifling summer nights my grandfather sat outside his home in the Manuel Acuña neighborhood singing songs like "Glass Eye, the Highwayman" and "Pancho Villa's Winged Horses" for anyone who cared to listen. Many Chihuahuans always did. On those nights everyone, even elderly women, shouted when my grandfather threw back his head, squared his shoulders and sang: "*Soy Mexicano, soy de Chihuahua. A mi bandera le juré honor.*" ("I am a Mexican, I'm from Chihuahua. I swore allegiance to my flag.")

And everyone laughed until tears came when he stopped in the middle of a song to imitate General Francisco Villa. Parral residents swore that no one else in Chihuahua State could imitate Pancho Villa the way my grandfather could. He puffed out his cheeks as though he were playing a trumpet, stroked his spiky gray moustache and shouted: "Boys, don't be afraid of Pancho Murguia's bullets. Just be careful of the holes they make."

My grandmother María de Jesús sang with him on those nights. So did everyone else. They cried "*Ay Chihuahua*" and "*Arribe el Norte*" when my grandfather sang the "brave" songs that northern Mexicans like so well.

Folk heroes like Heraclio Bernal and Valentín de la Sierra rode through my grandfather's songs on those nights. So did revolutionary leaders like Villa, Martin "Guero (Blondie)" Lopez, and Maclovio Herrera. Everyone made up new verses for the song "*La Cucaracha*" and the evenings passed all too swiftly.

These summer-night concerts became so popular that entire families from other neighborhoods came over to hear them. Some came from as far as the María Martínez neighborhood almost two miles away.

Wives of poor miners, without radios or money for shows, always thanked my grandfather after the singing was over. "May the dark virgin protect you and cover you with her mantle," they said. This made my grandfather uncomfortable. But my grandmother beamed with pride.

My grandmother liked Mexican music just as much as my grandfather did. She was a cheery, smiling woman, always laughing and joking with everyone. But sometimes she, too, lost her temper. "I like everyone who walks on these streets of God," she often said with pride in her good nature. But after she said this she bit her lip and added "except American blondies."

My grandmother showed her dislike for blondes every time American women asked my grandfather to sing "*Cielito Lindo*" for them on their sightseeing trips to Parral. He always did. But these street serenades made my grandmother so mad she wouldn't let him in the house. "This home is for Christians," she shouted when my grandfather knocked at the door. "It's not for shameless old flirts who serenade American blondies instead of being content with what our own nation produces."

My grandfather soothed her with music. He sang "*La Madrugada*" over and over until she finally let him in. After these outbursts my grandmother was always contrite. She did her best to make up for them by making *pozole*, *flautas*, and other foods my grandfather liked. And she even tried to compete with the chic blondes herself. She wore her best Zamora shawl wherever she went and even went so far as to pin a San Juan rose in her graying hair.

Except for these rare discords, my grandfather's work went along harmoniously. He liked the people he sang for and he made friends with them all. But he liked best the listeners who bawled and shouted when he sang Mexico's brave songs.

One of the most enthusiastic of his many admirers was a robust, middle-aged woman who ran the "Divine Strawberry" stand at the Hidalgo market. This was Doña Guadalupe Carmona, nicknamed "Lupe la Generala" because of her fondness for recalling the days when she fought for Pancho Villa. Lupe the General liked to tell my grandfather about her army days. "Ay, Don Trini," she sighed, "How gladly I'd give up my strawberry stand for a chance to hitch up my skirts and fight for Pancho Villa again."

The strawberry vendor was a fierce patriot. No military parade in Parral would have been complete without her. On parade days everyone cheered when the general marched by with a bandoleer strapped around her Amazonian torso and a 30-30 rifle on her shoulder.

A militant scowl harshened her dimpled face while she waddled along with the soldiers. A cornhusk cigarette was tucked between her chapped lips. She never threw it away until time to shout "Viva Madero."

Lupe the General wasn't one of those women who pray to St. Anthony for sweethearts. When my grandfather sang romantic songs like "*María Bonita*" for other market vendors, she always begged him to stop.

"Ay Mama Carlota not that one, Don Trini," she moaned. "Sing the brave one about how the federals chased Benito Canales instead." The songs she liked best were revolutionary ballads like the "Wet Buzzard" and the "Three Bald-Headed Women." But she liked songs about manhunts, shootings, and executions almost as well.

My grandfather's brave songs made the General wail and shout. They made her bawl: "Ay Chihuahua, land of brave men, where nobody gets shot in the back." Sometimes they even made her weep with fierce pride in Benjamin Argumedo and other heroes of the brave songs.

Once I asked my grandfather why Lupe the General shouted and cried when she sang and why she always marched with the soldiers. I hadn't been a Mexican very long when I asked this, for I was then not quite nine years old.

My grandfather, a veteran observer of our countrymen, smiled at me. "Every Chihuahuan kills fleas in his own way," he explained.

Eduardo Romero, the barber, liked the brave songs as much, if not more, than the fiery General did. Don Lalo Romero was a spindly, myopic man with a haggard face buttressed by bouldery cheekbones. Chihuahuans called him "Green Belly" because he came from the lettuce-growing center of León, Guanajuato.

Always timid and shy as a mustang when he wasn't listening to brave songs, he turned into a ranting patriot fierce as the General herself when he heard them.

He took off his bullseye glasses and defied his customers, Chihuahuans all, every time my grandfather sang "The Defense of Celaya, Guanajuato" for him. "I'm the only real man here because I come from Guanajuato," he boasted loudly. Then he glared challengingly at Chihuahuans waiting for haircuts as though daring them to deny it.

On crisp autumn nights my grandfather went to the old Juan de Dios market quarter with a Saltillo serape slung over his shoulder and his Ramírez guitar tucked under his arm. There he joined a working army of mariachi musicians who filled the old quarter with music all night, and never broke ranks until dawn.

The quarter's boisterous streets, so narrow and crowded that two people could hardly walk side by side, were jammed with outdoor food stands, fruit and vegetable stalls, and shouting vendors.

My grandfather wandered through streets named after poets and patriots, looking for countrymen to sing to. He usually found them near the "Meek Burro" bar. And always he sang Mexico's brave songs for them.

Sometimes he bought me steaming cups of vanilla *atole* at the "Beautiful Indian" refreshment stand. While I drank them he chatted with wandering musicians, street clowns, fire-eaters, magicians and other men who made their living on Parral's streets.

Then, too, on those chilly nights he told me how he used to wander over the states of Chihuahua, Coahuila, and Durango, sometimes on horseback but more often on foot, singing at the village fairs. Those were the days when he sang for such Mexican revolutionaries as Pánfilo Natera, Petronilo Hernández, and even Pancho Villa himself.

"Once General Hernández made me play for almost twenty hours in the plazas, streets, and bars of Santiago Papasquiaro, Durango, along with other members of the Agustín González orchestra," he told me. "He liked our songs so much he made us all travel with his army for a month giving campfire concerts out in the Durango Sierra."

Only once in his life did my grandfather ever try to make a living at anything other than music. This was after the Madero revolution when he went to Flagstaff, Arizona to work as a carpenter.

Many miners and housewives in the Manuel Acuña neighborhood said he could have been rich if he had stayed there. But even in Flagstaff my grandfather couldn't stop singing the songs that make Mexicans shout. He sang them for lonely countrymen and even for the American bosses. He had planned to save his money and bring my grandmother, my mother, and my uncle Rodolfo from Chihuahua to live in the United States. But the brave songs proved his undoing.

"They made me homesick," my grandfather said. "When I sang them I forgot I was earning more money and living better than ever before."

So after six weeks he went back to Mexico where he's been playing the guitar ever since. ★

Maceo Dailey

Historian Maceo C. Dailey was born in Norfolk, Virginia, and received his Ph.D. from Howard University. Presently, he is associate professor in the history department and director of African American Studies at the University of Texas at El Paso. He has taught at Smith College, Howard University, Brown University, Boston College, and Morehouse College, among others. Dailey is the co-editor of the books *Wheresoever My People Chance to Dwell* and *Tuneful Tales*. His scholarly essays and book chapters have appeared in such publications as *Digame*; *The Dictionary of Negro American Biography*; *Dictionary of the American Left*; *The Review of Black Political Economy*; *Harvard Business History Review*; and *Walking Integrity* among many others. Recipient of the 1996 Alex W. Bealer Prize by the Atlanta Historical Society, Dailey has received numerous citations of commendation from various local, state, and national organizations. Dailey has served on the board of directors of the Apex Museum and Hammonds House in Atlanta, Georgia, and has consulted at both the Atlanta History Center and the Smithsonian Museum. He served as chair for the board of directors of Humanities Texas for two terms, as a commissioner on the Texas Emancipation Juneteenth Cultural and Historical commission, and was a member of the Philosophical Society of Texas and an advisory committee member of the Texas Book Festival. Currently, Dailey is at work completing a biography of Emmett Jay Scott and the project *The Booker T. Washington Encyclopedia*.

From *Tuneful Tales*: Introduction

Bernice Love Wiggins was among the first African-American female poets to be published in Texas. Born in Austin in 1897 but raised in El Paso, Wiggins self-published her first (and perhaps only) book of poetry, *Tuneful Tales*, in El Paso in 1925. She wrote in an era of burgeoning national black literature as writers of the famed Harlem Renaissance and activists of the Universal Negro Improvement Association (led by Jamaican Marcus Garvey) achieved prominence. These new leaders and writers gave voice, passion, and direction to black Americans who sought relief from racism and endeavored to build their communities. Wiggins's poems were written with a similar intent, despite the fact that she was writing from distant Texas.

Though she lived far from any African-American metropolitan area, Wiggins emerged nonetheless in her poems as a brilliant and perceptive poet, capturing the many-sided black experience in El Paso, a remote Texas city perched on the U.S.-Mexico border. She could claim a spiritual and creative kinship with the larger black community through her poetry's illumination of African-American culture and consciousness. Thus her citation as a poet of note by the great Southern black folklorist and critic J. Mason Brewer, who proclaimed Wiggins the female Paul Laurence Dunbar.

Like Paul Laurence Dunbar, Bernice Love Wiggins used standard and dialect English in writing perceptively, sensitively, and humorously about black American life and her community. She focused on local personalities, women's issues, lynchings, African heritage, aesthetics, culture, literary writers, love, political and social growth, the family, the church, and the overall significance of black life in a racialized society of hope, hostility, bigotry, and persecution. . . .

***

Wiggins's poems were published significantly in the *El Paso Herald*, the *Chicago Defend*er, the *Half Center Magazine*, the *Houston Informer*, and J. Mason Brewer's *Heralding Dawn: An Anthology of Verse* (1936), but she remained unknown. There are several reasons for the obscurity of her book and the limited recognition she received as a poet. She was self-published; *Tuneful Tales* was her only book-length publication; El Paso was far from the centers of literary activity; and she disappeared from the historical record after her departure from the city in the early or mid 1930s.[1] Her life is still a great conundrum, though we are able to read her poems. These poems tell us much about black culture and consciousness in the west and southwest regions where small communities of African-Americans resided, and they manifest interrelationships of black life and another side of the flowering of black writers and artists coming out of the remarkable literary era known as the Harlem Renaissance.

Wiggins was born on March 4, 1897, in Austin, Texas. Her early childhood is shrouded in mystery. Her father, J. Austin Love, was a "laborer, a poet, and a state Sunday School director for the Holiness Church." According to J. Mason Brewer, the senior Love was "one of the most outstanding Negro writers of verse in Texas and the Southwest." One of Love's poems appeared in a compendium by Josie Briggs Hall of Mexia, the first known book by a Texas black woman. This is the extent of current information on J. Austin Love. The origins and life of Bernice's mother are an even deeper mystery. There is virtually no extant data on her life. Her background, family, interests, or childbearing age are all unclear, save that her young child Bernice is listed in 1902 and 1903 as orphaned at five years of age. In 1903, Bernice was moved to El Paso, Texas, to live with her aunt, and subsequently was given the surname of that relative. As did her father, Bernice Love Wiggins turned to poetry, and in the first grade was fortunate to have the inimitable matronly motivator Alice Lydia McGowan as an elementary school teacher. McGowan eagerly encouraged her young charge to express herself in rhyme and verse, and Wiggins showed early promise as a poet.[2]

Enrolled in high school when World War I erupted in Europe, Wiggins continued her poetry writing at El Paso's Douglass High School, the lone African-American secondary educational institution in the city. Douglass High School was similar to many other black educational institutions in a segregated America. Founded in 1883 to train black students to the best of their ability, sensitize them to racial matters, develop in them a sense of pride in their people and community, and spur them to leadership, the school's talented array of teachers and principals (some of whom had arrived in El Paso from as far away as Howard University in Washington, D.C.) ensured that the students would become what scholar W. E. B. Du Bois called for in his "Talented Tenth" cadre of blacks to uplift the greater black community. Douglass's principal, William Coleman, a Howard University and Brown University alumnus, was both a "Talented Tenth" educator and "race man" who made the El Paso black school a training ground for future black leadership and responsibility. With alacrity and much appreciation, Principal Coleman himself was proud to write in the preface of Wiggins's book, praising her effusively for "poetic visions born of holy passions, high hopes, and burning enthusiasms." Coleman showed himself to be a wordsmith of uncommon ability in his praise of Wiggins, noting that "the author is yet young. With the consciousness of a Higher Presence, and an imagination, divinely enlivened by a light that never was on sea or land, may she be inspired to sing still more touchingly." Beyond this first publication, however Wiggins is not known to have sung poetically "still more touchingly," but she demonstrated extraordinary talent and promise in this first book.

There are many interesting questions attending the publication of Wiggins's first book: What was the relationship between Wiggins and her father? Did he have any impact on her writing of poems? Did Wiggins, for example, take the opportunity in 1931 to attend an El Paso poetry reading given by the famed Harlem Renaissance writer Langston Hughes? Were Wiggins's poems, as scholar Frieda Werden surmises, written to be performed similarly to verses of a play or to the accompaniment of piano music?

Though these questions may remain mysterious, none can doubt J. Mason Brewer's statement that Wiggins's "deep knowledge of the psychology of her people is portrayed through the medium of her dialect verse which at times rises to heights similar to those attained by the immortal Paul Laurence Dunbar." The El Paso black community in which Wiggins lived offered much material for this poetic imagination. The black community expanded from 466 persons in 1900 to 1,330 in 1920 in an overall population increase from 15,140 in 1900 to 37,586 in 1920. Wiggins lived in a progressive and talented African-American community that had its origins as far back as Estevanico's appearance in the Southwest in the early 16th century. African Americans in El Paso, working largely for either the military or railroad industry in the late nineteenth century, built a solid community in the second ward in the southeast section of the city. Churches, schools, businesses, and professional services were all present in the second ward as well as prominent organizations ranging from the National Association for the Advancement of Colored People (founded in El Paso early in 1910), to the Sunset Lodge Number 76 of Free and Accepted Masons (Prince Hall affiliate). During the time that Wiggins resided in El Paso (1903–c.1933), the city also had its array of exciting and highly motivated African-American personalities. They included Florida J. Wolfe (Lady Flo), consort to an Irish Lord; Lt. Henry Flipper, the first black graduate of West Point and later a mining engineer; Zephyr Chisom Carter, a 1909 alumna of Douglass High School who went on to Howard University where she became one of the founding members of the Delta Sigma Theta Sorority; and Lawrence A. Nixon, a prominent physician who served persons regardless of race and capacity to pay. It should be noted that Wiggins published her book at the same time that Dr. Nixon led the historic struggle to challenge the state's all-white Democratic primary, taking the suit all the way to the U.S. Supreme Court. Drusilla Tandy Nixon, Lawrence Nixon's wife, organized the black Girl Reserves of the YWCA in El Paso in 1935.

Wiggins also lived in a city with a large Mexican-American community that additionally absorbed Mexican nationals fleeing the Mexican Revolution from 1910 to 1921. El Paso increasing became a terminus for immigrants and foreign workers seeking opportunity and jobs in a city now termed the "Ellis Island of the Southwest." One of the most significant events of this El Paso period was the Tejana laundry workers' strike of 1919, surprisingly supported by a number of the city's white male labor leaders and unions. Race, class, gender, and revolutionary issues were prominent in El Paso, driving poetic and political imaginations about the diversity and direction of the Southwest. In a city becoming increasingly urbanized and shedding its western heritage of cowboy images and occasional shoot-outs in local saloons, Wiggins found an abundance of inspirational topics and wrote accordingly.[3]

***

The poems in *Tuneful Tales* give full evidence of Wiggins's ability as a poet and a memorable view of black life in the Southwest.[4] Her characters defied the odds to build communities and carve out a palatable semblance of life free from persecution and pain. In the 1980s and 1990s, Wiggins's poems began to receive national recognition in literary biographies and encyclopedias of the black woman's experience.

Ruthe Winegarten was introduced to the works of Bernice Love Wiggins in 1979, when she was working as curator for the Foundation for Women's Resources, sponsor of the exhibition *Texas Women: a Celebration of History*, which toured the state from 1981 to 1982. She and assistant curator Frieda Werden came across Wiggins's work in J. Mason Brewer's anthology *Heralding Dawn*, and found Wiggins's self-published *Tuneful Tales* at the Center for American History. They included some of her work in the exhibit, and Werden's entry for *American Women Writers* (1982) brought national attention to Wiggins. During the 1990s, Dr. Winegarten featured Wiggins's life and work in several volumes about black Texas women.

During Black History Month in 1999, when she spoke at the University of Texas at El Paso, we were delighted to learn that we shared an admiration for the work of this great poet. Texas Tech University Press agreed to help us bring Wiggins's work to life again in this new edition, and we anticipate that students, scholars, and lovers of fine poetry will enjoy reading this wonderful collection.

This facsimile edition is made from one of two known copies of the original publication. When I first arrived in El Paso to join the faculty of the University of Texas at El Paso and serve as director of the African American Studies Program, I met Mrs. Leona Washington, the founder and executive director of the McCall Neighborhood Center, which is the epicenter of the cultural and community activities of the city's progressive African-American population. She casually noted to me a book in her possession, Bernice Love Wiggins's *Tuneful Tales*, drawing attention to the fine poetry, Wiggins's residency in El Paso until the 1930s, and the few remaining copies of the book to be found in the city. Upon taking the book of poems home and reading it, I was fascinated with the quality of the writing and sought to research the life of the poet and uncover the fate of the remaining copies of *Tuneful Tales*. No factual data were uncovered except that the El Paso Public Library had a copy and, according to several members of the black community interviewed, it was believed that copies of the book may have been destroyed in the late 1950s when the building of Interstate Highway 10 cut through a segment of the Second Ward community and razed the home where the copies of *Tuneful Tales* had been left. Still, some black El Pasoans have copies of the book, and McKinley and Bernice Griffin were kind enough to provide their copy for the reprint.

Maceo C. Dailey Jr.
El Paso, Texas
2002

Notes

1. We are indebted to the great African-American poet Mari Evans, who read and commented on the poems of Bernice Love Wiggins. Ms. Evans carefully reminded us not to think of dialect poetry in pejorative terms and other uncritical ways, and that she prefers labeling it idiom poetry. The point is, however, that black speech patterns, whether labeled as dialect or idiom, are to be taken seriously by scholars to ascertain worldviews, historical realities, and creative use of language, rather than dismissing that language usage as imperfect and inept. Gwendolyn Bennett left the state at a young age, but her girlhood in Giddings, Texas, influenced her writing, and her art, prose, and poetry sparkled within the covers of literary magazines in her day. She was the first female recipient of a Guggenheim Fellowship.

2. Trips to Los Angeles, searches in El Paso, and general birth and death records have failed to turn up any significant information on Bernice Love Wiggins and her kin. In the Texas Department of Health's Bureau of Vital Statistics there is a death certificate for Austin Love, Jr., born on March 9, 1909, and whose parents were Austin Love Sr. and Alberta Clark. This is the closest we could get to unraveling the mysteries of Bernice Love Wiggins's origins. It is possible that Austin Love Sr. may have been her father. A check of social security numbers did not produce a Bernice Love Wiggins in the records, but she may have married and obtained such a number under her new surname, assuming that she indeed lived through the late 1930s. In the early 1930s, Bernice Love Wiggins operated a kindergarten ("where the little ones work while they play") on Durazno Street in El Paso, charging ten cents a day per child. She listed herself then as B. Love-Wiggins. For information on Bernice Love Wiggins's activities in the 1930s in El Paso, see Maceo Crenshaw Dailey, *I'm Building Me a Home: El Paso's African American Community, 1539–1998* (Commemorative Black History Month Pamphlet published by Chase Bank: El Paso, 1998).

3. Maceo Crenshaw Dailey Jr. and Kristine Navarro, *Wheresoever My People Chance to Dwell: Oral Interviews with African American Women of El Paso* (Black Classic Press: Baltimore, 2000), 4-14.

4. Examples of the new and excellent literary and historical work to reconstruct the black experience in the West are Bruce A. Glasrud and Laurie Champion, *The African American West: A Century of Short Stories* (Boulder: University Press of Colorado, 2000) and Quintard Taylor, *In Search of the Racial Frontier: African Americans in the American West, 1528–1990* (New York: W. W. Norton & Company, 1998). Additional works that will prove useful in the discussion of African Americans in El Paso and the state of Texas: Alwyn Barr, *Black Texans: A History of African Americans in Texas, 1528–1995* (Norman: University of Oklahoma Press, 1996, 2nd Edition); Maceo Crenshaw Dailey Jr. and Kristine Navarro, *Wheresoever My People Chance to Dwell: Oral Interviews with African American Women of El Paso* (Baltimore: Black Classic Press, 2000); Ruthe Winegarten, *Black Texas Women: A Sourcebook* (Austin: University of Texas Press, 1996); and Ruthe Winegarten, *Black Texas Women: 150 Years of Trial and Triumph* (Austin: University of Texas Press, 1995). A selected bibliography, provided at the end of this book, is an additional guide to those interested in the larger subject of African Americans as well as those who resided in Texas. ★

Bernice Love Wiggins

Bernice Love Wiggins (1897-?), living far from the centers of literary activity during the era known as the Harlem Renaissance, was encouraged by her teachers as a child to write poetry. Her poems were published extensively in newspapers across Texas. *Tuneful Tales* is her self-published book of poetry that gives voice to the small, but active and distinguished African American community of El Paso during the 1920s and 1930s. When Wiggins left El Paso in the 1930s, no further information could be found on her whereabouts. Maceo Dailey wrote perceptively about Wiggins' work in his introduction to *Tuneful Tales* (See p. 131).

Grandmother Speaks

So that's what you youngsters call dancing,
  This shaking and twisting about,
You tell me that I'm a back number,
  I tell you I'm glad I'm left out.
You twist and you shake and you shiver,
  Yet call yourselves morally clean,
I tell you its low, and its wicked,
  The most vulgar thing I have seen.

And that hollow racket is music,
  You call it a "Jazzy refrain,"
I tell you theres far more harmony
  And music in thunder an' rain.
I'd much rather list when 'tis storming
  To the rough raging roars of the wind,

The night long, than listen an hour,
  To such music, this new "Jazzy' kind.

So thats a ball gown you are wearing,
  And lightly your bosom expose,
Your back is uncovered entirely,
  Don't you feel that you need on more clothes?
You call me old fashioned and fogy,
  But call me whatever you please,
I'll still hold 'tis brazen for women
  To wear dresses up to their knees.

You drink and you smoke and you gamble,
  You tell smutty jokes and you swear,
You have no respect for each other,
  Just strangers to shame and don't care.
It's more than a notion I tell you
  To think what the future will hold,
For its young generations when this one
  Today is so brazen bold. ★

The Poetical Farmwife

I think about all those sweet nothings
  I read, that the magazines buy,
I know I can write some that's better
  And so I sit down just to try.
I hear Billy call from the barnyard,
  "Ma! One of them hens got away,"
You can't mix up love lays and chickens,
  They don't go together, no, nay.

I've wandered away down the hillside,
  Carrying my book and my pen,
And there I would write just like lightning,
  To get all the pretty thoughts in.
The thoughts get all mixed up with turnips
  That Bill wants for dinner today,
You can't mix the cook pots and poetry,
  They don't go together, no, nay.

One day Billy came from the dairy,
  I said with my prettiest smile,
"Now, Billy dear, please don't disturb me,
  I really must write for a while."
"Come skim this milk, Janey," he blustered,
  "I've got to go help with the hay,"
You can't mix the sonnets with churning,
  They don't go together, no, nay. ★

Just Dreams

Dreams in sweet childhood
  Of fairies and goblins,
Dreams and air castles
  'Mid school books and toys,
Dreams when a maiden
  Of gay knights and lovers,
Dreams, happy dreams
  Void of griefs, only joys.

Dreams of a life mate
  And cozy wee cottage,
Of course not too tiny,
  But just the right size,
Dreams then of motherhood
  Far best, the sweetest,
Wondering what color
  Will be the baby's eyes.

Dreams of the future
  For mother's own darling,
Hoping that all things
  For him will be bright,
Thus are the dreams
  Of life's spring, summer, autumn,
Morn, noonday and evening,
  But what of the night?

The night and the winter
  When life is all hoary,
The sunshine is fading
  The future obscure.
Waiting, just waiting
  With naught but the memories
Of dreams that were sweet
  But so seldom came true. ★

Mimi Reisel Gladstein and Sylvia Deener Cohen

Mimi Reisel Gladstein was raised in El Paso. She earned a Ph.D. from the University of New Mexico and is a faculty member at the University of Texas at El Paso. She is the author of five books, including *The Ayn Rand Companion* and *In Search of Steinbeck: A Continuing Journey*, and co-editor of *The Last Supper of Chicano Heroes: Selected Works of José Antonio Burciaga* and *Feminist Interpretations of Ayn Rand.* Gladstein has been recognized internationally for her John Steinbeck scholarship and teaching. She has chaired several departments at the University of Texas at El Paso, was the first director of the women's studies program, and has served as associate dean of the College of Liberal Arts. In 2003 she received the award for Outstanding Faculty Achievement in the College of Liberal Arts and in 2006 received the award for Outstanding Service to Students. She is also head of the Content Committee for the El Paso Holocaust Museum and Study Center and was the director of the first Holocaust Remembrance Program in El Paso.

Sylvia Deener Cohen moved to El Paso from the Bronx and became aware of the resettlement of Holocaust survivors in her role as administrative assistant to Emil Reisel at the Rio Grande Sales Company. In 1986 she went to many concentration camps as part of the March of the Living project. She did survivor interviews through Steven Spielberg's Shoah Foundation and was the senior adult director of the Jewish Community Center. Now retired, Cohen was the first executive director of the El Paso Holocaust Museum and Study Center. She continues to work with survivors through Jewish Family and Children's Services and serves on the Advisory Board and Content Committee of the El Paso Holocaust Museum and Study Center.

From *Lone Stars of David*: The Wild West Welcomes Holocaust Survivors

El Paso, the international city that borders two countries and two states, has long been a crossroads of people and cultures, from nomadic Indians and migrating Mexicans to Jews who came as frontier merchants and later as Holocaust-era refugees. Both haven and highway, this city at the southernmost point of the Rocky Mountains is a natural passageway that diverse groups have traversed for centuries. Through this mountain pass, Spanish explorers journeyed from the Chihuahuan Desert to Santa Fe. The first Anglo settlers arrived shortly after the Texas Revolution in 1836, and Jewish entrepreneurs began setting up shop in 1849 after the U.S. Army constructed an adobe outpost named Fort Bliss. Outlaws hid in El Paso in the 1880s, the decade during which two Jewish merchants were elected mayor. Throughout the Mexican Revolution, from 1910 to 1920, El Paso served as a center of intrigue. Exiled leaders sought refuge there. Revolutionary general Pancho Villa—bandit to some, folk hero to others—contacted Jewish merchants and tailors to outfit his troops. One of those merchants, Rubin Cohen, recalled: "Whatever Villa wanted, Villa got!"

Since World War II, El Paso's Jewish population has held steady at around five thousand people. While the Jewish numbers remained stable, the city's total population nearly tripled to seven hundred thousand at the end of the century, making El Paso the largest American city along the Mexican border. Despite the Jewish community's shrinking proportion to the whole, El Paso's Jewish families maintained a high profile. Ever since the city's first rabbi arrived in 1898, Jewish religious leaders—along with a priest and a minister—have presided at civic occasions as if they represented a third of the populace. The city's long-time Reform rabbi, Martin Zielonka, who served from 1900 until his death in 1938, was among the founders of the College of the City of El Paso. Conservative Rabbi Joseph Roth, who served Congregation B'nai Zion from 1923 to 1953, headed the Philosophy Department at the Texas College of Mines, forerunner of the University of Texas at El Paso. A post-World War II rabbi, Floyd S. Fierman, wrote a series of colorfully titled history books—*Roots and Boots* and *Guts and Ruts*—that record experiences of the region's Jewish pioneers and demonstrate the degree to which Jews were among the mix of people that settled the Southwest.

When the Chamizal National Monument, celebrating the end of a century-old border dispute, opened in 1967 on an island in the Rio Grande, it evolved into a multicultural center with programs illuminating race and ethnicity. Chamizal became an avenue for understanding among Mexicans, Hispanics, native tribes, blacks, Anglos, and Jews. Logically, the Chamizal Memorial Theatre hosted the region's first Holocaust remembrance observance in 1976 produced by Sally Gilbert and Norma Geller—a standing-room-only multimedia production. The production closed in silence with survivors lighting memorial candles. Survivors were not yet ready to pour out their stories; however, the Chamizal Memorial programs, four in all, ignited a spark among the survivors and wakened the curiosity of the El Paso community to the *Shoah*—the Hebrew word, meaning "catastrophic upheaval," that is used to describe the Holocaust.

El Paso remained a sleepy town until after World War II, when many of the soldiers—both Jew and non-Jew—who had passed through Fort Bliss elected to settle in West Texas. A large number of soldiers had married local girls. Others chose to return to the Southwest after a cold winter or two in the North. In addition to the warm and arid weather in the foothills of the Franklin Mountains, what drew veterans to El Paso was the low cost of living and the abundant, affordable household help. Even lower-middle-class families could employ live-in Mexican housekeepers. Because everyone had a "maid," social life and entertaining in homes was quite active. Jewish women were freed from many household duties and often became active in social service organizations, in card-playing circles, and even in family businesses. The El Paso section of the National Council of Jewish Women, which served the community from 1917 until 2003, was instrumental in founding the El Paso Lighthouse for the Blind, the El Paso School for Emotionally Disturbed Children, and many other key community institutions.

Two of the newcomers to El Paso in the late 1930s were Emil and Regina Reisel, who had the foresight to leave Stanislav, Poland, in 1935 as Hitler was rising to power. They reached the United States in 1938 via Nicaragua and lived in Las Cruces, New Mexico, until 1945 when Emil began operating a wholesale warehouse in El Paso. Although a recent arrival, he headed up the El Paso Jewish Community Council's committee that resettled Holocaust survivors. Nationwide, approximately two hundred thousand Jewish refugees entered the United States from Europe between 1933 and 1945. Another one hundred thousand immigrated during the postwar period from 1945 to 1950. Of the latter group, around seventy-five ended up in El Paso—a small number percentagewise, yet a group that would have significant impact.

For many of the Jewish refugees who moved to El Paso, the city was an alien environment. Some survivors came to El Paso because they had relatives in the city. A few were recruited directly by Emil Reisel, who met them in New York when he visited the Hebrew Immigrant Aid Society (HIAS) offices. Other survivors decided to move to far West Texas after a brief experience with big cities and cold climates in other parts of the country. El Paso, with its 364 days a year of sunshine, felt like a more hospitable environment. It was an international city with manageable traffic, a low crime rate, and a small-town atmosphere.

Reisel's main task was to find employment for the men among the refugees. When he could not place an immigrant in a job, he put him to work in his own wholesale dry goods business, Rio Grande Sales Company. He gave many newcomers a start and then provided them with merchandise on credit to begin their own businesses. While Emil Reisel took charge of job placement for the men, an impromptu women's auxiliary—made up of his wife, Regina, her sister-in-law, Sally Rosen, and a friend, Ida Bendalin—oriented the women to their new environment. This entailed securing housing, furnishing homes, and showing them the ins and outs of shopping. After her first trip to the grocery store, one woman expressed confusion: "How do you know what to choose?" The array of soaps overwhelmed her. On the other hand, El Paso groceries did not have all the products the immigrants were used to. Bagels were unknown. One woman asked the manager for sour cream, which was not then generally available in the region. The grocer haughtily replied, "Madam, all our cream is fresh." On another occasion, as a woman was leaving a store, a checker said, "Thank you. Y'all come back." So the shopper walked back and heard the checker ask, "Can I help you?" She replied in her heavily accented English, "You told me to come back."

While Emil Reisel was finding jobs for the men and his wife was taking women shopping, the couple's two daughters got involved. "Here, teach them English," they were instructed. A refugee's age or country of origin did not matter. The sisters taught them English. There was no bilingual education in those days, yet the children of survivors felt driven to achieve and often became top students.

The Holocaust survivors who came to El Paso had varied backgrounds. Most exotic was Sarah Hauptman, a lion tamer active in the Belgian underground. Henry Kellen of Poland had studied textile engineering in Paris. Eva and Sigmund Weiser were pharmacists educated in Italy. Nathan Weiselman was a Polish tailor. Most built new lives, seldom continuing in their earlier professions. Many had a facility for language and quickly picked up conversational English and Spanish, enabling them to work among the border's bilingual clientele.

One of the most romantic stories is that of Rudy Burgheim (1891-1983), a diminutive man, about five feet tall, who escaped from Germany and spent the war years in Shanghai. By the time he arrived in the United States, he was close to sixty and had never married. When no work could be found for him in El Paso, he became a stock boy at Rio Grande Sales Company. Once established in Texas, he visited relatives in Chicago, where he met Beatrice, also never married and also diminutive, measuring all of four feet ten inches. It was a love match. The couple opened a small store in downtown El Paso, prospered, and bought a home. Their devotion to each other was legendary.

Ben Kandel, a Polish accountant, survived the Krakow ghetto, the Plaszow penal labor camp, and the Mauthausen Concentration Camp. He met Emil Reisel at the HIAS office in New York. Reisel offered him a job as a traveling salesman in the Southwest. After four years of life on the road and several attempts at operating businesses in Las Cruces, New Mexico, and Laredo, Texas, he settled in El Paso, where he successfully developed Ben's Men's Store downtown.

Drs. Sigmund and Eva Weiser received doctorates in pharmacy from Italy's University of Modena. Returning to their native Poland in 1939 to attend her father's funeral, they were trapped when Hitler invaded. Through connections in Italy—among them Grand Duke, nephew of King Vittorio Emanuel—they escaped on the last Italian Red Cross train leaving Poland. They hid in Genoa until an informer told police their whereabouts. Eva Weiser often retold the story of sitting at Genoa police headquarters, crying. The police captain told her not to weep, that she would be grateful later because he was sending the couple to the Ferramonti De Tarsia internment camp near Cosenza in south of Italy. It was one of fifteen internment camps Mussolini established in the summer of 1940. What she did not realize then was that the Nazis were demanding that some inmates in northern Italy be sent to death camps. Being in the south saved the couple's lives. After the war, both Weisers became active with the Haganah, procuring boats to smuggle Jews into Palestine. They also returned to their work as pharmacists. However, when they moved to El Paso to join Sigmund's cousins (Marcus, Paul, Sigmund, Leo, and Oscar Rosen), he went to work in one of the Rosens' retail stores, and Eva Weiser became a full-time housewife.

Dr. Larry Gladstone—the family name was originally Glattstein—enlisted in the Hungarian armed forces in 1941. Jewish soldiers were discharged quickly and put into labor battalions. Gladstone survived typhus, near starvation, and two death marches in Austria, first to Mauthausen and then to Gunskirchen, the site of mass graves. In 1946, with assistance from El Paso relatives, he resettled in West Texas, graduated from the College of Mines, then enrolled in Southwestern Medical School in Dallas, where he met his bride, Beatrice "Bitty" Marcus. He served at the U.S. Army Medical Corps' William Beaumont Medical Center in El Paso and then went into private practice, from which he retired in 1992.

Siblings Agnes and Ferenc "Frank" Klein arrived in El Paso in 1949 with help from their cousins, the Schwartz family, owners of the Popular Dry Goods Company. The Kleins survived Auschwitz, where their mother and aunt had been selected upon arrival for extermination. Ferenc and his twin brother, Otto, were taken to Dr. Josef Mengele, whose infamous experiments on human subjects are well documented. Otto survived and resettled in Switzerland. Agnes married Tibor Schaechner, also a survivor, whom she met in Brooklyn and brought to El Paso. Tibor had survived the war in safe houses in Hungary, ending up in the Budapest ghetto months before the Russian Army liberated it. In El Paso, he worked at the Popular Dry Goods Company from 1960 until it closed in 1995. Agnes earned her Master's Degree in social work and worked for the Texas Department of Human Services for twenty-two years.

A number of survivors who settled in El Paso have written memoirs about their experiences, replete with impressions of the Texas-Mexico border region. Among the published authors is Itzhak "Isaac" Kotkowski, who, as a teenager, served in the Polish Army, spent time in a Soviet prison camp, and wound up in a displaced persons camp in France. He immigrated to Israel, to Mexico City, and from there relocated to El Paso to go into an automotive business. Kotkowski's autobiography, *The Wiles of Destiny: Memoirs of Itzhak Kotkowski*, was published in English, Spanish, and Polish. He wrote that he adjusted quickly to Mexico because he had studied Spanish in Warsaw. His "interest in Mexican history and geography sparked an ability to quickly assimilate into the local cultural and business communities."

Mark Kupfer, who fled a Polish ghetto after the 1939 German invasion and survived the war in bunkers, attics, farms, and a forced labor camp, did not live to see his memoir published. His children completed *From Darkness to Sunshine: A Young Boy's Odyssey*. Initially, Kupfer resettled in Chicago, then Detroit and New York, where he met his wife, Rose Eisenberg. Together they moved to El Paso, his wife's hometown. He wrote that El Paso, with its small park in the center of town, reminded him of Europe. Describing his first day in El Paso, he recalled, "In the morning, the sun woke me up, and I couldn't believe what I saw . . . It was December 25 . . . yet there was no snow or ice. The weather there was glorious compared to the eastern cities . . . I said, 'This is beautiful, it's heaven on earth.'"

Among the Holocaust survivors who worked for Emil Reisel was Jake Beilinson. He and his wife Frieda came to El Paso because her uncle, Joe Ravel, lived there. Later, Jake and Frieda divorced and left El Paso, both resettling in California. Frieda's memoir, *Some Dare to Dream: Frieda Frome's Escape from Lithuania*, was published in 1988 under her new married name, Frieda Frome. In her book, she remarked that El Paso was interesting to her because so much of the population was of Mexican descent and spoke Spanish. "They seemed more like the natives of the Baltic countries than any of the people I had yet seen in America." Although her ex-husband was known in El Paso as Jake Beilinson, in her book Frieda identified him as Koba Yanovitch. His original name was dropped in the transition from Europe to the United States.

Among the most unforgettable refugees was Henry Kellen—whose original surname was Kacenelenbogen. A native of Lodz, Poland, Henry, his wife Julia, and nephew, Jerry, survived the Holocaust due to the kindness of a Lithuanian farmer, Andrius Urbanos, who hid them during the war years. In El Paso, Emil Reisel gave Henry Kellen two sample cases, a car, and a sales route that sent him out to remote towns such as Lovington, New Mexico (pop. 9,400) and Safford, Arizona, (pop. 9,000). Although he arrived speaking few words of English, Kellen became a top-notch salesman—evidence of the charm and persistence that would characterize his later endeavors.

Typical of refugees from Nazi Europe, Kellen and other survivors spoke little about their Holocaust experiences. They applied themselves to building new lives and community ties. Holocaust survivors the world over were slow to dredge up their experiences, although many, like Isaac Kotkowski and Elizabeth Vorenberg, quietly had begun compiling memoirs. They shared little of their past with their children, much less with strangers. Rabbi Floyd Fierman, who was adept at taking oral histories, attempted to interview the local Holocaust refugees. In the introduction to his 1983 book, *Insights and Hindsights of Some El Paso Jewish Families*, he wrote that the survivors were polite but unwilling to respond to queries. In his opinion, "they failed to cooperate because they did not want to leave any records for future Gestapo—secret police—who might conceivably seek them out to finish what the Hitlers of the world started. This is a psychological withdrawal with which I sympathize."

Throughout the fifties and sixties, popular culture paid little attention to the Holocaust, except for occasional productions such as Playhouse 90's *Judgment at Nuremberg*, telecast in 1959, and Sidney Lumet's film, *The Pawnbroker*, produced in 1965. The latter focused on memories of a survivor. The catalyst for transforming the *Shoah* into a topic of conversation across America was the NBC miniseries, *Holocaust*, televised in April 1978. In conjunction with its airing, journalists scoured their circulation areas for survivors who could put a local face on the highly rated television show, which attracted 120 million viewers. Writer Eli Wiesel, a Holocaust survivor and future Nobel Peace Prize laureate, criticized the miniseries for trivializing the deaths of six million Jews. He encouraged survivors to tell what had really occurred. Immigrants began to pour out their experiences. They were glad for the sympathy this evoked.

Seven months before the NBC miniseries, a group of Dallas survivors who worshipped at Shearith Israel had started to meet regularly. They called themselves Holocaust Survivors in Dallas. Their organizer was former physical fitness instructor Mike Jacobs, a native of the Polish town of Konin. He had survived five years in ghettos and concentration camps and emerged with optimism to start a new life. His group grew to include spouses and children who shared his dream, which he described in his memoir, *Holocaust Survivor: Mike Jacobs' Triumph Over Tragedy*, as a "place where we Holocaust Survivors could gather and memorialize our loved ones as . . . we had no cemetery to go to." Jacobs's vision of a Dallas Holocaust Center was so vivid, he had blueprints made as well as a mock-up model of the proposed museum.

In April of 1983, a national Holocaust Survivors Gathering convened in Washington, D.C. Jacobs brought his architectural model with him and was interviewed by camera crews from ABC Television's *Nightline*. The publicity inspired others to follow his example. It also spurred contributions to fulfill Jacobs's dream. In 1984, he became the founder of the Dallas Holocaust Museum and Study Center, which opened in the basement of the Dallas Jewish Community Center. It featured a fifteen-ton railroad boxcar that the Nazis had used to transport Jews to the ghettos and death camps. The Dallas Holocaust Center became a model for other grassroots museums across the country that would start through the efforts of one survivor and then gather momentum.

El Paso's Henry Kellen contacted Mike Jacobs in 1984, brainstormed, and developed a warm friendship. Soon, Kellen began collecting wartime artifacts and memorabilia that would become the core of a collection for an El Paso Holocaust museum. He returned to his native Poland to gather more materials. To exhibit them, he "shnorred" a display case from the Popular Dry Goods

Company, courtesy of Albert Schwartz, one of the department store's owners and a descendant of a pioneer El Paso family.

Kellen asked the El Paso Jewish Federation, the successor to the Jewish Community Council, to provide space for his display. At first, Federation directors allotted him one wall in a conference room, which Kellen filled with pictures and maps. Slowly, he began encroaching into other areas of the room. When the Union Fashion, a Jewish-owned men's store, gave Kellen a mannequin, he dressed it in an authentic concentration-camp-inmate uniform, bandaging and bloodying it for realistic effect. Another Holocaust survivor, Bernard Peregricht of Budapest, came upon the mannequin suddenly one day and was taken aback. "That's me," he said, pointing his finger. "That is what I looked like."

Kellen's quest for artifacts, memorabilia, and display cases grew. So did visitors to his Holocaust exhibit. Shortly after the first display was installed, Kellen began booking tours to the conference room. He invited schools, churches, and units from the Army's Fort Bliss. They came. Visitors sat on chairs, on the floor, and even on the conference table. Innocently, Kellen allowed children to handle the artifacts. A heavy Nazi helmet was passed around, and the children tried it on.

Needing clerical help, Kellen pulled in Sylvia Deener Cohen, the senior adult director at the Jewish Community Center. Cohen and Kellen had become acquainted years before when both worked at Emil Reisel's Rio Grande Sales Company. "Sylvia," he would often ask her, "could you write this letter for me?" She did. When a photographer from the nearby White Sands Missile Range in New Mexico arrived one day to photograph artifacts on display, Kellen steered him to Cohen. "Sylvia," he said, "you take care of it." She did. One day, when Kellen was hanging posters on a second wall of the conference room, Cohen admonished him that he had only been given permission to fill one surface. "Who cares?" he responded. Gradually, Holocaust materials engulfed the room. There were complaints from some Federation board members that the conference room, often utilized to plan recreational activities, was incompatible with pictures of death and devastation. Henry Kellen was unfazed.

His collection grew as retired military personnel who had fought in the European theater donated Nazi memorabilia. Among the donors was former

El Paso Mayor Peter de Wetter, whose Army unit had liberated concentration camps. Another liberator, Major General Raymond L. Shoemaker, former commandant of Fort Bliss, donated artifacts and spoke at events. Unfortunately, Nazi memorabilia attracts a certain type of thief. In 1987, the conference room was broken into. A Nazi saber was stolen. An investigation concluded that the motive was greed, not anti-Semitism, for such a saber could bring twenty thousand dollars on the open market.

With the theft and the burgeoning number of visitors, the need for a separate, independent Holocaust museum became obvious. There was no space to expand in the JCC building. More and more groups booked tours. A new organization, headed by Beth and Meyer Lipson, formed with the goal of constructing a local Holocaust museum and study center. Albert Schwartz, who had given Kellen his first display case, became president. He and the board continued to fundraise for a permanent space. Sylvia Cohen, by then drafted as a tour guide and lecturer, was spending so much time with Henry Kellen's Holocaust display that the fund-raising board picked up one-fourth of her salary. In 1988, the board assumed half her pay, and the exhibits consumed half her time. Once the museum was under construction in 1992, it consumed three-fourths of her working day as she conducted oral history interviews with survivors and trained docents from across the community. By the time the El Paso Museum and Holocaust Center moved from its single conference room into a free-standing building in 1994, Sylvia Cohen had become its executive director.

The modest, one-story building was designed with fifteen hundred square feet for the museum and another fifteen hundred square feet for the offices of Jewish Family Service, the social service arm of the Federation. Prominent local businessman Louis Rosenbaum and his wife Miriam donated the bulk of the funds for the $310,000 building, located on land in the Jewish Federation's parking lot. On opening day, the keynote speaker was Sister Rose Thering, the Dominican nun whose research led the Catholic Church's Vatican II Council in 1965 to reverse its historic doctrine holding Jews responsible for the death of Jesus. "The Holocaust was the culmination of the teaching of contempt," she often said. Her keynote address in El Paso signaled the focus of the museum. It would not only be a setting to learn about the Nazi era, but also a space for people of all religions and backgrounds to reflect upon the impact of intolerance.

When the tiny El Paso Holocaust Museum opened its doors in 1994, it was the only such museum between Dallas and Los Angeles. Two years later, the Holocaust Museum Houston opened. In 1998, Albuquerque launched the New Mexico Holocaust and Intolerance Museum and Study Center, with assistance from the El Paso Holocaust Museum. Also in 1998, San Antonio's Mazal Library, the largest private collection of books and records on the Holocaust, opened to the public by appointment. Two years later, San Antonio's Jewish Federation opened a Holocaust Education Center and Memorial Museum. By the beginning of the century, there were more than a score of Holocaust museums across the nation, including the U.S. Holocaust Memorial Museum in Washington, D.C., that had opened in 1993.

The proliferation of Holocaust museums, particularly in places like El Paso with relatively few Jews, is evidence of their relevance as a community resource for teaching tolerance. The local response to the El Paso museum demonstrates a hunger for knowledge in a region scarcely touched by the Holocaust. During the El Paso museum's first year, five thousand students toured the facility along with hundreds of drop-ins. By 2001, twenty-five thousand students a year were visiting the museum, and there was a waiting list. The museum became a component in the educational program of the public schools. At Fort Bliss, the Office of Equal Opportunity and the U.S. Army Sergeant's Major Academy incorporated tours and workshops into their curricula.

A larger museum necessitated more complex interior designs and displays than a single room with one showcase. Lucie Liebman, a Holocaust-era survivor who had fled from Vienna, stepped in as volunteer curator. She worked side by side with Richard Glass, a local artist. He put into artistic form her ideas for museum exhibits. Together, they maximized the use of educational tools. Professional librarian Mary Ann Plaut volunteered to arrange scholarly materials. Sylvia Cohen recruited a score of docents and speakers from the wider community. Among them were Sol Lederman, a former prisoner of war, and Ernesto Martinez and Gonzalo LaFarrell, two military veterans who witnessed the liberation of the camps. Eileen Licht, Toni Harris, Norman Farb, Phyllis

Saltzstein, and Trish Belbel were mainstay docents. Giving tours in Spanish was Dottie Grodin. Former U.S. Army photographer Neal Axelrod, who documented the liberation of concentration camps, gave tours. Professors from the El Paso branch of the University of Texas signed on as tour guides. They included humanities professor Robert Wren, who incorporated Holocaust studies into his classes; Robin Scofield, who assigned freshman English students to research the topic; Ilsa Irwin, who conducted many a tour in German; and David Hackett. Hackett is the Holocaust scholar who translated and annotated *The Buchenwald Report*, a volume filled with transcriptions of Allied Forces' interviews with concentration camp inmates.

One of the most unusual aspects of the El Paso museum is its relationship with the German military. Fort Bliss is home to the German Air Force Air Defense Artillery Center and School, which has 130 staff members and trains around six hundred soldiers a year. When the El Paso Holocaust Museum opened, German Brigadier General Eckart Wienss mandated that every soldier under his command tour the museum. One of Wienss's successors, Brigadier General Peter Merklinghaus, continued the policy. At museum workshops, he spoke about Germany's postwar efforts to come to terms with the Holocaust. Often, the general's driver would pick up Kellen, and the pair would travel to Cochise Community College in Arizona or to Western New Mexico University in Silver City to present seminars. The story of General Merklinghaus and Henry Kellen's friendship was featured in the *El Paso Times* on April 29, 2002.

The museum's second president, David Marcus, launched a series of high-profile dinners. New York Governor Mario Cuomo was the first big-name speaker. Subsequently, the museum hosted Mikhail Gorbachev, the former Soviet Union premier; General Colin Powell, former chairman of the Joint Chiefs of Staff and future U.S. Secretary of State; General Norman Schwartzkopf, commander in chief of U.S. forces in Operation Desert Shield; Christopher Reeve, the actor paralyzed in a horseback riding accident; and New York Mayor Rudolph Guiliani.

In early October 2001, seven years after the museum opened and a few weeks after the toppling of the World Trade Center towers, the El Paso

Holocaust Museum was destroyed by fire. Former President Bill Clinton, scheduled to address the annual fundraising dinner, visited the charred ruins. The fire destroyed 80 percent of the exhibits and artifacts. Because of the tense times, people could not help but wonder about the cause of the blaze. The fire department ruled it an electrical malfunction.

Although the original building was gone, the educational program continued. Shortly after the fire, the museum's new executive director, Leslie Novick, flew to Berlin at her own expense, along with a native Berliner who used her influence to gain access to the Topography of Terror Museum, the Resistance Museum, and the villa in Wannsee where the Final Solution was planned. Novick selected exhibit materials that were flown back to El Paso for display in a downtown bank. The Junior League of El Paso took on Holocaust training as a project, developing PowerPoint presentations, which its members took to the schools. One schoolteacher, Christina Vasquez, developed such expertise that she went to work at Holocaust Museum Houston heading its education program.

The big-name speaker program waned. Although bringing in world leaders focused the public spotlight on the museum, there was disagreement among the board of directors as to whether it was worth the considerable expense. In recent years, speakers have not been quite as high profile but have a closer connection to the Holocaust. They have included the chairman of the U.S. Holocaust Museum and the Danish ambassador to the United States, honored for his country's rescue of seventy-five hundred Jews during the Holocaust.

Even when the El Paso Holocaust Center became a museum-without-walls, it continued its mission. Three years after the fire, two El Pasoans—Sam Legate and Jim Scherr— donated downtown space at 101 Kansas Street for a temporary museum location. The space opened in October 2004 and began booking school tours and workshops.

There are plans for a new, permanent El Paso Holocaust Museum in an existing eighty-seven-hundred-square-foot building that will be gutted and renovated, with completion slated for the end of 2006. Henry Kellen, who was eighty-six when the museum burned, remains the driving force at the El Paso Holocaust center. He continues scheduling half-day, full-day, and two-day workshops for schools, community groups, and colleges in Texas, New Mexico, and Arizona. His calendar is full. He hopes to live to see the opening of the new museum. His original display on one wall in the Jewish Community Center has expanded into schools and colleges and inside the gates at Fort Bliss. The El Paso experience demonstrates that there is a need, an interest, and an audience for Holocaust studies not only in Washington, D.C., and New York, which have tens of thousands of Jews, but also in the American Southwest, at a cultural crossroads with relatively few Jews, in a remote corner of the Diaspora. ★

Mario T. García

Native El Pasoan Mario T. García earned his B.A. and M.A. from the University of Texas at El Paso and received his Ph.D. in history at the University of California, San Diego. He has taught at San Jose State University, San Diego State University, and Yale University where he also served as director of Ethnic Studies. García currently teaches at the University of California Santa Barbara. He is the recipient of fellowships from the NEH; the Ford Foundation; the Center for the Advanced Study of the Behavior Science at Stanford; the Woodrow Wilson Center in Washington, D.C.; a Guggenheim Fellowship; and most recently a Fulbright Senior Lectureship to teach in Madrid in 2009. García has written many books on Chicano history, several of which have been awarded prizes including the Southwest Book Award. He is the author of: *Desert Immigrants: The Mexicans of El Paso, 1880-1920*; *Mexican Americans: Leadership, Ideology & Identity, 1930-1960*; *Memories of Chicano History: The Life and Narrative of Bert Corona*; *The Making of a Mexican-American Mayor: Raymond L. Telles of El Paso*; *Padre: The Life and Spiritual Journey of Father Virgil Cordano*; *Católicos: Resistance and Affirmation in Chicano Catholic History*; and *Luis Leal: An Auto/Biography*. García is the editor of *A Dolores Huerta Reader*; *Ruben Salazar Border Correspondent: Selected Writings, 1955-1970*; *The Gospel of César Chávez: My Faith In Action*; and co-author of *Migrant Daughter: Coming of Age as a Mexican American Woman*. Recently, García completed an oral history of Sal Castro and the 1968 Blowouts in Los Angeles, and he is currently working on an oral history of the Chicano Movement in Los Angeles, as well as a biography of Father Luis Olivares and the Sanctuary movement in Los Angeles. García chaired the Department of Chicana and Chicano Studies at the University of California Santa Barbara from 1984 to 1990. Currently the director of the Latino Leadership Project at UCSB's Chicano Studies Institute, García is the recipient of a campus-wide teaching award from the UCSB Academic Senate.

From *Ruben Salazar: Border Correspondent, Selected Writings 1955–1970*: Introduction

Requiem 29

On August 29, 1970, in East Los Angeles, Chicanos staged the largest antiwar demonstration ever organized in the United States by people of Mexican descent. More than twenty thousand marched in a spirited Chicano moratorium against the Vietnam War. Demonstrators came from all over southern California as well as from other parts of the state and from the Southwest. Although predominantly young, the demonstrators included older Mexican Americans. They protested, like Americans across the country, a war that many of them had initially supported. After years of seeing their young men killing and being killed, Chicanos began to question the reasons for the bloodshed and the U.S. role in the conflict. It was an especially relevant issue for Chicanos since they, like African Americans, were being drafted in numbers disproportionate to their percentage of the total population. And once in the military, they were again being killed in numbers disproportionate to their representation in the armed forces.[1] Hundreds of Chicanos were returning in body bags or seriously maimed, both physically and psychologically. For young Chicanos now further engaged at home in a militant social movement for self-determination and self-identity—the Chicano movement—the Vietnam War represented one more example of the ongoing exploitation of Mexicans in the United States, beginning with the U.S. seizure of half of Mexico's territory—virtually the entire Southwest—in the mid-nineteenth century.

And so they marched and protested that fateful day in August, down Brooklyn and Whittier avenues until they converged on Laguna Park. They arrived by the thousands and were greeted with Mexican music and a festive atmosphere on a filtered sunny/smoggy L.A. day. As the first to arrive sat on the grass, watching the rest of the marchers streaming in, they listened to the entertainment and to the speakers. But apprehension soon began to set in among the crowd, and then intermittent police sirens were heard. Rumors began to spread about a disturbance on Whittier Boulevard: police were roughing up and arresting some of the demonstrators. As the crowd turned to look, they saw the ominous arrival of hundreds of helmeted police—Los Angeles County Sheriff's deputies—who were assembling at one end of the park, some wearing gas masks. Without warning (the Sheriff's Department would later claim provocation on the part of the demonstrators) they moved on the crowd. Pandemonium broke out as the deputies fired tear gas cannisters into the dispersing assembly of men, women, and children. Some of the Chicanos fought back. They pelted the deputies with their own tear gas cannisters and whatever else they could find. The deputies charged into the crowd. Flaying nightsticks found their marks. A young Chicana was struck on the back of her head and fell to the ground. Tears from the gas mingled with blood and streamed down the faces of the demonstrators. Moratorium leaflets were dropped and scattered on the streets.[2]

Out of the park, many Chicanos began to vent their anger and frustration at having their peaceful moratorium violently repressed by the police—another example of the oppression of La Raza. Windows were broken, cars were set on fire, and rocks were thrown. Reinforcement deputies arrived and joined in the beatings. That afternoon, East L.A. became a battleground.[3]

Ruben Salazar, a columnist for the *Los Angeles Times* and the news director of KMEX, the Spanish-language TV station in Los Angeles, covered the moratorium that day. He and his TV crew witnessed much of the disturbance. Later that afternoon, they retired to the Silver Dollar Cafe on Whittier Boulevard to relax and have a beer. According to cameraman Guillermo Restrepo, Salazar believed that he and his crew were being followed after the breakup of the moratorium.[4] Shortly after arriving, they heard a police radio outside the café. Through the window they saw armed deputies in riot gear. The deputies ordered everyone outside back into the café, and without warning, a tear gas projectile blasted through the door. Another cannister—a ten-inch missile—smashed into the café. Two others followed. The deputies would later claim that they had been told that an armed individual was inside the café, but no weapon ever turned up. Behind the café, Salazar's colleagues realized that Salazar was still inside. Their attempts to go back to find him were rebuffed by the deputies. Despite his friends' insistence that Salazar remained in the café, the deputies refused to check inside or to allow anyone to enter. When the deputies finally entered several hours later, Salazar's body was found. One of the projectiles, an inquest later determined, had torn through his head.[5]

Raul Ruiz and Joe Razo of *La Raza* magazine, a Chicano movement publication, happened to find themselves across from the Silver Dollar at the time. At the first signs of a disturbance, both began to photograph the actions of the Sheriff's deputies. Their photographs, later published in both *La Raza* and the *Los Angeles Times*, revealed that one of the deputies fired directly into the café. Ruben Salazar was forty-two at the time of his death. He left a wife and three children.[6]

Two other people died at the moratorium, and sixty-one were injured. More than two hundred were arrested, and property damage reached over $1 million.[7] When news of Salazar's death reached the Chicano community, its anger and hatred toward the police were mixed with great sorrow over the death of a journalist whom many in the community knew and respected. The inquest into his death was televised and lasted sixteen days. According to Los Angeles County Coroner Thomas T. Noguchi, whose office conducted an autopsy of Salazar's body, Salazar had died almost instantly from a "through-and-through projectile wound of the left temple area causing massive injury to the brain."[8]

The police, including Deputy Thomas Wilson, who fired the missile, were questioned, as were some of the Chicanos who were at the moratorium. One of the key issues was whether Wilson was acting in accordance with proper procedures when he fired the projectiles. This question, however, was never examined because the Sheriff's Department refused to turn over its training manual, which covered the use of tear gas equipment, and the manual was never subpoenaed by the inquest officer, Norman Pittluck. According to Sheriff Peter Pitchess, "There was absolutely no misconduct on the part of the deputies involved or in the procedures they followed."[9]

Instead the questioning turned into an indictment of the moratorium. The District Attorney's office, which was supposed to remain neutral so as to determine the facts of the case, in fact functioned as defense attorneys for the Sheriff's Department. The moratorium, it was suggested by Pittluck, was an unruly mob determined to do violence. And the Sheriff's deputies, furthermore, were there only to protect the community and restore law and order.

The demonstrators were also portrayed as subversives: "Is that Castro's man?" Raul Ruiz was asked about a photograph that showed some of the demonstrators holding a picture of Che Guevara. "Che Guevara," Ruiz responded, "was a great hero to the people of Latin America. He struggled against oppression and injustice." The Chicanos in the court cheered, and the jury ruled by a 4 to 3 vote that Salazar had met death "at the hands of another.[10]

However, District Attorney Evelle Younger concluded that the facts from the inquest did not justify criminal charges against Deputy Wilson or the Sheriff's Department. According to Younger, no criminal intent on the part of Wilson or the other Sheriff's deputies could be determined. Younger further concluded that the split decision by the jury suggested that it would be difficult to convince a trial jury that a crime had been committed. The Department of Justice added insult to injury when it also refused to investigate Salazar's death after requested to do so by twenty-two California state legislators.[11]

The case was closed for the police and the investigating officials but not for Chicanos, who held the police guilty of murder. A well-known Chicano attorney and subsequent celebrity, Oscar Zeta Acosta—aka the "Brown Buffalo"—accused authorities of criminal conspiracy to commit political assassination, another vicious example of police state tactics in America with precedents not confined to the Chicano community.[12] Acosta was twice forcibly ejected from the hearing room for protesting the injustice of the hearing. The ejections in turn provoked scuffles in the courtroom between Chicanos and courtroom deputies.[13] Danny Villanueva, who was then station manager of KMEX and Salazar's boss, perplexed to this day by the lack of prosecution of the officers involved in the Silver Dollar incident. "If there wasn't a conspiracy," he concludes, "it is an incredible set of circumstances."[14]

The protests continued, and the Chicano movement had another martyr. Yet, ironically, and despite the many dangerous assignments he undertook throughout his career, Salazar would never have conceived of himself in this way. Salazar was neither a martyr nor a politico but a hardworking reporter whose career and work needs to be appreciated beyond his tragic death.

Salazar can be seen as a "border correspondent," not only because he himself was literally a product of the U.S.–Mexican border or because he covered the U.S.–Mexican border as a reporter at one point in his career but symbolically as well. Salazar's career was marked by crossing new borders or frontiers. Although there exists a long history of Mexican American journalism in the United States primarily catering to a Mexican American or *mexicano* immigrant population, Salazar was the first journalist of Mexican American background to cross over into mainstream English-language journalism.[15] He was the first Mexican American journalist to work as a reporter for the *Los Angeles Times*. He was the first Mexican American journalist to become an important foreign correspondent. And he was the first Mexican American journalist to have a column in a major American English-language newspaper.

In his short career, ended too soon, Salazar crossed a variety of borders, certainly professional ones and undoubtedly personal ones as well. This work is dedicated to examining Salazar as a professional border crosser—a border correspondent.

Who Was Ruben Salazar?

While little is known about Salazar's early life, we do know some general facts. He was born on March 3, 1928, in Ciudad Juárez—"Juaritos," as the Chicanos on the other side of the border in El Paso called this notorious Mexican border town. When Ruben was eight months old his parents moved across the shallow Rio Grande and settled in El Paso, or "El Chuco," as it was known by the Chicanos and pachucos of the 1940s and 1950s. There Ruben became a naturalized citizen. His father worked at a downtown jewelry store, where he was in charge of the silver department. This job paid well, and apparently the Salazar family enjoyed a middle-class life in El Paso. After graduating from El Paso High School, Salazar served in the U.S. Army in Germany from 1950 to 1952. In the early fifties, as a result of his own ambition and the encouragement of his parents, Salazar became one of the few Mexican Americans to attend college. He chose Texas Western College, later to become the University of Texas at El Paso, where he majored in journalism and wrote a few pieces for *El Burro*, the campus paper. After graduation, he joined the *El Paso Herald-Post*, the first Mexican American reporter for that paper. The editor, Ed Pooley, had been a longtime champion of Mexican Americans, who, because they lacked education and a political voice (even though they represented the majority in El Paso), had few employment opportunities and most often lived in poverty.[16]

Cub Reporter

Salazar's work during his apprenticeship at the *El Paso Herald-Post* is obscured by the lack of byline articles carrying his name. Nevertheless, according to Earl Shorris, who began his career at the *Herald-Post* while Salazar was there, Pooley thought Salazar could do no wrong and considered him to be his best reporter."[17] What can be identified as Salazar's own work confirms his talent as a reporter and provides some fascinating reading, especially a short series of investigative pieces. Assigned to the police and Juárez beats and aware of the poverty and accompanying alienation of many Chicanos in this border city, Salazar volunteered to investigate the Chicano underworld. For one story, "25 Hours in Jail—I Lived in a Chamber of Horrors" (May 9, 1955), Salazar had himself booked on a phony drunk charge in order to experience conditions in the city jail. He was locked in Tank 6 along with several other Chicanos. Salazar reported on the filthy and repulsive conditions of the jail, where the prisoners had easy access to drugs. Under the influence of drugs and alcohol and almost totally unsupervised, the inmates committed violent acts against each other. After one night, Salazar had had enough. "I left the jail," he wrote, "knowing how it feels to live in a hophead Chamber of Horrors."

Shorris recalls that Arturo Islas, who was on the detective staff of the El Paso Police Department, remarked after the story broke that he had seen Salazar in jail but had assumed that Salazar had indeed been arrested for being drunk and therefore had done nothing to secure his release. Shorris further notes that the jail story quickly became the journalistic coup of the decade in El Paso. Before that story the local newspapers had carried very little investigative reporting. According to Shorris, Salazar's story and similar pieces helped change the nature of journalism in El Paso.[18]

In another investigative story (August 17, 1955), on La Nacha, the dope queen of the border, Salazar posed as a drug user. He hired a drug addict known as "Hypo" for $15 to demonstrate a purchase from La Nacha. Accompanying Hypo, Salazar visited La Nacha's home in the barrio and revealed to his readers how easy and open the trade in drugs, including heroin, was in El Paso.

It was just as easy for poor down-and-outs to purchase homemade liquor from one of the several speakeasies in South El Paso, the main barrio. On this story (July 3, 1956), Salazar met Chencha, the queen of the speakeasies, who was famous for her ten-cent shot of the potentially lethal "alky." "It rasped my throat like sandpaper," Salazar wrote. While these early Salazar pieces contain some stereotyping of Chicanos, they are also poignant expressions of the plight of the inhabitants of this Chicano underworld. They achieve an intense social realism, a kind of muckraking social reformism, and they reveal Salazar's willingness to investigate a story even under the most difficult conditions. According to Shorris, these stories made Salazar into something of a hero in El Paso. "Ruben was the best reporter El Paso had ever seen," Shorris concludes.[19]

Like many of the other reporters at the *Herald-Post*, Salazar, according to Shorris, possessed the ambition and the dream of eventually moving on to California, specifically, to the Los Angeles papers.[20] Consequently, sometime in 1956 or 1957, Salazar moved to California, where he first worked for the *Santa Rosa Press Democrat* and a short time later moved on to the *San Francisco News*. After moving to southern California in the late 1950s, Salazar found a position with the *Los Angeles Herald-Express*. In 1959 Salazar got his big break and joined the *Los Angeles Times*. It was with the *Times* that Salazar would mature as a journalist.[21]

Notes

1. See Ralph Guzmán, "Mexican American Casualties in Vietnam," *La Raza* (1970), Vol. I, no. 1,12-15.
2. On the Chicano moratorium, see special issue of *La Raza* (1970), Vol.I, no. 3. Also see Rodolfo Acuña, *Occupied America: A History of Chicanos*, 3d ed. (New York: Harper-Collins, 1988), 345-350; Oscar Zeta Acosta, *The Revolt of the Cockroach People* (New York: Bantam, 1974; orig. pub. 1973); and the film documentary *Requiem 29* (1970; produced by Moctesuma Esparza and directed by David García).
3. Ibid.
4. Interview with Danny Villanueva, February 8, 1994, by Mario T. García. Also see Edward J. Escobar, "The Dialectics of Repression: The Los Angeles Police Department and the Chicano Movement, 1968-1971," *Journal of American History* 79, no. 4 (March 1993): p. 1503.
5. See *La Raza* (1970), Vol. I, no. 3, and Acuna, *Occupied America*, 345-350.

6. Ibid.; Raul Ruiz, "August 29th & the Death of Ruben Salazar," in program for production of "August 29" produced by the Los Angeles Theatre Center Latino Theatre Lab and directed by José Luis Valenzuela in 1990 on the 20th anniversary of Salazar's death.
7. Ibid.
8. See José Angel de La Vera, "1970 Chicano Moratorium and the Death of Ruben Salazar," in Manuel P. Servin, ed., *An Awakened Minority: Mexican-Americans* (Beverly Hills: Glencoe Press, 1974), 274.
9. Ibid., 281
10. See *Requiem 29*; de La Vera, "Chicano Moratorium."
11. See de la Vera, "Chicano Moratorium," 279, 281.
12. See Acosta, *Cockroach People*. For transcripts of the Salazar inquest, see Oscar Zeta Acosta collection in the California Ethnic and Multicultural Archives (CEMA) in Special Collections at the University of California, Santa Barbara, Library.
13. See de La Vera, "Chicano Moratorium," 278.
14. Villanueva Interview.
15. Examples of such nineteenth- and twentieth-century newspapers exist in microfilm. These include *La Prensa* (San Antonio) and *La Opinión* (Los Angeles). Also see my chapter on the Mexican-American journalist Ignacio López, publisher of *El Espectator* in the Pomona Valley of southern California from the 1930s through the 1950s, "Mexican-American Muckraker: Ignacio L. López and *El Espectator*" in Mario T. García, *Mexican Americans: Leadership, Ideology, and Identity, 1930–1960* (New Haven: Yale University Press, 1989), 84-112.
16. See Ruben Salazar résumé in Ruben Salazar File with the *Los Angeles Times*. Interview with Earl Shorris, February 28, 1994 by Mario T. García. On Pooley and the *El Paso Herald-Post*, see García, *Mexican Americans*, 113-141.
17. Shorris interview.
18. Ibid.
19. Ibid.
20. Ibid.
21. Salazar résumé. ★

Ruben Salazar

Pioneer journalist Ruben Salazar (1928-1970) was born in Ciudad Juárez, Mexico, and raised in El Paso. In 1946, he enrolled in the Colleges of Mines and Metallurgy, now the University of Texas at El Paso, but left to serve in the army. He returned to school in 1953, earning his B.A. in journalism from Texas Western College, now University of Texas at El Paso, in 1955 while working as a reporter at the *El Paso Herald-Post*. Salazar's groundbreaking career was a series of firsts: the first Mexican-American reporter to work at an El Paso newspaper; the first Mexican-American columnist at the *Los Angeles Times*; and the first Mexican-American foreign correspondent when he covered the U.S. intervention in the Dominican Republic. The *Los Angeles Times* sent Salazar to Vietnam, and he served as bureau chief in Mexico City. He returned to Los Angeles in 1969 to report on the emerging Chicano Movement. In 1970, he became news director at the only Spanish television station in Los Angeles, KMEX. During his coverage of the Chicano National Moratorium on August 29, 1970, Salazar was killed when a tear gas projectile was fired into the Silver Dollar Cafe, striking Salazar in the head. Since his death, several parks, libraries, and buildings have been named in memory of him. He was posthumously awarded a special Robert F. Kennedy Award and was honored by the United States Postal Service with the issuance of a first class stamp in 2008. He was honored by his alma mater, the University of Texas at El Paso, with the creation of the Ruben Salazar Spanish Language Media Program in 2003. He was named a Distinguished Alumni in 2008.

From *Ruben Salazar: Border Correspondent, Selected Writings 1955-1970*: Speakeasies Sell 'Atomic' Booze in South El Paso

July 3, 1956

EL PASO, Texas—The age of the speakeasy is not over in El Paso.

Just recently I sat in one of those alcohol joints at 1217 South Oregon street and had a glass of tequila. It was cut with something which made it smell like kerosene. The taste is terrible. The effect on my stomach was atomic.

The man who took me to the speakeasy had the specialty of the house: an "alky." That, simply, is a drink of rubbing alcohol cut down with boiled water.

It all started when a South El Paso woman called me to ask: "Why don't the police do something about all these places down here that sell alcohol to bums?

"My kids are growing up having to observe the parade of alcoholics staggering up and down our streets all day long on their way to the speakeasies."

Bum Buys Booze

I went to South El Paso and started a conversation with a bum who looked like he needed a drink. He did. He immediately asked me for a quarter for a "pisto," a drink.

I followed him to an apartment house in the 500 block of South Mesa Avenue. The bum went in through the back and came out right away. He had a pint bottle of a smoky-looking liquid. He offered me a drink and I took a swig. It rasped my throat like sandpaper. A few minutes later I felt the results. I didn't get drunk— I was dazed.

I poured a sample from the bottle into a small container. Later I struck a match to the sample. It burned like gasoline.

The bum killed that bottle and announced he was going to "work" —that is, panhandle.

I went a little deeper into South El Paso and found another bum.

Queen of the Speakeasies

We went to three places where we were informed the supply hadn't arrived.

"Guess we'll have to go to Chencha's," the bum said. "It's the best place anyway."

Chencha is at 1217 South Oregon street. The speakeasy is in a basement apartment. Chencha, I am told, is the queen of the speakeasies.

A member of Alcoholics Anonymous told me later he used to drink there 18 years ago.

At Chencha's the alcoholic, if he has money, can satisfy his thirst with anything he desires: alky, tequila, mescal and beer. The specialty, though, is the 10-cent alky.

I had a tequila because I had had enough alky. The tequila cost me 25 cents. In Juárez you can get unadulterated tequila for a nickel.

Big Bruiser in Action

My bum friend had an alky. A woman poured the alcohol into his glass. Then she took a coffee pot from which she poured boiled water into the alcohol. We were told to pay when served.

A couple of men went in while we were at Chencha's and had an alky. They paid their dimes and left.

I left after a big bruiser, said to be a relative of Chencha, started asking a lot of questions. He didn't like me; I didn't like the polluted tequila so I didn't mind leaving.

According to information I gathered there must be about 20 speakeasies in South El Paso. Most of them do not offer as much as at Chencha's, but all of them specialize in the dime alky.

The respectable people in South El Paso don't like it a bit.

He Likes It

"Why do they get away with it?" a woman asked. "Doesn't the police or the Liquor Control Board care what happens in South El Paso?"

"My husband likes to drink. We have a big family to support so he doesn't have much money to spend on drinking. A few months ago he discovered he could get a drink of alcohol diluted with water for a dime."

"Now he drinks it all the time. I'm sure it's affected his health and mind. When I found out I even tried to get him to start drinking good liquor. He didn't want to. He says he likes that poison."

Why Not Raids

An irate man, who said it is hard to rear a family in the midst of speakeasies, commented: "I read in the paper that several policemen raided a bingo game in which old respectable people were having bare innocent fun."

"Why don't these policemen raid these speakeasies? Just because we're poor down here does it mean we're not entitled to police protection?"

Yes sir, the speakeasy is not a thing of the past in El Paso. ★

From *Ruben Salazar: Border Correspondent, Selected Writings 1955-1970*:
Militants Fight to Retain Spanish as Their Language

January 14, 1969

EL PASO — THE SPANISH LANGUAGE, SPOKEN in the Southwest long before Plymouth Bay and Jamestown were settled, is under fire in some quarters as being detrimental to Americanism.

The result is that militant Mexican-Americans, who prefer to call themselves Chicanos, are fighting back with a rising chauvinism which had begun to blur after years of conditioning by U.S. society.

Throughout the Southwest, and especially along the Mexican border, the old controversy of whether Mexican-American students should speak Spanish in school and on the playground is stirring racial sensitivities.

In the lower Rio Grande Valley, more than half of 150 high school students demonstrating against a rule that prohibited the use of Spanish on the playground were recently arrested.

Students Threaten Walkout

In El Paso, students threatened a massive walkout at Bowie High School, composed of about 95% Mexican-Americans, over a rule against students speaking Spanish. The rule was enforced with detention for any violations.

In both cases the defenders won the day—the lower Rio Grande Valley students were exonerated and the contested rule at Bowie was rescinded. Nevertheless, the issue, long an explosive one in the Southwest, is again out in the open with its complicated implications.

Shortly after the Rio Grande Valley and the El Paso incidents, Mexican-American high school students at Uvalde—the Texas hometown of the late Vice President John N. Garner* — staged a "Chicano happening."

Attending the year-end school dance, which is the semester's big affair,

Mexican-American students showed up in Mexican ponchos, while the rest of the students came dressed in conventional dark suits and long dresses. The Mexican-Americans then segregated themselves from the rest of the crowd and started making tacos with tortillas, chili and meat which the girls had brought in containers.

It caused a stir, not only among Anglo students, parents and teachers, but also among Mexican-American parents who couldn't understand why their children were "disgracing" themselves after they (the parents) had worked so hard to give them clothes like the ones the other students wore.

Puzzled by Youth

Mike Gonzales, an attorney and controversial Mexican-American leader in Del Rio, said: "Anglos and older Mexican-Americans just don't seem to know what is happening. Mexican-American kids are in the throes of self-identification."

Use of the Spanish language, say other leaders, is one thing that Mexican-Americans have over other students and they tend to exploit it.

The controversy centers on two arguments:

Mexican-American students should concentrate on English because speaking Spanish too much hurts their proficiency in the "national language," English. Besides, said a school psychologist, children growing up in a bicultural environment are more prone than others to neurosis and mental disorders.

Mexicans are indigenous to the Southwest, and so the Spanish language is part of their culture which should not be tampered with. Having colonized the Southwest, Spanish-speaking people refuse to abandon their traditions because of the advent of Anglo-American culture.

The controversy is not one of whether Spanish, or any other foreign language, should be taught in school. All educators agree that a person is better off speaking two or more languages. But some school officials object to Mexican-American students speaking Spanish in school and on the playground not only on the basis of it being detrimental to their English but because it irks other students who don't speak Spanish.

In south Texas, a teacher, commenting on the controversial issue, wrote a pamphlet which reads in part:

"They are good people. Their only handicap is the bag full of superstitions and silly notions they inherited from Mexico. When they get rid of these superstitions, they will be good Americans. Their schools help more than anything else."

Change Foreseen

"In time, the Latin will think and act like Americans. A lot depends on whether we can get them to switch from Spanish to English. When they speak English at home like the rest of us, they will be part of the American way of life. I just don't understand why they are so insistent about using Spanish. They should realize that it's not the American tongue."

This approach infuriates the growing number of militant Mexican-American leaders, many of whom now insist that meetings held to discuss the problems of this ethnic group should be conducted in Spanish.

Some education experts say that what is needed in the Southwest is for non-Mexican-Americans to become "Mexicanized"—not the other way around. Asked how the Mexican-American can find his way into U.S. society, Dr. Jack D. Forbes, research program director of UC Berkeley's Far West Laboratory for Educational Research and Development, recently told the U.S. Civil Rights Commission:

"The Anglo-American, quite obviously, is the new-comer." It is the Anglo-American, he said, who should learn more about the Mexican-American, his heritage and his culture. No one, he continued, can truly call himself a Southwesterner "unless he is a Mexicanized person to a considerable degree."

Not Enough

To the extremist Mexican-American leaders not even this is enough. What these leaders want for the 5 million Mexican-Americans in the five Southwestern states—California, Arizona, Colorado, New Mexico, Texas—is separatism not a "Mexicanized" society.

The controversial New Mexico Spanish-speaking leader, Reies López Tijerina, who preaches to his followers that they should speak Spanish as often as possible, is a prime advocate of a separate—but equal—state for Mexican-Americans.**

Though few take the separatist movement seriously, educators in the Southwest worry about Mexican-Americans retreating into a "Mexican shell." Not only are many Mexican-American students affecting Mexican rural dress but many have posters in their bedrooms depicting such Mexican revolutionary heroes as Emiliano Zapata and slogans reading "Primero la Raza" (the Mexican race first).

"Attempts to prohibit the use of the Spanish language, no matter how lofty the reasons, will only make things worse," says an El Paso teacher.

Those who would try to abolish the use of Spanish in informal situations in school and on the playground are guilty of the "cowboy-and-Indian viewpoint," says Harold Howe II, former U.S. Commissioner Education.

* John Nance Garner served as vice president of the United States between 1933 and 1936 under Franklin Delano Roosevelt.

** Beginning in 1963, Reies López Tijerina organized the Alianza Federal de Mercedes in New Mexico to renew claims to land grants stolen from Mexican Americans as a result of the conquest and annexation of New Mexico by the United States in 1848. ★

Part Two

Two Countries, One River: The People

Dos países, un río: la gente

"Life on the South Side is not contained soberly behind closed blinds; it is never a drawing room affair. Life here is a thing on the move—*persistent*, indoors and out . . ."

~Elroy Bode, "South of Paisano Street,"
from *Home and Other Moments*

Tomás Rivera

Tomás Rivera (1935-1984) was a poet, writer, and educator who was born in Crystal City, Texas. Along with his parents, Rivera worked as a farm laborer in Texas, Oklahoma, Missouri, Michigan, and Minnesota. Although he continued to work in the fields each summer, Rivera attended Southwest Texas State University and received a B.A. in English. He went on to earn two graduate degrees, an M.Ed. from Southwest Texas State and a Ph.D. from the University of Oklahoma. After finishing his graduate studies, Rivera taught English and Spanish at high schools in San Antonio, League City, and Crystal City, Texas. He began his university career when he accepted a position as associate professor at Sam Houston State University, and he went on to serve as the director of foreign languages and the vice president for administration at the University of Texas at San Antonio. When he moved to El Paso, Rivera assumed the role of executive vice president of the University of Texas at El Paso. He was the chancellor of the University of California, Riverside, at the time of his death.

Tomás Rivera's experience as a migrant worker was the context of his novel *Y no se lo tragó la tierra/ And the Earth Did Not Part*, which won the first Quinto Sol Prize for literature in 1970 and is considered a milestone in Chicano literary history. The novel was published during the height of the Chicano labor struggles and the rise of the La Raza Unida party, and its themes resonated with those who were suffering injustice. Rivera is also the author of five short stories, a chapbook of thirteen poems, and *The Searchers: Collected Poetry*. An anthology of his work edited by Julián Olivares, *Tomás Rivera: The Complete Works*, was published in 1992. Rivera's literary essays, including "Into the Labyrinth: the Chicano in Literature," have been cited as important critical texts in the study of 1970s Chicano literature. In addition to his literary and scholarly achievements, Rivera also worked for a number of non-profit organizations. He served on the boards of both the Carnegie Institute and the Corporation for Public Broadcasting and helped to establish the Tomás Rivera Policy Institute, which is now located at University of Southern California. Rivera was also appointed by presidents Carter and Reagan to serve on national higher education commissions. Rivera's legacy continues at the educational facilities that have been named in his honor, including the main library at UC Riverside, several public schools, and a conference center at the University of Texas at El Paso. A professorship at the University of Texas at Austin, as well as a Mexican American children's book award, has also been created in remembrance of Tomás Rivera's lasting impact on education and literature.

From *Tomás Rivera: The Complete Works*: The Searchers

I

How long
how long
have we been searchers?

We have been
behind the door
Always
behind screens and eyes
of other eyes
We longed to search
Always
longed to search

naranja dulce
limón partido
dame un abrazo
que yo te pido

We searched through
our own voices
and through
our own minds
We sought with our words

A la vibora, vibora
de la mar
de la mar
por aquí pueden pasar

How those words
lighted our eyes
From within came
the passions to create
of every clod and stone
a new life
a new dream
each day

In these very things
we searched
as we crumbled
dust, our very own
imaginary beings

Hey, ese vato, chíngate

A terrón lighted our eyes
and we watered it and made
mud-clay
to create others in

II

The search begun
so many years ago only
to feel the loneliness
of centuries

Hollow—soundless centuries
without earth

How can we be alone
How can we be alone
if we are so close to the earth?

Tierra eres
Tierra serás
Tierra te volverás

Una noche caminando
una sombra negra vi
yo me separaba de ella
y ella se acercaba a mí.

¿Qué anda haciendo, caballero?
¿Qué anda haciendo por aquí?
Ando en busca de mi esposa
que se separó de mí.

Su esposa ya no está aquí
su esposa ya se murió
Cuatro candeleros blancos
son los que alumbran allí.

III

Death
We searched in Death
We contemplated the original
and searched
and savored it
only to find profound

beckoning
A source that continued the search
beyond creation and death
The mystery
The mystery of our eyes
The eyes we have as
spiritual reflection
and we found we were
not alone

In our solitude
we found our very being
We moved into each other's
almost carefully, deliberately

Had we been here before?
What do we have, you and I?
Only our touch, our feeling
shared, that is all that we have
life in such ways, way
again, again, again
We found ourselves in ourselves
and while touching
we found other mysteries
that lay beneath
every layer of truth
unwinding each finding
another lonely vigil
another want, desire
to find
to find what?
What we always had?
Did anyone know that we

were searching?
That every look toward the earth
was a penetrating search that
had lasted for years
the mystery of time halted
and unknown without
itself discovery

IV

At night we searched each other
Somewhere was the soul
Somewhere in there was the heart
Somewhere in the night
was the lonely eye of the soul
Motionless
Waiting

Sometimes we found it
and slept with our lips
on it till the light fractured
everything

Can we find something every day
and every night?
We believed
yes, we had been finding
for centuries

Other beings?
We,
one,
the very same flavor
the very same

We looked behind heads
at the back of heads
The back of white heads
was less dangerous
Sometimes we turned the
heads around only to find
eyes that didn't see
who dared not see
who dared not be
within our own

No estamos solos.

V

We are not alone
if we remember and
recollect our passions
through the years
the giving of hands and backs
"dale los hombros a tus hijos"
We are not alone
Our eyes still meet with the passion
of continuity and prophecy

We are not alone
when we were whipped
in school for losing
the place in the book
or for speaking Spanish
on the school grounds
or
when Chona,
dear Chona,

a mythic Chicana,
died in the sugar beet fields
with her eight-month
child
buried deep within her
still
or
when that truck
filled with us
went off the mountain road
in Utah
with screams
eternally etched among
the mountain snows
We were not alone in death

VI

We were not alone in Iowa
When we slept in wet ditches
frightened by salamanders
at night
reclaiming their territory
and we
killing them
to maintain it as our—
then, our only—possession
or
in San Angelo
when we visited the desiccated
tubercular bodies of
aunts and uncles
friends and lovers

We were not alone
when we created children
and looked into their eyes
and searched for perfection
We were not alone
when taught
the magic of a smile, a kiss
an embrace each morning
and to feel the warmth
and quiver of a human
being

We were not alone
murmuring the novenas,
los rosarios, each night,
los rosarios we hoped
would bring joy and lasting peace
for Kiko
killed and buried in Italy in 1943
or
when we gathered each night
before bed
and waited
for the nightly sound
of the familiar cough
and the sweet/pan dulce
that it brought
Warm milk/pan dulce
opened the evening door
or
when we walked

all over Minnesota
looking for work
No one seemed to care
we did not expect them to care

VII

We were not alone
after many centuries
How could we be alone
We searched together
We were seekers
We are searchers
and we will continue
to search
because our eyes
still have
the passion of prophecy. ★

Abelardo "Lalo" Delgado

Considered one of the grandfathers of the Chicano literary revival of the 1960s and 1970s, poet, writer, activist, and community organizer Abelardo "Lalo" Barrientos Delgado (1931-2004) was born in Chihuahua, Mexico, but moved to El Paso at the age of twelve where he lived in a tenement in Segundo Barrio. After graduating from Bowie High School in 1950, he worked in local restaurants and construction. In 1955 he began his community outreach by helping the impoverished youth of the neighborhood to identify educational opportunities and to find jobs. Delgado entered Texas Western College, now the University of Texas at El Paso, in 1958 and graduated with a B.A. in Spanish in 1962. During the 1960s, he worked with César Chávez in the farmworker movement and went on a thirty-day fast to protest the living conditions on the south side of El Paso. During this period he also began to publish his poetry, which still resonates with Chicano/a writers today. Delgado's first book of poetry, *Chicano: 25 Pieces of a Chicano Mind* (1969), contains his iconic and widely anthologized poem "Stupid America." Subsequent volumes of poetry include: *It's Cold: 52 Cold-Thought Poems of Abelardo* (1974); *Totoncaxihuitl, a Laxative: 25 Laxatives of Abelardo* (1981); and the novel *Letters to Louise*, which won the Premio Tonatiuh-Quinto Sol Award for Literature.

In addition to writing literary works, Delgado became the executive director of the Colorado Migrant Council and taught Chicano studies for seventeen years at Metropolitan State College of Denver. He helped establish many Chicano studies programs at universities throughout the western United States. Delgado is recognized for his work in educating Mexican immigrants on obtaining U.S. citizenship. He is the recipient of the Lifetime Achievement Award by the Dr. Martin Luther King Humanitarian Awards Committee of Denver and was posthumously appointed as the first poet laureate of Denver.

From *Letters to Louise*: September

From my home to Bowie Junior High School was about a mile. Thirteen short blocks or so. Walking that distance four times a day gave me a good set of legs. I came home for lunch. The first day at Bowie I was sent home because evidently to the principal I appeared like a pachuco.

—We don't want your kind around here. You go home, get a haircut, a different pair of shoes and pants, and for God's sake wear a shirt. (I was wearing a coat without a shirt, weird)— he met me by the steps of the school building with these words which sounded a bit canned. He must have greeted hundreds of other weird looking students the same way. His name is Pollit. He and I, many years later, went round and round on the question of punishing students for speaking Spanish.

I did go home and returned a transformed student, at least in appearance. Going to Bowie represented a huge milestone in those days. It was a status symbol to go to Bowie. It still is. By going there, you, of course, felt grown up, even though you were a mere seventh grader. A couple of close friends came my way in Bowie. Ramón Gallardo, called "El Mon," or Monchis, and Victoriano Vásquez, called "Tolano." Actually there was a third one whom we called el "Chicken" or el "Smiley." His name is, don't tell me I've forgotten his name. It's Jesús, Jesús Mendoza. He is a retired army officer now, married a gringuita, a güera como él. The four of us plus my close camarada Ricash were the gang that stuck together through school. Except for Ricash, who dropped out and got killed in Korea, all of us conquered Bowie. We were as square as they came. None of us smoked or drank or went out with girls (or boys). By today's lingo we would be called jocks, except none of us went for sports either. There was a bit of brain competition but in the final analysis, at least gradepoint-wise, I took them all, finishing in the top ten and being the vice-president of the National Honor Society. Mon, I saw him just a few months back when I went to do a poetry reading at UTEP. He walks with a limp. I didn't ask why. His head is all white with canas. He had canas even de chavalo. He's also retired. Air Force, I think. He was attending UTEP, we talked a bit then he split, didn't even stay for the reading.

There is a good taste in my mouth/mind as I recall these days which for us were full of fun and challenge. We used to fool teachers by switching names around. She would call out,

—Ramón Gallardo.—

—Here.—I would answer one day and next day Jesús would answer to the name of Ramón. The teacher thought she was going crazy. We knew we had arrived.

I seldom project in these letters, as you may have noticed, Louise. This time I am looking forward to Labor Day. The V.W. in which I have been learning to drive stick shift was left to me for a week or so as the owner went to the Bay Area for some check up, a test with her family M.D., a female M.D. Anyway, I can borrow the car and go to Salt Lake Friday and return it to her on Labor Day, at three. It sounds like a date. It is a date. My insanity mounts. The human heart, for sure, is not equipped to love so much. All is yet in flux here at work. Either I finish this Friday and shelve the staff evaluation for lack of funds, or return after Labor Day to begin. Now you see why I hate to project. So many unpredictables always pop up in my plans. My daughter's accident a week ago had me on a plane which I hadn't at all planned to be on. Y nos dicen los gringos,

—Ustedes los mejicanos no hacen planes.—

—Pos con que ojos, divina tuerta.— Those who make plans usually have the wherewithal to carry 'em out. There is a wedding projected for my daughter Nancy. She's projected to get out of the hospital this weekend. I'm projected to become a granpa by November. I'm projected to go crazy, commit suicide, leave home, drop out of all existence. The only sure projection is death. I admire that certainty. Talking about projections, my boss Orlando has asked me to work on a time plan for his two programs, weatherization and C.F.N.P. Ford is projected to lose. World War III is projected. We Chicanos project revolution and liberation. In Mexico a single man projects to be the next president of the país. Anglos project him to be a bit too liberal and to the left for their liking.

***

Lean and proud of my size 28 waistline I began seventh grade at Bowie. I had ample choice of subjects and school began to take a bit more of my interest. I still could do my schoolwork without worrying about homework. This, in turn, allowed me evenings to fool around with my friends or to work. The latter was usually the case. I was, as I am now, always seeking the attention of teachers or classmates. I think it was around then that I was aware I could be witty in a Chicano way, la cabula, or at least I sensed people liked to be around me when I talked, even if it was merely cabula, pure bull. I renewed my interest in Lucy. The young girl I tried so desperately to date at Aoy was becoming a pretty "Junior Higher." Finally she agreed to go out with me. She was to be my real case of puppy love, discounting Espy. She used to work at the Upson Drug Store while I worked at Hotel Cortez. I had become a busboy and loved wearing my bow tie and white jacket. Since I got out about nine thirty it coincided well with going to pick her up at ten when she got through. I would walk her home and have my fill of kissing her. She lived at Campbell and Ninth, only a few blocks from where I lived at Seventh and Mesa.

This went on for only a short while. I don't remember if she quit her job or if we got angry at each other or broke up. Lucy was appealing to me because she was a little girl whom I thought I could teach about love. The first to make her reach love fever temperatures would then be me. It turned out that I was her primer jaino.

One night as we necked by an old beat up pickup her mother came and slapped her and took her home. It was about one A.M. I made fun of the approaching figure telling Lucy it was a huge ghost coming our way. She was kind of heavy. Lucy's brother once approached me on a threatening note and asked me to leave his sister alone. We turned out friends and he said it was ok to go out with her. He even borrowed a quarter from me to reinforce our new friendship. Lucy left for L.A. for a couple of months. After I lost her I wanted to commit suicide. I also was a proud little fool in that I refused to be the one to make up after our silly hassle.

One night, also about one, after I had left her home I got a good scare. I was crossing Stanton Street on my way home when out of an alley came a black donkey. I thought for sure the donkey was the devil himself who had taken that form to scare me for not minding my mother about getting home early. I ran and the fregao burro ran after me. I climbed the stairs, most likely flew up them, to avoid the burro who kept getting closer and closer. It turned out to be a real burro that had run away from its owner along the río. The burro hung around the barrio for a week or so becoming our football mascot and then disappeared as it had appeared, suddenly.

Just a few memory odds and ends, Louise, in my search for myself within the boundaries of time and distance. My egos play a poor second today to the heavy sadness produced merely from not having received my customary daily long distance call. Love is a hell of a disease. Worse, much worse than the worst drug addiction. It pulls, it tears, it disconcerts, it begs to be quenched at the same time deserts of desire pile on more thirst. No wonder love is attributed only to los locos. Normal people don't go around falling in love. They marry each other instead, establish relationships, share sexual experiences, become friends, but they know better than to fall in love.

I'm still in the dark about initiating the staff evaluation, but have moved one step ahead. The questionnaire, prepared and mimeographed, has been passed out to the office staff, some sent to the regional offices. I'm ready for next Tuesday, funds and God willing. I've been staying in the Idan-ha Hotel, a sort of museum downtown. I'll have to go register again as I had already checked out. I had in mind taking off for Salt Lake City today but have realized that my boss really needs me, if for nothing else than to help him think things out a bit more clearly regarding two proposals totaling almost half a million dollars. The bureaucratic hassles are enough to drive a saint to sinning. I am tired and puzzled. This is a rare state of being for me who is usually one of the most cool, calm and collected of individuals, at least that is the impression I give to people. Maybe I'm really tearing out my insides with anxiety and despair. I manage to smile, anyhow.

***

Seldom do I have the opportunity to get into heavy philosophical discussions, about life in general, about being Chicano, the movement to change America, the world. As it is, when I have the opportunity I don't have the desire, or, I'm not in the mood. Yesterday, about six, I experienced one of those rare occasions when all falls into place. My listeners were Orlando, Miguel, and "La Negra." The latter is a carnal from Texas staying with Orlando, he's a vet who just registered here at the Boise State. Miguel is a new IMC worker. Orlando is my boss and one of the prime movers within the IMC programmatic structure. We were pretty frustrated with the bureaucratic responses and games we have to play to obtain grants to serve the farmworker. The money is there by law, but once the regulations and limitations are attached it is hard as hell to obtain it and even harder to use it for its initial intent.

—It's all political. I wouldn't be surprised if they don't sit on the funding until after the November elections.— I ventured out with my two cents of political savvy.

—We take these programs too seriously. They are merely tools, vehicles to take us to total change, not merely reform.— I continued. Throughout an hour of discussion "La Negra" didn't volunteer a single comment but listened and occasionally smiled. Orlando was my main target. He thought about questions I raised, internalizing them and savoring their significance for his own personal position and life.

—Pos si, Santiago, but the Bible says somewhere we are always going to have the poor.— he baited me.

—Bullshit, carnal. The only thing of importance the Bible says is in Genesis, where all this damn mass was left at the domain of man, for his use and not abuse.— From that point on I personalized most of the statements pointing to my own life, to where I consider myself an utter failure, my family. I went on to say, it almost comes out like a cliche by now, that,

—You have to have some love for yourself, some respect, some faith that you can do almost anything you set out to do, including conquering bureaucracy, filling C.A.P. forms or initiating a revolution.— Thus the hour almost flew as we moved on and on, Such deep questions one seldom raises. We said our buenas noches. I would have forgotten the incident if it weren't that Miguel pointed out how the motivated mood continued as they drove the 20 miles to Nampa. Orlando had been touched. I would like to do much more touching like that, Louise. I guess that is why I enjoy my teaching at the U. and put up with all the related nonsense that comes with teaching positions at any U.

In some of those classes at Bowie I began to realize that when it came to thinking I had an edge even on my teachers. This gave me an early sense of self-confidence which has endured and grown. A while back I said to that new and final woman in my life that I no longer desired to think, but to feel life. Even such a statement emerged from the fact that I "think." About now I need a bit more of a balance to fulfill my life. To feel means exactly that. I want to feel life exploding, going through me, sense it with my eight or nine senses, without asking myself the millions of "whys" I always ask myself. Why does she love? Why do I love her? Why do we have to wait? Why do we have to hide? Why do we have to lie? Why am I jealous? Why? Why? Why?

I may not have painted a fair picture of my brief love for Lucy, brief and first. I really liked that chavala. Chavala means little girl, little bitty girl. It is an old Chicano word now seldom used. Mi chavala. My girl. I was even then a bit clever with words. For my friends I used the term camarada. This was long before I learned the communist implication in the term. In one of my jobs I was actually nicknamed "El Camarada." It does mean friend and not necessarily a party follower. Another nickname I was tagged with besides "Pelón" by Ricash, was "El Muse." Some in El Paso still ask occasionally,

—Y qué paso con "el Muse" quesque ya es un escritor, un profe en la universidad?—Thus I am an item of interest in the minds of those who, like myself, are beginning to live or search in los recuerdos. I know, Louise, it is extremely difficult to follow my thoughts.

***

In about one hour now the airplane from San Francisco will arrive. She will be coming then. After a very hectic weekend of husband/wife negotiations we're back at square one.

—There are the children to think of.—

—I'll go insane. I'll have a nervous breakdown.— can sound more like a threat than a declaration from a wife grasping not to lose a husband she had never really had. ★

Ramón Rentería

Born in Valentine, Texas, Ramón Rentería is a veteran reporter, editor, and columnist with the *El Paso Times*. Rentería attended Sul Ross University in Alpine, Texas, and the University of Texas at El Paso and went on to work for thirty-eight years in print journalism in Southern California, New Mexico and Texas. Over the course of his career, he has covered crime news, education, the courts, city politics, entertainment, and U.S./Mexico border issues. His feature story "Separate and Unequal: the story of Kelli, Veronica and school finance" about the inequities in Texas public school financing received a 1989 Texas Headliner Award and a 1990 Guillermo Martinez-Marquez award for journalistic excellence. Rentería received the 1980 Texas Headliner Spot News of the Year Award and a 1995 Texas Headliner Award for feature writing. The following selection is the last newspaper interview with Ricardo Sánchez.

Another Struggle

Famed poet fights deadly cancer

The powerful voice of the angry bull that was Ricardo Sánchez is hoarse and weak, barely audible now.

"I'm home for good," he says, whispering like Marlon Brando in *The Godfather*.

Sánchez—poet, maestro, ex-con, pachuco and gran rebelde—sits beneath a giant mulberry tree, an emaciated man sickened by an inoperable, deadly tumor in his belly.

The 54-year-old jefe of Chicano poetry is once again marching the front lines of another cause, this time fighting for his own survival.

In six quick months, the stomach cancer's destructive grip has chiseled down a stout 235-pound man into a frail 130 pounds.

"I came home from a trip one night and started spitting chunks of blood," Sánchez said.

Alone with his thoughts in the afternoon shade, Sánchez could be mistaken for a tired old man, not the literary icon described over and over as America's most prolific Chicano poet.

That he has come home to El Paso from teaching at Washington State University under a death sentence does not seem to bother Sánchez a great deal. For him, disease is another lucha—a fight worth fighting.

"Supposedly in two months I'll be dead," Sánchez said. "I'll be around fighting. I'm not afraid of living or dying."

"Cancer is just another struggle, not the first one, nor the last."

Fifty friends, compadres and admirers greeted Sánchez at the airport a couple of weeks ago. They embraced not a famous poet but a paisano, a humble vato who learned life's basics and its hostilities in El Segundo Barrio and El Barrio del Diablo.

"I always intended to come back to the barrio," Sánchez said. Sánchez has accepted his predicament like the countless other agonies in his life.

When schoolteachers told him Mexicans don't write poetry, he set out to prove them wrong. Eventually, he earned a Ph.D. without bothering to collect a bachelor's or a master's.

"Nobody will define me. I will define myself," Sánchez said.

Throughout the 1970s, Sánchez shouted against the indignities and injustices inflicted on the poor and Mexican-Americans.

Jailed for armed robbery, Sánchez defied hostile guards in a Texas prison camp.

And now, Sánchez contemplates death as if it was just another brutal intrusion in an intriguing journey that has driven him from the harshness of the barrio to Ivy League lecture halls and international respect as an authority on the Chicano experience.

His father died in 1967 while Sánchez was in prison. That turned his life around, he said: "I did it for him. He accepted me for what I was, but I wanted to show him that I could do something positive with myself."

Canto y grito mi liberacion, his first book, defined Sánchez as a major artistic voice in the 1970s Chicano movement. Colleagues call him a literary cyclone.

"I tried to talk about us as a Chicano culture, to say that we're a people that could do anything in life," Sánchez said, ever modest about his vast literary output.

Bruce Novoa, in his book *Chicano Authors*, said: "Ricardo Sánchez is one of Chicano literatures most talented creators of poetic narrative . . . he is the epitome of the artist: a person incapable of living anything without raising it into an aesthetic experience."

Sánchez ranks among major leaguers in Chicano literature: José Antonio Villarreal, Rolando Hinojosa, Sergio Elizondo, Miguel Mendez M., Avelardo Delgado, Jose Montoya, Tómas Rivera, Estela Portillo, Rudolfo A. Anaya, Bernice Zamora, Ron Arias, Tino Villanueva and Allurista.

Battling academia

Sánchez often shook up the establishment, thumbed his nose at academia and sought, most of all, to inspire young people. His extensive travels helped establish Chicano literature worldwide.

"It's been an honor to have been given a chance," Sánchez said. "I've enjoyed my life, a wonderful family and a lot of friends."

"I've written poetry, enjoyed it and touched people."

Sánchez inspired New Mexico author Denise Chávez in her early years as a struggling writer. Then he became a friend.

"He gave voice to the desert," Chávez said. "In my mind and heart, he is the father of Chicano poetry in the United States."

Poet Bobby Byrd, whose Cinco Puntos Press published Sánchez's *Eagle-Visioned/Feathered Adobes*, says Sánchez has the best ear for naturally jumping back and forth between English and Spanish in his work.

"It's a real pleasure to read his work not only for the meaning but also for the sound and the word play and the joy he has playing with both languages," Byrd said.

Muralist Carlos Rosas encouraged Sánchez to introduce Chicano poetry in Europe.

"A lot of people don't like him because he's too much of a free thinker," Rosas said.

Over the years, Rosas witnessed Sánchez's anger against institutions, the oppression of Chicanos and the lack of opportunities for his people.

Against the odds

Pete Duarte, chief executive at Thomason General Hospital, points to Sánchez as living proof that anyone can whip any multitude of obstacles—poverty, school failure, a prison record and cultural isolation—and become a writer, an internationally recognized poet and respected Chicano culture authority.

"The angry voices that Ricardo represents so well in his writings certainly need to be addressed as we see the increasing violence among our kids, the wanton destruction caused by crime, violence and drugs and the crumbling of the extended family as we knew it in our barrios," Duarte said.

Domingo "Nick" Reyes, El Paso radio talk show host, credits Sánchez with elevating Chicano cultural experiences. "If you put the total work of Ricardo Sánchez together, it is one of the more remarkable contributions to an understanding of what we are and who we can be," Reyes said.

Hope endures

Sánchez talks of recovering enough to lecture or teach again, maybe write the autobiography he hasn't written and establish a specialized creative arts school for barrio children.

"I haven't written all that I've wanted," he said. "Sometimes, I marvel at what I've done."

Some time ago, amid the thousands of words he has written, Sánchez said in harsher terms that premature death ought to go to hell.

"I've always accepted my mortality," Sánchez said. "What makes me so special that I can't get a human illness?" ★

Ricardo Sánchez

Poet, activist and academic Ricardo Sánchez (1941-1995) was born and raised in El Paso. His writing, which uses a blend of idiomatic phrases of English and Spanish known as caló, is influenced by his early years as part of the pachuco subculture of the Barrio del Diablo. Joining the army after dropping out of high school, Sánchez earned entrance into officer candidate school, but a series of events and tragedies led to self-destructive behavior that resulted in two prison terms for armed robbery. While incarcerated, Sánchez used that time to write and became a librarian and teacher. After he was paroled in Texas, he earned a high school equivalency certificate while his writings were already being anthologized and published. In 1969, Sánchez received a Frederick Douglass Fellowship in Journalism to write for an African American newspaper in Richmond, Virginia. With only a GED he was employed as a staff writer and humanities instructor at the University of Massachusetts, Amherst. He founded Míctla Publications in 1971 with the mission of publishing the works of Chicano writers who were ignored by mainstream publishers. When his first book *Canto y grito mi liberación*, an important work defining the Mexican American experience, originally published by Míctla, was published again by Anchor Books, Doubleday, in 1973, he received national attention. The recipient of several Ford Foundation grants, he earned his Ph.D. in American studies and cultural linguistic theory from the Union Graduate School, Antioch College. In his academic career, he was a professor at El Paso Community College, the University of Wisconsin, Milwaukee, the University of Alaska, and the University of Utah ethnic studies center. He became a full professor at Washington State University in the English department and the department of comparative cultures. Ricardo Sánchez is the author of *The Loves of Ricardo*; *Bertrand & The Mehkqoverse: A XicaAno Filmic Nuance*; *Selected Poems*; *Amsterdam Cantos*; *Perdido*; *Brown Bear Honey Madnesses: Alaska Cruising Poems*; *Milhuas Blues*; *Gritos Nortenos*; and *HECHIZOspells*. Widely anthologized, Sánchez is also the subject of the recent book *Timespace: The Poetry and Politics of Ricardo Sánchez*. His writing gave voice to a Chicano perspective of the world and the dynamics of living on the border.

From *The Loves of Ricardo*: "fragrance petals its presence . . ."

June 30, 1977
L Chukosburgo, Te(de)jaslum
cabulat/sufiteotls

"fragrance petals its presence . . ."

I. fragrance
petals
its presence
onto
realization;
love
is
that
which
permeates
life
with meaning…

II. you slide
almost quiveringly
into my arms,
your heated aroma
engulfs me,
you
blossom, woman,
while
liquidly
devouring
my tongue,
time
cannot exist
while

we pulsate—
one within
the other,
your breathing
is quick
and then slow,
builds up
and implodes
while
my essence
explodes
inside you,
each time is new,
each time a rebirth,
ay, yes,
you loosen up
then clasp me,
your eyes dilate
as sexuality
becomes
another shaking
of our earthiness.

III. streets filled
with swaying people
proud women
dance before my gaze,
all their womanliness
glides
palatably before my vision;
veils of hunger
dissolve
while mentally/spiritually

sexual games
promenade within,
no reservations hide
within
thoughtfeelings,
only awareness
of movement
and what movement
can portend . . . ★

From *Selected Poems*: Fridays Belong to Friends, Sometimes

trío de locos
in juárez bistros,
drinking/listening
to mariachis.

Fridays Belong to Friends, Sometimes

fridays belong to friends, sometimes,
when Horacio "Chacho" Minjárez,
Rafa "Chafa" Aguirre and I
can galavant all night
from cantina to cantina,
jiving with the pimps
as they shout:
"Say, can you spare a messican minute, fellows
and I'll take you to see the girls,"

and his mouth opens in surprise
as one of us shouts back jivingly,

"No, ese, we want to see the boys,
damn the girls,"

and we walk/saunter laughingly
up different streets,
stopping
with don cojón-chon,
buy little french rolls,
    sliced in half and stuffed
    with avocado, mexican cheese,
    jalapeños and a dash of salt,
and we continue
in our camaraderie
walking up juárez avenue
to carlos or the manhattan or the san luis
to hear mariachis and shout,
all the time eating tortas,
winking at the women,
alluding to ourselves
as being non-tourists
in this city on the border.

we enter the manhattan,
and mariachis serenade us,
and the tourist trade is thick,
aguirre squirms and says
let's go to another place
as young horacio bolts about,
splashing his tequila doble on his shirt,
and we walk down and cross the tracks,
get in the car and drive
across that stretch
of supertourist traps.

swarming streets
filled with hungers of amérika,
seekers of sexual bliss,
we laugh,
for we just came to drink
and shout and pay mariachis
for their art . . .
we enter the san francisco bar,
expecting music to blare out,
we drink and wait for them,
and then realize
that may 10th
is always
Mexican Mother's Day,
and good mariachis
make more money
        serenading
home to home
than in bars,
and these mariachis are the best,
so they'll play
out on the streets,
and we mope and start to talk.

Chacho is a youth
who wants to write
and film
and live
a legendary life
while creating sketches
of reality

on the canvas of our souls.
he is a poet,
            young and strong,
and full of vision,
and he reminds me
of garcía lorca and whitman
and rimbaud
and baudelaire
and lalo
and salinas
and more especially of himself,
and his quick mind
pounces on every word;
all night long rafa and i revel
in the magic
of the word worlds Chacho gives us,
he wants to go to yale
to whip it,
and he will,
and rafa is moved to tears
by Chacho's words,
and i feel strong/good
in meeting such a delicate/virile/affirmative mind/soul
as this young bato
who speaks of years at jefferson high
and the projects and the fact that he and his mother
survive somehow on about $1000, yes one thousand dollars,
a year,
yet, he believes in himself, in raza, in the struggle,
and
we sense him puffing out his chest,
he's gonna tell us something,

aguirre in his forty years of life
has learned patience
and he listens,
and i, in 33, have learned
how to bob/weave/and jive,
so i jive,
and we three laugh,
rap on
'til we tire
of the blandness
of music-less bars,
and walk out into the street
and as we rave and jive and galavant
we hear the far off strains
of inebriated music-makers,
over there
in that club on the corner,
yes, tontos, there,
sí, at the forum,
we enter, sit, order
bohemias for rafa and me,
a tequila doble for horacio,
he's beginning to get high,
"I really don't drink, I, ah er . . ."
we let it go at that and smile,
mariachis come on over,
toquen, we say,
something
for our friend Chacho here
it's mother's day, and for his age
he's a hell of a mothuh, he is,
so it's his day,
now play "Las Mañanitas,"

or something to that effect,
we laugh and jive,
and $23 later
we walk out of that joint,
drive over to max-fim's
and look at ballroom waltzers,
and drink a round or two and
drive back to el paso . . . ★

John Rechy

Native El Pasoan John Rechy is the author of the groundbreaking and controversial novel *City of Night*, the story of a gay hustler and the society that marginalizes those who are perceived as "the others." Continuously in print since 1963 and considered a modern classic, *City of Night* was published to great acclaim and outraged criticism; it has remained a best-seller. Rechy has written twelve novels including *Numbers*; *This Day's Death*; *The Vampires*; *The Fourth Angel*; *Rushes*; *Bodies and Souls*; *The Miraculous Day of Amalia Gomez*; *Marilyn's Daughter*; *The Coming of the Night*; *The Life and Adventures of Lyle Clemens*; the essay collection *Beneath the Skin*; and the nonfiction book *The Sexual Outlaw*. A memoir, *About My Life and the Kept Woman* (2008), is his most recent book. His essays and reviews have appeared in *The Nation*, *The Village Voice*, *The Los Angeles Times Book Review*, *L.A. Weekly*, *The New York Review of Books*, and the *New York Times Books* "Saturday Review." "Mysteries and Desire: Searching the Worlds of John Rechy" was produced by the Annenberg Center of Communications in a CDRom and *Outlaw: The Lives and Careers of John Rechy* is his published biography. He is an NEA Fellow and the recipient of the Publishing Triangle's William Whitehead Award for Lifetime Achievement. The first novelist to receive the Lifetime Achievement Award from the PEN Center USA, Rechy is also the first recipient of the One Magazine Culture Hero Award. His alma mater, the University of Texas at El Paso, named him a Distinguished Alumnus in 2007. He is a faculty member at the University of Southern California in the master's level professional writing program.

From *About My Life and the Kept Woman*

I WAS TWELVE, AND MY SISTER WAS ABOUT TO marry her football-captain sweetheart. She was sixteen, he was seventeen, and the approaching union was fraught with dangers whose effects, many years later, would multiply and spread into the core of San Francisco society and would, more years later, help to define my life.

But now it was 1945 in El Paso, Texas, and plans for my sister's wedding had aroused the wrath of the groom's father. A twig of a man, Señor Antonio Guzman, referred to only as "Señor," "Sir,"—bedridden for years and partially paralyzed—had sworn to stop the wedding "by whatever means may become necessary." His anger was meant to punish his son, who had, he declared, "strayed beyond decent bounds by intending to marry so young, a breach of decorum I will not condone." Being underage, the teenagers required permission of their respective parents. They had my parents' permission for a reason that Señor did not know.

Now, to understand the enormity of Señor's wrath at his son, and my mother and father's escalating anxiety that my sister's wedding proceed immediately, one must know that these implications of danger were swirling on the border of two juxtaposed cities—Juárez in Mexico and El Paso in Texas—cities separated only by a stretch of the Rio Grande, most often a bed of dry sand along whose banks lazy spiders spun their webs.

That geographical proximity had created in Texas a class of unique immigrants—men and women of education and means who had fled Mexico during the revolution of 1910, when Porfirio Díaz, the president turned dictator, was forced into exile, throwing the country into a chaos of shifting factions and loyalties. That class of formerly privileged Mexican immigrants often claimed ancestral lineage to "someone noble in Spain."

Displaced and impoverished by the revolution, they were drained once again by the Great Depression. They grasped onto a societal hierarchy, disdaining those Mexicans of Indian ancestry, a fact revealed, they staunchly claimed, by darker skin, by their "chicanismos"—crude mannerisms, the designation "chicano" being relegated then to a lower class of Mexicans—and by coarse down-tilted eyelashes. Not until years later did I understand why my mother so diligently and gently guided me, five or six years old at the time, to lie on her lap while we sat during stifling Texas nights on the unscreened porch of our dilapidated house as she curled my already long curly eyelashes with a saliva-moistened finger.

The two groups of Mexican immigrants had this in common: Spanish was the language of communication; English was practiced only as necessary among older Mexicans, though increasingly among the younger ones. My mother, like others of her generation and by announced choice, never learned English, considering speaking it to be a betrayal of the country her family had been forced by turmoil and circumstances to flee. At home, we spoke only Spanish.

During World War II, just recently ended, Mexican families with sons in the military had made a notable exception to their clinging fealty to Mexico. They were swept into patriotic fervor. Square signs—red, white, and blue—sprouted in windows: "Our Son is Serving America."

My mother went to church almost daily to recite tearful rosaries for the safety of my brothers: Robert, the older of the two, in the South Pacific; and Yvan, the younger, in Germany. Both would be returning soon, a fact that made me lament that that would not occur sooner so they might use their military skills to thwart the growing menace of Señor.

Through tumultuous times in El Paso, the class of once privileged immigrants, however poor they increasingly became like other Mexicans in the foreign state of Texas, retained from their previous culture, unbudging attitudes toward social propriety and morality. Those included a staunch belief in the Catholic church and in the sacred virginity of the Holy Mother, considered the Mother of God, not only of Christ. They held an equally staunch belief in the virginity of unwed women.

Señor's initial threat to stop the marriage of my sister Olga and his son Luis soon escalated into an overt declaration of war conveyed by his tiny wife in a second visit to my family—the first visit had announced his fierce opposition.

Señor's wife was a woman so small, so like a buzzing hummingbird, that it was difficult to believe what was generally known, that she daily dressed Señor in suit, tie, and shoes, and then carried him, coaxing, pushing him a little, and finally shoving him—gently—to a reclining couch, where, propped up, he glowered through a window and denounced the modern world's immorality. What she probably suspected and what had coaxed my father and mother to grant permission for the union was that my sister was pregnant by Señor's burly son and might very soon begin to swell.

Whether knowing of the pregnancy would have caused Señor to relent—or to fall dead—was something his wife and son preferred not to chance. "Any more revelations," the fluttery woman said after she had delivered Señor's emphasis on his earlier warning, "will enrage him to the point that we will all be in mortal danger, God help us!"

"Over my dead body he'll stop the wedding," my father proclaimed, launching a war of tyrants—he would not allow another tyrant to impose his will on his own daughter, and therefore on him. He, like Señor, ruled rigidly over his family; he did not permit anyone else to even question our conduct. (Once, he confronted a truant officer who had captured me leaving the Texas Grand Theater by the exit door that I used to squeeze in free—I had gone to see Claire Trevor and John Wayne in *Dark Command* during Revival Week, my favorite period, which came, too infrequently, once every three months or so and featured movies that, even then, had become "old." "Don't dare punish my son; only I can do that," my father warned the truant officer, who was already backing away from the short, red-faced Scotsman's fists, prepared to stress his words.)

Adding to the burgeoning dangers indicated in the alerts from Señor via his spindly wife was this equally grave one: The groom's sister, older than he by eight years, had conveyed her intention to travel from Mexico City and return to El Paso to attend her younger brother's wedding, thus challenging Señor, who had banished her years ago. That banishment had been accompanied by his vow that if she ever again crossed his path, or entered its environs, he would exile her not only from the city but from life. He had added to his harsh admonition one of his most emphatic curses—"a father's righteous curse"—because, he said, "of her vile association that my dignity will not allow me to clarify." He also demanded that she never again use his name as her surname.

Her banishment and the "vile association" had resulted from the fact that she was the kept woman of one of Mexico's most powerful and richest men (the "invisible president"). Marisa Guzman was often referred to only as "the kept woman of Augusto de Leon."

The kept woman! What did it mean to be kept? Not a wife, but belonging to—"the kept woman of!"—de Leon, a powerful man, a rich man whose wealth allowed him to choose among all others. To be kept meant—had to mean—that the kept woman was beautiful, didn't it? Being kept was special—and scandalous enough to enrage Señor so fiercely. Banished and cursed! Yet if the rumors were true, she was also brave to challenge the wizened little man who ruled like a despot from his couch. The enormity of it all sent my imagination spinning into vague but exciting conjectures.

All this acquired the fascinating taint of thrilling things forbidden, a matter underscored by my mother's despondent sighs and the loud epithets from my father each time a further message promising to block the marriage was issued by Señor through his frightened wife, who came next to gasp only this:

"What more? What more? *Ay, Dios mio*!"

The answer to "What more?" came in *El Continental*, the daily Spanish-language newspaper published in El Paso. Framed in an ominous black border, like a warning of obituaries, an advertisement, four inches by two columns, appeared in its pages, formally announcing Señor's grave displeasure.

> I, Señor Antonio Guzman, formally oppose the union of my son to a girl whose name I shall not mention in deference to her gender. I will banish from my esteem anyone who sanctions such a union, which will be stopped.

Since Señor's wife and my mother had once exchanged visits, I had seen the wizened mustachioed dictator on his couch as he shrank daily while his curses on the world and his uncannily dark mustache grew in fierce opposite proportion. When he barely glanced at me that day, I ran away, terrified, although I knew he was restricted to his couch.

"They'll have to marry immediately because God knows what Señor is planning and Olga looked plump to me today," my beautiful Mexican mother said as she conferred with my father in the dingy kitchen that defined his fall from grace. A gifted musician and orchestra conductor, my father had lived a privileged life in Mexico, the son of a Scottish father and a snobbish mother who proclaimed insistently that she was of "pure Spanish blood." The family had been regular guests at dinner with President Porfirio Díaz before his fall, sharing his vacation mansion in Guadalajara. My father had gone on to excel at the University of Mexico, to learn how to play "every musical instrument," and eventually to conduct his own orchestra, his own opera company. From the heights of artistic accomplishment and of Mexican society—and through the vicissitudes of disasters and poverty that the Depression had wrought in Texas—he had fallen to the rank of occasional musical tutor to untalented, grudging Texan children.

"We'll take them to Juárez, and they'll be married in a civil ceremony, but they'll have to agree not to live together until they marry in church, in a Catholic ceremony; and I will write the music," my father said, asserting his own moral qualifier to the wedding of the two teenagers, as well as his artistic participation in the nuptials.

Whether my mother thought that strategy was appropriate or not, she never dared challenge him. "Yes, you're right, Roberto."

We traipsed—there was no one to leave me with—my mother, my father, my sister, and her fiancé, across the border to Juárez, where any marriage or divorce might be obtained for a fee. A dowdy Mexican magistrate in a gray suit took a few hard-earned dollars from my father and pronounced the couple legally wed. They agreed not to live together until a church wedding could take place—quickly. Such a church wedding had now become possible without Señor's consent because the marriage was technically legal.

Another advertisement, even larger, appeared in *El Continental*:

> The claimed union of my son, and a young woman I will not name in consideration of her gender, is illegitimate, not sanctioned by the Holy Catholic Church, or by me. If this canard proceeds into the Holy Church, I shall appear at the sacred altar to proclaim the fraudulence of such a union.

"Does he intend to crawl to the altar?" my father said with a nasty chuckle, while my mother shivered at the prospect of Señor's carrying out his vow. "We'll see how he intends to interfere." My father's tone indicated that he was more than ready to meet the challenge in this escalating war. I envisioned the two tyrants entangled, exchanging blows at the entrance to the church, a sight that caused me to double over with laughter, which would have earned me a vicious smack from my father if I had not learned, though not always successfully, to dodge.

Rehearsals for the wedding ceremony proceeded in a private home, the address withheld as long as possible. Apprehensive bridesmaids and nervous awkward ushers gathered there, my future brother-in-law's fellow football players proclaiming their manliness by emphasizing their clumsiness. The stoutest among them was stationed at the door to make sure no invasion occurred. The wedding would take place next weekend in the Church of the Sacred Heart.

The tense silence that prevailed in our house was broken by a shrill little voice. Señor's wife had escaped from her husband's tightening scrutiny to appear again and warn us: "Señor intends to rise like Lazarus to stop the wedding!"

Whatever he did intend, I was sure that the man I had once retreated from in fear was capable of horrors, horrors that included my mother's and his wife's instant speculation that he would set fire to the church.

What's more—my mother expounded on added perils—if he learned that his daughter Marisa was indeed expected, then he would surely have someone carry him into the church on a stretcher to fulfill his terrible promise.

"Might your daughter be coaxed not to come?" my mother asked the trembling little woman, who gasped, "Oh, she's coming all right, nothing can keep her away, and she refuses to change her name, as he demanded—it's still his *and* hers!—and it will infuriate Señor to the limit of endurance because everyone knows she's the kept woman of Augusto de Leon."

The kept woman! Those words resonated from what I overheard. I tried to envision her, shape her. Nothing I could conjure satisfied the extravagant title. I knew only that being a kept woman had created scandal; and so I imbued all the secrecy and whispers about her with a glow of glamorous wickedness. I begged God:

Please let the kept woman come.

The time of the ceremony arrived. The church had been adorned with as much opulence as limited funds allowed, including paper flowers intermixed with real flowers gathered that very morning from outlying fields. In the balcony in back of the church, my father was directing his small band of enduring musicians playing the special music he had arranged with enormous care to further affront his adversary in this battle of wills.

Wearing a suit jacket that one of my brothers had outgrown and that draped over me like a cape, I sat in the front pew nearest the altar with my mother, who clutched her rosary as if it was a weapon she might hurl if the tyrant invaded. I had noticed that two hideous aunts—my mother's older sisters, whom I did not remember having ever said a kind word about anyone during their frequent unwelcome and unannounced visits to our house—were stationed like evil sentries by the entrance to the church, anticipating, I was sure, that Señor would somehow appear and that they would be able to egg him on to do his worst while they pretended to ask for God's succor for us all.

I was jolted by something else, strangely unexpected. I saw my sister entering the church wearing a white veil, while the groom, visibly uncomfortable out of his football uniform and in his rented tuxedo, awaited her at the altar. My sister? That was my sister Olga? My friend who had been a gangly tomboy who chewed her hair when she was anxious? Had I been so overwhelmed by the spiraling dangers, and so capable of ignoring my mother sewing into the late night on yards of white lustrous material—how purchased, only she and God knew—that I hadn't realized my sister was the cause of the main danger? *She* was being married?

How was that possible?—leaving me, her friend? Hadn't she given me my greatest moment of victory in baseball when, as a moony child of eight—she was twelve—I had been relegated to the "outfield" of a vacant weed-claimed lot to daydream while a neighborhood baseball game proceeded? As I had been imagining what lay behind the sheet of blue Texas sky, I heard her shout at me across the lot: "Jump and catch it!" Responding to her command, I jumped, my hand up, and I made the catch that won the game.

In church now, seeing her like a ghostly ship gliding away from my life, only then did I realize that my sister, who was not gangly anymore and was very pretty—would never again play games with me. I felt a sense of betrayal, deepened when she passed by in the procession of bridesmaids flouncing like lavender butterflies and she did not glance at me. Was she embarrassed by what she was doing?—there in white, getting married?

My mother, weeping, kept looking toward the back of the church, nervously, and then fretting with her rosary so absently that her fingers did not advance along its beads.

"God protect us!" my mother exhaled loud enough to be heard by those seated several rows away. They and others, stirred by her reaction, turned to locate the object of her shock at the entrance to the church.

Agitated whispers!

Señor! He had done it. He had been carried to the church on a stretcher, and then, with all the force of his meanness, he had pushed himself up. There he stood at the entrance to the church, the morning sun carving a threatening shadow along the main aisle as he paused, ready to unleash on us all whatever horrors he had plotted.

But it wasn't the tyrant that had cast such an imposing shadow. It was—

"The kept woman of Augusto de Leon!" my mother gasped. ★

From *Autobiography: A Novel*

(Editor's Note: This excerpt is from John Rechy's unpublished work in progress.)

"This is not what happened; it is what is remembered. Its sequence is the sequence of recollection."—John Rechy

My beautiful Mexican mother fled the City of Chihuahua during the revolution when word reached her family that Pancho Villa was sending one of his lieutenants to kidnap her after having seen her at a ball which he had invaded; and my Scottish father fled his wealthy home in Mexico City as his Spanish mother fired a gun at his heels to emphasize her act of banishment. Or so I was to learn from accounts of my family history as I inherited ghosts that roamed the memories of others and floated into mine.

My mother bore the grand name of Guadalupe Flores de Rechy, and my father bore the equally grand name of Roberto Sixto Rechy. The "Sixto," or sixth, was attributable not to any sequence of birth—he was an only child—but to a remote lord, the sixth, exhumed in versions of his aristocratic lineage, originating in Scotland but transferring to Mexico City, where he was born and where his Scottish father, a highly respected doctor, was a frequent guest, with his family, of President Porfirio Díaz, the Mexican dictator with European loyalties—all of which, years later, I would call, thrilling to the wonderful image, "mixed blood."

While the revolution raged across the Rio Grande, and having simultaneously fled their respective threats miles apart, both my father and mother—still unknown to each other—crossed the border into El Paso, Texas, at exactly the same time. In the new city my mother's youngest brother, playing, thrust a ball through the window of my father's house. Chasing the young destroyer, my father encountered my mother—and married her.

In the deep of the Depression, when Texas was swept by poverty, and winds gathered to devastate the crops of nearby Oklahoma into dust, I was born into a sea of clashing memories, the youngest of five children, two brothers, two sisters.

Now of course my father and mother did not flee at the exact time. Of course they did not cross the border at the same moment. Autobiography creates its own time in rearranged memories. It orders random accidents into inevitability. I am able to reconstruct my life from birth, even before birth through inherited memories, and so to provide structure to what is chaotic, reason to anarchy—and the only meaning possible, a retrospective meaning, imposed; the only truth, one's own. That is, autobiography as novel.

Oh, my mother was a conquering beauty, her dance card instantly filled during the balls she reigned over in Chihuahua. Her aunt, my great-aunt, *Tia* Ana (who practiced white magic and converted, through efficacious prayers and incantations, my first novel into a top bestseller) loaned me her recollections of my mother as a girl, of her beautiful green eyes, flawless fair skin and hair. My mother denied it all, but in tones which asserted happily, "Yes, it's all true, tell him more." And *Tia* Ana did, gave me such careful memories that in them, I become my mother's chosen escort! She draws a line cancelling out all others on her dance card, tied to her wrist by a pale-blue ribbon. I bow, take her hand, and gently remove her dance card to discard it along with all her other suitors. We waltz. Yes—and years later, she did teach me to waltz! Her skin remained flawless, her hair bright, her eyes truly green—until death attempted to close them; they remain in my mind, clear green, emerald green.

Death exists only for the living. It is a presence, not an absence, a new presence born at the moment of death. People gone, places left behind, continue to grow and change, are resurrected. And die daily.

My father willed me deep memories. His were of fortune and fame, then withering fortune, withering fame, finally assaulting loss. There was a tenuous reconciliation between him and his ferocious mother. She left me two paintings: one was of their family home in Mexico City, the horse-drawn carriage before it emphasizing their former high station in life; for me, years later, that carriage looked like a surrendered relic. The other was a portrait of herself, painted on glass: a handsome proud woman with stark-black hair and a white lace-ruffled blouse rising to her chin, deliberately isolating the face of the powerful woman who had banished my father with gunshots. Why?

My life as novel allows me to supply motives that satisfy me, adhering to autobiography by basing them on subsequent evidence, always allowing for mystery. Reordered memory at times discovers only a sharper shape of mystery. Explored too closely, though, that shape may shatter into fragments, revealing only shards of possibility.

At dinnertime while oppressed servants silently attended, my father announced, "I oppose the tyranny of the Dictator Díaz!"

"I forbid you to continue," says my grandmother.

My grandfather does not take sides—he was, after all, Díaz's physician—but, an emergent socialist, he quietly champions my father. My father goes on to assert sympathy for agrarian reforms. "And the revolutionaries!" exclaims one of the maids. (She was a pretty Indian woman with haughty brown breasts—my grandmother called them impertinent—and she had introduced my father to sex and the ways of social justice.)

"Yes, and them!" my father affirms. My grandmother grabs her jeweled gun. Yes! That is exactly how it happened; now it is lodged in my memory. I remember it! Reordered time, inherited memories, and imagination allow me to applaud my father's act while my grandmother glares at me, too, and my mother smiles approval—all within adjusted time. The Indian maid's name was . . .

Maria.

I have based that reconstruction on what happened subsequently. My grandfather, having located in El Paso, founded the first clinic for the poor in Texas, while his wife, pretending humility—with only moderate success—ruled over celebratory parades. Much later, my father was run out of a Southwest town for opposing municipal corruption by exposing it in a "radical" newspaper he printed by himself. Like his father, a daring pioneer against injustice, especially in bigoted giant Texas, he was defiant, courageous, talented—and, for me, cruel with the cruelty he inherited from the woman in glass.

Now jump across time as only memory can, and we encounter the spirit of Maria many years later. With two "Anglos" mistakenly proposing me for membership in a popular college fraternity, I went to visit the ranch of one of their families, in Balmorhea, darkest gothic Texas—where the only theater separated Mexicans from Anglos and never allowed Negroes. At dinner, a relative of my would-be "fraternity brother" expressed her dismay at eating while the Mexican maid "is still in the room." The maid was Maria's daughter! I didn't know it then but I know it now. Yes! And that is in strong part why I walked out of that house and began my various rebellions—furthering my isolation. Now—as I leave that Texan dinner of hatred—I say "buenas noches" to Maria's daughter. *Her* name was Maria, like her mother. *But why was she still in servitude?*

What is strongly imagined is finally remembered. Maria has become a living ghost, the first Maria—and an influence on my whole life! Yes, and when my father told my mother—and told her with some hesitation—about the first Maria, my beautiful mother glances up at him with her emerald eyes glinting, and she asks him, "Was she pretty?" "Yes." He paused, flirting with her—oh, how I long to believe that that cruel man once flirted and smiled—and so, yes, he flirted and smiled and said, "Yes, she was beautiful, but—" He wants to see my mother's green eyes flirting back and coaxing for long moments, longer. Too long. I finish for him now, "Yes," I tell her, "Maria was beautiful but not as beautiful as you." And immediately, I hear my father say, "Yes, Maria was beautiful but not as beautiful as you." He had to be truthful. "But why didn't you go back later to say goodbye to her?" my mother chides him, approving Maria's importance. "I did," he tells her, "but she had run away, too; to join the *Zapatistas*."

Autobiography changes from moment to moment. It is not what happened, but what is remembered. Its only sequence is that of memory. Alter the order of events and you change meaning.

Remember! Memory whispers.

In my memories I discover this: My father's eyes were always filled with tears!—perhaps unseen tears.

Before that discovery, I knew only this: he hated me.

Now that I remember—or have inserted tears—I find a new man bearing the same life. Early he became a notable figure in the world of music. He had been a child prodigy, learning to play "every instrument." He was intelligent, talented, educated—an education extended in travels to Europe, he moved in Mexico's high society, vacationing in often in the mansions of Guadalajara. He kept photographs of himself next to a baby-grand piano, in a performance before the Mexican President, photographs of an uncle, grandly mounted in impeccable riding clothes on a superb horse. He came to America, and the music faded. Aging memories were replaced by those of decline. He is no longer the conductor of his own celebrated orchestra, composer of musical scores, director of his touring theater, no longer even tutors untalented children. Now he spends dark hours re-orchestrating music no one wants, music filed in an old wooden cabinet eventually lost. Soon he will no longer be even the caretaker of a public park. Now he is an old gray man, mocked by ghosts. He gets up at dawn to clean the night's debris at a hospital, fragments of accidents and death. When he returns home, he lashes out with threats of fire and violence. Then he screams for recognition: "I am respected, known!" My mother soothes him, agreeing. When he died, telegrams came from important figures all over the country and Mexico, who had ignored his slow dying.

Truth changes with new memories. We do not move into the past, we bring it forward with new life. My mother and father speak words I heard long ago (or heard about) but hear now anew, spoken only to me, spoken through me. Tomorrow, if I find my father's anger wrenching my life, I may forget his tears, insist that I inserted them, revise the earlier truth, reinsert only cruelty.

Before that happens, I will remember this: After the rampages of anger, my father would bring me presents, lavish fresh flowers on my mother, flowers splashing the drab house of poverty with astonishing colors. He loved her! Shall I allow myself to believe that she loved him, too?

On her Saint's Day, December 12—the day of Our Lady of Guadalupe—he would serenade her at the tint of dawn, turning up with dashing *mariachis* to sing *Las Mañanitas* outside her window. She, pretending surprise but having gone to bed carefully arranged for her appearance at the window, would then invite everyone grandly to an already prepared breakfast of coffee, chocolate, *pan de dulce*. She reigned with her smile. He continued the yearly serenades even when he was old, turning up at her window with a band of increasingly ragged musicians.

Facts—what someone continues to remember—are reshaped by the growing past. Only the past changes. But for me this is constant: On the steps of a bandaged Texas house that has a tattered screened porch, five-years-old I lie on my mother's lap. The Texas sky multiplies a million stars. I begin to doze as my mother curls with her saliva my eyelashes, which were long and thick.

Poverty invaded our lives. We had moved from a pretty house we could no longer afford. Over fire made from wood and propped on bricks my mother heats tin tubs of water to wash our clothes. White sheets sway on wires. Memory washes them purer each time. My mother empties the tub, water carves mysterious shapes on the dry soil. I see her against the blue sky under a white sun.

A sharp memory asserts: In kindergarten Miss Stowe was showing us how to make butter in an old-fashioned churn. But the butter remained curdled liquid. Angered, longing for a vanished frontier, she kept us after school while she churned. I stand by the window knowing my mother is waiting for me—I see her across the street. She's thinking I've been stolen, she'll go through life looking for me while Miss Stowe churns passionately. Did the agitated teacher finish the butter? I don't know. I'm running out of the room, down corridors, out the schoolyard. Now I'm walking home holding my reward for defiance—my mother's hand.

There was another teacher. Miss Oliver. A Texas Cassandra. In El Paso Junior High she was a dreaded teacher because she was smart and demanded attention in class. Black, black hair, a pale, pale face, she seemed always on the brink of unendurable pain. Someone said that in her clenched fists she clutched secret pins. She walks into the classroom. She looks more pained and angered than ever. I hear her now. She says to us, all the children there: "You will always be as unhappy as you are now. Always!" A curse? A projection? A prophecy? A challenge? Her truth? A preparation. . . .

Years later when I denied God melodramatically, I was certain He was listening and caring. Did he hear Miss Oliver? Still later when I cherished the splendid indifference of cold stars in vast unseeing darkness, I hoped that she did, too.

The despised Texas windstorms begin in February, thrusting desert dust and tumbleweeds against budding trees taunted into resurrection by hints of spring.

We lived near railroad tracks. Dozens of men and women scattered by the Depression would ride through El Paso hidden in freight trains. Police raid the cars, bludgeoning crouching flesh. Tramps who escape sweep across the tracks in search of shelter, a sympathetic family. For me they sweep into ambiguous memories.

Mystery, too, grows in memory, providing more precise questions, not answers.

Lean men and women often handsome but dirtied, the wanderers would appear at our back door. My mother would seat them at a wooden table in the back porch. She serves them each a plate of rice and beans, a container of hot coffee.

Slides flash on the scrim of memory. Autobiography contains photographs. And silhouettes—shadows that exist only when exact light is at an exact angle.

A face: a man among the tramps. He was kind to me, a gentle figure, a dirtied angel. I was six years old. Memory jerks into a dark freight car of violent twisting shadows—Is this real? Imagined? Memory invents what it requires for tomorrow's truth, or conceals it.

I inherited dual Catholicism, Scottish and Mexican—but more Mexican because I was raised in El Paso. Pained saints with extravagantly painted tears like colored jewels writhe in gorgeous agony. Christ poses on his famous cross. Excessive, that religion burrows into roots of superstition.

Listen!

A spirit is telling *Tia* Ana that treasure is buried under the crawl space of our house. My mother says nonsense, my father says it's worth a try to find out—his background in opera allowed acceptance of the unseen. *Don* Ben, the pope of El Paso's good witches, a little twig of a man, is summoned—my aunt had contacts. The late sun waits in suspense on the purple horizon. My mother, my father, *Tia* Ana, and I gather in the yard. The old man becomes rigid! A trance! Something *is* buried nearby, he speaks. Only he and I—I was five—are small enough to crawl into the crawl space. We're in the dank darkness. No treasure, no sign. I decide to help *Tia* Ana and God. I twist two sticks into a hurried cross and put it atop a mound of dirt. "Look, the sign!" But in the dusky evening, a weary old man, coughing from the dampness, and cramped is already crawling out. He testily instructs that we must all pray 12 novenas each before he can proceed. He rubs his back to emphasize the necessity for the long devotional period. Only the Texas dust remained under our weedy house.

But perhaps I didn't make that cross. Perhaps it was there! Perhaps there *was* treasure! What is strongly imagined enters memory and becomes real.

I'll keep this memory in slow motion:

After my first novel was published, I bought my mother a house. Soon after, we drove to Los Angeles to visit my sister. Halfway there, so my mother will not grow tired, I rent for overnight a suite in the gaudiest and most expensive motel in Phoenix, Arizona. We collect stares as we enter the pretentious lobby, because I am wearing torn jeans, no shirt; my mother wears a lovely spring hat, white gloves, a faintly violet lace dress. I ask for the best accommodations.

Close up. Tight focus. The motel pool sprawls across a green lawn under pastel-haloed palm-trees, the water is colored silver in the desert night. My mother has taken her sleeping pill. She wears a summer robe, so light it sighs in a breezeless night. We sit by the pool. She tells me she would like a cool soft drink. I order it, and it comes on a platter. She sips it. She smiles her magical smile. "Thank you, my son. Now I'll have a restful sleep. Goodnight, my son." I see her tiny form moving in and out of pastel-tinted shadows, her robe sighing.

I want that mysterious moment to stay, to halt.

***

When I was told at age five that I had to start school, I refused to go. "What will happen to you if the robbers come or the house burns?" I ask my mother. "Who will save you?" "You will," she tells me. "You will know if anything threatens me and you will save me."

But did I?

Years later—after wandering the country from city to city—I did return to El Paso. Then love enclosed—locked—me and my mother in that new house, the love that occurs, when it does, only between mother and son, a love that defines itself. In wanting to make up for all her years of sacrifice, the demands placed on her love, I tried to give her everything I thought she needed, imposed it, demanded she vacation, visit distant friends, that we go out to lunch, dinner. But the unscreamed protests of her life had wearied her. She wanted now only to rest, just rest. And I raged. She pled once through her tears, "What do you want me to do?—become young again!" Yes!

Soon, she retreated to her bedroom, decorated like a doll's room, with delicate filigree, in shades of pastel, white golden-gilded drapes drawn so that the room glowed faintly. Her eyes grew even more beautiful, more luminous than ever. My beautiful beloved mother, who had waltzed with me in imagination and then in reality, had grown old.

After she died, and I stood alone in her house, I saw anew an old glass case she had cherished throughout the years. It contained delicate figurines, crystal angels, fragile handpainted cups and saucers, miniature white statues of the Holy Mother. In my memory, those objects seem imprisoned in a beautiful glass cage.

Of course nothing that I have written here is true. All of it is invented. All of it is remembered. ★

Bryan Woolley

Native Texan Bryan Woolley was raised in Fort Davis, Texas, and began his award-winning career in journalism as a stringer for the *El Paso Times* while a student at Fort Davis High School. Continuing to work for the *Times*, Woolley earned a B.A. from Texas Western College, now the University of Texas at El Paso. He holds a Master's degree from Texas Christian University and a Master of Theology from Harvard. A journalist in Kentucky, Alabama, and Oklahoma, Woolley returned to Texas and began working for the *Dallas Times-Herald*, then for the *Dallas Morning News*. He is the author of four novels: *Time and Place*; *November 22*; *Sam Bass*, which won a Golden Spur Award from Western Writers of America; and *Some Sweet Day*, which has remained in print since 1973. Collections of his newspaper feature stories and essays include: *The Time of My Life*; *The Edge of the West*; *The Bride Wore Crimson*; *Generations*; *Texas Road Trip*; *Where I Come From*; and *Mythic Texas*. Author of *We Be Here When the Morning Comes*, which won the W. D. Weatherford Award, and *Where Texas Meets the Sea*, Woolley has also published two children's books: *Home is Where the Cat Is* and *Mr. Green's Magnificent Machine*. He is co-author of the book *Final Destinations: A Travel Guide for Remarkable Cemeteries* and contributed essays to the books *Charreada: Mexican Rodeo in Texas* and *The Way Home*. Winner of the PEN Western Literary Award for Journalism, Bryan Woolley is also the recipient of four awards from the Texas Institute of Letters including the O. Henry Award for magazine journalism; two Stanley Walker Journalism Awards; and four Texas Headliner Awards. He was inducted into the *El Paso Herald-Post* Writers Hall of Fame. Past president of the Texas Institute of Letters, Woolley was appointed a teaching fellow in the Sam Donaldson Center for Communication Studies by his alma mater, The University of Texas at El Paso in 2007. His memoir will be published by Wings Press in 2010.

From *The Bride Wore Crimson and Other Stories*: Glory Denied

(Editor's Note: In 2006, the story of the 1966 UTEP Miners was made into a major motion picture Glory Road, *released by Disney Studios starring Josh Lucas as Don Haskins. Original team member Bobby Joe Hill has passed away and UTEP and El Paso lost their beloved coach Don Haskins, 1930-2008.)*

I graduated from Texas Western College in 1958, long before it was the University of Texas at El Paso. We had some good basketball teams in my day, but nothing like the Miners of 1966. I watched that NCAA final game on a black-and-white TV set in Cambridge, Massachussetts, where I was a graduate student at Harvard. I had to explain to my classmates who watched it with me exactly what and where Texas Western College was. None had ever heard of it. But they rooted for Texas Western, and I don't think they did it entirely for my sake. By then, the amazing Miners had captured the interest of the nation. When the 1966 Miners gathered in El Paso to celebrate the 25th anniversary of their accomplishment, Arturo Vasquez, the editor of Nova, *the UTEP alumni quarterly, invited me to attend the reunion and write about it for the magazine. A slightly different version of the story was published in the* Dallas Morning News, *and was reprinted in* Best American Sports Writing: 1992.

As they arrived one by one at the hotel, they shook hands, embraced, kidded each other about gray hair, bald spots, heavier bodies and slower feet. They marveled that a quarter century had passed since the remarkable thing that they had done. They were returning to celebrate the memory of it with their old school and the city. But first they would celebrate with their coach and each other.

"It's great to see all these guys in one place again, to tell the good old war stories," said Nevil Shed. "It makes us feel warm inside to have a city as great as El Paso still remember something that we did for them. And we don't forget what they did for us."

Twenty-five years ago, Coach Don Haskins said, it never entered his mind that they had done anything special. But few who saw it happen would forget it.

For the first time, an all-black team had played an all-white team for the NCAA national basketball championship. The black men had won. History had been made. The Texas Western Miners had changed college basketball forever.

But it was 1966. The march from Selma to Montgomery had happened only a year before, and the struggle for the rights of black people still held the country in turmoil.

Civil rights workers still were being shot. Arsonists still were torching black churches. Gov. George Wallace still was defying a school desegregation order in Alabama. A congressional committee was investigating the Ku Klux Klan. The Georgia Legislature was refusing to seat a newly elected black representative named Julian Bond. Rioting had broken out in a Los Angeles neighborhood called Watts. And Dr. Martin Luther King Jr. was promising to take the civil rights movement northward to Chicago.

A lot of people in the country didn't like the kind of history that team from Texas had made.

"I was so young and naive," Coach Haskins remembers. "I hadn't thought of it as putting an all-black team on the court. I was simply playing the best players I had. It's what I had done all year. Then we came home, and the hate mail started pouring in. I got them for months. Thousands of letters, from all over the South."

The letters were only the beginning of his bitter time. A dozen years after winning the greatest athletic triumph in his own life and the history of his school, he would say: "If I could change one thing about my coaching career, I'd wish we came in second in 1966."

***

On the night of March 19, 1966, the Texas Western College Miners walked onto a court in College Park, MD, to play the University of Kentucky Wildcats in the final game of the NCAA tournament.

Kentucky had compiled a record of 23 wins and only one loss during the regular season. It was ranked No. 1 in the nation. On the previous evening, in the game that most of the coaches and sportswriters attending the tournament thought would really determine the championship, the Wildcats had beaten the nation's No. 2 team, Duke. If the Wildcats beat the Miners, as almost everybody expected, they would give Kentucky and its legendary 64-year-old coach, Adolph Rupp, their fifth national championship.

The Miners were the "Cinderella team" of the season. Texas Western College—now the University of Texas at El Paso—was a small group of buildings perched on a desert hillside a few hundred yards from the narrow Rio Grande and Mexico. Some 6,000 students were enrolled there. The Miners' 36-year-old coach was in his first college job. A few years earlier, he had been coaching both boys' and girls' basketball at tiny Hedley High School in the Texas Panhandle and doubling as the school bus driver to make ends meet.

Until the 1965-66 season, no one in big-time college basketball had paid much attention to Texas Western. In its entire history it had won only one NCAA tournament game. And at the time it was an "orphan" team, an independent, belonging to no athletic conference. Since none of the major basketball schools had bothered to recruit any of Haskins' players, the Eastern and Midwestern press had dismissed them as "castoffs," "unknowns" and "nondescripts."

But the Miners also had compiled a 23-1 record during the regular season, and when the tournament started, they were ranked No. 3 in the country. After an easy victory over Oklahoma City University in their first tournament game, they had nipped Kansas and Cincinnati, both in overtime, and had beaten Utah in the semifinals to get a crack at Kentucky and the title.

They were upstarts. Traditionally powerful Kentucky and the arrogant Rupp, called "The Baron," were the Establishment. The underdog-lovers of America, watching the tournament on black-and-white TV in living rooms, bars and dormitories, became fascinated with the unknown team from nowhere. But most of the new fans knew absolutely nothing about the school the Miners represented.

"I run into people who remember that game, and they still think I went to an all-black school," said Willie Worsley.

Of course, Texas Western wasn't an all-black college. Far from it. A large percentage of the small group of black students on campus had been recruited from all over the country for their skills at basketball, football, and track. El Paso, where a majority of the citizens are Hispanic and Mexico's fourth-largest city lies over the river, had comparatively few black residents. So did the vast, nearly empty desert region around it.

But 11 years earlier, in 1955, Texas Western had been the first all-white college in Texas—indeed, in the entire old Confederacy—to admit black undergraduates. And in 1956, it had recruited its first black athlete—a basketball player named Charlie Brown.

These steps were taken without fanfare and without incident. And, since El Paso is isolated from the other big Texas cities by miles and miles, and since most of Texas Western's athletic opponents were Southwestern and Western schools that never had been segregated, nobody east of the Pecos noticed, and nobody west of the Pecos cared.

"We were so insulated out here in El Paso that we barely knew all that racial stuff was going on in other places," said David Palacio, one of the players. "We heard about it, I guess, but we didn't think about it."

Nor were the Miners really an all-black team. Of the 12 men on the squad, five—Togo Railey, Jerry Armstrong, David Palacio, Louis Baudoin and Dick Myers—were white. All had played in games during the season, and Armstrong had been instrumental in winning the NCAA semifinal game, coming off the bench to shut down Utah's star shooter, Jerry Chambers.

They and the seven black players were a close-knit group. "We used to drink wine in the dorm together because we didn't have the money to go out," Palacio said. "We used to play a lot of cards. It was friendship, pure friendship. I don't remember a single instance of race being an issue or a problem among us."

But the team's seven best players—Bobby Joe Hill, Orsten Artis, David Lattin, Willie Cager, Harry Flournoy, Nevil Shed and Willie Worsley—were black, and they were the only players who got into the game against the Wildcats, the only Miners seen on TV.

In its entire history, Kentucky had never had a black player. Neither Adolph Rupp nor any other coach in the Southeastern Conference had ever seriously attempted to recruit one.

"It was the first time such a thing had happened," Coach Haskins said, "and it was against mighty Kentucky and The Baron. Had it been against a team with some black players, probably nothing would have been said of it."

Midway through the first quarter, with the Miners leading by one point, Bobby Joe Hill stole the ball, dribbled down the court and made an easy layup. As Kentucky was bringing the ball back up the court, Hill stole it again, dribbled down the court and made another easy layup, giving the Miners a five-point lead. The Wildcats never recovered. Texas Western won, 72-65. For the first time, a Rupp team had been beaten in an NCAA championship game.

"They were a bunch of crooks," he said. "One was on parole from Tennessee State Prison. Two had been kicked out of a junior college in Iowa. Texas Western was suspended by the NCAA for three years after that."

After the game, the Kentucky players minus their coach—went to the Miners' locker room and congratulated them. "There wasn't any racial thing as far as the two teams were concerned," Artis said.

The next day, 10,000 delirious fans turned out at El Paso International Airport to welcome home the only team from Texas ever to win the NCAA Division I national championship. Willie Cager made a speech: "From all of us to all of you, No. 1 was the best we could do." The crowd went wild. There was a parade through the town.

"It was wonderfully crazy," Willie Worsley said. "The people of El Paso made us feel very special."

"It wasn't until later on," Nevil Shed said, "that we started realizing that this team had opened the doors, not just for blacks but for all minorities, to have an opportunity to play ball at some of the top-notch schools around the United States. What was so beautiful about it was that the very next year things began to open up."

***

Eventually, even Adolph Rupp would recruit a black player. But he was a sore loser. "I hated to see those boys from Texas Western win it," he told the press after the game. "Not because of race or anything like that, but because of the type of recruiting it represents." He hinted that several of Haskins' players had done sinister deeds in the past and that Texas Western had practiced recruiting most foul. A number of sportswriters fell in behind him.

"The title really should belong to Kentucky . . ." wrote an Iowa columnist. "I have heard that one of the top Texas Western players had been charged with a major crime at one time." Since Texas Western was an independent, he wrote, they "can do about as they please in recruiting. They can take rejects from other schools and make them immediately eligible. A school with such low ethics should not be allowed to compete for the national title. Rather it should be in the NBA playoffs."

Rupp's hometown newspaper editorialized that "there is no disgrace in losing to a team such as was assembled by Texas Western after a nationwide search for talent that somehow escaped the recruiters for the Harlem Globetrotters."

As Rupp got older, his loss to Texas Western seemed to gnaw more and more exquisitely, and his descriptions of his villainous opponents grew more and more lurid. In a 1975 interview he said the biggest disappointment of his long career had been losing to "all those ineligible players."

"It wasn't even as close as the score indicates," Orsten Artis said. "At one point we led by 17. Our easiest games in that tournament were the first one, against Oklahoma City, and the last one, against Kentucky."

David Lattin had transferred from Tennessee State University, not the state prison, and Bobby Joe Hill and a player on the Texas Western freshman team—not the championship squad—had transferred from Burlington, Iowa, Junior College. There were no ineligible players on the team. Texas Western had never been suspended by the NCAA for any reason. Indeed, the NCAA had investigated the allegations after the tournament and had given the school a clean bill of health.

"I didn't like us being called misfits, criminals and convicts," Nevil Shed said at the team's reunion. "My mother and father worked hard to bring me up, to make sure that I represented myself in a well-mannered attitude. The people who did that to us didn't really know us. If they had taken the time to look into what 'those seven blacks' were all about, they would have found some pretty impressive guys."

Rupp's vilifications dogged Haskins for years. "I would go to a coaching clinic," he said, "and somebody would come up to me and ask, 'Did you really get that guy out of the pen?'"

But the most serious damage was done in 1968, when *Sports Illustrated* published a five-part series entitled "The Black Athlete." Part 3, the centerpiece of the series, entitled "In An Alien World," was devoted entirely to the University of Texas at El Paso (the name of the school had been changed a year earlier) and its alleged exploitation of its black athletes, including the 1966 basketball champions.

"One might suppose that a school which has so thoroughly and actively exploited black athletes would be breaking itself in half to give them something in return, both in appreciation for the achievements of the past and to assure a steady flow of black athletes in the future," wrote its author, Jack Olsen. "One might think that UTEP, with its famed Negro basketball players, its Negro football stars and its predominantly Negro track team would be determined to give its black athletes the very squarest of square deals. But the Negroes on the campus insist this is not the case—far from it."

Olsen went on to describe UTEP and El Paso as a kind of racist hell in which the athletes labored in virtual slavery. The article outraged almost everyone connected with the university. Perhaps El Paso and UTEP hadn't achieved a racial paradise during the turbulent '60s, but, they contended, they had come closer than much of the country and many of its universities.

The athletes said that statements attributed to them in the article had been taken out of context and twisted. A flurry of rebuttal whirled through the local press. UTEP President Joseph Smiley ordered an internal investigation of the school's intercollegiate athletic programs. The investigating committee found no major racial injustices, but recommended a few small reforms, most of them having nothing to do with race.

Olsen and *Sports Illustrated* stood by their article, however, and that made recruiting very hard for Haskins. "Every coach in the country had a copy of that article in his back pocket," he said. "And whenever a black player would indicate an interest in UTEP, they would yank it out and say, 'You don't want to go to El Paso. It's a *horrible* place.'"

In 1975, Neil D. Issacs, a college professor, published a book called *All the Moves: A History of College Basketball.* Relying entirely on Olsen's article as his source, he cited the 1966 Texas Western team as the best example of the abuse of black athletes in America. "There was little in the way of social rewards for them in El Paso," he wrote, "none of them was ever awarded a degree from Texas Western, and they feel that they have lived out the full meaning of exploitation."

A year later, one of America's more famous authors took up the tune, adding a few licks of his own. In *Sports in America*, James A. Michener described the 1966 Miners as "a bunch of loose-jointed ragamuffins" who had been "conscripted" to play basketball in El Paso.

"The El Paso story is one of the most wretched in the history of American sports," he wrote. ". . . I have often thought how much luckier the white players were under Coach Adolph Rupp. He looked after his players; they had a shot at a real education; and they were secure within the traditions of their university, their community and their state. They may have lost the playoff, but they were the winners in every other respect, and their black opponents from El Paso were losers."

Years before Michener's book was published, eight of the 1966 squad—the five whites plus Nevil Shed, Harry Flournoy and Willie Cager—had received their degrees at UTEP. David Lattin had left early because he was drafted by the Phoenix Suns. "He had a year of eligibility left, but I encouraged him to go," Haskins said. "There was a lot of money in it for him, and I kept thinking, 'What if he plays another season for me and ruins a knee or something?'" The remaining three players—Orsten Artis, Bobby Joe Hill and Willie Worsley—had amassed between 78 and 115 semester hours of credit before they dropped out of school to take jobs. Worsley later graduated from the State University of New York.

Michener, who often brags of the amount of research that goes into his massive books, later admitted in a letter to Dr. Mimi Gladstein, a UTEP English professor, that his investigation of the 1966 Miners had gone no farther than the *Sports Illustrated* article. He had consulted neither Haskins nor the players nor even Olsen.

Haskins wanted to sue Michener for libel, but his lawyer talked him out of it. He didn't have the resources, the lawyer said, to fight the author and his publisher, Random House, in the courts.

"I had no fun after winning the national championship," Haskins said.

***

He's one of the winningest coaches in the game. During his 30 seasons at Texas Western/UTEP his teams have won 579 games and lost 256. Six of his teams have won the Western Athletic Conference championship, five have played in the National Invitational Tournament, and 13 in the NCAA tournament. Crippled by injuries and the scholastic ineligibility of a key player, the Miners didn't make it to the NCAA this year. It was the first time in eight years that they weren't there.

Today Nevil Shed is the director of intramural athletics at the University of Texas at San Antonio; David Lattin is in public relations in Houston; Harry Flournoy is in sales for a baking company in California; Bobby Joe Hill is senior buyer for El Paso Natural Gas in El Paso; Dick Myers is vice president of a clothing manufacturing company in Florida; David Palacio is vice president of Columbia Records in California; Orsten Artis is a detective on the Gary, Ind., police force; the others—Jerry Armstrong, Louis Baudoin, Willie Cager, Togo Railey and Willie Worsley—are teachers and school administrators in Texas, Missouri, New Mexico and New York state.

On the day of the 1991 Miners' last home game and the close of Haskins' 30th season at UTEP, fans by the hundreds would stand in line at El Paso's big shopping malls to have the 1966 champions autograph posters, pictures, pennants and basketballs. Later, during halftime of UTEP's game with New Mexico, the crowd would rise to its feet and cheer the aging heroes once more, and their school would present them with replicas of their old jerseys.

First, though, they would talk deep into the night, reliving their days of glory.

"We won some games while you guys were here," Coach Haskins told them, "but the thing that makes me the happiest is that each and every one of you has turned out to be a fine citizen and a good person and all of you are doing well. That's the most important thing of all."

He's in the twilight of his career, he said. He has mellowed, he said, and is no longer bitter. It's finally sweet to have won.

"It was all a long time ago," he said. "A lot of bridges have been crossed. The entire country has come a long way in the way people think. Tomorrow night, I'm going to start my best five, regardless. And that's what I was doing then."

March 1991 ★

South El Paso Street

(Editor's Note: Since this story appeared in The Dallas Morning News *in 2005, South El Paso Street remains one of the most vibrant streets in downtown El Paso. Even with ongoing construction and revitalization plans, it remains nearly unchanged. Shoppers still crowd the street to buy quinceñera dresses, long-stemmed red velvet roses, piñatas, and votive candles of patron saints in a lively mercado atmosphere despite increased border security.)*

Centuries before any Europeans showed up, the Manso Indians had worn a path down to the river. As the Spaniards and Mexicans and Americans came along, they used the same path. When the first permanent settlers arrived in 1832, they built their adobe huts along it.

Over time, the Manso path became known as El Paso Street. For a while it was the only street. It went south about half a mile from the village of El Paso to the Rio Grande. Across the river was an older adobe village called Paso del Norte, which now is Ciudad Juárez.

The present population of El Paso is about 700,000. More than 2 million live in Juárez. The desert cities, embraced by barren mountains, are separated only by a narrow concrete channel that more resembles a storm drain than the mighty river the Rio Grande used to be. At no other spot on the globe do the First World and the Third World live in such huge and intimate proximity.

As in many American cities, most of the department stores and shoe stores, dress shops and five-and-dimes that used to make downtown El Paso a busy shopping district have gone out of business or moved to the malls on the edges of the city. Only one large hotel remains downtown now, and only one good restaurant. There are many empty buildings.

"Back in the '50s, downtown was great," says Larry Baron. "Now it's decrepit."

But South El Paso Street, on which Mr. Baron's pawnshop has stood for 54 years, seems lively as ever.

In the morning about 8 o'clock, merchants along both sides of the street unlock the padlocks on their doors, drag samplings of their goods outside and spend an hour arranging them on racks and tables along the sidewalk.

One shop sells nothing but purses. One advertises four pairs of socks for $1. The marquee of the old Colón movie theater says it's now Abelitos Toys y Novedades. In a store called Gran Mercado, pictures of Jesus on the cross and angels in heaven are jazzed with colored flashing lights and flowing fake waterfalls and even the chirping of invisible phony birds. Everything is made in China.

Pinochio Ropa Para Niños y Niñas is advertising its *venta final* on garishly colored sneakers, made in China, too. $3.99 plus tax or three pairs for $10. At New York Trading, and at fragrant L.A. Perfumeria and Genesis Perfumeria, all along the half-mile, everybody is busy. Ruben Flores, proprietor of Dollar Store y Mas, says he has no time to talk now, even for a minute.

Then, when all is ready, the merchants switch on their radios and stereos and turn up the volume. Suddenly the bright morning is aquiver with sentimental Mexican love songs, ranchera polkas, Christian pop, a Spanish rendition of Handel's *Messiah* and the shrill, rapid cries of Juárez disc jockeys, all competing for the ears of South El Paso Street's first customers. They're just now trudging up the sidewalks from the Santa Fe Street port of entry from Mexico.

The noise, the bright, sunlit colors of the clothing and shoes and artificial flowers piled along the sidewalk, the aromas of fresh popcorn and tacos envelop the street in an air of carnival.

A Border Patrol officer in shorts and helmet rides along the sidewalk on his bicycle, watching from behind mirror sunglasses. He dismounts and goes into a store and buys a pack of gum. He curls two pieces into his mouth, remounts his bike and weaves northward along the sidewalk again.

"The business is becoming more and more people from Mexico," says Mr. Baron. He's 60 years old. He says he was at his shop—Dave's Pawn Shop at 216 S. El Paso St.—when his father opened it in 1950 and has worked there ever since. Now his own 18-year-old son, Clay, helps him out. "Monte de Piedad," the sign in their window reads. "Mountain of Pity." It's Spanish for "Pawn Shop."

"Eighty percent of the people who come in here speak Spanish," says the elder Baron. "Of the remaining 20 percent, 19 percent are bilingual. We know most of our customers by name. We see the same items over and over and over again.

"Most people bring in jewelry now. Small things. It's hard to bring a television across the river. Sales are terrible. It's so tough to get across the border these days."

But Clay and his friends, like many El Paso young people, cross the river often, he says, because the legal drinking age on the other side is 18 and nobody asks for ID anyway.

"Going from here to Juárez is quick," Clay says. "You just pay a quarter and walk across. Getting back is the problem. You have to wait in a long line. The heat in the summer is killing. They do random searches. You have to prove everything. If they get the slightest idea that you're lying, you get taken in the back room. They're just nasty about everything."

His father says, "People stand in line for two hours. And once they get across, the Border Patrol is now all over downtown. They stop people and ask: 'What are you doing? Shopping? How much money do you have on you?' They don't go to the malls and check people like that.

"During the height of the Cold War I went through Checkpoint Charlie in Berlin. It was easier to get into East Berlin than it is to get back into my own country right here five or so blocks away.

"So," he says. "Business is terrible."

Local historians say the block of El Paso Street where Dave's Pawn Shop now stands was the bloodiest stretch of ground in the entire frontier West. Many of its businesses were saloons and whorehouses. In the early 1880s, city marshal

James Gillett said the crowds on the wooden sidewalks overflowed into the street in the evenings. "Each drinking place had a gambling house attached," he wrote, "and if one wished a seat at a gaming table he had to come early."

Homicides were as common as headaches. Once in 1881, the year the railroads arrived in El Paso, a friendless homicide victim lay in the street for two days until a local merchant decided to pay for his funeral.

That same year, a gunfight on El Paso Street resulted in the deaths of four men in five seconds, including an innocent bystander shot dead by the city marshal, Dallas Stoudenmire. Mr. Stoudenmire himself died in an El Paso Street gunfight a few months later.

In 1894, John Wesley Hardin, the old West's most murderous gunman—he's said to have killed more than 30 men—was released from the Texas penitentiary and was admitted to the bar. In 1895 he opened his law office in the Wells Fargo building on El Paso Street. Later that year, Constable John Selman shot him in the back of the head. But that was over on San Antonio Street, a couple of blocks east.

This part of the border always has had a violent reputation. In recent years, wars between competing drug lords have lit up Juárez with gunfire more ferocious than the frontier gunslingers could have imagined. The bodies of more than 320 murdered women have been unearthed in its environs. In January, 12 corpses were discovered buried in a single Juárez backyard.

The stories scare away tourists. And El Paso, because of its symbiotic melding with Juárez, gets smeared, too. Unfairly, says Larry Baron. "El Paso is not a violent city. El Paso has always been a place where people shoplift. Lots of burglaries. But there's very, very little violent crime here."

Down the street, Elida Jackson, 37 years old, has just opened Sunrise Wigs for the new day. In the store, crucifixes share tables with bottles of aftershave lotion, rat and mouse and roach traps and bars of Irish Spring soap. Ranks of mannequins wearing wigs stare ahead over a table of stuffed kitties, bunnies, horses and feathery chickens. The radio in the store next door is blaring "Amazing Grace" in Spanish.

The business doesn't belong to Mrs. Jackson. She just works there, she says. "But I like to deal with people. Some people don't like me, but that's another story. A lot of people who come in here have problems. We get a lot of people from the cancer center. They're getting chemotherapy. So. No matter how you treat them, they still have problems. I tell them, 'Don't be upset. You're going to have a better day.'"

A glass case is full of rhinestone tiaras, necklaces and earrings. Hair extensions hang from the walls like rows of pelts, colored ash blond to black, from straight to very, very curly. There are also wigs in bright blue, orange, pink and purple.

"Out of 150 that come in here, maybe one don't like me," Mrs. Jackson says. "No matter how lovable you are, how friendly you are, there's going to be one in the crowd that's going to come and poop the party.

"Some of the cancer patients, they never had long hair, so this is their chance to have it. Some never had curly hair, and now that their hair fell out, they can have curly hair. They can have any kind of hair they want now.

"This is a fun store. You're supposed to come here and look at yourself in a way you never did. Know what I mean? I'm here to make you feel good about yourself."

Tammy Turner, owner of Sunrise Wigs, has arrived. Born in South Korea, widow of an American soldier, she has just celebrated her 61st birthday. But she isn't happy. A big street construction project is underway at the corner of South El Paso and Paisano, too near her door. It's blocking most of the intersection. It's hurting business.

"They say it will take 10 months," she says. "How are people going to keep their business up and pay rent money? Rent money downtown is very high. Some pay $5,000, $6,000, $10,000 a month. I use only a small space and I pay $2,500."

The construction is the least of it, she says. Everything is just pretty bad right now.

"A lot of Mexican people have no jobs now," she says, "because a lot of factories have moved to China, Indonesia. The Mexican factories are shut up. When Mexican people have money, they love to spend it. They don't look to tomorrow. They look to today. Mexican people are good people, you know. When they have money, they spend.

"But it's a sad story right now." She waves her cigarette toward the street.

"They have no jobs. After 9-11 it's hard for them to get across the bridge. I used to have two girls working for me. Now I have one. Right now I'm poor. It's the same everywhere.

"We need to get Bin Ladin today," she says. "We need to get him. Then everybody can relax. Yes?"

Whenever the government's terrorism alerts go up, the long wait to get across the bridge from Juárez into El Paso gets longer. People hesitate to try. But according to George Hernandez, Osama is only one of the problems facing the South El Paso merchants.

Mr. Hernandez and his family own Hernandez Fashions, a clothing store. Lately, their business hasn't been good, either. "Paisano Street is torn up," he says. "They've raised the tolls on the international bridge. They've raised security measures at the bridge. They've raised the amount of money you have to put in the parking meters. They're giving out more citations for parking violations."

His parents, Luis and Manuela Hernandez, established the business 20 years ago. They prospered. Eventually they owned three stores. Then in 1994 the Mexican government devalued the peso.

"In '95, a lot of the shops along here had to close," Mr. Hernandez says. "We fortunately didn't have to close our doors, but we did have to downsize. We shut down two of our three stores. In this one, we went from a 4,000-square-foot building to a 2,000-foot one. It took a good 12 to 18 months for all the shops along the street to fill up again."

But Mr. Hernandez is an optimist. He and his family remodeled their store last year. "Prices are lower on this side of the river," he says. "That's the reason the people come across. And there's a lot to look at on South El Paso Street. They'll come back.

"People react to everything with fear at the beginning. But when they get used to something, they accept it and come back.

"It'll be OK. It'll be OK."

Just up the street, Cordelia and Eszquiel Arciero are standing on the corner. Mrs. Arciero is 67. She's wearing a long black dress with colorful stripes, and a white poncho over her shoulders. She holds a large, worn Bible. Her voice is gentle, like a kind grandmother's.

"We go to a Christian church on Montana Street," she says. "The Lord brings us prophecy there. And he has said: 'Go tell my people that I love them. Tell them I'm coming soon. Tell them to repent and receive me while there's time.'"

She and Eszquiel, who's 69, have been standing on street corners for 28 years, she says, delivering this message, sometimes in El Paso, sometimes in Juárez.

Mr. Arciero stands quietly beside his wife while she speaks. "We're always together," she says. "When people speak in tongues, my husband can understand the messages. So we just enjoy ourselves, speaking to the people."

They ask for no money, but most who rush along the sidewalk look away from them.

"A lot of people respond to our message," Mrs. Arciero says. "I can see it in their faces. It's hard sometimes, but I see it."

She speaks softly, as if addressing each individual who won't look at her. "Jesus loves you," she says. "God bless you."

A few, not looking, make the sign of the cross.

Around 6 P.M., the merchants start bringing in their wares from the sidewalks. At 6:30 they switch off their music, padlock their doors and go home.

As darkness comes, kids are lining up outside Club Xcape, a few blocks farther up, where the bands Seven Dust and El Niño are about to play. ★

Rick DeMarinis

Award winning novelist and short story writer Rick DeMarinis was born in New York City. He taught fiction writing at San Diego State University, Arizona State University and at the University of Texas at El Paso from 1988-1999, where he retired as full professor. DeMarinis is the author of the novels *A Lovely Monster*; *Cinder*; *The Burning Women of Far Cry*; *The Year of the Zinc Penny*, named a *New York Times* Notable Book of the Year; *The Mortician's Apprentice*; *A Clod of Wayward Marl*; and *Sky Full of Sand*. He has published six collections of short stories: *Jack and Jill*; *Under the Wheat*, winner of the Drue Heinz Literature Prize; *The Coming Triumph of the Free World*; *The Voice of America*; *Borrowed Hearts*, winner of the Jesse H. Jones award for best fiction by the Texas Institute of Letters and the 2000 Independent Book Publishers Award; and *Apocalypse Then: New Novellas and Stories*. DeMarinis has also written *The Art and Craft of the Short Story*. He is a member of the Texas Institute of Letters.

From *Apocalypse Then: New Novellas and Stories*: Hell's Cartoonist

"Why me?" I said.

"Why not you?" Billie Blood said.

That's how it started, three months ago. Billie had a place downtown, a little studio apartment with a pull-down bed. I was like a kid with a new toy.

My wife, Ursula, noticed the change but it took her a while to make the connection. Why shouldn't it have? I'd been faithful as a dog for almost five years.

"You've lost weight," Ursula said, fingering my neck suspiciously. She worked in Denny's. We were in a booth next to the kitchen, having a 3:00 p.m. lunch. She went back to the unbusy kitchen and brought out another basket of steak fries for me. "You're not feeling well?"

I was eating more these days but weighed less. I was energized, the atoms of my body buzzed. I felt translucent, weightless, electrified.

Ursula saw the change. "Tell me her name," she said.

"Billie," I said. Lying is not my strong suit. Better to own up to it now than later.

"You love her, then?" she said. She was calm, steady. Tears rolled down her long face. She kept her hair dark. It looked black as wet tar against her pale skin. Her grave Bavarian eyes looked past me to our compromised future.

"Love is a strong word," I said, guilt-stricken. "The strongest, maybe. This thing with Billie Blood is just. . ."

I didn't know what it was. It was something I'd never experienced before even though Ursula was my third wife. I'd married women clueless as myself. I always thought it was love, but after a year or two I had no name for the thing that brought us together, held us for a while, then let us go. I was almost fifty and still feeling my way in the dark. It wasn't just women who mystified me. Everyone did.

"Billie *Blood*?" Ursula found some dismal comedy in the odd name.

"A *nom de peinture* she calls it."

She uttered a small dry laugh. "You think you're trading up again. You are going to be a wretched old man, all alone, full of regret. It's very simple. Anyone can see it."

"You're wrong about this, honey. Really."

"What would you like me to say? How nice for you, how wonderful you've found someone who stimulates you so much that you lose weight?"

I had put it all in jeopardy—wife, home, stability. And I needed stability. I couldn't work without it. What had I been thinking? But I hadn't been thinking. Thinking's got nothing to do with it. It was electrical, a surge, hidden amperes electrocuting good judgment.

Women don't hit on me. I'm not great looking, I don't radiate masculinity. I'm a little unkempt, even seedy. I don't send out flirtatious signals. And I'm preoccupied—mostly with my work.

I never expected it. I didn't see it coming, and when it came I had no defense. An image of Billie Blood on her queen size Murphy pull-down came to me. Graceful even in supine repose, sturdy igloo breasts refusing to slump, curves and planes tapering into each other, flaming masses of kinked red hair consuming the white pillow. More woman than a man like me has a right to expect.

She was magnetic north. The iron in my blood danced for her. "A true artist needs an active love life," she said. I didn't know whose state of need she meant, hers or mine.

We'd met at a gallery. We both had paintings on the back wall, next to the restrooms. Billie did levees, cotton fields and badlands. Sunlight like bloodclots thrombosed the flat brown skin of her west Texas skies. I do downtown decay—buildings, warehouses, the plaza with its fractured humanity: whores, transvestites, glue sniffers. Maids and gardeners waiting for the bus. Loafing pederasts, panhandlers, undercover cops. Cartoonist in Hell, Billie once said. "Not that that's a *bad* thing," she amended.

"No way I'm finishing my shift," Ursula said, lighting a tear-dampened cigarette.

I was between jobs. The free lunch I got at Denny's was my food for the day. I'd get the garlic-mushroom-Swiss-burger, and Ursula would pile on the fries until they spilled off the plate. Then two slices of French silk pie for desert. Unlimited coffee. It was like a date, and—I realized too late—not a good time to discuss Billie. As if there could be a good time.

Ursula slid out of the booth and took off her apron. The day manager, Derek Hubble, came over to us. "Please put out your cigarette, Ursula," he said. Derek Hubble is a suave black man. Tall and lean, goateed, manicured. He looked like one of the dark-suited Modern Jazz Quartet guys, elegant. I could picture him wearing shades behind a vibroharp, mallets poised, confidently cool.

"I'm sick, Derek," she said.

Derek Hubble looked at her, looked at me. "Uh-huh," he said. "Enjoy your lunch?" he said to me. He knew Ursula was feeding me gratis but let it go—another patron of the arts.

"Always," I said. "Thank you."

We both looked at Ursula as she moved careful as a drunk down the aisle and pushed her way through the double doors out to the parking lot.

"She coming in tomorrow?" Derek Hubble said.

"I don't know, Mr. Hubble," I said.

"She don't, could be her job."
"I'll smooth this over, Derek."
He looked offended by the uninvited familiarity.

***

Ursula is a UFO freak. Not crazy enough to claim abductions or encounters of any kind, but crazy enough to believe in them to the point of spending hours in internet chat-rooms with other UFO freaks. I took a generous position on it from the beginning, and looked at her obsession as a kind of harmless hobby.

When we first met I mentioned my UFO experience, which was really not my experience at all. It was Henry Russo's experience. It turned her on. It lit her up. I couldn't tell the story enough. She combed through it, pressing for details I might have left out or forgotten. When we got married I had the feeling that she had found, in me, someone to validate her life. I was living proof that UFOs were not a national joke.

Henry Russo and I were stationed at an Air Defense Command radar base in northern Montana years ago. I was working swing shift at the blockhouse—the concrete bunker where the radar scopes were kept. Henry was a radio technician. Before going on duty most of us "scope dopes" stopped by the chow hall for hot roast beef sandwiches and peach cobbler. Orson McCabe, the squadron psycho, was being a pain in the ass. He liked to stuff raisins up his fat red nose then pull them out with a disgustingly elaborate nose-picking gesture and toss them at other tables. Someone was yelling at Orson to knock it off but not in an "or else" way since Orson was a big mean bastard, when Henry Russo came stumbling in yelling Oh my God, Oh Jesus.

Henry was quiet and uncomplaining, the kind of guy who gets fast promotions because the Air Force needed to keep uncomplaining people who took their work seriously. He'd made Airman First Class in only two years and was squadron pinochle champ. Unlike most of us, Henry was goal-oriented. He knew computers were the coming thing and wanted to be on the ground floor when he got back to civilian life.

So when he said a flying saucer wide as a parking lot had hovered over the radio tower for maybe a minute, it was hard to laugh it off. Everyone in the chow hall looked at him in silence for a few seconds, trying to process what couldn't be processed, then started giving him a hard time. Henry never lived it down. But that night reports of UFO sightings came in from Yellowstone south to the Rio Grande. Casper, Fort Collins, Raton, Albuquerque, El Paso, all night long. Nothing appeared on our radar screens. That was my UFO experience. And now it was Ursula's UFO experience, which gave her prestige in chat-room freakdom.

When I first told her the story she was married to an army lifer but considering divorce. We were at a Halloween party in northeast El Paso, near the Fort Bliss artillery range. I was drunk enough to give up the UFO story, embellished a little with fictitious squadrons of Air Defense Command F-102s making Combat Air Patrol orbits in the general vicinity where the visitors from planet X had been sighted. Ursula Klock—her married name then—pulled me into the kitchen of the party giver's house and made me tell it again. Rum punch in hand, she backed me against the sink and leaned in recklessly—thigh to thigh, nose to nose, chest to chest, her excited blue eyes ferreting details. She shuddered orgasmically when I said the dark gray disk was big as a stadium and made no noise other than a windy whisper that Airman Russo would never be able to forget. I took her home and we made out in her driveway for half an hour while her soon-to-be ex-husband, drink in hand, stood on the porch trying to peer into the heavily tinted windows of my '73 Monte Carlo.

We eloped to Mexico, to Chihuahua City, took the train through the Copper Canyon down to Los Mochis on Mexico's Pacific coast. I was happy, I knew this was it, and when we got back to El Paso I found work at a greenhouse nursery and painted pictures mornings and weekends. Ursula took a waitressing job, which was all she'd ever done since coming to the U.S. from Stuttgart with her clueless lifer husband, Sergeant Major Maynard Klock.

***

After lunch at Denny's, I went downtown and crossed the Paso del Norte bridge into Mexico and had a fifty-cent shot of tequila in the Kentucky Club. I had my sketch pad with me. My idea was to go over to Boys' Town, the whorehouse district between Calles Ocampo and Mariscal, and do some sketches. I wanted a drink to loosen up. Sketching in Juárez made me a little self-conscious. I didn't want my sketches to be tight with strained intent. I had no point to make, no agenda. I just wanted to catch the unfiltered kinetics of doomed life.

Boys' Town was a mistake. The whores and pimps were off the streets and helmeted cops on horseback looked at me through their tinted visors as if they needed a gringo to walk on, so I took my pad and pencil over to Avenida Diez y Seis de Septiembre to the three-hundred year old cathedral and made some quick contour sketches of the beggars who sat or were otherwise propped up against the short walls of the old church's plaza, looking for turista coins. A man with no feet moved toward me on homemade crutches. He swung wildly between the crooked sticks like a suspended wind-up toy, grinning. He made almost no progress. I gave him two quarters, a dime, and a cigarette.

Midwestern tourists took digital pictures of him. One posed with him, then the other. They gave him paper dollars and everyone was happy. I sketched the tourists large and serene, Raybans hard as turtle shells against the relentless Mexican sun. A fast unpremeditated sketch: Ordinary doom surfaced in these transactions under my moving hand.

I thought: How were these people going to explain their photos back in Eau Claire? *Here's the grinning Indian with leather pads instead of feet. Those are his uneven crutches. Here is Georgette standing next to the Indian with no feet and uneven crutches.*

UFO's aren't the mystery. We are.

***

"We give birth to ourselves," Billie Blood said. "Over and over until we almost get it right, or we go wrong beyond help—either way."

We were out at the Hueco Tanks. She was painting the huge rock formations, I was sketching the rock climbers. The Tigua Indians were trying to put the rocks off-limits to the climbers but had not yet succeeded. The rock climbers claimed to have as much respect for the sacred rocks as the Indians, which severely annoyed the Tiguas. The dispute was going to the courts.

Billie's rocks, assembled on canvas, looked like a reclining Venus figure. Pregnant stone: milk rising in the pocked sandstone breasts; full, red stone belly tight with its stone child. She'd named it already. Bloodstone Madonna.

We took a break, walked up to the tanks where water collects under stone shelves in shallow depressions. Godsend water for thirsty travelers, Indians then whites, in this treeless west Texas llano.

We crawled in and sat next to the pool. "How you handle rebirth is the thing," she said.

For Billie there were no trivial aspects to life. She found intensity where most found stupefying dullness. She wore me out but she liked to have fun, too. But even fun had its risky non-trivial side. Once, on the roller coaster at Six Flags Over Texas, she screamed, "Gravity is God!" Later, at a hot dog stand she adjusted that. "Gravity is God's muscle. This is how we come to fear God, through gravity. Fear of falling. Everyone should be shot into space at least once, or take a roller coaster ride, to acquaint themselves with their center of fear by temporarily losing their center of gravity."

She made gravity visible in her landscapes. Light fell like lead bullets. Sky had density and weight, the sun always iterated as a string of bloodclots—Billie's signature image.

The important galleries had begun to show her work. She sold "Blood Moon" for two thousand dollars. Fame began to tease her. It made her cautious. "Fame's another kind of rebirth," she said. "A dangerous kind."

"I'll try to remember that," I said. She ignored the irony.

She knelt by the water. She cupped her hands and drank. She crafted a ceremony, her thirst not physical but spiritual.

"Drink," she said. "These waters have power. They might begin your transformation."

I went along with it. It was hard not to. To doubt Billie in the smallest things was to doubt her loftier ideas. She was fragile that way, and I didn't want to lose what I had. The water was slimy but sweet.

Before we crawled out of the crevice I found the graffiti some 19th century adventurers had chiseled into a narrow shelf of stone:

Thomas and Ondine Holland
August 12, 1851

Thomas and Ondine drank the ceremonial waters of the Hueco Tanks then headed for California transformed, ready for rebirth in the promised land.

***

"It's over, honey," I said. "Billie's gone. I don't know what came over me—temporary insanity, maybe. I take full blame, but honestly, I was swept up. I couldn't fight it. I finally realized what I was risking. I came to my senses."

This lie was not an adequate explanation of my two weeks in Santa Fe with Billie Blood. I made it seem as if breaking off with Billie had been my idea—a man realizing what was truly valuable to him. In fact, I never gave up hope of seeing Billie again.

When she said she was moving north I took it hard. A major Santa Fe gallery wanted to feature her work. She couldn't say no. She was headed for the big time. She asked me to help her move her stuff. She rented the U-Haul truck and I drove it north to the foothills of the snow-capped Sangre de Cristos. It took two weeks to move her into a tiny cabin that leaned into the wind on a blue mesa.

I said: "It's pretty small for two people."

Billie said: "It's fine for just one."

The silence between us held volumes of meaning. Even so she said, "It's time for both of us to move on, don't you think?"

"To new births," I said.

"You're learning," she said.

"You're right," Ursula said. "It's over."

There was another man at Denny's. Ursula had let him into our booth. He was a dark little man wearing a nice houndstooth jacket. He had perfectly combed hair, parted almost in the center. The part looked as if it had been made with the help of a carpenter's straightedge. His groomed mustache looked like a third eyebrow. Ursula brought him a bacon Swissburger stuffed with onions, tomatoes, lettuce, and sprouts. He had very small hands and he held the Swissburger in his napkin so that the makings wouldn't fall out.

"This is Basil Taks, originally from London," Ursula said. She sat down next to him. "Basil was abducted in 1988. Tell him about it, Basil."

Basil cleared his throat apologetically. He touched his skimpy mustache. "Perhaps he does not wish to hear it," he said.

"It doesn't matter what he wishes to hear," Ursula said. "Tell him."

Basil cleared his throat again. "I was in my vintage Saab Turbo, driving from Ithaca to the Saranac Lakes. I am a computer engineer. I say this to prove my seriousness as a person."

He waited for me to acknowledge his seriousness as a person. He was too small, too delicate, too politely British to cold-cock with the ketchup bottle. I nodded, assenting to his seriousness.

"An extremely bright light appeared in the sky above the expressway," he said. "Then my usually reliable Saab ceased to function. My mind became blank for minutes—perhaps it was hours. Then I found myself within a closed area, as in a shell of some sort. Small men—I call them men but in truth I did not have any way to determine their gender—examined me, head to foot. They probed my flesh. It was intensely painful. Then it was over and I was back in my Saab. I have told this story under the polygraph to prove its verity."

"There you have it," Ursula said. "First hand experience, not second hand." She sneered. The sneer was meant for me and Henry Russo and the entire United States Air Defense Command.

Ursula and Basil faced me like a triumphant debating team.

"Did you experience rebirth?" I asked.

Basil looked at me, puzzled. "I do not quite grasp your meaning, my friend."

"You know—did the experience change you in some fundamental way. Your outlook on things, I mean." I was actually interested in his answer.

He laughed, a musical little laugh that went well with his perfectly combed hair, his houndstooth jacket, and his small hands. "No, no! Not at all! I went back to my job, fit as ever!" His eyes widened with bemused merriment. He smiled and nodded his small head. "Oh, I see what you mean. Well, yes, it changed my perception in that I now know as a certainty that we have alien brethren. We are not alone. It is a very warm and comforting message. This is what I came to understand about our place in this grand universe."

"You on the other hand *are* alone," Ursula said. "I've packed your clothes. You'll find them on the front porch along with your paintings. I've never really liked your paintings. I tolerated them. But they are warped. They spill over with negative energy."

"I absolutely concur," said Basil jovially. "Ursula showed them to me. They are full of horror and misguided mockery as well as vulgarities of a distinctly sexual nature."

"Our alien brethren wouldn't approve," I suggested.

"Quite so," Basil said. "The galactic visitors are emissaries of good will, orderliness, and common decency."

Ursula put her long arm around his narrow shoulders. "Basil has invited me to his UFO abductee support group," she said. "It's a week-long session, up in Roswell."

"You're not an abductee," I said.

"No matter!" Basil said with full enthusiasm. "We are very democratic! Abductees and friends of abductees! Ursula would be most welcome!"

"I take it then," I said, "that you two are . . ."

"Lovers?" Basil said. "No, no, not at all! We are just excellent companions who share mutual interests!" He looked shyly at Ursula. Ursula looked shyly back. Her neck flushed red. His hands fluttered toward her, fluttered back. Lovers make bad liars. I should know.

Basil released a dainty burp and pushed his nibbled bacon Swissburger to the middle of the table. Ursula stood up and pulled Basil out of the booth after her. They left Denny's together, arm in arm.

Derek Hubble appeared. "He didn't pay," he said.

"Wasn't it a freebie from Ursula?" I asked.

"Ursula quit . . ." he glanced at his watch, "as of twenty minutes ago. No freebies since then." He dropped the check on the table in front of me.

I hadn't eaten that day and I saw no point in wasting three-quarters of a perfectly good bacon Swissburger. Basil had left most of the steak fries, too.

I paid the cashier with my last seven dollars, bought a newspaper with the change, then stepped out into the grinding city.

Life would be harder now without Ursula. But Hell's cartoonist had work to do. It was dirty work, full of horror, misguided mockery, and vulgarities of a distinctly sexual nature. But someone had to do it. ★

Dagoberto Gilb

Dagoberto Gilb is the author, most recently, of the novel *The Flowers*. His previous books are *Gritos*, an essay collection that was a finalist for the National Book Critics Circle award; *Woodcuts of Women*; *The Last Known Residence of Mickey Acuña*; and *The Magic of Blood*, the winner of the 1994 PEN/Hemingway award and PEN Faulkner finalist. He also edited *Hecho en Tejas: An Anthology of Texas Mexican Literature*. His *Winners on the Pass Line* was the first book published by Cinco Puntos Press. Anthologized widely, recipient of awards including the Guggenheim and Whiting, Gilb's fiction and nonfiction have appeared in a range of magazines including *The New Yorker*, *Harper's*, *The Threepenny Review*, *Latina*, and *The Texas Observer*. Dagoberto Gilb spent most of his adult years as a construction worker and journeyman high-rise carpenter with the United Brotherhood of Carpenters. Born in Los Angeles, he made his home for many years in El Paso. He now lives in Austin and teaches in the MFA program at Texas State University in San Marcos.

From *The Magic of Blood*: I Danced with the Prettiest Girl (a Tex-Mex song)

The best place for music is Austin, and that's where we were going. Both Lee Roy and I thought we were decent on the guitar, though Lee Roy surely did play it better than me, and, big man that he was, he had a voice somewhere between Hoyt Axton and Tom Waits, which was why I liked him to sing my songs. I wrote better music than he did, but Lee Roy was major star material and I knew my place. My success in the music business improved by my knowing him the same way it did when we did construction together—I'd work anyway, but with him around it was like having a guaranteed income.

I met him framing a Motel 6 in Tucson, where there was so much work and dry sunshine. My first sight of him was rolling 2x6 joists, grabbing up four or so and holding them rock-a-bye style and practically running with them and then running back for more. He took to the tops of walls like other humans do to sidewalks. I was stooped-over all that day banging treated sixteens and dripping sweat and listening to this foreman scream at us that we weren't going fast enough while that huge animal slopped around all lonesome slamming joist and blocking and decking and singing like to tell us that this ain't shit to him. He approved of what the foreman allowed musically, particularly Conway Twitty and George Jones. Once he started yelling, "What ever happened to Hank Snow?!" and single swatted nails to prove how serious he considered the radio station's failing to be. The first time we talked he'd come down to help us raise this long, double-studded party wall. He says, "They oughta hire a few more a you Mexicans to help do this, or else help me so I don't care." Sometimes I say things without thinking about who would win. I said, "They oughta hire one more big ugly white boy and breed singing cows."

We became friends and pretty soon learned to play music together. I've played lots of music, learned acoustic bass from a neighbor and sang in his mariachi band when I was still a boy. Love ballads were my strong suit. But I got ripped-off because I was the cute attraction at this Mexican restaurant and didn't even get an equal share. My revenge was to forget it all by twelve and listen to rock'n'roll which I preferred anyway. All this was about the same time my mother finally gave up waiting for my old man and remarried and we moved to a better neighborhood. These days I've got my favorites narrowed down: Ritchie Valens, Buddy Holly, early Elvis and Jerry Lee, Bobby Blue Bland, Jerry Jeff Walker. Lee Roy was into music young too. His old man played some bands and might have had a career if he hadn't been an alcoholic and done time for counterfeiting. Lee Roy still tells about going around different towns spending oily twenties on albums with his daddy waiting in a car. He likes any musician with redneck credentials.

The reason we stopped in El Paso was that I was driving and I got off the interstate and pulled into this bar's parking lot and kept hold of the keys. Lee Roy insisted that we should only get one beer and take a six-pack or two if I thought it was absolutely necessary, which of course for him it was. But he wanted to keep going until dark so we could make it to Austin the next day.

"This is where I was born, where my mother and father met," I explained, wanting to look around some.

Lee Roy wasn't much into my sentiment. "One beer," he said. "And besides, I thought you told me your old man *dumped* your momma without knowing you were gonna be *born*." He thought he had me between the legs.

"He was gonna come back. He was like a cowboy and had to follow the work."

Lee Roy got a kick out of that.

The Bullring was a modern bar with a big-screen TV and a happy hour. Even though Texas was playing Oklahoma there weren't many patrons, and they didn't seem too enthusiastic. Lee Roy and I changed this. It was like we kicked open the swinging doors. We took the stools at the counter, the bartender asked us what we gentlemen preferred, and Lee Roy tore into the free food.

"What's that music you got here tonight?" I asked the bartender.

"Progressive country, a little Charlie Daniels and Heart."

Lee Roy and I both laughed and ordered a couple more.

"Whada you guys do?"

"Lee Roy sings. Otherwise we play the hammer and nails."

We drank two for one and stayed on after the game ended and an evening crowd started in. We made acquaintances with the band members and in no time at all felt like regulars. We started getting free drinks, which stimulated Lee Roy to do his typical asshole routine, though nobody seemed to mind. He took center stage while I stayed put at the bar thinking about El Paso and trying to make up some verses to a tune I'd been playing around with. I put it down as the band warmed up, which was at the same time I fell in love with the prettiest girl I'd ever seen. She came in with this other female who might only be considered average looking in comparison.

"Look," I tried getting through to Lee Roy, "that other one's just right for you, and I'm in love. You gotta get ahold of yourself so we can work this as a team."

It was hopeless. He was too busy being drunk and I had to brave it alone.

"Um excuse me, but I had to introduce myself. May I sit down? Believe it or not I'm not good at this, but, well you're the best looking thing I've ever seen.

I mean it. You are the prettiest woman my sorry eyes have ever looked at. You already know that, don't you? You probably got guys under your feet when you walk, you probably had to get an unlisted phone number. Can I buy you both a drink? I'm just passing through town. Me and that big drunk white guy over there. We're on our way to Austin. We're musicians. Guitar. What else is new, huh? I was born here in El Paso. My parents are from El Paso. Well, you know, more or less. Really my mother. I'm not that sure about my father to be honest. But anyway that's why we stopped. Look, would you like to dance?"

Have you ever been on a dance floor with the prettiest girl? Let me tell you, your boots move differently, the world is a changed place. You sway to the earth and your animal heart beats young blood and your tainted eyes sparkle. You feel like a real man.

Her name was Alma and she was seventeen years old. She could obviously pass for legal age but she made sure by coming with her sister, Luisa, who really was harmed much more than she deserved by her sister's control of nature. I was convinced that it would all work out, that Alma loved me as much as I her, convinced that Lee Roy, despite himself, was making a good impression on Luisa, who had her own apartment.

"Lee Roy," I pleaded back at the bar, "her sister is very pretty. Don't you got eyes, man?"

"You take beautiful and I help you out with the other. You think I'm a dumb Mexican?"

Lee Roy ordered himself another beer. He and I had known each other for a while by then, and the truth was that much of our friendship was based on a truce: no racist talk at me. I'm sensitive and irritable about it for obvious and not so obvious reasons, and I've made it clear to him that I don't find it cute. Very seldom does he refer to "Mexicans" around me. Like any good old boy, he loves racial slurs and epithets and finds it very hard to refer to non-white people without calling them something. One time we were in a car and these black guys took a little too long in a crosswalk for Lee Roy—he'd been drinking of course—and he screamed something about niggers. I told him that time that if something came up as a result, he should know whose side I was on, that I wouldn't back nobody up for bullshit like that. I remember it made an impression on him and I was glad. Still, around a group of musicians, after a few shots and chugs, he'd sometimes refer to me as his little Mexican songwriter and partner. He meant it good-naturedly, and I tried to accept it in the same way he did when I talked about him as a white boy.

"Are you that drunk? You're lucky to stand a *chance* with the big sister. Look, *look* at her for a second. If Alma wasn't in the place you'd kill for her. And it's only a miracle that Alma seems to have taken a liking to me. I'm afraid she'll stop drinking and drop me cold."

"Maybe next time, little buddy. I ain't seen all the cards yet to fold my hand."

I should say this. I'm not so little. Lee Roy's about six-four and he's bigger, but lots of times that isn't big enough. I was pissed, but then I wasn't about to let him spoil my evening.

***

Everybody knows that fights don't start over a single incident, not even between strangers. The fight's already there, just waiting, just looking for something to fire it up. You always know when a guy in a bar is there to get into it. Well that guy was staring at Lee Roy, and Lee Roy, who probably wouldn't have cared any less anyway, was too drunk to pay him any attention. This guy was a tall, lean Chicano with a long reach, a man hard and strong in the spirit of Alexis Arguello. What he was saying was that he didn't like it that Lee Roy was drinking Coors. He would've found something else to not like if he had to, there was no question of that. The guy had some hair and he wasn't just in it to take *any* somebody out, he wanted to be challenged. He was also drinking beer, but in his case it was to chase his shots of either whiskey or tequila, I couldn't tell which for sure.

Meanwhile, things were falling in place for me. Alma and I danced and talked and she not only didn't seem to be getting bored, she was interested. Only Luisa wanted to leave. I wasn't sure how to handle this. There were certain questions of manners and taste to be considered, certain complications of Alma's youth. An easy "Let's you and me lose your sister" line wasn't gonna work. The game had to be played by old style conventions, so I had to convince Lee Roy to double date, to entertain big sister.

"Would you come *on*," I begged him. "As a favor to me if nothing else. I'm like having a dream come true here. I can't believe I've met her and that now she wants to be with me. And I swear to God, Luisa likes you, disgusting as you are."

Lee Roy finished a can and asked the waitress to bring him another. He'd won a couple games of eight ball for five dollars a rack. "Nah," he said, examining an angle. "Specially not right now."

I nodded my head and tightened my jaw. I shouldn't have been so surprised but I was.

The waitress came with the beer just as I was about to go back to my table.

"Dígale a su amigo que no compramos Coors aqui," that homeboy told me, "that here the people don't drink racist beer."

I decided to wait where I was a minute. "You can tell him, compa. He'll understand."

Lee Roy looked up. "I don't give a fuck what Mexicans drink or don't drink. They can swallow piss for all I care."

Guys moved away from the center of the room and got closer to the walls, made room. The Chicano's friends moved to his side.

Lee Roy had a pool cue in his hand and had casually brought the heavy end up. "I might need a little help here, partner," he said to me. "Looks like this boy don't think he can go it alone."

I'll be honest. Generally I hate this kind of shit. I dread it and feel very much like trying to work the problem out some other way, say by leaving. It's just not relaxing at all. But my heart pumped for this one. I took a long second. "I'll be there if any other guy jumps in," I told the ones behind the homeboy. "Otherwise," I wanted Lee Roy to understand, "que viva la raza, asshole."

Lee Roy tossed the pool cue onto the table. The Chicano came in first, popping Lee Roy twice with narrow-toe boots and a left-right combination. Lee Roy let him get through with a couple more and grabbed the Chicano by his shirt, unsnapping most of the buttons on it as he flung him and landed two solid blows into a mouth and against a nose. The two of them rolled around a bit and it was anyone's guess who was getting the worst of it. The Chicano was able to get up but missed, locking his boot under Lee Roy's neck, and went down again. They stood up together.

Of course, the excitement around this was intense and enthusiastic, except for the bar owner and his bouncer, who was a football player at the university. You knew that because it said so on his T-shirt. They obviously didn't appreciate the mess and were hollering about police. I really don't think he wanted to, but I suppose the bouncer, a heavy-set black dude, felt an obligation to grab someone, so he reached in for the homeboy, only because he was closer. That was probably a mistake. That Chicano made wind of his fists and the bouncer was against a wall, dazed, before he realized he should have been more polite. When he focused he was mad. Things got out of control at that point. Somebody hit me in the face and I hit him back and Lee Roy was fighting off three guys. Some white guy was helping him out, trying to pull a body off Lee Roy's back. I heard sirens.

I went to Alma and her big sister. They told me to follow them. Since I had the keys, I had the car, and right or wrong it didn't seem fair to leave Lee Roy behind. As tempted as I was, I went back for him. He was a mess, groaning as much as his pride would allow, but I think he was glad I was still friend enough to let him slump over in the back seat.

The fight enhanced things for me considerably. It gave me an excuse to go up to Luisa's apartment, it gave us a mutual story to share and drink coffee over, it made my interest in Alma seem more than just a one night hustle, which it was, but which it wasn't. I killed 'em dead when I got out my guitar and sang a few songs with that swelling, discolored spot on my cheekbone.

Much too forgivingly, Luisa tended to Lee Roy until he finally passed out on the couch. Then she excused herself and went to bed, though not before she gave her little sister a big sister warning about staying up. Alma and I went outside onto the balcony. El Paso's a quiet city under that load of stars and half-moon and wide black sky. Besides ourselves, we could only hear an odd rig on the avenue nearby and a rooster with a bad sense of dawn.

"That's where my dad works," she said, pointing to this unnatural blot of man-made lights on the horizon. "At the smelter."

"Right now he's there?"

"Almost every night."

"So he makes lotsa bucks anyway."

"There's too many of us, and they don't pay that good."

I took a second or two and I kissed her on the neck. "So how come we're talking about your dad?"

"I was thinking about him. He doesn't think I should stay with my sister even one night. He's afraid I'll get myself in trouble."

"Oh?" I wavered. "Have you been getting yourself in trouble?"

She took a second or two. "Tonight's the first time I brought a guy up here."

I had to think of something to say. "I'm telling you, it's true love."

"You always kid around, don't you?"

"I'm serious."

Finally we started making out. We kept at it. She acted seventeen, almost eighteen, about it.

"I gotta make love to you," I told her.

She didn't say anything.

"*Please*. You're so beautiful I can't stand it."

"How come you never write songs in Spanish?"

I moaned loud. She knew what I meant, but waited for my answer. "I dunno. I stopped when I was young. I hang around guys that sing in English."

"You should write some in Spanish."

I nodded. "Tonight's made me think about it." I kissed her again and we made out again. She was getting tired and she broke.

"We'll go in. Where were you gonna sleep?"

"Usually when I stay, on the couch, but Luisa said I should sleep with her."

We went inside and slid the glass door closed. I took one of the blankets off Lee Roy and then rolled him off the couch. I took the cushions. I laid the blanket on top of them, and Alma came back with two more.

"In the kitchen?"

"I'm hungry."

"I never slept with a guy before," she told me slyly.

"And don't you ever sleep with another."

***

Let me tell you, she was the prettiest girl. I was the happiest man to ever fall asleep. Is there any joy greater than sleeping with a woman you've fallen in love with? When she is still becoming one, when that wild sensation of innocence can still prey upon and consume a man's spirit? I had thoughts! My mind soared with possibility and hope, with certainties and destinies. I knew why the Lord put me on this earth, and I loved Him too.

"You won't come back, will you? Otherwise you'd stay."

"Alma, I'm telling you, I'll be back. We just gotta make this gig in Austin. It's a big break for us. Come with me if you want."

"You know I can't."

"It's only a couple nights there. Then I'll come back."

We both went back to sleep, and Lee Roy finally kicked me to wake up late in the morning. "Let's hit the road, Jack." Luisa came out of her bedroom when she heard us talking and offered to make breakfast. She woke up Alma and the two of them whispered and Alma kept the blanket around her and grabbed up her things and headed for the bathroom. I looked at Luisa guiltily. She told me it was love at first sight and I felt better. I offered to go to the store but she insisted that no, we only had to give her our first album when it came out.

"You know," Lee Roy told me, "you were right about big sister. She's a very pretty one. I missed out."

My thinking wasn't too clear about Lee Roy. His face was pretty messed-up though, and I did not feel sorry about that. "I'll have to drive the whole way. You better be able to sing tomorrow night."

"Don't be so tough on me, partner. You know I don't mean no harm."

It was an awkward goodbye. All of us were sleepy and exhausted, Lee Roy and I were hungover, I couldn't say for sure about the sisters, and Alma and I were trying to find the words.

I'll call you when I get there," I said. "It'll only be a few days."

As I drove off, I kept wondering how I was gonna go back, about how I could do it, about what I might be passing up in Austin. Then I got to thinking how all this was a good omen for us, how the muse was with me and wanted me to write my songs, how good it was to be wandering. I pulled over to the side of the highway and stopped in a dry, dusty cloud of desert soil. I took a piss on some hearty flora and told Lee Roy that he had to drive for a while because I wanted to write this tune about El Paso.

"About how I'm gonna go back for her," I told him.

He laughed.

"I'm not lying, man. I think I love her."

He howled out the window.

"You don't believe me?"

Lee Roy kept on laughing. I hopped in the back seat and stretched-out my legs and strummed the guitar with a pencil in my ear and a piece of paper on my lap. The song was about how I danced with the prettiest girl, and I wouldn't ever let Lee Roy sing it. ★

From *Gritos*: Pride

It's almost time to close at the northwest corner of Altura and Copia in El Paso. That means it is so dark that it is as restful as the deepest unremembering sleep, dark as the empty space around this spinning planet, as a black star. Headlights that beam a little cross-eyed from a fatso American car are feeling around the asphalt road up the hill toward the Good Time Store, its yellow plastic smiley face bright like a sugary suck candy. The loose muffler holds only half the misfires, and, dry springs squeaking, the automobile curves slowly into the establishment's lot, swerving to avoid the new self-serve gas pump island. Behind it, across the street, a Texas flag—out too late this and all the nights—pops and slaps in a summer wind that finally is cool.

A good man, gray on the edges, an assistant manager in a brown starched and ironed uniform, is washing the glass windows of the store, lit up by as many watts as Venus, with a roll of paper towels and the blue liquid from a spray bottle. Good night, m'ijo! he tells a young boy coming out after playing the video game, a Grande Guzzler the size of a wastebasket balanced in one hand, an open bag of Flaming Hot Cheetos, its red dye already smearing his mouth and the hand not carrying the weight of the soda, his white T-shirt, its short sleeves reaching halfway down his wrists, the whole XXL of it billowing and puffing in the outdoor gust.

A plump young woman steps out of that car. She's wearing a party dress, wide scoops out of the top, front, and back, its hemline way above the knees.

Did you get a water pump? the assistant manager asks her. Are you going to make it to Horizon City? He's still washing the glass of the storefront, his hand sweeping in small hard circles.

The young woman is patient and calm like a loving mother. I don't know yet, she tells him as she stops close to him, thinking. I guess I should make a call, she says, and her thick-soled shoes, the latest fashion, slap against her heels to one of the pay phones at the front of the store.

Pride is working a job like it's as important as art or war, is the happiness of a new high score on a video arcade game, of a pretty new black dress and shoes. Pride is the deaf and blind confidence of the good people who are too poor but don't notice.

A son is a long time sitting on the front porch where he played all those years with the squirmy dog who still licks his face, both puppies then, even before he played on the winning teams of Little League baseball and City League basketball. They sprint down the sidewalk and across streets, side by side, until they stop to rest on the park grass, where a red ant, or a spider, bites the son's calf. It swells, but he no longer thinks to complain to his mom about it—he's too old now—when he comes home. He gets ready, putting on the shirt and pants his mom would have ironed but he wanted to iron himself. He takes the ride with his best friend since first grade. The hundreds of moms and dads, abuelos y abuelitas, the tios and primos, baby brothers and older married sisters, all are at the Special Events Center for the son's high school graduation. His dad is a man bigger than most, and when he walks in his dress eel-skin boots down the cement stairs to get as close to the hardwood basketball-court floor and ceremony to see—m'ijo!—he feels an embarrassing sob bursting from his eyes and mouth. He holds it back, and with his hands, hides the tears that do escape, wipes them with his fingers, because the chavalitos in his aisle are playing and laughing and they are so small and he is so big next to them. And when his son walks to the stage to get his high school diploma and his dad wants to scream his name, he hears how many others, from the floor in caps and gowns and from around the arena, are already screaming it—could be any name, it could be any son's or daughter's: Alex! Vanessa! Carlos! Veronica! Ricky! Tony! Estella! Isa!—and sees his boy waving back to all of them.

Pride hears gritty dirt blowing against an agave whose stiff fertile stalk, so tall, will not bend—the love of land, rugged like the people who live on it. Pride sees the sunlight on the Franklin Mountains in the first light of morning and listens to a neighbor's gallo—the love of culture and history. Pride smells a sweet, musky drizzle of rain and eats huevos con chile in corn tortillas heated on a cast-iron pan—the love of heritage.

Pride is the fearless reaction to disrespect and disregard. It is knowing the future will prove that wrong.

Seeing the beauty: look out there from a height of the mountain and on the north and south of the Rio Grande, to the far away and close, the so many miles more of fuzz on the wide horizon, knowing how many years the people have passed and have stayed, the ancestors, the ones who have medaled, limped back on crutches or died or were heroes from wars in the Pacific or Europe or Korea or Vietnam or the Persian Gulf, the ones who have raised the fist and dared to defy, the ones who wash the clothes and cook and serve the meals, who stitch the factory shoes and the factory slacks, who assemble and sort, the ones who laugh and the ones who weep, the ones who care, the ones who want more, the ones who try, the ones who love, those ones with shameless courage and hardened wisdom, and the old ones still so alive, holding their grandchildren, and the young ones in their glowing prime, strong and gorgeous, holding each other, the ones who will be born from them. The desert land is rock-dry and ungreen. It is brown. Brown like the skin is brown. Beautiful brown. ★

Arturo Islas

Arturo Islas (1938-1991) was born in El Paso and graduated from El Paso High, earning a Sloan Scholarship to Stanford University. Although he planned to become a neurosurgeon, Islas soon realized his talent for language and literature and went on to earn a B.A., M.A. and Ph.D. from Stanford, becoming one of the first Chicanos in the United States to earn a doctorate in English. Islas remained to teach at Stanford, where he won the Dinkelspiel Award for Outstanding Service to Undergraduate Education in 1976, and became the university's first tenured Chicano faculty member the same year. His first novel, *The Rain God*, part of a planned trilogy about three generations of a Mexican-American family much like his own, won the best fiction prize from the Border Regional Library conference in 1985 and was selected as one of three best novels by the Bay Area Reviews Association in 1984. The second novel of the trilogy was titled *Migrant Souls*. Interviewed in 1990, Islas characterized the reluctance of East Coast publishers to publish Chicano literature as "a willful ignorance on the part of the machines that produce the books that we read." Islas was working on the last book of the trilogy when he died of AIDS-related complications. *La Mollie and the King of Tears* was published posthumously.

From *La Mollie and the King of Tears*: Just Like Romeo and Juliet

I ain't one to give up on things too easy, but leaning there against my brother's car with the pain shooting through my leg like one of them tracer bullets, I woulda given a lot for someone to tuck me in. It was the first time since they let me outta that V.A. loony bin that I missed it and wished I was back there chewing up pills like they was steak and sleeping my days away. I was gonna need more than Mr. Johnson's avocado to get me home to La Mollie's arms. I figured Tomás'd be my ticket if I could just find him in that after-hours joint up the alley. With about ten more motorcycles, parked in the alley and what seemed like all the leather queers this side of New York buzzing around the door of the place, I shoulda had some clue what was going on in there, but I wasn't thinking so clear. I headed down the alley, keeping myself together by saying the names of some of them sweet breads la Pixie used to buy at the Aracataca Bakery on the corner of Florence and Paisano Drive.

There are two important buildings in every barrio, man—the church and the bakery. Whenever I felt a lotta pain, I used to say bread names like a rosary. I been doing it for what seems like forever. It always used to make the guys in the gang laugh, though some of em coulda used their own homemade mantra, all cut up after a skirmish against the Fatherless Gang. The draft took care of mosta that, though there are still forty- and fifty-year-old gang members hanging around El Chuco. Them old Ace of Spades brothers still got their heads in the same place, man. And the younger guys' heads are all messed up with drugs. It's just ugly. Nothing stays the same, except them Mexican sweet breads.

That Aracataca baked magic. Mr. and Mrs. García got the bakery after her parents died and kept all the old recipes. They were good people. La Pixie knew the family real well so we got special treatment and free extras whenever we went there.

We never could figure out which one did the baking. One day she was out helping the customers and the next we saw him. Mrs. García looked like a pharmacist in a starched white apron and her hair pulled back in a bun. He looked like a *chamuco*—that's my favorite Mexican sweet bread, man, and there ain't no English word for it. He had a thick moustache and these big dark eyes that were always gleaming like he knew some secret we all needed to get into heaven, and it was gonna come to us in the very next bite. Maybe that's why at Christmas time he always played one of them Magi.

I wish I could tell you the names of them sweet breads in Spanish, man, cause changing em to English makes em lose their flavor. Don't get me wrong, neither. I think everybody needs to know English to get by in this country—the real English, not that liar's language the businessmen, lawyers, and politicians use. Don't even get me started on those dollar-bill words and sentences we're supposed to learn cause it ain't English. I'm glad Miss Harper ain't around no more to hear it. I know she'd say it was deader than Latin and nowheres near as beautiful. I even like Shakespeare's language better than that gobbledygook. Now that's a word, man. La Mollie taught it to me. Sounds like a description of turkey shit.

I don't want everybody to speak like me—that would be boring—but I don't want no one telling me I can't talk this way neither. And all this caca about which is the real mother tongue—our language is accents, man, like Virgil's and yours and mine. There's only one language that counts anyway. Ain't you gonna ask me what that is? The language of the heart, man, and most times you don't even need words to speak it.

That was the way them Garcías talked, man, with their hearts. Their bakery smelled like music. Right away you opened the door and took a whiff you left reality. Them smells was a jungle of delight—gingerbread pigs came out steaming on a tray, the egg bread knew exactly how far to rise, the Mexican rolls tasted better than any sourdough I ever ate.

The Garcías was wizards, man, and they could turn plain old flour, milk, and sugar into sweet breads called *novias*, *libros*, and *campechanas*. Get this. Them names mean "brides," "books," and "little old ladies you can talk to about your problems." Ain't that a kick? I love them names as much as the tastes of the bread.

So while I'm gimping over to the entrance of this Harley joint looking for Marlon Brando and his gang from *The Wild One*, I'm saying my Mexican sweet bread prayer to get me there. "*Chamuco . . . Laberinto . . . Pedo de monja* . . . And so on. I already told you about the first name. The second you can figure out. That third one means "nun's fart," man, ain't that something? And it's called that cause it's a real delicate, paper-thin tube that's filled with lotsa white goo. I never liked to eat em too much, but I sure got a lotta mileage outta the name. La Mollie, of course, don't believe that any bread would be called that. I wish I could tell you all the names, man. Too bad you only know English.

So taste by taste I'm getting to the front door of that place, which as I get closer I can see is called The Mind Shaft and where I'm deciding all the motorcycle fairies in San Francisco must be having their after-hours coffee and seeing who they're gonna hit on to help em make it through the night. I'm praying that Tomás is gonna be sitting at a table right near the front door so's I don't have to walk around giving everyone the wrong idea. Like I told you, man, I can't even think about sex without tits around. Real soft ones.

I got a friend named Lou and she knows what I mean. She's always teasing me and telling me I'm nothing but a lesbian trapped in the body of a macho man. Hell, man, I admit it. I love the taste of women. Lou was married and had three kids before she looked real close at herself and saw that where she wanted to be was with another woman. Her husband wasn't around too much anyways, so she took the kids and found this lady Sarah within two years. They're out in the Sunset district cause Lou wanted her kids to go to old-fashioned neighborhood schools and get that basic readin', writin', and 'rithmetic stuff. And she's had a good life with Sarah for almost twenty years now. Sarah is one of them gourmet cooks and even though La Mollie naturally don't understand two women making it with each other, whatever she pretends about it, she loves the way Sarah makes us this stuff you never even seen in restaurants and serves it to us on a plate that looks like a painting. To me, all that stuff tastes just like it looks, but I love them women cause they take care of each other.

I'm limping like a dog that just got it from some car by the time I get to the door of The Mind Shaft. There's this short, fat guy with a scruffy beard taking money and pushing back the crowd waiting to get in. I ain't got but a few coins in my pocket and I'm not about to give them away.

"One dollar," the fat guy says, pretending not to notice the way I'm dragging my leg.

"Hey, man, I just wanna see if my little brother's in there. I need a ride home."

This guy is even more round up close and looks like a ball in drag with handcuffs on the side. He looks down at my leg, then right into my face. I don't want him to think I'm interested in bouncing him up and down, but I know enough to look back real vulnerable.

"Sweetheart," he says in a Bogie voice, "we're all looking for our little brothers when we're not looking for Daddy. Go on in but I'm only giving you twenty minutes to find him and then I'm coming after you myself." He says something to somebody behind this big black vinyl curtain and then looks at me real hard one more time.

"Are you a cop?" he asks me.

"Me? Hell no, man. I hate the fuzz." I act real injured that he would even ask me that question.

"Too bad," he says all serious. "Cop types are my biggest turn-on. Leave your driver's license or drop your pants and show me your collateral," he says, like they're the same thing. "Your choice."

I dig out my license and leave it with him. "Cute picture," he says, and pulls the vinyl curtain aside so's I can go in.

I can tell pretty quick this ain't no pajama party at Hernando's Hideaway. There's a bar with a coupla guys drinking stuff outta styrofoam cups that glow in the blacklight. I don't see no tables or chairs, just benches along the sides where a buncha dudes are sitting or standing. Mosta the guys don't have hardly no clothes on, except for a couple in the corner dressed like Marines and one cowboy standing at the bar with his ten-gallon hat down low over his face. The only thing I can tell for sure is who's wearing contact lenses cause the light makes em glow green in the dark. I hate blacklight, man—it's even creepier than the lights in here. The whole place smells like leather and Clorox and guys working out in a gym. Sorta like the men's room in the Cathedral High swimming pool in El Chuco, man, where me and my buddies used to terrorize them middle-class Chicanas from Sister Abigail's catechism class.

Not even *cucuys* would walk into this place, man, and there I am clunking my cast across the room and trying not to have no one notice. I don't see Tomás nowheres and I probably wouldn't recognize him if I did unless he talked to me. I do one of them Wild Bill Hickoks and go for a corner where my back's covered. I figure I'm pretty safe where the bar meets one wall and nobody can get behind me unless they force it.

There's some real loud disco music coming from the next room with a coupla minutes of opera shit thrown in. Disco ain't music to me, man. It's nothing but electronic noise with a lotta screaming, and I hate it even more than opera. But after about a minute I figure out that what I'm hearing ain't coming outta no speakers. What I thought was a disco beat now's sounding more like somebody getting whipped, and that opera screeching is making me think of people dying. And not soon enough to suit me, man.

The guys reeling in from the other room are real sweaty and panting just a little. Most of em don't even bother to put no clothes back on. I'm starting to catch on that they ain't just dancing in there and I just hope Tomás don't got no part in it, cause no way am I gonna leave my spot against the wall to go next door and look for him. I'm beginning to be glad that la Pixie ain't alive to see that her boys spend their nights lost in some south-of-Market Babylon for fairies.

Somebody has sent me this icy mug of beer and even though I could use one right now more than a footrest, I don't even leave a fingerprint in the frost. I don't look up to see who the bartender points to as my benefactor, and I just barely have the nerve to take a peek at the guy that's standing next to me. I don't remember that he was there before. I'm sure I woulda noticed, cause what I see just about does me in, man. He's all naked except for a pair of boots, a cowboy hat, and about a dozen clothespins clamped onto diffrent parts of his body, even down there, where I never dreamed I would see one.

We used to have some pretty crude initiation ceremonies in our gang, man, but nothing like this. We only pretended we were gonna hurt guys where it hurts the most—we never actually did it. This dude made me thinka them stories about Indian tribes and the kindsa rituals they put young bucks through before they'd make it to manhood. He made me forget all about my own pain just thinking about what it must feel like to be pinched like that in the you-know-what. He noticed the look on my face and asked real matter-of-fact, "Are you into pain?"

"Actually," I tell him, trying to sound just as casual and like I don't really care what's going on or what he's got on, "my leg hurts like hell. I just broke it."

"Oh, too bad. You're serious. I thought that was your costume for the night and that you were just looking for some one to play doctor. I thought it was pretty clever and told myself I might try that next time so I could get somebody in this hole to notice me." He's telling me all this as calm as calm can be, sipping from a beer bottle and looking towards the vinyl curtain and not missing nobody that walks in. "I like doctor scenes, especially when they include water sports."

"What're water sports?" I ask him. I need to hang onto words cause I'm starting to really see and hear and smell what's going on around me. I feel about as ignorant as Sonia's mom in that confessional, man. Oh, Virgil, where are you now?

I like to think there ain't nothing I can't say, but I ain't gonna talk about that Mind Shaft. I'm only gonna tell you that them dudes weren't just standing and sitting around chit-chatting. They were getting right down to business there in front of everybody like it was the most natural thing in the world, and I'm thinking I better get outta there before I do run into Tomás and embarrass him and me. But I'm telling you, man, what them sissies can take is more than any straight guy I ever known could take or would want to. I gotta hand it to them fruits—they can handle pain better than me.

"You don't know about water sports?" Mr. Clothespins asks me with a real amused look on his face, the first expression I seen on it since we started talking. "Come on in the back. They have a water sports room here. I'll show you what they are."

Well, I figure he ain't talking about no tubs and rubber duckies and so I stay as cool as I can. "No thanks," I say. "Maybe next time." And I start thumping my way back to the door cause I'm hearing the twenty-minute clock ticking away and I can see Mr. Ball's head peering around the vinyl curtain looking for me.

I wanted to make a quick exit, or as quick as I could manage in my condition, so naturally I tripped and bumped into guys all the way out. I started sweating real heavy like everybody else there and then, at the door, I ran right into Mr. Ball's round, round belly.

"It's real hot in here," I tell him, not knowing what else to say except what's under my nose. And outta nowhere he's blowing three breaths, real quick and real cool and not bad smelling neither, right into my sweaty face. They kept me from passing out, man, I really believe it, cause I was on the edge. I shoulda thanked him probably but all I wanted to do was get my license and fade away.

"Did you find your little brother?" he asks, like he really cares.

"No, but that's okay. I'll find a way to get back home. Don't worry about it." I'm feeling real uncomfortable about everything, man.

"Well, honey" Mr. Ball says, giving me the once over and squeezing my biceps. "If I wasn't on duty, I'd take you home. I can play little brother real good and wouldn't mind showing you how good it can be. Or how bad, if that's what you're into."

"Thanks," I tell him. "But I got a woman waiting for me."

He lets out a big whoop, louder than the opera singer, who's still screeching away, and helps me hang on to the slippery curtain—there was grease all over it, man—to keep from tripping. At the door he tells me real confidential, "That's what they all say when they look in the mirror baby. You come back soon."

Maybe I didn't hear him right cause I was fighting with that stupid curtain, but I been thinking about what he said about looking in the mirror and I can't come up with what he meant.

"Yeah, sure," I tell him, not knowing what to say. "Thanks, man." The fresh air hits my lungs like a baseball bat.

Fast as my leg lets me, I move on down to the end of the block. All outta breath and trying real hard not to pass out, I sit on the curb, put my head on my knees, and wait for my soul to drive by and pick me up, cause I was more tired than I ever been in my life. That dumb comet was making me look at things I ain't never seen or ever wanna see again.

When I was making all them phone calls this morning trying to keep the *cucuys* away before you and your listening machine showed, I called Tomás to tell him where I was and I asked him about them sports. He laughed real loud and told me I didn't wanna know.

"I seen your car near that place, Tomás. Were you there?" The big brother in me couldn't keep from asking.

"It's none of your business, Louie," he say real tough. "But if you want to know, no, I wasn't. I loaned my car to a friend and as a matter of fact, he hasn't brought it back. Maybe he's still there."

I was relieved. I wanted to tell him how it really was with la Mollie but I knew I'd start crying and then he'd start worrying about me and I didn't wanna upset him. So I told him she was doing okay and that we was just waiting to get the release papers and some pills for her pain.

"I can go get groceries for you and Mollie," he said. "Just tell me what you need."

"No, it's okay. We'll stop at the Safeway on the way home." I was trying to be real light but I could tell he knew something was going on.

"Well, let me know," he said. "And Louie, forget about the water sports, okay? Cause if you ask me about them again, I'm going to tell you what they are. You won't like it. Call me if you need anything."

"I will," I told him, but I didn't wanna be asking him for help right then cause I was still so sad about what I'd seen in that bar. I needed Virgil Spears to talk to me about this, man. I know he coulda told me how come them guys needed to get into each other's guts like that. And I was thinking about Tomás, too, and having a real hard time figuring out how he lived his life. I didn't hate him or feel disgusted, just real sorry, man, sorta like my heart'd been busted by that drum stead of my shin.

I kept seeing pictures of all them dudes connected to each other in these weird ways, like their bodies were machines and could be bent and stretched in all directions. Nobody was laughing, neither—just making noises like the kind people make when they ache or want something. Kinda like being hungry, only the kinda hunger you feel when you ate plenty but you're still starving. Like there's lotsa food in front of you on the table and you don't really wanna eat no more, but you just put the nearest goodie in your mouth and chew away til it's gone anyways. And then you find the goodies are still there even after you eat em, so you start again.

It was eerie, man—not *cucuy* eerie but human eerie— and I recognized the old demon lust winking in the background of all them pictures I couldn't erase from my head. That monster was the one putting oil all over that vinyl curtain, I'm sure of it. I had to keep telling myself that it was only a buncha guys doing all that stuff and not no extraterrestrials. Maybe the whole thing felt strange to me cause there weren't no women around and women always bring something mysterious into any room. They don't even have to say nothing. Just one woman in a room fulla guys will change everything. Ever notice that?

I still don't know what it was that got in my skin about that place, but it had me stuck there in the alley so's I couldn't of moved if Sherman's army'd showed up. I sat on the curb breathing deep til the world began to turn to the sun again and that white soft light before dawn chased any ghosts or *cucuys* around the block and back to where they came from. There wasn't even any fairies on the street by that time. I was alone, just sitting and breathing. I knew then that my soul weren't coming for me in no stretch limo, man. I had to go and claim it. So after awhile I got up and tried putting some weight on the broken leg. It hurt but I knew I could make it as far as Market Street and catch the trolley that would take me outta this end-of-the-world night.

You can count on Market Street to be there, man, cutting across San Pancho from the Ferry Building to Twin Peaks. We call them peaks *las chi-chis*, so you can figure out what that makes Market Street. Market don't care that the streets that run into it are forced to make ninety-degree turns and still keep the same name. If that confuses everybody, that ain't its fault. It just goes its own way, man, and lets the rest of the town readjust.

You know what? I think the earth gods put San Francisco on a fault line to keep it from ever getting too stuck on itself. Anything that beautiful would get spoiled real fast without nothing to threaten it. To lotsa people, San Francisco is a beautiful woman floating face-up on the Pacific. When she ain't floating, man, she walks on water and turns into clouds carrying you along. She's better than a fairytale city, specially in the morning when the earth and the light are meeting again after being separated so long by the night. Then she shines in the sun with a tender glow.

Down on the flat part of Market Street near the Tenderloin, where I dragged myself onto it like a injured wet rat on a dry drunk, I could start making out the winos. They were stretched out against doorways where the warm air coming through the cracks from inside them big buildings kept em from catching pneumonia. Some of the real old people that live in them run-down hotels between Mission and Market were out for their stroll of the day cause dawn's the safest time for em to take it. A couple of em across the street looked like fat birds all wrapped up in Salvation Army coats. Others just looked like slow-moving bundles of blankets. One of them little old ladies took one look at me clunking towards her and said, real cheery like she knew me, "Good morning. You look like you had a real good time, you handsome devil," and she passed on by, like an owl on its way to some church in the branches. Them old people are the real extraterrestrials, man. Most of em are ready for outer space. Anything's better than living on Social Security in one of them rooms in the Anglo Hotel.

The Muni stop is your world's headquarters for trashy newspapers, man, with one vending machine after another lined up all along the street. And that morning la Mollie coulda written the headlines for em all: WORLD ENDS TODAY, and COMET TO COLLIDE WITH EARTH, and THE END IS HERE, KAHOUTEK KONQUERS; with a "k"—not too bad, you know. I like "k's." I didn't have no extra change to buy one for la Mollie and still pay for the ride back to her, even though I wanted to let her read about it before it happened. The first coupla paragraphs I could see through them little vending windows don't tell me more than what I know already from la Mollie, but it was like them newspapers were glad the world was gonna end.

I don't get it. It's scary, man, the way a lotta people really believe we're all gonna get blown up so why bother. Since it says right there in the Bible that it's gonna happen, they spend all their time getting prepared stead of thinking about if they might be able to change things. I think they're making it happen, man, living their lives waiting for the end like that. I wonder if they're gonna have time to say "I told you so" when the first missile or comet or whatever hits em.

I didn't even look to see what the headline on the *Chronicle* was. That paper's just one giant cartoon. The ones in El Paso ain't no better, but at least they don't pretend to care about what's going on in the rest of the world, and their letters to the editor are a lot more fun cause every one they print is written by some wacko survivalist high on patriotism or on some candy cane picture of Jesus.

But a coupla minutes before the Judah Street trolley opens its doors to let me in, I'm standing behind some guy who's holding up the *Chron* in front of his face. And he's reading something about a high school girl in the East Bay who was saved by the heart of the boyfriend she turned down. He managed to off himself just to will her his heart so she'd never reject him again and they'd go on ticking away their days together forever. I tell you, life and the *Chronicle* come up with some doozies. I started wondering how the old boyfriend managed to kick the bucket just to convenience her.

"Musta been a Mexican," I said to the driver, who just ignored me and was only interested in seeing I put exactly the right amount of change into the collecting machine. Only a Mexican can love like that. Even if you reject me, I'll still die for you and see that you get my fresh and pounding heart so's you can go on to other lovers. It comes from our Aztec background, man, and all them sacrifices we made to get the sun to come up every day. We knew it wouldn't do it without us.

There was only two old guys in long black coats on the bus and they're sitting near the rear exit and looking like they just came from a flashers' convention. I gotta confess that I mighta seen anything then I was so delirious from being so tired and the feeling that I was finally on my way back home. Unless Kahoutek hit us before we got through the tunnel, I was gonna hold my sweet sweet honey close to me again.

The trolley moved like one of them slow-motion shots of a marshmallow melting above a low flame. It stopped at every single corner like it was waiting for permission to cross the street. Once, it got unhooked from its connection and the driver got out to fix it and everything else that was wrong on the planet Earth. It took him ten hours to get back in. And when I finally got off and hit the sidewalk just two blocks from la Mollie's bed, I heard something snap near my left hip.

But I was too close to worry about that none. Them blocks was definitely life in dream-time, man. Every love scene in every movie I ever saw went running through my head in wavy ripples that made me feel like I been drinking again and didn't know where or how or what. The scenes and the characters and the movie stars got all mixed up, and I was playing in em all. It was a giant Mexican mural of Hollywood starring me, Louie Mendoza, of course!

I was Rhett Butler saying goodbye to Scarlett and asking her to kiss me like she was sending me off to war. I could feel the sting of her slap across my face. I was even that flake Ashley Wilkes coming back to Tara with Melanie running towards him down the road. I got the goose-bumps, man. Then I was Rick in Paris with the Kid, and then looking at her at the Casablanca airport, their two big hats kissing each other above their eyes cause they couldn't never kiss each other's lips again. That movie is the love story of them two hats, man.

I was Paul Henried handing Charlotte Vale a whole branch of camellias, then lighting both their cigarettes, handing her one over and over til they both took a puff and the smoke came between them like sex. Nicotine addicts in love. I turned into Gregory Peck and Jennifer Jones hunting each other down in the desert and killing their passion cause it was too hot for them to handle. The desert faded into a jungle and I was Tarzan swimming towards Jane with Cheeta on the shore doing back-flips and going into a chimpanzee ecstasy.

Right as I reached the bottom of the front steps—miracle of movie miracles—everything and everybody dissolved into Elizabeth Taylor's eyes. Them eyes are the reason the movies were invented, man. There I was, Monty Clift before his accident, looking into them and hearing Angela Vickers say in the biggest and greatest all-time close-up ever, "Come to Momma. Come to Momma." I thought my heart was gonna jump outta my chest and rush up them stairs ahead of me.

I put the key in the door real quiet and got my leg in without banging it on nothing. It musta been about 7 or 8 A.M. so I thought la Mollie was still asleep upstairs. I didn't know nothing about her night and what she found out, or thought she did, about what happened at Big Eddie's.

After all I'd been through, I didn't wanna try and call out cause I wanted her to see me first in all my glory. But I needed a drink of water real bad before I tried climbing the stairway to heaven and her, so I made my way slow and quiet to the kitchen at the end of the hall, dragging that cast along the floor so's it seemed to whisper.

When I got there, man, I saw la Mollie standing at the sink. She had her back to me and was in that see-through robe she had on a million hours ago back yesterday morning, with that pink skin of hers showing all hazy through the gauzy stuff. She was looking into them dishes piled up in the sink like she'd lost something. I could tell she was hanging on to the front of the porcelain real tight, like for dear sweet life, but still I didn't know why. All I could see was that I'd made it back to my woman, where I never wanted to leave again. Even Elizabeth Taylor's eyes weren't nothing to la Mollie's back shining at me through that shady wrapper of hers. ★

Denise Chávez

Novelist, short story writer, playwright, and actor Denise Chávez has her roots in New Mexico, Texas, and Mexico. Born in New Mexico, she calls Las Cruces and El Paso her "two home towns." Chávez received an M.F.A. in Drama from Trinity University and an M.A. in Creative Writing from the University of New Mexico. Her novels include *Face of an Angel*, which won the 1995 Premio Aztlán and the American Book Award, and *Loving Pedro Infante*, recipient of a Lannan Foundation grant. She was the 2003 Hispanic Heritage Foundation Award Honoree at Kennedy Center. The title story of her short story collection *The Last of the Menu Girls* has been published in the *Norton Anthology of American Literature*. Her play *The Flying Tortilla Man* has been published extensively in anthologies for young people, and she wrote a children's book entitled *The Woman Who Knew the Language of Animals*. Growing up in a family of storytellers, she identifies with that oral tradition and calls herself a "performance writer." In her writing, she refuses to italicize Spanish words, not wanting to set them apart in any way. She is a regular contributor to *New Mexico Magazine* and *Latina Magazine* and a former newspaper columnist for *The Ink*, a Las Cruces art newspaper. Her essay "Crossing Bitter Creek" was published in *Writing Down the River*, a collection of essays about rafting down the Colorado River. She has toured her one-woman show Women in the State of Grace throughout the United States. Chávez is the artistic director of the highly successful Border Book Festival and is also the founder of Sin Fronteras, Writers Without Borders. Her latest book is *A Taco Testimony: Meditations on Family, Food and Culture*, published in 2006. She is currently at work on a novel *The King and Queen of Comezón*, a collection of stories called *El Inglés Tan Bonito*, and a screenplay based on *Loving Pedro Infante*.

The McCoy Hotel

Here's your key, Mrs. Chávez. Mrs. Madrid is in 417. The elderly clerk handed the usual key to my mother. Room 415. The McCoy Hotel. El Paso, Texas.

It was a key that signified so much to the women in our family. To my mother this key was a grateful respite from her duties as a third grade teacher, a divorced mother of three children, two of us still at home.

When she had this key there was no rushing to her charges, no small children crowding around, waiting to be soothed. There was no return to feverish midday meals or anxious waits for that long awaited child-support check, the one that never came.

My mother's every day worries disappeared on those days at the McCoy Hotel. Her life there was not like her other life, which was always rushed, and filled with disappointment and disillusionment.

My mother's days started with early morning mass after which she would return home to get us out of bed and make our breakfast. Oatmeal is what we ate every day; there was never any change. My sister Margo and I always left our oatmeal untouched, complaining about its texture. It was always cold, lumpy as well and could literally be lifted out of the saucepan like an unbroken grey mold.

Time not having improved its taste, and barely noticing it, mother would eat the oatmeal hours later, sitting in front of the television set during her lunch break from school, her keen ears tuned to the news of the world's ever-altering events.

To my sister and I, both scrawny, underdeveloped and sensitive teenagers who craved all of life with its experience, its awakening mystery and passion, the McCoy Hotel meant freedom from the confines of our female-only home, our girls-only school, and our angry, unresponding Father-God dominated religion that clouded and affected every aspect of our lives which always seemed to be on hold, waiting prayerfully for some better day, some happier time, when the three of us women would know completion, transformation, not of a self-determining kind, but one dependent on someone else, someone who would ease us out from the unspoken prison of our lives, decidedly male.

All of our lives turned ever so delicately upon this unspoken tenet of unshakeable faith. To be happy you must be loved by a man. This is what my mother yearned for. That is what she taught us to desire with all our hearts.

What I wanted at that time was freedom from that inescapable world where one man, invisible, irresponsible, unpleasant and selfish, ruled our every waking thought, and determined every future action.

When my mother was released from her daily chores or her weekly responsibilities and discovered herself at the McCoy Hotel, her bowed back at once straightened up. She became another woman, lively, even more beautiful than she was, her long, dark-brown hair in a bun, her intense face, with its burning, deep-set brown eyes that of another woman, someone I barely knew. This new woman was open to possibility, joyful with hope.

At these times my mother was not the driven, burden-tormented, long-suffering warden of our misery, a divorced mother of two growing, demanding young woman who struggled every inch of the way for individual freedom. She was someone else, almost a stranger.

My mother, having stood so much for so long, now bore the physical and emotional scars of all those years of suffering: a hunched back, bad legs with inflamed, pulsating varicose veins, an inability to sleep throughout the night, an over-reactive fear of men, all men, who could only hurt and deceive, as well as a sense of overriding anxiety that all her worst fears would come to pass. She worried if my sister and I were too close to the edge of a stairway, if we were too hot, too cold, if we were in the bathroom too long, or not long enough, if our hair was up or down, and if we did go somewhere, who we were with, for how long and why.

Our weekends at the McCoy Hotel, in downtown El Paso, were freedom to the three of us from our life in the small southern New Mexico town of Las Cruces, city of Christian martyrs, ever-present crosses.

The McCoy Hotel was just off the plaza and Mesa Street. A structure of only six stories, it seemed much taller in those days. It was situated south, facing away from the plaza toward México and the many liquor stores and Tiendas de Rebajas, discount clothing stores that lined the street that became the Old Bridge we used to cross into Juárez at ten cents a car.

The hotel, while old, was quite respectable. The rooms were plain, but unusually clean for all the wildness of the border life outside its walls.

Our room had double beds that faced a moderate-sized mirror on the opposite wall, underneath which was a small basin with an overhead ledge that held two glasses turned upside down. They were wrapped in transparent, shiny, semi-waxy paper and stood next to a small pitcher of lukewarm water. That good "Texas water" my mother always bragged about.

To one side of the mirror was the bathroom door, connecting our room to that of my Tía Chita, my mother's young sister. She lived in Redford, Texas, a town of around fifty people, where she owned, along with her seldom seen, less often heard husband, a small, but prosperous grocery store.

When we stayed at the McCoy Hotel, we invariably stayed with my aunt, who'd come into town only the night before to see her doctor, or to check up on some insurance policy or other business matter.

The two sisters were always happy to see each other, sharing among themselves memories and stories of their days on the farm in West Texas, in a town called El Polvo, the Dust.

To my Tía Chita, El Paso was like New York City. For us, it was a new and novel, ever-expanding civilization that existed before our time and would be there long after we were gone.

In the McCoy Hotel, the rooms were shared by two sets of sisters, one young, the other much older, both still working on their relationships to each other, always at odds. In the shaded darkness of those rooms, both groups of sisters sought respite from the intense summer heat, the inescapable sun, tormentingly male.

The McCoy Hotel was a meeting ground between family, a place we all came to further knowledge of our separate lives. Here we found those secret sins we now confessed to each other. No matter how much we fought, quietly and then with anger, or how much we cried, hard to ourselves and then softly to our other sister half, the McCoy was always for us a place we loved, a place of love, despite our waning youth.

Our room and my aunt's was connected by a white and black-checkered tile bathroom. It contained an old fashioned tub with heavy knobby gold splayed feet that lifted the tub high off the floor.

During the daytime, both doors leading to the bathroom remained open, allowing free access to either side of our mutual suite. At night, either side of women closed the door that led to the bathroom. When the bathroom was in use, whichever side happened to be inside locked the door as well and ran the faucet to muffle any sounds.

I rarely went into my Tía Chita's room. It seemed very far away, despite its close proximity to us, our side, centered by those familiar double beds, sheets crisp with starch, the blankets thin but soft.

In all the years we'd stayed at the McCoy, it never changed. The lobby was always the same, with its red high-backed metal chairs, the paneled reception desk near the elevator, small end tables scattered here and there, with months-old magazines. The ancient, still functional elevator, with a creaky metal door you had to swing sideways, to the left, to open, locked into place once it was closed.

EEEEEEKKKKKKKKRRRRRRR! The metal door slid shut, the tired machine slowly revved up and creakily it ascended, coming to a not uncommon jumpy false stop as the elevator sought the right stoppage point, finally resting midway between floors. Through the firm doors with their ornate black grates could be seen a hallway, indistinguishable from the other five, with dark carpet, chairs and ceiling fan.

All those weekends visits to the McCoy Hotel melded into two strong memories. One of them was the magical time of my eagerly sought, never truly won, adolescence. I was a child then, still under the rule of my mother, who dictated my life. The other memory is as strong, and defined a period of setting forward into young adulthood, with its time of rebellion. Each of those phases marked a chapter in my life as discovered at the McCoy Hotel.

As a young teenager, I was very agitated by most everything. I felt trapped in a world I could never escape, confined to mediocrity, a pale, thin, over-protected girl to whom imagination was both fearful and a blessing. When we were at the McCoy, I became, like my mother, a new person, startled, and then emboldened by my budding maturity, and then challenged by possibility.

One afternoon, in summer, when I was thirteen, just learning to assert my growing adulthood, I left our room and wandered down the long, grey hallway.

I peered down the mysterious stairs, then ran quickly, breathlessly, back to get my sister, who sat in bed, reading. My mother was in Tía Chita's room. She lay across her sister's bed, stripped down to her brassiere, wet towels holding her uncomfortably large breasts in place.

There was no air conditioning, and all the windows were open. The ceiling fan swathed a circular path near the top of the high room, displacing and then correcting the hot air. Tía Chita, as relaxed as she ever became, wore a dark blue cotton robe and slippers, her knee-high hose held up by her soft, pink rubber-covered ligas, or garters. The two women talked quietly to themselves, the way people do in extreme heat, slowly, with as little breath as possible, conserving what energy they have.

Eagerly, I begged Margo to join me in my wanderings, and just as enthusiastically she replied that she would.

I liked to sneak around. I loved to be afraid. We both did. We liked to imagine things that would never come to pass. What if the building caught on fire? Who's the man in the far end room? I think he's in love with me. What if the elevator didn't work and stopped between floors and we were trapped in there with the man from the far end room? How many floors are there? Are there really only six? What if there was a secret floor that no one except us knows about? Imagine living in a hotel!

My questions grew bolder and so did my movements. Slithering through the cool, darkened hallway to the stairway, I climbed up one flight of stairs, then another, urging my little sister forward.

Afterwards, we ventured down the elevator to the lobby, controlling the lever manually. Amazement, terror, and joy ruled us as we stared at the open floor moving past us. Fighting to control the lever led to us coming to a bumping and prolonged stop. Landing between floors, Margo jumped out. More afraid, despite my age, I followed her, a somewhat timid explorer who tiptoed through the silent, tunnel-like hallway to the guest sitting room, where a solitary old man sat staring out into space.

There were no television sets or radios in the sitting rooms, much less in any of the guest rooms; the only form of entertainment was watching other human life. Few children stayed at the hotel with their parents. I never saw anyone near my age. The clientele was older, monosyllabic, long past their fecund time. The lobby clerk and his wife were elderly as well, ever polite to us, in a dry, stiff-smiling, girdle-harnessed, yellow false teeth sort of way. We jeered and made fun of them behind their backs, because we didn't know to react to courtesy and deference from people so much older than ourselves. So, with a cruel and rude cynicism we allowed them to wait on us, little princesses come in from the heat.

In the presence of the older clerk and his wife, I felt mature, comfortable with myself, not just another person, but one younger, stronger, more alive, not exhausted and frustrated by a life nearly over, like theirs, or my mother's or my aunt's, both passed over in quiet and relentless desperation; lives lived not in the present, but in a never-arriving future, with heated nightly dreams and a what-might-have-been past.

I knew I wasn't so well behaved, or so nice, but what I did know was how special I was, if only to myself. I felt my life full of meaning. Surrounded by so many people, so many stories, feelings, I couldn't exactly explain why I felt so different, in the body that I wore then, an ill-fitting outer skin that wasn't really me, not the inside of me that was hidden to everyone, even myself: the spirit of the woman I longed to become.

I got off in the lobby. Margo followed. Sitting in a stiff chair, I looked out into the street, half-shaded by a set of merciful blinds, the hot sun boring small holes into my consciousness. Unable to effect longed-for freedom, I returned to our room, to rest from all that longing. It tired me like nothing else ever did. Unable to explain my bad mood to Margo, I said nothing as my mother came out of the bathroom, trying on a new dress.

Pulling it over her head, the bodice stuck halfway and she called frantically to me to help her. She was trapped. Her large, humid breasts were caught in a vise of cloth. Flattened and punched down, at that moment they seemed more of a bother than something to be proud of. I was glad to be myself then, flat-chested, without that burden of softened flesh to drag around, continually subdue.

Extricating Mother from that already zippered dress took some time and was embarrassing for all three of us. Breathy, with tiny beads of sweat near her hairline, Mother was finally freed with one last tug.

My mother's large impressive body was something she could never escape, try as she might, day or night.

Nights she slept in the nude, and it was not uncommon to walk by her room to find her, head facing the window, swaddled like the statue of a carved Greek torso in her thin sheet, her wet towel draped over her prominent chest that heaved and sighed.

Did everyone's mother sleep in the nude? I didn't think so.

In that second phase of the McCoy Hotel when I was older and had begun to define myself, we stayed at the hotel for the last time.

My mother, ever-devoted chaperone, now served as a group mother to eight thespians who earlier had participated in a speech tournament in El Paso. She assigned rooms. My friend Ellen and I drew a room connected to my mother's, much to our dismay. Ellen and I slept in one adjoining room, my mother and sister in the other. The six girls were spread out between two nearby rooms, all interconnecting, with promises to behave.

I wondered: would Mother sleep in the nude this night? I hoped not.

I whispered to Ellen in the darkness.

My mother sleeps in the nude.

She does?

Yes. She sleeps with her head at the foot of the bed, her legs facing the headboard, her head near the window, so she can feel the breeze, a fan on the chest of drawers aimed at her head, her long hair fanned out on a small, soft pillow like a baby's under her head. Like that, nude. And when she's alone, she locks all the doors and does her housework in the nude.

No!

Yes, she does! She's told me.

No!!

She says it feels good that way.

Reaaallly?

In the summer she'll open all the windows and sleep nude with her door open all the way, the fan going all night long, forget the cost!

Really?

She gets up early before anyone gets up and goes to sleep long after anyone.

She sleeps naked?

Does your mother?

No . . . I don't . . . I don't . . .know . . .

Suddenly from the other room came a voice in the darkness. Mother had heard us!

Yes, Ellen, I sleep nude. Want to come see?

Nothing Mother said ever surprised me. I was used to her loud half-whispers, her scathing, but honest asides, her candid and profound announcements. See that woman, she needs a good bra! Look at that girl in the bathing suit, you can see her sex outlined like a man's. Ese hombre, that man, he smells! Puuuuuccccchhhheeee! Excuse me, but your child is very fat, don't you think you should do something to help him?

Can't you Can't they do something about their skin, their hair, their clothes, their bra, their skirts, their pants.

Hey, you there!

No one could ruffle her, no hostile salesman or rude saleslady. Mother would turn to them placidly, and with great sweetness say: You don't feel well, do you?

Nothing ever surprised me about my mother, the woman who lay in the darkness of the McCoy Hotel, a wet washrag on her head, a damp towel on her breasts.

She was two people to me: the potentially dangerous woman who slept in the nude, who loved to shop, try on clothes, and hit a good sale. She was also the woman who didn't feel guilty about tipping, the woman who loved going to the movies and still yearned for romance. The other woman was the woman who was my mother, preoccupied with the person she thought I should be.

The first woman I knew was bitter, hard with arthritis, never really defeated, but in constant pain of one sort or another. This woman bravely moved through her every day with actions calibrated to insure our good, pronouncing by her strict, fearful ways a burden of relationship. Her Hope or Heaven, Her Garden of Eden, was centered by that inescapable tree of life and love, surrounded as it was by slithering, tempting, always male serpents.

But this tormented woman, and this other life was always forgotten when we approached the McCoy Hotel.

***

To the immediate right of the hotel was the Plaza Theatre, constructed in the luxurious style of those days gone by. The lobby was just as elegant as the exterior. When we entered the theatre, all cares left us; we forgot the harsh brightness of late afternoon El Paso.

Inside the Plaza Theatre we were transported to a world of make-believe. The theatre has a large screen that was flanked on either side by a painted façade that was lit by painted turning silver lights that blinked on and off. On either side of the screen was a mural. The one on the left depicted a beautiful Spanish señorita standing on a balcony, a rose in her hair. The opposite mural showed her suitor, a handsome, dark-haired man playing a guitar. There was an aura of yearning, unconsummated passion about the scene, as they stood separated by the huge white picture screen. There was a great and touching sadness as the viewer realized that throughout eternity the lovers would never get any closer to each other, for all the imminent drama and romance.

We usually sat in the balcony on plush red, very comfortable seats. It was an intimate and special place, as opposed to the larger lower main floor. In the cavernous darkness, I sat next to my mother, who placed herself between Margo and me, "so you won't fight," to watch double features, and one day, four movies in a row! The movies alternated between the family type, like *The Swiss Family Robinson*, the nature or animal variety, *Ole Yeller*, the religious, *The Robe*, or there were comedies or romances like *Three Coins in A Fountain*, with an occasional hair-raising drama like *Imitation of Life* thrown in.

Mother loved the movies and so did we. Her interests extended to buying all the *Silver Screen* and *Photoplay* magazines she could afford, poring over them and passing them on to Margo and me. In our room at the McCoy Hotel we read them voraciously, never wanting anything more than to be a part of that world of glamour, intrigue and veiled intimation.

One block away was El Colón, the Spanish-speaking movie theatre, where we went to see comedies with Cantinflas or drama with Dolores del Río, or

Pedro Infante, who was the famous Mexican singer turned movie idol. My mother loved him, and I also came to revere him. Pedro was very handsome with his thin mustache and his serious eyes. He sang to his women beautiful, wrenching songs of undying love, and they were grateful, succumbing always to his emotional, heart-filled fervor that captivated and then overcame them, but never against their wills. While I sometimes missed much of what he was saying, too embarrassed to listen closely, I secretly longed to hear those same desperate relentless words.

What El Colón gave us was passion, another form of possibility and way of living. Crying with Dolores, or Pedro, laughing with Cantinflas, I embraced my mother and her dreams, as well as those of all my people, the Mexicans and Mexican-Americans of La Frontera, the Border world that was my own. When we sat in the darkness, all our faces were familiar, laughing, crying, in the same way, and the same language. We were brothers and sisters united in our world away from the Plaza Theatre, with its stately red carpets and elegant balustrades, where red-costumed blond ticket-takers greeted you in crisp English and promised you, at least momentarily, the great American dream. Somehow in Spanish, our dreams seemed purer.

At El Colón we made our way alone, of course, no usher to guide us to the sticky, paper-littered balcony, where we carved out by our insistence a comfortable place with people like us who never had to pretend who they were or how much money they had. The emotions that we experienced at El Colón were more real than those we felt at the Plaza, the stories more familiar, the language rooted in things we had experienced as women, waiting on men, one man, never quite sure if we would ever be truly loved. For an hour and a half, we could be caressed by Pedro Infante himself, who proved to all men and women that it was good to be a man, a state of being that demanded respect, especially from woman. I never questioned anything then. That was in the early days of the McCoy Hotel.

In later years, I was to remember Pedro Infante, his untimely death in an airplane crash. Whenever I wanted to run away with someone, this tragedy of his stayed me. I couldn't explain to myself why Pedro's death had permanently touched me. He who struggled so long in celluloid to find true love, who seemed to have found it at last in real life, only to have it snatched away so abruptly and mercilessly by a jealous God who could not condone hard won happiness, come where it had, lead where it might. An elusive attempt at joy, what others called adultery, was now a tragic character in his own life's movie.

Leaving El Colón, I always found myself immensely hungry. I begged Mother to take us down the street to the chicharrón place, a take-out restaurant where hot, greasy, dripping sides of pork skin hung from racks to dry. The chicharrónes were real, not the type with some sort of artificial preservative staining the corners with red or orange dye. They were fat, juicy, the kind I could suck for some time with enthusiasm and then crackle with my teeth. A large greasy bag went a long way. A whole side of pork skins would be broken up, and holding a treasured dollar's worth, we'd walk back to the McCoy. We'd eat them until we could eat no more, drawing the coolest water from the tap and pouring it into our glasses when we got thirsty.

From the hotel we'd walk down to the plaza to watch the alligators that occasionally lurched outside in the hot Texas sun and then ponderously and painfully crawled back into the tepid wetness of the murky green pond, its flagstone slabs scraping their crusted, dried underbellies. The pond, located in the center of the plaza, was inaccessible to all except those three or four closed-eyed, nearly inert alligators that inhabited that space all seasons, a displaced curiosity.

In later year, this same dusty plaza was transformed at Christmastime by an incredible display of holiday tableaus. In one, cheerful elves cavorted merrily in artificial snow while Rudolph and his cohorts pulled a smiling pale-skinned Santa through the cool desert air.

This is the plaza we'd drive forty-two miles to see when we were young, a tradition that in later years had little meaning. Rituals had delighted and sustained us then, like having breakfast at the Oasis Restaurant next to the McCoy Hotel, where I'd order pancakes with hash browns or corned beef hash.

Sitting in a booth facing the street, my mother would contemplate her day: I need some comfortable walking shoes, a new brassiere, and my support hose, we'll go to the White House first, and then we'll have lunch at Kress' or Newberry's.

At Kress' Five and Dime, the majority of my time was spent in front of the makeup or jewelry counters. Mother roamed the store, usually ending up in the bargain basement. She'd have already picked up her supply of hairpins, hairnets, Kapok to stuff pillows, as well as some gum, and either candy orange slices or yellow gum drops that made the inside of my mouth rough if I sucked too hard.

Returning to the McCoy Hotel with our purchases, we'd rest a short while and maybe change our clothes. Shyly, and with a muffled voice, Tía Chita would call my mother from her room, someone having accidentally closed either bathroom door, to see if we were hungry. I always was. Down the creaky elevator we'd descend, my aunt included, to eat dinner at the cafeteria around the corner.

It was at this cafeteria I was first looked at as a woman, or so I imagined. Flirting with a young man over my fried fish filet, I felt him looking at me as well. Burning with embarrassment, I turned away, attempting to ignore him, and when I looked up, he was gone.

Later on, I wondered if I really had this exchange or not. I was in my teens, skinny-chested, wild-eyed, with a thick mop of unruly curly hair, straddled on either side by two imposing women, my mother and her sister. Could a look have gotten through?

When we returned to the McCoy, Tía Chita returned to her room. Mother closed the door to the bathroom and emerged in a flowing nightgown she'd made, one size fits all. It wasn't long before she was in bed, and the night gown was on the floor, her window open to the noise of late night El Paso: the metal rattle of trucks, the screech of passing cars on their way to Juárez, and later, the constant, soothing distant lull of that border night life, that coming and going between countries, states of mind.

But before my mother's always troubled sleep, she would ask me to pull her toes. As the older, stronger one, I was inevitably asked to do this favor for her. She was arthritic, with no circulation in her battered legs, and she told me it helped her to relax, just like taking hot baths from which she said she emerged ten years younger.

Taking her fleshy, bruised feet in my hands, her long second toe draped over the rest of her large feet, her Morton's toe, that had genetically become part of me as well, I would begin from the big toe and work down, pulling and popping as I went, now and then returning to a stubborn digit. Sometimes I was cruel and held my nose as I approached her, lifting her corn-filled calloused feet irreverently as if I were holding a leprous limb.

Tired from my day, I would later join my sister in bed. We sparred awhile, fighting for control of our sleeping space.

My nights were peaceful at the McCoy, dreamless too. The days were so full, so complete, so full of variety and stimulation, that my nights were a release from the never-ending hum of El Paso, La Frontera.

After a sigh of contentment, my aunt's snores from another part of the suite would cease. I would fall asleep, under imaginary silver stars, a Spanish señorita serenaded in the moonlight.

The next morning I would wake up Mexican, glad to be myself, and yet wanting more from myself at that time that than could ever be. I was my mother's vassal, my sister's companion, my father's faraway, forgotten little girl, no man's sweetheart.

Sunday morning Mass awaited me, my retribution unholy, complaining thoughts. My mother, sister and I visited many El Paso churches, never settling on one. Each unprecedented visit to an unfamiliar church allowed me one special prayer. Mother said every time you visited a new church, you could ask God for a new wish. So, I left my hopes and dreams that way, all over town.

After church we returned to the McCoy, where we left off our prayer books and gloves, and adjourned to the Oasis Restaurant for more grilled cheese and tuna fish sandwiches. Afterwards, Mother drove us home to Las Cruces, our city of myriad crosses.

In phase two of the McCoy, when I was older and in high school, a car full of failed debaters crowded, exuberant, if not exultant, in our blue Ford after the speech tournament. To hell with our defeats! Led by my mother we prayed the rosary. Mysterious Glory Bes led to stately Our Fathers, and onto interminable Hail Marys.

We arrived forty-two miles later, the rosary completed, merry but with crippled limbs. Never before had we fit so many girls into one car. We had set a record.

That was my last visit to the McCoy Hotel.

It's fitting that it should have been at a time of celebration for my emerging adolescent voice, a voice that then was always prone to laryngitis. I didn't know how to speak then, what to say. I was untrained, too eager to hear myself out loud, not caring whether I modulated my voice or damaged it in my fury to be heard.

My mother's voice now comes from another room. In my dreams I see her: proud, naked, dancing. She is not her seventies as I last knew her, but young, with the beautiful full body I knew she'd always had when she was younger. She wasn't hunchbacked, as she later was, with red, always bruised feet and legs. She wasn't that anxious woman who was always wondering if my father would ever call or write, or maybe even return home. His return to us never seemed a reality. He did in fact return, the year before my mother died, and in a strange way, I believe he hastened her death, a process that had begun twenty-eight years before when he left home.

In my dreams my mother sits in our room at the McCoy Hotel brushing her long dark hair in front of an open window. I can see her from my aunt's room and yet I cannot get near. I wonder if ever, when I least expect it, she will walk into the room, and sit next to me. I will be able to smell her skin the way it was, sweet, smelling of dried flowers, overripe fruit. That is how the dying smell. It does not terrify me. I breathe in with gratitude and exhale my passing sorrow.

Some years ago the Plaza Theatre was to be destroyed. The local citizenry saved it eventually, calling it an architectural landmark.

The chicharrón place isn't there anymore, or has moved, or become one of the many Casas de Cambio that line the street leading to the bridge that will take your dollars and convert them into pesos.

After that last time at the McCoy Hotel, we visited El Paso shortly afterward to see a visiting President Kennedy, who was staying at the Cortez Hotel, the fancy, removed stepsister of the McCoy Hotel.

If I were to go inside, I would surely meet the ghosts of that past life, perhaps the solitary old man staring into space in the guest sitting room, or the phantom clerk and his wife, both aged specters, with haunting, faraway voices. Can I help you? Do you need a key?

Yes, the key!

I would see my mother inside her room, staring out the window to the oppressive heat, her ears inclining to the shouts of Viva, Que viva, and there he is, the President! The hearty waves of President Kennedy are an intimation of bygone grandeur, of a mythical life, once acted out, now barely remembered, and then always with a struggle.

But I do remember.

To go back to that time is to go back to the heart of the McCoy Hotel; it is to remember those thrilling, but small adventures full of imagined danger. Today they seem as lugubrious and absurd as the overheated alligators in the plaza pond. Poor creatures so far away from home!

I grew up in a world of people who were always remembering the past. When you grow up this way, time has a different significance to you than to others.

Pedro Infante, dark rebel, but that one tragic flaw of his, was everybody's lover. He sings to me, larger than life, on the big screen in the timeless darkness of the balcony of the El Colón Theatre. . . . Solamente una vez . . .

At the Plaza Theatre the Spanish señorita demurely hides her eyes while her handsome suitor sings and strums a haunting song on his guitar. . . . Solamente una vez . . .

Life is spooky, but not in the ways you'd ever expect. ★

Ana Castillo

Poet, novelist, essayist, and short story writer Ana Castillo was born and raised in Chicago. She earned a B.A. from Northeastern Illinois University, an M.A. in Latin American and Caribbean Studies from the University of Chicago, and a Ph.D. in American Studies from the University of Bremen, Germany. Her most recent academic appointments were the 2001-2005 La Sor Juana Inés de la Cruz Chair created for her at De Paul University, Chicago, and the 2007-2008 Martin Luther King Jr. Outstanding Visiting Scholar at M.I.T. Castillo is the author of several poetry collections including: *Women Are Not Roses*; *My Father Was a Toltec*; and *I Ask the Impossible: Poems*. She has published the novels *Sapagonia*, a 1994 New York Times Notable Book; *Peel My Love Like an Onion*; *The Mixquiahuala Letters*, winner of the 1987 Before Columbia Foundation's American Book Award; *Water Color Women, Opaque Men*, a novel in verse; and *The Guardians*. Additionally, she is the author of *Massacre of the Dreamers: Reflections on Mexican-Indian Women in the United States 500 Years after the Conquest*; a children's book, *My Daughter, My Son, The Eagle, The Dove*; and the plays *Psst . . . I Have Something to Tell You, Mi Amor*. Castillo is the recipient of the Carl Sandburg Award; a Mountains and Plains Booksellers Award; the 1998 Sor Juana Achievement Award by the Mexican Fine Arts Center Museum in Chicago; and the 2006 Independent Publisher Story Teller of the Year Award. Her essays and columns have been featured in newspapers and magazines across the United States. She has been interviewed and profiled for National Public Radio and the History Channel. Currently, she makes her home near El Paso.

From *The Guardians*: Regina

It was raining all night hard and heavy, making the land shiver—all the bare ocotillo and all the prickly pear. In the morning we found a tall yucca collapsed in the front yard. Everything is wet and gray so the day has not made itself known yet. It is something in between. As usual, I'm anxious. Behind the fog are los Franklins. Behind those mountains is my brother. Waiting. On this side we're waiting, too, my fifteen-year-old nephew, Gabo, and his dog, la Winnie.

Winnie has one eye now. She got it stuck by a staghorn cactus that pulled it right out. Blood everywhere that day. By the time Gabo got home from his after-school bagger's job at el Shur Sav, I was back from the vet's with Winnie, rocking her like a baby. You couldn't blame the dog for being upset, losing her eye and all.

I kept Gabo this time around because I want him to finish high school. I don't care what the authorities say about his legal status. We'll work it out, I say to Gabo, who, when he was barely walking I changed his diapers, which I also tell him. He's still embarrassed to be seen in his boxers. That's okay. I'm embarrassed to be seen in mine, too. Thirty years of being widowed, you better believe I dress for comfort.

"Stop all this mourning," my mamá used to say. "You were only married six months. The guy was a drug addict, por Dios!" She actually would say that and repeat it even though Junior died fighting for his country. That's why we got married. He was being shipped off to Vietnam. If the coroner suggested he had needle tracks, well, I don't know about that.

Mamá always had a way of turning things around for me, to see them in the worst light possible. It's probably not a nice thing to say you are glad your mother's dead. But I am glad she's not around. Can I say that and not worry about a stretch in purgatory? Then I'll say that.

We've been waiting a week, me and Gabo—for his dad to come back. He's been back and forth across that desert dodging the Border Patrol so many times, you'd think he wouldn't even need a coyote no more. The problem is the coyotes and narcos own the desert now. You look out there, you see thorny cactus, tumbleweed, and sand soil forever and you think, No, there's nothing out there. But you know what? They're out there—los mero-mero cabrones. The drug traffickers and body traffickers. Which are worse? I can't say.

So the problem is Rafa, my brother, can't just come across without paying somebody. Eight days ago we got a call. It was a woman's voice. She said in

Spanish that Rafa was all right and that he was coming in a few days so we had better have the balance of the money ready. Who did those people think they were, I asked myself. That woman on the phone acted so damn cocky. I swear, if I knew who she was, I'd report her to the authorities, lock her up for five years. How dare she treat people like that? Take advantage of their poverty and laws that force people to crawl on their bellies for a chance to make it.

Truth is Rafa should have just stayed here last time he came to work the pecans. That's when he finally let me keep his son. Someone in the family's got to finish high school, I said to him. Poor Rafa, all alone like that now, going back and forth, even though I think he has a new wife down in Chihuahua. He won't say nothing out of respect for Gabo's dead mother. Just the mention of Ximena and the boy falls apart. It's been almost seven years now but Gabo was just a child. His mind sort of got stuck in that time when his mother didn't make it. He was here with me that winter, too. When Rafa and Ximena were returning they got separated. The coyotes said no, the women had to go in another truck. Three days later the bodies of four women were found out there in that heat by the Border Patrol. All four had been mutilated for their organs. One of them was Ximena. It was in all the news.

I've been fighting to keep my sobrino since then but my brother gets terco about it and keeps insisting on taking him back to the other side. What for? I tell him. Because he's Mexican, Rafa says. As if I'm not, because I choose to live on this side. He's got to know his grandparents— meaning Ximena's folks. He's not gonna become a gringo and forget who he is, my brother says of his only son, as if getting an education would erase the picture the boy keeps in his head of how his mother died.

I stayed and worked here in Cabuche, first in the pecans and cotton. Because of marrying Junior, I got his army benefits. I could stay and not hide in the shadows no more. This meant no more picking, no more peeling chiles, and no more canning. Instead, I got up my courage one year and signed up for night classes at the community college. I did pretty good in my classes. I really liked being in a classroom. I liked the desks, the smell of the chalk and erasers, the bulletin boards with messages about holidays like Valentine's Day and Martin Luther King Day. So later I got more courage and applied for a job as a teacher's aide in the middle school. That's how I bought my casita, here on the mesa, where I can't see los Franklins this morning. But I know they are out there, playing with me. Like giants, they take the sun and play with people's eyes, changing colors. Like shape-shifters, they change the way they look, too. They let the devoted climb up along their spines to crown them with white crosses and flowers and mementos. They give themselves that way, those guardians between the two countries.

I do not know what Rafa is talking about his son becoming a gringo. These lands, this unmerciful desert—it belonged to us first, the Mexicans. Before that it belonged to los Apaches. Los Apaches were mean, too. They knew how to defend themselves. And they're still not too happy about losing everything, despite the casinos up by their land. "Keep right on going," they'll tell tourists when they try to pull over on the highway that cuts across it during dry season.

Ha. I wish I could say that out here whenever some stupid hunter wanders near my property. It's just me and the barbed-wire fence between the hunter and government land where he can do what he pleases, all dressed up like if he was in the National Guard.

One day we heard some shots. It wasn't even dawn yet, that Sunday. Winnie went nuts—the way heelers do at the sign of something amiss. Gabo got up—pulling up his jeans, tripping on the hem of them, barefoot. "What was that, Tía?" he said, all apurado and the dog, meanwhile, barking, barking. This was before the accident, when she could practically see in the dark. I let her go out, and la Winnie ran toward the fence that divides my property and BLM land. "HEY, HEY!" was all my poor nephew called out. He always freezes up. I think he remembers his mother.

Over in El Paso people have asked me if I'm not afraid of the coyotes and rattlers living right next to the wide-open spaces kept by the Bureau of Land Management. The worse snakes and coyotes, I always say, are the ones on two legs. People think that's funny.

"Hey-Hey," Gabo called out again in the dark of the new day out there, with a little less conviction the second time. But la Winnie kept right on barking-barking. I went in the house and got my rifle. When I came out I went up to the fence and pointed the rifle somewhere I couldn't see. What were they shooting anyway? We don't got any deer around here. "YOU ARE WAY TOO CLOSE TO MY LAND!" I yelled like I was Barbara Stanwyck or Doña Bárbara or somebody and I took a shot that rang out like a 30-30. It must've woken up la gente all the way in town. A little while after that I heard Jeeps taking off.

We couldn't go back to sleep after that so I made us some atole and put on the TV. I needed to fold up the laundry I'd left in the dryer anyway. Winnie didn't come in like she would have normally, ready to be fed. She stayed outside roaming the grounds.

"Your father will came back," I said to Gabo that morning at the table about my kid brother who you'd think was way older than me, his mind full of the beliefs of another time, another era, belonging to the Communist Party and all that. He's so proud of it, too.

Gabo's older sister ran off a long time ago with a guy over there in Chihuahua and no one's heard from her since then. So all Gabo has to count on is his father.

And me, of course, his tía Regina.

But he's lost way too much already in his short life to know that for sure. So that's what I'm doing right now trying to do something good— for my brother and Gabo but for me, too—to see that my sobrinito gets a chance. One day I'm gonna take him to Washington, D.C.

"What the hell for?" Rafa asked me when I mentioned it.

"To see where the Devil makes his deals," I said.

One day I'm gonna take my nephew to New York, too, where I've never been but it's on my list—my very long list—of places to see in this life. I may even take him to Florence, Italy, to see the David. Well, actually I'm the one that wants to see the statue of David but it won't hurt for Gabo to know a little something about great art. What? Why not? All our lives we have to be stuck to the ground like desert centipedes? My nephew doesn't show any signs of interest in the arts. He don't talk about girls. He goes to Mass every Sunday down in Cabuche. If I don't drive him or let him take my truck, he walks. He observes all the holy days of obligation. My biggest fear is he's gonna become a priest. Wait 'til Rafa hears about it. He'll be so disappointed.

***

The truth is when I fired that weapon I was trying to show my sobrino not to be afraid. I wanted to show him that if a middle-aged woman like me could confront things that went bump in the night, he could do it, too, that he could face anything.

Actually, I had used my .22-caliber rifle only once before in the ten years I owned it. It was when a coyote was getting at my chickens. For a while I had it in my mind that I was gonna get rich selling fresh eggs. Everyone started asking me for eggs, all the neighbors, the teachers at the school, but no one really wanted to pay for them. Then I started feeling for the poor familias I worked with at the school and I gave them free eggs. The coyote ate three of my hens before I caught up with it. After that, I said, What do I need all this for? And I sold the rooster and the hens I had left.

I've never been very good at get-rich-quick schemes anyway. But it don't stop me from trying. The only thing I will not do is gamble, go down to Sunland Park or up to Ruidoso and throw my money away in the casinos the way some of the ladies in town do. Oh sure, now and then they win a couple of hundred bucks. They get all excited. They forget how much they lost to begin with. They forget the dinner or the motel and gas money they put out to be there. And I surely will not play the lottery. Millions and millions in the pot some weeks. So I figure, what are the chances?

Instead I take that dollar and buy two avocados if they're on sale. Avocados, the food of the gods, are the only things I can't grow on my land—too arid; avocado trees don't grow in sand. Another thing I've done with one dollar is send a fax to the White House on that number they give out to people in case you got a complaint about how things are being run up there. I tried to send the fax out of the school office but Mrs. Martínez, the head secretary, said no, nothing doing. Plus, she voted for the president. So I took my letter of complaint to the place on the corner of Main Street and Washington in Cabuche where you can send out faxes, buy phone cards, or have your taxes done. It took five minutes and one dollar and I felt much better afterward. I know I am nobody; no one has to tell me that. But I still vote like everyone else. So if I feel like sending a fax and complaining about the president's latest pick for a Supreme Court judge, that's my prerogative.

That's a word I use with the students all the time: *prerogative*, as in "It's a lady's prerogative to change her mind." The boys say they know all about that—about girls changing their minds. You cannot get a gallon of gas for a dollar these days. You might still get yourself something you don't need, like a thirty-two-ounce can of beer at the package liquors across the street from the "business" tienda where I send out my official faxes. Sometimes I have actually sat and thought out what you can and cannot buy with a dollar no more and it's very interesting—because you think you can't buy much, but in reality, if you think about it, it all depends on your priorities.

That's another good word I've given the students and my nephew. "What are your priorities in life, anyway? Go to jail or go to college? Get drunk with your friends or get a job and make a little money to get ahead?" Things like that. You would be very surprised at how little thought any of them have given those choices until I start telling them about priorities. Gabo's priorities are very clear and I am very proud of him for it.

He says he is going to college. That is, if the government lets him. If he can't get residency he won't be going nowhere but back to México. They don't give scholarships to migrant kids without papers.

We do the dollar game sometimes. I used to do it by myself, but now that my Gabo is with me we do it together. He's come home with a big bottle of shampoo for one dollar. Of course, you can get a whole lot of stuff at the Dollar General for a dollar or what shouldn't cost more than a dollar; it's so cheap and falls apart so quick. But this was the champú bueno that Gabo bought at el Shur Sav with his employee's discount. Shampoo is just a small example of how our dollar game works. We've gotten all kinds of things for a dollar.

What we won't get and what we'd never do with our dollars, we have agreed, because we got our priorities straight, I tell him, is nothing that would be harmful to our bodies or our souls. That's why I made him take back the pound of chorizo he bought for us one time. He felt so bad and I felt so bad because the truth was that we both love our chorizo with eggs for breakfast. But we know that spicy greasy sausage is no good for your health, and what's bad for your arteries cannot be good for your mental well-being neither.

Gabo and I are figuring these things out—he, with his suspicious signs of priest potential and me, a woman who has been living alone so long I may as well become beatified. Santa Lucia, who cares for blind dogs. Santa Barbara, whose father locked her in a tower because he desired her so much. When I've thought of the martyrs and saints, I told Padre Juan Bosco down at the church one time when he reprimanded me for hardly going to Mass no more, it seems it would be very, very hard to become one these days. It isn't because we don't have diehard virgins, but because these days the pope is not about to proclaim every girl who fights a rapist a saint. As for the martyrs you don't get thrown in the den of lions for refusing to renounce your faith as in early Christian times. I wonder why I always think of things like that—imagining myself tied to a stake, scalped, Roman soldiers demanding I give up on God. Mamá used to come and slap me on the head when she'd catch me daydreaming.

"Maybe you used to be a martyr or a saint in another life," Gabo said when I talked out loud about these ponderings.

"According to the Church, there is only one life and this is it," I told him.

My sobrino looked very disturbed by this reminder. The rest of that day he kept to himself, listening to his John Denver cassette in his room.

He got it for a dollar at the flea market.

***

Gabo found a hawk. It was young, you could tell. It was the most beautiful thing you ever saw, brown and near-white with dashes of black on the wings. Nature is so geometrically precise. If you look real close at birds and fish, too, you see how everything—every feather, fin, wing, gill, is colored just so.

Somewhere I heard that baby hawks have a high mortality rate. This one didn't make it. It must've been trying to take flight when it got hit on the road. Its neck was broken but otherwise it looked like it was sleeping, as they say about people when they're in their coffins. (Except for Mamá. The mortician had painted on such bright-orange lipstick and powder too light for her complexion she looked dead for sure.)

"What are you going to do with it?" I asked my nephew. He looked so sad. You'd think he had killed the hawk himself. He'd found it on the road. He was driving my truck back from work. I let him take the truck since he comes home after dark. When he saw it, he pulled over and put it on the passenger seat. "I'm going to bury it, Tía," Gabo replied solemnly, the way he speaks most of the time, "with your permission."

My nephew is so polite to the point of being antiquated. True, humble Mexican kids have better manners than American Mexican kids, but Gabo sounds like a page out of Lope de Vega. Lope de Vega, the prince of Spain's Golden Age. I haven't read anything of his; I heard the Spanish teacher at the school talking to the students about him. But Spain's Golden Age of literature is on my list of things to read—my very long list. I've done some reading on my own, García Márquez, for example. *One Hundred Years of Solitude* was assigned in one of the classes I took at the community college and then I looked for other books of his, like the story of Eréndira and her wicked grandmother, that, in some ways, reminded me of my own life with Mamá in the desert. I read the newspaper every day. But now with Gabo here I have become more conscious of the importance of broadening the mind through reading. The next book fair the school has I'm going to buy us everything we see that we think we'll like. We'll treat it like a candy store. I'll have to assure my considerate nephew, who behaves as if he may be overstaying his visit—the way he tiptoes around and hardly eats, although I'm not sure why; it's not because of anything I've said or done, I hope—that I have saved up for such a splurge. Otherwise, he'll hesitate to get anything, even if he sees something he really wants.

The hawk was on Gabo's dresser. He brought home a white veladora. He got it for a dollar with his discount at work. It took exactly seven days to burn through. When the candle was done, Gabo said he would bury the hawk. Every night he prayed over it. "You look like some kind of shaman," I told him when I peeked in to say good night and there he was, standing in the glow of the flame, head bowed, hands suspended just above the dead bird. It looked as if he were trying to resurrect it, although I'm sure that's not what he was trying to do.

When the candle had burned out I found it in the trash. Where was the bird, I asked Gabo. Had he buried it already? Where? When? I thought we were going to hold a funeral for it. I felt a little left out of his ceremonies.

"Yes," he said.

Later that day, I saw a hawk perched on the fence post by the gate. The front gate is about an eighth of a mile from the front door, It was brown with near-white feathers, black dashes on the wings. It looked a lot like our dead hawk. Maybe it was its mother or some other relation.

"Where did you say you buried that bird?" I asked Gabo when he came to the kitchen to make a sandwich for his school lunch. He refuses the money I offer so that he can eat in the cafeteria or go out with some of the kids. He saves his work money, spends only on what he needs. He offered his whole check to me at the beginning, but I looked at him as if he were crazy and told him to use it on himself. His sandwiches are very frugal, too—one slice of meat between two slices of ninety-nine-cent whole wheat bread.

"I didn't," Cabo replied.

"You didn't what?" I asked. "You didn't say or you didn't bury it?"

"No," was all he said.

"Maybe that bird was carrying that virus, Gabo," I said. "How much did you handle it anyway?"

"Do not worry yourself so much, Tía," he said.

As far as teenagers go, from what I hear at the school and from the students' parents, Gabo could get a lot worse on my nerves.

This is not why I am so anxious all the time—having a teenager to look out for now. It was not even part of the Change, like the doctor down in Juárez told me last year. The anxiety is just part of me. On any given day, a person can find several reasons to be anxious. If you don't find it in your own life at that moment, all you have to do is pick up a newspaper and read the headlines. Being a fifty-plus-year-old woman alone for so long, widowed thirty years, that could be cause enough. Every paycheck covers the bills to the penny—when I'm lucky.

Every three months or so I come up with another get-rich-quick idea that ends up not making me much money and sometimes ends up costing me some. I've delivered groceries for people out here in the boonies who can't or don't want to drive into town every week. I've taken orders for curtains and sewed quite a few up. Over the years, I've dog-sat, old people-sat, house-sat. I sold

Amway, Avon, and Mary Kay products, even though I am allergic to most anything with a chemical scent. I had Tupperware parties. I sold red candy apples and pecan bread in the parking lot of el Shur Sav. For a time, I had a little business out of my troca selling pizzas. I'd buy them wholesale down the road at a place across from the police station. Then I'd drive them to an empty lot on Main Street and put out my sign. People didn't really want to bother ordering a pizza ahead of time. Just drive up and I hand them one into their car or troca or maybe they were on foot. On weekends I'd make a killing. Then a guy started doing it, right next to me, out of his car. He gave away free Cokes, so he ran me out of business. A long time ago I went door to door selling bibles, the King James version. Then my mother found out and told Padre Juan Bosco and he had one of his talks with me, so I felt morally inclined to quit. All these jobs I had in addition to whatever other full-time work I was putting in somewhere. And all of it caused me anxiety.

I keep almost nothing from my nephew now, except what I might look like in a swimsuit, but why he would care to see his fat old aunt half naked I wouldn't know, but nearly everything in my heart or that crosses my mind I share with him. He's been God-sent that way, I think. I had no idea how lonely I was until one day I found myself at my Singer stitching up his jeans, talking my head off, and he, so patiently, sitting nearby listening to it all. Or at least he looked like he was listening.

One thing I won't tell Gabo about is my money worries. He'd run off so as not to be another burden on me. The other topic I cannot bring myself to approach is the fact that we haven't heard from his papá yet. It isn't as if Gabo himself hasn't noticed. I heard him crying into his pillow one night. He probably envisions his father being killed by a coyote and left in the desert like what happened to his mother. It isn't like Rafa not to get word to me somehow, but then again, I wouldn't be terribly surprised if he changed his mind about coming. That coyote woman on the phone was horrid—he may not have wanted to pay them all that they wanted. The fact is, all Gabo and I can do is wait.

In the meantime I discovered where he buried the hawk. It was right near the fallen yucca. La one-eyed Winnie, or Tuerta, as I am calling her now, dug it up. My Mescalero Apache friend, Uriel, told me over the phone that Gabo's finding the hawk was very good luck for him. She said the hawk is good protection medicine. I wonder if finding where it was buried and digging it up was good tuck for la Tuerta. Poor little hawk— with so many now trying to benefit from its death. I reburied it this time between two huge chollas, where I don't think the dog will go, seeing that she's cautious now about getting too near anything with thorns.

***

I'd rather be pricked by a thousand thorns than have to think about what my little brother may have endured. The fact is, however, that I don't know what exactly he had to endure. Sometimes I like to think he is back in Chihuahua with a pregnant wife and that we just never heard from him because he became too selfish and didn't care about Gabo no more or his past life with Ximena.

Another week went by when a foco went on in my head and I realized that the phone number of that nasty coyote woman that called me might be on the caller-ID box. We don't get many calls. All the numbers of anyone who has ever called since I put in the caller ID right around the time Rafa left my nephew here were still on there. We never erased them. Most of the time we didn't even pay attention to it. Without saying nothing to Gabo, I checked and, sure enough, there was a call from El Paso the very same day la coyota had called me.

"Bueno," she answered when I tried it. I knew it was her. It was a voice full of intriga and bad tidings.

I went on to tell her who I was and that we were still waiting for Rafa. "I don't know what you are talking about," she said and hung up on me, proving all the more that she very well did.

My heart started breaking with the sound of the dial tone on the other end and I knew that my brother had been done some awful wrong. Still, without mentioning my concern to my nephew, the next day I took someone into my confidence at the school. I consider most of the teachers much more intelligent than me, with their college education and all. One of them could give me some advice, I thought, but it would have to be someone I could trust, since my brother trying to cross without papers was obviously against the law. Most of the teachers at the school are Mexican or at least of Mexican heritage although half of them call themselves "Hispanic," which means they don't want to be considered Mexican. Or at least that is how Rafa and I feel about the word. It is one of the few political points we agree on.

Mr. Betancourt, the history teacher, calls himself "Chicano." He wears a long ponytail and while he obliges the system with a nice shirt and tie, he always has on jeans. All this about Betancourt told me I could trust him with my fears about Rafa, so I pulled him aside the very next day and told him what I thought.

"We might be able to find an address for that phone number," Betancourt told me. He said there was a phone number that you could call where, if the number you had was listed, you'd get a name and maybe an address. I thought I would try it when I got home, but he took out a cell phone from inside his jean jacket and, to my surprise, within ten minutes had obtained the woman's information for me.

"Will you go to her house?" he asked me.

Betancourt is about thirty-five but most of his hair has gone white. He looks old and young at the same time. I remember when I was in my thirties, I felt like that—old and young at the same time. Now I'm middle-aged and I feel old and really old at the same time. Yes, I told him that I would, that I would have gotten in my truck and gone right then and there but that my nephew would need it for work in an hour. Betancourt nodded. He looked at his watch and then he said, "Let me move some things around. I can meet you somewhere in an hour or I can go pick you up at your house. I'll take you. It's probably not wise for you to go there alone."

Miguel. That's his name. He told me to call him Miguel or Mike but to please not call him Mr. Betancourt no more. I never called him just plain Betancourt to his face but that's how the teachers called him in the lounge. Especially a couple of the young women teachers said it like they meant something more by it. Sometimes a single man is as likely to be the object of a lot of unprofessional interest as a single woman, in particular the attractive ones, of which, at the school, I can count only four. I look around, too. I may not say nothing, being a fifty-plus-year-old widow, but I still look.

Miguel was handsome in his own way but more important, for the purposes of our errand, tall and very strong-looking. When he showed up at my house he was still wearing his tie. He decided to keep it on, he said, because it made him look like he might be someone of authority. "I mean, I'm not gonna say I'm with La Migra or anything but it wouldn't hurt if they think we have some pull." The woman's house was very close to the customs bridge going into Juárez. It was a little house like others on that block, nothing special about it, and if my brother was in there, if they were holding him for ransom, never in a million years would I have guessed it would have been in such an ordinary place and right there in the middle of everything. The woman herself opened the door. She looked us up and down, especially Miguel, who did start to look like some kind of agent all of a sudden, with his Serpico long hair and bigotes.

At first she denied knowing anything, even the fact that she was the one who had called. Then Miguel took me by surprise. He pushed her, and next thing I knew, we were all in the house, in a dark, tiny, crowded living room with a dirty beige couch and two little kids, one in Pampers, in a playpen. "Listen," he said right in her face, "you are going to tell us what happened to this woman's brother or you are going right to jail— today. Do you understand? Do you understand?" He pushed her again so that she went reeling back until she hit a wall. She started crying. She might've been around thirty or so, with a bulging midriff from babies, and her breasts already sagging. The house smelled of stale cigarette smoke. The TV was blaring a Spanish channel. I felt sorry for the babies who looked startled but hadn't started to cry. It was funny that they didn't cry when the mother was crying. Then she got hold of herself and looked me up and down. "What would I know about your brother?" she said to me with that same sneer I imagined that time she had called me. "Have you tried calling your family back in Mexico? He's probably there."

Before I could even say nothing, Miguel took her by the shoulders and shook her so hard her head went back and forth like it was on a spring. "I'm only going to ask you one more time," he said. And before he asked again, she looked at me and with spittle coming out of the corners of her mouth and with more hate than I have ever felt from a human being, she seemed even glad to tell me, "Your brother must be dead, stupid. Why else do you think you never heard anything again? Do you think they come and tell *me* what goes on out there? I only know about the ones who make it. They come here until their people pay what they owe. Your brother? What do I know of him? They most likely left him to rot out in the desert because he was a tonto or maybe for being a pendejo he got himself killed. What do I know? Now get out of here before I tell my husband you were here and you'll both be sorry you came."

It was like a movie. In movies about drug traficantes they have women like that, in their nightgowns in daytime in gloomy rooms and living an obscure existence. And they have guys like the one who drove up just as we were leaving, wearing a big anchor on a chain around his neck and a diamond earring in one ear. They—everything, even their frightened little kids who wouldn't cry—looked like they were right out of a bad drug video.

El coyote looked at Miguel as we left as if he was memorizing him, taking a mental photograph in case he ever saw him again. But neither said a word to the other.

I turned around and took a last glance at the woman, who stayed inside in the shadows. She knew something about my brother's fate. I felt it in my heart. She could have given me some piece of information, however small, a gold nugget to take back to Gabo so that the poor boy would somehow, someday find closure.

I wanted to go back in and shake her myself. Shake her until her stupid head fell off. Until her neck snapped and we'd carry her lifeless body to Gabo so that he could pray over it for seven days. Then he'd find a place to bury it even though his father had gotten no such consideration. And when la Tuerta Winnie sniffed up the corpse and started digging, fine; she could dig all she wanted. I'd let her dig up that estúpida's body so that all the coyotes that wanted to come on my little bit of land that I protected so well could feed off of her stupid flesh and lick her stupid bones clean. And then we'd all, me and Winnie and Gabo and Miguel, too, if he wanted, and even the coyotes with four feet, could go out to the BLM land and scatter the bones out there to dry in the sun, for sands and wind to wash over. And Rafa, wherever they had left him, would no longer be alone out there.

Then I felt Miguel take my hand. He had to pull me with him. "Come on," he muttered close to my ear. "We'd better get the hell out of here while we can." ★

Manuel Vélez

Poet Manuel Vélez was born in Salinas, California, and moved to El Paso at the age of sixteen. He earned a B.A. in theatre arts and an M.F.A. in creative writing from the University of Texas at El Paso. Vélez was assistant professor of English at El Paso Community College where he established the Chicana/o Studies Program and served as an adjunct professor at UTEP. His collection *Bus Stops and Other Poems* was the first publication of Calaca Press of California. Currently, he teaches at San Diego Mesa College in the Department of Chicano Studies, where he has also been project director for an NEH-funded lecture series.

From *Bus Stops and Other Poems*: Memories Fade

Night descends upon the room
like thick blankets, covers light
with a cold that comforts my skin.
Abuelita in her room whispers
a rosary, its soft words escape her
lips, brush like wind through walls,
settle on my bed like dust.

In the kitchen papá's voice raises,
carries with it the pain that has landed
like blackbirds on his chest, tries
desperately to reach the voice inside
the phone. Still, it cannot hide the sound
of mamá's tears like waves crashing on
a distant beach.

I lie on my bed, stare into the nothing
of my room, think of the tío who visited
only once a year like a circus; full of color
of smells, of toys. I think of how he would
arrive only at night, a quiet knock on the back
door. Then the laughter that exploded from
his body once he saw mamá, as if it had been
trapped inside for so long and finally found
the strength to escape. How his pants were
always wet, how he smelled of fall,
fresh and cold. How Papá always told me
to keep an eye on the migra. *Pon ojo, mijo.*
No dejes que se lleven a tu tío. How I would
smile at this, feel important. Nod *si papá* with
the deepest voice I had. I would take care
of my tío, watch out for him while he was here.

How every March I would count the days,
wait for them to pass like rusted boxcars
on trains, until that last week when I knew
he would come, pick me up with a grunt
and say, *ya eres hombre, mijo.* How we'd
walk together down the street, me with
my chest up trying hard to keep up with his
steps, he with a smile big as the sun and
a *buenos días* for everyone we passed. How
he always sighed when we entered the cool
of Lalo's groceries, as if the heat outside
was too much, and walk straight to the cooler
for a six-pack of Bud. I would run down
the familiar aisles until I found my section
and pick my candies.

Memories begin to fade, are not as bright.
Their colors stolen by mamá's tears, by Abuelita's
prayers. Papá's voice still on the phone, begins
to shake as his own tears drown his eyes. He knows.
Has heard the news he didn't want to believe.
Alfredo left his home three days ago. Said
he would call as soon as he got to El Paso.

Now there is no doubt. The story on the news.
The body wrapped in blue and carried into
a white truck by two men while others dressed
in cold green look on. The cold voice of the
newscaster who announced that the border patrol
had found yet another body in the Rio Grande.
The fourth one this year.

Now there is no doubt that mamá's scream,
her hands flying to her face, her eyes widening
like two full moons were right. They knew
what we refused to believe. They knew even after
Papá said it couldn't be true. It could've been
someone else. Alfredo was still in Casas Grandes.
Papá would call to show her he was right.

But something in his voice betrayed him. Something
in the way he ran to the phone, tried to dial the line
of numbers, dropped the phone, tried again until
he finally put it to his ear and waited with heavy breath.
Something told me that I would never hear my tío's
laughter, walk with him down the street, hear his
voice or see his colors again. ★

Alicia Gaspar de Alba

Alicia Gaspar de Alba was born and raised in El Paso, receiving a B.A. in English and an M.A. in English-Creative Writing from the University of Texas at El Paso. She earned her Ph.D. in American Studies from the University of New Mexico. In 1994 she began her academic career at UCLA and was a founding faculty member of the César E. Chávez Department of Chicana and Chicano Studies. Gaspar de Alba is the recipient of numerous fellowships, including a Chicana Dissertation Fellowship from the University of California, Santa Barbara; a Ford Foundation Dissertation Fellowship; and a Minority-Scholar-in-Residence postdoctoral fellowship at Pomona College. In 1999 as the Roderick Endowed Chair at the University of Texas at El Paso, Gaspar de Alba was named a Distinguished Visiting Professor. UCLA awarded Gaspar de Alba the Shirley Collier Prize for Literature and the 2008 Gold Shield Faculty Prize for Academic Excellence. She is the author of the poetry collections *Beggar on the Cordoba Bridge*; *La Llorona on the Longfellow Bridge*; the novels *Sor Juana's Second Dream*, winner of the 2001 Latino Literary Hall of Fame Award for Best Historical Fiction; *Desert Blood: the Juárez Murders*, winner of the Lambda Literary Foundation Award for Best Lesbian Mystery of 2005 and a Latino Book Award; *Calligraphy of the Witch: A Novel*; the short story collection *The Mystery of Survival and Other Stories*, the recipient of the Rudolfo and Patricia Anaya Premio Aztlán Award; the essay collection *Velvet Barrios: Popular Culture & Chicana/o Sexualities*; and the cultural study *Chicano Art Inside/Outside The Master's House*. Her work has been included in numerous publications and has been translated into Spanish, German, and Italian. Currently, she is full professor and chair of the César E. Chávez Department of Chicana and Chicano Studies at UCLA and affiliated appointments in the English and Women's Studies departments.

From *The Mystery of Survival and Other Stories*: American Citizen, 1921

Alberto Morales looked in the plate glass windows of the *El Paso Herald* and saw that his hat was crooked again. He straightened it, mumbling to himself that he couldn't touch his hat during the interview. He would lay it on his lap after shaking the man's hand firmly and being asked to take a seat. He would slide his hands under his thighs as he answered the man's questions, sitting straight and sure of himself and never looking down at his hat.

These had been his wife's instructions. It was she who had convinced him to come. *You're an American*, she'd said. *You have a right to apply for any job you want. Here, put on your shirt. See how nice I starched it for you? Just remember to keep your hands off your hat, Albert. Sit on them if you have to. And don't worry! You're an American citizen. You can be anything you want.*

When Rosemary spoke to him like that, Alberto could almost feel the brown draining out of his skin, could almost imagine that his father was a conductor for the Southern Pacific instead of a worker who laid the track for it, and that his mother had never borrowed money from the principal of his school. Alberto could see his daughters growing up without fear or shame, nobody pitying them, nobody laughing at their accents, nobody denying them a library card or a high school diploma.

He straightened his hat again, wiped around his mouth with the handkerchief Rosemary had made for him, and walked in.

"I would like an application, please," he told the receptionist in the front office.

The receptionist looked surprised. She told him to go out and wait in the foyer while she got her super. Alberto did not even have time to sit down before the receptionist, followed by a redheaded man in funny glasses, joined him in the foyer.

"Now, what exactly is it that you want?" the man asked. "Thank you, Miss Lind," he said to the receptionist. The young woman looked over her shoulder at Alberto just before stepping back into her office.

"I've come to apply for the job," Alberto said, burying his hands in his trouser pockets. "I read the advertisement—"

"You mean the *reporter* position?" The man pinched off his glasses and stared at Alberto with bulging eyes. "You're . . . why, you're Mexicano, aren't you?"

Alberto took out his right hand and held it in front of the man. "Albert Morales," he said, waiting for the man to notice his hand. From the graduating class of '17, El Paso High. I'm an American citizen."

The man shook the tips of Alberto's fingers, the frown on his face telling Alberto that he didn't believe him.

"Can I get an application?" Alberto said.

"Well," the man said, scratching his head with his glasses, "just a minute. Let me see what the boss has to say. Just a minute."

The man disappeared behind the glass door. Alberto unfolded his handkerchief again and wiped his whole face. He could smell his nerves stinking up his armpits.

You've got to stop thinking of yourself as a peon, Albert, Rosemary had said. *You have talent. Remember what Miss Foster said. If you put your mind to it, you could be a writer. Show 'em your stories, Albert. The ones with Miss Foster's comments.*

Alberto touched the envelope curled in his coat pocket.

Besides, Rosemary had reminded him, *the* Herald *stands up for people like you. You remember that article last week about how the mayor should clean up the barrios, how unfair it is to let people live in those conditions.*

That doesn't mean they want people like me writing their articles, Alberto had told her.

Well, you just tell 'em to practice what they preach, then! They want people to be fair to Mexicans, let them set the example. Go on, Albert! You're a high school graduate. You're no ditchdigger. My dad would give us that property in Five Points if you got a real job.

That's not all he wants me to do, Alberto had said. *And I already told you, I'm not going to become a Mormon.*

He didn't say you had to convert for him to give us the land. But he won't do it unless you get a decent job. It's half an acre, Albert.

"Would you follow me, please?" Miss Lind was calling him from the doorway. Alberto's knees bounced a little as he followed her into the clatter of typewriters and the bittersweet smell of old coffee.

"All the way down the aisle and to the left. You'll see Mr. Gaines," she told him.

Alberto felt his hand fidgeting with his hat again, and he took it off as he walked to where Miss Lind had pointed. The noise of the typewriters died down. He knew that every eye in the place was glued to the color of his skin. Alberto did not look around. *Tell 'em to practice what they preach*, he heard again, but he felt like a coyote sneaking through somebody's backyard.

"Here he is. Come on in, muchacho," said Gaines. "Say hello to Mr. Corbitt, editor-in-chief. Sir, this muchacho wants to be a reporter."

Mr. Corbitt was fat and bald. His shirt was open at the collar, and his T-shirt and fingers were stained with ink. "You say you graduated from El Paso High School?" Corbitt spoke with a twang.

"Albert Morales." said Alberto, sticking his hand out, "from the graduating class of—"

"You got your diploma with you?" Corbitt interrupted.

Alberto didn't know what to do with his hat. He stuffed it under his arm and then took out the envelope that held his diploma and stories. "Right here, sir." He slipped the parchment out of the envelope and presented it to Corbitt. "My brother joined the Army, so I'm the one that got to finish high school."

Corbitt scrutinized the diploma. "How do I know this is yours?" he said. "Where's your birth certificate?"

"Birth certificate?" Alberto echoed. "My mother has that, sir. But I could go get it right now and be back in half an hour. If you need to see my writing, I do have these stories from my senior English class." Alberto offered the envelope to Corbitt. "The teacher said that I . . ." He swallowed the spit that had suddenly turned to salt in his throat, ". . . that I had talent. That I could be a writer someday."

"Where does your mother live?" Corbitt asked. "Chihuahuita?"

Alberto nodded. Corbitt looked at Gaines, ignoring Alberto's envelope. Alberto put the stories away, took his hat from under his arm, and punched it back into shape. Why didn't he have the guts to talk to them the way Rosemary would? He was the man of the family, but Rosemary was the one who knew herself. Knew that she didn't want to be called Mexican American, ever. Even though her mother was Mexican, her father and her skin were white, and that's why she would have insisted Corbitt read those stories. She would have read them herself, out loud, so that both Corbitt and Gaines could hear the talent that had written those words. Alberto didn't have Rosemary's advantages, and he didn't really want them, either. But Rosemary wanted the property that her father had offered, and Alberto had promised that he would try.

"Well, Mr. Moralees," the fat man started, "the problem is that that reporter position is filled. We hired a man just an hour ago."

Alberto shrugged. He started to put his hat on, but Gaines held up a hand to stop him.

"I don't think the chief is finished," Gaines said.

Alberto spun the hat by the brim and looked back at Corbitt.

"But we do have an opening for an office boy—"

"Office *assistant*," Gaines put in.

"Yes, an office assistant," said Corbitt. "Something along your line of experience."

"If you play your cards right," Gaines stepped in again, "you might even get to help the reporters out. You do any typing?"

Alberto shook his head. Inside, Rosemary was screaming: *I starched your shirt so that you could get hired as a janitor?*

"Mr. Moralees?"

Alberto blinked back his humiliation. "Excuse me?" he said.

"Mr. Corbitt was saying you might be able to do some research for the reporters."

"In your barrio, especially," added the fat man. "The *Herald* needs an anchor in the barrio, but your people don't trust us. They won't give us any information."

"I don't live in Chihuahuita anymore," said Alberta. "We have an apartment near St. Patrick's."

"Of course you do!" said Gaines. "Mr. Corbitt meant you could go to Chihuahuita and communicate with the folks. That would help the *Herald* out quite a bit. Why, you could move up from office assistant to research . . . research specialist mighty fast. Your salary would go up, too, naturally."

"What *is* the salary, sir?" Alberto asked, but he was thinking about that title: research specialist. Sounded like a fancy name for a spy. Or a vendido.

That's what his father would call him, a *pinche vendido*, selling out his people for half an acre of land.

". . . that's about standard for office boys," Corbitt was saying, "I mean office assistants, these days. Once you started doing research for us, we'd move it up from fifteen to eighteen a week."

Alberto took a deep breath and let it out through his nostrils, slowly, so that his indignation wouldn't show. "I'm afraid I can't be an office boy, Mr. Corbitt. I can't support my wife and two little girls on fifteen dollars a week. If you want, I can start being a research specialist right away. For twenty dollars a week. That's standard for high school graduates, isn't it?"

Alberto's eyes felt like lead. His father had once told him, *They can crush your heart, hijo, but don't let them break your huevos. That's the only advantage we have.*

Corbitt was looking at Gaines again. Finally, Corbitt said, "Call Peters in here, will you?"

Gaines stepped out of the office and yelled the name. A young fellow in a striped jacket limped into the room.

"What's up?" he said. He had a pencil tucked behind one ear, a cigarette behind the other.

"Peters," said Corbitt, "meet Albert Moralees. He's going to be your research specialist."

Alberto felt a pinch in his chest.

"My what?" said Peters, eyeing Alberto from hair to socks.

"He's going to be your link to Chihuahuita," said Gaines. "Your inside man."

"Chihuahuita ain't my beat, Chief," Peters said to the fat man.

"It is now, Peters," said Corbitt. "We're giving you a column. *Barrio News*. And Moralees here, he's going to get the news, and you're going to write it. Any complaints?"

"Hell no, Chief! A column? Hot tamales! Hey, Moralees, your name rhymes with tamales!"

"My name is Alberto Morales, Mr. Peters." The pinch had moved down to Alberto's groin.

"Show the man around, Peters," said Corbitt. "Then give him an assignment. Might as well break that column in *pronto*. When you bring your birth certificate in, Moralees, we'll get your contract ready."

"Congratulations, Moralees," Gaines said, slapping Alberto on the back.

Alberto did not thank the men. He followed Peters out of Corbitt's office, wringing his hat like a mop. Research specialist. Rosemary would like the sound of that.

"This here's *my* desk," said Peters. "My typewriter. My chair. My ashtray. You're gonna work on the street. Go get yourself a notebook from honey pie over there." He jerked his thumb in the direction of Miss Lind, who was filing her nails in the front office.

"I need a notebook," Alberto mumbled to her.

"No kidding?" she said, her file suspended.

"No kidding," Alberto said. She opened the bottom drawer of her desk, took a long thin notebook from a pile, and handed it over to Alberto. On the cover, it said *Reporter's Notebook.*

"Go out and get me some news," Peters said behind him, the man's tobacco breath hanging on Alberto's neck. "But don't be giving me any opinions, Moralees. All I want from you is facts. Information. Keep your tamale-brained opinions to yourself. Flunkies don't give opinions, do they, Miss Lind?"

No señor, thought Alberto, gripping his hat in his fist. He was no ditch-digger. A ditchdigger would've already punched this cabrón's teeth out of his mouth. But he could hear Rosemary already. She would want to go down to the drugstore right away to telephone her father and give him the good news. *Albert got a real job, Daddy. He's training to be a reporter for the* El Paso Herald. *They even gave him a reporter's notebook.* ★

Abraham Verghese

Born and raised in Ethiopia, Abraham Verghese immigrated to the United States after obtaining his medical degree. He has served on the faculty at East Tennessee State University; the University of Iowa; Texas Tech University in El Paso, where he was Professor of Medicine and Chief of Infectious Disease; and at the University of Texas Health Science Center, San Antonio, as the founding director of the Center for Medical Humanities and Ethics. A graduate of the University of Iowa Writer's Workshop, Verghese has written short stories and essays that have appeared in *The New Yorker*, *The New York Times*, *Sports Illustrated*, *The Atlantic Monthly*, *Esquire*, *Story*, *Granta*, *The New York Times Magazine*, *The Wall Street Journal*, and elsewhere. He is the author of *My Own Country: A Doctor's Story*, a 1994 National Book Critics Circle Award Finalist and one of five books chosen as Best Book of the Year by *Time Magazine*; *The Tennis Partner*, a New York Times Notable Book; and his most recent book and first novel *Cutting For Stone*. He is currently Senior Associate Chair for the Theory and Practice of Medicine at Stanford University School of Medicine.

From *The Tennis Partner*: March 17, 1994, St. Patrick's Day: El Paso, Texas

I DASH OUT OF THE HOSPITAL INTO THE BRIGHT sunlight. It is two in the afternoon and windy. Other than the police, at this moment, as I cut between cars in the parking lot, I am the only one who knows that David is dead. For the people who haven't heard, David's death is yet to happen. For them, he is still alive.

I run into an intern, a big, affable El Salvadoran sporting a bright green tie.

"Dr. Verghese, about Mrs. Escobedo—"

"Not now." I grip his arm. "I have to go to the morgue."

Then I say it: "David Smith is dead."

His face goes slack and his head lolls back as if I have hit him. He stumbles, reaches to support himself against a car that is not there. I grab him. I have a moment of perverse pleasure in seeing how he reels and totters, imagining how his day is now unhinged. I picture how the shock waves will spread through the rest of the staff— David's fellow interns in particular—and leave them frozen in doorways. They will rack their brains for the memory of the last time they saw him, the last thing he said to them. They will play the before-and-after game that I am now playing.

***

On Alameda Street, leading away from the hospital, there is a procession of hopeful signs: LUCKY CAFE, GOOD LUCK BAR, LUCKY TAVERN. Between the hospital and these neighbors only the cemetery intervenes, claiming four city blocks. From the hospital's upper floors, patients look out through their windows over a sea of crosses.

The morgue, which I have never visited before, seems to sit *in* the cemetery even though it is not of the cemetery. With its mirrored glass front, stepped skylights, and large panels of marble and stone, it resembles a giant mausoleum.

Inside, it is cold. The orange carpeting, the modular furniture, and the ficus plants of the atrium have been imported directly from a Scandinavian furniture showroom. No echo here. No green tile. I sniff like a bloodhound, but not a whiff of formalin escapes.

The coroner's secretary is pretty solicitous, experienced in these matters. She offers me coffee and a chair, but with her eyes she takes my pulse. I thank her and decline both. Yes, his next of kin are in Australia and are unlikely to come for at least a few days. A few code words into an intercom and then she weaves down a baffle of short corridors. I follow into the labyrinth, my eyes on her shoulder-length black hair that bounces with every step. Suddenly we are in another room. She positions me in front of a large glass partition and then she disappears.

I bring my hand up to shield my eyes from the glare of my own reflection. I see into a spotless, darkened chamber. My eyes fix first on the tiled floors—at last something morguelike here—and then, almost hidden in shadows, swinging double doors to the right. David will come through them. No, David's *body* will come through those doors.

I try to picture how it will look. The police have asked me to identify David's body. They need me to be certain it is he. They are pretty sure . . . I am pretty sure . . . still—

***

Wait, wait, I want to say when I hear voices and sense movement on the other side of the glass partition . . .

Overhead lights click on and chase away all shadows. The tiles become lustrous. The swinging doors bulge open and disgorge onto this stage-lit scene the backside of an attendant, then a stainless-steel gurney, then another attendant.

I have seen both the attendants around Thomason. One of them is a ringer we sneaked on to our internal medicine soccer team, a left-footed, fluid striker. They are surprised to see me. I raise a hand and then am embarrassed by this gesture. They are wearing thick rubber gloves, the kind you use to attend a mare in labor.

The attendants jockey the stretcher back and forth until it is right below me. I push against the glass and look down at the body on the gurney.

***

David's face is intact.

I feel a huge relief. I worried that I would carry away a horrible and lingering vision of him, of a face blown away, a grotesque *after* picture, a gaping hole of a death mask that would terrorize me at night, distort and supplant the memory of the real face of my friend. A stored-up breath leaves my body in a long exhale.

Still, the bony scaffold behind David's face is shattered, causing it to sag back as if it were a deflated football. The right eyeball has popped neatly out of the orbit and dangles by the optic nerve, staring at the toes of the corpse. It is, strangely, not repulsive to me: A splendid anatomical specimen has been delivered from its housing by a careful dissector. The eyeball is undamaged, a perfect sphere, shiny still, with a tinge of blue to the sclera and turgid from the vitreous fluid within.

From the back of the eyeball, the optic nerve gathers its fibers together like a carefully combed ponytail and slips back between the closed eyelids.

There is a bloody pool at the back of David's head where it meets the metal of the gurney, a pottage of hair, sero-sanguinous fluid, brain. David put the muzzle of the shotgun in his mouth, pointed it up and back against the soft palate, perhaps shading to the right just a hair. The eyeball must have been forced out by the explosion that went off within the confines of the skull. This same dangling eye witnessed the shape and form of the treason about to unfold. And then he pulled the trigger.

A memory from when I was a medical student, a fragment of text from a forensic book, appears in my head. Criminologists of the late nineteenth century tried to dissect out eyeballs of murder victims, hoping to find the image of the killer preserved on the retinae. Now, in the presence of this body, I can see how that silly thought was formed.

***

I pull my gaze away from that eye and start again, clinically, through the glass, to examine this face. My hands reflexively reach for the instruments in my coat pocket. Their touch against my fingers is reassuring even though they are completely useless in this building. I see the blond hair, the small jaw that is so much like Rod Laver's . . .

The body looks smaller than how I remember it, perhaps because the oversized gurney dwarfs him. He wears boxer shorts and an El Paso Tennis Club T-shirt.

This looks like the T-shirt Emily gave him two days before he died. Yes. I had seen it in her car. She had been carrying that T-shirt and a tracksuit and a Bible for him in the backseat, just in case she spotted him a third time walking on the street. Each evening I had driven up and down Mesa Street looking for him, but it was Emily, on her way to and from school, who had run into him three different times. The last time he again told her to get away. He didn't want to talk. And he wouldn't tell her where he was staying.

But he accepted the change of clothes and the Bible and the fifteen dollars she put in the Bible, weeping suddenly, she told me, at this act of thoughtfulness and concern on her part.

"Why are you doing this for me?"

"Why are *you* doing this, David?"

He trotted out his worn excuse: She had left him, he couldn't do emergency medicine, he hated internal medicine.

"I wish you'd get your crap together and quit this," she said.

"I want you to know, I never, ever cheated on you." It seemed terribly important for him to tell her this, even though by now I knew that this was not true.

"You're going to be fine one day," he said. "You're going to have a husband and you'll be happy." He pushed away all her other offers of help. "Tell everyone thank you," he said.

Off he went, heading in a different direction each time, never toward the motel he was staying in.

***

One moment I was eating the lunch special, dipping into a bowl of *caldo de res* rendered fiery by home-canned serrano chilies being passed around the cafeteria table. The next moment, sweating slightly, my mouth on fire, I answered a page and was told David was dead. When I could speak, though not make my words come out straight, I had confused the sergeant with my questions.

Now, as I stare at the body, I reconstruct David's last moments: He was in bed. The Bible was on the nightstand. The TV was silent on its pedestal. Perhaps he was asleep. Or staring at the exposed rock wall that ran the length of his room, a feature of this motel that, when it first opened, must have seemed as radical as the wood-patterned Formica on the nightstands, or the bright yellow vinyl on the chairs. The tennis bag I had seen him disappear with, and which had surely held his shotgun, sat on the shaggy green carpet along with seven bottles of unused Vaseline Intensive Care hand lotion, each representing a bad check, a trip to Furr's where he would buy lotion and pay for it with a twenty-dollar check, pocketing the difference.

The cops knocked at the door of his motel room, ignoring the PRIVACY PLEASE sign. There was no peephole. David got up and cracked open the door.

Are you Dr. David Smith?

Yes.

We have a warrant for your arrest.

What for?

Bad checks.

That was our doing, we the friends-of-David. After checking at every motel on Mesa, we had tracked him to this one. He was registered in his own name. We sent the cops after him. To catch him and take him straight to the El Paso County detox, bypass jail, get him off the street.

David closed the door, as if to slip the chain off. But instead, he turned the dead bolt.

One cop ran to the back of the motel, thinking he might be diving out the window. The other cop banged on the front door. David made a phone call. "Mickie? MICKIE!" Mickie, his former landlady, was out and only her answering machine recorded the despair in his voice, the pounding in the background . . .

And then came the boom of a shotgun, a deafening blast that reverberated down the corridors.

The cops took cover.

Motel guests were flushed from their rooms.

The SWAT team arrived and with them the press and every other scanner hound nearby.

It was a while before they stormed into David's room and found his body.

***

The coroner's assistant materializes beside me. I am petulant. Where was she all this time? I am resentful of her tidy appearance, her perfume, her professionalism, her matter-of-factness, the way she wears the reserve and severity of this building. There is a process here that she is comfortable with but that hasn't been explained to me sufficiently.

"I can't be sure it is him," I say finally. "Can I go in there?"

She goes out to ask the coroner.

I wait.

The two attendants stand deferentially on the other side of the glass, their hands resting on the gurney. I know how they feel: This is just another body to them, and yet they have to act a certain way in the presence of the living. Once I'm gone they can resume their chatter, the Tex-Mex Spanglish patois that I caught from behind the closed door before the stretcher came through.

The assistant returns. "You can go in."

She escorts me out and around and through the double doors and then she leaves.

***

Suddenly, I am on the other side of the looking glass, under the theatrical lights, in the tiled room, beside what is left of my student, my intern, my tennis partner, my friend.

There is a visceral smell now, the miasma of a freshly opened cadaver, not unpleasant but leaving me feeling as if I had stumbled on to someone's most intimate scent, the kind left on their bath towel or that wafts up from their laundry hamper. There are so many odors in medicine; if I had students next to me now, the pedant in me would recite the list that I have memorized: the moldy-hay smell of typhoid, the mousy odor of liver failure, the sweetish acetone odor of diabetic coma . . .

But this odor is not in my canon of odors.

I move closer and lean over the body. My hands come out of my coat pockets, restless again, an instinctive response when you put me close to a recumbent figure. David's face is as I saw it from behind the glass. The skin is dry and flaking, there is three or four days of stubble around his chin, the fine wrinkles at the corners of his eyes are exaggerated by the light. But, as a face, it yields no more clues. My fingers want to reseat that eyeball in its socket.

Instead, I lift up his T-shirt. The scaphoid belly and the thin, hairless chest look like David's. A loss of at least fifteen pounds in the last two weeks. I run my fingers down his arms. There is a salmon-colored bruise and a pale puncture mark in the crook of his left elbow. Before I am aware of it, my fingers are rooting reflexively on the inner side of his biceps tendon. A cold, pulseless, brachial artery submits to my touch.

His hands are ensconced in brown paper bags. I reach to remove them.

"Don't!" one of the attendants says. "Sorry, Doc. *Es que,* they need to do the gunpowder test."

"Like there's some doubt as to who pulled the trigger?"

He shrugs and smiles.

I leave the paper bags alone. I inspect the lower torso, the thighs, the knees.

***

I turn at last to the feet.

And then I know for sure it is David.

His feet are pointed down and turned out at the heels to make a V. I see the toes with the prehensile curl in them, toes I recognize from the locker room, and from when he padded around my apartment barefooted. I see the pearl-like calluses over the joints of his second and third toes, and the knobby excrescence of hardened skin on the side of the big toe of the right foot. The toe cap of his right sneaker would wear out long before the left, from his dragging that foot to the line as he launched into his serve.

***

His battered toes carry the stigma of his past life, before he was a doctor, when he was a professional tennis player. Those toes were shaped by scuffing on ant-dirt courts in Australia, sliding on clay and skidding on grass in Europe, pounding on American cement and Har-Tru. They are surprisingly coarse when contrasted with the grace of his movements on the court.

I laugh. The attendants have been watching me with concern and now they are positively alarmed. I want to tell them how he said when he was playing college tennis his feet ached so much that he would limp off the court after a match, then limp around all week, limp during practice, eventually limp back onto the court for his next big match where he would leap and pivot and scramble brilliantly only to limp off again . . . it was a running joke among his teammates. And I remember the way he told me this, laughing at himself, his smile so broad that his eyes were buried in the crinkles that formed around them.

I straighten up. I don't say any of these things.

I adjust his T-shirt, pull it back into place, tug it down so it covers his boxers.

This is undoubtedly David. But I am reluctant to leave. This is the picture I have been left with: a deflated face, a wasted body . . . the familiar curl of his toes. ★

Lee Merrill Byrd

Born and raised in New Jersey, Lee Merrill Byrd has made El Paso her home since 1978. She is the co-founder of Cinco Puntos Press, established in 1985, a publishing house with the mission of bringing the multicultural literature of the American Southwest, the U.S./Mexico border region, and Mexico to a national audience. Cinco Puntos publishes nonfiction, fiction, poetry, and children's literature. Byrd is also an award-winning author of fiction for adults and children. Her novel *Riley's Fire* was named one of the Top Ten Best books of 2006 by *People Magazine* and her collection of short stories, *My Sister Disappears*, received a 1993 Texas Institute of Letters award. Byrd is the author of two children's books: *Lover Boy* and *The Treasure on Gold Street*, which received a Skipping Stones Honor Book Award, a Southwest Book Award, a Paterson Poetry Center Prize, and the Teddy Award from the Texas Writers League. A recipient of the 1997 Dobie-Paisano Fellowship, she also received a Cultural Freedom Fellowship from the Lannan Foundation in 2005.

From *My Sister Disappears: Stories and a Novella*: When He Is Thirty-Seven

When he is thirty-seven, it will snow in El Paso. His wife and his children will be in bed. It will be early still, nine or nine-thirty.

At that hour there are clouds lying over the city, pressing down around the mountains at the top of his street. The night is filled with the heavy electric stillness that brings rain. No one expects snow. It is nearly March and the winter has been mild. After supper his kids play outside as if it were summer and in the morning when he goes to work his wife and the woman across the street sit on the front stoop of his house and talk, the way women do at the first sign of spring. In the back yard, the peach tree he planted three years ago, framed in the window of their bedroom, has buds and from the buds faint tokens of the white petals soon to ignite in the brooding air.

He will stay up late, way past midnight. It is a Friday night and from long habit he will drink red wine, sitting down to read at the old dining room table, the newspaper spread out before him, a dim light overhead. He works his tongue in his mouth while he reads just as, were she here to see him, his mother would remember he read as a boy; the same way his son, who is seven, reads now. The paper is full of stories and he leans forward, squinting, letting himself disappear inside them.

But they do not hold him. Then for a long time, he studies the things in this room that is partly a living room and partly a dining room—the couch with the orange and brown stripes in it, the stuffed chair, the unmatched rugs, some pictures drawn by his children and framed carefully by his wife. His son sighs in his sleep. The dog stretches, stands up and shakes, turns around, lies back down on his blanket. The refrigerator clicks on, hums.

He gets up, restless, walking back and forth, goes to the front door and opens it. It is then that he sees the snow. It covers the trees and the bushes, the grass and the sidewalks and the houses of all his neighbors—elegant, silent, a special grace.

***

Are you coming to bed?

His wife calls out sleepily, hearing him as he rummages through the hall closet, looking for the red winter coat and the dark brown wool cap that have been stored there since the days when they lived in colder places, when they were first married. He goes into their bedroom and kneels down beside the bed so he can talk to her.

It's snowing, he says.

It is? Oh no. She smiles, her eyes open for just a minute. For his sake she pretends to raise up on one arm and look out, but she cannot. It's pretty, she murmurs, rolling over onto her stomach.

The red coat buttoned, the collar turned up, the cap covering his ears, he goes outside, standing on the front porch for a long time, looking south toward the lights of Juarez. There are no cars moving on his street. Only an occasional one creeps along the bigger, busier street a block away. Everyone is sleeping, their houses dark and quiet.

Across the street a light comes on. It is Mrs. Miller's house. She is a widow lady. Her nephew, a boy of fifteen or sixteen, has come for a visit from Oklahoma. Now the boy has turned on the light in the glassed-in porch at the side of Mrs. Miller's house, the little crowded corner where she stores newspapers and jars and flowerpots. From where he is standing, the man can see the boy preparing to set out from his aunt's house. The man's wife has told him that Mrs. Miller's nephew is a nice boy, a little too serious perhaps, very shy. Of course, says his wife, that may be because he has no one to hang around with. He is only visiting. Imagine his trying to make friends with the Lopez boys who live two doors away from them. Ha! They are so coarse and rough; they like to drink and swear and sit around talking to girls all night. This boy, Mrs. Miller's nephew, is not like that, his wife has declared.

The boy switches off the porch light so that his aunt won't miss him if she wakes up. He shuts the door carefully behind him. On the top step he buttons his long overcoat. From where the man stands, hidden in the shadows on his front porch, it looks like a good coat, a formal one, the kind that you would bring with you when you visit your aunt because there is no room in your suitcase for two coats and your mother will insist you bring one that will not embarrass your father's older sister, one that will do for church, for shopping, for going out to visit or for play. Although your mother knows that this last is not possible, knows that a boy cannot "play" in a long formal overcoat, knows that a boy cannot consider it when he is visiting his aunt.

It is all right though. For the boy, when he comes to visit his aunt every year, foregoes play of any kind. He stays inside, sleeping late and watching TV. Sometimes he reads and sometimes he helps his aunt cook and sometimes he gives her a hand with the spring cleaning that she likes to save up for when he comes. Though he would never admit it, he likes to be with her, he likes to listen to her talk. Secretly it pleases him to go through his aunt's storage closets in her annual cleanups, to look over the stacks of old magazines she saves and all her old pictures, the funny dated shoes and hats, and to listen to all the old stories that go with them.

There is a great pleasure in hearing his aunt's stories. There is something about people's lives laid out the way his aunt lays them out, like a suit of clothes, that makes him feel as if he is about to understand something very important.

The lives she tells about have a beginning and an end, not just an infinite middle, like his own. They can be looked at and studied, conclusions real and fantastic drawn.

But his aunt has her boring moments, too. She is going on sixty-two. She likes to go to bed early. Up alone in her maidenly cottage at night, he feels nervous and restless. He remembers that he is almost sixteen, almost a man. He peers out across the street at the Lopez house where the boys gather in ominous crowds on their front steps. His aunt, he knows, would dislike it intensely if he ever approached the Lopez house where boys of all ages congregate to laugh and curse and make themselves useless. Overcharged with energy, they spill out into the street, playing football or baseball, depending on the time of year, always screaming and yelling. Every night, late at night, the older boys will sit on the front porch with their girlfriends and tease them. The sound of their excited laughter worries the boy, makes him wish he were older than he is and had more courage than he has.

But tonight the street is silent. The stoop where the Lopez boys crowd by day is covered with snow. Their house is dark. He is safe then. He walks down the porch steps and out onto the drive, placing his feet down slowly in the clean white snow. At the street he pauses, looking first one way and then another. He sets out toward the main road a block away.

The man watches the boy. Sometimes he is just a dark shadow. Sometimes he is hazy with light and snow, standing beneath the cone of light from the streetlamps. Then for five or ten minutes, Mrs. Miller's nephew is gone.

From out of a side street near his aunt's house, he appears again. He comes to the bottom of her drive. He doesn't want to go in. There is more to do this night. The snow excites him, the silent empty street fills him with power. He starts in the other direction toward the park on the next block but in ten minutes he is back again, his hands jammed into the pockets of his long overcoat, the collar pulled up around his neck.

Now the man, watching the boy, will remember something he had forgotten.

***

I am sixteen.

I live in Memphis, a river-town.

My father is dead. My mother supports me and my brother and my two sisters by selling real estate.

People want to help us. Is everything all right? they ask. Is there anything we can do? They are always so sad. They fuss over me. How sullen Bobby is, says Uncle John to Mother. Don't you think a boy that age should have a job? Why, when I was his age, I had already been working for five years, helping out my mother and father.

I want to be like my father. Far away from all their voices. Now his life can go on undisturbed. I want to be like him, away from all their voices and all their help. I am sixteen and I don't want any help.

I want to be like my father because he can study life. He is no longer held by it. He can look at it and understand it. A dead man could write a book.

I would like to write a book. I would like to write a book about Memphis and the way it is, about the river, about the black men in the Dew Drop Inn, about Beale Street and the white women in their flowered hats, about the young girls, about my friends, about my friend Walker.

Walker is the only one I can talk to. He walks along down beside the river. He is young and skinny like I am. He stands beside the river and lights a cigarette. He smokes it, the river at his back. When Walker stands beside the river, I can read it, like a book. Where there is an empty space, the river comes to fill it. Where the land will let it, the river moves in. The South is like that, like the river, like a woman. Women are like the river, moving into all the empty spaces that we, through neglect or fear or lack of time, have failed to fill up. The only thing a woman will ignore is a dead man.

My mother is anxious for me to do well in school, to get good grades, to begin to take out the daughters of the best families in Memphis. My mother has the connections through her father that will make a good match possible. But I have already been thrown out of two private high schools and I am not interested in the daughters of good families. I am surly and intractable. In the afternoons Walker and I go down beneath the bridge by the river and drink red wine and smoke Camel cigarettes.

Besides my mother, I have a mammy, Tula. The only ambition that Tula has for me is that I will not worry Mother. A young boy will get hisself into all kinds of trouble, she says to Mother, to soothe her.

Mother and Tula sit up late in the kitchen on Holmes Street that in the afternoon is laced with light and shadow. My mother does not know the kitchen shadows of the afternoon. All day she sells real estate. Her shoulders are stooped. She grinds her teeth in her sleep. She sighs and it rips through us the way a saw might rip through flesh, cutting deep memory in our hearts, tearing at the idea we have sometimes that everything will be all right.

Even after all these years my mother's sighs come to me like blows, heavy and irrevocable. Even after all these years, my mother remarried, a fine house and plenty of money, the sight of her alone, with folded hands, staring straight ahead, makes me afraid.

I am sitting in the kitchen with Tula. I have just turned sixteen. I have my driver's license in the wallet in my back pocket. Outside the clouds lie heavy and pressing over the city, as ominous as women. It will rain.

Do you think Mother will let me have the car? I ask Tula. I watch her hands. She is making biscuits, patting out the dough.

Tula and I sit in the kitchen in the afternoon. She talks to me. She never says anything about my fingers that are yellow from the cigarettes or about my eyes that are sometimes bloodshot or about my friend Walker who Mother says is not a good boy. We do not talk about everyday. She doesn't tell me about her husband she goes to see on Thursdays, her day off, or about her kids. For all we know, we are her kids.

In the kitchen Tula pats the dough and she tells me stories. They are stories that begin when a person is born and end when a person dies. She lays them out like the dough, rolling them flat on the table for me to see and draw my understanding from. She requires nothing from me but that I do not worry Mother.

Where you going? she wants to know.

Caroline Gage is having a party, I tell her, and though she knows I might not go, she is satisfied. She is satisfied because she has no ambition for me other than that I do not worry Mother and Mrs. Gage is Mother's friend. Knowing I was at Caroline Gage's house would bring a certain amount of peace to my mother's heart.

And I haven't lied. Caroline is having a party. Walker and I may even go there. Sometime. Maybe early, maybe late. We cannot tell. It will depend. On how soon we get started, on whether we want to have a beer first, on how much we enjoy driving along in Mother's car, on the black men at the Dew Drop Inn and on the stories they tell. It will depend on whether the night is very fine and if it is, we will go looking for girls. It is spring and the smell of dogwood will drive us nuts and then no stories the black men can tell will hold us at all.

Or, if it rains, maybe we will go to Caroline's.

It is hard to tell.

You be home early, Tula says. Hear? Your mother needs that car.

I watch her hands and do not answer.

Your father wouldn't let you have the car, says Tula. If he was here, he wouldn't let you have the car. She means that if it were up to her, she would not let me have the car, not because she cares one way or the other about it, but because she knows it will worry Mother.

She flours the table and puts the dough down on it, patting it flat. Your mother wanted your daddy to find another job, she begins, as she has begun every time the subject of my father comes up.

She told your daddy she don't like him to fly. And your daddy says he'd quit. He says soon he won't even go up in the air at all, he'd move on to the factory where they make the planes and get him a job as a manager.

She takes a glass and cuts the biscuits out round and separate from the flat sheet of dough.

Said he only have two more times, then he'd quit. That was when Patsy was seven months old. We was in the kitchen, right here, talking about the dinner, waiting for your daddy to come home and the phone ring. They say the plane crashed and your daddy is dead.

She pushes at the last bit of dough.

You crying around the house all day. Daddy. I want my Daddy. Worrying your mother. When you get bigger, when you was five, you never did shut up, you talked all day, you was full of plans. You be in and out of this kitchen all day. Telling me, Tula, I'm going to build a fence. Tula, if we fix the toolhouse this way or that, then we could put more of the rakes in it or more of the hammers.

Or how you was going to fix the car. The kind of things a boy tells his daddy, coming in and telling them to me.

She shakes her head back and forth, wiping her hands on her apron.

Can't you walk tonight? she says.

I got my license, I tell her, going to the back door and looking out. I'm a good driver.

I go and sit out on the front porch, waiting for Mother to come home with the car. It is five-thirty and I told Walker that I would be at his house by seven. When Mother gets home, she'll be tired. I'll have to wait awhile before I can ask her to be certain that she'll say yes. I'll have to wait awhile more for her to tell me how important having a car is in the real estate business and how it is real estate that puts food on our table and how she would rather I find another way to go.

I see her drive up the street. My mother is a small woman. I can barely see her head above the steering wheel. She is leaning forward and holding on tightly to it. She pulls into the driveway and her face doesn't relax. It is full of contracts and openings and closings and what will she do to help her children and how will the bills get paid.

It would be so easy to make her laugh. I could say, How are you, Mother? and I could kiss her on her cheek. I could tell her all about myself, about what I want and what I dream of and how well I would like to do in school and the plans I have for my future. But I cannot give her that. Not now, not when I am sixteen and I want the car.

Now all I want is to get away from her, to go out with Walker and get drunk, stay out all night racing up and down the dark wet streets of Memphis in her car.

The car stops by the porch and she sits for a minute, thinking. I don't like to watch her sit and think. I get up and go out.

We carry in the groceries. She is tired and sits down in the living room. Mother, I tell her, Caroline Gage is having a party tonight.

Oh! Oh! she says, as excited as a little girl. I wonder if Ann Gage will want me to send over my punch bowl.

No, I say quickly. She has everything. She said everything is fine.

Well, isn't that wonderful? she says. What will you wear? Your suit?

No, Mother, I tell her. It's not like that. We don't need to dress up.

You need a bath, she says. And a good white shirt.

Yes, Mother, I say. Mother, can I take the car?

Now she is not so excited. I'll drop you over there, she says. And then later, around ten or so, you can walk back.

She gets up and walks out of the room and then comes back. Why, I think that's just marvelous, she goes on. Isn't that nice of Caroline Gage to invite you to her party?

I sit down in the chair in the corner of the room and stare straight ahead of me.

What's wrong with me taking you over, Bobby? she says. That's the only car we've got. That's all we've got.

I only just want to go over there and back, Mother, I say.

Now, all of a sudden, I believe in my story. God, I only just want to get in the car and drive over to Caroline's and come back. You'd think I wanted to go all over Memphis, I yell at her.

No, she says, I can't let you do that.

She sits down in the chair across from me. By now it must be six and Walker will be calling over soon to see what is going on. If Mother knows that Walker is going, I'll never get the car.

I shut my eyes. I know what she is doing, even with my eyes shut. Her hands are clasped and she is rubbing her palms together. She is biting her lip and remembering what Tula remembers and remembering what only she can know. If I look up, if I open my eyes, her eyes will have tears in them. I put my hand over my own eyes to hide from her.

I want you back by eleven, she says finally. At the latest. She sighs. She takes her purse up from beside the chair where it is lying on top of piles of contracts and brochures. She unclasps the handle and searches inside for her keys. I hear them jingle. She turns them over and over in her hands, as if they are beads and she is saying the office of her trials. She holds them out to me. I try not to grab them and run.

You can't go looking like that, she says. You go and clean up. And I'm sure Ann Gage will need the punch bowl. I will get it in its box and get the glasses wiped out and you may carry it over in the car to Caroline's.

I pull out of the driveway at a quarter to seven, the box with the punch bowl and its glasses in the trunk, put there by Mother and Tula. They are standing at the door and watching me. I am wearing a white shirt and have a sport jacket hanging in the back seat and I have promised to be home by eleven and promised to see that Mrs. Gage understands that Mother is in no hurry to have the bowl returned.

***

Mrs. Miller's nephew shuffles up the sidewalk, his head bent against the snow. He turns back and stares down the street, looking first in one direction and then another. Certain that he is the only one awake at this hour, that the street and the snow are his alone, he begins to run, gathering speed and sliding, making long trails in the untouched snow, falling down and getting up again, dizzy, ecstatic in the sweet dark and empty night.

***

That night, Walker and I went early to Caroline's, just to get rid of the punch bowl. Mr. Gage was there. He wore a suit and stood at the edge of the living room, checking his watch every few minutes. Mrs. Gage said she was thrilled with the punch bowl. She said that Mother was the most wonderful woman she knew and so brave. Walker and I stuffed ourselves on boiled shrimp and slipped out without saying thank you. It had gotten colder some and the air hung heavy, wrapped around the city like a blanket.

The Dew Drop Inn was packed. After a few beers, me and Walker came out of the back room where you drink if you're white and underage. We sat down in the bar and nobody seemed to care.

An old man sat playing the blues on his guitar. You got to fan it, he sang.

Oh my, yes, said a black woman in a wide-brimmed hat.

You got to fan it to keep it warm, sang the old man, till your baby come home.

The black men were laughing, telling stories, one right after the other, about the women, how they come and go and make them spend, about the work they were doing, working in the white man's yards and houses, about picking up and moving fast, about people living and dying, and Walker and I got drunker and drunker and I forgot all about my promise to Mother to be home by eleven.

The bartender came over after a long while and said, White man coming, boys, to warn us about the cops, and Walker and I got up and went out the back door, but it was a whole different night outside than the one it had been when we'd first come in.

It had snowed. Goddamn! yelled Walker and we stood, leaning against the back of the Dew Drop Inn, and stared at it for a long time. Then we peed and got into Mother's car and drove ever so slowly out of the alley behind the Dew Drop Inn where we always parked and set out through town, slowing down even more to stare into the empty stores, leaning out of the windows of Mother's car to look with astonishment at the long empty lunch counters where there were no people. The streets were empty, the sidewalks were empty, everything was covered with snow and Walker and I were so drunk, we were astounded.

The clock over a pawnshop said it was twenty to two.

My God, Walker, I said to him. Mother will kill me. I've got to hurry home.

Yeah, he said, hurry.

We got onto Central, heading east, away from the river. It had two or three inches of snow on it and, for as far as we could see, it was wide and straight and empty.

Hurry, hurry, Walker said. I pressed down a little on the gas to get up some speed. Not too much in case someone should see us and think we were drunk. But I was so anxious suddenly about Mother's car that I slammed down on the brakes. The car began to spin. I heard Walker moan. The back end came around to where the side was and Walker and I turned in surprise to watch it. It spun slowly, as if it were in a dream, and when it came to rest, we were heading west again toward the river.

I thought we were going to die, Walker said.

So did I, I told him.

See if you can do that again, he said. Spin around the other way.

I got the car going fast, maybe a little too fast, because when we spun the next time, it turned full circle and we were right back where we started.

Here, said Walker, let me try it. He got out of his side and I got out of mine. We stopped for a minute to pee again in the fresh snow. He lit a cigarette and got behind the wheel.

Okay, he said.

That night Walker and I spun all the way down Central, taking turns, going first in one direction and then in the other, getting up some speed and slamming on the brakes. We must have spun thirty or forty times that night in Mother's car, going all the way down Central to home.

***

The boy is beginning to get cold. The spell of the snow and the quiet night is over for him. He trudges up the street, toward home. The bed in his aunt's house will be warm and he is ready to go back to sleep.

The light at the side of Mrs. Miller's house comes on. It is Mrs. Miller, holding the neck of her bathrobe closed, peering out. She sees her nephew coming up the drive and opens the side door for him. The man can almost hear what she is saying. Can imagine it, anyway.

The boy and his aunt stand face to face on the glassed-in side porch while Mrs. Miller finds out where he has been and what he has been doing. The man can see the two of them talking, the boy sleepy, his aunt wondering if it is all right to believe what he has told her. She turns to look out across the street, toward the Lopez house, anxious to see if they are up. Satisfied that they are not, she turns back.

The light on her porch goes off. Lights appear throughout the house while Mrs. Miller adjusts herself to this strange whim of the nephew she thought she knew so well and while the boy, not caring if she believes him or not, falls asleep.

The last light goes out in Mrs. Miller's house. The street lies silent and dark, no cars to wake it, no commerce to engage it. The man stands quietly on his porch, watching, thinking about his mother, and then now his own children, letting his memories and his dreams, like the snow, drift down slowly and surround him. ★

Estela Portillo Trambley

Estela Portillo Trambley (1936-1999) was born and raised in El Paso. She earned a B.A. and M.A. in English at the Texas College of Mines, now the University of Texas at El Paso. She is considered a pioneer in Chicana literature with her themes of women rebelling against male domination, and her writing has been the subject of scholarly and critical study. Her play *The Day of the Swallows* won the Quinto Sol Award in 1973. Her plays have been widely produced throughout Texas, New Mexico, California, and Mexico. In 1975, her collection of short fiction *Rain of Scorpions and Other Stories* was published, followed by the novel *Trini*, published in 1986. Portillo Trambley taught English at the high school and college level, hosted radio and television shows, and was resident dramatist at El Paso Community College. She was the Presidential Chair in Creative Writing at the University of California, Davis.

From *Rain of Scorpions and Other Stories*: Pay the Criers

Chucho had gotten home before the storm broke. The act of apologizing to Juana for staying away for three days was heavy on his mind. When he went into the house, he found his wife crying over the body of her dead mother. She had rushed into Chucho's arms from the back room where Refugio lay dead in her own bed. She had left her work as a maid in El Paso because she was feeling bad, only to die of a heart attack in her daughter's arms. Chucho thought of Juana grieving in loneliness; he thought of his mother-in-law who had died like a warrior in the midst of the daily battle for bread. The old woman's life had been nothing but work. Sure, she had had her share of good times and had enjoyed them fully, but the duty of the daily struggle had always been foremost in her life. That's why she had been a tiger, wearing a shawl, carrying a rosary in her hand, ready to pounce on him for being what she called "shiftless."

The old woman had disliked him because he couldn't keep a job, because it had been up to her to support the household. The fifteen dollars a week she earned in the American city were enough when she crossed to Juárez on the Mexican side. It was enough to feed them and pay the rent on the lot where their house stood. More important, Refugio was able to save a dollar a week for a grand funeral. She had been saving for seventeen years, and the more she added to her little nest egg, the more she planned for the festivities that were to take place at her wake. Chucho was thinking of the money at this moment as Juana broke out tormentedly in sobs. She had loved and depended on her mother all her life. Now the security was gone.

Refugio had always resented giving Chucho even a nickel. Once in a while she had opened up her purse strings to send him out for beer, and she had graciously not asked for the change. When his mother-in-law came home for weekends, they locked horns like bulls. Well not all the time, for they had shared some good times together. The money . . . He tried to put the thought out of his mind, but the thought would not leave. All that funeral money somewhere in the house! Or else, she had given it to Juana before she died. Certainly Juana would know where it was. While he held his weeping wife, he imagined the money in his pocket. He could coax Juana to give it to him. Money was never meant to be wasted on the dead. He knew he was planning something low and underhanded, and he fought the idea within himself for a minute or so, only to give way again to his unprincipled ways. His life had been lived so far without creed or rules. Juana and Chucho looked at each other, a look that held them together. It was time to comfort.

He led his pretty little wife to their bed in the front room and held her close as he stroked her hair. Suddenly there was a burst of thunder and a flash of lightning nearby. It frightened her, and she nestled in the haven of his arms. He kissed her in sympathy at first, but then the rain began to fall hard, fierce and exciting. His kisses became passionate and she did not resist. She was the hungry earth after a dry spell, wanting rain. And like the parched earth welcoming rain, Juana welcomed love. Temporarily the thoughts of her dead mother were forgotten.

Afterwards Chucho felt the warmth of her happiness. Juana lay on the bed, breathing softly, her eyes closed; she had loosened her neat braids until they were undone to please him, for he loved her hair soft and wild. Chucho stood by the bed looking down at Juana with great fondness, then he went to the door to watch the falling rain; the jarros outside the house were already half full with rainwater. There was a newness in the world outside. Death could wait for a little while.

He felt Juana's small hands caressing his back, then she pressed her lips on his bareness as if to claim him. He felt the warmth of her tears. "She's dead in the other room, Chucho. What am I going to do without her?"

He turned and gathered her in his arms. "I'm here, querida."

"For how long?" It was asked in anticipated fear; it was not a condemnation.

"I'm just the way I am, Juana," He said it with a certain guilt, the rainbow lights of rain were beckoning.

"What about her? The burial, the arrangements . . . Oh, Chucho, I can't." She was yielding to timidity, to indecision, to the inability of accepting that her mother would no longer be.

"I'll take care of everything," Chucho offered accommodatingly. It was a craving now, wanting that money. "First to Domínguez's Funeral Home, then the plot, and of course, the criers. She wanted criers."

"No! I can't let you take care of the funeral. She made me promise—"

"—Not to give me the money." Chucho interrupted. He concluded matter-of-factly, "Then you'll have to do it. There's no one else."

"She said you would just steal it, get drunk and go whoring." She was sobbing in abject desolation. "But I can't—I can't go to the funeral home. I can't . . ."

"If I can't be of help, I'll just go," he insisted perversely, then he paused and waited for her to give in.

She grasped his arm in desperation. "You do it." He could feel her distress over giving him the money, but he paid no heed. He tried to be kind. "You don't have to give it to me. That way you've kept your promise. I'll look for it myself. It's in the house isn't it?" She nodded, helpless as a child.

Now that the rain had stopped, the jolt of life sounds from the barrio made his blood race. He left the door, looking around for his clothes. As he dressed he started opening drawers. With one hand he zipped his pants while with the other he rummaged through paper bags and boxes piled in a corner. Juana watched him, her face a conflict of loyalties. The only place the money could be, he decided as he put on his shoes, was in the room where Refugio lay. Juana seemed to sense what he was going to do. "Don't go in there, Chucho."

"Why not? It's my house."

"It's her room."

"Does that make sense, woman? In that room, Refugio and me, we'd drink ourselves to sleep in there, we planned our destinies in there, she cured me of the fever in there with her incantations, her curandera ways. It's really—our room."

Juana began to cry, remembering her own jealousy watching her husband and her mother—sharing drink, talking crazy, or beating each other half to death; then, the joking—the laughing at themselves after all the havoc. She never understood how two people who hated each other so much could have spent so much time together, in that little room no bigger than a chicken coop. She hated those times because she was always the outsider. Juana offered resignedly, "I'll get you the money."

She went into the room where her mother lay. The money was in the rag clown. Many years before, when Chucho and Refugio had had good feelings, he had come home one weekend with a life-size clown; he wore all the colors of the world. Chucho had given it to her mother as a gift. He had joked, "Now you have a man. You don't have to sleep alone." Juana had been embarrassed by his crassness, and her mother had cursed him at first; then she had laughed, obviously delighted with the rag man. Chucho and her mother had gone out for wine to celebrate. They had drunk half a dozen bottles that night, joking and singing to the clown until the wee hours of the morning. Juana had found them the next morning with their arms around the clown, fast asleep. The daughter had learned to accept all their craziness because they were the only two people she had in the world. Refugio, in time, had slit the back of the clown's suit, taken out some of the rags, and hidden the shoe box with the funeral money. Every time Refugio added money to the box, she opened up the slit, then sewed it back.

The rag man hung on a hook in the corner by her bed. As she reached for it, she glanced at her mother's face. How peaceful death was! She did not look like a woman who had battled a lifetime. The tumult of living had been erased. Juana felt the brightness of her love for the woman in whose womb she had been cradled thirty-two years before. Now her mother was gone; the womb was gone . . . Juana felt an inquietude as she took the clown from the hook, ripped opened the now-worn seam, and found the box. She used a large safety pin to close the rag man's wound, to keep the stuffing safe. She sat the clown on the bed at her mother's feet, as if to give her the company of an old friend.

Juana found Chucho drinking his mother's beer, memories in his eyes. She handed Chucho the box and reminded him, "You must pay the criers." Chucho took the money. Juana shivered with dread apprehension growing. She was still warm with love, but the money was now in Chucho's hands. "You must keep your promise, Chucho."

He kept quiet, averting his eyes, as he put on his only coat and took the box under his arm. Then he was gone.

The money was gone; her mother was gone. Juana's sobs began again, slowly at first; soon they were hard and painful. Instinct flared. The lost child from the womb went to her mother. She dropped by the side of Refugio, flinging one arm around the body as if cradling a nonexisting safeness, a nipple of security with no nourishment for her. She remained thus for a long, long time, the clown smiling at her with a special kind of sympathy.

***

Chucho walked out of the two rooms he had built with Refugio. The old coyote was dead. He touched the box under his arm as he went down the hill. The small adobe house was surrounded by fruit trees, flowers, and all kinds of plants. The land belonged to Don Tiburcio, the junk man, who had refused to sell it to Refugio. It had been a huge hole next to the junkyard. That's why the owner rented it cheap. But Refugio had seen the possibilities. It was close to a canal (water for trees!) and to the bus stop where she caught the bus that took her to the bridge between Mexico and the United States. Refugio decided to fill the hole and make a level surface on which to build a house. For three years Chucho and Refugio had worked filling in the hole with discarded tires which they begged, stole, or paid for until the land was level. The top was filled with soil from the canal and with horse manure. "I want rich soil," Refugio would say, "for around my house I shall bring to life the Garden of Eden." She sure did, Chucho thought, looking up at the only patch of green in the whole barrio.

He quickened his step, smelling the aroma of cooking food mixed with the fragrance of wet earth. Yes, the first thing he would do with the money would be to buy a good supper for his best friend, Chapo, and himself. The most expensive on the menu: he could afford it now. He felt rather lightheaded and a shout of gladness escaped from his throat. Whoever heard him slammed an open door. The whole world would be his for the next few hours. He imagined that the lighted lamps were happy eyes belonging to the houses; they too, anticipated the good times he was going to have. He would treat everybody tonight. What a beautiful thought. His friends would not believe it, for he was always broke.

As soon as he could he'd fill Chapo's old car with gas. After supper they'd go to the poker game behind Chen's Laundry and gamble the way he liked to gamble, with money in his pocket. He would then go to the Red Chapulín, and he and Chapo would drink with all their friends. He had to break the news of Refugio's death to Don Tiburcio, owner of the bar and of Refugio's land. After all, Don Tiburcio was his landlord and his friend. After that, a visit to Adela's girls.

He was not far from Chapo's house. Chapo washed cars all day long with a trancelike vigor. This was the pattern of his day: soap, rag, mop, water—soap, rag, mop, water—car after car. Poor Chapo! He was a machine. His soul had been numbed. His life was a desperation, working for a few pesos to feed his family. Chucho knew he would never give up his own life for a few pesos. The whole world looked upon him as shiftless, worthless, no-account; that was the price of freedom.

The old dead witch had been the worst one. He remembered her wild roars and accusations. Why tell him what he already knew? He had made that choice in life and was well satisfied with it. The old woman's venom had been the fuel for many battles, but she was well aware of why she hated his ways. She had been jealous, jealous of his freedom. "You pay for that freedom with my money, desgraciado!" she would scream at him. True, true, she was tired of the money responsibilities, but she had chosen her life, just like he had chosen his. What could he do? Beneath it all, he respected her sense of respectability, her honesty, and most of all her generosity, especially after a few drinks.

Some time back he had gone to watch some ice skaters at the coliseum across the border. Chapo had a job cleaning up the place after the Ice Capades, and Chucho had gone along to help. He had been overwhelmed by the skill of the skaters. Their skill was freedom, making something hard seem so easy, so effortless. He had decided with a happy sigh, *that* was beauty. For some reason his brain could not make a clear connection, but he kept thinking their skating had something to do with the way he wanted to live. He knew those skaters had worked very hard to achieve that beauty, the easy, swift, graceful gliding on the ice. Chucho wanted to work like that at living—to make an art of enjoying life, a constant celebrating, to be a spectator to the freedom of others, to share the openness of that freedom. Every man in life must know his part well in that life, develop the skill in what he could do best, then skate through life enjoying, spreading beauty like confetti, or the joy of circus balloons. He had remarked to Chapo while watching the skaters, "I want a skill like that, Chapo."

"You want to be a skater, eh?" Chapo was never surprised by anything Chucho said.

"I want a skill for living, so I can skate smoothly into freedom, so my friends can see that I can see." Chucho was well pleased with that thought.

"Oh, you have a skill in life, Chucho. You drink more, fight harder than anyone I know. You've been in jail more times than anyone I know."

"Oh, shut up." Sometimes it was useless trying to explain anything to Chapo.

"You can afford the freedom. You have a mother-in-law to support you. Look at me. The bastard without balls that I work for, the thief pays me slave wages, but I need the money to feed my little ones. I would like to spit in his face, but I don't think about it. I just wash cars until they shine, then I get my centavos and I go home to my family. We eat one more day."

"I want to skate through life like a god," Chucho had wished.

"You're full of beans."

He reached Chapo's house. Next to it stood Chapo's bright green car like a sentinel against total decay. The lamps were lit. His friend must be sitting down to an early supper. Chucho whistled, loud and shrill, calling, "Hey, Chapo!"

Chapo stuck his head out of the door, then came out hurriedly closing the door behind him. Chucho was not welcomed at Chapo's house.

"Ese, Chapo, let's go buy some new tires for your car and fill it with gas." Chucho grinned, moving about, jabbing right and left, in a dance of delight.

"Hey, paisano, you won the lottery?" Chapo scratched his head.

"The old lady died today. I got the funeral money!" Chucho informed his friend with some gravity.

Chapo crossed himself. "May her soul rest in peace . . . all the money?"

"All the money . . ." Chucho relished the thought.

"Jaaaaaaaa!" Chapo grabbed Chucho and they began to wrestle like bears. They fell to the ground laughing, rolling about on the grass. When their play was done, they lay face up, feeling good, and watched the first stars of the evening. Chucho broke the silence. "What a night we're going to have!"

Chapo jumped to his feet and kicked Chucho who was still looking at the stars. "You see anything special, you old dog?"

"It's all so big, isn't it?" Chucho was awed by a thousand stars.

"Let's go!"

A short time later the old green car was rattling off toward town where city lights spoke of temporary lightning dreams.

***

Juana sat in her neighbor's kitchen. Her voice was tired. "I'm waiting for Chucho." She had waited for Chucho for one whole day. Now it was another day, and in her house there was the growing stench of death.

She blamed herself. "Why do I wait for him? I should do something about my poor mother, but I don't know what."

The neighbor looked at her skeptically. "You really think he's coming back when he has all that money? Ha!"

"But he has a responsibility to me, to my mother. He promised to make all the funeral arrangements."

"Poor child. God sure made you pretty, but decided to hold back on brains. He's not coming back. You should get the police after him before he spends all of your mother's hard-earned money. Pobrecita!"

"What am I going to do?"

"Well, you better do something. Someone told the authorities about your mother. You know what they're going to do if you don't bury her soon."

"I won't let them." Juana began to cry painfully.

"That's all you know how to do, Juana—cry. That crematory was built by the city at great expense. According to the municipal president, it is the clean, efficient way to get rid of the dead, of the ones who can't pay."

"The church says it's a sin to burn a body. Father Vallejo will not allow them to take her." Juana felt her betrayal.

"What can he do? He's just a poor priest. If she can't afford a funeral, she'll go into the ovens."

Juana's crying became hysterical. "Chucho has to come! He has to!"

"I wouldn't put my hopes on that. He's probably passed out somewhere."

"If he spent all my mother's money, he's feeling guilty. He always comes back when he's feeling guilty."

"The devil he does!"

"He's always full of remorse when he drinks." Juana remembered the many times Refugio and Chucho had cried with a bottle between them.

"If I were you I'd just accept that your mother will be ashes in the wind." The neighbor was a realist.

Juana put her head down on the table. "Mamacita, forgive me. Why did I give him the money?"

"Why do you think? Because you're putty in that man's hands, because you love it when he gets into your pants. Animal."

"I was talking to my mother."

"I know, I know. You poor little thing." She smoothed out Juana's disheveled hair in sympathy.

They heard Chapo's car. Juana rushed out of the house. She saw Chapo following Chucho, and all she could do was stand at her neighbor's door and cry. Chucho and Chapo were now making their way to the house. She would let him. He should smell the stench, so he could see what he had done.

Chapo was remarking, "Thanks for the tires and the good time."

The two men disappeared into the house, then there came a long, drawn-out bellow. Juana knew it was Chucho, who probably had forgotten about the body. The two men ran out of the house, Chucho looking like a wild man. He was shaking his head in disbelief, then he let out another bellow like a wounded animal. He fell to his knees and began to pound the wooden planks of the porch. Chapo stood by helplessly, looking as if he wanted to throw up.

Chucho moaned, "She's dead. Oh, God, she's still here, rotting . . ."

"We have to do something, Chucho," Chapo clumsily suggested, walking nervously around Chucho's kneeling body. Chucho was hitting the planks again. "It's not fair, it's not fair that life should rot!"

Juana could not bear it any longer. She ran across to him, kneeling by his side, taking him in her arms and kissing his forehead to stop his suffering. She had to tell him right away. "Chucho, the authorities are coming to take her body if we don't bury her right away."

"I looked at her face, Juana, She looked so peaceful, so young—but the stink!" There was a cosmic bewilderment on his face. Then it sank in. "To the crematory?"

"Yes . . ."

"I will never let them do that."

"Do you have any money left?" There was a ray of hope in Juana's voice. Chucho shook his head in despair, not only because the money was all gone, but because he could not bear the thought of Refugio being burned. He raised himself to his feet and picked up his clinging wife. He turned to Chapo. "She must not be burned."

"What can we do? There's no money left. We can return the tires."

"If we take the tires back, it wouldn't be enough even to buy a lot to bury her in, much less a coffin. You know what we can do? Let's go back to all the places we visited last night. Someone's bound to give us some of the money we spent on them."

"They were mostly strangers." Chapo was not optimistic.

Juana pleaded, "You can't leave me. The authorities will come. We can't leave her body in the house. Something has to be done now, right now."

"All right. We won't leave her here. We'll take her with us." Chucho knew it was an idea born of desperation. But what could he do?

"In Chapo's car? With both of you? Where are you going to take her?" Juana thought Chucho had gone out of his mind.

"We'll put her in the trunk." Chucho was serious.

"The stink, Chucho, the stink," Chapo reminded him.

Chucho remembered how, long ago, Refugio had talked about las yerbas de los yaquis which she kept in her herb bag. She had bragged that her medicine could cure anything, even the stench of death. He told Juana what they had to do. "Her herb bag, Juana, the one with the Yaqui herbs, do you know where it is?"

"Hanging in her closet."

"All right then, you and me are going back into the house, take some sheets, sprinkle all the herbs on her, wrap her up. Chapo and me, we'll put her in the trunk and tie her down real good. Come on!"

Juana could not move. The neighbor, taking her by the arm said, "Come, it's something. Better than the authorities. I'll help you wrap up the body."

The three of them went into the house and an hour later a mummylike bundle was tied securely in the trunk of the car. The trunk remained half open; it was the only way. So Chapo and Chucho used an extra rope to tie the open trunk to the rear fender. That way she wouldn't be left behind somewhere on the road. Chucho didn't waste any time; he got into the car and turned on the ignition. Chapo jumped in beside him and crossed himself. "¡Que Dios nos bendiga!"

Chucho stuck his head out of the car window. "If the authorities come, you know nothing. Do you understand? You know nothing."

The neighbor nodded her head in disbelief. Juana bit her lip and whispered, "Yes. I promise. I won't tell them anything."

When the car disappeared around the bend, the neighbor offered, "You can stay with me if you want."

"I have to clean the house before Chucho comes back. Put things away."

The neighbor walked away shaking her head in sympathy, and Juana sat down on the porch steps to watch the glorious colors of the dying sun. Her mother was gone. The traces of rain were gone. The sun had drunk all moisture in the desert. She looked at her mother's fruit trees. They needed water. The plants too. It was Chucho who watered the trees. He never failed to tend to them, bringing the water up the hill from the canal in huge white plastic milk bottles. It was a tedious and exhausting job. But he had done it for Refugio, for her Garden of Eden. Juana reflected how the trees would be there even after she herself was gone, as they were now that Refugio was gone. There was no mother now, no weekly ritual of waiting at the bus stop for her to come home from her job, no more stories from her mother about the outside world, no Chucho fighting with Refugio and laughing and talking to the rag man while they shared a bottle of wine. The trees grew in beauty with her mounting loneliness. Tears came to her eyes. She opened the palm of her hand to catch the tears. Little wet drops glistened in the glory of the sun's last rays, colors found in soft whispers. She looked for a jewel in her teardrops. She was lost in a world all her own.

***

Chapo's face was fiercely red with anger. He threw a finger in the direction of the store. "Ladrones, not even half of what we paid for the tires. Let's twist the tires around their necks. You want to take the money?"

"What for? It's not enough. The tires get us around." Chucho had expected just that.

"Where to?" asked Chapo, truly discouraged.

"To El Chapulín Colorado. I have to pick up the deed for the land."

"What deed?" Chapo's eyes widened.

"Last night when I told Don Tiburcio about Refugio, he took it hard. I didn't know he liked the old battle-ax that much. He cried," Chucho explained.

"I don't remember any of that. Where was I?"

"Dead drunk."

"I remember you dancing flamenco on top of the bar."

"That was before your first hundred drinks."

"I lost count. You kept buying free drinks. Everybody was your friend last night."

Chucho felt the warmth of good memories. "Nice, nice." Chapo was curious. "Deed for what?"

"The land under my house."

"You bought it from him?"

"Didn't have to offer him a penny. Seems Refugio had asked to buy it many times and he had refused. He liked to have her beg cause she looked so soft—that's what he said. So, last night, he just confessed to me that he was giving it to her."

"But she's dead."

"Don't be stupid, Chapo. When people touch each other in life, they touch each other in death. He was going to sign over the deed to Refugio. He said that Refugio would know up in heaven where she is."

"There's the answer. You can sell the deed or borrow money on it for her funeral."

"Never! The deed belongs to Refugio. It is her land now . . . No."

"Are you going to ask Don Tiburcio for money, for the funeral?

"Not him. He is doing something generous already. We don't ask him. We'll just look around for some of the people we bought drinks for last night."

They went into the Chapulín Colorado and found Don Tiburcio at the bar. "Two drinks on the house for my friends." Don Tiburcio was remembering the night before when Chucho had spent so much money at his place.

"Gracias, Don Tiburcio."

"I'm glad you came around. Here's the deed for Refugio. I know she knows. You say goodbye to her for me at the funeral. I can't go. I want to remember her alive. But you tell her, I will visit her on Sundays, take her some flowers, and we can talk about the days." Don Tiburcio's face revealed how very fond he had been of Refugio. Chucho did not have the heart to look around for familiar faces. He did not want Don Tiburcio to know that it was Refugio's funeral money that he had spent the night before. Chapo came up to Chucho and nudged him as Don Tiburcio went to take care of another customer. "Look, the Red Beard. He borrowed fifty pesos from you last night, remember? You want me to explain the situation?"

"No," Chucho protested nervously.

"No?" Chapo did not understand.

“I don’t want Don Tiburcio to know I took her money. I’m just a thief, that’s all I am. I took money from a dead woman. May the heavens strike me dead if I don’t give her a decent funeral. I’ll find a way.”

The gypsy who had played the guitar for Chucho’s dancing the night before came over. “Now it’s my turn to buy you a drink. Two tequilas, Don Tiburcio.”

Don Tiburcio came back with two tequilas while the guitar player strummed the song about the Mountain of Sorrow in Andalucía. The song was a plaintive melody about a lost love who followed fireflies into heaven. Don Tiburcio took out his handkerchief. He blew his nose and told the musician, “We lost a loved one only yesterday. Chucho’s mother-in-law. She used to come on weekends and sit right where you’re sitting. A fine, fine woman. I’m going to miss her.”

There was a faraway look in the musician’s eyes. “In Andalucía we not only sing about the loved ones who have left us, but we dance about them with the passion of our feet.” He begun to strum a flamenco tune, the very one Chucho had danced to the night before when he had been quite drunk. But he was sober now. Too sober.

Red Beard came up to the bar and ordered a drink for his two friends. The guitarist asked Chucho, “Did you love your mother-in-law?”

Chucho had no idea why he said what he did, but he did. “Yes, I loved her very much. She was a warrior. She scorned dreamers like me because we don’t take reality between our teeth. We don’t face up to the struggle. She was a coyote balasiada, a bullet-scarred coyote who was not afraid.”

“Dance it!” commanded the guitarist. Chucho jumped up on the bar and proclaimed, “I dance for Refugio. I dare life and pain and fear with my feet, as she did with her guts and her heart. I dance her passions! Her laughter! Her spirit!” Faster and faster, Chucho dared with his feet for the love of Refugio. The dance became unrelentless until both Chucho and the guitarist were spent. Then silence, until Don Tiburcio blew his nose again and commented, “That was a good thing you did for her, Chucho.”

“I should have done things for her when she was alive.”

“No one cares about the living.” These words of wisdom came from Chapo.

"You know that her favorite season was autumn? Because it was a time of realness, of harvest. Fruits were gathered and flowers gave the last of their bloom." Chucho's memory of Refugio was full blown.

"I never heard her say that, Chucho."

"That's because she never confided in you. Only in the rag man, Chapo."

"What rag man is that, Chucho?" asked Don Tiburcio.

"A clown I bought for her made out of rags."

Don Tiburcio started to cry again. Chucho put his arm around Don Tiburcio and comforted the bartender. "She told me many times how much she liked you, but that you were a dreamer, like me."

Don Tiburcio nodded. "I am."

"You know why she didn't like dreams?"

They all listened intently to Chucho's words. "She used to say that dreams were cruel because the waiting sometimes had no end."

"You talk as if you loved your mother-in-law."

Chapo could not believe Chucho's reply. "You are very right . . ."

A stranger came into the bar asking, "Who owns a green car parked outside?"

Chapo and Chucho looked at each other while the stranger continued, "There's a bunch of dogs sniffing and howling around it. I think someone went to call the police."

Chucho and Chapo jumped off their stools and ran outside without a word. Outside, the neon lights were playing fiercely with the white bundle tied to the trunk of the car, as dogs tried to take a grab, then sniffed around it. Off and on, on and off, off and on, blue and red, green and yellow, neon lights claiming the body of Refugio. The two jumped in the car and rode off after kicking a dog or two.

"Where to?" Chapo asked.

"To Adela's."

"Chucho, she's stinking terrible."

"Not her life, Chapo, not her life."

"You know, they were right back there. You talk as if you loved her."

"I loved her—that's why I hated her so much."

"She used to call you a coward."

"She called me every name in the book. She had a big mouth. She was jealous of my freedom. She had a right to resent me, I suppose."

"I remember the time she cracked your skull."

"Why do you remember only the bad things?" Chucho shouted in Chapo's ear.

"I just don't think we're going to get the money," Chapo answered despondently.

"Adela has a heart." Chucho was not about to give up.

"She's a businesswoman."

At one time Adela had catered to the best clientele. The powerful police commissioner had been her protector and best client. Or at least that's what she claimed. Now in less prosperous times, she housed six girls in a dilapidated two-story building at the south end of the red-light district. One of the girls opened the door, then went to call Adela. The room where Chucho and Chapo waited was dimly lighted. It was not a busy night by the looks of the place. The madam came in, smiling in recognition. "You must have fallen in love with my girls, you came back so soon."

"I'm not here as a customer tonight," Chucho explained.

"Oh? Your friend, perhaps?" She turned to Chapo.

Chapo stood doggedly behind Chucho, who reminded her, "He was here with me last night for the show. We only saw the show, Adela."

"That's not like you, Chucho—just the show?"

"I've got a favor to ask, Adela."

"Favor?" Adela was now on guard.

"I tipped your dancers last night, a lot of money. I was very generous. Don't you remember?"

"I remember. My girls remember," Adela said pleasantly.

"Well I'm in a little trouble. I was generous with money that wasn't mine. So I thought, since you've known me all these years, you could make me a loan—mind you, not give the money back, just make me a loan, and I'll pay it back as soon as I can."

"For you, Chucho, I would do anything. But money? It is an ironclad rule in this house that we do not give money or lend money to any clients. It would be our ruin. We can't afford the luxury. Sorry."

"Just this one time." Chucho felt awkward begging. But it was for Refugio.

"Nope. Can't do that. If I break the rule once, I'll do it a second time. That's the way it goes. You understand. It's a hard life." It was a businesslike refusal.

"I see your point." It was Chucho's attempt at a gracious out.

"Here, a few pesos, since you were so generous last night." She handed him some money.

Chucho was too embarrassed not to take it. Out in the street, Chucho and Chapo put up the collars of their coats, for the wind was raw and cold. They got into the car without a word and drove around for a while.

"Well, our last bet is Chen's. We dropped a bundle there last night. There's another poker game going on." Chucho was still hopeful.

When the two drove up to Chen's Laundry, the place was in total darkness. Chucho jumped out and went to ask at the bakery next door. He came back with bad news. "Place was raided. Our last hope." The two men sat numbly, staring out into the darkness.

Chapo's voice had a finality. "We can't pay the criers, Chucho. No funeral for Refugio, no wake, no dancing, no eating . . ."

"To hell with all that, Chapo, what's so great about paying criers to moan and scream at your funeral?"

"We better do something about the body. They'll throw us in jail if they find it in our trunk."

"To hell with the criers. They're not good enough," Chucho concluded.

"They go with the grand funeral and that's what she wanted," Chapo sighed, waiting for Chucho, for an answer. Far off in the distance the howl of a coyote mixed with the laughter that spilled from a doorway.

"We are going to bury her ourselves, Chapo," Chucho decided.

"Now don't get crazy. Where? Not the cemetery. . . ." Chapo was not up to that.

"Up there. The hill behind the church." Chucho was imagining the climb.

"Go up that hill? Who's going to dig a grave in this freezing weather?" Chapo was skeptical.

"You and me . . ." Chucho squinted in thought.

"We don't even have a shovel," Chapo protested weakly.

“I’ll borrow two from the shed behind the church. Father Vallejo won’t mind.” Chucho had the whole plan in his mind.

“He’s asleep, Chucho. We can’t wake him up at this hour.”

“We’ll borrow them anyway.” Taking the shovels without asking was the least of Chucho’s problems.

“Now, Chucho?”

“Yes, now. But first we buy a couple of bottles with the money Adela gave me.” He winked at Chapo.

***

It was close to midnight when they started the climb up the hill with two shovels and Refugio. The biting wind was torturous but most welcome, for it lessened the overpowering stench of the body. Their fingers and noses were numb with the cold. Up, up, they climbed, huffing and straining. The body was cradled in two huge horse blankets that Chucho had taken from Father Vallejo’s shed. They supported the weight high on their shoulders, holding tight with both hands. The two shovels, alongside the body inside the blankets, would clank against a rock every so often. Chucho was very careful not to let the body drag. At intervals they would stop to rest and to drink tequila for warmth. The rest was brief, for it was better to keep moving, creating some body heat against the bitter wind. It took what seemed like an eternity to reach the top of the hill. Chucho’s throat felt bruised with cold.

They scrambled to the top. The lights of the city shone bright against a dark horizon. Somehow distance diluted their glaring vulgarity. Chucho felt as if his nose and fingers were going to break off. The climb was over, and now they could build a fire to thaw themselves out. They laid the body down gently and began to gather sagebrush and branches broken by the wind. There was no protection from the swift and biting wind. Building a fire was next to impossible on open ground. Chucho led the way to a huge boulder that broke the wind; in time, they had a fire blazing.

“I’m one great big icicle, Chucho.” Chapo put his hands out to pick up the scattered warmth of the fire. He kept his gaze on the fire, once in a while blowing on his hands. Chucho was already looking for a good burial ground.

He soon found a high spot, next to a clump of trees. It was on the edge of the hill with a full view of the town. Refugio's town. Chucho walked the area round and round and dug his foot into the earth.

"We'll dig the grave here," he finally decided.

They took turns digging and, at times, they dug from opposite ends. Every so often, they stopped and rested from their labor to drink from the bottle. The warm glow of the liquor sent new vigor into Chucho's tired body. He looked down into the town that spoke of many lifetimes. Then he resumed his digging, his body aching from fatigue. He insisted that Chapo rest for longer intervals. After all, this was Chucho's way of asking forgiveness from a woman who had given so much to his life. He finished the digging himself, letting Chapo scoop earth out of the shallow grave. When the grave was deep enough, they went to the body where it lay, close to the boulder where the fire blazed. They moved it with great care and laid it next to the open grave. Chucho rested a hand on Chapo's shoulder. "Now we wait."

"Wait?"

"For the sunrise. I want her to see it one more time." Chucho felt the excitement of life's conspiracy with death.

Chapo did not answer, but took out the bottle and drank, then he handed it to Chucho who drank also. Chucho took a knife from his pocket. He squatted to pick up the upper part of the bundled Refugio, and laid her head on his lap. He carefully cut the cloth that covered up her face. "There, now she can see."

The two men sat and watched the lights of the city disappear gradually as they waited for the sunrise. Chapo rubbed his arms vigorously. "Let's wait by the fire. Too cold here."

"You go. I want to stay with her. We must see the sunrise together."

Chucho's mind flashed with memories—Refugio's face full of softness when she talked of good things, of Juana as a child, of the seeds she had planted breaking through the earth, of the men she had loved. The softness had been for the realness of things that smacked of life.

Chapo stayed, taking another drink. "You think where she is, she knows there are city lights?"

"She's still here with us. She hasn't gone anywhere yet." Why would she? thought Chucho. She had never been in any hurry to go.

"I suppose soon she'll be in heaven."

"I hope heaven is half as wonderful as earth." Chucho really doubted it.

"What do you think?" Chapo waited for Chucho to answer, knowing his friend had answers for everything, but Chucho's mind was still cushioned in the memories of Refugio.

"She suffered a lot, Chapo. When we drank together, she talked about her husband. She cleaned houses for gringos on the other side since she was thirteen. When she got together with a man, she kept on working. She never stopped working. Before we built the house, she had never had a house. She rented in a presidio all her life. She would buy furniture, and her old man kept selling it for money, to get drunk. But in spite of the bad things, deep down, she understood how precious life was. We men are a bad lot, Chapo. Women are much better creatures."

"Where are your balls? We are men!" Chapo looked like a little rooster, posing manhood.

"We whore around, drink too much. That husband of Refugio's kept selling every stitch of furniture, so she took after him with a two-by-four, beat him up bad. He left town awfully scared. Went back to his mother in Coahuila. Refugio saw him years later when she went to visit her family. He recognized her. He was selling fake watches to American tourists, but when he saw her he ran the opposite way. Ha!"

"She was a fighter all right."

"Didn't have a man for a long time, that's why I gave her the rag man. Something to hug at night, after a few drinks."

"Why didn't you do her the favor?"

"Sometimes when we talked about life and joked all night, and she would grow soft in wisdom, I had desires—but I couldn't. There was this respect I had for her . . ."

"You were scared of her." Chapo got up and danced about. The warmth of the fire had dissipated. "I'll get more wood. Fire's dead. I'm freezing just sitting."

The first light rose in the east. The city did not have long to sleep. Chucho sat Refugio up against his shoulder to face the east. "Look, Refugio, morning.

Your face is the sunrise, mother-woman-friend . . ." He called Chapo. "Come back, Chapo. Her face is beautiful."

Chapo was looking down at Refugio's face. "She was a fine-looking woman."

Chucho held the stiff, dead weight of the woman in his arms. The stench had been forgotten. Tears filled his eyes. "Refugio, I couldn't give you your fancy criers, or the kind of wake you had in mind with five kinds of meats and candies and all the wine flowing free. I couldn't give you musicians and fireworks, and all your friends singing and dancing for you. I'm so sorry. There's only me, the poor fool who stole your money. This is all I can do for you. I wish I could do more. You deserved so much."

"She can't hear you, Chucho,"

Chucho bent his face and kissed her fully on the lips. "Listen, I promise to keep the rag man company when I'm feeling blue. I'll get me a couple of bottles, and the rag man and I will wait for you. Don't forget. I love you, Refugio, for having lived."

With great care he laid the body gently down on the ground, then he jumped into the grave, took off his coat and made a pillow for Refugio's head.

"That's your only coat, Chucho," Chapo reminded.

"Here, help me." With effort and care, they got Refugio in the grave until her head rested on Chucho's coat. Then the two scuttled out of the grave, dirty, tired, half-frozen, Chucho looked down at the still form and became very conscious of death. The crying of the morning wind was the expectancy of something more. There was the morning and sunrise unexplained, like the life of each day. These things are better not explained, surmised Chucho.

The grave had to be covered. Then there were the coyotes. "Let's shovel the dirt, then we'll look for rocks to cover her grave," Chucho exclaimed with a note of finality.

They took different paths to find enough large rocks, each making a trip to the grave with their arms full. The rocks were finally gathered. The sun was high when they finally filled the grave and then sat down to fix the rocks in a mound. Again Chucho was pensive, thoughts spilling over to try to understand the coming of the sun, the waking life, the atmosphere diffusing light, all a song like the currents of a river, all beyond his understanding. If a skill is a form of freedom, thought Chucho as he formed a small mountain of rocks, then it belonged to death as well as life. Chucho became euphoric. slapped Chapo on the back, and both men laughed. Then they wrestled like bears around the grave. Chucho took out his bottle and peered into it. "Hey, there's some." He took one gulp and handed the bottle to Chapo. A thought came to Chucho. "A plain cross with two good pieces of wood and her name on it. That will please her."

They found the wood, then sat down near the grave again to make a cross, sharing the rest of the drink. ★

Sergio Troncoso

Born and raised in El Paso, Sergio Troncoso graduated from Harvard, was a Fulbright Scholar to Mexico, and studied international relations and philosophy at Yale University. In 1999, his book of short stories *The Last Tortilla & Other Stories* won the Premio Aztlán for the best book by a new Chicano writer and the Southwest Book award from the Border Regional Library Association. His novel *The Nature of Truth* was published in 2003. Troncoso's stories have been widely anthologized in books such as *The Norton Anthology of Latino Literature*; *Latino Boom: An Anthology of U.S. Latino Literature*; *Once Upon a Cuento*; *Hecho en Tejas: An Anthology of Texas-Mexican Literature*; *City Wilds: Essays and Stories about Urban Nature*; and *New World: Young Latino Writers*. His work has also appeared in *Encyclopedia Latina*; *Newsday*; *El Paso Times*; *Pembroke Magazine*; *Hadassah Magazine*; and *Other Voices* among many others. Troncoso is a member of PEN and currently lives in New York City.

From *The Last Tortilla & Other Stories*: The Abuelita

The old grandmother glared into the hot street. Her lazy eye wandered about while the fierce eye centered her steady gaze. Damn that man, she thought. Es un coyote bien hecho. He always tries to get through the day by doing nothing, yet he still pretends to be tired from all the work that he did. Damn him. Just wait until I see him—he'll wish that he was somewhere else then. We'll see what excuse he mumbles out today.

"Here is the chicken and the milk," he said, giving her the paper bag with groceries, four bills, and coins. She looked at the money, and then she stared at him. She could not count, and the American bills seemed the same to her, although she usually recognized Lincoln's beard. This afternoon he was being honest, because he already had enough money for his cigarettes.

"Where's the rest of it? I know you took more money today. Cabrón. Bastard."

"Here is the receipt, señora. That is what I bought, and that's how much it cost. Esta señora no le tiene conflanza a nadie. You don't believe me, but there it is. I took nothing." He looked away: his arched back shielded him from the gleaming gray eyes.

"Why did it take you so long? You brought nothing, yet it still takes you half the day to run an errand. Come here!" she shrieked while her head trembled. He was in the next room, where he had quickly shuffled away in search of a quiet reprieve.

"Go bring me a dozen eggs and some vegetables. I forgot the vegetables. Here. Take it and go!" She flung the money at his dark, outstretched hands. Not quick enough, he watched the coins fall to his feet. Almost daring to challenge her for this reckless impatience, he jerked up and shook his tiny bald head in disgust. But he only condemned her silently.

"¡Ándale! ¡Levantalos! Pick them up and get going!" her voice exploded into the hot afternoon air. Slowly he placed his right knee on the floor and then his left, while his beady green eyes scanned the floor for quarters, pennies, and dimes. Finally he shuffled toward the door and yanked his sagging brown pants over his belly before stepping outside. Otra vez, he thought. Again I must go to Paisano Market; but I'd rather be out there than in here.

"And don't take all day!" he heard from behind the fuzzy gray of the screen door just when he dropped his weight on the throbbing corn in his left foot. Yes, it's much better out here under the hot summer sun.

***

In El Paso, the heat of the day lingered within the black asphalt of the streets after the sunset. This radiant heat reminded people of the day's difficulties and of the need to endure them for only a while longer. The nights were cool and dry, however, and often a desert breeze joined the distant clanging of a freight train to welcome a deep, forgetful sleep. This soothing repose was the night's contribution to the vitality of the coming day.

The old couple lived in downtown El Paso, slightly north of El Segundo Barrio, the area of the city that passed for the poor district. Yet it was not really poor like Harlem or South Boston; it was only comfortable and familiar. The proper and proprietary sons and daughters of the city could not understand the concept of a neighborhood, and they certainly could not understand this neighborhood. They lived in suburbs that had sprung forth from the desert with the guiding hand of the developer. The matching barbecue pits, rock walls, and cactus landscapes betrayed a cold and barren land where people merely existed next to each other. A nastily self-righteous individualism pervaded the fashionably new neighborhoods, and rightfully freeway restaurants and drive-up gas stations engulfed them. But the area of El Segundo Barrio lay, as did all of downtown El Paso and central Juárez, at the ancient pass that cut through the pyramidal Franklin and Chihuahua Mountains. The heart of El Paso had always been at this mountain pass.

The history that created the progressive Sunbelt city from the Old West town of mining and railroads was eagerly overstepped by the modernists, and only El Segundo Barrio lived reluctantly with this whole history. Red brick warehouses, cracked streets, and abandoned apparel factories were girdled by clothing-by-the-pound stores, foreign exchange houses, and tenements. Old people abounded: grandmothers, grandfathers, viejitos, and solitary oldsters. Some owned modest homes that were built forty or fifty years ago, while others stayed in government housing or inexpensive apartments. Here in El Segundo Barrio, the street life burst with a peculiarly patient mortality forged out of a life that was present as history. This life expected and understood the present as if this moment was at once disarmingly familiar and, yet, still alive with a newly aroused power. At any second, it seemed, the mortality of the barrio could hurl itself heavenward, into laughter, or toward death. Each way could just as easily rip away the looming seriousness. And only then could history seize the present.

Intermixed with this place were the glossy outposts of the Sunbelt city, and Lolita's favorite was La Gallina, the fast-food chicken restaurant on Paisano Street. She would send José to the restaurant on the third day of each month when the government checks arrived in the mail. She liked their crispy wings.

"¿Qué está pasando, qué quiere ahora el maldito viejo?" she asked, pointing to a television picture of Ronald Reagan on the evening news.

"They are saying," José's eyes beamed with a distant pride, "that el Presidente wants a war with a country called Iran." He had learned English while laboring in the copper and gold mines of Colorado during the 1920s.

"Parece que está loco. Why doesn't that crazy man go fight himself? What does he have against these poor people? This man talks too much and does nothing. He reminds me of you, José. I remember el General Villa riding into Chihuahua City with his revolutionary troops when I was a little girl. Villa would hang men like this Ree-gaan on the spot. El General hated politicians and bankers.

"Pobrecitos. These poor people look as if they have nothing to eat. How can they fight the Americans?" she said, looking at a news report on the famine in Ethiopia. "They seem in worse shape than the Mexicans. Look at the eyes of this child: he is crying without tears. The mother must think this world is only for terrible suffering. You know who's at fault? The governments, they're to blame for not helping the people. They steal everything from you, and then they step on you to keep you in line. It's just like Mexico."

José went into the kitchen to wash the dishes. She watched the television silently for a few minutes and then turned it off. In the bathroom, she began to clean her aged face. The left side of her mouth drooped, and it just quivered whenever she spoke. Recounted repeatedly by her older sister, the story of the drooping mouth began when Lolita was a young woman working on her father's cattle ranch. Apparently, a bolt of lightening had struck the ground nearby and shocked Lolita into this facial disfigurement. Since strong hands and a sturdy back were the most important tools to have in those days, nobody thought twice about a doctor's cure. Anyway, the nearest healer was in Chihuahua City which was 112 miles from El Charco. Now she not only had that mouth and the lazy eye, but also her back was arched into a hump. The stoop forced her to look up into the mirror whenever she wanted to see her reflection in the bathroom. Slowly she stroked her bluish gray hair with a comb, and her steady gaze dominated that mirror.

The sounds of the summer crickets alternated with José's heavy breathing. They lay on a folding bed that provided them with just enough room to turn in their sleep. Lolita was still awake, however. On her back she was quiet, and she attempted to distinguish the various sounds of the night, her eyes twitching nervously from left to right. Her frail and crooked body was resting, and the leg that was injured last week when she misjudged the curb on Olive Street had only a weakly pulsating pain emanating from the bruise.

Her mind jumped from a worried thought about her grandson, Arturo, to a faith in a God who resolved all the problems of the world. Arturo se va volver loco. ¿Para qué estudia tanto ese muchacho? That combative and moody child, now a young man, studied too much, and he would go insane, she thought, if he did not stop working. He should begin to enjoy the sweetest fruits of life. Usually Arturo called whenever he was deep within a frenzied state, and he would ask his grandmother for advice. Sometimes he called just to hear a steady voice imbedded in the world of pot-boiled chickens and mashed sweet potatoes. He was studying at Yale, where he was homesick and alone, and the phone bills to Texas only added poverty to his miseries. ¿Por qué no te vienes a la casa? ¡Ya no te mortifiques! She told him to come home and forget his self-imposed torment. Why was he suffering when he was handsome and had a college education? Arturo, the one blessed with such bounty, did not listen to his beloved abuelita. She worried about him tonight because he had not called her in two weeks. Tomorrow, she thought, I will say a prayer for him at the Church of the Sacred Heart, and I will ask Lupita to say one for him too. Esa señora es una santa. Lupita's prayers are always answered. That woman is God's angel of mercy.

***

When the sun erupted over the stark desert landscape and filled the morning shadows with an orange glow, a courageous enthusiasm often overtook the solemn solitude of the night and pushed the staggering heat of the day into the distant future. With a creaking stiffness in her back, Lolita removed the safety pins that closed the living room curtains. Then she dislodged the wooden boards that jammed shut the windows. The cool morning air soon swept into the room.

"¡Levántate! ¡Vas a llegar tarde con la señora Smith! Hurry up and drink your coffee! And get dressed for God's sake!" she yelled to José. Today he would work for Mrs. Smith, who had a ten-acre farm on the east side of town. Each week José waited eagerly for this day. For years he had worked regularly for four days during the winter, and six days during the spring and summer. Everybody was impressed with this kindly, hardworking old man who defied time with a toothy grin and a viselike grip. Yet eventually, time slowed him. Soon the people looking for someone to cut their grass, or trim tree branches, or pull weeds called young kids or professional gardeners for the job instead. After José smashed into a slow-moving locomotive on the Saint Vrain tracks, his 1956 Chevy station wagon was destroyed. Distraught and fatalistically angry, he called his grandson, who took him to Legal Aid Services. José finally received nine hundred dollars from the C & O Railroad Company after two months, yet this was only a bitter recompense: his working life had ended, even in his hopeful eyes.

The people who had already contemplated his replacement quickly dismissed him when he could no longer move his yard equipment after the accident. He was an old, slow man. They patted him on the back and gave him a farewell bonus, but they saw only their escape from a difficult decision, and not his plaintive eyes. Finally José even lost his job with the ornery, but loyal Colonel, a sixty-five-year-old stocky ex-marine. After much dillydallying, which ended when loneliness overcame the need for independence, the Colonel decided to move north to Missouri with his grandchildren. He had always looked at José with the begrudging respect that military men gave other survivors. This respect was like a rough sympathy toward another. The Colonel saw the uncommon vigor in José's work, and like a battle leader who admired the sacrifices of his men, he responded to this nobility with unflinching loyalty until the end. To give was to be needed. Now Mrs. Smith did the same. Tuesday was another work day. Another day for uncommon vigor, another day for uncommon respect.

"All right. I'll be done in just one minute, señora. Stop hurrying me! I'll catch the bus with plenty of time to spare," he said, bending over his shoes and pulling up his socks.

"¡Viejo roñoso! When you come back today, I'm going to wash those filthy pants. You look like a street bum. Don't you feel any shame for looking like that? At least pull your pants up, so everybody doesn't stare at you as if you have some disease." She handed him his sack lunch, which contained two jelly-and-cheese sandwiches and one ripe black banana.

"I'll be back late. After work, I have to get a loaf of bread at Safeway. Do you want anything else?"

"Get some cigarettes and a box of doughnuts. They're on special today."

The screen door slammed shut, and she was alone. She sat down in the living room, holding her mug of black coffee, and looked out into the street. From there she could watch the entrance of her two-story apartment building and still enjoy the breeze. She stared at the sparrows that drank water from the two plastic bowls under the shrubs. She worried about Arturo. Why did he enjoy being separated from his family, why did he go away to attend that school? I know he is suffering, she thought, because he is alone over there; he is without his familia. The jobs and the schools in El Paso are not as good as the ones over there. But the family is here, and he needs to be with his family. I do not understand why he is over there. Mi Dios lo va a cuidar. El verá que Arturo no se vuelva loco. She asked God to care for her grandson and to keep him near the Holy Spirit.

Without warning, a sharp pain ripped through her lower abdomen. She uttered a soft cry as she clutched herself, and stooped over in the chair as if she were plunging into an abyss. Her eyes watered while the abdominal pain intensified to a peak. Hoping that the pain would quickly leave her body, she tried to remain still in the chair. "God, please help me," she whispered. "Help me now with this pain, please help me." Her grimace further distorted her bloodless face, and the perspiration covering her neck and shoulders so cooled her spotted brown skin that she lost her bodily sensation. She was dizzy. She reached for the nearby sofa with her left hand. "God, I don't want to die, please help me. Ayúdame Dios, por favor, ayúdame." She collapsed onto the sofa and lay there breathing heavily. The stillness in her apartment was interrupted only by the whirring of passing cars, the squeaky chirping of the birds, and the spasmodic gasps of her guttural breathing. Soon the pain receded, and she fell asleep exhausted.

"Señora, wake up, Lolita," said a high-pitched voice from behind the screen door. It was Margarita, a good friend who lived next door.

"No, Margarita. I can't go today. I don't feel very well."

"The girls will be disappointed. We are starting to make our plans for the Christmas celebration, and since you are the second oldest member at El Centro you will be a princess in the parade this year."

"I know. But today is not a good day for me. I need to rest," Lolita said. Finally she lifted herself from the sofa and sat in the chair, her legs quivering after the sudden motion. "Can you please ask Lupita or Maria to finish my side of the quilt? I'm falling behind and I don't want everybody to wait for me."

"Of course. Do you want me to bring you food from the cafeteria? I'll just ask Rodrigo to give me a plate for you. I'm sure he'll give me double portions too, you know how much he likes you."

"You are an angel of God, Margarita. Thank you for helping this poor old woman." Margarita left, and through the window Lolita saw her friend disappear into the brightness of Saint Vrain Street. She enjoyed seeing everybody at El Centro, and for many years she had never missed a day. There the oldsters were taught how to make stuffed animals for their grandchildren, colorful quilts, and dolls. Each month they also went on field trips, to the zoo or to neighborhood parks. The best part of each day at El Centro was lunch, when Lolita and her friends sat in the corner of the cafeteria next to the coffee machine. She led the largest and most popular table during lunch, a boisterous gathering of real friends. When she had first gone to El Centro, however, she had sat alone, and later with Elsa, a pretty widow who had just retired and moved into the government housing on San Antonio Street. Unlike others at El Centro, Lolita easily ignored or dismissed the notions that became the tenets of the day in the reinforcing swirl of the demagogic cliques. Her jokes and ready smile were interrupted by quick and pointed comments that seemed to cleanse the musty air. This critical gaiety surprised the shy and controlled people who sought only quiet company, and alienated those cynically lonely victims who came to El Centro only to suffer before an audience. Soon, most of the señoras and señores, the gray-haired and the dark-skinned, began to seek Lolita's table at lunch. Some came timidly hoping to be near the merriment and irreverence, while others sprang forth into the tumble with their dormant personalities enticed by her laughing eyes. Last year she had ceased her daily visits to El Centro because she was often tired. This month she had already missed one week. Today she did not go.

She sat still as the pain lingered in her abdomen like a faint pulse. The late morning yielded to midday, and the enlivening freshness gave way to an intensive heat that subdued the day. She concentrated on the pain, which focused her on the fragility of her body. Her eyes, glazed and tearful, first stared at the floor and then glanced outside at the birds splashing in the water. When she shifted her body in the chair, the remnants of the pain suddenly sharpened into prickly points against this deep and dull vagueness inside her body. Even the tilt of her head became a concentrated, gentle motion haunted by a lurking distress. "Dios, no quiero morir. Pero cuando me muera, espero estar en Tus manos y en Tu gloria," she repeated in a breathless chant. Knowing that the time to face death was not now, she prayed to God. She prayed because that time was not now, and thus she could still hope. The attacks her failing body endured, however, could only remind her of this irrepressible time that would soon come. This horrible time that was no time at all.

The desperation and the fear finally surrendered to a time where she could wait for death again. A time and a place where death was not here now, although it lurked nearby. She prayed after these attacks because praying was the best way to unveil and to confront the waiting. Usually, pain constricted the body and the mind like a foe attacking the ramparts. The self retrenched. In the young, however, the healthy presence of the body overran the self's embankments and spilled out into the world in a euphoric wave of pride. For Lolita, her waiting anticipated death as an important event in a vigorous life. But this anticipation was not a morbid ideal in a life dragging itself through an abyss to live, strangely and gloriously, within a kingdom of defeat. Lolita's waiting came from her life's roaring engagement with the world. A worthy life faced death like one confronting an unkind intruder who demanded a severe review of the past: the melancholy and fear in the response to the dreaded inquiry were joined with the joy and fulfillment of having acted already on these questions in life. Most never wanted to die, but a few were ready.

Lolita prayed to be able to face the time when the pain reached an apex of intensity. Amid the overflowing and uncontrollable pain, she would sense a stillness that eventually ceded to a soothing return from sheer pain. During several attacks, she eagerly anticipated this stillness: it was the beginning of the end of the ordeal. Today, for the first time, she contemplated the possibility of not returning from this peak. She thought about the time beyond the stillness. She did not know what to think; she did not know how to comprehend the time when the waiting was not proceeded by a return. She prayed and asked God to help her. She asked not for life but to be in the time after death. I am in your hands, she thought, please let me enter your kingdom of justice so that I can live in your glory forever. Slowly she lifted herself from the chair and walked to the kitchen. She heated chicken broth on the stove for lunch. As she sipped the broth from a cup, she was tranquil. I know that I will die, and when the Lord calls me to heaven, I shall go into His hands. I hope that José remembers my cigarettes.

***

The cool air of the evening brought back the vivid life of the morning. Soaking his callous feet in salty hot water, José was in the kitchen. His limp and dusty trousers gently unrolled into the steamy water while his bald head reclined against the wall. His rigidly concave back almost pushed him onto the floor. He was sitting on a kitchen chair and resting. His eyes were closed.

Pobrecito, she thought, the poor man is tired. She looked at him for a moment and quietly shuffled to the bathroom, where she was scrubbing his foamy work pants on an aluminum washboard. I hope he already ate dinner and washed the dishes because the news will be on soon.

"José, José!" she yelled from her supplicating position in front of the tub. "Levantate y prende las noticias. No te quedes dormido en la silla como un perro. Get up and turn on the television. You can sleep after the news!" José grumbled something about the need to pace yourself, yet rose to his feet to finish the dishes. His soggy trousers left a trail of water droplets across the kitchen floor. The telephone rang, and Lolita answered it in the bedroom.

"Hallo," she said.

"¡Abuelita loca!" screamed a man's voice. "How are you and El Tigre? Have you been good, señora? I miss both of you."

"Arturo," she responded with a sigh. "Why haven't you called? I was worried about you. How do we know you are okay when you don't answer the phone? We called you about two days ago and nobody answered."

"¡Ay, señora!" he said enthusiastically. "I've been working almost as much as the Tiger works under the hot sun. Instead of pulling weeds, I've been sitting in the library reading and writing. I was probably in the library when you called. Usually I stay there until it closes at midnight. I am the nocturnal gremlin who explores the darkness, you know. But don't worry about me, abuela, I'm fine. I'm just tired of studying so much." Actually, the solitary Arturo was fighting off desperation. The mixture of an intense academic burden with his longing for the simplicity of life at home caused him to almost suffocate some nights, when matter seemed to torment even his quietest movements. Add to that his insistence on studying philosophy and his use of this critique as a relentless self-destruction of beliefs, and the world of Arturo thus fluctuated violently. He used his uneasy self, like a bustling laboratory, to foment and experience new ideas. But periodically, the experiments went awry, beyond his own nature, and his world rocked dangerously on the edge of an abyss, almost ready to fall.

"Where is the Tiger?" asked Arturo, the pace of his bouncing right leg even quicker than before.

"Aquí estoy," José said firmly, "your abuelita is in the bedroom and I have the kitchen phone."

"How are my parents and the rest of the family?" Arturo asked after a short silence.

"Everybody is fine. Your mother and father were here two days ago. They were going to the movies in Juárez. They're always out, having fun and enjoying themselves. I hope they don't neglect your brother," she said.

"Don't worry about Rudy, he can take care of himself. I am also well, but I'm tired and I miss being at home. Sometimes I feel so lonely that I can't read another page. They give us too much work at this school. Sometimes I want to give up on everything," Arturo said, resting his head on the cool wood of his writing desk. He needed to hear their voices to feel calm. By appreciating the worth in their lives, Arturo indirectly searched for and found self-respect. To care was to see the fragility of this ephemeral world, where man sacrificed himself in order to possess the good life. When he called his abuelitos, Arturo felt needed, and they felt needed too.

"Well, if you don't like it there, get out," Lolita said, "just get out. Didn't you finish school already, didn't you tell me that? What are you doing there anyway?"

"Yes, señora, but this is for another degree. I want to improve myself and I want to learn more things so I will be an educated person." Arturo explained simply so that his grandparents understood why he was still in school at the age of twenty-five. "Remember what you told me: El que adelante no ye atrás se queda." He who does not look forward is left behind.

"That's right, but why are you killing yourself with all that work? Why do you want to read all the time? You're going to drive yourself crazy."

"I'm studying because I think I have important ideas. My schooling is important to me and I must do it," Arturo responded in a loud, nearly shrill tone. When he studied furiously, he was isolated from the world, and he called them to claw at his loneliness. "I'm studying some German philosophers. One of them is called Heidegger. That is, HEI-DEG-GER," he repeated clearly, so that they could understand the name.

"Who is this Hi-ger?" Lolita asked. "Aren't these Germans hated by many countries, are they not a bad people? Why are you studying them?"

"No, abuelita. Not all Germans are gente mala. They're often very intelligent. This HEI-DEG-GER writes about death and about how it should be important to people during life. What do you think of that?"

"Ese viejo está loco. That man is a lunatic. How can death be important during your life when you have so many reasons to live? If you continue to read those philosophers, you're going to be as crazy as they are. That idiot Hi-ger probably never had a happy day in his life.

"Look, my son," she continued, "drop those books, and go outside for a walk, or go out with some of your friends. Stop studying too much and don't be a crazy hermit. Remember what I told you: El que adelante no ye atrás se queda. Do you know what that means? It means that you should stop waiting for death and let the Germans worry about that. Find contentment and happiness in your life before you realize that your time to live is almost over. Use each day to make yourself and others happy, and then you will never have regrets in your life. I'm an old woman now, but I will only stop when the good Lord brings me down with his own two hands."

"Gracias, abuelita. I'll be okay, don't worry about me. I just felt lonely and depressed, but I feel better now," he answered.

"Arturo, you are only beginning to live. You're young. Enjoy the rest of your life. And don't waste it by studying all the time. The only things that you'll get from plunging into your books are depression, blindness, and insanity. Have faith in God and he will show you what is life. I will pray for you on Sunday, and I'll ask God to help you when you are lonely and afraid. I'll also ask Lupita to pray for you. She is an angel of mercy," said Lolita.

"Go out and have a beer, or go to a party," José interrupted, his tight skin yielding to a grin.

"Don't pay attention to that drunken old fool! How can you tell him to do that? That may be the answer for a useless old man like you. Go ahead, go out and get yourself drunk. I'll leave you out there in the streets with the stray dogs! And if I don't punish you first, the Lord will surely toss you into the dark pit with the horned one. Don't pay attention to him, Arturo," she said.

"Ay, señora, you always take everything I say the wrong way," José responded resignedly.

"Please don't fight. I didn't call to listen to a fight. I have to go now. I have a lot of work and I also don't want to stay up late," Arturo said.

"Okay. But remember what I told you. Don't drive yourself crazy. Relax and enjoy yourself," she said. "And call us again whenever you can. I'll tell your parents that you are well. Do you want me to send you more hot chocolate packets and homemade cookies? I'll wrap them up and I'll tell your brother to put them in the mail. And Arturo, please don't suffer all the time. That is no way to live."

"Thank you, señora. Don't worry about me, I'll survive. I miss the family. Please say hello to everyone. Goodbye, Tiger. Don't let la abuelita get the best of you. You know how she is. Hasta luego, we'll talk again soon."

***

Lolita walked into the kitchen while José was placing the leftovers in the refrigerator. She looked at him and almost said something, but returned to the bedroom and undressed. She was happy after having talked with Arturo, yet as she pulled her airy white nightgown over her knees, her eyes looked plaintively at the ground. How can he be preoccupied with death at his age? That Hi-ger is probably a poor bastard with nothing to love; maybe he doesn't have a God, she thought. Poor lonely bastard. I'm not surprised he writes all the time; he probably thinks writing is all there is in life. And my pobrecito Arturo, alone and separated from his family, he must be digging himself into an early grave of insanity by working too hard. That damn German is the only companion he has over there.

She folded the bedspread and uncovered the soft white sheets. José was washing his face and shaving. Both were soon in bed, and the apartment was dark and quiet. Yet Lolita was still awake.

Death.

She remembered the abdominal pain. She could pose the question about death but did not know how to answer it. Without knowing how to find an adequate answer, she asked about her life and the end that would be death. The dark stillness of the room seemed to crush her into an existence where she faced herself alone, although she also seemed everywhere. She remembered Arturo and the anxiety that he felt when he studied too much and when he was alone. Why does he do that? He only needs to live his life and to enjoy it. I am old—what choice do I have? I must think about death because I know I will not live forever. I feel old, she thought, my body reminds me each day that I will be here for only a while longer. I think about death because I can see clearly that it will soon be a part of my life. When you are young, you can live forever, and you can make a life that is as ferocious as an angry lion's life. When you are old, however, you must retreat from this ferocity and become an old child: you live each day with your eyes open to the world, knowing that this wonderful creation will soon be taken from your hands. Why does Arturo plunge himself into these pits of torment? He needn't worry about death. Of course, he will also die, but not soon. And with the Lord's help, he will live a long life. Then why think about death now? Why?

She closed her eyes, attempting to impose rest by command. There must be something else that Arturo is trying to do, she thought. I can't believe he is tormenting himself for nothing. Well, whatever it is, it seems a waste of time. That crazy Hi-ger just put some notions into poor Arturo's head.

She shifted her weight to find an elusive comfort, yet a persistent tenderness spread through her body like a gentle wave. The pain in her abdomen slowly swelled from a gaseous sensation to an intense pain that drained her mind. She braced herself for the attack, rigidly fixing herself and hoping this posture would discourage the agony assaulting her body. The pain was now a roaring, evil wave, and she began to choke, her larynx contracting with one giant spasm. Her extremities twitched with the convulsions reverberating throughout her body. José stirred, yet remained in a deep sleep. On the bed with her hands clenching her stomach, she winced at the blinding light pounding her exposed face. Her forehead was pale, and the loose skin under her neck tightened as she pushed her head into the pillow.

Damn death.

I'm going to fight you; energy to kill is energy to live. Damn this pain. Stop, God, please stop. If I die, God help me, please help me God. She reached the apex of intensity. Everything in the world was still while she was uncontrollably spinning, and then suddenly she was motionless while the world itself was shaking violently. Nausea. The darkness of the room became a life of specificity and sheer intensity—she could discern the minutest detail in the mass of darkness. She breathed deeply, and the pain finally receded. Her pillow and gown were soaked. Attempting to regain her balance and trying to quell the rising vomit in her stomach, she lay in bed for a moment.

Damn, she thought, as she slowly rose from the bed. Tomorrow I will go to El Centro, and I will get ready for the Christmas parade. She lit a cigarette on the kitchen stove and sat quietly puffing away great clouds of smoke. Tomorrow I will get someone to take me to Licon's Dairy; I want asaderos and cheese for my chile con calabazas. Gently the night yielded to the dawn, and Lolita sensed the cold desert breeze coming in through the open window. ★

Tanya Maria Barrientos

Born in Guatemala, Tanya Maria Barrientos came to El Paso with her family in 1963. After graduating from the University of Missouri School of Journalism, she was a reporter, editor, and columnist for twenty-five years at the *Dallas Times Herald* and the *Philadelphia Inquirer*. She has taught writing at the Stonecoast MFA program in Maine, Bryn Mawr College, and the University of Pennsylvania. Author of two novels, *Frontera Street* and *Family Resemblance*, as well as numerous essays and short stories, Barrientos was awarded the prestigious Pew Fellowship in the Arts in 2001. She is currently a writer at the National Constitution Center in Philadelphia.

From *Frontera Street*: Dee

"This is your third week, and if you're gong to stay you have to take this off."

Septima peeled back the strip of masking tape that I'd been using as a name tag since my arrival. Everybody else had their names sewn permanently into the left side of their red smocks, and it was clear they had put considerable thought into the designs. Septima had created a large *S* out of baby rickrack and had embroidered the rest of her name between the curves. Pilar had wrapped yellow ribbon around a needle and, with a few nips and tucks, had made a vine of roses bloom in a wavy border around the five letters of her name. Alma, of course, had used buttons.

I hadn't considered what I was going to do—whether I should use colored thread or simple white stitches, whether I should brighten the apron with sequins or get creative with patches and rivets. None of the options had occurred to me because, when I began working at the store, I was convinced the same stray wind that delivered me to Frontera Street would just as unexpectedly carry me away. But I kept coming back. I kept parking my car in the underground garage near the bank and walking five blocks to the fabric shop every morning. Soon I was a regular on the sidewalks near the downtown plaza, such a regular that the kids waiting for the school bus didn't even look up when I walked by. Such a regular that I knew exactly when the smoky smell of the breakfast chorizo sizzling on the greasy grill of La Indita luncheonette would lead me off Main Street, across Empresario Avenue and straight into the heart of a neighborhood I had ignored, or at least conspicuously avoided, for most of my life.

On my way to the shop I walked by Flores by Dolores, where the front window was decorated with a selection of cemetery wreaths and Barbie doll centerpieces with puffy gowns made out of pink and yellow chrysanthemums. I passed an appliance store that kept two loud air conditioners displayed on the sidewalk. The owner tied red and white ribbons to the machines' plastic grilles, and they flicked and snapped at passersby like lizard tongues.

Half a block from Septima's shop I passed the blind man selling Mexican lottery tickets on the honor system and the Quick Snap Photo Studio, offering a green-card-and-passport-picture package for twelve dollars.

It was the same every morning, and it wasn't long before I began to chuckle at how my momma used to say the barrio had nothing to offer people like us, except trouble. The fabric shop seemed like the perfect place to start over. Nobody there needed to know more about me than what they saw. Septima and Alma must have thought I was divorced, or even abandoned by a lover, and I didn't bother to tell them otherwise. I felt safe leaving their unspoken questions unanswered, and I wrapped the silence around me like a big black cloak.

***

Officially, of course, Mexico doesn't begin in downtown Los Cielos. It starts a few miles away, where the Monterey Bridge straddles the Rio Grande. Halfway across that uninspired arch of concrete a sign reads: You Are Leaving The United States Of America. Two paces farther a different sign offers: Bienvenidos a Mexico. Nobody is sure who owns the steps in between, but just like that, the nations divide.

Anyone who has ever lived in West Texas knows the real border has nothing to do with that bridge, or the Rio Grande, or even the government. People have drawn their own lines for as long as they've been able, and in Los Cielos the true border has always been at some invisible point near Frontera Street, just past Schuster's Department Store, directly across from the downtown plaza.

That's where shop names abruptly change from Bobby O's Factory Discount Boots to Castillo de Zapatos. It's also where, every weekday as the first red ribbons of daylight stretch across the shallow Rio Grande, four tired Mexican buses limp over the Monterey Bridge's hump, down Texas Avenue, and across Main Street, hauling cheaper-than-American day workers from *el otro lado*, the other side. Like old horses following a well-worn trail, they pull up to the south side of San Elizario Plaza, where shimmering purple oil stains coat the hot pavement like melted wax. The engines shudder and sigh, as weary of the repetitive route as the dozens of dull-eyed passengers riding inside.

It is the same scene every morning. You can set your clock by it, and for decades lots of people have. Especially the Westside ladies who drive down to the plaza for the Pick-and-Pray. That's what the housewives call the once-a-week trips they make to fetch their maids. Pick a woman and pray that she won't steal the family silver.

The caravan begins early on Tuesdays with the wives rushing out of their front doors by six-thirty in order to make it downtown by seven. Any later than that and all the good ones will be gone. Plus, nobody wants to be on the road at eight o'clock, when the men get tangled up in rush hour. The entire thing is so precisely timed that by half-past seven they will all be home again and the maids will be busy stripping bed linens. Then the mothers who don't have toddlers tugging at their knees will fill their long days with round robins of tennis or golf at the Westside Country Club, or luncheons sponsored by groups that pride themselves on their devotion to civic duty.

Whenever a new family moves to the neighborhood, the Westside wives fill them in on the going Pick-and-Pray rates. Forty dollars a week from Tuesday to Saturday afternoon. Saturday evenings are negotiable, especially if there is entertaining involved. But all the *muchachas* are to be back home by Sunday morning, in plenty of time for church. Because there is, after all, a right and wrong way of treating people.

My family's longtime maid, Serita, used to stand just beyond the four iron benches at the north side of the plaza. I can't remember a time during my childhood when she wasn't there, waiting for us. As a girl I loved Serita's sturdy roundness for the comfort it offered. Her ample shoulders melted directly into the folds over her elbows, and her generous hip line was as inviting as a feather bed, especially when she sat down and offered her lap along with a blanket and her soothing Spanish lullabies.

***

The downtown plaza started out as the throbbing heart of a hopeful frontier town. The men who founded it set out to create a sophisticated cross between a Mexican *zócalo* and a Victorian town square. Old photos show them wearing black suits, tall black hats, and fine pocket watches, their faces weathered but triumphant, as they dedicate their creation to the blue skies of the future. They show lots of trees, too, probably the same sun-bleached and water-starved cottonwoods that the maids lean up against now. But in those photos from 1864 the trees look lush and shady, and underneath them, in the center of the old plaza, stands a glorious fountain made of hand-painted Spanish tile. Momma used to tell me that even when she was a little girl, entire families would stroll down Main Street to gaze at that fountain after Sunday services at First Baptist. Restless children would climb onto the iron fence that surrounded it with curls and dips that looked like a fine lady's handwriting. She said most folks let the children play, assured that the swirling iron gate was strong enough to keep even the rougher boys away from the two Louisiana crocs that crawled around the bottom of the fountain bowl. The plaza has never looked like that again, not since the 1950s, when the better neighborhoods of Los Cielos migrated westward and left the founders' little piece of determination behind.

By the 1970s, when I was growing up, the fountain was long gone and the plaza had become the meeting place of *los Mexicános*, with Spanish being tossed across the scrappy lawn in rapid fire and tinny radios blaring music that was broadcast from the other side of everything. The Mexican songs would seep into our cars when the maids slid into the backseats, and for a few moments the rushing currents of sad ballads, weeping accordions, and trembling voices clinging to a single note would wash over us.

Mitch grew up in New Orleans, where the past and present were allowed to simmer into a rich gumbo, and he never understood why one side of Los Cielos pretended that the other didn't exist. He always wanted to visit the plaza, to take a walk into the neighborhoods I'd never been allowed to enter, saying that I'd left the best part of my own hometown undiscovered. I let him go on his border safaris by himself, and my family would chuckle when he would return and tell us about discoveries that he believed were cultural diamonds but we knew were just mangy pieces of the barrio.

***

Not long after Septima told me to decorate my apron she announced that Alma was going to be late getting to work and that Pilar was going to be busy all morning stocking the new polyester blends.

What she was saying—without coming out and actually saying it—was that for the first time since I was hired, I was going to be alone in buttons. I walked behind the counter, but instead of feeling comfortable, I felt like I had wandered into someone else's house. For three weeks Alma had allowed me to stand back there with her, but she always made it perfectly clear that I was an uninvited guest taking up room that could have been put to better use. Without her there, the narrow space suddenly seemed big enough to get lost in.

Selling buttons wasn't a hard job, we both knew that, but it did require a certain eye for detail, and Alma took pride in her ability to complement a fabric's weave and pattern with her selections. She could convince even the most skeptical seamstress that choosing the best buttons she could afford would make her feel better inside her clothes.

I looked for something to do, but there were no button cards in the plastic tub for me to return to the drawers, and there were no customers waiting for service. For a moment I considered taking the time to study more Spanish verbs and grammar from the little book I kept in my handbag, but when I saw Septima glance over her shoulder, checking on me, I gave up on that.

Alma kept a scrap of last year's green Christmas velvet around to use as a dustcloth. I pulled it out of the cardboard box she'd tucked under the counter and wiped everything around me. I dusted the craft magazines featuring do-it-yourself pillows covered with buttons and wiped down the diameter display cards taped to the countertop.

When I put the dustrag back under the counter, my hand brushed against something pushed far into the corner. It was a square box the size of a notebook, made of wood. I pulled it out and saw that the lid and sides were decorated with uneven carvings, vines and flowers that someone not at all comfortable with cutting tools had sliced into the grain. The tiny brass clasp—a latch shaped like a question mark—was bent and, instead of sliding into the hook underneath it, passed just over it, keeping the lid slightly ajar. I knew the box probably belonged to Alma and she was keeping it secret for a reason. Still, I opened it,

Septima was at the other end of the shop, holding a clipboard and checking off each bolt of polyester blend that Pilar pulled out of a shipping crate. Only two customers were in the store, and they were sitting at the tables near the Ultra Suede, slowly leafing through pattern books.

Inside the box I found some unopened letters, two photographs, and a tarnished silver *milagro* medal shaped like a tiny hammer. I'd seen the miniature medals before, nailed onto crosses and, more recently, decorating high-priced furniture that designers sold as Santa Fe style. But I knew Alma wasn't using this one as a piece of art. In Mexico the medals are used as religious charms, a cross between a voodoo doll and a prayer card. People find a medal that represents whatever they are praying for and when their prayer has been answered they nail the medal onto a crucifix in their home, or they sometimes place it at the feet of their favorite saint.

Lots of crosses for sale in antique stores along the border are encrusted with a lifetime worth of prayers, in the shapes of arms and legs and houses and baby carriages. But I couldn't recall ever seeing a tiny hammer like the one Alma had stored away in the box, clearly still waiting for an answer.

I put the medal down and picked up the sealed envelopes. They were all addressed to the same person.

Paul Walker, P. O. Box 529, Scottsdale, Arizona.

The handwriting on the blue-tinted paper was cramped and lurched to the right. I had never heard Alma mention the name, but that didn't mean anything—she never told me about her life anyway.

I wanted her to like me, and I think that is why I kept coming back to the fabric shop, why I stood behind the button counter and kept quiet when she spoke to her friends as if I weren't there. It was why I asked her if she would explain some of the more confusing rules of Spanish grammar that I came across in the paperback that I carried around like a worn Gideon's Bible. And why I didn't push when she refused, saying that people who grow up speaking a language don't ever know the rules, they just speak.

It wasn't unusual for us to get through an entire day with conversations built on two words or less.

"Black crescents?" I'd ask.

"Wood or plastic?" she'd answer.

"Glass."

"Fifth row."

At first I thought she was shy because her English wasn't very good, but I learned soon enough that she both spoke and understood English better than she let on. She wasn't shy around her friends at all. When they came into the store her entire bearing changed. She gossiped with gusto, and as she spoke I watched her shoulders soften and her cold glances thaw.

Of course, I knew she wouldn't appreciate that I was poking through the contents of the little box. I was trespassing on property that I wasn't even supposed to know existed, trampling a trust I hadn't even won yet. I knew I should stop. But I couldn't.

I picked up the photographs. One curled in on itself like a cocoon. I smoothed out the corners. It was an old black-and-white snapshot of two people—a dark-skinned man with a heavy mustache in a crisp, dark suit with a rosebud pinned onto the narrow lapel and a delicate-boned woman in a satin Marilyn Monroe-type dress that pinched at the waist and clung all the way to the middle of her calves. The woman had her hair up in what must have been a loose French twist, and her hands were clasped around a limp pair of white gloves. Uneasy in front of the camera, the young couple were touching only at their elbows and shoulders, yet their eyes were electric with emotion. Something important had just happened, but neither the man nor the woman managed to smile about it. It was, I decided, a wedding portrait, taken at the very instant the young lovers conceived the enormity of the promises they'd made. I recognized the look in their eyes.

The second photograph was lodged inside a small frame made out of Popsicle sticks held together by dried clumps of schoolhouse glue. Bits of green glitter shed onto the counter like dandruff as I pulled the color snapshot out of the box.

I'd never seen Socorro, but I knew the picture was of her. She was beautiful and completely different than I had imagined. I had envisioned a wide-bodied girl because of the stories I'd overheard Alma tell her regular customers—stories about her headstrong daughter's adolescent stubbornness, her unpredictable moods, and her drive to shove harder, shout louder, and even fight tougher than the neighborhood boys. Yet the child in the photo was hardly more than a puff of smoke.

She was looking over her shoulder at the camera, as if somebody had just called out her name. A breeze had lifted her long hair and sent it flowing around a Valentine-shaped face. Her skin color was what people called olive when they didn't feel like saying dark brown. She looked like lots of other Mexican American girls, except for her eyes, which set her apart. They were clear instead of dark, not a gem green but the wintry tint of sagebrush leaves, surrounded by thick crowns of dark lashes.

Alma had, of course, never spoken directly to me about Socorro. But she told Septima everything, from what Socorro did or didn't eat for breakfast, to how she found her in the kitchen late one night, shaving her legs for the first time with one foot propped up against the kitchen sink and a handful of green Palmolive liquid smeared from ankle to thigh. Her stories were buckets full of pride and exasperation, pulled up daily from a deep well of tenderness.

The most recent news I'd heard about Socorro was that she and a boy named Peeps had been awarded scholarships to Arts High School. Alma mentioned it to Septima on a Monday morning, and by that same afternoon she was accepting congratulations from customers who came in to say they'd heard all about it from their children, who had heard it from someone else's kids.

"Elena *me dijo* that Socorro sang with a voice *tan fuerte* that all the windows rattled," one customer boasted.

"No! That's not the story," another one argued. "I heard that she sat down and sketched a bowl of fruit so detailed that you could see the juice inside the green grapes."

Alma and Septima laughed at how the simple facts had been passed from one woman to another and whipped like a bowl of egg batter. Out of politeness, or maybe curiosity, Alma patiently listened to every version of the story, no matter how exaggerated, before setting the record straight.

"What else did you hear?" Septima prodded.

"She has a full scholarship, that's what I heard," yet another customer reported, adding: "Richard the music teacher said he already has plans to try and get more scholarships next year. And Benita Quintanilla says her daughter, Norma, is practically guaranteed a spot because she cleans house for the vice principal. But I don't know who she thinks she's fooling, because that girl walks like an iguana, and is starting to look like one, too!"

"Well, I don't know about that," Alma jumped in, rescuing the discussion from sliding into a debate over what other reptiles poor little Norma might favor. "Most of what you heard is right," she confirmed, "except her scholarship is for dance."

"Dance?"

Alma nodded.

"I didn't know Socorro could dance."

"Me either," Alma answered, raising her eyebrows and throwing her hands open.

She explained that Socorro had gone to the audition only to keep Peeps company. He had asked her to be there because whenever he gets nervous his lips go numb and he can't press them together properly to play his French horn. He thought if Socorro could be in the audience he might stay calm, but when they got to the school Peeps was told to line up with the other musicians and Socorro wasn't allowed to even stand next to him.

Alma had everyone's attention as she continued to tell, in both English and Spanish, how it happened.

***

A teacher told Socorro that she would have to wait for Peeps outside, and got another student to walk her to the door. On her way out, Socorro glanced back over her shoulder and saw poor Peeps standing at the end of the long line of trumpeters, trombonists, and baritone players, smacking his lips in sheer terror.

Socorro had never seen a school like Arts High. The buildings were spread out over a huge island of green grass, watered by automatic sprinklers, and tended so carefully that if it weren't for the dusty desert hills just across the street, you'd never know you were in West Texas. There were tennis courts and greenhouses and even a swimming pool with not just one but two diving boards.

Inside each building, different auditions were in progress. Socorro walked from one to the other, observing. She saw students pacing in the hallways as they mumbled lines from plays they had memorized. She heard waves of violin solos and snippets of piano pieces escaping from behind closed doors. Alma said Socorro eventually walked into the gymnasium to take a seat in the bleachers and wait for Peeps. There, she saw girls in pink tights and black leotards taking turns leaping and twirling diagonally across the floor. The teacher was dressed in the same outfit, except hers included a black chiffon skirt that brushed against her knees. She walked from one end of the gym to the other, keeping time by pounding a black cane against the floor.

The teacher stopped in mid-beat when she saw Socorro walk in. "You're very late!" she yelled at her.

Socorro tried to explain that she wasn't there to audition, but the teacher, who spoke with a heavy Russian accent, didn't understand.

"Shh. Shh. Shh. Clothes? Shoes? Where are they?" the angry teacher demanded.

Socorro walked down onto the dance floor to try and explain, but the teacher hooked her walking cane into the crook of Socorro's elbow and pulled her into line with the other dancers.

"Take off shoes. Take off! Take off!" the teacher commanded, clapping her hands impatiently.

Socorro tried to speak up.

"No. No speak. Shhh. We continue," the teacher said, resuming the steady pounding.

Going through the movements, Socorro felt like a cow on ice compared to the other girls, who not only could slide their feet into awkward positions without falling over, but could move their heads and arms in different ways at the same time. The only two things Socorro was good at were the split-legged leaps and a balancing exercise that required her to stand on one leg while raising the other as high as possible.

After each exercise the teacher walked up to one or two girls, tapped them on their shoulders with her cane, and said, "Thank you." They left the floor immediately and either sat in the bleachers silently watching the test of the audition or dashed into the locker room, crying. Socorro said she waited for the Russian to tap her on the shoulder, but that never happened. Every time the teacher dismissed somebody else, Socorro felt that girl aim a dirty look her way. At one point, according to Alma's version of the story, Socorro tried to walk off the floor. She'd had enough. But the teacher scolded her again.

"No. No quit. You dance now!"

The audition took an hour, and in the end Socorro was left standing with five other girls. The sweat she'd worked up made her shorts and T-shirt cling to her back and thighs.

"Congratulations," the teacher told Socorro and the five other finalists, handing each of them a manila envelope filled with forms.

"Fill out. See you in class," the teacher said before she turned and walked away.

The other girls squealed and hugged one another. Socorro took her envelope and went to find Richard and Peeps.

She found them standing by Richard's car, worried that she had gotten lost. Peeps had an envelope in his hand, too.

Richard told Alma that the ballet teacher believed Socorro had enough natural talent to catch up with the test of the dancers within a year.

"All I know," Alma told the customers listening to the story, "is that Socorro wants to go, so I'll let her."

***

I looked at the photograph of Socorro in the Popsicle stick frame and understood what the dance teacher saw—a willowy strength coiled up like a tight spring inside elastic arms and legs. She was the kind of daughter Mitch and I used to whisper in the dark about having—chosen by God to move like a melody. I studied her picture closer and began to hear Mitch whispering something to me that I couldn't make out. His voice was tempered, deep and low, but his words were as murky as unsettled water.

"I said, what are you doing with that?"

It wasn't Mitch who was speaking to me at all. It was Alma. She was standing at the far end of the counter, her arms crossed and her face raw with anger.

Her eyes dared me to explain why I had her things spread out like a casual game of solitaire.

"What the hell are you doing with that?" she demanded as she snatched the photograph out of my hand.

"I found it," I murmured in weak defense.

"You think you can walk in here and do whatever the hell you want, don't you?"

She grabbed the wooden box and glared at me as she put each of the items back inside it.

"Septima might feel sorry for you, but I don't. You got that? I don't give a damn what sort of trouble you got yourself into. We've got plenty of our own troubles around here. So don't think I'm going to protect you *para nada*! If somebody comes in here looking for you—I don't care what sort of *cabrón* he might be—I'm just gonna point straight at you and say, here, you can have her."

Startled and unsteady, I stood back as Alma pushed her way behind the counter to put the box back where she'd hidden it.

"Around here you're not better than anyone."

I thought she was going to slap me, and I prepared myself for the sting.

I backed up against the button drawers and saw her raise her fists.

I gulped mouthfuls of air to try and stop the wrenching sobs that made my rib cage ache. I wiped my face with the tail of my red apron, and then I felt my knees give way as a tidal wave of nausea swept over me. A sharp pain in my abdomen knocked me to the ground.

The vomit burned like acid and then everything went black. ★

Christine Granados

Born and raised in El Paso, Christine Granados is a graduate of University of Texas at El Paso and the MFA creative writing program at Texas State University at San Marcos. The 2006 winner of the Alfredo Cisneros del Moral Foundation Award, a grant given by Sandra Cisneros to further the aspirations of new writers, Granados is the author of short fiction that has been featured in both literature anthologies and periodicals, including *Hecho en Tejas: An Anthology of Texas-Mexican Literature*, *The Texas Observer*, and *El Andar Magazine*. Her collection of short stories *Brides and Sinners in El Chuco* was a 2006 finalist in the short story category for the Foreword Magazine Book of the Year and received a notable book mention in the 2006 Pima County Public Library Southwest Books of the Year awards. In addition, Granados' story "Inner View" was a Spur Award finalist for Best Short Fiction from Western Writers of America in 2007, and she was named one of the Top Ten "New" Latino Authors to Watch (and read) by LatinoStories.com. Her stories have been featured in *Not Quite What I was Planning: And Other Six-Word Memoirs by Writers Famous and Obscure* and *Big Tex[t]* and *the Newspaper Tree,* as well as in the *Austin American Statesman*, the *Dallas Morning News*, the *El Paso Times*, *Hispanic Magazine*, *El Paso Magazine*, *Latina Magazine*, *People*, *People en Espanol*, *Teen People*, NPR's *Latino USA*, *American Book Review*, and the *Rockdale Reporter*. Currently, she is a freelance journalist and a lecturer at Texas A&M University.

From *Brides and Sinners in El Chuco*: The Bride

When the month of June rolls around, I have to buy the five-pound bride magazine off the rack at the grocery store. The photographs of white dresses, articles with to-do lists, and advertisements for wedding planners remind me of my older sister Rochelle's wedding. She had been planning for her special day as far back as I can remember. Every year when she was a child, Rochelle dressed as a beautiful, blushing bride for Halloween. She sauntered her way down the hot, dusty streets of El Paso, accepting candy from our neighbors in her drawstring handbag. The white satin against Rochelle's olive skin made her look so pretty that I didn't mind the fact that we had to stop every three houses so she could empty the candy from her dainty bag into the ripped brown paper sack that I used for the journey. She had to drag me along with her—a reluctant Caspar—because Mom made her, and because I could hold all her candy. Her thick black hair was braided, and she wore the trenzas in an Eva Perón-style moño. She spent hours in the bathroom, with her friend Prissy fixing her hair just right, only to cover her head with a white tulle veil.

As Rochelle did this, Mom would prepare my costume. Spent and uninspired after a long day at work, Mom would drape a sheet over me and cut out holes for eyes. It happened every year without fail. The fact that I couldn't make up my mind what I wanted to be for Halloween exasperated my already exhausted mother even more. In a matter of minutes, I would list the Bionic Woman, a wrestler, a linebacker, a fat man, all as potential getups before it was time to trick-or-treat.

Ro, on the other hand, had her bridal dress finished days in advance, and she'd wear it to school to show it off. When people opened their doors to us, they would say, "Ay, qué bonita la novia, and your little brother un fantasma tan scary." I'd have to clear things up at every house with "I'm not a boy." They would laugh and ask Rochelle if she had a husband. She would giggle and give them a name.

When she got too old for Halloween, she started getting serious about planning her own wedding. She bought bride magazines and drew up plans, leaving absolutely no detail unattended. When it finally did happen, it was nothing like she had expected.

Rochelle was obsessed. Because all those ridiculous magazines never listed mariachis or dollar dances, she decided her wedding was going to have a string quartet, no bajo, horns, or anything, no dollar dance, and it was going to be in October. It was going to be a bland affair, outside in a tent, like the weddings up North in the "elegance of autumn" that she read about in the thick glossy pages of the magazines. I wasn't going to tell her there is no "elegance" to autumn in El Paso. Autumn is either "scramble a huevo on the hood of your car hot," or wind so strong the sand it blows stings your face and arms.

In the magazine pictures, all the people were white, skinny, and rich. All the women wore linen or silk slips that draped over their skeletal frames, and the men wore tuxedos or black suits and ties. She didn't take into account that in those pages, there was no tía Trini, who we called Teeny because, at five-foot-two, she weighed at least three hundred pounds. The slip dress Rochelle wanted everyone to wear would be swallowed in Teeny's cavernous flesh. And I never saw anyone resembling tío Lacho, who wore the burgundy tuxedo he got married in, two sizes too small, to every family wedding. The guests in the magazine weddings were polite and refined, with their long-stemmed wine-glasses half full. No one ever got falling-down drunk and picked a fight, like Pilar. He would get so worked up someone would have to knock him out with a bottle of El Presidente. He was proud of the scars on his head, too, showing them off just before the big fight started.

Rochelle wanted tall white boys with jawbones that looked like they had been chiseled from stone to be her groomsmen; never mind the fact that we knew only one white boy, and he had acne so bad his face was blue. She also wanted her maid of honor to be pencil thin, although she would never admit it. Still, she was always dropping hints, telling her best friend, Prissy, that by the time they were twenty all their baby fat would be gone, and they would both look fabulous in their silk gowns. Never mind the fact that I, two years younger than Rochelle, could encircle my sister's bicep between my middle finger and thumb, and that Prissy rested her Tab colas on her huge stomach when she sat. My sister was in denial. And it wasn't just about her obese friend but about her entire life. She thought that if she planned every last detail of her wedding on paper, she could change who she was, who we were. Her lists drove me crazy.

She kept a running tally of the songs to be played by the band, adding and deleting as her musical tastes changed through the years. She carefully selected the food to be served to her guests. She resolutely decided what everyone in the family would be wearing. She even painstakingly chose what her dress would look like, down to the last sequin. But in order to marry, she needed a groom. And she was just as diligent about finding one as she was about the rest of the affair.

Every night before going to bed, she would pull out her pink wedding notebook and scratch a boy's name off her list of potential husbands. She went through two notebooks in one year. She was always on the lookout for husbands. One time, Rochelle and I spent an entire Saturday morning typing up fake raffle tickets to sell to Mike, who lived two blocks over. Ro had never met Mike, but she liked his broad shoulders thought they'd look good in a tuxedo. So she made up a story that she was helping me sell raffle tickets for my softball team. Ro didn't let little things, like the truth, get in the way of her future. All the money raised would go into the team's travel budget. She even made up first-, second-, and third-place prizes. First place would be a color TV, second place, a dinner for two at Fortis Mexican Food Restaurant, and third, two tickets to the movies. She said Mike was going to win third place, and when she delivered his prize, she was going to suggest he take her to the movies since she was the one who sold him the winning ticket. I thought my sister was a genius, until we got to the door and knocked. When Mike answered, Ro delivered her lines like she had been selling raffle tickets all day long. When he told us he had no money we were shocked. Ro didn't have a Plan B. Then, when his older brother came to the door and offered to buy all ten of the raffle tickets, we were speechless. All we could do was take his money, give him his stubs, and wish him luck. Ro was so upset her plan was a failure that she let me keep the ten dollars. Needless to say, Mike got scratched off her list.

Her blue notebook was where she compiled her guest list and either added or deleted a name depending on what had happened in school that day. I got scratched out six times in one month: for using all her sanitary napkins as elbow and knee pads while skating; for wearing her real silver concho belt and losing it at school; for telling Mom that Rochelle was giving herself hickeys on her arms; for peeking in her diary; for feeding her goldfish, Hughie, so much that he died; and especially for telling her the truth about the food she planned to serve at her wedding. That final act kept me off the list for two months straight. She wanted finger foods like in Anglo weddings—sandwiches with the crusts cut off.

"Those cream cheese and cucumber sandwiches aren't going to cut it, Ro," I said through the cotton shirt I was taking off.

"My wedding is going to be classy," she yelled at me from across the room, where she was sitting on top of her bed, smoothing lotion on her arms. "If you don't want to eat my food, then you just won't be invited."

I laughed. Her nostrils were flaring pretty steady, and she was winding her middle finger around her ponytail. Then she reached under the mattress for her notebook, and my name, Lily, was off the list, just like that.

"I wouldn't want to go spend hours at some dumb wedding when I was half starving anyway. Everybody's going to faint before the dollar dance starts."

She stopped writing, "There isn't going to be a dollar dance." Then she wrinkled her wide nose, "Too gauche."

When I came back into the room after I had looked up the word, I told her, "I'm telling Mom you think she's tacky. You're carrying your gringa kick too far." Before shutting the bedroom door, I poked my head in and yelled, "I'm glad I'm not invited. I don't want to go to no white wedding."

Later, I asked her how she expected to go on her Hawaii honeymoon without a dollar dance. "You plan on selling the cucumber sandwiches at the wedding?"

She wiped the sarcastic smile off my face when she said, "No. I'm going to have a money tree." I told her that she was ridiculous and that she was going to be a laughingstock, not knowing how close my words were to the truth.

She didn't care what anyone thought. She said her wedding was hers, and it was one thing no one could ruin.

She kept up her lists as usual, but stopped physically adding to them in tenth grade—dropped and discarded as "too childish." By then, the lists were committed to memory, and I knew that she mentally scratched ex-friends and ex-boyfriends off of it. Lance, Rubén, Abraham, Artie, Oscar, Henry, Joel, and who knows who else had all been potential grooms.

It turned out to be Angel. He was beautiful, too—the Mexican version of the blond grooms in her magazines, right down to the cleft in his chin. He was perfect as long as he didn't smile, because when he smiled, his chipped, discolored front tooth showed. Rochelle worried about it all the time. She'd pull out photographs they had taken together, and the ones he had given her, to study them, trying to figure out the right camera angle that would hide his flaw. Anytime she mentioned getting it capped, he would roll his large almond-shaped eyes and smile. They would kiss and that would be the end of the discussion.

I knew this because Rochelle always had to drag me along on her dates. It was the only way our mother would allow her out of the house with a boy. I was a walking-and-talking birth control device. When we got home, I would replay the night's events for my mother. Funny, Ro relished the details of her wedding, but she never could stand for my instant replay of her dates. She would storm out of the living room when I would begin and slam the door to our bedroom. I usually had to sleep on the couch after our dates.

On prom night, Rochelle was allowed to go out with Angel alone, and she was so excited that she let me watch her dress for the big event. Tía Trini came over and rolled her hair, Prissy was there with her Tab in hand for moral support, and Mom was making last minute alterations to her gown. It was a salmon-colored version of her wedding dress. After she was teased, tweezed, and tucked, she looked like a stick of cotton candy from the top of her glittered hair down to her pink sling-back heels. When Angel saw her, he licked his lips like he was going to devour her.

Because I, her birth control device, wasn't in place during this date, the two got married when she was only a junior in high school, and she was four months pregnant. Rochelle and Angel drove thirty minutes to Las Cruces to be married by the justice of peace, with Mom in the back seat bawling. Even though Rochelle didn't get her elegant autumn wedding, she stood before Judge Grijalva in her off-white linen pantsuit, which was damp on the shoulder and smeared with Mom's mascara, erect and with as much dignity as if she were under a tent at the Chamizal. It didn't matter to her that the groom wore his blue Dickie work pants with matching shirt that had his name stitched in yellow onto the pocket. She looked at him like they were the only two people inside the closet-sized courtroom.

She didn't even blink when a baby began to wail in her ear during "Do you take this man . . .

And she never took her eyes off Angel when the woman next in line to get married, who was dressed in a skin-tight, leopard-print outfit, said, "Let's get this show on the road already. Kiss her, kiss her already."

And it didn't bother Rochelle that after Angel kissed her, he looked at his watch and said, "Vámonos. I need to get back to work," because he needed to get back to Sears before the evening rush. ★

Octavio Solis

Playwright and director Octavio Solis was born and raised in El Paso. He earned a B.A. and M.F.A. from Trinity University in San Antonio. Solis has received a National Endowment for the Arts 1995-97 Playwriting Fellowship, the Roger L. Stevens Award from the Kennedy Center, The Will Glickman Playwright award, the 1998 TCG/NEA Theatre Artists in Residence Grant, the 1998 McKnight Fellowship Grant from the Playwrights Center in Minneapolis, and the National Latino playwriting Award for 2003. His works, *Lydia*; *June in a Box*; *Lethe*; *Marfa Lights*; *Gibraltar;* *The Ballad of Pancho and Lucy*; *7 visions of Encarnacion*; *Bethlehem*; *Dreamlandia*; *El Otro*; *Man of the Flesh*; *Prospect*; *El Paso Blue*; *Santos & Santos*; and *La Posada Mágica*, have been mounted at the Oregon Shakespeare Festival, the Denver Center of the Performing Arts, the Dallas Theater Center, South Coast Repertory Theatre, Shadowlight in San Francisco, the Venture Theatre in Philadelphia, the New York Summer Play Festival, Teatro Vista in Chicago, Latino Chicago Theatre Company, and the Imua Theatre Company in New York and Cornerstone Theatre, among many others. His collaborative works include *Burning Dreams*, co-written with Julia Hebert and Gina Leishman; *Shiner*, written with Erik Ehn; and *Great Highway,* written with Wendy Weiner. Broadway Play Publishing recently released a new anthology of Solis' works, entitled *Plays by Octavio Solis*. He has also completed *Prospect*, an independent feature film, which he wrote and directed. Solis is a Thornton Wilder Fellow of the MacDowell Colony, alumnus of New Dramatists, and a member of the Dramatists Guild. His many directing credits include *Prospect,* at El Teatro Campesino and the Magic Theatre; *El Paso Blue*, at Intersection for the Arts and the San Diego Repertory Theatre; *Dreamlandia* and *June in a Box*, at Thick Description. He is currently writing an adaptation of Cervantes' *Don Quixote* for the Oregon Shakespeare Festival.

From *Lydia*

ACT I

(AT RISE: The living room of the Flores home. CLAUDIO slumps on the La-Z Boy watching TV. Ironing his white shirts and pants is his wife ROSA. In the pad lies CECI in sweats, a long thin scar rising from her eyebrow and disappearing into her hairline. She lies very still, her eyes on the flickering light of the TV. After a moment, an awareness dawns on her and she starts.)

CECI

She touched me and I flew. Touched my fault-line. And I flew. With her hand, laid holy water on my scar. And I flew on wings of glass. My body como una bird racing with the moon on a breath of air. Flying out of range of pain, purpose, this thing we call Vida, soaring into the blueness of memory, closing my eyes for the thud to come.

(She closes her eyes. Opens them.)

I wake to this. Life inside my life. No wings, no glass, no moon. Only Loteria which means Bingo which means chance which means play. So I play the cards into view.

(She looks down at her arms and legs curling under her as a light falls on her cot.)

A card with me printed, La Vida Cecilia, rag doll thumbing the stitching in her head, forms the words in her vegetable tongue, what happened to me, porque no puedo remember, I must remember.

(The light bears down on Claudio.)

There. A card called El Short-Order Cook. Broken man drowning in old rancheras and TV. I hear voces antiguas calling his name, Claudio, my poor Papi Claudio in your personal winter, drowning out the will of Mami saying come with me across the rio, give up that lie you thought was you and live mine, live American with me. So the dish ran away with the greasy spoon and a girl jumped over the moon but you don't spikka the English, only the word No, which in Spanish means No, No at work in bed in your dreams in your cantos perdidos.

(The light shifts to ROSA, ironing clothes and muttering silent prayers to herself.)

Aqui, the Mami Rosa card, dressmaker of flying girls, sewing up my unfinished seams; a beautiful woman losing beauty by the day, see it gathered at her feet like old panty hose, ay Ama! You were Rosie Flores, clerk for the County, making your life here, Anglo words like lazy moths tumbling out your mouth, you were toda proud, but now. You're Rosa Reborn holy-rolling me to sleep with the prayers of your new church. Your prayers for us to be family which hasn't really been family since they stopped putting cork in soda bottle caps.

(Rene comes in from down the hall. He goes to the front door and retrieves the day's mail. He goes over it carefully.)

CECI

Ayy. My wild card, El Carnal Mayor, Rene, my elder volcano, bustin' noses just by looking at 'em, both hands fulla middle fingers for the whole world, checking every day for hate mail, but always nada. Cars go by and honk Puto-Puto-Rene-Puto! but cowards, my brother is invincible.

(He throws the mail on the coffee table and stares at Ceci.)

The army recruiter don't want you, huh, not like those other flag-draped Chicanos on our block, even those that come back alive look like they gave up the ghost, that's kinda what you want, that damned ghost taken out of you. 'Cause you're all messed up with some hard-core macho shit nobody gets.

(He finally looks at Ceci and slowly comes to her.)

Andale, plant a kiss on my head like that saint in church with the chipped nose—

(He kisses her and leaves out the front door.)

dry-kiss and move away. Simon, carnal, before the disgust starts to show.

(Misha enters with his books. Flops down on the couch.)

Misha? ¿Eres tu? Card with the inscription Little Shit. Carnalito Misha bringing to my nariz fragrances of the street the school his body, yes, the musk of you coming of age, coming into yourself, coming all over yourself. I hear your little secrets like crystals of salt in the pockets of your eyes, sad-boy Misha, sad for me, for us, the things that darken the day, King and Kennedy, the killings of students, the killings of Nam—

¡Aguas! I see her again. . . in her own card. . . her face in a mirror looking back. . . showing me her own scar—ggghn mmm her—own—mmgfmhm . . .

MISHA

Mom, what's wrong with Ceci?

ROSA

Alomejor she went poo-poo.

MISHA

She doesn't smell like it.

ROSA

Maybe she wants her therapy. Could you do it, Misha? I'm pressing your father's shirts for work.

(Misha sits by Ceci and runs her through a repertoire of delicate physical exercises, shifting her position from time to time.)

MISHA

Orale, carnala. Let's get the blood pumping.

ROSA

Con cariño, okay?

MISHA

Always gentle, Ama. Hey Dad.

ROSA

He can't hear you.

MISHA

Dad!

ROSA

¿Que te dije? What are you doing home so early? Don't you have practice?

MISHA

(as he rubs Ceci's arms and hands)

I dropped out of the squad. Football ain't my game. You hear that, Dad? I'm a woose and I don't understand what all those little circles and arrows mean. I can't hear the quarterback in the huddle. He grunts uhh twenty-uhhh on huuu-uuhh! But I go on huuu and Coach yells at me. At the scrimmage today, a touchdown got called back on account of I was off-sides. I told them it wasn't my fault. I told them we need enunciation in the huddle. In the showers they all towel-whipped my bare ass.

ROSA

Watch your language.

MISHA

So you know what, Dad, I quit. I turned in my equipment and walked. I'm sorry, Mom. I just feel I'm needed here.

ROSA

It's okay, mijo. I never liked you playing with those brutos. You're my special boy. That's why I named you Misha.

MISHA

You named me Miguel.

ROSA

But after I saw that Baryshnikov on TV, I started calling you Misha.

MISHA

I don't even like ballet.

ROSA

The point is a brown boy named Misha in El Paso is special. I got my hopes pinned all over you like dollars.

MISHA

Is there anything to eat?

ROSA

There's albondigas on the stove.

MISHA

Meatballs? From last night?

ROSA

They're a little dried out, but still good. You want some?

MISHA

¿Jefita?

(Rosa looks. He opens Ceci's arms wide.)

I wuv you this much.

ROSA

Sangron.

(She laughs and goes into the kitchen.)

CECI

Huuh onhuu-uuh.

MISHA

You sound like my quarterback.

CECI

Shhghgm.

MISHA

The truth is when I'm on the field, I don't pay attention. I watch the yellowing grass and the zip-zip-zip of the sprinklers and the clouds making ponytails in the sky.

CECI

Uhh. Ghhh. Gngngm.

MISHA

Mom. There's something different about her.

ROSA

What?

MISHA

I dunno. Something. Are you still giving her her meds?

ROSA

(returning with a bowl of meatballs)

Of course!

MISHA

'Cause I know you don't sometimes, Mom. I know how you "forget" sometimes.

ROSA

I don't forget, never!

MISHA

Where are they? Where're the pills? How much did you give her today? How much, Mom!

ROSA

Oye, it's not drugs she needs but faith! Faith! Mijo, the doctors said it was over, remember, she's a vegetable para siempre, they said. What are these pills supposed to do then?

MISHA

Give me the pills. Or I'm telling him.

ROSA

Tell him. Andale. Dile todo.

(Misha turns to his father. Claudio takes off his headphones and stands.)

CLAUDIO

Que paso, Miguel. ¿Como te va en el football?

MISHA

Good.

ROSA

I'm almost done here. Just a few more shirts.

CLAUDIO

¿Como?

ROSA

Nomas estas camisas, Viejo.

CLAUDIO

Miguel, una cerveza.

(Misha nods gravely as Claudio goes down the hall to the bathroom.)

ROSA

Praise God.

MISHA

I wish you'd keep your religion to yourself. It's not doing Ceci any good.

ROSA

Oyeme, Misha. When your sister got hurt, I prayed to the Virgen Santa, la Patronesa de todos los Mexicanos. La Virgen de Guadalupe herself. And she failed me. That's when I knew. Us Catolicos, we worship the wrong things. Idols can't make miracles. Only God. So I go to a church with no other gods but God.

MISHA

Has that done her any good? Has it?

ROSA

Today. While your father was sleeping. You know what I did? I took her to Our Church of the Nazarene.

MISHA

What? You took her to those holy rollers? Are you kidding me?

ROSA

Misha, she loved it. All the peoples adored her. And Pastor Lujan himself baptized her.

MISHA

What?

ROSA

He put her in this big glass tub and laid his hand on her, mijo. Right here where her precious brains came out, and he prayed to God for her soul. He dipped her backward in the water and her face came alive! Eyes bright as nickels and her mouth wide open, taking in the light of heaven! Pastor Lujan said very clearly: Cecilia, prepare you! Your redemption is knocking on your head. And he took her pills and poured them all into the same tub.

MISHA

Oh no . . .

ROSA

He said we don't need them anymore! He said it's evil in our hearts that makes her sick.

MISHA

No more saving her soul. I mean it. Leave her soul alone.

ROSA

Don't you lecture me on how I care for mija! Who stays home with her day and night, changing her when she needs to go, making her special food, rubbing her joints y todo? Who?

MISHA

I help.

ROSA

Por favor, Misha. You're in school all day.

MISHA

I know.

ROSA

Well, I know more. Nothing happens without me in this house. I see to Cecilia's needs. That's how come we're getting a maid.

MISHA

A maid? Like to clean the house?

ROSA

To clean the house, to cook the food, to watch your sister. I asked your Tia Mirna, and she said her maid knows this chavala from Jalisco who just came over and she needs work and she's cheap.

MISHA

What about you?

ROSA

They called from the county office and told me my old position is available if I want it. Well, I want it. I'm tired of staying in this house all day. Plus we need the money.

MISHA

Is she legal?

ROSA

I don't ask about such things. I just ask her to come tomorrow.

MISHA

Tomorrow? Dammit, why didn't you tell me?

ROSA

I did. Watch your tongue. Last week. I mentioned it at dinner. But you never listen. You and your brother only hear what you want to hear.

(Claudio returns from the bathroom.)

CLAUDIO

¿Y mi cerveza?

MISHA

Mom dice que we're gonna have a maid, una criada.

CLAUDIO

Asi lo quiere.

MISHA

¿Y tu, que quieres?

CLAUDIO

Mi pinche cerveza.

(He sits and puts his headphones on again. Misha watches him.)

ROSA

You heard him.

MISHA

What am I, his mesero?

(She glares at him. Misha goes off to the kitchen and reenters with a can of beer.)

Ask yourself, Mom. Do we really want this? Do we really want a stranger coming into our house?

ROSA

What's wrong with our house? What don't you want her to see? What are you ashamed of, Misha? Your sister?

MISHA

Not her.

ROSA

I promise you. When she comes here, she will find a close, caring Mexican familia trying to make it in this blessed country.

CLAUDIO

(impatiently waiting for his beer)

Miguel . . .

ROSA

Get over your verguenza and give your father his beer.

MISHA

Mom . . .

ROSA

Do it, Miguel.

(Claudio suddenly gets up, takes the beer, and slaps Misha across the face.)

CLAUDIO

Tres veces te lo pedí, cabrón. Tres veces.

(He sits, rips off the pull-tab and drops it on the floor by Ceci. He watches TV as Misha's eyes well with tears.)

ROSA

¿Que te dije? Pick up that thing before your sister cuts herself with it.

(Misha picks up the pull-tab, his cheek reddening with the heat of the blow, and goes.)

CECI

I hear your face clapping against the way things are, and I know it hurts, 'cause I feel it too. I feel my face smashing against the mad will of God, but we can't let that swelling block us off, we can't, we gotta believe that it passes, bro, it passes. Sure as day passes into night. ★

Daniel Chacón

Daniel Chacón, born in Fresno, California, earned a B.A. in political science, an M.A. in English at California State University, and an M.F.A. in fiction writing from the University of Oregon. El Paso has been his home for the past twelve years. He is the author of the short story collections *Chicano Chicanery* and *Unending Rooms*, winner of the 2007 Hudson Book Prize; the novel *and the shadows took him: A Novel*; and the plays, *King of the Fruit People*; *Speak Thru the Wind*; and *The Finest Tastiest Carrot, Ever*, which have been produced in California and Oregon. Chacón is also co-editor of the book *The Last Supper of Chicano Heroes: The Selected Works of José Antonio Burciaga*. His fiction has appeared in such journals as *Americas Review*, *Bilingual Review*, *Colorado Review*, and *New England Review*. Currently, he is associate professor in the bilingual creative writing M.F.A. program at the University of Texas El Paso. He is now working on his latest novel *The Cholo Tree*.

Boat Sailing Over Juarez

Marisol goes as a mad scientist, black-framed glasses and a white lab coat splotched with blood. Since we live in El Paso, which is legally in Texas, I go as a Texas Ranger with a white cowboy hat. I pin a badge onto my shirt pocket. A real-looking gun hangs on my hip.

"Kind of scary," she says, walking in, framed by the light in the door, looking at me in the mirror. She's dark-skinned and very short. She crosses her arms over her chest and stares at me. "I mean, you really look like a cop," she says.

We stop at 7-11 for some wine. The clerk sees my badge and gun and calls me "sir." Shortly after arriving to the party, Marisol and I stand against the wall watching people dance. I'm about two feet taller than her. Some tall blonde girl dressed like a white seal comes off the floor, grabs my red wine away from me, takes a sip, and licks her lips. She says, "Why officer! You're drinking on duty."

"You got a problem with that?" Marisol says.

The girl looks down on her, noticing her for the first time. She looks at me. She understands and walks onto the dance floor, into the blur of bodies. "You *better* get lost," Marisol says to her departing shadow, as if she would kick her ass.

Later, the hostess of the party, dressed like a pirate, spots us and kisses Marisol on both cheeks. This woman is from Argentina, light hair, green eyes, and talks Spanish so fast that I have to concentrate to understand her. When she kisses me, she whispers into my ear, "Where's your handcuffs? I've been bad." I could feel the moist brush of her lips.

Marisol doesn't hear that.

Marisol and I dance.

She lets her hair down, and she closes her eyes, her arms reaching, twisting up, like dangling ropes, her face calm, as if she were somewhere other than the Halloween party, maybe back in Guatemala. She is a graduate student, a Ph.D. candidate in sociology. We dance all night long, forgetting to drink our wine, forgetting to talk, our eyes mostly closed, our minds free to wander.

I see a ship sliding slowly along the horizon, but the surface in which it glides is not the sea, but the air over the city, the poor side of Juarez, the Mexican border city, a barrio in the hills of the desert, where they found those women. I see shabby shacks painted pastel colors, dirt roads, rickety busses. I see this great boat—with sails like a pirate ship—floating through the air, over the city. It's a ghost ship, and I cannot see anyone onboard, just the slow flapping of the worn sails and the rapid whipping of the tattered flag on the topmost mast. The music pumps with energy, intensity, and it runs through me like a chemical. I don't want to stop dancing. When the DJ plays a slow song, we're disappointed. We stand side by side, waiting for the music.

***

It's late. We're still dancing, but the party crowd has shrunk. Marisol and I are sweating through our clothes, wet, but full of energy. Even after every one else quits and the DJ is yawning and only our silhouettes tremble in the shine of the dance floor, we still want to dance.

We groan when the music stops and lights come up.

We drive around the city for two hours looking for a club. We're like crack junkies looking for rock. I have to take off my badge and hide my fake gun, because we cross into Mexico to find an after hours club. We dance all night. When the place closes, we're still not satisfied. We stand by the car, the sun already shining, the desert mountains lit up.

***

When we get home, I take off my clothes. I forget to take off my Texas Ranger cowboy hat. Walking down the hallway to the shower, I see myself in the full-length mirror, naked, with my cowboy hat still on. "Howdy, pardner," I say to myself.

I suddenly remember my sixth birthday party. I remember flashes from the camera and my father walking toward me on his knees, clicking photo after photo. I remember our little kitchen table was scattered with Tupperware glasses of Kool-Aid and a half-eaten white cake.

I remember that my parents got me a cowboy hat and holster and sheriffs badge. I played cowboy all day. After the neighborhood kids left, my mom told me to take a bath, but I didn't want to quit playing cowboy. I got naked, but I didn't take off my holster and hat. In the photo that still exists, I'm naked, running through the house, shooting my cap gun into the air, my little penis vibrating like stubby rubber.

My mom crooned, "How cute!" her hands on her cheeks, and my older brothers and sisters were laughing.

The camera flashes.

I see myself naked with my Texas Ranger cowboy hat in the full-length mirror. I'm a tall man, six three, but I feel like a child. An idea comes to me. I giggle as I tiptoe to get my toy gun on the nightstand next to the bed. I hold the handle firmly and run into the living room.

Marisol sits on the couch reading something on the screen of her laptop, perhaps another email from Guatemala. She has been getting a lot of emails from home, or maybe she just re-reads the one she got last week from her sister telling her about it. This must be the fourth or fifth time she has read it, or at least that I've seen her read it. Once she read it to me, but she read so fast, her voice cracking with so much emotion, that I just listened to the sweet, sad sound of it. I lost track of the meaning. It was in Spanish, and I was too embarrassed to tell her I didn't get it the first time. All I know is that it has to do with home, something about her town, and that it isn't good, and that there isn't anything she can do about it.

I jump in front of her.

It dangles.

"This is the police!" I yell.

I run around the house shooting my toy gun, yelling, "Bang bang! You're dead!"

I run through the dining room, into the kitchen, into the library, through Marisol's office, where I flick on the lights so I don't trip over her map-tables and globes. On the wall above her computer hangs a map of the Americas. All over her desk are articles and tapes about the Juarez women, her dissertation research.

I run out of her office and back into the living room. I expect her to be giggling, maybe looking for the camera so she can take a shot, maybe yelling things like, "Oh, honey, that's so cute!"

Instead, I see that she's still reading the letter. Her indigenous face is still as stone. "Hey, you're under arrest," I say.

She slowly raises her head to look at me, the blue screen of the laptop glowing on her chin. "You can't," she says. "You can't." ★

The Crazy Chicken

My mother saw herself in the mirror, her face sunken from not eating. She was lying on her hospice bed in the middle of our living room. "I look pretty bad," she sat touching what was left of her hair, as if all she had to do was arrange it and she could grab her keys, go out of the house and have a regular day. My brother Bobby stepped in front of the mirror, covering her image, a tall and heavy man. He took her hand and said, "You're beautiful as ever."

"Don't say that," she said. Then she ran out of energy and plopped her head back on the pillow, closed her eyes.

I was sitting on an armchair editing a story I had just written. I was a new writer, or suddenly thought that I might become one. My very first story was going to be work-shopped by the creative writing class that evening. I was pretty proud of it, my first ever, and I was sure that the people in the workshop would like it. I couldn't help but reread it, over and over. *Who was this chicken? Some giant bird from Mexican folklore that came out at night and endowed good boys and girls, the ones who obeyed their parents, with intelligence and ambition?*

The story was about a Chicano boy, a young man my age, who like me, didn't really fit in with the Chicanos and didn't fit in with the whites either. One day, he was attending the Chicano graduation ceremony at the university, because he was graduating with a B.A. in Political Science, like me, and like me he didn't know what he would do next.

He (my character) didn't speak Spanish, and when some of the students took the stage and said their speeches in Spanish, he could have sworn that he heard many of them thanking the *Pollo Loco*. What they were really saying (unknown to him) was something like *gracias por su* ***apoyo, lo que*** *me ayudó,* but he only heard the ***poyo lo que***, which he thought was *Pollo Loco*. He knew some Spanish words, not a lot, only what his mother had taught him when he was growing up, things like mi'jo and ven acá y te quiero y vámanos y porfavor ¡no me dejes solo!—he knew enough Spanish to know that Pollo Loco meant Crazy Chicken. As he heard some of the graduates who spoke Spanish thanking the Crazy Chicken, he suddenly felt as if he had been left out of a great source of power that everyone else had but him. It was a source of magic from Mexican lore, this Crazy Chicken, this chicken who helped so many young Mexicans, but never him, because he didn't speak Spanish.

Now, it was too late.

I looked up from my story and across the dimly-lit living room. I could see in the mirror. It had a gold-colored frame like an old painting. I saw myself sitting on the chair. I saw Bobby standing before my mother's death bed. Red pillows. I saw my mother's head slowly move, and then she moaned.

"She's in pain," said my sister Betty. She was standing in the doorframe to the kitchen. "We should give her more medicine."

"Let's wait," said Bobby. "She's sleeping. When she wakes."

"You guys want to hear my story?" I said.

They both looked at me. My mother lightly moaned, like she was having a bad dream (Surprise, Mom! Wake up and it'll be worse than the dream) and she moved her head slightly. My sister came into the room and stood between me and the mirror. "Sure, let's hear it," she said.

"It's called *The Crazy Chicken*," I said.

"I like that title," Bobby said.

"It's intriguing," my sister said. "Makes me want to read it."

"It's not too long," I said. "I'll read it."

"The Crazy Chicken." I said, as if proclaiming it.

"By me." (I said my name.)

He remembered hearing his aunts and uncles and his mother talking in another room, at a party, all of them laughing and joking, but in Spanish, a language he didn't understand. He would pretend like he knew what they were saying.

I read most of the story, almost to the end, when my mother moaned. The shot of pain must have been pretty bad, because I could see in the mirror the way her body contracted, and her bones curled up like dry weeds. She beat her fist on the bed, a fist she could barely make, barely clench, her fingers too tired. She cried out. Bobby and Betty surrounded her and started saying stuff to her.

Betty regressed to childhood and said, "Mommy? Mommy?"

The relatives, who were in the den or in the backyard smoking, came into the living room, one by one, slowly, respectfully, like spirits, quiet, as if they were entering church after the mass had already started. They filled the frame of the mirror with shadow and dark colors.

"No, no, no," my mom said, presumably to the pain, or maybe she saw death standing there, waiting to take her.

Then there was a slight shift of bodies, and I could see in the mirror. I could see within a space between two hips of two people that my mom could see herself in the looking glass. She saw her dying face, her dying eyes, her dry, wrinkled lips.

"Mom?" Bobby said, leaning down, squeezing her hand. "You want some medicine, Mom?"

Suddenly my mother looked in the mirror, right at me, with clarity, it seemed. She looked into my eyes. You may not believe what I saw next, what I'm about to tell you, but it's true. I don't think I'm making this up. This isn't the fiction part.

My mother looked right at me, and her face suddenly became soft. She looked young. Then she mouthed to me, "The Crazy Chicken." She chuckled. She closed her eyes.

I figured she wanted to hear the rest of my story.

So I read.

"Who was this Crazy Chicken?? How could he have not heard about it all his life, when he knew of the others, the Tooth Fairy, Santa Claus, Los Reyes Magos, the Easter Bunny, Father Time, and he knew the bad ones, too, the ones you needed to fear, the Boogey Man, La Llorona, El Cucuy, he knew of all of them, but not this one. Not this Crazy Chicken." ★

Pat LittleDog

Novelist, short story writer and journalist, native Texan Pat LittleDog spent her teenage years in Wiesbaden, Germany. She received both an undergraduate degree and masters from the University of Texas at El Paso. As Pat Ellis Taylor, she published the novels: *Border Healing Woman: The Story of Jewel Barr*, the winner of a 1981 Southwest Book Award; *Tonics, Tears, Roots and Remedies: A Selection of Poems*; *How It Happened That I Came to Live in the West: Diary of Coyote Pat*; *The God Chaser*; and *Afoot in a Field of Men and Other Stories from Dallas' East Side*, which won an Austin Book Award. In 1991, as Pat LittleDog, she wrote the novel *In Search of the Holy Mother of Jobs*. *The LittleDog Reader* will be published in 2009.

What Cecilia Reveals

One day the Christian missionaries come, a group of them—old friends, once rock musicians and marijuana dealers, turned religious all at the same time by a blinding light they mutually witnessed at an A. A. Allen revival meeting on an Arizona Indian reservation, which caused them to give themselves over to a particular god, this god being the one that wants no others before him. So they tell me how Jesus came to give a higher law than the Maharishi's, which they know I have been following for a little time, and therefore they want me to give up my ways and go to church with them. Which I finally do. So the altar call comes and I am standing by myself at a railing and the golden light comes down and the tears, and my heart stops and my jaw chatters and someone calls out *Thank you Jesus* while hands come down on my head.

When I go home I start wearing only dresses and no pants, and stop putting make-up on my face, just stop. Just stop every little thing that might come in the way of salvation. Become serious and read the Bible. Just stop the flirtation and concentrate on the Laws of God.

That's about the time that Cecilia comes into my life and starts doing my ironing. She has worked as a maid for many years in El Paso homes where many women are available from across the border for cheap pay and no questions asked about illegality. Although Cecilia works in the days and goes home at night to South El Paso as she is a United States citizen born in the Upper Rio Grande Valley in a little town where her own mother was also born and her grandmother, nevertheless she will never cross the bridge into Juarez afraid as she is with her broken English and her lack of valid identification that she would never be let into the country again. She is very old. I don't know how old but she has been working as a maid and looking very old since I first married when she was ironing all the clothes once a week for my mother-in-law. And my mother-in-law told me when she first spoke about Cecilia that the woman was old and very slow and that she was exasperating. Yet she had been ironing for the family for several years and if I ever needed ironing done I should remember her. So for many years I had a full-time maid when I was working full-time myself. But then when I stay at home and do my own housework my mother-in-law calls me one day and says that Cecilia could really use the money and that I would be doing her a favor if I let her come and iron for me one day a week. Five dollars.

So Cecilia comes on the bus on the mornings scheduled for my ironing and she is very fat and loaded with a black bag and lumpy sacks and moves like a huge full moon through the atmosphere, her hair greased down to her neck and tied and her mouth always open, a silver crescent capping a front tooth. She fixes a cup of coffee in the kitchen, makes herself a little egg, sets up the ironing board and already it is noontime. She sprinkles the pieces. She spends a great deal of time in the bathroom—there is only one in the house—and sometimes I wait my turn for her to come out as long as half an hour. Then when I go in after her the little room is filled with the smoke of incense and the smell of oil of some kind, very strong, and a little perfume and then the underlying rich manury smell she has left in clouds.

I wear a cross around my neck and I have been making a Christian tapestry to hang on my wall which depicts a mannikin with a beard and felt arms outstretched while a large white felt bird is rocketing down on his head out of the upper lefthand corner. I read the Bible. I say Praise-the-Lord a lot, even to Cecilia. In turn she tells me how Cecilia was a saint who saw Jesus one time, it was the second day when he was still in the tomb, or so people thought. But instead he was already hiking down the road toward Europe away from Gethsemane and into Spain somewhere, which was where this beautiful Cecilia had had a dream about him and was waiting . . . "and so he came down the road and she got down on her knees and she says my Lord my Lord and she kisses his feet."

I frown when Cecilia gets finished telling me this story.

"Now where did you hear that?"

"Oh, it's in the Bible," she says.

"I don't think it's in a regular Bible."

"Oh everybody knows that story," she says.

She has ironed the iron over and over the same sleeve of the same shirt while she tells the story. I wash the dishes, put them away, start cooking a chicken. Cecilia takes another sprinkled shirt out of the ironing bag.

She makes a little café y leche for Pearl. Pearl sits down daintily at the bar, her little girl legs dangling from the chair where she watches Cecilia run the iron back and forth.

"Oh a bad thing happen last night," Cecilia tells Pearl, "to a girl, a teenager. . . ."

"What happened?"

"Oh there was this party last night and this girl wanted to go to it, see, even though her mama said no. So she slipped out the window and went anyway and today this morning they found her—" Cecilia rolls her eyes back and clucks her tongue "—with chicken slashes—" Cecilia swings the iron across her wrists and bosoms "— all the way here, everywhere. . . ."

Pearl has stopped drinking her coffee. Her mouth is open.

I am frowning again. "But I don't quite understand—chicken marks. . . ."

"The devil!" Cecilia says. "This girl, she probably thought she was with a young man, see, but it was the devil. That's how you can tell, you look down at the feet and instead of shoes he has big chicken feet, that's how he tore that young girl apart. . . ."

The stories continue as long as anyone listens. It may be slow but the clothes are well-pressed. If Cecilia irons too slowly she will miss the last bus, but then I have a car so that I drive her home when she asks.

"Oh don't throw that away," Cecilia tells me when I put a wine bottle into the garbage sack. She pulls it back out and washes it, then shoves it into one of her own sacks.

"Can I have this too?" She pulls out a sock with a hole in it I had thrown out earlier.

"You can have anything that you find in there," I say. I wonder what I should save of my garbage to give to her. She becomes serious and pokes through the coffee grounds.

At the end of an evening she holds up a piece of bread with butter she has wrapped up in waxed paper. "Can I bring this with me? For my evening snack when I get home."

"Of course." Whatever she asks for I say yes, but I am embarrassed with all of this asking.

Each time I drive her home she directs me along a different route through streets that run in and out of tenements and low-income housing projects in the south part of town close to the river.

"This is where my daughter/friend/aunt lives, I'm going to spend the night with her tonight," she says.

Cecilia's own apartment is in a neighborhood where the houses are older, where the apartments are long rows of crumbling pastel plaster and exposed mud arranged in a horseshoe. One day she calls me. "Can you pick up this mattress for me? With your car? Someone has given it to me if I can get it to my place."

I go to the address she gives me over the telephone and two boys tie the mattress to the top of my Volkswagen, then I drive very carefully the few blocks to Cecilia's apartment number. She is waiting on the curb with another young boy. He unties the mattress and carries it down the sidewalk and into the courtyard on his shoulders. I follow the two of them passing a row of screen doors with bits of cloth hanging over each one of them. Arranged near the doors are crates with tomatoes, garlic, and onion growing out of them, and in the middle of the courtyard a concrete outhouse with black and brown streams coming out of its door puddling near the sidewalk I am following. And then there is Cecilia going into a door with the boy and I follow.

We are in a fairly large room with dirt floors. The ceiling is high because it is the tin roof of the apartment itself. There is a wood stove and a table piled with jars and scraps of rotting food, much of it uncovered, bold black roaches running up and down and around. A piece of cloth covers a door to the back room.

"You want to sit down for a minute?" Cecilia pushes up a chair.

"Here. You sit and rest yourself for a minute—I'll be right back."

She disappears with her black purse behind the cloth to the back room and the boy follows her. The faint unintelligible sounds of their conversation come to me while I sit facing a wall covered—I now notice with my eyes' adjustment to the room's muted light—with pieces of clothing, men's, women's and children's, all sizes, as well as indefinable bits of rag and cloth, and I think that maybe Cecilia is running some sort of rag business on the side. My eye suddenly fastens on a brown and white washcloth halfway down the wall which I know has come from my bathroom.

The boy is laughing in the other room and Cecilia's voice is becoming louder and more animated. And I think of Cecilia's black bag, how she carried it so carefully into this back room as if she planned on giving the boy some money, but now I realize it might be full of many things I believe are forbidden, possibly marijuana, possibly some kind of voodoo, some witch kind of herb or something like a black book, a wad of gum, or toenails taken from a bathroom. . . .

"Listen Cecilia," I call out to her while the cloth is still between us, "I think I'll go on home, Cecilia, I'll see you Wednesday."

My washcloth! I think about it driving back home, the shock of the stinking outhouse and the dirt floor and the bits of food, but the washcloth! Then I wonder if it is really mine or simply like one of mine. When I go home I study the closet where I keep washcloths and towels. There seem to be some missing but I can't tell for sure.

"You hear that they're going to throw all the houses away down there?" she asks me next Wednesday.

I had read something in the newspaper. "They say they're going to tear down the substandard housing and make newer apartments, Cecilia, that's what I read in the paper."

She nods decisively. "Yep, they're going to throw them all away—good houses. Where we going to go now?" She shakes her head and sprinkles one of Pearl's pinafores. "It's too sad—now they want to throw away my house."

"I'm sorry to hear that, Cecilia. Maybe you can go and live with your daughter."

"No, she don't really want me now. You know that old lady, she lived across from me in her apartment, she has lots of cats, see, she has twenty-seven of them. And the people come and they say to this woman they're going to throw her house away and she has got to go. And they take every one of her cats away because there can't be any cats in these new apartments where they take the lady to. And these new apartments have everything—shiny new stoves. New kitchens. Hot water. Bathroom inside of them. But that old lady, she didn't stay there more than a day. She just went back home."

"Did they come back for her?"

"No. She went to find some more cats. She's living somewhere with them."

Cecilia spends more time in the bathroom than usual. She goes in twice, then three times. I take a nap in the afternoon and when I wake up she is still in the bathroom. I think of the washcloth. I listen to her movements through the wall—is she stuffing things of mine down her dressfront? Is she picking slivers of soap out of the garbage can?

It is almost nine o'clock when the last shirt is ironed. As she starts to go out the door to my car I stop her.

"I want to see what's in your grocery bag," I say.

She clutches it to her. "Oh no señora.

"Yes I want to see." I pull the sack from her hands, my teeth clinched suddenly furious. The bag spills between us so that now there are three washcloths and a towel of mine on the floor that I recognize.

"Oh señora—" she tries to pick them up. I knock them out of her hands.

"Now you know that those are mine, Cecilia."

"No they're not señora."

"You know they are Cecilia!"

"No they're not!" She puts them in the bag, then leaves the whole thing behind her, walks out the door and gets into the car.

I get in and drive toward the river. She sits silently staring out of the windshield. Then her head slumps and she starts crying. "Oh señora, I'm sorry, I'm so sorry, God will forgive me, please, for what I have done."

I stop the car by the curb. She gropes for me above her other grocery bag and her black pocketbook, her fat arms come shivering around me, the smell of fat and incense.

"The Lord will forgive you," I say somewhat formally because I myself am still indignant.

She sniffles, then she stops crying. "I want to go to my friend's house," she says, "turn this way."

She directs me east along the freeway that follows the river. We turn right, then left, down an alley, then left again, and the streets are dark, overgrown with vines, and as we drive Cecilia composes herself.

"This woman who is my friend," she says, "lives with so many birds. She has a parrot in her bedroom, see, and it always sleeps there. And so finally her husband says, I am tired of so much bird caca in my bed! and so my friend says, Well get out of the house then! And so he leaves after all that time, but she is very happy because he was always beating her up, so she still sleeps with the parrot and now it is a much happier home."

We pass through a gate and down a driveway through heavy bushes and sounds of clucking and bird calls.

"Okay here we are now." Cecilia gets out on her side.

I fight through the bushes and around the car in total shadow which wraps over us at the moment I turn the headlights off. But soon I can feel my eyes grow large and black with adjustment and begin to make out the shapes of boxes and coops piled high on top of each other. Then a dim porch light appears and a small woman comes down the driveway led by three ducks. One she swoops up and holds it flapping against her.

"This is my friend Hermina," Cecilia tells me, "don't you like her ducks?"

I hold out my hand and touch the head of the one peering at me from under her chin no longer flapping. "This one is beautiful."

I turn back to the car, but Cecilia suddenly pushes me to one side into the shadowy bushes and puts her head close to mine so that she can whisper:

"I promise you, señora, I promise you *on the Bible* that I never took anything of yours."

Her face is as large as a house shadowed by leaves, she is so close to me, yet neither of us can see the other's eyes because it is too dark. Then she lets me go and I slide behind the steering wheel again. There is a whir of wings and her friend's duck begins to quack as I back the car out of the driveway, then up and down the maze of alleys, lost now in the strange neighborhood without Cecilia's direction, unable to figure out how I came, my heart loud and fluttering with stolen birds. ★

Lex Williford

Born in El Paso, Lex Williford holds an M.F.A. from the University of Arkansas and has taught at Southern Illinois University, the University of Alabama, and the University of Missouri, St. Louis. His book, *Macauley's Thumb*, was co-winner of the 1993 Iowa School of Letters Award for Short Fiction. Both his fiction and non-fiction have appeared in such publications as *American Literary Review*, *Glimmer Train Stories*, *Kansas Quarterly*, *The Novel and Short Story Writer's Market 2002*, *Poets & Writers*, *Prairie Schooner*, *Shenandoah*, *Southern Review*, *Tameme*, *Virginia Quarterly Review*, and *Witness*. His stories have been widely anthologized in such publications as *W. W. Norton's Flash Fiction*; *The Iowa Award: The Best Stories 1991-2000*; *The Best of Witness 1987-2004*; and *The Eloquent Short Story*. Williford has been the recipient of fellowships from the National Endowment of the Arts, Bread Loaf Writers' Conference, the Blue Mountain Center, the Centrum Foundation, and the Djerassi Foundation among many others. He is co-editor with Michael Martone of the *Scribner Anthology of Contemporary Short Fiction* and most recently the *Touchstone Anthology of Contemporary Nonfiction*. Lex Williford is currently the director of the online M.F.A. program and teaches in the bilingual writing program at the University of Texas at El Paso.

My Mother's Wedding Dress

For My Mother

The first time she could remember my father ever striking me, my mother told me forty-five years later, I was just learning to crawl on the hardwood floors of my father's cramped officer's barracks at Fort Bliss, and when—just bathed and powdered-pink and still naked on hands and knees—I reached out to touch a scorpion, carrying her young on her back, dozens of them, her hind end up, pincers out, flicking her tail at me from the shadows of my mother's closet, my father jumped from their bed, shouting, "*No!*" then slapped me across the back of my tender knuckles, picking me up like a football under his arm as I howled, then stepped the scorpions into a long blond smear with his boot.

***

That's what Maricella, my mother's best friend from Juarez, the bullfighter's daughter, called them: "Little blondies. *Güeritos*." Tiny scorpions the vanilla color of *calaveras*, candy skulls for *el Dia de los Muertos*, the Day of the Dead. The day I was born, William Barret Travis Truitt, III. November second, 1954.

"*¡Los alacranes son güeritoscomo tu!*" Maricella said the next day, helping my mother hang two-dozen Boraxed diapers on a clothesline in our backyard of blond sand and prickly pear and creosote bush. *The scorpions are little blondies like you*! Maricella pointed at my beautiful, fair-skinned mother and told her how much she looked like that *gringa* movie star Marilyn Monroe now that she'd bleached her dark auburn hair blond the first time.

"¡*Como tu niño tambien*! Like your baby, too!" Maricella laughed and made faces at me in my stroller, ruffling the thin blond curl at the tender pons still peaking my skull till I squirmed and sweated, squinting in the sun, drooling as I sucked at my fisted knuckle. "But your husband was right," Maricella said, shaking her head, a good Catholic woman. "This isn't Dallas!" Then she laughed and waggled a finger at my mother for not knowing better than to let a naked baby crawl on the hardwood floors of a home in the middle of the desert.

My mother was twenty years old.

That afternoon, when she heard my diapers flapping outside like flags in the wind, she looked out the kitchen window to see a blue-black sky and a great wall of dust rolling south toward the officers' barracks down from the flats at Oro Grande—where my father spent weeks at a time blistering in the sun and taking stinging saltwater showers after he'd spent all day shooting off 120-mm artillery shells and anti-aircraft missiles at the Army's desert artillery firing range—and my mother rushed outside, the screen door slapping hard behind her as she choked and squinted her sand-stung eyes, then pulled down all my once-white diapers fast as she could, each one brown now as the suffocating sky, and she brought them back into the house, where I was crying in my crib, so she could wash them all over again as the thunderstorms rolled in.

***

The pregnancy with me had been hard, my mother said, her second, and with all that time alone to think in those cramped tar-paper barracks while my father was gone, she'd convinced herself that she'd lose me like her first.

"There was one before me?" I said—her first born—but she just looked down into her coffee on the kitchen table.

"Please be quiet about it," she said. "Not even your father knows."

For two years after they'd moved from Dallas, they'd tried everything—my father going AWOL in the middle of the night sometimes, ordering his jeep driver out of his bunk and swearing him to secrecy to drive him two hours south from Oro Grande so my father could get a real shower in El Paso and leave my mother standing naked on her head just before dawn, laughing, in my great grandmother's canopied feather bed—and after all that trying, then nothing, for months, my mother came to believe she'd never conceive again. So when she'd missed her cycle for the third month, she walked around for weeks with a smile frozen on her face like the one she'd worn in her white silk wedding dress on the steps of St. James in east Dallas, my father, William Barret Travis Truitt, Jr., standing there on the steps with her in his khaki jodhpurs, his commissioned second lieutenant's uniform and cap, a perfect spit shine on his Texas A & M senior boots.

Nothing like a man in uniform, my mother told me, smiling, and he had such a handsome face, square-jawed, with that strawberry blond crew cut and such intense blue eyes you wouldn't believe it, like the wide New Mexico sky, like that actor Jeffrey Hunter's in *Seven Cities of Gold.* The man, she knew the moment she saw him, who'd make all her beautiful babies.

"Helen, why are you so happy?" my father asked her, taking her face into his rough palms, caking blisters on his knuckles and sunburned nose, his fatigues still dusted from a week-long stint of shooting off missiles in the desert.

"I just am," she said. And then she told him.

***

On Halloween two days before she went into labor, a diphtheria epidemic broke out in the Fort Bliss hospital—three newborns dead—and when my father rushed her there, her water breaking in the back seat of my father's 1950 Plymouth Coupe, the hospital, in quarantine, turned them away at the last minute, then sent them on with a Military Police escort to the Emergency Room at Biggs Air Force Base. Born there on a gurney, headfirst, ten pounds, seven ounces, I was a big baby boy, my mother told me, with a bright red nevus across my forehead, from where it had pressed against my mother's spine for months, a pink spot on my forehead that still glowed red at forty-five whenever I grew angry or hot from too much work in the sun, a birthmark shaped like the scorpion that never stung.

Six days after my mother returned home, she grew sick, a piercing pain in her side like Maricella's father's, gored once by a huffing bull. Then a terrible odor arose from under the sheets as she rolled moaning in their bed, and my father rushed her back to Biggs Air Force Base, where the doctors removed the sponge they'd left inside her for over a week.

Thirty-five years later, when her gynecologist had removed everything in a radical hysterectomy, she said, he found one of her ovaries collapsed in on itself, as if it had been crushed, from a terrible infection decades before, shrunken like the sun-pruned husk desert pomegranate, and the nurses all marveled at how she'd managed to have six healthy children.

***

When my father struck my knuckles that first time, my mother said, it was as if he'd struck *hers*—she could *feel* it, a sympathetic pain as real as the stabbing labor she felt when she'd begged for a spinal block in the emergency room, when the doctor held me upside down by my ankles and slapped me across the backside screaming into the world—but when she raised her hand to slap my father's face, she couldn't.

She took me from his arms and held me, squalling, at her shoulder and screamed "Don't you *ever*! *Ever* do that again!" But, of course, he did and would many times over the years, as if it was his god-given right and duty, as if there was nothing she could do or say to stop him.

"I'm his father," my father told her, "and I have to teach him."

"Teach him what?" my mother said.

***

"Fort Bliss," my father always joked. "So where's the bliss in it?" But those were blissful days, my mother told me, the most blissful days of her life. Before they had me to keep them up all night, blissfully free of their own parents and of being parents themselves, long before they had to worry about mortgages and bills and sick children and bankruptcy and war, they drove weekends to the mountains in Cloudcroft and Ruidoso and threw snowballs at each other when they'd fallen skiing, then cut down their own Christmas trees from the Lincoln National Forest. Weekends in summer and spring, they crossed the bridge over into Juarez with Maricella and her husband Juan and they got so smashed at Martino's on the best martinis in the world they could barely walk back over the bridge, and when she watched the bullfights, all that blood bothered my mother so much she almost got sick, and so they left *la Plaza de Toros Alberto Balderas* before the bullfight was over and spent hours at the *mercados* haggling for cut-tin mirrors and *calaveras* and tequila with the worm floating at the bottom and bullshit cigarettes the Mexican clerks sold only to tourists and stupid *gringo* soldiers out for a night in Boy's Town.

But after I was born, they were blissful, too, my mother said, my father and mother both staring down at me for hours in my crib, their faces unable to unsmile themselves, till I was awake and crying to be fed and my mother would breast-feed me, and then my father would lift me up, smiling, and toss me so high into the air that I almost hit my head on the ceiling, squealing with laughter, and though it terrified her to think my father might not catch me as I fell, my skull cracking on the hardwood floor, she swore to me she could never remember a time in her life so full of pure and simple bliss.

***

For months after my father struck me, my mother said, I held my hand in a tiny fist she could never unclench. "Like now," she said and reached across to touch my knuckles fisted on the kitchen table.

"All those years," my mother said, "I should've protected you."

I palmed the back of my mother's hand. "No, Mom. Don't. You don't have to—"

"Yes, I do. *He* won't apologize to you—can't admit he was wrong, too goddamn stubborn and proud—but *I* can. It's the least I can do for my son."

My father was upstairs asleep now in one of the houses I'd grown up in, just a white-haired old man—a little pitiful, if you want to know the truth—mellowed in his own way, I suppose, completely harmless to me now.

"How could you protect me?" I asked my mother. "How?"

***

The night she cut open their boxes of clothes after they'd moved back to Dallas, into a new house with hardwood floors my father had just bought on the G. I. Bill, his stint in the Army over, my mother pulled her wedding dress out of its moth-protected plastic and held it up in front of her in her new vanity mirror.

My mother was seven-months pregnant with my sister Hannah then, and I was just walking, tottering, as I reached up to the bathroom counter for my father's box-cutting knife.

"No, no, honey," my mother said, "you don't want to touch that." Then she pulled my hand away and put the knife up higher, out of my reach.

"I wonder if this thing would still fit me now?" my mother said. Then, smiling as she had on her wedding day, she slipped her wedding dress on over her head, hoping to surprise my father.

When she began to scream from the bathroom, my father ran to her down the hall from the kitchen.

"Get it off!" she screamed. "For god's sake, get it off me!" And she screamed and screamed and screamed, till I was screaming with her, and she slapped at her shoulders and neck and thighs, her back and breasts and stomach, still bulging under her dress, stuck there so tight in the middle she couldn't get it off, till finally my father took the box-cutting knife and ripped her white silk wedding dress down the back, till it fell torn and shredded to the floor.

Inside the dress my father found a nest of baby scorpions, dozens of them, all of them little blondies, like the mother carrying her young that had almost stung me, and my father swiped what was left of them off my mother's naked back and shoulders and stamped them into the hardwood floor.

***

"You don't remember, do you?" my mother asked me.

"No," I said, "I don't."

Well, it was the strangest thing, she said. When she and my father had first moved to El Paso, she'd threatened to leave him, if only for just a moment, just one of the many times she'd threatened to leave him in all the years I was growing up, and never did.

"Who'd ever want to live in such a god-forsaken place?" she'd told him. "Nothing but cactus and rattlesnakes and scorpions!"

But for months after they'd moved back to Dallas and the scorpions' stinging welts had all disappeared, she still found herself missing the dry air that made her nose bleed sometimes and the intense blue sky, like my father's eyes before he was my father, and the clean, sweet smell of creosote bush in the arroyos after rain. But the thing that surprised her most, my mother told me, the thing she would always love and miss the most about the desert, was that all the young and tender things grew thorns. ★

Richard Yañez

Richard Yañez was born and raised in El Paso. He received an M.F.A. from Arizona State University and teaching fellowships at Colorado College, the Center for Women's Intercultural Leadership at Saint Mary's College, Indiana, and was a visiting writer at New Mexico State University. *El Paso del Norte: Stories on the Border*, his first book, was a finalist for the Texas Institute of Letters first book award. His work has been published in *When I Was a Loser: True Stories of (Barely) Surviving High School*; *U.S. Latino Literature Today*; and *Our Working Lives: Short Stories of People and Work.* A founding member of Con Tinta, a coalition of Chicano/Latino writer-activists, Yañez is also a contributing editor to *BorderSenses*. He is currently an assistant professor at El Paso Community College and organizes community writing programs through the PaPaGaYo Literary Center.

From *El Paso del Norte: Stories on the Border*: Rio Grande

Kmart

One second we're picking up lunch at Chico's Tacos. The next, Steve's speeding through a red light, nearly taking out a Datsun.

I braced myself.

"What the hell are you doing?"

"Check it out, man."

"What?"

"There."

He screeched his van to a stop in the parking lot of a Kmart. One of who knows how many in El Paso.

Trays of rolled tacos in soupy salsa splattered all over the place. Rivers of red cheese sauce ran down the dashboard onto my jeans and canvas high-tops.

Not sure what he was worked up about, I watched Steve bolt over to the side of the store. And like so many times before, I decided if it's good enough to incite my best friend, it must be worth seeing. I got out of the van and sloshed behind him.

About ten yards away, there was a crowd of blue shirts—Kmart employees, I figured—checking out la migra. One Border Patrol agent herded men and women and children into a bile-green Suburban while another rummaged through the illegals' belongings: limes, gum, candy, cigarettes, the usual stuff you see them selling in parking lots and at intersections around town.

Just when I thought that things were going very business-like, a man and a teenage girl slipped out of the Suburban and took off running. One of la migra, a gringo, went after the man, and the other agent, a Chicano, chased the girl. While the man was slow and an easy catch, the teenager was quick and darted in and out of the Dumpsters behind Kmart, scurrying like a scared rabbit in the desert.

I edged closer to the scene. The Chicano agent was closing in on the girl when he tripped. Before he got up, he yelled. The girl froze. I couldn't really see everything from where I was, but I bet he drew his gun.

The gringo agent had already locked away his man and saddled himself in the driver's seat by the time his partner led the girl back to the Suburban. The Chicano agent, who sized up like the welterweight Roberto Durán, jabbed the girl with his baton in our direction.

I was about to grab Steve, who was eyeing some blond Kmart babe, and put his ass in the van when the Chicano agent struck the girl. She screamed and swung a sack of limes that she hadn't let go of. Agent Durán got real angry. He smacked her again. Her limes spilled onto the ground. The Chicano agent stomped them as he kicked her with his black Tony Lamas. A wild dance.

The girl balled up on the asphalt and endured the Chicano agent's beating as the other illegals witnessed it from the caged Suburban. The girl was about to take the last blow before, I was sure, she was going to pass out when the gringo agent jumped out of the Suburban. He clashed to the scene, snatched his partner's baton, and knocked him to the ground. "That's enough. You crazy?"

Just like John Wayne in *True Grit*, the gringo agent sauntered over to the girl, who'd taken refuge under the Suburban. Tears cleaned streaks down her face. Her blouse was ripped of its buttons. Before he reached her, the Chicano agent rushed up behind him and jumped on his back, mounting his partner like a bronco. The next thing I knew they were going at it.

MANOS DE PIEDRAS vs. THE DUKE. A helluva match.

A mass of green uniform rolled around in the oil stains and gravel of Kmart's parking lot. Arms and legs and boots flew into each other's bodies. If their Stetsons hadn't been knocked off, it would have been hard to tell exactly who was who. The Chicano had a brown bald spot. The other agent's hair burned gold in the Texas sun.

The illegals jailed in the Suburban rocked it back and forth, making all kinds of noise, presumably rooting for the gringo. A first, I'm sure.

While my body cramped watching the beating of the girl, I was exhilarated by the Border Patrol agents beating the hell out of each other. The bout excited me so much that when both men collapsed from exhaustion I wanted to jump in and start them fighting again.

I might've done something, who knows what, while the agents were at their weakest if I hadn't been distracted by the Mexican teenager. She crawled from under the Suburban over to some keys that had fallen out during the fight. When she noticed that I was watching her, she paused, for only a second—met my eyes with hers—and hurried to set her friends loose.

Like fans at a track meet, Steve and the rest of the crowd cheered the illegals' exodus from the Suburban. The two Border Patrol agents remained on their backs—faces bloodied, chests heaving, uniforms drenched in sweat. They didn't move until ambulances arrived and carted each one away separately, the Suburban left behind like a robbed safe—an empty reminder of the day's losses.

Many members of la migra showed up on the scene. By the way one of them barked orders at other agents, I guessed he must've been the Border Patrol chief. I didn't say shit about anything, especially about the illegals; that would be included in some official report. They were long gone by then and had probably found another Kmart to resume their business.

Rio Grande

Hours later Steve drove west on the levee road that ran along the Border Highway. A full moon hung over the Sierra de Juárez on the other side. Its dirty-orange reflection played in the full river that cut us off from the Third World, a whole other time zone.

I absorbed each bump in the levee road as if I was one of the van's shocks. Steve was doing his best to miss the holes. At least that's what he swore he was doing. A few times, a tire slipped off the narrow road, jolting me to notice that he was drunker than I thought. He kept insisting that our buddies were having a bonfire out here.

While I was used to his wild driving, especially on nights when we'd both had lots to drink, the earlier scene in the Kmart parking lot had left me nervous. A feeling had crawled under my skin. A chilling numbness, like when one of your limbs falls asleep. My whole body felt this way.

"Slow down, fucker." I snapped on my seat belt. "You're gonna put us in the river." I had to yell so he could hear me over Van Halen. We'd unbolted and removed the rear seats to make room for his latest score—four huge speakers.

"Don't worry, Joe, I got it under control." He flashed me his white-Chiclet smile.

"Just don't kill us."

"Ah, c'mon, would I do that?"

This is what I remember: He popped a cigarette in his mouth, pulled out a lighter, which dropped between his legs, the road there one second, gone the next, a sharp decline, gripping the dash, an approaching tree, yelling, and thud.

I might've also reached for the steering wheel when Steve took his eyes off the road and his hands off the wheel. All I know for sure is that we were lucky to have gone right not left, cottonwood not Rio.

It took all of "Best of Both Worlds"—Eddie Van Halen's guitar screeching like cicadas in the night—for my head to stop somersaulting and realize we'd crashed. The van was kissed up against one of the many trees next to the levee road.

My door was jammed, so I escaped through the side window. When I landed outside, I spotted Steve teetering in front of the van. I might've told him I was okay and asked how he was if he hadn't seemed more concerned about taking a piss. Head leaned back, he stared at a starless sky. A river of piss flowed with the fluorescent antifreeze gushing out of the van's radiator.

"You could've killed us," I yelled. "You had to—you had to reach for the fucking lighter. What the hell are we going to do now?"

"I don't know, Joe, but I'm pretty sure this is the last brew"—he toasted me as if it was New Year's—"so we definitely have to restock." He chugged his beer, still holding his dick in his other hand although he was done pissing.

"Oh, shit." I kicked the van's bumper and hammered my fist on the hood, not to leave any doubt of how mad I was.

I scampered down from the wreck to the Border Highway and tried to figure out where we'd ended up. I was still a little drunk but sobered enough from the accident to know we had to get the hell out of there. La migra was more than likely to swarm all over us. The last thing we needed was to be mistaken for wetback smugglers or drug runners.

The buildings downtown were beacons. I decided I'd find a phone, call my brother to come pick us up and call a wrecker for the van. Not telling Steve my intentions, I just started walking. I figured he'd follow.

Neither of us said anything as we made our way west along the Border Highway. There was hardly any traffic, so there was no chance of us hitching a ride. I took a drag from Steve's last cigarette as a sort of truce. We said nothing.

I'm pretty sure we should've embraced the day's earlier events as a sign. We should've taken our teenage thirsts to the isolated desert, like every Friday night. The acres of sand hills surrounding the Lower Valley always cradle our bonfires like a good hostess.

We walked down the desolate Border Highway for nearly an hour. Before we even reached downtown, I had to convince Steve that it was a totally bogus idea for us to swim across the river when the Santa Fe Bridge was just minutes away. I told him that anyone who might catch us wouldn't be so thrilled with a güero and a pocho—two *drunk* Americans—washing up on their side of the Rio. While you have a fifty-fifty chance of the U.S. Border Patrol being professional, I'm certain, the odds are less with the Mexican police.

Avenida Juárez

As I had loyally done for years, I followed Steve to the Atomic Punk, one of several bars on "the Strip." This J-town bar catered to hard rock fans: mostly El Paso high school students and Fort Bliss GIs. Steve immediately made himself the center of attention at the bar and challenged others to drinking matches. I stationed myself by the jukebox, a watch guard, daring anyone to pick songs that would further screw up my Friday night.

I kicked back with a bucket of Coronas on ice and invited Van Halen into my head. My hopes were that Eddie's guitar riffs and brother Alex's drumbeats would settle my nerves. Just like the time Steve and I road-tripped to see them in Cruces.

After many beers and the day's misadventures still too vivid, I finally surrendered the jukebox to some rocker chick who was trying to start a conversation. Something about a guitar player killed when a plane landed on his band's tour bus. She wore a Cheap Trick T-shirt and did a decent air guitar. Good signs despite my suspicion of her white-and-purple mohawk. I lied and told her that I didn't know who she was talking about.

I joined my prized drinker at the bar. A row of yard-long glasses, crystal trophies, was lined up in front of him, an ashtray buried in butts and bottle caps nearby.

"Check this out. I think I got more than enough for a carton of smokes and a whole week of Chico's." Steve flashed a wad of bills. I didn't let him know I was impressed.

Unlike El Paso, closing time in Juárez is usually when people decide to go home. Another thing you can count on is that the later it gets the more the Atomic Punk brews excited energy.

My gut was in knots. Like when Steve would switch off the van's headlights and laugh as we drove by the moonlight of the Chihuahua Desert.

"Hey, man, let's call it a night," I proposed.

He grinned, turned back around, and placed his palms flat on the bar. Who did he think he was? An outlaw gambler, John Wesley Hardin or some shit? Ready for the next hand, he said, "C'mon, Joe, a couple more rounds, and I'll have cab fare for us and Marlene."

I assumed the blonde with dark roots and her tongue in his ear was Marlene.

"Do what you want," I said, as the bartender happily set him up again. A pug-nosed GI who resembled the bar's mascot, a ceramic bulldog behind the bar, claimed the stool next to Steve. The GI had already lost a few rounds. And the hardness of his eyes said he was ready to get even. One way or another.

"My amigo, Ho-say, can be such a tight-ass," Steve told Marlene. She ran her hands through his David Lee Roth mane.

I gave Steve the finger. "Okay, pinche gringo. Later."

He knows better than to call me anything but "Joe."

I was prodded out the door as much by half-sober instincts as by the song playing on the jukebox. I definitely wasn't in the mood, especially this night, to hear Heart whine about dogs and butterflies.

I figured Steve would be there when I got back—either drunk or beat-up and broke, possibly all three—and I wandered out onto the Strip.

Shoeshine boys bragged their expertise.

Tarahumara Indians peddled pottery.

Countless vendors sold food along Avenida Juárez.

The smell of meat and chile and onions cooking on homemade skillets enticed my empty stomach. However, Steve's stories about doggie burritos and kitty tortas spiced with pico tie gallo and avocado steered me away. I dropped my ass on the sidewalk. Thinking of the spilled tacos rolling around Steve's van, I scraped hardened Chico's cheese sauce off my high-tops. The sights and smells of the Strip stimulated my senses.

"¡Riiicas¡ . . . ¡Tooorrrtas! . . . ¡Deliciiiooosas!"

An old man in a never-washed apron called out to passing throngs of wasted teens. The viejito chopped his ingredients and flipped his spatula with the skill of a samurai. He stuffed many tortas for his willing customers.

The flashing neon signs of the Copacabana and Tequila Derby hovered on the other side of the street. This is the world of dance music Steve and I avoid like the Duran Duran styles and Flock of Seagulls haircuts that many of our classmates mimic. I busted up at guys applying eyeliner, using mousse, and wearing anything other than jeans and T-shirts.

I could've sat there till daybreak, witnessing other MTV posers stumble out of the Juárez discos, if a roaring noise hadn't drawn my attention.

Soccer game? Parade? At this hour?

I left the viejito selling his late-night lonches, and I joined the pedestrian line on the Mexican side of the bridge. At the turnstile, a shoeless girl put a hand in my face and begged in Spanish. As much as I understood, she wanted something to eat—not for her but for her dog. A rheumy-eyed mutt licked its balls nearby. I was glad when a Boy George-wanna-be handed her some coins.

Santa Fe Bridge

Pursuing the noise, I began the steep walk over the bridge back to the U.S. side. I was tired, and it felt like I was carrying someone on my back. Numbness still chilled my limbs. All the drinking had only made my stomach feel emptier. I gripped the handrail, hoping its firmness would pass through me and give me strength, allowing me safe passage to the other side.

A credit to the torta-selling viejito, my sense of smell was most awake now. The exhaust from the long line of trailer trucks waiting on the bridge was like the smoke-filled Atomic Punk. The moldy stench of the river rivaled the thick cloud over the bridge. I inhaled my surroundings.

The noise that had drawn me off the sidewalk grew louder the closer I got to the top of the bridge. It's here that I always utter a reminder: "I just lost my rights" if I'm going to Juárez, or "I just gained my rights," if I'm coming back to El Paso.

From the bridge's peak—where the U.S. and Mexico flags rested motionless, a safe distance apart from each other—I spotted the ever-present star on the Franklin Mountains. It's supposed to be a symbol of some kind, "El Paso's Sign of Hope," as written on billboards all over town. But it always reminds me of hostages. That was when the tradition of leaving it on every night began.

I thought all this, very aware of the high fences topped with barbed wire surrounding me. I might've contemplated this more if the scene below, the source of all the noise, hadn't distracted me.

I walked down to the U.S. side of the bridge. All ten lanes were blocked off. Traffic was at a standstill. Forty to fifty demonstrators faced the INS checkpoints. A woman with a megaphone made a speech. The crowd shouted its approval. Signs danced above their heads.

2 Cities =1 People	Justicia Para Todos
No More Fences	Free Bridge

I'd seen parts of these same slogans in headlines as I dug out the sports section, the only part of the *Times* I ever read. Although I still didn't know what the demonstration was about, I was drawn to the partylike gathering.

"Not that 'No Grapes' thing again." A couple of tourists also observed from the bridge's walkway. They sported straw sombreros and clutched margarita glasses.

"Here, take this. Sign it." A Chicana wearing a T-shirt that read BORDER RIGHTS COALITION handed me a clipboard.

She didn't appear much older than me, so I reluctantly glanced at the petition. The bold type outlined a proposed barrier—"a steel wall"—along the river to replace the present chainlink fence, the Tortilla Curtain, as it's popularly known. I signed the petition, playing it safe, using Steve's name and address.

The Border Rights Chicana asked if I wanted to carry a sign; WILL YOUR CONSCIENCE BOTHER YOU? Although I liked the way her braided hair pointed to her butt, I shook my head. Her tight jeans asked me to change my mind as I backed away.

My sobering instincts demanded my immediate attention when a fleet of Suburbans drove up to the U.S. side of the border checkpoints. The white vehicles had Border Patrol seals on the doors and what looked like federal license plates. Something bad hid behind the tinted windows.

The officials in suits and ties handling the scene communicated on walkie-talkies and directed security guards in every direction. All eyes on the demonstrators.

I'd had enough.

There are some things, I told myself, that I just don't want to take part in. None of my business anyway. I decided to cross the bridge back to the Mexican side. I'd get Steve, with or without Marlene, and we'd catch a taxi. Time to go home.

Many teens were returning to their cars parked on the American side. Going the wrong way, I went head-on with a drove of partiers and was almost swept up in their drunkenness. I stumbled and hugged the handrail to keep from falling into the border traffic.

The moon that loomed earlier was lost behind rivers of clouds. Whether I looked right or left, El Paso and Juárez appeared the same—dark and dirty and dwarfed by mountains. I didn't know if I was losing or gaining my rights.

I was about to turn my back on the mountain star when I heard what I first thought was thunder. A redhead fell back into my arms. She wore a silky blouse that smelled of tequila and lime. I disappointedly pushed her on her way.

Clouds of smoke sprouted up around the U.S. side of the bridge. The crowd of demonstrators below dropped their signs and covered their mouths. Most of them frantically hurdled the waiting vehicles and sprinted past the checkpoints.

The Border Patrol agents wore black riot gear: helmets, boots, batons, shields. An army ready for action.

I ran back down the bridge and pushed scared teens out of my way. By the time I reached the bottom of the bridge, a group of cornered protestors had torn the posters off their signs and stood poised with wooden stakes.

The woman with the megaphone pleaded with everyone to drop to the ground and lock arms: "Don't fight back! You won't get hurt! Don't fight back!"

A showdown: the demonstrators and the Border Patrol.

No one dared move.

Seconds passed.

Someone lit the fuse.

The scene exploded.

For a moment, I considered running to get Steve. But when I saw an agent running toward the Border Rights Chicana, I didn't hesitate. My left forearm over my head, I charged.

"Goddamnpinchimigra..."

Bodies. Punches.

"Fuckingputonazis . . ."

Screams. Sirens.

I had the Chicana right in my sights and thoughts of being a hero when I was grabbed from behind. I hit someone—I hope it was the right someone—before I went down. Withstanding countless blows, I managed to turn over, face the border soldier, and see my reflection in her helmet's shield.

The last thing I remember is her kicking me before I was cuffed and dragged to a Suburban. There was little hope that the Mexican girl from Kmart, or, hell, even John Wayne, would come and set me free.

"El Corralón"

After hours at the INS detention center, I was let out of an individual cell that smelled worse than the infested Rio. I couldn't even imagine the condition of the other cells, where they corralled hundreds of illegals.

I signed some papers, and when I asked for my watch and ID, a Border Patrol agent said they'd been misplaced. I know I'll never get them back.

I thought about calling home, where my mom would be finding an empty bed soon, but decided I didn't want to do any explaining.

Across the street, in a gas station's bathroom, I plugged up the sink with paper towels and dunked my head in cold water. I managed to see in a graffiti-covered mirror what had become of my face: cuts on my forehead, a black eye, a red lump above my left cheek, a swollen lip.

Inside the gas station, the attendant sat behind a copy of the *Times*. I glanced at the headlines when I asked if he could give me change for a dollar. I scored a Dr Pepper and a lemon pie from the vending machines.

I walked over to this bus stop, which advertises El Paso's annual festival: FRIJOLE FIESTA—BEST BEANS ON THE BORDER.

I know I'm in a bad way when I can't even laugh at the event's mascot: a cartoon pinto bean dressed in a sombrero and serape and sporting a long mustache and huaraches. "Señor Frijole" usually cracks me up.

I arch my back and stretch my arms, trying to work out some of the soreness. My ribs hurt when I breathe in. The rest of my body stiffened with aches and pains.

I squint at the rising sun as I scarf down my breakfast. I'm not sure how early the buses run. Or, for that matter, which one to take. The only thing I'm sure of is that yesterday's numbness is gone. ★

Sheryl Luna

Born and raised in El Paso, Sheryl Luna holds a Ph.D. in American literature from the University of North Texas and an M.F.A. from the University of Texas at El Paso. Her first poetry collection published in 2005 by Notre Dame University Press, *Pity the Drowned Horses*, won the Andres Montoya Poetry Prize and was a finalist for the national poetry series and the Colorado Book Award. Luna's second poetry collection, 7, forthcoming in 2010 from Notre Dame, was runner-up for the 2008 Ernest Sandeen Poetry Prize. She is the 2008 recipient of the Alfredo Cisneros del Moral Foundation Award. Her poems have appeared in *Georgia Review*, *Amherst Review*, *Feminist Studies*, *Borderlands*, *Margie*, and *Poetry Northwest*, among others. She currently teaches at the University of Colorado at Boulder.

From *Pity the Drowned Horses*: Bones

Once, as a girl, she saw a woman shrink
inside herself, gray-headed and dwarf-sized,
as if her small spine collapsed. Age
and collapse were something unreal, like war
and loss. That image of an old woman sitting
in a café booth, folding in on herself, was forgotten
until her own bones thinned and hollowed,
music-less, un-fluted, empty.

She says she takes shark cartilage before she sleeps,
a tablet or two to secure flexibility and forget
that pain is living and living is pain.

And time moves like a slow rusty train
through the desert of weeds, and the low-riders
bounce like teenagers young and forgiving
in her night's dream. She was sleek in a red dress

with red pumps, the boys with slick hair, tight jeans.
She tells me about 100-pound canisters of lard
and beans, how she could dance despite her fifth
child, despite being beaten and left
in the desert for days, how she saw an angel
or saint glimmer blonde above her, how she rose
and walked into the red horizon despite
her husband's sin.

I'm thinking how the women
in my family move with a sway, with a hip
ache, and how they each have a disk
slip. The sky seems sullen, gray, and few birds
whisk. It's how the muse is lost
in an endless stream of commercials, how people
forget to speak to one another as our ending skulks
arthritically into our bones, and the dust
of a thousand years blows across the plain,
and the last few hares sprint across a bloodied
highway. Here in the desert southwest, loss
is living and it comes with chapped lips,
long bumpy bus rides and the smog of some man's
factory trap. And there are women everywhere
who have half-lost their souls
in sewing needles and vacuum-cleaner parts.
In maquiladoras there grows a slow poem,
a poem that may only live a moment sharply
in an old woman's soul, like a sudden broken hip.

And yet, each October, this old woman rises
like the blue sky, rises like the fat turkey vultures
that make death something beautiful, something
towards flight, something that circles in a group
and knows it is best not to approach death alone.

Each October she dances, the mariachis yelp
and holler her back to that strange, flexible youth,
back to smoky rancheras and cumbias, songs
rolling in the shadows along the bare Mexican hills.
She tells me, "It's in the music, where I'll always
live." And somehow, I see her jaw relax,
her eyes squint to a slow blindness
as if she can see something I can't.

And I remember that it is good to be born of dust,
born amid cardboard shanties of sweet gloom.
I remember that the bare cemetery stones
in El Paso and Juárez hold the music, and each spring
when the winds carry the dust of loss there is a howl,
a surge of something unbelievable, like death,
like the collapse of language, like the frail bones
of Mexican grandmothers singing. ★

From *Pity the Drowned Horses*: Learning to Speak

I forgot how to speak. The old man with a gray
beard eyed me, waiting for Spanish.

Years of English rumbled something absent, forgotten.
The Tigua Indian Village, men at the corner bench eating

tamales. Indoors, tables with white formica,
floor-tiles peeling. In the steam of cilantro and tomato

children sit cross-legged and sip caldo de res.
Men smoke afterward in faded jeans, and T-shirts lightly rise

around their pecs in the wind. It is how home is all
that's left in the end. The way we all return forever exiled.

History in mud houses and shady river-trees. Canal water
drifts. Children poke crawdads with dry branches. I spoke

Spanish broken, tongue-heavy. I was once too proud
to speak Spanish in the barrio. He waits for my voice.

His eyes generations. My brown skin a scandal on the hard streets
of El Paso. But, everyone loves a resurrection. Mauricio on a red

motor bike; Bob, a green-eyed white war hero, spits tobacco.
The sunlit desert and its gold light falling upon us. *Quiero*

aprender español, I whisper. He smiles. Blue hills
in the distance sharpen in an old elegance; the wind
hushes itself after howling the silences. ★

Pat Carr

Novelist and short story writer Pat Carr was born in an oil camp in Wyoming, but grew up in Texas. She earned a B.A. and M.A. from Rice University and received a Ph.D. from Tulane. Carr taught literature and creative writing in several universities and taught for ten years at the University of Texas at El Paso where she became a full professor of English before she left academia to write full time. Carr has published fourteen books, including *The Women in the Mirror*, winner of the Iowa Short Fiction Award; *If We Must Die*, a finalist in the PEN Book awards; *The Death of a Confederate Colonel*, winner of the 2008 PEN Texas Southwest Fiction award; the short story collection *Night of the Luminarias*; and *Border Ransom*, both set in El Paso. Carr has published over one hundred short stories in such publications as *The Southern Review*; *Yale Review*; and *Best American Short Stories*. Her other awards include the Texas Institute of Letters Short Story Award, a Library of Congress Marc IV, a National Endowment for the Humanities, and a Fondation de Ledig-Rowohlt Writing Fellowship in Geneva, Switzerland. She is currently at work on her book *A Perfectly Splendid Time*.

The Anatomy of a Victim

She read about the shooting the day after it happened. "The well-known El Paso lawyer, B. J. Turner," the reporter called him and detailed how the shots, five in the chest, had been fired by an unknown assailant in the law offices, in a manner so reminiscent of, and so close upon, the Chagra murder that one might well wonder about the violent influences of Southwestern sunspots or the howling desert wind.

The story included a photograph—-one of those not taken by the newspaper staff photographer but, as is the case with the dead, one of those retrieved from some forgotten album—of a man who knew where he was going, of a man in control, but it was the photograph of a man much younger than the one she remembered.

He had probably looked more like that the first time she'd seen him, but she was no longer certain. She'd walked into his office, the same brown furnished rooms described in the account of the shooting, having selected his name from the list of lawyers in the yellow pages, having decided that "Turner" was sufficiently down the page to avoid the commercialism of the AAA Legal Services and the opportunism of the Acme Law Clinic.

"Well, hello." He'd stood up in his expensive gray suit whose coat had been flung casually into the chair opposite the desk, and his blue eyes had glinted appreciatively—"dilating," her psychiatrist would have explained drily, "the way pupils do during sexual arousal." He came toward her with a sleek, large animal motion, took her hand in both of his. "I can't believe anyone as stunning as you could need a lawyer," he said with such an ingenuous smile and such an artless creasing of his eyes that it avoided any hint of a leer.

"I think I need a divorce."

"If you think so, maybe that's the first step," he said, appraising her kindly, sounding rather fatherly like her psychiatrist, but then tossing the gray silk jacket from the chair to the brown couch with the exuberant gesture of a teen-ager slinging jeans off a kitchen stool. He released her hand and pulled a legal pad toward him on the desk. "Probably everyone tells you this, but if I don't say it, I'll sit here unable to concentrate on what you're going to tell me, so I'll say it the way every man you meet must. You're one of the most beautiful women I've ever seen. There, now we can get down to business. Let's start with your name."

She sat looking at him, the heavy, but handsome features of square, solid lines, the cleft chin that barely missed being too theatrical, the dark wing of hair across his forehead. She couldn't remember meeting anyone with his intensity in years, or perhaps ever.

"Your name," he prompted gently, a gold pen poised.

"Lucia Apodaca."

He glanced at her as everyone always did to reaffirm his initial impression that she wasn't Chicana. "Any relation to the heart surgeon?"

"My husband."

"From whom you think you might need the divorce?" He had written her name in a large script so careful as to appear childlike.

"Yes."

"O-o-o-kay." He took a deep breath and in a very businesslike tone began a series of very businesslike questions, the answers to which he numbered and recorded in that meticulous child's hand that gave him a charming and youthful earnestness.

When she nodded affirmatively to question number 23, "Has he ever struck you?" he paused to glance at her with concern. "I guess y'all just might need that divorce."

The questions continued for page after long page in the yellow legal pad until at last he said, "Well, that ought to be enough for openers. I guess we both have earned the right to a double martini on the rocks."

She was distinctly attracted to him, to the way he listened, to the way he gazed sympathetically at her, and she heard the echo of her psychiatrist explaining that sometimes people in vulnerable situations too rapidly transfer their affections to an authority figure who seems able to take charge of their shifting lives. "Isn't there something about a conflict of interest if lawyer and client get intimate?" she stalled.

He grinned. "We're only getting better acquainted so I can be of more help to my client, Lucia Apodaca. That's not the same thing."

But as they sat in the dark murkiness of the Chaparral Club, he asked more probing questions and listened attentively to her answers, then finally shook his head. "I take that back. There may be a conflict of interest here after all. Y'all definitely need a divorce, sweetheart. But you don't need that psychiatrist, you need me."

"Aren't you married?"

"Separated. I haven't quite figured out how to give myself that definitely necessary divorce."

"What does the B. J. stand for?"

"I'm from East Texas, from a little town on the coast by the name of Palacios. where the sewer meets the sea, and it stands for Billy Jewel." He signalled for a third round of martinis. "I'm also a Scorpio, a Vietnam War ex-helicopter pilot, have a Phi Beta Kappa key that really doesn't open beer cans like everyone assured me it would before I ordered it, and have an obnoxious teen-aged son whom I've indulged too much because I was poor as a kid and had one pair of winter shoes that had to last the school year no matter how short they got for my toes. And after this drink I'm taking you to the Motel Flamingo in Juarez because they rent rooms by the hour, your famous surgeon husband would never imagine anyone taking you there, and it's too early yet for us to go to dinner."

She sipped the third martini and gave herself up to the pleasure of having transferred, too rapidly, her vulnerable affections that liked to hear his East Texas accent and liked to watch his appreciative blue eyes.

At the Motel Flamingo on the highway to Chihuahua, a shabby motel of cracking, flaking adobe, that smelled as well as looked illicit. Billy Jewel poured cognac from his silver hip flask into the spotted motel glasses, and they lay side by side on the warm motel sheets.

"Damn, you are undoubtedly the most beautiful woman I ever saw." He stroked her cheek, traced her collar bone with his finger. "You seem so . . . delicate, I guess, so fragile, like fine crystal or china."

"I'm not."

He smiled. "I never met a woman yet who knew herself." He kissed her lingeringly, the taste of cognac mingling on their lips. He lifted the water glass from her hand, set it on the damaged dresser, then kissed her again, again, their teeth clashing together with increasing passion, his hands gripping her shoulders.

Her breath quickened, shallowed, for the unaccustomed thrust as his tongue sought hers fiercely. The pressure of his palm on her flesh intensified, and his rushed breathing was like steam against her throat, but no thrust came, and after a surprised wait, she opened her eyes.

His face was close to hers, sweat beading his upper lip, the veins on his forehead bulging thickly blue. His hair was plastered like a sodden wing to his scalp, and his eyes were clenched, his teeth set above the cleft in his chin.

She quickly closed her eyes again.

Possibly three double martinis and half a sterling flask of brandy were too much for a Vietnam veteran's performance. Or perhaps the first time for a man like this, a man of such acute sensibilities, was difficult with any new partner. She hadn't had enough affairs to make any hypotheses, to draw any conclusions.

She didn't know how long he struggled above her with his impotence, how long she lay, lids closed against his agony, before he at last rolled aside, lay back, his arm across his face.

There was a silence in the shoddy little room, and she could hear faint sounds of traffic on the Chihuahua highway.

"Sometimes I think I should quit screwing on my lunch hour," he said.

She smiled with relief. "You're supposed to take *in* calories, not expend them all on lunch hours."

He took his arm away from his blue, blue eyes and grinned at her. "Yeah, I keep forgetting."

As they were dressing again, he said, "Did you know that Ibsen kept a scorpion in a jar on his desk with an orange so the scorpion could sting it and get rid of his venom?"

She glanced at his reflection behind hers in the dresser mirror as she applied a charcoal line to the roots of her lashes. "How about that."

"I wonder if Ibsen was a Scorpio." He fastened his belt buckle, a gold disc with a centered Texas longhorn steer. "Want to take in the bullfights next Sunday? Have you ever seen one of the illustrious Juarez corridas?"

"Carlos always thought they were rather lower class."

"Now I *know* you need that divorce."

At the bullfight, he stared across the sunny arena, urging with his shoulders both the bull and the matador, his eyes not appearing to blink against the vermillion blood, the horns grating an inside thigh. She found the heat oppressive, the sun too harsh, but every time he glanced at her, he smiled. "Beautiful," he murmured. "I've never seen any woman quite as beautiful as you." And at the finale of the sixth bullfight, when he ushered her from the plaza and said, "How about a date on Thursday? I'll have those papers ready for you to sign if you want to drop by about three," she assumed that their second rendezvous at the Motel Flamingo would be different.

But it wasn't. And on the following Thursday when he picked her up in his silver Porsche with "I've got us reservations at the Villa del Mar," she was vastly relieved.

He settled back in the curtained booth, lit them each a cigarette. took her hand, and they sipped the dry martinis.

"I thought this might be a change from our weekly screwing," he said.

And as he smiled at her, she knew with terrible certainty that he was impotent with everyone—including the separated wife he never mentioned.

"Don't you think?" He clasped his fingers and thumb around her wrist like an oversized bracelet. "You certainly have delicate bones, sweetheart." He clamped his hand, twisted the wrist slightly.

"Hey, that hurts."

It was dusk in the booth, a ruddy dusk that filtered surreal, darkly scarlet through the red drapes of the restaurant, but she could see the white square teeth of his smile. She stared at him in surprise as he twisted her wrist again.

"Billy Jewel, that hurts," she said. "Take your hand away."

He continued to smile in the artificial ruby twilight. "Don't threaten me."

"I'm not threatening you." She moved the lighted cigarette closer to his hand. "But take your hand away."

He sat motionless except for his fingers and the thumb that pressed against her wrist bone, tendons, and twisted them again.

She touched the glowing coal of the cigarette to the back of his hand.

He didn't move, not the flick of a muscle in his face or hand. He didn't even glance down as she felt, heard, the flesh burn.

Shock pounded inside her chest and she lifted the cigarette away. He was smiling faintly, just the edge of his white teeth showing. His hand tightened on her wrist. She touched the tip of the cigarette to his motionless hand again, again.

She'd never seen anyone with that kind of control, that kind of determination to carry a game so far.

She was to see it one more time

The following weekend he drove up to her apartment and knocked quietly on the door. From her bedroom window she'd caught the silver gleam of his Porsche, and she was tempted not to answer the door.

"Lucia?" He knocked again, quietly. "Lucia. I've got to see you." His voice was subdued. "You don't know how sorry I am. I just want to see you for a minute. Lucia?"

He sounded so forlorn. She gave a sympathetic sigh.

"Hi, sweetheart." he said as she opened the door. His eyes held hers with a pleading blue gaze. "Could I talk to you for a couple of minutes?" He stood there in a snowy tennis outfit, his tanned legs stocky, bare, his hands in the pockets of the shorts like a sturdy, punished child.

The harsh, unrelenting glare made his stance even more painful, and she stepped aside for him to come in out of the sun.

"I know how you must feel about that whole stupid episode the other day, Lucia. It was ludicrous, downright insane I guess, but. . . ." He was studying her face closely. "I wasn't myself. Not anywhere near myself I guess. I'd just heard that Arnold had been picked up with a carload of marijuana near Phoenix. Six hundred pounds. I'm a damned good lawyer, but he's just turned eighteen and that takes him out of juvenile, and I don't know if I can get him out of it this time."

She saw him waiting for a reaction, and she stood watching him, thinking how sad he was.

"I know I should've said something, not just acted like some demented idiot, but I guess I knew it wasn't your problem. He'd promised me he was going to shape up, and I guess I was just so damned hurt that he'd been lying through his teeth, right to my face. . . ." He shrugged, "But to have hurt you in turn. . . . If you could just put that whole thing out of your mind. . . ."

An abject sadness radiated from him.

"It's all right," she said and put out her hand toward him.

He caught it. "If you'd just let me make it up somehow. Lucia, let me try to blot out that. . . ."

"It's all right," she said again.

He drew her to him and she felt him take a long shuddering breath.

"Would you let me take you on a picnic?" he asked against her hair.

"I was just about to. . . ."

"I brought some pâté de foie gras and a bottle of French wine in case you could bring yourself to forgive me. We could drive out of town a little way, maybe just beyond the pollution, have some pâté and white wine and I'd have you back in an hour or so."

"Billy Jewel. I. . . ."

"Please, Lucia, just an hour to let me. . . ."

"All right," she said quickly, her better judgment submerged by her need to have him stop talking. "But I do have to be back by one."

"I'll have you back by one." He gave her a tight hug and then grabbed the purse that lay on the table beside the door. "Your keys in here?"

"Yes, but. . . ."

"No 'buts'. Come along before you change your beautiful mind."

He pulled her after him, slammed the apartment door shut, and ushered her hurriedly into the convertible. There was an elaborate woven picnic basket in the back seat.

He drove expertly, without talking, only glancing at her occasionally to smile fondly and gratefully. Once he put his hand over hers, pressed it gently, and she noticed then the five burnt round holes in the back of his hand. He'd dabbed them with a tincture of some indigo antiseptic and they were startlingly obvious. She stared down at them, remembering that when she and Carlos had honeymooned in Rio, he had explained carefully that the beggars painted their sores to elicit more sympathy from the gringos but that medically no one really had that kind of azure hued disease.

She looked away from his hand, watched the center of town flow past, then the drive-in food kiosks and used car lots of the outskirts, then the open highway, a straight black crusted scar on the desert landscape. She regretted having given in to her sympathy, regretted not having brought some kind of hat against the sun.

After what seemed a long time, he turned off the highway, sped along a dirt road into mountainous sand dunes. The dust billowed behind the Porsche, obscured the road, and obliterated the tire tracks with the fine dirt spume as if they hadn't passed at all. He whirled the car into an open space beside the ten foot dunes and braked to an abrupt stop.

Her eyes were still stinging with the motor and the speed.

"Where are we?"

"Where does it look like we are, sweetheart? We're in the desert." He grinned at her, his youthful exuberance beginning to return, and tousled her short hair. "God, but you're beautiful. Here, hop out. We haven't much time, remember." He leaned across to open the door on her side and shoved her gently with his shoulder. His eyes were a glittering luminous blue. "And now I'll show you a surprise before we break open the French wine."

She got out, knowing he was watching her and feeling her knees stiffen with his close observation. She closed the car door behind her as he unlocked the glove compartment and took out something she couldn't see but that was obviously a heavy, bulky object.

Then he reached into the back seat for the picnic basket, climbed out of the car, and came around the silver hood.

She saw that what he'd taken from the glove compartment was a pistol.

He was watching her face, and when he grinned delightedly, she knew her startled expression had been unmistakable and had been what he'd anticipated. He seemed to have regained all of his former assurance.

"I don't like guns, Billy Jewel."

"You'll take to a gun like a duck takes to water, sweetheart. I can guarantee it." He put the picnic basket on the hood and extracted a box of shells from his shirt pocket. "If there's anything I know, it's people." he said. "Most women don't have the foggiest idea who they are, but I know you're the type who'll take to shooting a gun like you'd done it all your life." He fitted the brass shells with their silver tips into the gaping holes of the cylinder, clicked it shut. "You'll love it, sweetheart."

She watched him and felt slightly dizzy under the cloudless sky.

"O-o-o-okay. Now you just do as I show you," he was saying as he came to her side, lifted her limp arm with the hand she'd burned, and put the handle of the gun in her equally limp palm.

It was heavy, warm, and the wood of the slick stock was oily, almost as if it had been sweating in the glove compartment.

"Now, hold it up like this, sight through these—see how they line up—and when you get your target right in the center of these little metal points, you just squeeze the trigger like this." His hand was around hers and his finger pressed hers against the trigger, drew it slowly back.

The gun went off with a quiet bark, not the loud crack she'd expected. The barrel jerked slightly upward, then steadied under their two hands.

"Now you try it. Aim at those old bottles over there."

She looked across the empty dunes, saw three brown bottles in a row, and recognized that he'd been at the site with the pistol before, that he'd planned the picnic to bring her there.

She raised the gun. It was too big, a pistol for a much larger fist, but not as heavy as she first thought. Nor was the trigger as hard to pull back as she'd assumed with Billy Jewel's hand over hers. She sighted, aimed, and the gun barked again, quietly, like a discreet cough. The brown bottle in the center of the line suddenly flew apart on the sand.

"Good girl! See there. You're a natural. Try it again."

She hadn't lowered the pistol and she aimed at the next bottle, pulled the trigger, and at the short hacking sound, the bottle exploded.

"Bravo!" he shouted jubilantly as he had at the bullfight when the bull had slammed into the padded horse of the picador.

He swung his arm around her shoulders and gave her an approving hug as he took the gun from her hand. He broke open the cylinder, jammed three more cartridges into the emptied spaces.

"Look how easy that is." He grinned and wiped at his forehead glistening with perspiration. He tossed her the gun, barrel first, and she barely caught it.

Then he walked over the sand to the single remaining bottle and kicked up two cans rusted almost black. He stood them up precariously, dented, beside the bottle.

"Think you can hit these, sweetheart?" He was squatting beside them, his bare knees toward her, and seemed to be calling from a long way away. "Can you get them in your sights? How about me? Can you line up those little metal points so they aim right here?"

It was as if she were looking at him through a telescope as he tapped a stubby finger of the blue burned hand against his white shirted chest. His teeth were a dazzling white in the sun.

And she realized how easy it would be to pull the effortless trigger, hear the gentle cough of the gun. It would be no more than shooting at the useless cans or the empty bottles. He was as hollow, and as she held the metal sights around the finger on his chest, she was sure if she had pulled the trigger, he would no more have bled than the deserted bottles had spewed out stale beer.

He knelt motionless, as if he were posing for a photograph or an oil portrait, and only a sparkling rivulet of sweat on his jaw gave the impression of moving.

He was right. Without compunction, almost without feeling, she could have shot him.

She lowered the gun.

"Sorry, Billy Jewel. You'll have to find someone else to help you commit suicide." But she didn't know if she'd said it, or only whispered it from her vast distance. She flung the gun at one of the dunes, and it skidded heavily, dug its barrel into the sand as if trying to burrow out of the sun.

"Hey, you can ruin an expensive gun treating it like that."

She'd opened the car door and got in. "How about that."

***

She folded the newspaper over the photograph of his deceased strong square face and gazed out the window into the dry still air. He should have kept a scorpion in a jar and watched it punch venom into sweet oranges. Five shots in the chest. Five neat round holes he'd never have the chance to paint blue. ★

Lucy Fischer-West

Born in Catskill, New York, Lucy Fischer-West was raised in El Paso and attended school on both sides of the border, receiving her B.A. from the University of Texas at El Paso. A career educator, Fischer-West has taught classes at the university and high school level and was a finalist for the Mary Jon and J. P. Bryan Leadership in Education Award for the Texas State Historical Association in 2008. Her articles and essays have appeared in such publications as *BorderSenses*; *Password*; *The Family Saga: A Collection of Texas Family Legends*; and *Both Sides of the Border: A Scattering of Texas Folklore*, both published by the Texas Folklore Society; and an essay on audiotape from Writer's Audio Workshop titled *The Best of Texas Folklore Volume I.* Fischer-West's book, *Child of Many Rivers: Journeys to and from the Rio Grande*, evolved from a 2003 presentation for the Texas State Historical Association and has won a varietiy of awards, including a Southwest Book Award from the Border Regional Library Association, a WILLA Literary Award Finalist Award from Women Writing the West, and a Violet Crown Special Citation from the Writer's League of Texas. Fisher-West was the associate editor of the American Folklore Newsletter from 1972-78 and is a member of Women Writing the West. She has presented papers at the Southwest Popular Culture Association, the Texas State Historical Association, The Border Regional Library Association and the Texas Folklore Society, where she serves as vice-president and program chair for the 2009 centennial meeting.

From *Child of Many Rivers: Journeys to & from the Rio Grande*: Food Between the Waters

Whatever time of day it was, whether you were walking, skipping, or roller-skating up and down my street in El Paso in the mid-1950s and 1960s, the aromas wafting out of most homes were unmistakably Mexican. Freshly rinsed rice hitting hot skillets sizzled;

comino- and *cilantro*-seasoned *caldo de res* was a weekly staple; *menudo* with its dried oregano and freshly chopped onions was the Saturday or Sunday special; and when you smelled *caldo de pollo* you knew someone was sick. There was a *molino de nixtamal* within walking distance if you had a craving to make *gorditas* or your own *tortillas de maíz*. You got the *masa* to make tamales for Christmas from the same place. It was in my mother's kitchen in that small adobe home that I learned to cook. There that she passed down to me her knowledge of foods and herbs; there she fed my body and nurtured my soul.

The house I grew up in sits on a former riverbed. Paisano Avenue, the main thoroughfare to go downtown, and the site of the river's old channel, was the first street beyond ours, the last street before the fence separating El Paso from Juárez. The Rio Grande had changed courses several times over the years. Those occurrences flooded the poorest parts of the city, particularly the *Segundo Barrio*, and wreaked havoc with international boundaries. In time, a concrete channel contained the Rio Grande, and the Chamizal Treaty resolved the issue of where the border lay. A park with rolling hills of grass came to commemorate the peaceful settlement, but most of the time I lived in that house, the desert beyond the fence was our only vista. The Franklin Canal behind our house carried the river's water from the base of Mount Cristo Rey down the valley to feed the farmers' cotton and chili crops. The fertile riverbed we lived on explains why everything my mother planted grew. From the trees alongside the house she picked peaches, apricots, plums, and apples. All of these had sprouted from seeds or pits she had nonchalantly tossed out. Against the wall of the canal she built a raised bed to grow vegetables. What time she didn't spend on the garden, she spent inside, mostly in the kitchen because she loved to cook.

The kitchen was about eight feet square and on the east side of the house. Outside, between it and the chain-link fence, was just enough space to walk sideways, holding your breath. One day when I came home from school she was standing inside the sink, with chalk and yardstick in hand, marking out an outline on the wall where she intended to put a window. There would be nothing to see from this window save the neighbor's back screen door. Even so, my mother wanted light in the room where she spent so much time. The house may not have been very big, and it lacked many creature comforts, but it was solid, built in the early 1930s. Keeping her property in Juárez in rentable condition had taught her a lot about home repairs, but when it came to knocking a sizable hole in an outer wall, I had to wonder whether she really knew what she was doing. She did. She was never one to wait for things to be done for her and she had the guts to attempt practically anything that needed doing around the house. After outlining the space, she got a chisel and a hammer and dug deeper and deeper, following the adobe lines. Someone with more strength would have probably taken a crowbar or sledgehammer and saved some time, but she knew what she was capable of. From time to time, she'd use a small pick, like miners use. As she took out chunks, she put them on the counter for me to carry out to the yard when I got home. Somewhere along the line, an itinerant worker happened by and she hired him to help her frame the hole with two-by-fours and put in a casement window. That is how there came to be light in our kitchen.

My father took no interest in home projects, but he was well used to my mother's. When he bought the house, its kitchen had no cabinets. My mother bought them, one at a time, from the Union Furniture store downtown. They were metal, plain white, and heavy. She chiseled into the adobe and secured a two-by-four at the height she wanted to hang them and did it, once again with whatever help happened by. Once they were securely hung, she and I took a long walk to the neighborhood Winn's about a mile-and-a-half away, where I got to pick out decals to dress them up. She let me place the decals wherever I thought they should go. Such a smart woman my mother was, in so many ways. I was invested in all her projects, so proud when we finished one, always looking forward to the next.

After she got through paying for the cabinets, she bought a kitchen table, red and gray, with a faux-marble Formica top and chrome frame all around. The matching red chairs had a marble design on their vinyl seats. That table and a freestanding cabinet were her work spaces. The purchase of the gas stove came next, one with an oven on top and storage on the bottom. That stove kept painstakingly clean, was a source of pride for her. My mother knew exactly how it was put together, took it apart on a regular basis, and cleaned every bit of it until it shone. Eventually she replaced the sink, since she had put in a few dents and knocked out a few chips when she opened up the wall above it.

Resurrecting the tastes, sounds, sights, smells, and feel of my mother's kitchen doesn't take much effort. The small kitchen was devoid of many gadgets to help her cook, but her solid metal, heavy-ribbed, glass-container Oster blender got daily use. It whizzed through the fresh tomatoes and garlic that were the basis for so much of what she cooked. She chopped onions expertly and without tears, frequently singing or whistling as she worked. The memories of my mother's kitchen date back half a century and are a vivid, continuing source of pleasure for me. The aroma of the garlic, the sizzle of pureed tomato mixture hitting the hot cast-iron skillet in which she had browned her rice—these, happily, I can replicate in my own kitchen, whose drawers, I must confess, hold a gadget for every task imaginable.

Three times a day we sat down together for meals. Most of the time she didn't set the table but just casually flung the utensils on it. My father often said that if he ever opened up a restaurant, he would love for her to cook, but her waitressing skills left a lot to be desired. He was meticulous about his eating habits; my mother was just the opposite. She would scoop up food with her hot—often burnt crisp—tortillas and rarely use utensils except for soups. She rarely finished a meal without finding an excuse to lick her fingers.

My first recollection of cooking is of being lifted up onto a step stool by my mother so that I was waist high to the stove top. There sat a *comal*, a flat, round, cast-iron griddle with a handle, always ready to heat tortillas for at least two of the three meals. On days when she was not too harried, those tortillas did not come out of a plastic bag from the corner grocery store, but rather were hand-patted from lime-soaked, finely ground *nixtamal.* I would get a child-sized ball of *masa* to pat out my own less-than-perfect *tortillas de maíz*. Occasionally, my mother would use either a wooden or cast-aluminum tortilla press lined with wax paper to speed up the corn tortilla-making process. I had a smaller version of hers.

It goes without saying that our mainstay foods were Mexican. I've eaten corn tortillas since my four front teeth came together to bite into them. There is something ineffably elemental about the aroma of a freshly made *tortillas de maíz* browning on cast iron. That smell of the earth's corn cooking on the fiery hot metal evokes a treasured childhood in the kitchen working beside my mother. For her flour *tortillas*, she would use a red-handled rolling pin that she found at the old *Mercado Cuauhtémoc* across the border in Juárez. I had a child-sized rolling pin with which to turn my portion of flour dough into a lopsided *tortilla de harina*. Proudly I watched over our *tortillas*, mashing down both my mother's and mine when they puffed up. I developed a healthy respect for the hot *comal* on which I placed my creations, both corn and flour.

If there is another aroma that takes me instantly to the kitchen on the riverbed, it is pinto beans simmering in a day pot. My mother's *olla de barro*, which I still have, has a reddish-brown glaze, with designs painted in cream and dark green. I wouldn't know how to cook beans in anything else. That John liked her *frijoles de la olla*, beans straight out of the pot, was probably one of the reasons that she came to like him as fast as she did, even though she objected strongly to our marriage. I never could understand why he would want to put salt pork or a chunk of bacon in the beans, except that it was a tradition in his Southern family. My mother's beans never had anything except a good amount of garlic and salt. They were a staple of our diet, along with Mexican rice garnished with canned carrot cubes and peas.

Not all of her dishes were so simple. On her stove, over an open burner, my mother toasted *chiles verdes*, then wrapped them in a cool, moist cotton towel. At the table she would peel and deseed them, then fill them with cheese or ground meat. With her bent-tined wooden-handled fork and a shallow bowl, she produced a rhythmic, musical clinking that turned two egg whites into a mountain of froth. After adding the egg yolks, she dipped the flour-dredged chilies in the fluffy eggs and fried them. In a process that seemed like magic to me, she transformed those skin-scorched wrinkled green chilies into plump, flavorful *chiles rellenos*. Her sauce was simple: garlic, sliced onion, and pureed, simmered fresh tomatoes, which she drizzled on top. Invariably, my fair-skinned German father would get the hottest one on the plate, and even though his ears would turn bright red and his forehead would break out in perspiration, he wouldn't trade his *chile relleno* for another that might be milder. Even today, my efforts with the wooden-handled fork are a dismal failure, the egg whites rising for an instant and then going limp in the bowl. Only in my mother's hand was that fork ever magic.

We crossed from one of the river's banks to the other to get the food to prepare in my mother's kitchen. It was a good thing that we lived in a neighborhood where the basics were available within walking distance, because my mother never learned to drive. But with her roots so strongly embedded in Juárez across the border, and my grandmother still in residence there, all the vegetables we used, and a lot of canned goods, beef, fish, and cheese, as well as herbs, medicinal and culinary, we brought across week after week. We carried groceries first in sturdy handwoven dyed hemp bags and later, with the advent of plastic, in bright plaid mesh bags. The rituals connected with our finding the *materias primas* for food preparation were an adventure. It was a hunting and gathering expedition.

The walking required in our Saturday trips totaled at least four miles. We started at the far end of downtown, at the *Mercado Cuauhtémoc* beside the *Misión de Guadalupe*, where we shopped for vegetables and herbs. The endless array of produce, sold by merchants of every age, was a palette of rich reds, varying yellows and oranges, and multiple shades of greens. The merchants' calls in the market were as colorful: "*Marchantita, marchantita, venga. Aquí tengo ricos tomates, aguacates, calabacitas. Ándele, pruebe este melón jugocito y dulcecito. Ándele, llévese estas tortillitas recién hechecitas.*" It will lose something in translation, but it goes something like this: "Lady, Lady, here. I have delicious tomatoes, avocados, zucchini. Come, taste this juicy, sweet cantaloupe. Take some of these freshly patted tortillas." For cooking, she bought *hojas de laurel*, *orégano*, *canela entera*, and *cominos*—bay leaves, oregano, cinnamon, and cumin—a few kilograms at a time, in *alcatraces*, small squares of newspapers shaped into cones and folded at the top. We always got chamomile and spearmint to keep on hand for sleeplessness or stomachaches. And because my mother was as much a nurturer of the soul as the body, she bought an occasional jasmine plant, which she would carefully take out of the coffee can it was planted in with just enough soil to protect the roots, cradle it in a small plastic bag or a newspaper *alcatraz*, and tuck it carefully in her purse, or sometimes even her bosom, to smuggle across the border. These plants would flourish under her care, and the aroma of jasmine blossoms mingled with cooking food to fill our small house. After I started driving, she got more brazen with her smuggling. I thought for sure I was going to have my car confiscated when she bought a canary to bring home one summer. Right before we got to the inspection station, she tucked the paper bag under the seat. The claustrophobic bird poked through one of the airholes, got loose, and the next thing I knew I felt his feathers on my feet. When the customs official asked what we were bringing across, I recited the litany—tomatoes, onions, cheese, bananas, papaya, avocados without the pits. I guess I must have looked honest, although I was terrified. Fortunately the bird had enough sense to sit still and not go flying into the inspector's face. My heart skipped a few beats during that escapade, and we never tried anything that bold again.

Our load from the *Mercado Cuauhtémoc* in hand, we trudged another three-quarters of a mile downhill to *La Florida*, a Chinese-owned grocery store and butcher shop where we bought beef. The store was a long corridor, with the butchers' area in the back. The area was small, with three chopping blocks and an ample supply of sharp knives in several sizes to cut through the quarters of beef hanging from well-worn hooks. Chava, the butcher, was quite fond of my mother. As a matter of fact, everyone she ever encountered on our shopping outings developed a fondness for her. Anyway, she would ask Chava for a *kilo* of this or that and he would raise an eyebrow ever so subtly to tell her whether or not she should stick to her order, suggesting other cuts that were fresher. Subtlety was called for, because from the end of the corridor, perched on a tall stool, the owner kept a watchful eye on all the goings-on. Whatever she bought in the way of canned goods and sugar was always rewarded with a *pilón*, a little something extra thrown in for regular customers. Another perk from the store owner was the yearly calendar at Epiphany, one with all the saints' days indicated, and illustrated with a scantily dressed Aztec maiden about to be sacrificed, or perhaps rescued, by a handsome, muscular warrior.

If we were out of cheese, it took another mile to get the only one she would use, at the *Mercado Juárez*. For *enchiladas* and *chiles rellenos*, we bought cheese made by the German Mennonite community near Casas Grandes, Chihuahua. For the sheer delicious pleasure of it, we bought *azaderos*, thin hand-swirled tortilla-shaped cheese, brought from Villa Ahumada, a small town 180 kilometers from Juárez. The *azaderos* from Villa Ahumada have a texture unlike any other and make mouth-watering *quesadillas*. Sometimes not all of them made it home. To give us energy for the return journey we often slapped one on a fresh hot tortilla with a little salt we carried with us and part of a scooped-out avocado. Throughout my childhood, I do not remember ever getting anything in El Paso that we could purchase in Juárez. Beyond saving her money, the trips enabled my mother to immerse me in the world in which she had grown up and the culture she held so dear.

Once home, my mother would slice onions and toss them into a hot cast-iron skillet. While they browned, she would season thin slices of filet, which she cooked just long enough to leave them pink and juicy. Removing the meat and onions, she laid in fresh tortillas to soak up the juice. She called this dish *carne aventada*—tossed meat—and served it with some of the avocados and fresh jalapeño chilies we had bought at the market. It is still one of my favorite meals, although I don't alternate a bite of raw jalapeño with a bite of a beef-filled tortilla like she did.

The strong aroma of *caldo de pollo*—chicken soup—wafting out of any house on our block was a strong indicator that someone was sick. For her *caldo*, my mother boiled the chicken with garlic cloves, onion, and bay leaves, skimming it as necessary. When the chicken was tender, she added carrots, potatoes, zucchini, cabbage, and corn, usually in that order, the hardest vegetables first. Adding fresh cilantro at the end gave the *caldo de pollo* a little color and surely speeded up recovery. Smelling *caldo de pollo* coming from a neighbor's house was a signal to check to see who was ailing. Even on our limited income, my mother would bake something, then put it in a basket lined with a clean, well-ironed—usually hand-embroidered—cup towel and send me to deliver it while it was still warm. Sometimes she came along to see if she could offer any assistance to the family. Baskets, as well as pots and pans, circulated up and down our block, were never returned empty, and gave all the women who were lucky enough to stay home with their children ample opportunities to visit.

In our predominantly Roman Catholic neighborhood, you knew when it was Friday because households smelled of fish. And if you somehow missed seeing foreheads marked with crosses from Ash Wednesday, the forty days of mostly meatless foods left no doubt that it was the Lenten season. Even though our household was half Baptist and half Unitarian, the kitchen was all Mexican Roman Catholic. On the shopping trips to Juárez, we added a stop at the fish market, buying whole fishes when my mother's pocketbook allowed, or fish heads for soup when it did not. At either market we bought *chacales*, cracked corn to cook with onions, garlic, and *chile colorado*, and sprinkled with a little cheese; *lentejas*—lentils that my mother would turn into a very soupy soup and serve with chopped raw onions, fresh *cilantro*, and diced hard-boiled eggs; and *camarones secos*—dried shrimp—which she would combine with whipped eggs and a bit of flour to make *tortitas de camarón con tomate*—shrimp patties with tomato sauce. The Friday fish days were topped off with *capirotada*, Mexican bread pudding with as many variations as there are cooks. My mother's had *francecitos*—French rolls—toasted, then layered and drenched with *almíbar de piloncillo*—syrup made from dark brown sugar that came in solid cones and had to be wrapped in a towel and hit with a hammer to break it up before being melted over a low flame—each layer sprinkled with whatever nuts she had in the house, plus raisins, cheese, sometimes coconut, and topped with *grajeas*—colored sugar sprinkles for the final garnish. Seasoned with cinnamon and cloves, melding with the brown sugar and the other ingredients, *capirotada* baking in the oven was as much a treat to smell as it was to eat. For me, the Lenten season did not mean being deprived of meat, but rather being treated to foods not prepared the rest of the year.

Typically the word *tamalada* evokes the happy image of women who come together to share in the making of tamales for big family gatherings at either Christmas or New Year's. As the only child of a mother whose sisters did not like the kitchen, the *tamaladas* I remember were not gatherings filled with the raucous laughter and bustling but quiet, intensive collaborations with my mother. Instead of one joyous day of tasks split among many, it was two or three days of chores divided between just the two of us. It started with soaking the corn shucks and then cleaning them, which was my responsibility even when I was too small to reach the sink without a step stool. My mother cooked the pork, shredded it, and made the chili the day before the assembly; while it was cooking, she washed the pots that had grown dusty from lack of use since the year before, laundered the towels that she was to spread over the tamales to aid in the steaming process, and laid out all her utensils in the manner of a surgeon preparing for an operation.

The day before cooking day, usually several days before Christmas, we would either walk a mile or two to the neighborhood *molino de nixtamal* or take the bus downtown and at the same time shop for other groceries needed, mostly at the Canton Grocery Store, which would deliver whatever we bought. The *molino* downtown had a gleaming light blue chrome grinder. It was operated by a tiny woman, who even in her youth had difficulty transporting the buckets of lime-soaked corn from the back room to the grinder. She emptied the buckets, flipped the switch, and knelt at the end of the chute, waiting to test the coarseness and moisture of the *masa*. She would make any adjustments necessary, finish grinding, wrap the twenty or thirty pounds of *masa* in butcher paper, and send us on our way with a *pilón* of finely ground *masa* for making *champurrado*, a corn and chocolate hot drink seasoned with stick cinnamon and cloves that accompanied the meal.

Once home, we divided the *masa* into manageable piles, added Snow Cap lard, seasonings, and baking powder, then kneaded it and kneaded it until it was fluffy enough and light enough that a drop of *masa* plunked in a glass of water came floating to the top. With everything arranged efficiently, we would take a moist, clean corn shuck, spread a thin layer of *masa* on it, put a generous dollop of prepared meat in the center, fold the sides in toward the center, fold the tail in the opposite direction of the seam, and arrange the tamales around a cone in a dark blue speckled enamel canning pot. After filling the pot, my mother would cover the tamales with several clean towels and pour a liter of boiling water in the pot, just enough to steam them. In about an hour, the tamales were ready to eat; some were kept on hand for holiday visitors. Mr. and Mrs. White two doors down always got a dozen. After Johnny came into our family, he took part in all of the *tamal*-making rituals, including putting chili or *masa* on each other's noses when we spread it on the countless shucks. Whatever tamales didn't get eaten over the holidays were frozen for future meals. One of the hardest things to do after my mother died was to eat the Ziploc bag full of the last tamales she and Johnny and I had made together. Over the years that we all cooked together, Johnny developed a love for the kitchen, a fine-tuned sense of taste, and a respect for the rituals connected to our meal preparation.

Some of the day-to-day dishes my mother cooked were not what you would call epicurean cuisine, but it was all comfort food. For breakfast she often cooked oatmeal, and purposely let it stick to the pan to scorch for me. I have yet to find a pan that will burn oatmeal (yes! truly burn—so delicious, as long as you don't scrape too much off the bottom) to my satisfaction. When she didn't do that, she made *huevos con tortillitas*—small squares of tortilla fried until crisp, with an egg or two scrambled into it, seasoned with salsa. On Sundays we usually had bacon with Aunt Jemima pancakes smothered in dark Karo syrup, or *huevos rancheros* with mashed beans, or *huevos con chorizo*. When I came home from school for lunch, we had *fideo*, *sopa de estrellitas*, or some other kind of soup. For supper it was a piece of beef, pork, chicken, or fish, and the two vegetables, one green, one yellow, as prescribed by the food pyramid of the era. A lot of the vegetables came from cans; after all, we could not carry enough on Saturday to last the whole week. For variety she would sauté slivered almonds in with the green beans, or throw in a scrambled egg. She made elbow macaroni with ketchup or enhanced a couple of cans of Campbell's Pork & Beans with sliced wieners; our biscuits always popped out of cans. Her desserts consisted of Jell-O with whatever kind of canned fruit she had in the pantry, using their juice instead of water to make the gelatin. If she was too busy to make dessert, Libby's canned fruit cocktail in a little Pyrex bowl would suffice.

Two men infiltrated my mother's Mexican kitchen. One lived in the house; the other one merely visited from time to time, peddling his wares. My father was easily pleased with everything my mother cooked, and although he loved her Mexican food, she often tried her hand at some of the German dishes he liked. There were always potatoes fixed in some manner or another for him, usually to go with pork, his favorite meat. When she could find pig's knuckles at the nearby Big 8, he considered it a delicacy, particularly if she had the sauerkraut to go with them. Those bones glistened when he got through with them, but he never picked them up with his hands. Given a choice of sauces for his mashed potatoes, he would pick not a gravy made from the drippings in the meat pot, but the same sautéed onion and fresh tomato sauce my mother fixed for the *chiles rellenos* that she cooked regularly. Up until the day he died, when my mother put a plate of food on the table before him, my father kissed her hands.

The other man was Morton Kolleeny He worked for the Watkins Company, which has been in existence since 1868. In my child's eye I can still see him—tall with broad shoulders, possessing an abundance of dark brown hair, and wearing horn-rimmed glasses that set off his dark eyes. I cannot tell you how often he came to the neighborhood, but I do remember that not many people on the block encouraged him to visit regularly, either because the women in other kitchens were less adventurous than my mother or because money was more scarce than at our house. Like the rural peddler in a wagon laden with treasures, he came with a car full of everything a well-equipped pantry could ever hope for—spices, extracts, prepared mixes for lemon meringue pie and chocolate and banana puddings. And cookbooks.

In my mother's kitchen there were only two cookbooks: the *Watkins Cookbook* and the *Watkins Salad Book*, purchased, for $2.00 and $1.50 respectively, sometime in the late 1950s. Published in 1948 and 1946, and in my possession still, their pages are spotted and splattered, as all well-loved cookbooks should be. In those cookbooks she found ideas for all the potluck suppers we attended at *Primera Iglesia Bautista Mexicana*. My signature cookie is a variation of a recipe found in the *Watkins Cookbook*. To be historically accurate, it should be made with Watkins vanilla extract, which had a trial mark on the back of the bottle and indicated that if you were displeased with the flavor by the time you got it to that point of emptiness, Watkins would refund your money. Watkins still makes great vanilla, but they no longer adhere to their trial mark guarantee.

Morton Kolleeny's intrusion into my mother's Mexican kitchen was a mixed blessing. To be sure, it lent greater variety to her cooking, but her thrown-together meals were not only tastier than those with artificial flavors and ready-made mixes, they seemed to emanate from her hands in the same way my grandmother's meals and her grandmother's before hers did. Time spent in my mother's kitchen instilled in me a love for cooking. When I miss my mother most, I cook *huevos con tortillitas*. A fresh *azadero* melted between two fresh tortillas with a little *aguacate* on the side is a feast for my palate as well as my memory. I share meals, both simple and elaborate, with friends and strangers in my house, just as my mother did in our kitchen between the waters of the Rio Grande. ★

Gloria López-Stafford

Gloria López-Stafford was born and raised in El Paso and graduated from Austin High School. She received her B.A. from the University of Texas at El Paso and an M.S.W. from LSU Baton Rouge. López-Stafford began her teaching career in the remedial reading program in the El Paso Independent School District and was the head of a team of social workers in the Gadsden School District in New Mexico. She was a visiting professor in the department of social work at Texas Tech University in Lubbock and served as a special education teacher in the autistic unit of the El Paso Independent School District. Her book *A Place in El Paso* has been widely anthologized and adopted for university courses. An important memoir of growing up in El Paso during the 1940s and 1950s, *A Place in El Paso* is in its third printing.

From *A Place in El Paso: A Mexican American Childhood*: The Trouble with English

In the Segundo Barrio during the 1940s, people spoke Spanish. They spoke the Spanish they brought with them from their *ranchos*, villages, and cities. They also brought the music of their accents. You could tell by the quality of their speech whether they were country or city people. Spanish in the 1940s in south El Paso was formal and polite. People apologized if they said a word like *estúpido*. I would often wonder why that required an apology. And I would be told that people from rural areas are not open with criticism and do not want to offend with what they consider vulgar language.

When people left the barrio, they began using English more. You still spoke Spanish at home because that was what your family used. Then when you spoke with someone who also spoke both languages, the language evolved to a mixture of English and Spanish that became an art form. Sometimes sentences might be in one language with certain words in the other. Other times whole paragraphs might be in one language and only a few sentences in the other.

It was a living language, a musical score that conveyed the optimal sense, meaning, and feeling from both languages that a single language might not achieve. The combination drew criticism from purists and people who did not speak both. They accused the bilingual person of being lazy or undisciplined. But I think it was a love for both languages that made it impossible to be faithful to just one. On the other hand, cussing or profanity were best in English. The words were just words to me. Cussing in Spanish was painful and created emotions that led to guilt. And, it was unacceptable to our parents and priests.

The first time I remember having problems with English was the year before Carmen came to live with us. At least once a week Palm and I would have a talk about why I wasn't learning English. I saw no reason to. I had to experience a need for it, and that is what happened.

"You have to learn English, Gloria," Palm would say.

"I don't want to. I don't have to. I don't need it," I would stubbornly refuse.

"I suppose you didn't need it at the border on Saturday when immigration held you after you were in Juárez with López and you couldn't answer their questions?" he said firmly. "I had to leave the store to go and get them to release you. All because you can't carry on a conversation in English."

I had created problems for Palm and myself, but I didn't want to learn English and that was that.

On this particular morning, I waited for Palm to get tired of the topic and to move on to something else. But he didn't. He continued.

"The note the teacher sent home says that you will not speak English. She says that everyone speaks for you. And she says that you talk all the time, but in Spanish! It's been a month since school started and she says you will not cooperate. She says she is going to have to punish you. She wrote to inform me that she is at the end of her patience with you," Palm said.

"So that is what the *mugre*, dirty, note said. I thought she liked me," I said as I thought of how she and I grinned at each other every day. I didn't understand what she was saying and she didn't know what I was saying. She could have been speaking Chinese just like the Chinos near the Cuauhtémoc market in Juárez. I just didn't want to speak English.

"It sounds ugly. And I look stupid speaking it," I admitted when I saw the look on Palm's face.

"It's because you don't use it enough to get used to it," Palm tried to explain.

"My friends and I don't need to speak it. We have our own way of speaking." I continued the argument until I noticed that Palm was frustrated and quiet. I decided to play. I put my left hand on my hip and shook my right index finger menacingly.

"Wo do bo to do ri ra do fo, da mo, meeester!" I said in gibberish. "Ha, no, meezter?" I raised my eyebrow and looked at Palm. "That's English!"

"*Payasa*. You are very stubborn. You need to learn English." Palm started up again. "My son is coming to visit and he speaks English."

The last remark caught my attention. I turned my eyes to the picture of Palm's son, which was displayed in a large oval frame. He resembled Palm. I wondered why he was only my half brother. When I was younger, I thought it was because only the upper part of his body was in the picture. Palm corrected me. He told me his son had a different mother and was the only one of his children who stayed in touch with him. He loved Palm very much and would write to him every week. He was the youngest child and had been in college when my father went to Mexico. Palm's son's light eyes seemed to follow me around the room.

Palm was still talking about a visit from his son when I found my voice and said. "¡*Que suave*! When he comes, I'll tell him all about me and the neighborhood." Palm just nodded his head and gave me a strange look.

The next week, when I got home from school, I was frightened because I thought someone was in the apartment. But Palm called to me when I pressed my nose against the screen to look inside.

"*Entra, mi'ja*." Palm's voice was happy. I pulled the screen door open and entered the living room. A man was with my father. He looked like my father but he wasn't old; he looked familiar. Then, suddenly, my eyes turned to the picture on the wall. I looked at the man and I looked at the picture. They were the same!

"¡*Hola*! ¿*Cómo estás*?" I yelled with happiness as I ran to hug the stranger. He returned the hug. I was overjoyed. Palm was telling the truth about his son coming to visit. Here he was . . . all of him!

Palm's son opened his mouth and said something to Palm who was telling him something too. They were speaking Chinese!

"Apá, tell him that I speak Spanish," I told my father.

"Yoya, he knows." Palm spoke slowly because he knew how I would react. "He doesn't speak Spanish. He only speaks English. I told you many times."

I was speechless. What a dirty *trampa*, trick!

"Didn't you tell him I didn't speak English? Did you forget?" I questioned my Palm as the other Palm looked on with the biggest and sweetest smile. How could he not speak Spanish? I started to cry, but the other Palm understood as my father told him in Chinese what the problem was. Palm's son laughed as he picked me up and kissed me as he said something to my father. I looked to Palm for a translation.

"He says you're as precious as he knew you would be. He's sorry that he can't speak Spanish. He has never been able to learn," my father said.

I hugged his son and just watched them as they talked. Occasionally, Palm would tell me what they were saying if he thought it might interest me. I just kept looking into our visitor's beautiful face. My little chest was heavy with the weight of my broken heart. I had so wanted to be able to talk with him. I couldn't believe it. And I knew Palm had warned me.

When the sunset, the color of a West Texas sweet potato flesh, began to spread across the barrio, our visitor said he had to leave. We went outside. Palm's son picked me up and kissed me. Palm softly told me what his son was saying to me.

"He says he loves you, Yoya. He hopes that when you meet again, either you'll know English or he'll know Spanish."

I hugged and kissed my favorite visitor back. It would be many years before I would see him again and it would be long after our father's death. But on this evening, my father and I watched him as he walked to Virginia Street where he had parked his car. Palm and I sat on the cement step. As the car pulled off with my half brother, I turned to Palm and said with determination and sadness,

"It's time I learned English, Papí."

"*Sí, corazón*, yes." He understood.

***

English continued to be a problem for me for the next few years. In September of 1945, after Carmen came to live with us, my friends helped me with a clever solution.

The morning glories in the widow's garden were the true sign that September was here. The little blue-purple flowers were spreading and growing anywhere they could. The roses were also in bloom, which indicated that it was not a hot September in El Paso. The nights were cool and the windows of the two-story apartments were open all day. School started and my English was not as good as it had been when school let out in May. During the summer, I lost some English vocabulary because I didn't use it. I had only been back in school two weeks and the teacher and I had already gone around and around about my speaking Spanish.

"English is spoken in school . . . even when you are speaking to your friends, young lady!" the teacher snapped when she eavesdropped on a conversation I was having in the closet of our classroom. I had just commented to Raquel that I wished I could get a new coat this winter just like the one she had last year. The teacher appeared from nowhere and caught us speaking Spanish. So, Raquel and I had to each stand in a corner of that stupid closet during recess. You may as well have put me in front of a firing squad because it hurt just as much to miss recess. "*Dísparen*, fire!" said the teacher *commendante*, in my fantasy. "Only English is spoken in school, in El Paso, in Texas and in America, *entiendes*, do you understand?"

My pledge of allegiance had already earned me a note home to my father. In the note, Palm was informed that my version of the pledge was a mockery. How was it possible that he could not teach me such a small task? Would he or his wife please teach me the pledge? The note said, "Gloria enjoys the laughter and disruption she causes each morning." Palm smiled when he read the part about Carmen teaching me the pledge.

"Gloria, let me hear the pledge." He wanted to hear for himself what the problem was. Palm listened with interest and smiled a couple of times. When I was finished he put on a serious face and talked to me about my presentation.

"You mix the words around . . . you move the words in your pledge." Then seeing the puzzled look on my face, he said, "You take a word out and put the wrong one in its place." He struggled to explain. "You don't know what you are saying. Didn't the teacher explain?"

"I guess that she did . . . but I didn't understand her Chinese." I replied, trying to be clever. "You explain it to me."

"Stop clowning! And stop calling English Chinese. You're not funny anymore," he said, annoyed. It took a long time but he tried to explain what each of the words meant and in what order they went. But each time I tried to say the pledge I would make new revisions. I couldn't get it right.

"I will give you a *tostón*, a walking Liberty fifty cent piece, if you learn it by your birthday. That gives you a week. Practice saying it with your friends and you will get the fifty-cent piece." He knew that I loved the walking lady silver coin because I loved what it could buy. That would encourage me to learn the pledge. For that much money, I agreed immediately. I started thinking of how I would spend the money. My dreams were full of fifty-cent pieces that night: beautiful silver ladies dancing with silver stars all around.

The next day, I met the boys at the jalopy. I told them what the teacher had done and what Palm had promised me if I learned the pledge. They were impressed with the money. We quickly made plans on how to spend it. It could easily buy us all *raspadas*, ice cones, and some gum. Or it could pay for all of us to go to the movies on the Saturday after my birthday. It was endless, what we could do with fifty cents.

Then my brother Carlos, who was the oldest and a fourth grader, reminded me that I had to recite the pledge correctly in order to get the money. We all agreed that it was a problem since I didn't understand the words. So each of them proceeded to recite the pledge slowly and carefully, right in my face. They put a great deal of acting into the words. Still I didn't say it correctly any of the times I tried.

"I guess you want to put me in front of the firing squad just like the teacher would like to," I said, explaining my fantasy to them. They liked the idea and said why didn't we take time to play the scene. They would shoot me down if I didn't learn the words.

Carlos and I went home to get broomsticks and hats. Flaco was to get a handkerchief to put across my eyes. Pelón was to bring back his cowboy holster for Carlos, the *commendante*. We agreed to meet after lunch. I hoped that Carmen had something for us to eat because all the pledging had made me hungry.

After lunch we gathered at the jalopy. Carlos was in charge. The other boys were the soldiers who helped me learn and they were also the members of the firing squad. It was agreed that we would break the pledge into parts. As soon as I learned a part, we would move on to the next part. They were very relieved when they discovered that I had no problem with the first part. "I pledge allegiance . . . ," I began well. "To the republic . . ."

"No . . . No! To the flag . . . the *bandera*, Yoya!" Flaco would yell. "*A la pared, to the wall.*" We walked over to the jalopy. I stood in front of it. Prieto put the handkerchief around my eyes and said a prayer for me with his head bowed.

"That is not necessary!" barked Carlos as he yelled for the men to ready themselves. "Shoot! *A toda ametralladora*, like a machine gun."

"We only have rifles, Commander," Flaco yelled sharply.

The rest of the afternoon went like that. Each time I made a mistake, I faced the firing squad. It was a lot of fun. By the time the sky started to turn the color of a Sinaloa mango, I had thoroughly exhausted the group. I didn't want to play any more. Let Palm keep his *tostón*. But the boys said we would try again the next day. Carlos would think about the problem.

"Palm said you have to learn it by your birthday?" asked Flaco. "When is that?"

"In a week, I think," I answered. "It's September the 12th. Pretty soon, no?" Carlos nodded yes.

"Are you having a party?" asked Prieto.

"I have never had a party. Not that I know of," I said.

"Don't you want one? A party with a piñata," Carlos added. "We can ask Palm."

"Yes, but I don't think I am going to have one," I said sadly. "It would be nice. Don't people bring gifts?"

"Yes, let's plan a party. We'll make invitations and take them to the neighbors," Flaco said excited by the idea. "Palm will have to give you a party!"

"Yes, *cómo que no*? He got a new wife and a new car. He can give me a party," I said bravely. "And we'll tell everyone to bring a present. No gift . . . don't come!"

The next day we met at the jalopy. No one could find any paper to make the invitations, so we simply went to all the neighbors' houses and invited them in person. Flaco was in charge of telling them to bring a present. I felt it might be *falta de educación*, lacking manners, for me to say it. Then we agreed that I had to tell Palm that evening. I became a little uncomfortable with that idea. But who cares, that's how he told me he had a new wife and a new car.

We got back to the problem of the pledge. Once again, we set up our scene. Carlos encouraged me with whispers and yelled at me when I missed. The rest of them loved it when they had to execute me.

"Young lady, that is not right!" Carlos would imitate his teacher. "Now, say it after me. Indivisible is what you should say, not invisible. Invisible means you can't see it, Yoya!" Then he gave up. "Let me explain it to you in Spanish, but you must say it in English. Spanish will not be right." Soon, we stopped the play and talked about the party until I saw Palm coming home. Carlos and I turned to meet him.

"Tomorrow we'll sing the pledge . . . for sure you'll learn it then," said Pelón. He was inspired by the idea as he went off singing the pledge to play with Flaco in his apartment.

After dinner, Palm and I were sitting in the living room while Carmen was cleaning up the dishes. Palm took out a pack of cigarettes that he had bought at the store. Carmen didn't like the smell of the ones we made so he bought Lucky Strikes just to please her. They were so fat and smooth, unlike our homemade ones. And she didn't let him fix his one drink anymore. He didn't complain. She certainly had changed things.

Palm asked me how my pledge was coming along. I told him about the game the boys and I had made of it. He smiled as he always did when I would tell him about our plays. He explained the word indivisible with the box of cigarettes he had just opened. And he explained the word invisible by telling me it was like the ghosts I saw that no one else saw. I softly hit his arm for saying that, but I finally understood. When he asked me to recite the pledge to see if I had learned it, I refused. I told him that I wanted to surprise him on my birthday. And speaking of my birthday, the boys and I thought it would be nice if I had a party. We invited the neighbors today. What did he think?

"A party, Yoya! Whose idea was that?" He muttered some nasty words under his breath. "I don't have the money for a party. Where am I going to get the money?"

"You had the money for the car. All we need to have is a piñata, candy for the pinãta, a cake and some Velvet ice cream. The big people will want some *cerveza*. I will ask López to bring some from Juárez. Everyone will be happy. Especially me." I tried to solve the problem. When Palm didn't answer, I continued to give him ideas as to where to get the things for the party. "The cake can be bought at that bakery at the corner from you. Lopez can bring the piñata from Juárez."

The poor man couldn't answer. Then Carmen came into the living room. She saw how Palm looked and asked what was the matter. I didn't really want to tell her, but I didn't know what to do about my father's long face. So I told her about the party. She started laughing, something I had never seen her do before. It made her seem real. She told Palm what a clever child I was. She said that she had always felt bad because she didn't have a party when she was eight. Her family and some friends in Juárez could bring the cake. Carmen's excitement lifted my father's spirits. I was grateful to her for that, but at the same time I was surprised. He laughed. After a while, he said that since I had already told the neighbors and since Carmen was so happy to give the party, that it would be all right. He just didn't like parties that he couldn't afford.

"Your birthday is in a week, but we can't have it then because it is a Wednesday. We'll have to wait until Saturday September 15. That is also the night before Mexican Independence. You remember how many people were in the neighborhood last year?" he groaned. "Now for sure I know I can't afford it."

I started thinking about the year before. The terrible thing that happened to Luisito in Juárez. I hadn't thought about it in months. It seemed like it was so long ago that we went to sit with his family. I wondered if Señora Olga would join us in the backyard. It was ten days until my first birthday party. It seemed like a long time.

The next day at the jalopy, the boys and I tried singing the pledge and making each of the boys represent one of the words that I couldn't get. Pelón had a small flag that his rich cousin had given him when he went to visit him on the 4th of July. The boys formed a line that represented the flag, republic, nation, liberty and justice. The flag was in Pelón's hand and he was also the republic. Flaco was one nation and indivisible. Prieto was liberty and justice. Pelón was the first, then Flaco and then Prieto. All I had to remember was the order of the boys by their age. Carlos, the commander, was in charge and the one who thought of the idea. By the second time, I could say it without any mistakes. I jumped around and fought an invisible boxer just like the Brown Bomber did. Then we started planning how we would spend the money.

On Sunday, the widow came over and talked to Palm. She told him that Eduardo was coming home next week and that the rest of the neighbors wanted to help with my party and get together with the boys home from the war. She said the whole neighborhood wanted to do the midnight cry that begins Mexican Independence. Everyone was going to pitch in with the grownup part of the party after Yoya and the children had their piñata. Palm was relieved and thanked her for her help.

I was so excited for the next couple of days. The teacher was happy that I could recite the pledge and had stopped clowning around. On my birthday that Wednesday, I said the pledge for Palm and he was proud of me. He gave me the fifty-cent piece. I also said it for López, who did not speak English. He kissed me and said that I looked pretty saying it. Because I wanted Carmen to make me a good party, I was on my best behavior. Friday afternoon, the boys and I bought *raspadas* and gum with my money. On Friday night, I went to sleep wondering if Señora Olga and Señora Alma would be at the party. The two women detested the war; no medals made up for their losses. Only the widow's son came back without any wounds. ★

Selfa Chew

Selfa Chew is a poet, playwright, translator, graphic artist, cultural promoter and teacher, who was born in Mexico City and raised in the El Paso/Ciudad Juárez area. She holds an M.F.A. in creative writing and M.A. in borderlands history from the University of Texas at El Paso, where she taught history and Spanish American literature. An editor for the literary review *BorderSenses*, Chew also coordinates the Mexican Contemporary Literature Conference held annually in El Paso. In 2004, Selfa Chew was awarded a fellowship by the Smithsonian Institute for the Interpretation and Representation of Latino Cultures. Her work has been published in Peru, Spain, Argentina, Mexico, Holland, and the United States in various journals including *Rio Grande Review*; *Upstreet*; *Versal*; *Bilingual Review*; and *Common Ground Review*. Her books include *Azogue en la Raiz* and *Mudas las Garzas*. Currently, Chew is a visiting instructor in the department of global studies at Saint Lawrence University, New York. The English translation of "Chio Sam" is by Noli Chew.

Chio Sam

Dice mi madre que no es posible
que yo recuerde el olor a pan
ni el bambú sosteniendo el vapor que se escapaba
de la cocina de mi abuelo.
No es posible que recuerde su canto en cantonés

en su mirada delgada y orgullosa
en su bastón y sus zapatos quietos.
Veo todavía el olor a cigarro y sus dientes amarillos
la vitrina, el nombre rojo del lugar
en que mi abuelo cocinaba
y los trajes, los immóviles sombreros

contemplando el pan blanco
almohada tenue que envolvía
el sabor definitivo del almuerzo.
Veo la penumbra y sus palabras cortas
como las galletas adivinas
que ahora dan en restaurantes chinos
y que mi abuelo no supo ganarían algunos clientes

y una expectativa más
de lo que debemos ser o dar los orientales.
Crecerás
Construirás murallas
olvidarás la marcha detenida
en el café de mesas rojas
y la cascada de cubiertos a lavar
interminable detergente al fondo
el vapor del pan blanco
suave
tibio.
Pero mi madre dice es imposible
quc yo cntendiera los avisos del abuelo:
yo no hablaba aún y él
sólo cantaba cantonés. ★

Chio Sam

My mother says that is not possible
that I remember the smell of the bread
nor the bamboo sustaining the steam that was escaping
from my grandfather's kitchen.
She says that it is not possible that I remember his song in
Cantonese
his slip and proud glance

his cane and quiet shoes
I still see the smell of his cigarettes and his yellow teeth
the display cabinet, the red letters of the place
where my grandfather used to cook
and the suits, the unshaken hats
gazing at the white bread
delicate pillow enveloping
the familiar breakfast flavor.
I see the penumbra and its short words
like those in fortune cookies
that nowadays are given in Chinese restaurants
and my grandfather did not know they would bring some
clients
and one more expectation
of what we, the Orientals, should be or give.
You shall grow
you shall build great walls
you will forget the long march nested
in the coffee shop of red tables
and the cascade of chinaware to be washed
endless detergent in the backroom
the steam of white bread
soft
warm.
But my mother says that it is impossible
that I could understand my grandfather's warning:
I did not speak then
and he only sang Cantonese. ★

Part Three

This Favored Place

Este lugar favorecido

"What I've tried to do as a painter is to express,
when it comes down to it, the great privilege of
living in such a majestic and mysterious
world made by the Almighty.

We have the privilege of living in this life in
this marvelous place. And writing and painting to me
don't have anything to do with who I am and what I do,
but with what is so wonderful about what's out there."

~Tom Lea, interview with Adair Margo

José Antonio Burciaga

José Antonio Burciaga (1940-1996) was born in El Paso and attended the University of Texas at El Paso and the San Francisco Art Institute. He began his career as a graphic illustrator in Mineral Wells, Texas, and later worked in Washington, D.C. Under the pen name El Indio Hispanic, Burciaga was the creator of cultural and political cartoons, many of which were published in magazines across the United States and were syndicated through *Hispanic Link*. Burciaga was also a founding member of the comedy troupe Culture Clash and was a talented and accomplished muralist. The critically acclaimed mural "the Last Supper of Chicano Heroes," featuring images of César Chávez, Che Guevara, Sor Juana Inés de la Cruz, Frida Kahlo, Robert Kennedy, and Martin Luther King, Jr. is located at the Casa Zapata at Stanford University. In addition to his work as an illustrator, Burciaga produced a large body of writing. His many books include *Restless Serpents; Weedee Peepo; In Few Words; Spilling the Beans; Drink Cultura: Chicanismo;* and *Undocumented Love*, which won the American Book Award from the Before Columbus Foundation. Burciaga received the 1995 Hispanic Heritage Award for Literature, a 1989 Short Story Fellowship, and Honorable Mention for Journalism from the World Affairs Council, San Francisco. Burciaga's articles were published in *The Los Angeles Times, Texas Monthly, Vista*, and *Hispanic Magazine*. Long considered one of the most important voices of the Chicano/a Movement of the 1960s and 1970s, Burciaga is an integral contributor to the Chicano/a literary canon. He is widely anthologized and was most recently the subject of the 2008 book *The Last Supper of Chicano Heroes*, edited by Daniel Chacón and Mimi R. Gladstein.

"Like a flower, we also don't last long in this desert called life"
—José Antonio Burciaga

From *Drink Cultura: Chicanismo*: Memories of a Juarez Nightlife

SOME NEWS TRAVELS SLOW. ON SUNDAY, November 27, 1988, Ciudad Juarez, Chihuahua, Mexico, began closing its bars as early as 11 P.M. It seem incredible to those of us who knew the wide-open town near the Rio Bravo, across from El Paso, Texas.

For millions of G.I.s who served at Fort Bliss and other military installations around the Southwest during World War II, the Korean War, the Vietnam War or peacetime, Juarez was their first introduction to a foreign country, to drinking, brothels and fiesta time.

Adolescent adventures abound in a Mexican-American grafitti style of life on the border. At the tender age of sixteen, young El Pasoans could discover Juarez, the wildest town south of Las Vegas. The shock of discovering a brothel and porn flicks was a bad dream for the innocent. High school football games and proms often ended in trips to Juarez, where puberty, a fake ID card and money would get you into any bar.

Naively, we bought cheap, cherry-flavored alcohol and snuck it past the U.S. customs officers at the bridge. As we grew older our tastes became more sophisticated, but we continued to smuggle the liquor in lowered 1950 Chevys and Fords. Today it would be extremely unadvisable to smuggle or taunt the customs officials like we used to.

Tijuana may have been more famous because of its proximity to Hollywood but Juarez was unique because of its desert mountains, international trolleys, quickie divorces and Pancho Villa's historic struggle with General John J. Pershing. Juarez's strip was born as a result of prohibition. To drink, Texans had only to cross the bridge. Even after prohibition, the state remained dry. Except for private clubs, only beer and wine was sold in El Paso bars.

Forget Gay Paree! Avenida Juarez was the Champs Élysées complete with its own "Follies" and *El Lobby*, where the meanest dancers boogied through the '40s, rhythm-and-blued in the '50s and rocked through the '60s and '70s to "made in the USA" bands.

A block down from El Lobby was Carlos' Bar, a.k.a. The Mex-Tex, where the best *mariachis* played sad *corridos*, ballads, wild polkas or classic symphony pieces. Some argued that the mariachis at the San Luis Bar down the street were much better. They had a mariachi singer with such a great voice that opera lovers came to hear him sing corridos—until a group of civic-minded El Paso women sponsored his study of opera and he was never heard from in Juarez again.

During the wild and crazy '50s, people spilled from the sidewalks along the Avenida Juarez drinking from bottles of José Cuervo or Bacardi, meeting strangers as friends, long-forgotten amigos, single women and exchanging toasts. New Year's and football victories were celebrated in the streets. Juarez was Mardi Gras everyday of the year.

It was in the '50s that Juarez achieved international acclaim for its "quickie" divorce laws. The internationally rich and famous, from Elizabeth Taylor to Marilyn Monroe, had only to take a quick trip to El Paso to shed so many pounds of ugly husbands and thousands of dollars in a matter of minutes. The end of quickie divorces came on October 10, 1970, as Mexico sought a better image. Right up to that date, men swarmed the hotels and bars looking for women celebrating their new-found freedom.

In the New Yorker Bar with its 1920s Mexican tiled decor, I was arrested and jailed for having punched a young drunk who had insulted me. My supposed friends went to bail me out only to run across some girls and forget about me. In jail, I ran across an uncle, who was serving time for shooting and killing two ex-mayors of Juarez at the Mint Bar, a few feet from the International Santa Fe Bridge. After being wounded and lying on his back, Mexico's champion target shooter had pulled out his 45. caliber with his left hand and shot them dead in self-defense. He then tried a run to the bridge but was captured halfway across. He was brought back to trial and a seven-year sentence while the *pueblo*, the people, turned him into a hero with ballads, poems and essays. Through their power, wealth, and arrogance, the two ex-mayors had abused and robbed across the state of Chihuahua for years.

Crossing the International Santa Fe Bridge back to El Paso was a ritualistic process. First you paid the toll of three pennies, then you passed on to a U.S. Customs officer who first asked for declaration of citizenship and then what kinds of products you were bringing into the country. Fruits, plants and meats were strictly forbidden. Delicious Mexican avocados could be passed if the big seed was taken out.

My father recalled those days when the bridge was wooden and the banks were lined with old Alamo trees from which Pancho Villa hung many men. Even earlier, my grandmother recalled the boats, the rafts, and the floods. In those days before the turn of the century the river was untamed and wild. My aunt, *tía* Elena inherited valuable Mexican property on land that had shifted to the U.S. side when the river had changed course. She gave up hope of ever receiving compensation for her property and so she threw away her property title—only to live through the day when the U.S. Government agreed to settle the Chamizal land dispute with Mexico and compensated those who had lost their lands.

I still recall the river banks lined with trees and wild shrubs. But they obstructed the *Migra's* vigilante ways and so the river was defoliated. In the '50s, Mexican boys poised themselves below the bridge on the river bed, with long poles in their hands, At the top end of the poles were cardboard cones to catch coins pitched by *turistas*. Hundreds of pennies, nickels, dimes and dreams were lost in the muddy current.

In Juarez, bars that never closed encouraged drinking marathons. Some started on Friday night in El Paso, closing up El Paso at midnight, driving a few miles into New Mexico where they closed at two, then on to Juarez, where the bars never closed. Then it was back to open up El Paso's bars, close them, close New Mexico and return to Juarez. The marathon's grand finale would take place Sunday afternoon at the Monumental Bull Ring in Juarez, sitting on the cheap, sunny side with a pail of Cruz Blanca beer. Then it was back to El Paso only to pass out under some freeway bridge.

Behind the bright lights district in dark streets and alleys were the *Maestro* Bars where Mexican blue collar workers relaxed. Once in a while Tarahumara Indians would venture into a bar only to be refused service. From bar to bar, a boy escorted his blind father who played the guitar, sang and collected pesos and quarters for haunting melodies of love gone sour. Old women selling flowers, dancing dogs and men with electric shock boxes made their way from bar to bar. These electric shock boxes had two cables that ended with two steel rods to be held in each hand. An electric current would then be turned on and increased until the rods were dropped.

There was the famous Tommy's Bar where my uncle, Francisco Morales invented the most popular drink of all time, the Margarita. There was the Manhattan Bar, with its thousand-drink repertoire and a seven piece marimba band.

Curley's Bar began as a high-class soft music lounge. Then Curley's changed owners and it was named the Noa Noa where young Mexican bands came to imitate the best rock hits in mimicked English. The Noa Noa was made famous by Mexican composer and singer Juan Gabriel, born in Juarez and influenced by El Paso radio pop music.

Some El Paso high schools claimed their own bar. Such was Fred's Rainbow Bar, where El Paso High and Cathedral High schoolers hung out. There we drank sweet mixed drinks or cheap Corona and Cruz Blanca beer along with the delicious Mexican sandwiches we called "cancer sandwiches" because eating Avenida Juarez street food was not advisable.

The Submarine, the Caverns and so many other bars all had first-rate bartenders who personally catered to their clients and became friends, confidants and counselors: "Stay in school, go to college." The sidewalks were lined with hundreds of *curio* stores and stalls selling everything from beautiful silver and gold jewelry to black velvet paintings and "horse shit" cigarettes. Shoeshines went for a dime, while artists and pre-Polaroid photographers stalked vain customers who took their photographs and then ran to develop the photos that would soon turn a sepia color. Cheating husbands and wives kept their distance from popular hangouts and photographers.

Cabdrivers forever wanted to take you to Irma's or Cherry Hill, mansions of ill repute with pseudo-Greek plaster of paris imitations of Corinthian columns and Venus sculptures.

Once, a friend we called Baby was robbed by a cabdriver in Juarez. The next night, Baby had a friend hire the same cabdriver to bring him back to El Paso. Once in El Paso, Baby jumped into the cab and at gunpoint forced the driver to a deserted mountain road overlooking the bright lights of both cities. There he was left naked and his cab keys thrown into a brush-filled arroyo,

Because of Juarez, El Paso was a natural convention city for everyone from LULAC, the League of United Latin American Citizens, and the GI Forum to firemen, barber shop quartets, Sun Bowl football teams, fans and the ever faithful turistas.

But that was long ago. The death of Juarez nightlife began with the end of quickie divorces in 1970.

Meanwhile, El Paso, like the rest of Texas, was as dry as a bone in the desert, although bars could serve beer and wine. Then private clubs began serving liquor by the drink and they proliferated. The drought was officially drenched with the passage of a liquor-by-the-drink Texas Law in 1969.

The nightlife in Juarez had already begun to change. Few El Pasoans crossed over for fear of Mexican police and their *mordidas*—bribes—or the bridge delays and closings that ran anywhere from one hour to several days depending on the time of day, season, U.S. customs searches and Mexico's political climate.

The statewide order to close bars early came from Chihuahua Governor Fernando Baeza as a crime prevention measure. The cost of crime was more than the income from the night life industry. *Maquiladoras*, U.S. assembly plants, have replaced the Juarez night establishments as its main industry. But I'll always have memories of when we helped build that nightlife industry. ★

From *Drink Cultura: Chicanismo*: A Mixed Mex-Cal Marriage

According to Cecilia, my wife, we have a mixed marriage. She's from California, I'm from Texas. Though we have no regrets, this truly proves that love is blind.

When Cecilia and I first met, we thought we had a lot in common. As young, professional Chicanos in Washington, D.C., we both supported the United Farm Workers' grape and lettuce boycotts, the Coors boycott, the Gallo Wine boycott, the Farah Pants boycott, and the Frito Bandido boycott. We still boycott some of those items, for many reasons: health, habit, nostalgia or plain, ordinary guilt if we indulged in any of these.

As first generation Mexican-Americans, we both spoke *Español*, graduated from Catholic schools and had similar politics.

But, as we were soon to discover, the vast desert that separates Texas and California also differentiates the culture and style of Chicanos. Because we met far from Texas and California, we had no idea at first at the severity of our differences.

We both liked enchiladas—the same enchiladas, I thought, until the first time Cecilia prepared them. They looked like enchiladas, and they smelled like enchiladas. And then I bit into one.

"These are good, *corazón*," I said. "But these are *entomatadas*. They have more tomato than chile. *Mí Mamá* used to make them all the time."

She threw me a piquant stare as I chewed away. "Hmmm, they're great!" I stressed through a mouthful.

Californians, like her parents who immigrated from the coastal state of Jalisco, Mexico, use more tomatoes than Texans like my parents, who came from the central states of Durango and Zacatecas and use more chiles.

Cecilia grew up with white *menudo*, tripe soup. White menudo? How could anyone eat colorless menudo? And not put hominy in it? Ours was red-hot and loaded with hominy. In Texas, we ate our menudo with bread. In California, it's with tortillas. Texas flour tortillas are thick and tasty, California flour tortillas are so thin you can see through them.

She didn't particularly like my Tony Lama boots or my country-western and Tex-Mex musical taste. I wasn't that crazy about Beach Boy music or her progressive, California-style country-western.

In California, the beach was relatively close for Cecilia. On our first date she asked how often I went to the beach from El Paso. Apparently, geography has never been a hot subject in California schools. That's understandable considering the sad state of education, especially geography, in this country. But in Texas, at one time the biggest state in the union, sizes and distances are most important.

In answer to Cecilia's question, I explained that to get to the closest beach from El Paso, I had to cross New Mexico, Arizona and California to reach San Diego. That's 791 freeway miles. The closest Texas beach is 841 freeway miles to the Gulf of Mexico.

Back when we were courting, California Chicanos saw *Texanos* as a little too *Mexicano*, still wet behind the ears, not assimilated enough, and speaking with either thick Spanish accents or "Taxes acksaints."

Generally speaking, Texanos saw their *Califas* counterparts as too weird, knowing too little if any Spanish and with speech that was too Anglicized.

After our marriage we settled in neutral Alexandria, Virginia, right across the Potomac from the nation's capital. We lived there a couple of years, and when our firstborn came, we decided to settle closer to home. But which home, Califas or Texas? In El Paso we wouldn't be close to the beach, but I thought there was an ocean of opportunity in that desert town. There was some Texas pride and machismo, to be sure. It was a tug-of-war that escalated to the point of seeking advice, and eventually I had to be realistic and agree that California had better opportunities. In EPT, the opportunities in my field were nonexistent.

The rest is relative bliss. Married since 1972, I'm totally spoiled and laid-back in Northern Califas, but I still miss many of those things we took for granted in Texas, or Washington, D.C.—the seasonal changes, the snow, the heat, heating systems, autumn colors and monsoon rains; the smell of the desert after a rain, the silence and serenity of the desert, the magnified sounds of a fly or cricket, distant horizons uncluttered by trees, and the ability to find the four directions without any problem. I do miss the desert and, even more, the food. El Paso *is* the Mexican-food capital of this country.

Today, I like artichokes and appreciate a wide variety of vegetables and fruits. I even like white, colorless menudo and hardly ever drink beer. I drink wine, but it has to be a dry Chardonnay or Fume Blanc although a Pinot Noir or Cabernet Sauvignon goes great with meals. Although I still yearn for an ice cold Perla or Lone Star beer from Texas once in a while, Califas is my home now—mixed marriage and all. ★

Benjamin Alire Sáenz

Benjamin Alire Sáenz was born in the small farming village of Old Picacho outside of Las Cruces, New Mexico. He received a B.A. in humanities and philosophy from St. Thomas Seminary in Denver, Colorado, and an M.A. in theology at the University of Louvain in Louvain, Belgium. He earned an M.A. degree in creative writing from the University of Texas at El Paso and continued his studies at the University of Iowa on a fellowship. While at Iowa, he was awarded a Wallace E. Stegner fellowship in poetry from Stanford University, where he continued his coursework toward his Ph.D. in English and American literature. During his time at Stanford, Sáenz completed his first book of poetry, *Calendar of Dust*, which won the 1992 American Book Award. Sáenz returned to the border and began teaching in the bilingual M.F.A. program at the University of Texas at El Paso. He is the author of the critically acclaimed novels *Carry Me Like Water*, which was translated into Dutch and German; *The House of Forgetting*, translated into French and German; *In Perfect Light*; and *Names on a Map*. Sáenz is also the author of the poetry collections *Dark and Perfect Angels*; *Elegies in Blue*; and *Dreaming the End of War*. The young adult novel *Sammy and Juliana in Hollywood* won the Americas Book award, the Patterson Book Prize, the J. Hunt Award, was named one of the top ten books of the year in 2004 by the American Library Association, and was a finalist for the *Los Angeles Times* Book Prize of 2005 for the Best Book for Young Adults. *He Forgot to Say Goodbye* is another of Sáenz's young adult titles. He is also the author of three bilingual children's books, *A Gift from Papa Diego*; *A Perfect Season for Dreaming*; and *Grandma Fina and Her Wonderful Umbrellas*, recipient of the Texas Institute of Letters award for the best children's book of 1999. He is the recipient of a Lannan Poetry Fellowship and is currently a professor in English and creative writing at the University of Texas at El Paso.

From *Elegies in Blue: Poems*: Elegy for Burciaga

(Written in an undocumented language)

O YES, BURCIAGA, FIJATE QUE I WAS LISTENING to 93.9 "Caliente" and I thought of you. Porque las voces en ese radio station comienzan a decir algo en español and all of a sudden they're speaking in English and, hombre, que te cuento, dicen unas cosas that would drive any monolingual person to question the meaning of language. Tanto a los Gringos como a esos Mexicanos orgullosos que también nos odian because we're such pochos and have no real appreciation for the structure, beauty and grammatical nuances of the Spanish language. Nos tiran unas miradas como fueran balasos. So nice to be hated by both sides. Bueno, la Chicanada's used to this.

¿Y sabes qué? We may need papers to cross the river, but la cosa es que we don't need papers to talk. And that's a good thing, because if we needed papers to talk, the Migra would never give us those papers and the barrio would be as quiet as a twelfth century monastery which the gringos and the Republicans would like, because even though they love our food, chiles rellenos, enchiladas, arroz con pollo, they're not so sure about the people who make it. It's funny ¿verdad? They like to name streets in Spanish, "Vista del Sol" y "Calle de Sueños" y que sé yo—no the moral is, it's okay to have a Mexican surname if you're a street. But if you're a person, bueno, maybe that's not so okay. Pero, tu ya sabes estas cosas and you're resting now. You've earned your rest, I know. You were so tired before you left us. And I hate to bother you. Pero, hermano, your door was always open. And you and Cecilia, you were always muy listos para recibir a cualquiera que les caía alli en Casa Zapata. And I don't forget. Bueno, I lock myself out of the house, because I forget the keys, and I forget where I'm going sometimes when I'm driving down the freeway. And I forget English Department meetings all the time. But, Burciaga, you, I don't forget.

Oyes, when I get tired of listening to the tonterias on "La Caliente" I listen to K-B-N-A, "Que Buena," and on that station they also like to bathe in linguistic impurity. Code switching is a soap we use to clean ourselves, sabes? I think there are monitors from the English Only movement all over El Paso.

They walk around taking notes. This town really pisses them off. El gusto que me da. Que se vayan mucho a la you know where. Bueno, they still think que somos medios rústicos—unless of course, we act exactly like them, speak like them, vote like them—in which case we're suddenly considered civilized, upstanding citizens who've managed to overcome our gene pool. When we toss out our icons and worship their gods, all of a sudden we're evolved. Makes me want to run out and get a tattoo. Except I hate needles. Anyway, I'm too old for body art.

Burciaga, we'll never be good enough. Or as you liked to put it, they think we're una bola de pendejos o mas bien they are the broom and we are the dirt on the floor. They keep sweeping us up, but we keep coming back inside the house every time a good wind storm comes along. Somos tercos. We keep coming back. Show me a locked door and I'll show you a Mexican who can figure out a way to open the door. Imagination's on our side. ¡Que barbaridad! Y aunque uno pasa unos corajes tremendos aqui en la frontera, tambien pasamaos unas curadas chingonometricas. I mean, baby, the talk of the border's the best. I want to die listening to all this. Lie down and die. I swear. God. The talk of our people, it's like listening to the rain. You know it and I know it, and the reason we know it is because we are both insanely and illogically in love with mestizaje. Bueno, what can you expect? Somos hijos de la conquista. Pero siquiera nunca fuimos agachados. Okay, so we're always fighting with the wrong ammunition. That doesn't mean we're not fighting—it just means we're not winning.

Mira, yo sé que tenías tus quejas con El Paso. Bueno, the whole world está en pleytos con esta ciudad tan dejada. Pero, we're still here. They call us dead—pero fijate que no. After all the funerals, we're still here. Making tamales and eating menudo at two o'clock in the morning on Alameda at the Good Luck Café. Don't believe everything you read in the newspapers. We're still here, Tony, so put in a good word for us. Remember, you were ours from the very beginning. And you will always be ours. No se te olvide de nosotros. El Chuco loves you, baby. ★

From *Elegies in Blue: Poems*: The Blue I Loved

Maria de Guadalupe Cenizeros, citizen of Smeltertown,
sings a lullaby explaining the color
of the headstone on her grave

I loved the August rains, I loved the calm October
days. I loved the sound of thunder as it echoed
in the nights; I loved the breeze that made my curtains
dance a waltz. I loved the water in the river,
chocolate as my skin.
I loved the smell of beans,
the smoothness of the masa in my hands. I loved
the stacks of fresh tamales on the stove, the
taste of yerba buena on my tongue. I loved
the rows of chile in the fields.
I loved the look on Mama's face
before she closed her eyes and never woke again.
I loved the worn wood rosary she left to me, her
only child to live past thirty years. I loved the
picture of her wedding day. I placed it next to mine.
I looked like her. That is what I loved: I had her
face, her eyes.
I loved the stove where I cooked meals
as simple as the wood I walked on with bare feet.
I loved those pisos made of wood, and loved the Little
Flower of Jesus. She made me hers. And just like me
she loved the smell of candles and copal. I loved
the afternoons we talked, just she and I.
I loved to wake
the house each dawn. I loved my children's grumbling
as they rose to meet the sun. I loved their look

of hunger as they ate. I loved their loving me.
I loved their look of pain when I grew sick.
Their tears burned like the sun the day I died.
                    I loved my husband's eyes. Green
as apples growing on a branch. I loved his
hand upon my back. The roughness made me tremble.
Forty years that man could make me tremble. He's
buried next to me. In death I swear he snores.
We sleep the way we lived: in peace. And one
more thing I loved. I loved, I loved the color blue,
the color of the room where we made
love and slept. Where we made love and slept.
I loved the color blue. ★

Tom Lea

Old Mount Franklin

I first wrote this in order to speak it on a radio broadcast in December of 1951. Two years later I revised it a little, to accommodate the speaking to the requirements of television cameras which had joined the microphones at KTSM. Since then the words here written seem to have become an invariable part of an annual ceremony, an affectionate salute repeated each year, spoken in a December dusk when a star is lighted on a mountainside and Christmastime comes again at the Pass of the North.

Old Mount Franklin is not a part of any fabled range of Delectable Mountains graced with green trees and softened by the fertile rain.

Mount Franklin is a gaunt hardrock mountain, standing against the sky like a piece of the world's uncovered carcass.

Mount Franklin is a ridge of rock rising like a ragged wall along the flank of a desert river.

The shape of Mount Franklin is a jumbled set of wedged pyramids, broken and interlocked, buttressed and bastioned together in a massive long line of heights and hogbacks.

Mount Franklin is built of humped twists and folds of mother rock, laced and interleaved with a little thin soil, pushed up in some primal birthpain of the earth, and then tilted above the desert's floor.

The plants that grow along Mount Franklin's slopes are tough plants, with thirsty roots and meager leaves and sharp thorns that neither hide nor cover the mountain's rough rock face. Mount Franklin is a lasting piece of our planet, unadorned.

The bulk and substance of it stand changeless, immortal to our mortal eyes. Yet the color of Mount Franklin is as various, as transient, as its shape is eternal. Let your eye follow the speckled sandy fold and slope of the hills to the level lines of the mesa tops, up the ridges, along the mountainsides, to where the bare rock stands faintly stained with red of iron, touched with subtle ochre, ribbed with rich blue of shadow, paled with high blue of distance. In the air of the desert, sun and shadow and cloud and haze change the monotone of tawny tan ground and gray rock into bluing hues of an infinite subtlety, as if soil and stone might borrow the magic airiness of the sky.

Under the journey of the sun whose shifting slants of light are never still, whose slowly shortening and lengthening shadows are always various, the passage of each moment of time casts its own color upon the mountain's face. The hours write upon it with light and space in an evanescent hand, from the first reaching sunrays pink on the summit stones lifting from deeps of shadow, to the flat and formless glare of noon glittering on the grain of granite and hot in the dust, to the last glow of cloudlight touching down at day's end upon darkening slopes. Above the black loom of Mount Franklin at night, the stars wheel the never pausing mark of time.

The seasons touch at the mountain's rigid face. Spring winds make a brown ghost of Mount Franklin under the gritty amber of the sand-filled sky. Summer rain brings a burgeoning green velvet fuzz along the rounded tilt of the sun-worn slopes. Autumn haze shrouds Mount Franklin's feet and touches canyons with a blue and violet mystery. Winter snow traces with a delicate white the lift and turn of the ridges.

Above the Rio Grande's ribbon of green, forming one side of the portal of the Pass of the North, Mount Franklin is a presence and a personality. Standing above us, above the build of our town, Mount Franklin is the landmark and the trademark of where we live.

And it is more.

"A mountain," Carl Sandburg said, "is something that's fastened down, something you can count on." By that token, a mountain is a talisman in our hearts. In looking at Mount Franklin, up there, we lift our eyes toward the sky. ★

Elroy Bode

Native Texan Elroy Bode was raised in Kerrville. After graduating from the University of Texas at Austin and serving in the military, he made El Paso his home in 1959. He taught in the Texas public schools in Kingsville, Garland, Bandera, and El Paso for forty-eight years, more than thirty years at Austin High School in El Paso. While stationed in San Antonio as a second lieutenant in the air force, Bode began writing what is called his inimitable "word sketches" after his short stories were rejected. He decided: "I would never again write anything the way I thought I was 'supposed to.' I would never write in order to make money and I would only write about those things that I cared about. If I never got published—fine. I would write strictly for me about those moments of intensity that would not let me alone—that seemed to be the very stuff of my life." Rooted in the geography of West Texas, these word sketches vary in length from a few paragraphs to essay length and are sensitive observations about the moments that are often ignored in everyday life. His critically acclaimed books include: *Texas Sketchbook*; *Sketchbook II*; *Alone: In the World Looking*; *Home and Other Moments*; *To Be Alive*; *This Favored Place*; *Commonplace Mysteries*; *Home Country;* and *In a Special Light.* Two-time recipient of the Stanley Walker Award for Journalism from the Texas Institute of Letters, he also served as a contributing editor for the Texas Observer. Elroy Bode is a member of the Texas Institute of Letters.

From *Home Country: An Elroy Bode Reader*: Sunset Heights after Dark

In the late 1950s, when I moved to El Paso, I walked in Sunset Heights, just west of downtown, and tried to get a feel for this city at the edge of Texas—so far from home, so close to Mexico.

At nightfall I walked along Porfirio Diaz Street. The porch lights were on and lamps shone within living rooms behind thin curtains. It was romantic to me—nothing less: the faint smell of October-night dust, the cool air, the chinaberry tree on the corner; the sounds of children's voices—their Spanish words, their laughter—as they played on the dimly lit porches. The moon had risen in the east, a train was rumbling at the station below the hill, and as I stood on Porfirio Diaz it was as if I were in Paris, in Madrid, in some fabled city of the earth.

I look back, and I think of how crickets and shadows and children and barking dogs set the tone of that time of my life, my twenties, more than philosophies and ambitions. As I walked at night I was constantly pleased by the sides of the half-darkened buildings and small front yards—as if they held, somehow, important answers to my as yet unformulated questions. I was looking—constantly—but I had no idea what I was looking for.

So I kept walking—roaming through the streets of Sunset Heights, past the red-brick homes that for decades had been facing west toward the desert, south toward Juárez and Mexico. It was as if they were still faintly hushed from the dramas of the past, and now, though solemn and decorous in the early-night darkness, their burnt-red bricks carried within them the fever of memory, the warm crimson trace of history.

Prospect, Upson, Mundy: they were strange streets to me, but as I walked them those first October nights I knew I wanted to know them, wanted to stare past their lighted porches and learn of their hidden lives. ★

From *Commonplace Mysteries*: Going to Juarez

I LED AN IDIOSYNCRATIC LIFE. I PURSUED singular paths.

Or to put it another way: I liked going to Juarez and walking around on a summer day. And the going was as enjoyable as the getting there.

I stopped first for coffee at Victor's Cafe in downtown El Paso. I liked Victor's—maybe it was just the simple, understated invitation of C A F E printed in the window. I took a seat at a side table with its red-checkered cloth. The cook whistled bouncily in the kitchen; the waitress stood in the middle of the room, looking out the doorway at the people passing by. She talked in Spanish to a man seated at a nearby table, having his midday glass of beer. The woman was not a real waitress—that is, she didn't wear a uniform and white shoes and she didn't have a ticket pad at her hip. She was just someone's mother who finally brought me a cup and spoon as she would have brought them to a guest in her own home.

I sipped the coffee, gazed out to the street past the E F A C on the window glass, listened to the whistle-gymnastics of the cook while the small portable fan turned back and forth above the cash register. I sat, blending into the mood of the cafe as easily as the salt shaker, the toothpicks, the coiling cigarette smoke.

After paying for the coffee I eased on past the Greyhound bus station toward the bridge—past the loan shops and dry goods stores; past the Hollywood Cafe and, above it, the bulging eyes of the apartment bay windows that for a century had stared down on the swarming life of South El Paso Street and never blinked.

Before crossing Paisano Drive I went into the Plaza Grocery for a package of gum. The Plaza: a store to dally in for sure, one that still had the tone—the flavor—of the small neighborhood grocery stores of the past. No Muzak there: no swathed, computerized goods lying in state. It was cramped, crowded, narrow-aisled, and it smelled of laundry soaps and brooms and meats from the butcher counter. I could have spent the whole afternoon there, sitting on an apple box and smelling the cleaning compounds.

At the old Colon Theatre I was in the full flow of pedestrians headed toward the bridge. In every block the people, the Mexican people were walking south—carrying, clutching, clasping, moving with their sacks and packages towards home.

I paid my dime at the toll booth; then, with the others—with old women in scarves and canvas sneakers who had already walked miles and would walk miles more before finally putting their shopping bags down—I started up the incline of the bridge. At the top I paused a moment, letting the others go by. There it was again: the whole hypnotic sweep of river and mountain range and blazing summer sky; the meeting place, the Pass.

In Juarez, on a side street, I watched a woman close a door. I was struck by the care, the consideration, the sense of propriety with which she had opened and closed her old screen door at one o'clock in the afternoon. It was as if the proper functioning of society—indeed, the orderliness of the universe—depended on how well that door was opened and shut.

On Calle M. Ocampo Norte two men walked along pushing a cart of melons. The cart had a microphone attachment and one of the men called out to the neighborhood: "*Sandias . . . sandias!*" They pushed toward a brown and white dog sleeping in the sidewalk beneath a chinaberry tree. "*Sandias!*" the man called, but the dog did not move.

It was an ordinary hot afternoon. Naked children sat on the cracked, broken sidewalk playing with wooden spools. Women walked in 100-degree heat, holding up their purses to shade their eyes from the sun. Pigeons on the nearby roofs preened and postured to one another. A man strode smartly along in cracked, run-over shoes without socks, holding out his cellophane sacks of limes for sale.

Now and then vans came by, the *maquiladora* workers seated inside as subdued as prisoners. They were two rows of profiles in the windows, staring ahead.

A girl passed—a young mother carrying her baby. Flap, flap, her rubber thongs slapped the sidewalk past the small yards, the doorways, the bougainvillaea here and there, the unpainted fences and gates.

An ice cream man in a straw hat pushed his cart down the sidewalk, up and over the curved bridge of the canal, and on beneath the line of willows where men had gathered to talk. In front of them, on the canal fence, a woman's washing dried in the sun.

Other men, in undershirts, sat in chairs in their doorways, leaning forward on their knees to watch the afternoon. Above them, voices of women drifted out from shadowed, second-story windows. The brown, debris-filled canal water flowed past fading advertisements for Sky sodas and beneath the bar windows where prostitutes had already gathered for the afternoon trade.

On Avenida Juarez I leaned against a store front. Tarahumara Indian women were seated on the sidewalk—palms up, begging. Their sleeping babies were sprawled nearby.

Three Mexican girls walked past and I turned to look at them. They were teenage children with freshly painted and shining lips, high heels, thin bodies, tight jeans. Newly pubescent, they wore men's-style white undershirts with no bras. They stopped for a moment in the middle of the sidewalk—to talk, to laugh, to listen to the drum-and-saxophone combo blaring from an upper-story window across the way.

As they stood there and as I watched them, my first thought was a vaguely patronizing one, something along the lines of: How little they know of *anything*, such girls—how incongruous they seem in a country of such poverty and need.

But what finally struck me was: Just because they live in Juarez, Mexico, why should they wear serious looks, be grave and weighted down? *They are doing the first living they have ever done.* . . . Sure, they were as innocent of the world and its awesome dimensions as reeds along a river bank. They knew nothing of *The Iliad* and ICBM's and the curve of time—but that was their dignity and their strength. They had a right to be young and to be frivolous.

It was as if each girl standing there in her high heels and skin-tight jeans carried a message—wore a placard: Life, wherever it is found, is to be respected.

I could have been leaning against a building in Havana—or Rio de Janeiro or Hong Kong—and the millions, walking there, would be carrying the same message. ★

From *In a Special Light*: Love in Smokey's Barbecue

I WAS SITTING NEAR THEM AT A REAR TABLE. His arm was across her back, and his hand rested at her neck beneath her long black hair. She sat pivoted in her chair, facing him. They had finished with their barbecue, and now they were free to resume being young lovers, content in their talking.

She smiled often; sometimes she laughed. He sat composed, unmoving, attentive to her. Half-turned, he murmured assent to what she had to say: she, his pleasant-faced companion; she, with her bright eyes, dark eyebrows, dark eyelashes; she, with her strong and classic profile, a face on a coin.

As she moved her hands from time to time—shaping her ideas there between their faces that almost touched— he would give a light little laugh in agreement with a point she had made. But even then he did not move, did not alter his rapt focus on her.

Romeo and Juliet—doomed—did not make it into old age. But as I looked at these two lovers—he with his Nordic blond hair and eyebrows, she with her Hispanic dark hair and light brown skin—I thought they surely would. I could see them years from now: his yellow tufts of a chin beard faded into white, her dark hair still flowing across her shoulders but streaked with gray. She would be talking, of course; she would still be bringing him her vitality. And he would be there beside her: staunch, unwavering, the fixed planet to her ever-circling moon. ★

From *Home and Other Moments*: Orange Marigolds

It was Sunday morning just before noon, with elm leaves falling in the yard and a breeze of mid-October moving casually about. The El Paso sky was a rich, cloudless blue. I was seated on the steps outside my kitchen door, eating an apple, half-daydreaming, half-listening to my eight-year-old daughter picking out her simple tunes on the piano.

As I chewed the apple I gazed about at familiar sights of the yard. The two pet chickens, one glossy black, the other light brown, were seated on top of a small table, resting in the shade after their morning's foraging in the dirt and grass. Flies were moving here and there in the sunlight, occasionally settling on the bright chicken droppings left on the concrete walk. A pink bedsheet waved a little on the clothesline. The four cats, recently fed, were sleeping now on top of the high rock wall. I could see the tip of Smokey's tail among the green vines.

It was a casual, undramatic Sunday morning, much like any other, yet as the elm limbs swayed and the cats slept and the orange marigolds wobbled to themselves against the garage—as I sat there, looking and listening, with everything around me immensely relaxed—the morning gradually entered one of those vacant stretches of time when all the ragged edges of existence seem to come together, simply, artfully, as one.

It was as though the halting notes of the piano, the pink bedsheet, the brilliant-faced marigolds—all the bits and pieces of the yard—were trying to say, This is it, my friend; this is how things are. Struggle as you will, think and brood and worry as you will, you can never know more about why you are alive than you do right now. For this is that elusive moment of truth, that subtle little vibration from the world's mysterious rhythms, and if you remain still enough you might be able to feel it: the silent pulse of creation, the steady breath of life. ★

From *In a Special Light*: Earth-Life

I NEED THE EARTH-LIFE, THE ORDINARY COUNtryside moment, but I cannot make this deep affection seem important to others. On occasion friends look indulgently with me toward the trees or fields that I am showing them, my arm thrown out expansively as we take in the view. They nod, they make affirming comments—try to seem tolerant of my preoccupation with "nature," as they tend to call it—but clearly what is there before us does not mean very much to them, will never count as anything fundamental to their lives.

I need the El Paso countryside. I need to hear the call of redwing blackbirds from salt cedars along an Upper Valley canal. I need to stand in a pecan grove and feel the breeze that moves through it—a breeze that reminds me of other breezes in other trees in other, almost forgotten, times. I need to see stretches of plowed land where, in the distance, humans are reduced in scale and become of no greater importance to the eye than a rooster in a yard, a tractor in a field.

I walk about on farmland roads and I have an urge to say, We are together, these, my silent friends under the sun: the yellow jackets investigating the fenceline grasses, lightly touching—almost kissing, it would seem—the stems and seeds; the leisured, midafternoon drifting about of white fluff from the cottonwood tees; the green June corn and the yellow squash in an old man's backyard garden; the flock of pigeons wheeling upward, coasting, settling again in their smooth formation to sit together in their pigeon community on a telephone wire; the rows of early summer cotton spread across a field like green spokes of a gigantic wheel.

I look, too, at distant trees bordering the fields, and they seem to be offering quiet respirations to the countryside. Their tree-shapes lift, flow, move about, shimmer in the ocean swells of warm summer air, then settle back within the contours of their passive greenery.

The earth: it is as though I were born to be next to it, to see what is growing there—to feel friendly toward the grass on the ground, limbs on a tree.

I walk, I smile, I am rewarded. This valley land—these fields within their mountain borders—is my sun-blazed heaven. I need no other. ★

From *Home Country: An Elroy Bode Reader*: The Day the Earth Stood Still

If there had been a declaration of war, or an earthquake, or perhaps some shocking new turn of political events, people in El Paso would have felt that they had a reason to remember Sunday, November 11. Editorial writers would have pounded out editorials. Commentators would have commented. News analysts would have analyzed. And people would have agreed that something significant had happened in their lives that day.

Something did happen in El Paso on November 11: it was a day the earth stood still. But no history book will ever record the fact that it did. That particular Sunday passed unheralded by headlines on Monday morning.

Yet it was as important a day as ever comes into a person's life, even though that's all it was—a day. A non-historic, non-newsmaking day.

If you were alive, you surely remember it—that perfect, rare, autumn Sunday when the earth stood still and let men and women and children and animals and all other breathing and crawling and flying things move about in the sun as if they were eternal creatures of the universe and would never die. . . . That day; surely you recall it: how the sun came casually down and the afternoon shadows gathered like old friends and the air touched the skin like a lover.

That day: when boys ran and cats curled in the warmth of the afternoon grass and couples walked about and there was no sense of tragedy, of excess, of unmet needs anywhere.

That day, that impossibly friendly and lovely El Paso day—just right for human living—stayed a perfect day all day long, and then it ended.

But such a day—a day worthy of gods and editorials—will not go down in the history books because nothing happened. It did not make any news; it only made life worth living. ★

Pat Mora

Poet, writer, and literacy advocate Pat Mora was born and raised in El Paso and received a B.A. from Texas Western College and an M.A. from the University of Texas at El Paso. Mora held the Carruthers Chair, Distinguished Visiting Professor at the University of New Mexico. Recipient of a Kellogg National Leadership Fellowship in 1986, she also received a 1994 National Endowment of the Arts Creative Writing Fellowship in Poetry and a 2003 Civitella Ranieri Fellowship, Umbria, Italy. Mora was elected to the Texas Institute of Letters, inducted into the *El Paso Herald Post* Writers Hall of Fame, and named a Distinguished Alumna at the University of Texas at El Paso. She is the author of six poetry collections, including *Chants* and *Borders*, which both received Southwest Book Awards from the Border Regional Library Association, and is the author of the non-fiction books *House of Houses*, winner of the Southwest Book Award, Border Regional Library Association, and *Nepantla: Essays from the Land in the Middle.* Additionally, she has published books for children and young adults including: *A Birthday Basket for Tía*, winner of the 1994 Southwest Book Award, Border Regional Library Association and was twice awarded the Tomás Rivera Mexican American Children's Book Award—in 1997 for *Tomas and the Library Lady* and in 2003 for *A Library for Juana: The World of Sor Juana Inez. This Big Sky* won the 1999 Texas Institute of Letters Best Children's Book Award. *Confetti: Poems for Children* was the winner of the 2004 Arizona Governor's Book Award and *Yum! MmMm! Qué rico!* was the winner of the 2008 Américas Award. Mora was awarded an Honorary Doctorate of Letters from State University of New York (SUNY) Buffalo in 2006 and an Honorary Doctorate of Humane Letters, North Carolina State University in 2008. She was named an Honorary Member of the American Library Association. Mora is also the founder of El día de los niños/ El dia de los libros, Children's Day/Book Day, a family literacy initiative, now housed at the American Library Association. Annual culmination celebrations occur nation-wide on or near April 30, encouraging what she calls "bookjoy."

From *Borders*: Desert Women

Desert women know
about survival.
Fierce heat and cold
have burned and thickened
our skin. Like cactus
we've learned to hoard,
to sprout deep roots,
to seem asleep, yet wake
at the scent of softness
in the air, to hide
pain and loss by silence,
no branches wail
or whisper our sad songs
safe behind our thorns.

Don't be deceived.
When we bloom, we stun. ★

From *Agua Santa: Holy Water*: Corazón del corrido

1
En la Frontera de Tejas,
miren lo que ha sucedido,
venían los mexicanos,
buscaban lo prometido.

2
En mil novecientos quince,
de Chihuahua Moras llegaban,

buscaban paz pa´-sus hijos,
al Paso Norte mudaban.

3
Venía Raúl Antonio,
llegó de niño chiquito,
a siete ya trabajaba,
lechero con caballito.

4
Buscaba otro trabajo,
periódicos él vendía,
después de ir a la escuela,
tantas tareas tenía.

5
De chico iba a los pleitos,
—Soy de la prensa, decía,
en periódicos se sentaba,
gran boxeadores veía.

6
Jugetón desde muy joven,
a su hermana asustaba,
vestido en sábana blanca,
como espanto gritaba.

7
Su padre, sastre paciente,
su madre nunca paraba,
esa familia tan grande,
Raúl lo necesitaba.

8

Decía Raúl Antonio,
y sin pistola en la mano,
y sin caballo melado,
—Soy luchador mexicano.

9

Un hombre bien aplicado,
gerente pues lo nombraban,
su sueldo daba a su madre,
amigos lo admiraban.

10

Pero llegaban los güeros,
que ojos malos le daban.
—Jamás podrán insultarme,
¡Adiós! Ya no lo abusaban.

11

—¿Qué haré? pensaba ese joven,
cuando lavaba su coche,
—Te ocupo, dijo un viandante.
—Iré al taller día y noche.

12

Los lentes bien él pulía,
y las medidas tomaba.
—¡Muchachos, prisa! gritaba.
Ni pa´ comidas paraba.

13

A veces dando un paseo,
bonita joven veía,

sentada frente a su casa,
—¡Qué linda! Raúl decía.

14
—Con esa voy a casarme.
Pronto con ella salía,
mandaba muchos regalos,
y ella se sonreía.

15
Esposo de bella Estella,
de piedra casa fincaron,
y cuatro hijos tuvieron,
los cuatro bien educaron.

16
Fue dueño de su negocio,
al pobre siempre ayudaba,
por años de día y noche,
los lentes él trabajaba.

17
Decía Raúl Antonio,
y sin pistola en la mano,
—Yo cuidaré a mi familia,
Soy luchador mexicano.

18
Al fin las cuentas montaban,
se fue buscando dinero,
a Houston, Gallup, Califas,
se mudó entre el güero.

19
Jugetón desde muy joven,
con nietos siempre guasaba,
les daba pues su domingo,
y luego los pellizcaba.

20
¡Ay! Murió en California,
y sin pistola en la mano,
y sin caballo melado,
gran luchador mexicano.

21
Aquí se acaba el corrido,
y como él lucharemos,
ya con ésta me despido,
¡Ay, Papá! te cantaremos.

for my father ★

From *Adobe Odes*: Ode to El Paso

Stubborn mountain,
rock anchor,
you grew from cuentos carried at night
in the wind's dry hands,
seed pebbles
that became your wide-hipped,
unmovable contours, curves
where finches and secretive
spiders nest.

Poet of ancient seas
and baritone fossils,
of trilobites and cephalopods,
lyric cantadora of horn corals,
ammonites and crinoids,

impatient, gray historian
lured by the whir of a pen,

its tip, a top whirring,
dancing on the page,
you write until your fingers cramp
and your shoulders knot,
weary at the echoes of grief
still moist beneath the boulders
of prejudice.

You wake
stung, eye pierced
by an angry, red thorn,
burning struggles,
embedded in your pupil.

Stern mother,
venerable sentinel, impervious
to sand thrashings,
you close your face,
head thrown back,
you rise rooted in memory,
and when the storm limps away,
hoarse, gasping,

you hum, unpack your rose shawl
and again toss the lace
    over your bare, wrinkled shoulders,
wear your rippling silver
    bracelet, el río grande.

    Poised to protect,
you sleep standing,
    wrapped in your black rebozo.

    Cada primavera,
lizards play between
    your toes and young again,
you sip the yellow breeze,
    desert fountain of youth,
your breath soft as dawn. You blush
    at the wind's whispered invitations
at the feathery caresses
    of ruby-throated hummingbirds
    and begin your slow spin.

Your skirts ripple for miles
    encrusted with cactus pads,
magenta cholla flowers, needle-gold spines,
    poppies fluttering Like glorious sunsets

At night, your long, glinting hair streams
    skyward, among the stars. ★

Ray Gonzalez

Ray Gonzalez was born and raised in El Paso. He is the author of ten books of poetry, including five from BOA Editions: *The Heat of Arrivals*, a 1997 PEN/Oakland Josephine Miles Book Award; *Cabato Sentora*, a 2000 Minnesota book Award Finalist; *The Hawk Temple at Tierra Grande*, a 2003 winner of the Minnesota Book Award for Poetry; *Consideration of the Guitar: New and Selected Poems*; and the forthcoming *Cool Auditor*. *Turtle Pictures*, a mixed-genre text, received the 2001 Minnesota book Award for Poetry. *The Religion of Hands*, the second volume of the *Turtle Pictures* trilogy, was published in 2005. He is also the author of three collections of essays: *Memory Fever*; *Renaming the Earth: Personal Essays*; and *The Underground Heart: A Return to a Hidden Landscape*, the recipient of the 2003 Carr P. Collins Award from the Texas Institute of Letters, named one of the best non-fiction books of the year by the Rocky Mountain News and one of ten best southwest books of the year by the Arizona Humanities Commission. Gonzalez has written two collections of short stories: the *Ghost of John Wayne*, winner of a 2002 Western Heritage Award for best short story and a 2002 Latino Heritage Award in Literature, and *Circling the Tortilla Dragon*. His poetry has appeared in the 1999, 2000, and 2003 editions of *The Best American Poetry* and *The Pushcart Prize: Best of the Small Presses 2000*. He is the editor of twelve anthologies, most recently *No Boundaries: Prose Poems by 24 American Poets*. Poetry editor of the Bloomsbury Review for twenty-two years, he also founded the poetry journal *Luna* in 1998. Currently, Gonzalez is full professor in the M.F.A. creative writing program at the University of Minnesota in Minneapolis and also teaches in the Solstice M.F.A. program at Pine Manor College in Boston.

From *Memory Fever*: White Sands

It was like playing on the moon as we rolled down the white sand dunes when we were kids. By the time we came to a stop at the bottom, we were covered in white dirt, looking like ghost children.

The memory of family picnics at the White Sands National Monument near Alamogordo, New Mexico, in the fifties is blurred now, but I still cling to a few vivid images of miles and miles of a white world where I had fun playing in the dunes, building white sand castles without knowing we were only a few miles from the government test site where Trinity, the first atomic bomb, was detonated on July 16, 1945.

Until I studied World War II in high school, I did not know the white desert playground of the park distracted visitors from the fact that they were near the historic site. After seeing what I was reading, my mother casually told me that she and my father, along with thousands of El Pasoans, had seen a bright flash in the sky on July 16. My parents were high school students at El Paso Technical when the test bomb went off one hundred miles to the north. No one knew what the flash was until years later, but she told me that day felt very unusual. The sudden light made many people nervous because the war was still on.

My parents had witnessed a turning point in history by seeing that bright light in the sky. As a child, I spent many weekends playing in the white sands of the future, just another kid amazed at the endless horizon of white hills and dunes, the light falling from the desert sun to wither everything in 95-degree heat, making us play harder as the light intensified.

I can't forget the first day we walked through the park museum. Besides the usual geological charts and raised maps, I saw displays of mounted white mice, white rabbits, and white coyotes—even white tarantulas. These creatures had adjusted to this white world so that they could survive in the heat and desolation of the bleached landscape. Each species evolved to take advantage of an endless camouflage. When I learned about Trinity, I wondered how many of the animals had been affected by the radiation of history. Had they truly changed color to blend into the white sand for protection and survival against predators, or was this ivory land, and its creatures, a mutation from the first blast?

Concerns over nuclear fallout were not hot topics for high school students in an isolated, west Texas town during the sixties. No one thought about it. It was not an issue. I knew nature had created the white sands thousands of years ago and the evolution of white animals had nothing to do with the atomic bomb, but as I remembered that day in the museum, I sensed the whiteness of every living thing around me was connected to the darkness of the brilliant flash of 1945.

I first read Leslie Groves' eyewitness account of the Alamogordo explosion when my American History class studied the development of the atomic bombs the U.S. dropped on Hiroshima and Nagasaki. As director of the Manhattan Project, a top-secret government program, Groves described what he saw across the white sands as an intense and blinding flash of light, a tremendous ball of fire that turned into the first mushroom cloud that any of them saw. He watched as the steel tower vaporized in the 15,000 to 20,000 tons of explosives.

When I read this in high school and recognized the area as the place we enjoyed family outings, I had not been to White Sands in years. Groves' account did not really strike me until a decade later. In high school, it was just another assigned chapter to read. For whatever reasons, my high school friends and I never went to White Sands, even though it was less than two hours from El Paso. I enjoyed the white fields only as a small boy.

I didn't make the connection between the bomb, my parents seeing the flash, and my naive childhood in the sand until 1977, as I drove alone across southern New Mexico. I was on my way back to El Paso after living for two years in San Diego, California. I drove south past Albuquerque. But instead of taking the straight, short route to El Paso, I headed east from Las Cruces over the Organ Mountains.

The high pass took me to the eastern side of the range, directly above the vast flatness of the desert floor and White Sands, forty miles away. I don't know why I chose to return to El Paso from that direction, but driving past White Sands brought it all back. Perhaps I thought of those days because friends of mine in San Diego had mentioned their participation in antinuclear groups protesting at the nuclear power plant near San Clemente. The last demonstration had taken place a few days before I said good-bye to them and headed home.

It was an early evening in April when I headed down the long stretch of highway bordering the eastern end of White Sands. The setting sun ignited the peaks of the Organ Mountains and washed the miles of white sand with a peach-colored hue. I drove past fenced-off land whose barbed-wired barriers held small signs every few hundred feet. "Property of United States Government. No Trespassing."

A simple warning like that was enough to keep people away and draw them to the park instead. Thousands of visitors came each year to gawk at the white sand dunes, miles and miles of them. Roads had been cut to get into the interior dunes. After the shock of the white world wore off, families could eat at the picnic tables scattered throughout the park.

I spotted the museum building about a mile down the road and began to relive our family picnics. It must have been 1958. As a six-year-old, I thrilled in climbing the steep dunes to pretend I was going to get lost out there and scare my parents into coming to look for me. When I stood at the top of the dunes, my father and mother looked tiny and far away as they sat at the picnic table at the bottom.

I waved and yelled until I caught their attention. They waved back, but I couldn't hear what they were saying. I turned and started hiking across the deep sand. The white powder seeped into my sneakers and pant cuffs. I never hiked more than a hundred yards before I began to get scared at the realization that I was standing in an endless sea of whiteness. I would turn and retrace my deep footprints back to the family.

Now, as I drove past the museum, I had the urge to stop and find out if the display of white animals was still there. I slowed down and saw the "Closed" sign on the doors. Twenty years after my first visit to the museum, I couldn't go in to look at the white kangaroo rats, the snarling white coyote, or the huge albino rattlesnake that was the most vivid, shocking animal mounted in the museum.

I sped past the closed building and continued toward El Paso, remembering how the white rattlesnake had startled me as a boy. After peering into the glass-enclosed exhibits of rats and lizards, I came upon the coiled body of the rattlesnake. The sight of a white reptile, and the fact that it had come from the sands where I loved to play, increased my wonder and was one of the first times I felt I belonged in the desert.

My nose barely cleared the top of the display, so I had to stand on tiptoe to get a good look. I stared at the huge snake and couldn't believe the sight of its pale skin and transparent rattler. Its head was a dirty, milky white with tiny black eyes, the only dark spots on the body. I had seen rattlesnakes in El Paso, but I never guessed they could turn white to live in these sands.

The rest of that day is a blur. I think I ran out of the museum to find my parents and sister walking back to the picnic area. I didn't say a word to them about the white rattlesnake. I sat at the table and kept looking up at the walls of white sand as we ate, wondering if I had rolled over any snakes in my adventures in the dunes. I can still see the sudden brightness of the white sand as it intensified while we ate. It must have been noon on a hot day because I see myself sitting at the table, sweating and biting into my sandwich as the blinding sunlight draws the white earth closer to me.

***

I drove toward El Paso and the heat of the picnic faded. I couldn't recall the last time my family took me to White Sands. As I approached Alamogordo, the image of the white rattlesnake changed from a coiled shape to a mushroom cloud rising above the desert.

I have never been an antinuclear activist or protester, and have never even read books about Hiroshima, but as I drove through the area where Trinity was detonated, I thought about those childhood picnics, the white animals in the museum, and the brilliance of the sands. I discovered a certain light, a clarity of understanding, a radiance burning through the dunes of family history.

Its energy came from many sources. The innocence of childhood produced the light on those white hills. Our family outings generated the heat because they were part of growing up with a sense that the concept of family could never be broken. Those picnics on the dunes represented the idealism of a small boy growing up in the late fifties, a boy who thought the world was made up of nothing but good times.

The energy of the blinding desert also came from the fact that the U.S. government chose this area in which to conduct experiments that would change world history. If someone had interrupted my fun on the dunes to tell me that the Manhattan Project had reached its climax a few miles away, I couldn't have comprehended it. As a child, I would have thought the idea of a big bomb in the desert was kind of neat. Nothing could have destroyed my playground.

Twelve years after my solitary drive past the dunes toward home, the first test of a Star Wars laser weapon was successfully completed at White Sands. In 1989, the U.S. government finally shot down a missile with a laser. The flight and destruction of the missile took place over White Sands. Forty-four years after the first atomic flash startled the people of El Paso, another turning point had taken place over the white dunes.

As before, the energy for the laser weapon came from the white desert, from energy spilling over from the atomic bomb. Yet it was a power derived from the desert itself.

In *Masked Gods* (Swallow Press, 1984), his classic book on Navajo history, Frank Waters writes about the *kiva* ceremonies of native people and he reflects on the future of mankind and how studying native religions gives many clues to our turbulent century.

He describes a visit to Los Alamos, the town near Santa Fe founded in 1945 to house scientists working on the Manhattan Project. The atomic reactor constructed there was named Clementine after the miner's daughter of the folk song. Waters states that the Clementines were also an Egyptian religious sect in the first century A.D. who believed in the female spirit. He compares this female power to the same force rising out of the kivas near Los Alamos. He points out that the Sun Temple at Mesa Verde is the most intense example because elaborate ceremonies of light and fire were held there, ceremonies to end life cycles and begin new ones, the whole process forming out of the sheer power of Mother Earth and her underground forces.

Waters writes about the Sun Temple of Mesa Verde and its parallel to the atomic reactor. He feels it is not farfetched to see the parallel in their meanings. He compares the physical energy locked inside the atom to the psychic energy inside our psyches. They both involve the transformation of matter into creative energy. This creation arises from a dependence on what he calls "the reconciliation" of the primitive forces of life. This fusion results in a new birth of energy.

Tremendous conflict—from the smallest, insignificant act of a small boy rolling down the white dunes, to Trinity exploding nearby—detonates past the spiritual kivas toward the end of the twentieth century and the Stars Wars forming high above the desert. If Frank Waters is correct, and if the white rattlesnake is my most vivid memory of the White Sands museum, then the first atomic blast that startled my parents was destined to take place in the desert of New Mexico. It is a transcendence of light from the ancient people to the builders of the test tower melting at ground zero, to me rolling down the white dunes as rattlesnakes coiled undetected nearby—all the way to the final act of driving past the closed museum.

***

As I drove past Alamogordo and neared El Paso, the white sands were left behind. The familiar brown and red desert covered the horizon. To my right, the Franklin Mountains rose in a purple haze. I was coming home to again live in El Paso.

I made my way through the northeast suburbs of my home town and tried to picture what it must have been like to see the flash on July 16, 1945. My mother said it lasted only an instant and life went on. I stared at the mountains and noticed how new housing developments were creeping up the canyons. It meant cutting into the desert, disrupting the ancient landscape, uprooting cactus, and forcing wildlife to readjust. It also meant that many new homeowners in the foothills of the Franklins would find rattlesnakes in their yards. I wondered how many they would kill, or if any of those people in the new suburbs would get bitten. It was a small ecological problem. The snakes would disappear.

I drove into El Paso knowing that none of those homeowners would ever be startled or frightened by a white rattlesnake. They would never learn albino rattlesnakes lived one hundred miles to the north of their new homes. These new residents of El Paso had no reason to discover the secrets that lay hidden in their magnificent desert. It was too vast, too much property. They would have no urge to explore beyond the city limits of their dreams. Retirees from nearby military installations and new high-tech company employees weren't interested in local history. It's not part of the dream. After all, the stark, brown mountains a few miles from their backyards gave off a beautiful light each evening, enough heat to satisfy them in their moment under the Southwest sun. ★

(Editor's Note: The following poems are unpublished.)

The Rio Grande Near Flood Stage, Summer 2006

"You can't forget a river before crossing it."—a stranger

When I crossed it, I was home.
When I stayed home, I was close
but could not count the cracks
in the adobe walls.
The less I say about cracked walls,
the more you will know.

I crossed the water
and the bridge was still there.
I made it to the other side
and didn't know where to go.

When vulture shadows painted
the town from overhead,
I wasn't there.
This was long ago, when people
left the dirt streets, dying
and singing, the muddy
waters changing course.

I wandered past the river
and learned to swim.
I was given bread and medals,
but never allowed to wash
and find a place to sleep.

When I crossed again,
I was lost.
When I left, a man over
my left shoulder picked up
a white stone and I saw
the river stretch where
neither one of us
could cross.

The more I traced the current,
the closer the mountains rose.
The darker the river grew,
the farther I walked
in search of a way to
find the other side.
Someone followed me
and disappeared by the bridge.

He must have been the man
who told me to never pause
before a river without having
to take a drink or two.
The only time I understood
about this raging, I could not
raise my lips to the brown water.
As it dripped and glowed
off my open palms, I knew
it was the last time the flood
would recede and the drops
from my hands formed
tiny patterns on my shoes. ★

Somewhere Outside El Paso

Somewhere outside El Paso, there is a mountain
that marks the place where it happened.

This mountain is made of canyons and cliffs
that hide their rocks well, the road into

their red flesh the last line drawn
before it happened.

There is a tree that shadows the spot
where it took place.

This tree is dying and its gray trunk is opening
like the arms of the only witness, the empty

branches drawing blood from the sky.
A monument is cracking under the weight

of the concrete cross, the broken slab hiding
its language in the dirt so the sun can move

in the opposite direction without giving
away its historic message.

Somewhere outside El Paso, a man watches
the tree fall on the other side of the cross

before he can find his way to the river
and bow down to take a drink. ★

Bobby Byrd

Bobby Byrd grew up in Memphis, Tennessee, but made El Paso his home in 1978. In addition to his numerous books of poetry including *Get Some Fuses for the House*; *On the Transmigration of Souls in El Paso*; and *The Price of Doing Business in Mexico*, he is also co-editor of two award-winning non-fiction border anthologies: *The Late Great Mexican Border: Dispatches from a Disappearing Line* and *Puro Border: Dispatches, Snapshots & Graffiti from La Frontera*. His latest volume of poetry, *White Panties, Dead Friends and Other Bits and Pieces of Love*, received the 2008 Southwest Book Award. Byrd is the recipient of a National Endowment of Arts Fellowship, the D. H. Lawrence Fellowship by the University of New Mexico, and a 2005 Cultural Freedom Fellowship from the Lannan Foundation. He is the co-publisher of Cinco Puntos Press, which the Byrds founded in 1985 in their home in the Five Points neighborhood of El Paso. It has grown to become an important independent publishing house that draws national attention to the border region and its writers and artists.

From *The Price of Doing Business in Mexico*: The Gabachos in the Photograph

They'll tell you when you're growing up
that water goes under the bridge,
but they don't tell you about the bridge
that goes over to Avenida Juárez
where Martino's Restaurant is
two doors down from the Kentucky Club.
The imagination opens those doors,
and there I am,
the big bearded gabacho in the straw hat,
the coral necklace,

drinking Dos XX Oscura
and thinking I will have enough riches in my pocket
to nourish my heart in case of love.
It's Lee's 32nd birthday, 1977,
a year before we moved to El Paso.
Isn't she beautiful?
I am 35.
We sit in the corner booth by the windows
where the tiny Tarahumara children stand forever
with their outstretched hands
reaching into the emptiness of the 20th Century,
and a kaleidescope of people walk
back and forth
looking for ways to lose themselves
in the dwindling twilight.
Glittering mirrors.
Hard-crusted bolillo rolls.
French onion soup.
Chateaubriand for two fried in butter French-style.
We become stuffed and drunk and happy.
We wander the streets holding hands,
we climb a rickety staircase
to a small $10 room with clean sheets,
we make love like resplendent wild beasts
in search of something Jesus said,
and then we walk back into
the jingle-jangle of Avenida Juárez.

That was twenty-one years ago now.
Nothing has really changed except us.
Pedro Ruelas Alvarez,
the street photographer who took this picture
is dead now.

Like my mother is dead.
My sister Patsy.
My brother Bill.
Like Lee's mother and father.

"Water under the bridge, ¿verdad?"

Another gabacho couple is sitting in that booth tonight.
They are looking out the window
at the Indian children with the large black eyes,
and they are afraid
of what they see in that confusion.
Give them a quarter, mister,
give them a dollar,
give them back the secret places
in the mountains where their spirit thrives.

That's what I always want to do,
to give away something to make myself whole,
but it seems so impossible,
even to give something to myself.
At least I feel like I am at home now,
here in El Paso,
walking back and forth across the bridge,
and I'm hoping to find enough riches in my pocket
to cure some of the ache in my heart.
This is my prayer—
May God grant us all love
and a little bit of peace on Avenida Juárez.
Amen. ★

From *Get Some Fuses for the House: Householder Poems El Paso, Texas*: One Way for Middle-Aged Persons to Meditate

Like my neighbor Berta Alemán has taught me,
one way to meditate
is to hold a water hose in your hand.
Paradise is right around the corner.
But you should not expect too much progress at first.
There is plenty to do, standing there,
watering the lawn.
It could be a Wednesday night,
maybe right before September, right before
the kids go back to school.
Some times you hate them.
They don't listen.
That's okay.
You might even be out of milk.
There's plenty of time for milk and kids.
You are outside now.
That's what counts.
Like it's a real hot night, hotter than usual,
a good night to water the back yard,
it's been so scraggly lately,
especially in spots.
You maybe think that you have forgotten so much
this last month, this stretch
of the summer which seems so much like waiting.
This is okay too.
This is the physiology of the summer,
the way it insists that all is not done,
will never be,
the autumn and the winter comes,

over and over,
a snake with its goddamn tail stuck in its mouth.

So forgive yourself.

This is essential to the act of meditation.
You must remember you are watering the yard.
That is all you are doing.
Stand out there,
your left hand on your hip
in perfect repose, your right hand
carefully, gently,
grasping the water hose.
Be careful to watch the spray of the water
shine in the light of the full moon.
The water is perfect.
The moon is also perfect.
As is the grass, even if it is dying.

Your back should be straight,
but at ease
so that you can drink in the darkness of the night
without worrying about tomorrow.
If you are a man, you might want to
scratch your nuts, cradling them,
or if you are a woman,
shake your hips back and forth
slowly.
Whatever, the purpose is
to feel the sex of who you are.
You might hum a tune,
some sort of nursery rhyme
like you heard growing up

wherever that was.
It was a long time ago.
Your mother was so beautiful.
You can finally understand that now.
Stretch your legs.
Rock your body back and forth.
But concentrate on the water.
Be grateful.
Life is not what you imagined.
You have friends that have better,
others that have worse,
still others who are dead.
Breathe in and breathe out.

Maybe your lover is inside.
It will be a good night for love-making,
so warm and fine,
the drone of the swamp cooler
so the kids won't hear.
The bright moon.
You can tell your lover
about standing here in the moonlight
watering the yard.
But there is time before that.
You should think about your children again,
their bodies,
how they have changed
since they first squirmed through the door of flesh,
and your parents too
who are close to their death,
waiting to take the other journey.
So this is what life has been about.
It may seem so right now,

so clear,
to come to this point
exactly
and to think that a certain spot in the grass
has been dry for too long.
You have forgotten some things.
You have remembered others.
You have come this far.
Before you go back inside
be certain that the grass is watered completely. ★

Leslie Ullman

Poet Leslie Ullman was born in Illinois and graduated from Skidmore College. She received an M.F.A. from the University of Iowa and is the author of three poetry collections: *Natural Histories*, winner of the 1979 Yale Series of Younger Poets Award; *Dreams by No One's Daughter*, and *Slow Work Through Sand*, co-winner of the 1997 Iowa Poetry Prize. Recipient of two National Endowment for the Arts Fellowships, she has had poems published in magazines such as *Poetry*, *Hayden's Ferry Review New Letters*, *The New Yorker*, *Poetry Miscellany* and many others, as well as numerous anthologies. Her poetry reviews have appeared in *Kenyon Review*, *Poetry Magazine*, and *The Denver Quarterly*. For twenty-seven years she was a professor in the creative writing program at the University of Texas at El Paso, where she established and directed the bilingual M.F.A. program. Currently, she is a professor emerita at UTEP and teaches in the low-residency M.F.A. program at Vermont College of Fine Arts. In 2008, Ullman was featured in *Writing across Texas*, a television series for PBS.

From *Slow Work Through Sand*: The Way Animals Are

Sometimes I'm startled to find myself
in this white skin, this blankness,
time's drawings erased
the way highways have levelled
the land's natural drift.
I'm distracted by the history of rain
in a single cactus. I wonder
how heavy the mountain is.
Sometimes I feel the earth tilt
on a great magnet while I sleep
and a man with a history of his own

leaves his wife's body parts in boxes
all over town, while a building is blown up
in another state and 20 children die,
now 30, now 95, not just children, some
still missing, and the numbers
flash across the world in slender cables.

Yesterday I walked the border bridge
into Juarez, where time had stopped—women,
children, begging or selling candy,
their bare feet tough as roots
and their skin streaked with weather.
Such patience in their faces—
the shadow of the Andes,
broad cheek and burnished braid,
rain over terraced slopes,
the breath of childbirth and sorrow
keening through bamboo. Across the river
the windows of my city gleamed.

I stepped into a cathedral
where matrons one by one knelt
by the altar, their privacy
a brief and deepening well,
to speak with someone I wish
I could love. Or fear. Then they rose
and returned to their used bodies,
vessels shaped to gentle fullness,
broken and mended again and again.

Across the blowing litter
of Avenida Juárez, an old man
sat on a curb playing a violin—

a tuneless song that fed
on its own exhaustion.
Once he stopped and put his head
in his hands. Traffic rushed
between us. My eyes touched him
but I didn't cross the street.
This morning he is slow rain
passing through me, waking in the same
grey clothes, tightening his bow

and still I try to sing
in any language I can,
sing to you one at a time
which is all I can do;
there's a slow tongue that some days
runs through me unbidden,
in rhythms I am part of
the way animals are, even when
they're standing still. ★

From *Slow Work Through Sand*: Gourd

Baked the color of sand
and fitted with hemp, it holds
rainfall. It is carried over the adobe
land and hung against sand-colored
walls, inside or out, while the sun beats
water to sand, and the sky
thrums overhead, endless
and deep, a great exhalation of breath.
When I run my hand along the once-green

skin, I can feel it breathe. I can
feel sky running through its veins.
When I drink from its heart
and eat the bread baked in the smooth
clay ovens that rise here
like temples, I can taste sunlight
ground against sand-colored rock
and saltwater flaked from dried
oceans, where men and women formed
a ragged line from the Bering Strait
pulled by a god for whom they had no name—
each night along the way must have been
like no other, a grain of rest
inside the dome of firelight.

Here the very fields know how to wait.
They flare green when they can.
They subside and flare green again
the way this brown fruit holds rain
for months in its fortress shell
until a man's or woman's hands
lift it into use, sand-colored hands
with sand in their creases.
They offer water to the land, they
shape the land into bricks and tilt more
water to their faces, containers of silence
warmed to fine leather from looking
at sky, looking down, looking
at sky again. ★

Marian Haddad

Marian Haddad was born in El Paso to Syrian immigrants, growing up between three languages and cultures: English, Arabic, and Spanish. She earned a B.A. in creative writing from the University of Texas at El Paso and an M.F.A. in creative writing from San Diego State. As a recipient of a National Endowment for the Humanities Fellowship, she pursued further graduate study at the University of Notre Dame. Her chapbook of poems, *Saturn Falling Down*, was published at the request of Texas Public Radio in connection with their Hands-On Poetry Workshops. Haddad's poetry collection *Somewhere between Mexico and a River Called Home*, was an *El Paso Times* Top Five Book in October 2004 and is recommended reading by the *Small Press Review* and the *Valparaiso Review*; it is currently in its third printing. Haddad has taught creative writing at Our Lady of the Lake University, Northwest Vista College, and St. Mary's University. In San Antonio, she works as a visiting writer, manuscript and publishing consultant, and a creative writing workshop instructor. Her current book projects are two collections of poetry and a collection of personal essays about growing up Arab American in a Mexican American border town.

From *Somewhere Between Mexico and a River Called Home*: Somewhere Between Mexico and a River Called Home

> *I walked near the river that went beside our town . . . I was there in that place . . . I was alone in the two o'clock silence of the world—It wore a groove in me as deep as memory . . . It was the heart of my childhood. . . . and the moment would be so good and deep and so very much ours—our family's— that it was as if time had stopped and we were fixed there forever: the eternal familiar . . .   —Elroy Bode*

I.

Mama,
I've always wanted
to write a poem about you
but didn't know where to begin
all I remember now
are the pink strawberry floats
you would buy me on the mezzanine
at The White House downtown

we would ride the bus
and you would hold my hand
and tell me stories
tell me what to say
when someone came in
tried to teach me the words

every Saturday
like a prayer
we would walk down that quiet street
past Mr. Lopez's house
to meet the green bus on the corner
and drop the change in the bin
walk down a row of unfamiliar faces
brown and looking like Indian winds
and we would find a seat
I would always sit by the window

Mama   you knew I liked to pull the rope down
when it was time to land
on that same corner we saw
every Saturday like the sun

you would let me pull
that dirty heavy string
and the buzzer would go off
and you would smile
because I was smiling

II.

were you trying
to show me the world

were you the opener of the sky
revealing the light

or were you seeking a friend
someone to talk to
to walk with
on these streets
on this black pavement
in front of Kress's
and the Walgreen's Grill

and there I was
this miracle child
that came from nowhere
but the ground

you were forty-five
your face flushed
when you proclaimed to the world
you were having another
some kind of mistake
and the world caught you

red-handed
and for a small instance
that seemed like ten miles
you were ashamed

these rivers nailed into you
that you could not release
and you passed them down to me
notions of man and woman
and what sex was about

and I was surprised to find out
a few months ago
in a restaurant where we sat
by a window looking out
on the blue rain
that you liked it
that you really liked it
that you were a woman
in every sense
that you were wise
and regal
and a woman

who delivered ten children
and lost two
in a bleeding womb—puddle
on the kitchen floor
or in a field

and the first died young
but we are left
nine stars falling

Mama		I heard you cry
when he screamed
and you sank into yourself
like a wounded calf
and I never forgot
the fear in your eyes
that tired wail
that kept coming up
like a forbidden flower
against some white wall

and you lay there
crying voiceless—
a lifetime
of misunderstanding

Mama
you love pretty things
flowers and well-lit rooms
sunshine flooding in
and pretty china with pink flowers
etched like ribbons on a porcelain cup

you love drinking coffee
fresh
and telling stories about love
and listening to mine
you know so much
even though you are from another world
another time
it's as if you are here
in me

I remember once I looked up in the mirror
and I saw your face
and I died a moment in that light
I was you
that black and white photo
on your green passport
in your old black wallet
filled with receipts
crumpled and torn
hair parted in the middle
and these formless eyes
and I turned the water off,
touched my hair,
made sure I wasn't dreaming

III.

what were you like in Italy
when you brought your children over
from Syria on your way to this America

walking the streets of some foreign land
six children at your side on a boat
asking for bread and water

and when you were a child
did you sing
atop a thatched roof
with your friends looking down
at these boys
hardly men
in their black *ilbaysees*
fluttering with every stride

or gust of wind
and their crisp white shirts
some stark sheet wrapped around each head
tied with a rope—
they stood under their sun
smoking long brown cigarettes
they rolled themselves
and there he was
you said you told your mother
how handsome he looked
and how you loved
that bump in his throat
that moved when he talked
his sun-baked skin
a life in the field
that would be yours

and you went and swept his mother's small house
making yourself known
putting yourself up for sale
like a good girl
and she thought you were good
a child-bearer
strong

and she became your friend
for the greater part of your life
lived under the same roof
kneaded the same dough
talked behind his back
as she rolled grapeleaves with you
on that brown formica table

you sitting on a vinyl orange chair
and grandma bent
over the table just beneath
her black scarf falling

this marriage of three
and when the garage door would open
you both went quiet
like a country street at night
nothing but crickets chirping

IV.

Mama   your pink pajamas
and your fat gold bracelet
this life you shared
with a man
who stomped the earth
dust dried around his mouth
who knocked on doors
sold blankets   *cobijas*
tennis shoes
rose colored couch covers
olive green at times
he pulled out his *tarjetas*
entered $5.00

thanked them
as they shut their doors
and he walked with a step in his feet
like hooves against the ground
to his dark red Impala
goods piled high in the back

where I heard he made my brother ride
like a camel over desert mounds
'til he dropped him off at school

Mama were you proud
when Daddy would come home
did you know he made his money today
by selling his life
he drove up a wind-swirled dirt road
high and curving
until he stopped by the levy
put it in park
looked out the window
and saw a train of white muscle shirts
and blue bandannas

and he had two choices
to drive off
or to step out onto the same dust
as these men
and he chose to open his door
enter this den
of beer-drinking
penny-pitching
tobacco-chewing
brown men
whose skin shined in the sun
like bronze gods from Inca

and he walked over to them
like a leopard
quiet, graceful, strong
a brick in his throat

he thought he might have to swallow
and he made himself known

he was fifty
a man
earnest   firm
and handsome
and he let them know
he sold *pantalones*
and things for the bedroom
and they offered him a beer
compadre
every Saturday he drove up
those dirt roads
blue and pink houses
lining that place behind the river
to pick up his seven dollars
payment on his land he left behind
orchards blowing
green grapes clustered on the vine

and now he tends his backyard haven
his fruit trees
tomatoes red with life
his little forest
where he finds that young man
strong as a rock
who dug the earth beneath him
and made it rise again ★

Beatriz Terrazas

Born in El Paso, Beatriz Terrazas received a B.A. in journalism from the University of Texas at El Paso. She began her career as a writer and photographer at the *Fort Worth Star-Telegram*, then at *The Dallas Morning News*. In 1994, she was part of a team of journalists at the *News* that won a Pulitzer for a project on violence against women. Her work has won first place in contests sponsored by the National Association for Hispanic Journalists, the American Association of Sunday and Features Editors, the Society of American Travel Writers, and has been a finalist in the James Beard Foundation awards, Pen Center West and others. A Nieman Fellow at Harvard University, class of 1999, Terrazas is also a member of the Macondo Writing Workshops. A veteran writer and photographer, she now freelances and is based in the Dallas area.

The River That Runs Through Me

I MISS THE RIO GRANDE. IN MY MIND I SEE IT, and I smell menudo spiced with oregano. I see it and I hear the clop of horses' hoofs outside my grandfather's house in Juárez, feel the beat of a corrido lifting my feet.

I've been away from El Paso/Juárez for 20 years now, but I still call it home. Early this year, driving along Interstate 10, I caught a glimpse of the Rio Grande. The river lay there between the two cities where I grew up, dry and bare in spots, looking more like a snake that had slithered up to the wrong end of a farmer's hoe than the mighty force implied by its name. It lay there, broken, totally passable for anyone wishing to cross it either north or south but for the white border patrol vehicles planted like sentinels along it.

The river—and all it stands for to me—has become invisible despite being in the background of our daily political discourse. I read or hear story after story about international border fences in Texas: The town of McAllen agreed to reinforce its flood walls rather than submit to new fencing to deter trespassers. A federal judge ordered Eagle Pass to surrender more than 200 acres of land for fence construction.

I keep hoping others will see what I see: not borders and fences and illegal immigrants but the Rio Grande itself. To those of us who love it, the river is not merely a boundary with Mexico, it's a living thing. And to those of us who carry it in our veins, it is the story of our lives. The river haunts me. Several years ago, I traveled long stretches of the Rio Grande from its headwaters in Colorado to its mouth in South Texas. Meeting others along its trajectory was a lesson in how this bony, nearly 1,900-mile channel has shaped and influenced people. I came to see how the river is irrevocably intertwined with the child I was, the woman I am. It tethers my soul to the arid landscape in West Texas, and to Mexico. But today's Rio Grande is oh so different from the river I once knew.

The river of my youth flowed deep and strong near Las Cruces, N.M., where my family used to picnic. Once, when I was 6 or 7, my mother commanded my siblings and me to stay on the bank and wait for our father before jumping in to play. While he unloaded sandwiches and chips from the trunk, she stepped into the water for a quick swim. Then she was shouting, and in just seconds, her voice sounded far away and she looked tiny, her arm a matchstick floating on the water. She was drowning! I shouted to my father: "Mi mami se está ahogando!" My father, all white skin and plaid trunks, leaped into the water, but by the time he reached her, she was standing on a sandbar. Later, she told us that la corriente, the current, swift and unseen beneath the river's surface had carried her away from us, but shhhh, it's okay now.

Another memory: I was about 10 and in Juárez playing quinceañera with my cousins on a packed-earth patio. We dreamed about that first dance and the white pearly dress like an upside-down tulip that would signal our passage to womanhood. We shuffled our feet to the song we sang aloud, our budding hips bending to the beat of the cumbia: "Ven a bailar quinceañera. Ven a gozar, quinceañera." And though we couldn't see the river, as dusk fell, coloring the neighborhood purple and gray, its ghosts beckoned us. You know La Llorona drowned her children in the river. You know that, right? Now she wanders the river crying, looking for other children, so watch out!

In high school, some Latino boys threatened to throw into the river a white kid one of my friends was dating. Looking back, I wonder: Were they thinking of the deep symbolism of drowning a white boy in the waters that embodied their different ethnic histories? Probably not; they were just angry, disenfranchised in the way that brown-skinned boys were then, looking for a way to vent their feelings.

But what some people fail to understand—about me, about those boys—is that for us the river wasn't a barrier. An inconvenience, perhaps, when we had to cross the international bridge to visit our abuelas and primos or wait in long lines of chugging, overheated cars on the way back to our American lives. But the river was our connection, a witness to our attempts at straddling two cultures—to the fact that we could learn U.S. history in school during the week and spend Saturday nights celebrating weddings al otro lado. To the struggles of navigating two languages, two collective histories, and finding that with the passage of time, we were completely at home in neither one nor the other.

That's why seeing the disappearing Rio Grande fills me with such longing. I see it and taste the cinnamon coffee of mornings in my grandmother's kitchen. I see it and feel the sweat trickle down my back on a hot day, while my grandfather is lowered to his final resting place in a dusty cemetery. I see it and hear it calling my name as only a loved one can. It is the mirror that reflects the middle space between cultures and countries where I spent my formative years. Yet, for several months out of the year, even Google Earth would be hard-pressed to find this river between El Paso and, say, Presidio. During the summer it is dammed upstream for irrigation, its flow so greatly compromised that it dries up in some places and disappears.

The river seems to be vanishing just as I've realized I can't live without it. I worry that for all of our border talk, we are so blinded by political and economic issues that we don't really see the Rio Grande. I worry that we won't be able to control the invasive salt cedar breaking up its banks. I worry that we will divert its waters to the point of no return.

What happens then? La Llorona, the restless spirit whose existence calls for water, will have a tough time calling forth a chill by a dry channel. As for me, would losing the river mean losing a part of myself? Sunday picnics, high school raft races, crossing into Mexico to watch my grandfather die—would all these memories dry up as well? I hope and pray the river outlives my family as the natural world is supposed to do.

And if I'm lucky, the Rio Grande will have been the great witness I think it is and will have carried the bones of my memories to be cradled in the sea. ★

Howard McCord

Poet, novelist and essayist Howard McCord was born and raised in El Paso. After his service in the navy during the Korean War, he received a B.A. from the University of Texas and an M.A. from The University of Utah. McCord has taught at Washington State University and at Bowling Green State University, where he directed the creative writing program for many years. McCord is the author of more than thirty books of poetry, fiction, and travel writing including: *Maps; poems toward an iconography of the West; Mirrors*; *The Selected Poems of Howard McCord, 1955-1971*; *The Fire Visions*; *Swamp Songs & Tales*; and the *Duke of Chemical Birds*. His short novel *The Man Who Walked to the Moon* was published in French translation in 2008. He is the recipient of two fellowships from The National Endowment for the Arts; two from the Ohio Arts council; a Fulbright award; a Woodrow Wilson fellowship; the D. H. Lawrence Fellowship from the University of Mexico and a Research Fellowship from Bowling Green State University.

From *Howard McCord: The Poems*: Ysleta, Texas, 1947

My theology began
with a whistle made of a bird's wing.

Unthinking, I had killed
a buzzard,

    he had settled to the ground
    like a mountain
    in a great exhaustion

and above the stench
had stripped the bones of flesh

I dried them in the sun,
cut four holes
in the big wing bone

One for lips
Three for fingers

The bird was made of death,
with wooden eyes,
and the flute hissed more
like a snake than it sang
and the blowing made me dizzy.

But I was young
and full of nonsense
and thought the dizziness
was to dance to.

I did not know that it was a blasphemy
of death, or that the steps
spelled out I was condemned
and would know fiercer lips
on my own bones before I died. ★

From *Howard McCord: The Poems*: Covenant

Each gentleman of the party
shall possess a decent respect
for art, poetry in particular,
a pair of stout boots, a pistol
in .45 Colt (that we may share
the burden of ammunition)
and a rifle in .30-06.

His clothing will be twill
or loden, the colors of earth
and foliage. A good knife,
a dictionary of his other tongue
or so, three or four texts
too rich to be remembered,
and a bed as he wills it.

Toiletries, his own kit
of nesting pans, and two
canteens, for the way is long.
Dried food, not forgetting
fruits and sweets, which
make steep ascents more bearable,
if never less hard.

Let each bring a huddling
sack should it rain of a night,
or be wet.

It is not the mountain we climb,

nor the creatures we hunt, not
the crag-leaps.

It is the distance, the purity,
the completeness, the forgetting
          we cherish. The clarity.

Each dream is his own,
the dreamer's, to share
or to hide, but each poem
as open as eyes. ★

Carolina Monsivaís

Carolina Monsivaís was born and raised in El Paso. She received her M.F.A. in poetry at New Mexico State University. Her book *Somewhere Between Houston and El Paso: Testimonies of a Poet* received the Premio Poesía Tejana award. Her poetry is anthologized in *U.S. Latino Literature Today* and *The Wind Shifts: New Latino Poetry*. A dedicated advocate and activist in the field of violence against women and children, she co-founded The Women Writers' Collective, a community-based group that showcases the talents of women writers while raising awareness for issues related to women and their allies.

From *Somewhere Between Houston and El Paso: Testimonies of a Poet*: Summer Day Spent Filming Areas of El Paso

It's late afternoon and the air rung
of all its liquid is beginning to cool.
I'm at the edge of the city watching,
the sand through the lens unfurl
from flatness into dunes. A lizard
scampers under a shrub, not far
from encroaching quick-built houses.
Far off, a gray rabbit moves across
my lens, it stirs trash strewn
about. I can hear a train headed
for a nearby ditch where it will
unload its latest toxic harvest.

I make my way towards mountains
to watch the sunset.
I pass
barbed wire fences lining a muddy river
shaped by concrete banks.
I pass,
Tigua's bright lights in danger
of being dimmed by law, even though
many are finally getting by.
I pass
empty factories left like refuse,
like the women buried in pieces
beside buildings.
I pass
the oldest mission in Texas,
now crooked with age, built over what
Apaches called "Home of the Ancients"
which to them was like an apartment
building with water in pipes.

I catch the sunset, just as light lowers
in a weaving of purple, red, and orange.
It breaks
across the jagged rocks.
These mountains guard
against heavy storms and whirling warm air.
They keep the calmness and traditions
of the city safe. But they would be
helpless against any weaponry aimed
at the military base near the center
of the city. ★

From *Somewhere Between Houston and El Paso: Testimonies of a Poet*: Un Día de Verano filmando en El Paso

Muy entrada la tarde.
después de que el aire
se ha librado de la humedad,
comienza a refrescar.
Me encuentro a orillas
de la ciudad observando
a través del lente
como la arena se transforma
de superficie plana en dunas.
Una lagartija corretea bajo un arbusto,
no muy lejos de las
de casas construidas al vapor.
A lo lejos, frente a mi lente
se mueve un conejo gris.
Revuelve la basura que se encuentra
tirada por ahí.
Puedo escuchar el tren
que se dirige a una zanja cercana
donde desechará su ultima cosecha
tóxica.

Me dirijo hacia las montañas
a observar la puesta del sol.
En el camino paso por
los cercos de puas
a orillas del túrbio río
moldeado por paredes do concreto.
Paso por las brillantes luces
de los Tiguas en peligro de

ser atenuadas por decreto legal,
a pesar de que finalmente
varias estén lográndose.
Paso por las fábricas vacías
abandonadas como desecho,
como mujeres
enterradas a pedazos
junto a los edificios.
Paso por las misión más antigua en Texas,
ahora torcida de vieja,
construida en el lugar que los Apaches
llamaban "La casa de los antepasados"
que para ellos era como un edificio
de apartamentos con agua de tubería.

Alcanzo la puesta de sol,
justo cuando la luz
toma tonos morados, rojos y anaranjados.
Se parte en los picos de las rocas.
Estas montañas protegen de las
tormentas y de los remolinos.
Mantienen a salvo la calma
y las tradiciones de la ciudad.
Pero se encontrarían inermes
frente a proyectiles lanzados
contra la base militar
cerca del centro de la ciudad. ★

Duane Carr

Born in eastern Kansas, Duane Carr left for Colorado at the age of eighteen to work as a telegrapher on the Denver and Rio Grande Western Railroad. He moved to El Paso in 1969 to begin his graduate work at the University of Texas at El Paso. He is the author of the novel *The Bough of Summer* and the nonfiction book *A Question of Class*. He has published numerous articles, poems, and stories in literary magazines, and his poetry has been anthologized in such books as *The Texas Anthology*.

An El Pasoan Returns from Galveston

The way the sea rolls in and then retreats,
Sifting out the shells of life it holds
In seminal indifference makes you feel
At times the urge to swim and let it cull
Your final life breath, then spew back the bones.

But in the desert death is much too slow
And so holds no attraction as the heat
Descends in long unceasing days of dry
Relentless suns that do not yield to clouds
And blind you with their piercing rage of light.

For in the desert you must wait the time
When night's extended shadow cools the earth
And gods demand a strange affinity
With sky and stars that span the universe. ★

Christmas Eve in Juarez

I watch below the now-stilled ceiling fan
As waiters clear a table near the bar
For celebrants whose youth betrays escape
From country club and parents who exact
A momentary stop at midnight mass.

The man behind the bar, striped towel in hand,
Holds goblets to the light in disregard
Of empty table talk. I rise and leave.

Against the curb outside a woman sits,
And on a dirty shawl beside her lies
A child. I toss a dollar in her cup
And see infection in the baby's eyes
And know the sleeping promise of this world
That cradles sons of man unrealized. ★

Robert Burlingame

Robert Burlingame was born and raised in Kansas. Educated at Wichita University and the University of Arizona, he received his B.A. and M.A. from the University of New Mexico and his Ph.D. from Brown University. He was a Fulbright Scholar to Queen Mary College, the University of London. After teaching at the University of New Mexico, Brown University, the University of Wyoming, and Kansas State University, he came to Texas Western College in 1954. Robert Burlingame retired from the University of Texas at El Paso as emeritus professor in 1989. He has published two books of poems: *This Way We Walk* and *Eighteen Poems* and three chapbooks. His poems, essays and reviews have appeared in such publications as *Saturday Review*, *Texas Observer*, *Bloomsbury Review*, *Massachusetts Review*, *Sin Fronteras/Writers Without Borders*, *Blue Mesa Review*, *New Mexico Quarterly*, and *Borderlands* among many others. His work has been widely anthologized in *Pushcart Prize III*; *Washing the Cow's Skull*; *Borestone Mountain/Best Poems*; *The Weight of Addition: an Anthology of Texas Poetry*; *Inheritance of Light*; and others. His most recent work has appeared in *Sin Fronteras*; *Texas Review*; *Baltimore Review*; *Samsara Magazine*; and *Big Land, Big Sky, Big Hair: Best of the Texas Poetry Calendar*. A new collection of his poetry will be published in 2009.

After Bird Watching Near the Mexican Border

I am slow moving.
Like Mexico, the land we walk next to.
But we're not, in truth, lazy. I gaze west, south.
Mexico, always.
I feel passionate music grip my thighs. I sing.
I feel purposeful as milk in a summer breast.

All morning, in this bosque, we watched birds.
Birds irreverently flying across the uniformed border,
ruled line guarded by balloons, patrols, or by
worms with eyes hidden in their genitals;

Painted bunting, yellow billed cuckoo, burrowing owl,
grackel, air-widening swift, small finch. We watched them,
elegant trespassers of man's ignorance.
We drank from our canteens. A heron flew crazily into Mexico,
Mexico—white wall beneath the shadows of ascension.

Birds dovetailed, broke apart in a scattering of seconds;
vivid as women at the moment of spasm, they delivered
themselves from the green caves of June
We are denied their adventure. We must imagine.
So tell me, my friend, where is the woman with our coffee,
that one with a smile like a deliberate, slow wing? ★

Walking to a Halt in Ciudad Juarez, Near the International Bridge

He is walking north on Ramon Corona.
It has been a decade since he walked this street.
Peso devaluations and red Marches of blown sand
have not made the low roofs look any better.

He carries a white and yellow copy of Popol Vuh
and a 45rpm of Augustin Lara's "Aventurera." He walks,
respectable turista, past doorways hungry as those
of the Lords of Death. Near the corner he sees a boy,

his right hand gone, and other sights of grim dignity.
He asks, "Where, wise old story, are the helping animals?
Mankind, is it doing so well?" but no animal—
not ant, louse, rat, or toad—steps forward. That one—

next to a woman, her face like a seared field—dog all
ramshackle bones, is too weak to join any human crisis.
He stops at the corner and looks around. He sees
yesterday's newspaper on fire warming the woman's hands.

She laughs "Ai!" across the traffic. At him. At no one.
He can't look. He can't look away. He steps back. This
flow between them, between laugh and look, is all there is.
The dog has gone. Cars crowd the bridge. He stands rooted. ★

Permissions

Barrientos, Tanya Maria. "Dee" from *Frontera Street*, copyright © 2002 by Tanya Maria Barrientos. Used with permission of Dutton Signet, a division of Penguin Group (USA) Inc.

Bode, Elroy. "Earth-Life" and "Love in Smokey's Barbecue" from *In A Special Light* by Elroy Bode, copyright © 2006. Reprinted with permission of Trinity University Press. "Sunset Heights After Dark," "Going to Juarez," "Orange Marigolds," and "The Day the Earth Stood Still," reprinted with permission of Elroy Bode.

Burciaga, José Antonio. "A Mixed Mex-Cal Marriage" and "Memories of a Juarez Nightlife" from *Drink Cultura: Chicanismo*, Joshua Odell Editions, copyright © 1992. Reprinted with permission of Cecilia Burciaga for the estate of José Antonio Burciaga.

Burlingame, Robert. "After Bird Watching Near the Mexican Border," *Blue Mesa Review*, Number two, Spring 1990; "Walking to a Halt in Ciudad Juarez, Near the International Bridge," *Sin Fronteras/Writers Without Borders*, Journal Dos/Two, 1997. Reprinted with permission of Robert Burlingame.

Byrd, Bobby. "One Way for Middle-Aged Persons to Meditate" from *Get Some Fuses for the House*, copyright © 1987 by Bobby Byrd, published by North Atlantic Books, Reprinted with permission of North Atlantic Books. "The Gabachos in the Photograph" from *The Price of Doing Business in Mexico*, copyright © 1998, published by Cinco Puntos Press. Reprinted with permission of Bobby Byrd.

Byrd, Lee Merrill. "When He is Thirty-Seven" from *My Sister Disappears: Stories and a Novella*, copyright © 1993 by Lee Merrill Byrd, published by Southern Methodist University Press. Reprinted with permission of Southern Methodist University Press.

Carr, Duane. "An El Pasoan Returns from Galveston" from *The Texas Anthology*, ed. Paul Ruffin, copyright © 1979 by Duane Carr. Reprinted with permission of Duane Carr. "Christmas Eve in Juarez," from *Transitions*, copyright © 1980 by Duane Carr. Reprinted with permission of Duane Carr.

Carr, Pat. "The Anatomy of a Victim," *Sundog* 1984. Reprinted with permission of Pat Carr.

Castillo, Ana. "Regina" from *The Guardians*, copyright © 2007 by Ana Castillo, published by Random House. Reprinted with permission of Susan Bergholz Literary Service, New York, NY, and Lamy, NM. All rights reserved.

Chacón, Daniel. "Boat Sailing Over Juarez" and "The Crazy Chicken," copyright © 2008 by Daniel Chacón. Subsequently published in *Unending Rooms* copyright © 2008 by Daniel Chacón, published by Black Lawrence Press, 2008. Reprinted with permission of Daniel Chacón.

Chávez, Denise. "The McCoy Hotel," copyright © Denise Chávez. Reprinted with permission of Denise Chávez.

Chew, Selfa. "Chio Sam" from *Azogue en la Raiz*, copyright © 2006 by Selfa Chew, published by Ediciones Eon. Reprinted with permission of Selfa Chew.

Dailey, Maceo. "Introduction" from *Tuneful Tales*, copyright © 2002 by Texas Tech University Press. Reprinted with permission of Texas Tech University Press.

Delgado, Abelardo. "September" from *Letters to Louise*, copyright © 1982 by Abelardo Delgado, published by Tonatiuh-Quinto Sol International. Reprinted with permission of Dolores Delgado.

DeMarinis, Rick. "Hell's Cartoonist" from *Apocalypse Then: New Novellas and Stories*. Copyright © 2004 by Rick DeMarinis. Reprinted with the permission of Seven Stories Press, www.sevenstories.com

Fischer-West, Lucy. "Food Between the Waters" from *Child of Many Rivers: Journeys to & from the Rio Grande,* copyright © 2005 by Texas Tech University Press. Reprinted with permission of Texas Tech University Press.

García, Mario T. "Requiem 29" and "Who Was Ruben Salazar," from the Introduction to *Ruben Salazar, Border Correspondent: Selected Writings, 1955-1970*, edited with an introduction by Mario T. García, copyright © 1995 by Regents of the University of California, published by the University of California Press. Reprinted with permission of the University of California Press.

Gaspar de Alba, Alicia. "American Citizen, 1921" from *The Mystery of Survival and Other Stories* published by Bilingual Press/Editorial Bilingüe, 1993, Tempe, Arizona. Reprinted with permission of Bilingual Press/Editorial Bilingüe.

Gilb, Dagoberto. "Pride" from *Gritos,* copyright © 2003 by Dagoberto Gilb. Reprinted with permission of Dagoberto Gilb. "I Danced With the Prettiest Girl" from *The Magic of Blood*, copyright ©1993 by Dagoberto Gilb, published by the University of New Mexico Press. Reprinted with permission of the University of New Mexico Press.

Gladstein, Mimi Reisel, and Cohen, Sylvia Deener. "The Wild West Welcomes Holocaust Survivors" from *Lone Stars of David: The Jews of Texas*, copyright © 2007, published by Brandeis University Press in association with the Texas Jewish Historical Society. Reprinted with permission of Mimi Reisel Gladstein and Sylvia Deener Cohen.

Gonzalez, Ray. "White Sands" from *Memory Fever*, copyright © 1993 by Ray Gonzalez, published by the University of Arizona Press. Reprinted with permission of Ray Gonzalez. "Somewhere Outside El Paso" and "The Rio Grande Near Flood Stage, Summer 2006," previously unpublished poems, copyright © Ray Gonzalez. Reprinted with permission of Ray Gonzalez.

Granados, Christine. "The Bride" from *Brides and Sinners in El Chuco,* copyright © 2006 by

Christine Granados. Reprinted with permission of the University of Arizona Press.
Haddad, Marian. "Somewhere Between Mexico and a River Called Home" from *Somewhere Between Mexico and a River Called Home*, copyright © 2004 by Pecan Grove Press. Reprinted with permission of Marian Haddad.

Haines, Cynthia Farah. "Spanish Language Movie Theaters" from *Showtime! From Opera Houses to Picture Palaces in El Paso*, copyright © 2006 by Texas Western Press. Reprinted with permission of Texas Western Press of the University of Texas at El Paso.

Hamilton, Nancy. "El Paso's Pioneer Women," *Password*, El Paso County Historical Society, vol. 50, no. 3, 2005. Reprinted with permission of the El Paso County Historical Society.

Hertzog, Carl. Memo to Bob Wells, January 16, 1956, Carl Hertzog Collection. Reprinted with permission of Special Collections of the University of Texas at El Paso Library. "El Paso's Durable Sinner," *Password*, El Paso County Historical Society, vol. 25, no. 2, 1980. Reprinted with permission of the El Paso County Historical Society.

Islas, Arturo. "Just Like Romeo and Juliet" from *La Mollie and the King of Tears*, copyright © 1996 by Arturo Islas and Jovita Islas, published by the University of New Mexico Press. Reprinted with permission of the University of New Mexico Press.

Lea, Tom. Chapters I and II from *The Wonderful Country* © 1952 by Tom Lea; "Old Mount Franklin," reprinted with permission of James Lea for the estate of Tom Lea.

LittleDog, Pat. "What Cecilia Reveals" originally published in the *Texas Observer*, later in the anthology *New Growth, Contemporary Short Stories from Corona Publishing Company*, 1989, copyright © Pat LittleDog. Reprinted with permission of Pat LittleDog.

López-Stafford, Gloria. "The Trouble With English" from *A Place in El Paso: A Mexican American Childhood*, copyright © 1996 by the University of New Mexico Press. Reprinted with permission of the University of New Mexico Press.

Luna, Sheryl. "Bones" and "Learning to Speak" from *Pity the Drowned Horses*, copyright © 2005 by Sheryl Luna, published by the University of Notre Dame Press. Reprinted with permission of the University of Notre Dame Press.

Mangan, Frank. "The Twenties Roared" from *El Paso in Pictures*, copyright © 1971 by Frank Mangan, published by Mangan Books. Reprinted with permission of Frank Mangan.

McCord, Howard. "Ysleta, Texas 1947" and "Covenant" from *Howard McCord: The Poems*, copyright © 2002 by Howard McCord, published by Bloody Twin Press. Reprinted with permission of Howard McCord.

Metz, Leon Claire. "El Paso" and "Four Sixes to Beat" from *John Wesley Hardin: Dark Angel of Texas*, copyright © 1996 by Leon Metz, published by Mangan Books. Published with permission of Mangan Books.

Monsivaís, Carolina. "Summer Day Spent Filming Areas of El Paso" and "Un Día de Verano filmando en El Paso" from *Somewhere Between Houston and El Paso: Testimonies of a Poet,* copyright © 2000 by Carolina Monsivaís, published by Wings Press. Reprinted with permission of Carolina Monsivaís.

Mora, Pat. "Desert Women" from *Borders*, copyright © 1986 by Pat Mora, published by Arte Público Press. Reprinted with permission of Arte Público Press, University of Houston. "Corazón del corrido" from *Agua Santa: Holy Water*, copyright © 1995 by Pat Mora, published by University of Arizona Press. Reprinted with permission of Curtis Brown, Ltd. "Ode to El Paso" from *Adobe Odes,* copyright © 2006 by Pat Mora, published by University of Arizona Press. Reprinted with permission of Curtis Brown, Ltd.

Muro, Amado. "Sunday in Little Chihuahua" and "My Grandfather's Brave Songs" from *The Collected Stories of Amado Muro*, copyright © 1979 by Thorp Springs Press. Reprinted with permission of Robert Seltzer for the estate of Amado Muro.

Rechy, John. Chapter One from *About My Life and the Kept Woman*, copyright © 2008 by John Rechy. Used with permission of Grove/Atlantic, Inc. Chapter One from the unpublished manuscript *Autobiography: A Novel,* copyright © by John Rechy. Published with permission of John Rechy.

Rentería, Ramón. Interview with Ricardo Sánchez: "Another Struggle: Famed Poet Fights Deadly Cancer," *El Paso Times,* May 30, 1995. Reprinted with permission of the *El Paso Times.*

Rivera, Tomás. "The Searchers" from *Tomás Rivera: The Complete Works*, copyright © 1992 Arte Público Press, University of Houston. Reprinted with permission of Arte Público Press.

Romo, David Dorado. "Music Across the Lines" from *Ringside Seat to a Revolution: An Underground Cultural History of El Paso and Juárez: 1893-1923,* copyright © 2005 by David Dorado Romo, published by Cinco Puntos Press. Reprinted with permission of Cinco Puntos Press.

Sáenz, Benjamin Alire. "Elegy for Burciaga" and "The Blue I Loved" from *Elegies in Blue: Poems,* copyright © 2002 by Benjamin Alire Sáenz, published by Cinco Puntos Press. Reprinted with permission of Cinco Puntos Press.

Salazar, Ruben. "Speakeasies Sell 'Atomic' Booze in South El Paso" and "Militants Fight to Retain Spanish as Their Language" from *Ruben Salazar: Border Correspondent Selected Writings 1955-1970*, edited with an introduction by Mario T. García, copyright © 1995 by Regents of the University of California, published by the University of California Press. Reprinted with permission of the University of California Press.

Sánchez, Ricardo. "fragrance petals its presence" from *The Loves of Ricardo*, copyright © 1997 by Ricardo Sánchez, published by Tia Chuca Press and distributed by Northwestern University Press. "Fridays Belong to Friends, Sometimes," from *Selected Poems* copyright © 1985 by Ricardo Sánchez, published by Arte Público Press, University of Houston. Reprinted with permission of Maria Teresa Sánchez for the estate of Ricardo Sánchez.

Seltzer, Robert. "My Father, Amado Muro," from the unpublished manuscript, copyright © 2009 by Robert Seltzer. Published with permission of Robert Seltzer.
Solis, Octavio. From Act I of the play *Lydia,* copyright © 2008 by Octavio Solis, published with permission of Bret Adams, Ltd. For performance rights, please contact the author's agent, Bret Adams Ltd., 448 W. 44th St., New York, NY, 10036 (212) 765-5630.

Sonnichsen, Charles Leland. Excerpts from "Six Shooter Capital" from *Pilgrim in the Sun: A Southwestern Omnibus,* copyright © 1988 by Texas Western Press. Reprinted with permission of Carol Sonnichsen for the estate of C.L. Sonnichsen.

Terrazas, Beatriz. "The River That Runs Through Me," *The Washington Post*, July 7, 2008; copyright © 2008 by Beatriz Terrazas. Reprinted with permission of Beatriz Tarrazas.

Timmons, W. H. Excerpts from "El Paso and Ciudad Juárez, 1910-1945" from *El Paso: A Borderlands History,* copyright © 1990 by Texas Western Press. Reprinted with permission of Texas Western Press of the University of Texas at El Paso.

Trambley, Estela Portillo. "Pay the Criers" from *Rain of Scorpions and Other Stories,* copyright © 1993 Estela Portillo Trambley, published by Bilingual Press/Editorial Bilingüe, Tempe, Arizona. Reprinted with permission of Bilingual Press/Editorial Bilingüe.

Troncoso, Sergio. "The Abuelita" from *The Last Tortilla & Other Stories,* copyright © 1999 by Sergio Troncoso, published by the University of Arizona Press. Reprinted with permission of the University of Arizona Press.

Ullman, Leslie. "Gourd" and "The Way Animals Are" from *Slow Work Through Sand,* copyright © 1998 by Leslie Ullman, published by the University of Iowa Press. Reprinted with permission of the University of Iowa Press.

Vélez, Manuel. "Memories Fade" from *Bus Stops and Other Poems*, copyright © 1998 by Manuel Vélez, published by Calaca Press. Reprinted with permission of Manuel Vélez.

Verghese, Abraham. Pages 329-336 from *The Tennis Partner*, copyright © 1998 by Abraham Verghese. Reprinted with permission of HarperCollins Publishers.

Walker, Dale L. "The Mencken-White Letters," *Nova Quarterly* Winter 1968-69, Vol. 4, No. 2, copyright © Dale L. Walker. Reprinted with permission of Dale L. Walker. "The White Sands Mystery" first published as "Murder in the White Sands" from *The Calamity Papers: Western Myths and Cold* Cases, copyright © 2004 by Dale L. Walker, published by Macmillan/Forge Books. Reprinted with permission of Dale L. Walker.

West, John O. "The Weeping Woman: La Llorona" from *Legendary Ladies of Texas*, Texas Folklore Society publication XLIII, edited by Francis Edward Abernethy, copyright © Texas Folklore Society. Reprinted with permission of the Texas Folklore Society.

White, Owen. "The Passing of Stoudenmire" from *Out of the Desert: The Historical Romance of El Paso*, copyright © 1923 by The McMath Company.

Wiggins, Bernice Love. "Grandmother Speaks," "Just Dreams," and "The Poetical Farmwife" from *Tuneful Tales*, copyright © 2002 by Texas Tech University Press. Reprinted with permission of Texas Tech University Press.

Williford, Lex. "My Mother's Wedding Dress," *The Prairie Schooner*, Special Fiction Issue, Summer 2003, copyright © 2003 by Lex Williford. Reprinted with permission of Lex Williford.

Woolley, Bryan. "Glory Denied" from *The Bride Wore Crimson and Other Stories*, Texas Western Press, copyright © 1993 by Bryan Woolley. Reprinted with permission of Bryan Woolley. "South El Paso Street, copyright © 2005 by the *Dallas Morning News*. Reprinted with permission of Bryan Woolley.

Wright, Bill. Excerpts from *The Tiguas: Pueblo Indians of Texas*, copyright © 1993 by Texas Western Press of the University of Texas at El Paso, published by the Texas Western Press. Reprinted with permission of Bill Wright.

Yañez, Richard. "Rio Grande" from *El Paso del Norte: Stories on the Border*, copyright © 2003 by Richard Yañez. Reprinted with permission of the University of Nevada Press.

Index